THE SON OF MARIETTA

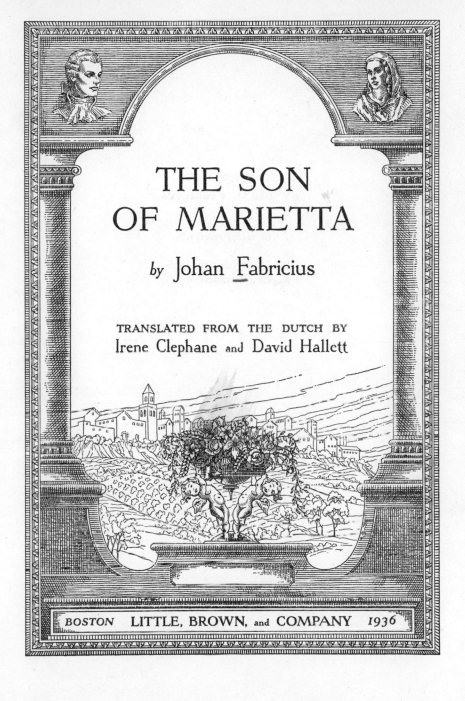

THE SON OF MARIETTA

by Johan Fabricius

TRANSLATED FROM THE DUTCH BY
Irene Clephane and David Hallett

BOSTON LITTLE, BROWN, and COMPANY *1936*

TO

MY WIFE

CONTENTS

CONTENTS

BOOK THREE
CARNIVAL AND CONFESSION

CONTENTS

Decorative Drawings by CONRAD G. ROBILLARD

PLAYERS
PASSED BY

THE

PLAYERS

ARRIVE

I

RAGGED CLOUDS WERE DRIFTING ACROSS CENTRAL
Italy. A harsh west wind blowing over the sea from Spain was
driving them through the night across the bare autumnal landscape. They were gathering in the west behind the dark Umbrian mountains, as if an unseen shepherd sat there calling together his flock of gray-
white cloud sheep. The moon was almost at the full. Mysterious, in a
mysterious shifting world of silver cloud and illimitable sky, unbelievably
blue, it cast white gleams over the bare mountainside, over the valleys in
which moved wisps of mist, over the winding road on whose uneven surface
a procession of some dozen vehicles traveled towards the hamlet of Pontecutini.

Some among them must have done service for at least fifty years — old-
fashioned caroches, each with high twisted wings and a little seat at the
back for the groom, who had to make room for the piled-up luggage bound
together with cords; calashes with oft-mended awnings; a coach packed to
capacity and drawn by three mules; a peasant cart full of boxes and
junk.

The first carriage stopped in the middle of the bridge across the Tiber;
and the coachman, his three-cornered hat pulled down over his eyes, his
nose muffled in a red woollen scarf over which the little tail of his black
wig was flapping, stood up stiffly. He opened the coachman's box, took
out a pail, clattered down the wheel with it and descended to the riverbank. Other coachmen, slowly making up their minds, followed suit. The

thirsty horses and mules, sensing what was awaiting them, stood looking on impatiently, their haunches turned towards the wind that twisted their tails and blew their manes about their ears.

Before long, a carriage door opened first here, then there. Figures enveloped in wide, dark cloaks sprang onto the road, and on stiff legs walked to the stone parapet of the bridge. Then, still adjusting their clothes, they gathered into a group, offering snuff boxes to one another under the protection of a hollowed hand and casting glances at the magic reflection of the moon down below in the fast-flowing water.

From the carriages, which were hastily closed again, came light, laughing, women's voices. A little hand with tapering fingers wiped a windowpane clean, and from it peered a small smiling face under a white wig. But immediately the window grew dim again, from the warmth of stoves and crowded bodies inside the vehicle. Then, behind the curtains, sprang up flickering flames of candles and oil lamps, giving to the shaky old vehicles the appearance of important carriages.

Peasants from the hamlet, awakened by the barking of their dogs, approached, and were so busy looking at all there was to see that they were very slow to answer the questions showered on them. These began by being seemly: How far was the little city of Todi? Did it contain an inn and a theater? Then the gentlemen in their wide cloaks grew childish, and tried to get some fun at the expense of the peasants of Pontecutini.

From one of the vehicles issued animal sounds such as nobody had ever heard before. In the coach, a nursling baby was whining — its tiny voice still like the trembling, helpless whimper of a newborn lamb.

The horses had finished drinking. The travelers had returned once more to the lighted vehicles. The coachmen jumped up onto their boxes, and cracked their whips.

The peasants still stood gaping on the bridge when the last vehicle turned the corner. One of them stepped forward and picked up from the ground a pink silk bow that gleamed in the moonlight — a lost silk bow, attached to a garter. Involuntarily his clumsy hand carried the fragment of material to his nose, and, as he sniffed in the soft mixture of perfume and intimate femininity, his eyes bulged with astonishment. The others wanted to share his experience; but with a sudden sense of shame, mingled with a selfish impulse to keep his discovery for himself, he threw the garter over the parapet of the bridge into the water, and smiled at them obtusely. They grinned in response, concealing their envy and curiosity. One of them made a coarse remark. All guffawed, then fell silent again, and tried to look sly, as if full of understanding.

As they sought their miserable beds, they carried with them a dim realization that to-night, in a strangely confused form, sin had passed through Pontecutini.

II

Silent and dying, the old episcopal city of Todi slumbered in the sleeping mountains. Its streets of gray stone buildings were like narrow clefts cut out of the rock; the entrances to the somber houses were like caverns. Nowhere within the walls of the city rustled the dark velvet foliage of a single tree. The only live thing was the murmuring fountain on the narrow piazza. The gleaming silver water spouted from the curved mouth of a dolphin into the glittering basin. But when a cloud sailed before the moon, the fountain also sank into the darkness of the overhanging Gothic houses. Then only its monotonous voice, that had the timelessness of all falling water, revealed its presence.

Suddenly this dark peace was disturbed. A procession of strange vehicles came rolling along, rattling over the uneven cobblestones under the stone arch of the city gate. Clattering hooves echoed from the walls of the houses.

Gaetano came running out of the tollhouse. Drunk with sleep, he failed at first to understand that a company of traveling players wished to put up in Todi.

"Where is your permit? Have you a permit?" he demanded, fearful of being punished if he let them in, but not at all clear himself as to what sort of permit was required.

"Permit? We shall get a permit to perform from the podesta to-morrow. You wouldn't turn us back, surely? There are ladies with us. They need rest. *Per Bacco*, you surely don't take us for brigands?"

Gaetano scratched his dazed head. He tried to take in the entire procession in one sweeping glance; ran outside the gate, came back; was conscious that a lira was being pressed into his hand — and suddenly to his own surprise he found a way out of his difficulties.

"All right, these can go through." With a gesture of the arm, he indicated the first nine vehicles. "The rest must wait here until it's light."

"But those carry only scenery, costume boxes, and theatrical stores."

"We shall see about that soon enough to-morrow."

While the horses and mules were unharnessed from the last carriages, Gaetano, well pleased with his solution, started to rummage through the lighted carriages in front. They contained gay, painted ladies; a cloud of sweet perfume emanated from their colored-silk presences. They addressed roguish, risky remarks to the toll-collector as he faithfully carried out his duties — no respectable citizen's wife would ever have given such free rein to her tongue. So that he could search under the benches, they laughingly stretched out their dainty legs in front of them, lifting up with gracious hands the lace hems of their skirts. His face a fiery red, Gaetano carried out this dangerous official inspection, and was about to bring it to a conclusion by casting a cursory glance into the half-darkness of the coach, where they were all busy trying to calm the wailing infant; but just as he opened the door an innocent pair of woman's hands was turning a napkin inside out, and with a mighty oath he jumped backwards.

Before re-entering the tollhouse, he gave permission for the tenth vehicle to go through. In it, besides performing dogs and cats, traveled animals — monkeys and parrots — that could not endure the cold because they came from distant hot countries.

A little later, the procession came to a standstill on the piazza opposite the sleeping cathedral, and Vacca, the squinting landlord of The Three Popes, almost broke his neck as he stumbled hastily up and down the steep wooden staircase of his inn. His wife and his two maids prepared the bedrooms upstairs. He himself, dragging his left leg, brought out the beakers of wine. With clenched teeth he hoisted himself onto a chair to light the lamps, while he counted up the number of available beds.

"We have eleven, gentlemen, but in two of them three can sleep easily."

"And two in all the others. Then four-and-twenty of us are fixed up. But we number thirty-one."

"Leave it to me, gentlemen. I will borrow blankets and mattresses from my neighbors. Only have a little patience."

"We're patient enough; but we're anxious about the heating. And where is your larder? We'll choose what we should like."

Lights sprang up in some of the neighboring houses. Sleepy-faced servants who had jumped hastily into their clothes came and looked into the taproom, and remarked timidly that their masters could place one, two, or more beds at the disposal of the strangers. But the innkeeper, who was reluctant to lose any of his guests, growled at these servants and sent word by them to their masters that he had room — what he needed was the loan of mattresses and blankets, if they would be so kind. One or two of the actors, however, realizing that, by great good luck, they were being offered free lodging in comfortable houses, had already disappeared — to the amazement of the innkeeper, who snarled like an angry dog as he ran to fetch logs for the fire.

In the low-pitched taproom, a fire had speedily been kindled. Sitting near to its brightness and warmth, on chairs, benches, and tables, the players ate and drank and stared with dark eyes into the glow of the flames. The innkeeper's wife, whose blooming, opulent form contrasted pitifully with the expression of helplessness and suffering on her face, appeared with a candle at the door to announce that some of the rooms were ready; whereupon the actresses, hastily emptying their glasses of wine, sprang up and, lifting their trains, followed her with little screams up the narrow, badly lit stair. Quarreling among themselves, they allotted the beds. The mother with her infant was given a bed to herself, after a certain amount of consultation and protest.

The innkeeper's wife looked on appalled at the innocent mite already compelled to travel through the cold night: it seemed so thin, so very, very thin. Was it a girl? she inquired. She herself had a boy, about ten weeks old; he was sleeping restfully in her bed, keeping it warm for her. He was a regular little bed-warmer. Would the ladies perhaps care to see him?

Certainly, the ladies would be delighted to inspect this living bed-warmer. Cracking jokes in strange dialects, they followed the innkeeper's wife to her room, where they peeped into the bed, and immediately fell into ecstasies over the charms of the bouncing boy. Anxious to show him off in his full glory, his mother remembered that it was his feeding time. As her dainty guests at once expressed an ardent desire to witness this ceremony, she picked up the baby and demonstrated how the little rogue seized her heavy white breast as a field worker seizes his earthen wine-jar. He was already a regular little man.

The suffering disappeared from her round face, which took on a look of youth and comeliness. The enthusiastic amazement of these strange ladies, who, by way of a change, were reveling in their own enjoyment of this spectacle of respectable maternal happiness, had gone to her head. Smiling vaguely, mysteriously as a Madonna, she looked down at her child. It was her first. Luigino was his name, after his father, Luigi. . . .

The trembling cries of the other infant across the passage penetrated to them. The comely features of the mother became fixed in commiseration as she suckled her child. "Just listen to the poor lamb," she murmured.

"It's always crying," said the ladies in confidence. "We're all bothered by it. It keeps us awake. Sometimes you feel furious; but then, when you see the miserable little wretch, it breaks your heart. It isn't strong. It hasn't chosen as fine a mother as this one here."

The innkeeper's wife, silent again, looked down upon her suckling child as though she were only half listening. She was struggling with an idea that had come to her out of the fullness of her happiness, an idea that seemed to her simple and obvious, but that she was ashamed to express, for fear the ladies should imagine a certain pride lurked behind it. At last, however, the pitiful wailing from across the passage compelled her to speak. Her eyes were vague and the blood rose darkly into her cheeks as she looked up at them standing there in their silks and finery, and said, "Perhaps it would be quiet with me?" And with her hand she touched her full breast, in a gesture infinitely expressive.

The ladies, ready for anything new, cooed with astonishment. "What a splendid idea! But it would be all right, because she's the same age. You'll get it to keep quiet — it's only hungry. We'll go and ask Corallina. She'll cry when she hears the suggestion, of course — she's a bundle of nerves."

Downstairs, the men sat on round the fire. They had pushed forward a long table, and were leaning on it comfortably. As they ate and drank, they told the innkeeper many things he had never heard before — truth and lies so closely interwoven that they themselves could not have unraveled one from the other. The servants from the neighboring houses, after listening from a distance, had drawn closer and sat down near the strangers, their ears wide open as they drank their share of the wine — this wine that had caused the storytellers to forget the time, to forget even the beds that were waiting for them, to contrive which half the piazza had been turned upside down.

Felt-covered cages stood on the table. Before the fire lay some half-dozen dogs, their heads upon their paws.

The company had come from Naples. *Bella Napoli!* In the south, autumn is friendlier than in the Umbrian mountains — there you had the blue sea, and smoking Vesuvius. And now they were going to Venice for the carnival. Madonna! what a life, this perpetual traveling. They could not expect much in the way of receipts until they reached Bologna; and there was so much competition in Naples that the cash box was practically empty now. It was to be hoped they would get a permit to perform in Todi.

When the morning came peering gray-white through the windows, those who were still awake decided to go upstairs and try to find a vacant place. Several of them had fallen asleep by the table, their heads buried in their arms. They slept on even when the first inquisitive morning customers, having heard the report of this unexpected and surprising visit, slipped into the inn to have a look at them.

Vacca alone showed no sign of fatigue. It would never have occurred to anyone watching him, as he hobbled backwards and forwards behind the counter, serving customers, satisfying their curiosity, and reckoning out what they owed him, that he had been up all night.

III

Later in the morning Garotti, the director of the company, attended at the podesta's house, accompanied by his principal actress, La Bella Marinetta. Signor Orlandi, small and jovial, turned graciously in his worn mayoral chair to cast a brief glance at Marinetta. She responded with a challenging little smile and, as she sat opposite him, allowed her white hand with its pink nails to rest accidentally on the table, so that the city father might lay his hand on hers, confidentially and unobtrusively, as he talked.

"Signor Garotti, if it depended upon me . . . ! But without the permission of the ecclesiastical authorities, we can do nothing. Go and try on the other side of the piazza: if the bishop gives his consent, you can put my name down for a box at once. It's not often we have the honor of a visit from Thalia. To tell you the truth, it has never happened before during my term of office. Earlier in my youth . . . in Florence . . . Oh, *Dio!*" With a vague melancholy, his smiling glance met the velvet eyes of La Bella Marinetta again. Softly she lisped, "Perhaps the Signor Podesta would be kind enough to give us a word of introduction to Monsignore?"

"If that's all . . ." He stretched out for a sheet of paper, dipped his quill in the ink, and under Marinetta's encouraging gaze wrote the date with a flourish: October 18th, Anno Cristi 1720. Then he hesitated, and asked abruptly, "But what kind of play are you going to give?"

Garotti and his principal actress looked at one another questioningly. Then Garotti said, soothingly, "We have chosen 'The Venetian Looking Glass.' You will certainly be satisfied with its tone, Signor Podesta."

"Oh, that's all right so far as I'm concerned! That's all right so far as I'm concerned!" protested the city father in embarrassment, and, reassured, began to inscribe his note to the bishop of Todi. But halfway through he halted again. "I assume that all the same you'll place the script before Monsignore?"

Only after Garotti had dispelled his apprehension on that point did the cautious podesta append his signature to the epistle, pour sand over it, and fold it up, not without a certain satisfaction.

"Till to-night, Signor Podesta!" said Garotti, confidently.

"Steady, now. That remains to be seen!" Hesitatingly, he took Marinetta's lovely hand. Then, relinquishing it with a sigh, he added, "But you make haste, for Monsignore is in the habit of conducting the second morning service himself."

Before asking an audience of the bishop, Garotti crossed quickly to Vacca's inn, and went thundering through all the rooms on the first floor, clapping his hands and shaking the beds. "Get up! I insist! Everyone must attend eleven o'clock Mass!"

A few refused to open their eyes, or actually did not wake. Others vented their bad temper in oaths that were warmly reciprocated by Garotti. In the end he succeeded in getting most of them to crawl out of their blankets; drunk with sleep, they huddled into their clothes.

In little groups they sat scattered about the dark cathedral, sulkily returning the inquiring glances of the pious; yawning and with streaming eyes, they gazed upwards towards the windows, blazing with color, on which the sun was playing. At the Te Deum that concluded the service, they came alive, and the full jubilant tones of several of the women's voices, the deep metallic bass of a man's — sounds such as rarely reverberated in the walls of the little cathedral — caused the bishop to lift up his gray-white head and listen.

Garotti knelt in front, in full view of the roaming eye of the prelate, who sat in his chair of honor enthroned like the god of Todi, with choir-boys at his feet.

After Mass, the prelate received the director of the players and Marinetta, now modestly attired, in a small room in his palace. He made his secretary read aloud to him from the soiled script of "The Venetian Looking Glass." The secretary, a young abbé, who was anticipating a pleasurable evening, emphasized the moral ending and tactfully slurred over those passages that seemed to him open to question. When he had finished and was waiting almost as tensely as Garotti for his master's decision, the bishop picked up the script himself, and, bringing it to his failing eyes, appeared to attempt by the help of mystic powers to read something hidden that had eluded his listening ear.

Then he returned the script to Garotti, and his words fell heavily in the expectant silence. "There seems to me to be nothing objectionable. But no women must take part in the performance — Todi lies in the Papal States, as you are no doubt aware."

Marinetta heaved a deep sigh. The bishop, surprised, turned his eyes slowly towards her, and let his gaze, not without good will, rest on her a moment as he went on, "I trust that the actors in their improvisations will refrain from uttering anything that might offend the ecclesiastical and temporal authorities or public modesty."

Garotti hastened to assure him that his actors were without exception artists possessed of the highest moral conceptions, who, in the fluency of improvisation, always knew how to bridle their tongues; his actresses might well serve as models of virtue and modesty. They, too, were artists of the first rank, and they would consider it an infinite privilege to be allowed to reveal their gifts before art-loving Todi.

Marinetta re-enforced this last point by throwing herself down before the bishop and kissing his hand respectfully and imploringly. With the same friendly good will, he looked down on her, requested her in a gentle voice to stand up, and with quite unexpected gallantry said, "Your beauty, Signora, makes me regret that as the humble servant of the Church it is not in my power to modify the regulations of the Holy See. Forgive me. My affairs call me elsewhere. . . ."

He rose, supported by his secretary, who had come forward hastily; blessed his visitors, and left the room. A moment later, while Garotti and Marinetta were still waiting doubtfully for somebody to show them out, the secretary returned and, with a wink, called Garotti mysteriously on one side. Marinetta dried her tears while the two men whispered by the window. Her gaze wandered inquiringly up and down the narrow, lank figure of the young abbé, and when he turned round she met him with her sweetest smile. He flushed to the roots of his hair, and involuntarily nodded to her encouragingly, thus adding to his own confusion.

"Well?" asked Marinetta, when they were once more outside in the blinding sunlight of the piazza.

Garotti did not answer immediately — he wanted to prepare his effect. Then he said laconically: "Monsignore goes to bed every evening at nine o'clock."

In the end, it was Vacca the innkeeper, proprietor of the only hall that lent itself to a theatrical performance, who turned out to be the most serious stumbling block. For the use of the draughty shed behind his inn, he demanded no less than a hundred and fifty lire.

"Are you crazy, you idiot?"

"I should call myself that if I let you have the hall for less. Half the city will come running, and if you charge — "

"We know perfectly well what we ought to charge, and that we shall have to be content if our total receipts are double what you demand for the hall alone."

"Good! In that case, we shall both earn the same thing," answered Vacca, defying the righteous indignation of the players with the glare of his shameless, squinting eyes.

"The same thing! You don't seem to take into account how many people have to live off the other half. Have you no heart at all?" asked one of the women.

"At least I have a hall," was Vacca's clever retort.

Garotti said importantly, "Fortunately the podesta is on our side. We shall go straight to him and lodge a complaint. Wait for me here, the rest of you."

"It is my hall, not the podesta's," Vacca reminded him calmly. He was sure of his position: he had them in the hollow of his hand, as certainly as a street urchin has a captive sparrow.

And of course they had to give way. After further consultation, they chose the only solution Vacca had left them: they raised the price of admission to the unheard-of level of four lire a head, and hoped that the citizens of Todi would not take it amiss. Angrily they wrote on the notice-board that had been posted up in front of the inn: —

OWING TO THE BOUNDLESS GREED OF VACA THE INNKEEPER,
WE ARE COMPELLED TO CHARGE FOUR LIRE AS THE PRICE OF ADMISSION

When the curious collected in front of the notice, Vacca himself went out to read it and, winking at the bystanders — who did not return his smile — he inserted with a piece of chalk the C that had been omitted from his name.

IV

Piety reigned in the old and stately episcopal city of Todi, small though it was. The sound of the bells was the voice of God, to which the citizens listened every hour of the day. But when on this evening the Angelus sounded from the towers, and the citizens betook themselves obediently to vespers, many pious hearts were filled with worldly unrest. In the prayer books of the well to do lay the expensive tickets they had just fetched from Vacca's inn — the tickets for the first and last performance of "The Venetian Looking Glass" to be given at Todi by the far-famed Garotti Company.

And in the evening, in their best attire, they streamed into the hall, where a stage had been constructed out of boards. They filled the lower space with the buzzing of their laughing, excited voices, with airy greetings, with shuffling of feet, with the rustling of silk clothes. All this noise was hushed for a moment as a distinguished family took its place in one of the primitive boxes. The atmosphere was already stifling, owing to the sickly sweet smell of sweat and powdered wigs. It became worse as the audience endeavored to make good the absence of oxygen with snuff and perfume.

But every discomfort was forgotten when, the podesta with a party of ladies having taken his place in the principal box, the sound of stamping feet from behind the torn and faded curtain caused the tension to rise to breaking-point. A stagehand lit the footlights with a torch. Garotti, already in the costume of his part, came forward and extolled in a graceful address the local authorities of Todi, the celebrated past of the city, and the artistic sense of its citizens, who had so graciously paid for the privilege of meeting together in the temple of Thalia. Then the curtain rose on the first act.

A strange emotion ran through the audience, many of whom were witnessing a performance by professional actors for the first time. As they went through their parts on that wretched little stage, the actors seemed to possess a fluency, an elegance of manner, a ready wit unattainable by the ordinary mortal. They knew how to give each word its precise value. They could flatter and stimulate the vanity of the spectator. They could move him, and then make him feel ridiculous in his own eyes for being moved; and if perchance their cleverness wounded, they healed the wounds they had made by their gay and comical inconsequence.

There they stood as large as life, the famous figures of the commedia dell' arte. First, Harlequin in his parti-colored clothes, symbolizing poverty so lightheartedly; the still innocent human being who, unperturbed by hard experience, continues to follow his instincts, only to be painfully astonished that life will not back him up. He is a bundle of mischief, cowardly and boundlessly inquisitive; a filcher of sweets, and a wanton; cruel, and sometimes kind. This kindness, however, is but the illegitimate sister of self-adoration; and still one cannot help loving him, for the sake of that one second when his kindness was pure kindness. His part is to show how punishment follows sin, how contrition and good intentions follow punishment, and how the way to hell is paved with such good intentions. And all realize this, except himself. On winged feet, he dances through the piece, and at the end is the same Harlequin as in the beginning. He is stupid, as stupid as mankind. Only his dancing body is wise, with a wisdom that can express through its mad capers the sadness as well as the joy of life. So that his body may be the more expressive, his face is hidden behind a mask with surprised, turned-up eyebrows and narrow slits through which his wily eyes glint. On his close-cropped head is planted askew a hat decorated with a feather. Should one pity or laugh at Harlequin, who has sprung from the inner self of humanity onto these crazy boards, in order to show humanity itself?

Around him were ranged the others: the half-educated *dottore* from the university town of Bologna; the raffish Pulcinella from the disreputable town of Naples; the cynical Brighella, iniquity incarnate from Bergamo; Pantaloon, the greedy, pitiable, old spouse, a thousand times cuckolded of a young and beautiful woman, and Capitano, the blustering braggart and adventurer — both from Venice, city of unfaithful wives and of adventure. Almost every city of Italy has provided the commedia dell' arte with a figure crystallizing some characteristic of its citizens. Each of them represents some human weakness, but not one of them enthralls as does Harlequin, who is mankind itself.

At moments, the citizens of Todi who had sacrificed four lire to enjoy themselves were vaguely aware of Harlequin's alarming resemblance to themselves, and it was with a feeling of relief that they turned to watch with proud superiority the villainy of Brighella who, in the midst of intrigue and murder, of hair-raising wickedness, thoughtfully strokes his formidable mustaches and winks behind his olive-colored, wart-studded mask: only a moment later to whisper honeyed words under the window of a merchant's virgin daughter. The prudent, thrifty paterfamilias of the audience smiled disdainfully at the prudent, thrifty paterfamilias Pantaloon, who is tyrannized over and exploited by his young wife and half-washed daughters, and who, unperturbed, carries the most formidable antlers. And those who themselves knew a little gibberish Latin roared with laughter over the pidgin Latin of the Bolognese quack, whose proximity to the university had gone to his head.

The company's performing animals not only amused the public in the intervals, but also played a part in the performance itself: for instance, when greedy Pantaloon dismissed his servant Harlequin just before the midday meal, the rogue in revenge opened the doors of the cages containing a half-dozen hungry cats and dogs, which immediately flung themselves onto Pantaloon's well-garnished platters and refused to be driven away even with sticks. And in Pantaloon's parlor hung a cage of parrots that grotesquely imitated their unhappy master's cries of distress when he discovered at last upon what rickety foundations reposed his domestic bliss.

But long before the screeching of the brightly feathered parrots was reached, there was an unexpected interruption. The play had been in progress for scarcely a quarter of an hour when, over a small portion of the audience, came an anxious, exciting feeling that to-night they were enjoying forbidden fruit. It was unthinkable that the bishop could have given his consent to some of the scenes. Furthermore, there could be no doubt that women were taking part in the performance. True, the notice had allotted all the parts to actors, but no eunuch could have tuned his voice to such charming, roguish intonations. Such warm, living femininity was inimitable. The soft flowing lines half-hidden by the pink bodices were unmistakably feminine. So too were the dainty wrists and the hands and the fingers, the pretty noses and charming mouths, the coquettish chins and shell-like ears. From the tops of their heads to their little satin shoes, these figures were certainly feminine; and their clear, sinful laughter seemed to mock the righteous assembled in the hall.

Yes, there they were, the undaunted guardians of morality, the enemies of pleasure and of sensual happiness. They were at their posts, finding compensation for the cost of their tickets in the satisfaction of their curiosity. As the play progressed, they sought support from one another by the exchange of glances charged with conscious virtue. When the scene in the moonlit park was reached, where the lovers Lelio and Smeraldina, Pantaloon's unfaithful wife, were depicted resting after love's sweet delights, and the marble Diana and Venus and Apollo and Hermes and other half-naked pagan gods stepped down from their pedestals and danced hand in hand round the slumbering pair, then the moralists felt that the moment for intervention had come. They cast a hail of indignant glances towards the podesta, who till that moment had been in an extraordinarily good humor, and who now felt that the burdensome official honor that ought to compel him to outrage his healthy human nature had been laid upon his shoulders by the devil. In irritation, he affected not to see the indignant glances cast at him; but when the play was held up by the stamping of feet, and by hissing and whistling, he was compelled to take some action. He nodded reassuringly to the interrupters and sent a note behind the scenes requesting an explanation for the unauthorized appearance of the ladies. A moment later, Harlequin bounded to the front of the stage, solemnly unfolded the note, and, to the great success of the evening, publicly read it aloud.

No mortal could have believed it possible that the mayor's short note could contain so many pitfalls for the reader. Three, four, five times Harlequin bounded forward preparatory to reading aloud the mayor's missive with the necessary dignity and respect; but ever and again he got confused in some turn of phrase or other, and not one member of the audience could in the end make head or tail of it. He put in commas and full stops where they did not occur. He ignored the end of a sentence, noticed his mistake, stopped, reread it, missed a line, which he afterwards put in in the wrong place, and ended in despair on a mysterious note of interrogation. He made it quite clear that there was no malice in the proceedings — on the contrary, he was so grimly determined to read it correctly, he addressed so many sincere apologies to the mayor's box, that no one could possibly take offense; and in the end, when half the audience was already in convulsions, the podesta himself could no longer restrain his laughter. But the more laughter he provoked, the more nervous grew

Harlequin. He implored them to respect this missive, which had been in-spired by virtue itself. He begged for careful attention once more, read the letter against the light, got upon his knees to read it, peered at it be-tween his outspread legs, in his despair even read it backwards, standing meanwhile upon his head. Now the words fell in complete chaos, like the tiny pieces of colored glass in a kaleidoscope — a waterfall of words that might all have occurred in the letter, but had lost the last connecting thread.

When at long last Harlequin succeeded in gathering them up again and stringing them together intelligibly, he wiped his sweating forehead with his sleeve and ended with a suggestion that finally disarmed the con-vulsed audience: the suggestion that the podesta in person should come onto the stage to convince himself that no woman stood upon the boards — at which all the actresses promptly *sat*.

The audience greeted this exhibition of virtuosity with thunderous ap-plause. Breathless with laughter, the podesta waved away Harlequin's in-vitation. But the moralists got up from their seats in a body and ostenta-tiously left the hall. As soon as he knew that all present were on his side, Harlequin no longer concealed his real anxiety as to what might follow; but, with half an eye on the mayor, who remained sitting in his box, the audience set Harlequin's anxiety at rest. "Go on! Go on with the play! They'll find the bishop in bed. To-morrow, Monsignore will have you turned out, but by then you'll be on your way in any case." Delighted, Harlequin laid his hand upon his heart, while the guilty actresses sprang to their feet and threw charming kisses to the audience.

No, to-night they were not to be deprived of their sinful pleasure. En-tranced and grateful, they stared at the beautiful, gaily dressed women. They listened to these gifted strangers who, with free and sparkling humor, could express in half a dozen words more of the things that matter than a man could experience in his whole lifetime. The company of strolling players carried the torch of truth, whose wonderful light they held aloft for one single night in the old, dark city of Todi.

Its glow was reflected on the faces of all in the hall. Right at the back, between two broad backs, bobbed a red young face from which the sweat was pouring: Monsignore's private secretary was praying, praying with all the power of his belief, that he might escape notice.

V

Early next morning the players rose. Short of sleep and shivering in the chill of dawn, they entered their traveling carriages. Gone was the

glorious aura that had surrounded their persons. Now they were a band
of tired, ill-humored men and women. Sad, expressive, furrowed faces
peered from the carriage windows; and the wanton beauties of yester-
night who, with their saucy cooing, had brought disquiet into the hall,
now held weary hands before yawning mouths still soiled with grease
paint.

Garotti was settling the bill with the innkeeper, and several of the others
still stood about abusing the limping man for the extortionate price he was
demanding for his rooms.

"You'd better pay," said Vacca. "You've done good business here, and
you won't get your carriages outside the city gate until you've settled your
account."

The previous evening Vacca had made no comment when Brighella
the villain had appeared wearing an apron and dragging his left foot. People in the audience had laughed, but Vacca had kept quiet, deciding
silently to double the charge for the rooms; and now it was his turn to
laugh. Finally, with a curse, Garotti paid him. The actress Corallina, who
had been too unwell to play, was behaving hysterically: ever since her
pregnancy began, she had worried the whole company with her hysteria,
and Garotti had allowed her and her child to travel with them from
Naples only out of compassion — he intended to get rid of her in Venice.
She was addressing a sort of homily to Vacca, the scoundrel. She stood
on her toes in front of him in order to be able to reach up to his face,
which stared down at her cynically while she conjured him thus: "Why
are you so bad? How can you be so bad? When you see yourself every
day in the innocent eyes of your child. And such a nice wife as you have,
too! The nicest woman I know, even though I did see her for the first time
last night . . ."

She was trembling in her whole slim body, and stopped as though she
were waiting for him to say something; but he remained silent, winking
towards the others who, irritated, were calling to her. She paid no attention, only said with an imploring gesture, "Just a moment longer! I've forgotten something. Don't drive off yet!"

She flew up the creaking wooden stairs, and was back again in a moment, deathly pale, in tears. Nervously, she nodded to the others who,
shaking their heads, were waiting for her. She pressed a little packet into
Vacca's hand. "Give this to your wife . . . from me," she said, and then
suddenly, completely losing her senses, she flung her arms round Vacca's
neck, kissed him, and tottered away. "I'm coming, I'm coming now."

Her friends drew her into the coach, and the procession got under way.
Unable to comprehend the meaning of this curious leave-taking, and of

the little packet in his hand, Vacca stood before the door of his inn, trying to save his face by adopting an attitude of brutal defiance. With a smile, he let the curses that came from the departing vehicles roll over his head, observed with silent mockery that fists were being shaken at him and that he was being spat at through the open windows. That little woman must have been quite mad: crying still, she was throwing him kisses from the coach. Slowly he nodded in response. "Good-by, ladies and gentlemen," he thought sarcastically, "it has been an honor and a pleasure!" Corallina's friends now seemed to be holding her back: it looked as though she were trying to get out again. He was very curious to know what precious thing the little packet contained.

The carriages had turned the corner. The clatter of hooves, the rattle of wheels was dying away. A strange silence crept over the inn. The two serving maids, who had stood by the vehicles up to the last in order to say good-by and to hand over this, that, and the other, came back into the inn. It was still early, and as they were far too excited to resume work (for whom, now that the strangers had departed?), they sat down by the fire to warm themselves, and to talk about these strange, wandering folk. You couldn't tell what they were really like. They ran you off your feet and snapped your head off into the bargain. They mocked you with grand words when they asked for shaving water; and yet they seemed to feel for you, asked you things about yourself. Whether you wanted to or not, you quite liked serving them, they were so plain and simple with you, and they really gave very good tips into the bargain. Camilla, who was to marry within the month, had received some ribbons and bows to sew on her wedding dress. Look, Nana! And also some delicate perfume to turn the head of a person called Cesare, a carrier on the Rome road. Ha! ha!

Turning his back towards them, Vacca went behind the counter and opened the little packet. A coin fell jingling from it. He stooped down hastily to pick it up and to examine it at close quarters, but the sound had already told him it was gold. There were more in the little packet. Also a few more or less precious ornaments. Stunned, he stared at the things, trying to understand. Slily he looked round, slipped the packet into his breeches pocket, and decided to go round to the hall to see what sort of state it was in. There he pulled the little packet out again, and reconsidered its contents, looking round suspiciously in the half-darkness of the empty hall.

What did she want from him? Why had she given him this? People do not give things away unless they expect something in return.

Perplexity drove him back to the taproom. While he was crossing the dark inner court, a feeling came over him very forcefully that perhaps, after all, he had been the one to be cheated that morning. He swore uncertainly.

Then he stumped upstairs, through the rooms which were topsy turvy as a result of the visit of that accursed brood of actors. Blankets lay about, empty grease paintpots, a pair of forgotten shoes. . . .

Nothing, nothing.

Downstairs he went again, his useless left leg bumping over the wooden stairs. He leaned heavily upon the rickety banisters. Halfway down, he stood still and pondered again on the fact that she had kissed him upon both cheeks. He broke out into perspiration. In the taproom once more, he snapped at the servants, telling them to go upstairs and clear up. Conscious of his bad temper, they obeyed. A little later, one of them came rushing downstairs again, and, out of breath, burst out with, "Padrone! Come quick!"

"What's the matter?"

"The child! They've left the child behind!"

Vacca's only answer was a convulsive laugh. Now he saw everything. They had left the child behind. They had saddled him with the child. If only he had realized that woman was the mother of the miserable brat! That explained the little packet, those kisses, here on his cheek.

He hoisted himself upstairs. In spite of everything, he could not help feeling more at rest now that uncertainty had vanished. His feelings had been justified. Now he was in front of the bed, where the child lay sleeping so restfully that he had overlooked it during his tour of inspection. He tried to make up his mind what he must do.

It was really simple enough. He could order the calash from the posting house and overtake them with the child. They could hardly have got beyond the city gate. Yes; but then she would demand the return of the little packet with the gold coins. Yes. . . . After all, he could also leave the child at the city hall. Nobody could expect him to turn his inn into a home for foundlings. And the maids had not seen the little packet.

Hastily he cast a look at the sleeping brat. Then he grinned at the serving maids. Raising himself by self-mockery above the ridiculousness of his position, he muttered sardonically: "They've put me in a fine fix."

The eyes of the servants were full of tears; and they did not know, themselves, whether it was from pity for the poor child or from indignation against its mother. Camilla felt such indignation that it was as if she herself had committed the deed, and as if strangers were now bending over *her* child. She clung to the bed, white as a sheet. Nana, the elder, said: "We'd better take it to the padrona. After all, she fed it yesterday."

Vacca looked at them, attentive and questioning.

"To keep it quiet! We were all watching. It drank the breast empty, and was then so satisfied that its mother stood by crying. But who would have thought she'd leave her child behind?"

"Only the padrona can save it," sobbed Camilla, and looked round at Vacca with hatred.

So only his wife could save it. To-day his wife was as indispensable as his hall had been yesterday.

He caught sight of a slip of paper that had been pushed half under the pillow. He took it towards the window, flattening it out to read what was written on it.

She is called Maria. She was baptized in Naples on the Feast of the Assumption of the Holy Virgin. My heart is bleeding for this deed. I shall never recover from it. Why is life so terrible? I cannot feed my child. This traveling is killing me, but I must follow him, her father. Rather than see her pine away in my arms, I prefer to let her go and know her contented and healthy. Curse me, but save my child. There are clothes for the first months. God alone knows what this is costing me. He will forgive me, just as He will bless the savior of my child, just as He will bless the milk that will nourish my baby.

The baby, awakening with a start at some noise, began to whimper. Nana and Camilla threw themselves down beside it. "*Poverella!* Poor little lamb!" Vacca closed the letter and limped downstairs.

As he had given no instructions yet as to what was to be done with the child, Nana was at liberty to pick it up and take it to the padrona. Oh, but if he had forbidden her to do that, she would have done it just the same!

A few hours later, Vacca crossed the piazza and asked urgently to speak to the podesta. Although the innkeeper related his discovery of the morning with anything but humor, the mayor could not help smiling when he heard with what these lighthearted birds of passage had saddled Vacca. He was still under the enchantment of yesterday's performance, fully prepared to bear Monsignore's displeasure. He was still thinking of Marinetta's dark mischievous eyes, and found it impossible to view the morning's events in a too pessimistic light.

"Vacca, show yourself a Christian, and rejoice that the Lord has given you the opportunity to perform a good deed! He will reward you, as this note says. For the time being, the only person who can do anything for the child is your wife. Afterwards, the City Council must decide what is to be done. Perhaps you'll be prepared to give the infant lodging at the city's expense?"

Yes, Vacca might be prepared to consider that idea, but he was gravely disappointed at being allowed to go away now empty-handed.

"But will you be put to any expense?" asked the podesta, and glancing at the letter added humorously, "It would seem that for the first months the baby is already provided for."

Hesitating, a subacid smile on his face, Vacca stared in front of him. He made the discovery, to his own unpleasant surprise, that he simply did not dare to charge the city for the milk with which bountiful nature had provided his wife. For one moment, he felt again the embrace of the slender, desperate mother, he felt her Judas kiss upon his cheek. It gave him a pain. It made him sick with himself and the whole world.

He dragged his leg back across the piazza. He was well aware that nobody was keen upon speaking to him in the street. But he did not care. He accosted people and told them the morning's news. He gave them secret satisfaction by making himself ridiculous in their eyes as he deplored this unwanted increase to his household — why *his* household? Then he roused their indignation by making it clear to them that greed for money had almost eliminated his humanity. He insisted that the city would have to fork out for the keep of this cuckoo egg — he wasn't going to spend a soldo on it. He had just been to tell the podesta so. Who had ever heard of a poor innkeeper turning himself into a charitable institution? So far as that was concerned, those ladies and gentlemen, the strolling players, might have acted more wisely if they had not chosen just him for the honor of receiving such a souvenir.

DOWN
THE CELLAR
STEPS

I

THE COUNCIL DID ACTUALLY MEET A FEW MONTHS later and voted Vacca a monthly grant of fourteen lire for the care of his foster child. For this sum he was to feed it, clothe it properly, and educate it in the spirit of Holy Mother Church. For the expenses of its first communion, and for its wedding trousseau, a modest amount was at the same time set aside by decision of the Council; but these sums Vacca was not allowed to touch. Fourteen lire a month — that was all. Vacca protested that he could not make both ends meet, especially as the child would gradually grow up, would wear out its clothes, and would soon be eating him out of hearth and home. For a whole year he did his utmost to get the grant raised to twenty lire. He wrote request upon request, he wore down the step of the city hall, until in the end nobody listened to him. The very clerks jeered at him as he came limping up the marble steps, dragging his left leg. But Vacca had the hide of a bull, and jeers were nothing to him.

In the course of time, the podesta could barely remember the alluring eyes of La Bella Marinetta. Five or six years had elapsed, and those eyes of hers would again be glittering at the Venetian carnival — unless they had lost their gleam. But in Todi the everyday routine of life had gone on steadily since that one magical night. Life was gray and monotonous, and must have appeared bitter to a man who had passed his student days at Pavia and Bologna. Besides, that famous October evening had brought in its wake a great deal of trouble and annoyance for the podesta. He had been blamed for his demeanor in the box — indeed, it had almost cost him his mayoral chair. He no longer smiled when he inquired about the child those vagabonds had left behind. After being obliged to listen to a half-outspoken reprimand in the Council, he had gone to some trouble to overtake the mother. He had sent several letters to Venice, but nobody there had cared a fig for the troubles of Todi's City Council. At last, an answer had come back, to the effect that the mother was no longer a member of the Garotti company and her address was unknown. . . .

"What's wrong now, Vacca? Have you come about that child again? I thought we were in agreement on the matter. You can't make ends meet on fourteen lire, and the Council refuses to pay more. Why do you keep coming to bore me about it?"

"You may be bored, but I feel it in my purse," insisted Vacca. "She costs me more every month. She's seven now."

"I have an excellent solution: regard her as your own child, and the fourteen lire as a recurring gift from heaven."

"I only need to look at her, Signor Podesta, to know she's no child of mine."

In spite of himself, malicious insinuations — plentiful as blackberries, and inspired by Vacca's not very attractive appearance — came into the mayor's mind. However, he refrained from giving expression to them, with some difficulty, and merely said, "Very well. Refuse to house the child any longer, and the Council will be compelled to use the fourteen lire to provide her with a roof elsewhere."

Vacca pulled a wry face, and suddenly lost something of his assurance. "Apart from the fact that you won't find a suitable home for her elsewhere for that money, I don't want to upset my wife. She's attached to the child."

"Then keep the child for your wife's sake, and stop worrying about a few lire," said the podesta, irritably.

"Keep it for your wife's sake," sighed Vacca, as he picked up his hat and departed aggrieved. The podesta rang his bell, and gave instructions to his clerk in unmistakable terms, that that was the last time that fellow was to be shown up.

But Vacca ceased his visits of his own accord — he had been silenced by the podesta's suggestion that another home should be found for the child. No doubt it was foolish, and perhaps the child really did cost him more than fourteen lire a month, for the amount was small enough, but everything in him revolted against losing this monthly allowance; and after all it was impossible to reckon up exactly what the child did cost. It was a vague sum that you scarcely noticed, and fourteen lire were certainly fourteen lire. Put into your hand once a month, in the course of a year they amounted to a hundred and sixty-eight lire, a hundred and sixty-eight lire.

But the little Maria knew nothing of all this. She played with the other children of her age on the steps of the cathedral opposite the inn. The marble pavement lent itself admirably to the drawing of lines for the game of hopscotch. At home in the counter there was a pigeonhole where chalk was to be found. Unobserved, she broke a little piece of it off and slipped out through the door. Her little friends waited impatiently for her, for she was the only one who had chalk. Sometimes the sexton chased them away because, even during Mass, they would not be quiet; and on Saturdays he scoured the chalk marks from the steps and threatened them with hell because they were desecrating the temple of God. The old bishop took a milder view of their play. He watched them smilingly from the windows of his palace hard by the cathedral, and nodded kindly to them when they looked up at him. The bishop was on their side, and therefore they cared not at all for the angry sexton's threats.

"Monsignore doesn't mind our playing hopscotch here," they said to him.

"I'm master in the church, and not Monsignore," growled the surly sexton.

The children were perplexed by this grotesque assertion. "You're a liar," they called out indignantly.

The little Maria was now seven years old. She was slender, and had thin but muscular arms and legs that were always torn and bruised. Playing hopscotch with little girls on the steps of the cathedral soon became too childish for her. She sought the companionship of boys, fought with them on occasion, and climbed walls with them. Her raven black, slovenly hair flowed in heavy curls over her frank forehead and her cheeks, bobbing carelessly up and down as she moved. In her bronzed face glowed a pair of great, wild eyes whose gaze it was disconcerting to meet. Vacca at least found it so when he sat in his domineering way at table. He held out against her direct gaze as long as he could, and then suddenly threw down his spoon and bellowed at her, "Look in front of you!"

The culprit grew pale and stared straight in front of her at her plate, as she had been ordered, but she could not control her glances. She simply had to watch him as he wolfed the titbits from the dish. With a frightful curse, he made as though to jump up, but she was already out of the door into the inner courtyard. Like the little Luigino, she was too quick for Vacca. Despite her haste, she had had time to seize her plate: though she might just as well have left it behind, for it was empty. Only when she was outside did she realize the full extent of her unhappiness. With anger and despair, she flung the plate against the stones. His face congested, Vacca bobbed up behind the window. Marietta fled through the alley by the inn and up the street, until she felt herself safe. Haughtily she brushed away her tears, and gloried in the plate smashed to smithereens.

After an hour of aimless wandering, she could resist her hunger no longer, and began to rage and curse at Vacca. She had already learned to repeat his curses — words full of a vague, bewildering menace that echoed like thunder within her and made her shiver even as she uttered them against him in her thoughts. Hunger drove her through the whole city like a mad rat. She wondered whether she should go home again, and take the beating that awaited her, with the prospect that afterwards she would get something to eat from Nana in the kitchen. The difficulty of coming to a decision brought the sweat out on her forehead. Suddenly she re-appeared at the door of the inn, trembling in her whole body, and looked at Vacca with that same glance that had infuriated him at table — if she had not been so terribly afraid of him, she would have looked at the ground in contrition.

"What? You've dared to come back?"

"I'm hungry."

"Hungry? You come along with me." He seized her arm, which he could have encircled twice with his hand, and dragged her to the cellar. Marietta tried to bite and scratch. When she was alone in the frightful darkness, she kicked against the bolted door with all her might. "Let me out! Hangman! Murderer of children!"

In the taproom sat customers, and they would have been deaf if they had not heard the loud cries coming from the cellar. Vacca grew purple with rage, wrenched the door open again, and kicked at her viciously with his stiff left leg as she escaped. But she was too quick for him, and slithered into the kitchen — where Nana received her with open arms, ready to defend her if necessary with her own life. Vacca, however, vaguely realiz-ing as his rage subsided that the little devil's incredible quickness had prob-ably saved him more than once from seriously injuring her, went back to the taproom, and remarked, half-ashamed of himself, "And *I* must be saddled with this devilish brat!"

Meanwhile, in the kitchen, the little Maria hungrily devoured what Nana had saved from her own plate for "that poor lamb." Nana had called her that on the fatal morning that saw the departure of the players, and she had had no occasion to revise her opinion since. With a doting expres-sion, she stood watching Marietta as she ate her supper.

"Nana," said Marietta, as she gathered up the last bit from her plate, "I love you better than Mother."

Fearful, Nana made the sign of the cross. "You mustn't say such a thing, Marietta. It's sinful to say such a thing. . . ."

Marietta did not look up as she continued obstinately, "Mother would not have stood in front of me, as you did, when he came in."

This was too much for Nana. She wanted to say something more, but suddenly began to cry instead. Calmly Marietta got up from the table, flung her arms round Nana's neck and gave her a flood of kisses of unexpected warmth. The strangest feelings came over Nana. At last she pushed her away, and said, "Stop! Please stop! I won't listen, the way you talk about your mother. She's afraid of him. She looks stout and big, but she's not strong, and soon you'll have another little brother or sister. Didn't you know? He's more afraid of me than he is of her, because he's always afraid I may run away, or talk to people. Go away now, Marietta."

Marietta sprang panting and laughing towards the door; her dark eyes were gleaming. Perhaps she had heard nothing of what Nana was saying. She pulled a grimace, and was off up the street, suddenly carefree once more, now that hunger no longer tormented her.

II

It would soon be autumn again. Marietta knew every nook and cranny of the little city. She was the youngest of a band of young rascals who filled the summer evenings with their pranks, and she it was who always carried out the most daring of their exploits. She did not steal fruit for herself, but for the band; proudly she handed over the booty, and proudly she listened to the exaggerated praises with which it was received.

"Marietta, how *did* you get away with it again? You're so devilish quick."

But in the sharing out of the booty she was always forgotten, until one day this fact dawned upon Marietta, and she said timidly as she watched the distribution: "And what about me? Don't I get anything?" The others looked at her in astonishment, as they sucked up the juice of the peaches from their dripping fingers. Giuseppe, the leader of the band, grinned at her as he answered: "You? A little tot like you can have its share another time."

Marietta paled with indignation. She stood on tip toe in front of Giuseppe, intending to give him a piece of her mind, but the words refused to come, and instead she gave him a ringing slap on his cheek and immediately fled into the twilight. In vain he went raging after her.

During the days and weeks that followed she had to be perpetually on her guard to avoid meeting him and his band. She found herself compelled to fall back upon the companionship of her brother; but Luigino was a difficult playfellow. He was as silent as a fish, and as unfriendly. The children who played on the piazza said he was a sneak, and refused to let him join in their games. Marietta was completely his master. She was a leader among the children of her own age, whereas he was nothing. Once she felt herself personally injured by the contempt in which he was held, dragged him along with her, and insisted, "If you don't mind, he's going to play with us. He's my brother." But she soon saw how useless he was, and she herself sent him home: "Go away!" she commanded, "run along home! If you can't do anything, go and play with your dull old bottles. Idiot!" Silently, Luigino obeyed, and went home to play with the empty bottles of the inn, dragging them about behind him in a row, one after the other, all over the cellar, or up the stone steps. He didn't seem to mind that the others refused to play with him. He was accustomed to being alone, even at home, where Nana invariably chased him out of the kitchen whenever she found him there.

But now Marietta was forced to seek his companionship. He knew well enough that she came to play with him for want of something better, but he said nothing, and they went together into the cellar. That was his kingdom, and there he was king. Marietta was not allowed to move a bottle without his permission, and even then she did everything wrong and he had continually to put things to rights. She was absentminded and unhappy, and looked on timidly while he showed her how to play his games with these hundreds of empty bottles. They could be turned into armies, processions, funeral companies. Marietta stood looking dreamily at these masses of bottles.

In the late afternoon a silent, mysterious dusk crept into the cellar. The outline of the bottles grew vague, and a feeling of oppression came over Marietta, as she helped Luigino to clear up the muddle they had made without listening to his instructions as to where this kind and that kind must stand. Then she slipped out of the cellar, out of the inn, and thankfully breathed the evening air outside in the street.

It was the hour of the daily plundering expedition, and restlessness forced her, in spite of danger, to the usual meeting place of the band. She found them gathered together outside Racioppi's watching Racioppi and his two sons, Carlo and Romano, pressing the grapes with their bare feet, their backs bent so that they should not knock their heads against the ceiling of the low stone vault. His wife stood by holding a stable lantern.

Marietta too watched, fascinated. Suddenly, Giuseppe seized her by the neck. "So you've come back again, you little vermin!" he shouted.

She made no movement to free herself, merely said, "I want to join in this evening!"

Giuseppe burst out laughing. Satisfied that he had shown his authority before the others, he released her, and said: "All right, you say what we're to do!"

Grapes were lying there ready to be seized, but the band had already eaten so many that they were satiated with them — the sour smell of the wine presses hung about in every street these days. Marietta knew a better scheme. "Let's go and take corn cobs from Brogi, and roast them somewhere."

Her scheme met with general agreement. Half an hour later, they were roasting heavy yellow-gold cobs stolen from Brogi, the grain merchant, over a fire that had been kindled just outside one of the city gates. An invigorating smell as of warm bread rose round their unwashed, uncombed heads. This time, Marietta did not have to ask for her share of the booty. "Here, Marietta, here are two for you" — just as though that had been the usual thing.

Meanwhile, Vacca had gone to the cellar — and slipped over a bottle left lying on the stone steps. His right foot skidded on the smooth, rolling bottle; his weak left leg gave way. He fell, striking the back of his head so hard as to lose consciousness. In his loosening grasp, he still held the candle he had brought to light the way. The flame continued to flicker, licking round the greasy horsehair of his wig: it really looked as though he were deliberately setting himself on fire.

Only Luigino, who was making water in the alley, heard the soft thud of his falling body and the rattle of the bottle as it rolled away down the steps. Full of fear, he rushed into the kitchen and confronted Nana. As usual, she went for him. "Heavens above! You're always giving people a fright! Get out! I won't have you here." But Luigino held his ground, and when Nana ran to him and tried to push him out of the kitchen, he suddenly found his voice and shouted, "Father's on fire!"

Nana shrieked and hurried towards the cellar, to find that Vacca had regained consciousness through pain, had shaken off the burning wig, and was trying to stand up. Luigino shouted to them, "It was Marietta who was playing with the bottles!" and then fled upstairs to his mother.

Groaning loudly, Vacca hobbled with Nana's help into the taproom and sat down. He stared before him with dazed eyes. His close-shaven head was covered with blisters, and a customer, in an effort to be helpful, imprudently bathed it with wine, which caused Vacca to roar aloud with pain.

Convinced that he was about to die, he repeated to everyone who came near him, "I've seen death! I've seen death!" The surgeon barber from the piazza was hastily summoned. He bandaged his head, and tried to console him by reminding him that it might have been worse. Gradually Vacca grew calmer, and then he began to relate to the customers gathering in the inn exactly how the accident had happened. Despite his mortal anxiety, he seemed to have heard what Luigino had shouted from the corridor, for he kept saying: "That little cuckoo they left in my nest wanted to murder me! I've thought as much for a long time. She put the bottle on purpose so that I should break my neck. When I get hold of her, I'll break every bone in her body! To think that such a thing can happen to a man under his own roof, done by a child that isn't his, either . . ."

Nana, realizing suddenly the danger in which Marietta stood, left the inn and waited outside in the gloaming for her return.

When Marietta, warm with running, reached the piazza and was stopped by Nana, she knew at once that something unusual must have happened, for Nana never left her kitchen except to go to early Mass.

"Child," gasped Nana, kissing her nervously, "you mustn't go home. He'll beat you to death."

"What have I done?" asked Marietta rebelliously; her voice had a contemptuous ring that made her, for a moment, seem older than Nana.

"You left a bottle on the cellar steps. He slipped over it, and set his wig afire, and now his face and head are covered with blisters. The barber had to bandage him up."

Marietta stood speechless. "I want to see for myself," she said, when she found her voice again. "Where is he?" She escaped from Nana, flew to the inn, and, jumping on the bench outside, peered through the window. Nana, coming up behind her, seized her frock. "Marietta, come away! He'll beat you if he sees you!"

Marietta took no notice. She could see that she was in no immediate danger, for Vacca sat helpless in his chair, surrounded by a sort of guard of honor of solicitous customers. His head was swathed in white bandages, and his appearance was half-dignified, half-ridiculous. Under that odd headdress, his eyes had lost their power to terrify her. Fascinated by the whole scene, she could not tear herself away. With a sly, mischievous snigger, she looked round at Nana, and her eyes wandered over the piazza: little playmates might enjoy the spectacle too, and it was her handiwork — at least, if what Nana said was true, that it was she who had left the bottle

on the steps, and not Luigino. Now they were all looking at something. What could it be? Wild with curiosity, Marietta stretched out her thin little body, pressing her nose and lips flat against the windowpane in order to see. Oh, it was his wig. A great hole had been burned in it, and the queue, bound in black worsted, was twisted by the heat like a pig's.

At last, she paid attention to Nana's nervous insistence. She jumped down, and beginning to realize the punishment that threatened her on her home-coming, said, "Can't you hide me in your room, Nana?"

"Lord, no! That would never be safe. Suppose he found you there. But go to Camilla's and ask her if you can sleep there. She won't send you away, for she cried over you when you were only ten weeks old . . ."

As she stared into the dusk, Nana saw all over again the finding of the infant Marietta. "Quick," she exclaimed, "run! Just tell Camilla I sent you."

Camilla, long married and the mother of several children, had ceased to cherish the same vivid memory as did Nana of that fateful morning when the players departed. Other deep impressions — births, sickness — had passed over her like waves, almost eradicating the memories of the years before her marriage. Nana, whose life had passed gray and monotonous, and whose whole repressed maternal feeling went out to Marietta, had not thought of that. It was with some misgiving that Camilla saw the small, excited Marietta storm into her home and listened silently to her plastic story of what had happened. When Marietta had finished, Camilla said, "All right, come along with me. We'll go to him together. I'll put in a good word for you."

Terrified, Marietta realized that Camilla had no idea of the extent of her danger. She clenched her teeth in wild anxiety, and, suddenly seeing how well fed Camilla was, how stupid and self-satisfied her eyes, she exclaimed, "Nothing will make me go to him."

"Then you must have told me a pack of lies, and you're afraid I'll find out."

"Ask Nana if I've told lies. Ask Nana what he'll do if I go home. It was she who sent me here."

Still doubtful, Camilla looked at her, as if trying to probe the truth be-hind her words. Finally she said, "All right. My husband will be home soon . . . You'd better have something to eat with us."

Without more ado, Marietta sat down to table, where the macaroni stood ready. Hungrily, she devoured more than the other three children put together. Camilla watched in silence. She was vaguely disquieted by the emaciated little body, the thin little face; but she was not far-seeing enough to guess the simple reason. Instead, she thought within herself, "It's easy to see that the child came from no ordinary cradle, and hasn't been properly brought up either. She's only eight and she talks like a grown-up, and her eyes are almost frightening."

She made several commonplace remarks, to which Marietta gave commonplace answers, eating the while.

"How's your mother?"

"Fine!"

"I've seen nothing of her lately."

"No, she's always upstairs."

"Why doesn't she come down?"

"Oh, she's waiting for another baby."

Camilla wondered if this was meant as a joke, but Marietta's remark was due merely to childish ignorance. In case Camilla was still in doubt as to why her mother remained upstairs, she added between two bites, "She's always ill."

Camilla changed the subject. "And Luigino? Do you get on with him all right?"

"Oh, fine!"

"I never seem to see you together."

"No, when he plays in the street he plays with girls."

"And you?"

"I play with boys."

"Yes, I've heard about the mischief you're all up to," said Camilla, severely.

At this moment, her husband Cesare came in. He looked at his guest with astonishment.

He was a great, hulking fellow with heavy, hairy wrists, and a kindly bulldog face to which formidable bristling eyebrows gave an air of involuntary menace. All four little heads looked up and nodded in response to his greeting; it was the first time that Marietta had heard his voice. He was famous for saying little, but it was rumored that, as he sat on the box of his freight wagon, he sang lustily on his weekly journey to Rome, thereby frightening away the robbers of the Campagna.

But Camilla talked enough for two. With much repetition, she told him why Marietta was there, but he already knew the story — it had flown round the city, greatly exaggerated in transit. He had called at the inn, and gave it as his view that things were not as bad as had been made out, and that Marietta could safely go home.

"I wanted to take her back," said Camilla, "but she says Nana sent her here."

"Oh, she says that, does she?" He looked at his wife in perplexity, waiting for her to decide.

Marietta, trembling at their indecision, said emphatically, "If you won't let me stay here, I know something will happen."

Anxious in spite of themselves, the two grown-ups looked at her. "What would happen?" asked Cesare doubtfully.

Marietta could not well tell what might actually happen. She said nothing, and merely looked at Camilla and her husband with her great dark eyes.

"But surely you can tell my wife," said Cesare softly. "Did you leave that bottle intentionally?"

"If anybody did it, it was that sneak of a Luigino!"

Camilla shook her head disbelievingly, and exclaimed, "Luigino? His own father?"

"And if not Luigino, why should I?" broke in Marietta indignantly.

The two grown-ups looked at each other. For the first time, there rose clearly before Camilla's eyes a vision of that autumn morning of eight years ago. Her closed heart, completely absorbed in her own domestic cares, suddenly opened, and this wild-eyed child, cruelly abandoned by her own parents, found a corner in it. After all, Marietta too was one of God's creatures, and as such had a right to pity.

"All right. Let her stay for to-night," she decided. Cesare nodded, and said, "Then we can see what happens to-morrow."

When she heard this decision, Marietta had difficulty in restraining her tears, so intense was the reaction after the anxiety and emotion she had gone through. Without a word, as if she had lost the power of speech, she allowed herself to be put to bed with the other children, and immediately fell asleep.

Camilla and her husband continued to discuss her situation: evidently the poor little wretch did not even know yet that Vacca was not her father.

It came back to Camilla now, how *she* used to tremble before Vacca. By the side of her strong Cesare, she had forgotten her old fears. She went and looked at the children, and the sight of Marietta's curly head lying upon the pillow among the others, as if she too were one of them, brought a swelling to Camilla's heart that astonished and impressed her. Strangely agitated, she fled from the bedroom and, creeping up to her husband on tiptoe, threw her arms about him. He turned his head in astonishment. Then, understanding, he looked up at her suddenly with a vague, happy emotion. But she was immediately seized with the fear that came over her every Saturday and Sunday evening, when Cesare was not on the way to Rome, but at home, and the time had arrived for them to go to bed together — fear of his power over her heart, of his silent, hungry love, and of what might again result from it, the cowardly fear that was destroying the happiness of her marriage, and made her go about with a chronic sense of inferiority.

She eluded Cesare's outstretched arms and turned away from him, to look for her mending. But she still felt the drunken, bashful, lustful look with which he regarded her.

III

That night, Vacca was tormented by the pain of his burnt head and his twisted back; and his pregnant wife did not improve his temper by fits of nervous weeping for the absent brat who had nearly succeeded in breaking his neck. At last, he could stand it no longer. With a curse, he got up, put on his slippers, and staggered with a candle towards Nana's room.

Nana was awake, and heard him come. She thanked heaven that she had not hidden Marietta in her room. From the open door Vacca, clad in nightcap and shirt, bellowed, "You know where she is. Don't deny it!"

Nana was surprised to discover how little she feared him at the moment. She snarled back at him, "All I know is that the poor child is too terrified to come home."

"As if she could have had any idea what had happened here!"

"Any idea! She would have known nothing, if I hadn't waited for her and told her!"

"Oh, you did that, did you? That's a fine piece of work. The little brat makes me almost break my neck, and then you send her off up the street in the night, and I shall have to answer at the city hall for that."

This was a new aspect of the situation. Nana looked at him hesitatingly, and, taking advantage of her uncertainty, Vacca said meekly, resting his hand upon his burning head, "Well, now, tell me where she is. I can then at least put my wife at rest."

"I'll see if I can get the child home to-morrow morning; but I won't unless you promise not to beat her," said Nana decisively.

Nana's half-promise was a great relief to Vacca. "All right," he conceded. "She deserves to be beaten black and blue, but I'll let her off lightly. Tell her that. Tell her I've too much here," pointing to his head, "to think of thrashing her into the bargain." He tottered out of the room, reported his conversation with Nana to his wife, and then dropped off to sleep like a log.

Nana in her attic pondered long on what he had meant exactly when he pointed to his head. She saw again in her mind's eye his swollen, bandaged skull, and came to the conclusion that he must have meant that it gave him too much pain when he lifted his hands for it to be worth his while to beat Marietta.

There was something almost grotesque about their meeting next morning. Yielding finally to the united pressure of Nana, Camilla, and Cesare, Marietta appeared, white and in tears, at the inn. She could not believe in the forgiveness she was assured had been accorded her. She could not imagine that Vacca had suddenly become as gently disposed as a lamb, and was prepared to fly at his first suspicious movement. Vacca was at his post behind the counter. The bandage round his head had lost its freshness. He had pushed it up untidily, and it had become a sort of turban under which he glared distrustfully at Marietta.

Several customers were in the taproom.

"So there you are again, idiot! Have you come back to see if I'm dead? You wouldn't have cared. I knew you were capable of a lot, but not of this" — pointing gravely to his head. "Well, say something."

Marietta had nothing to say. His conciliatoriness reduced her to silence. There he sat, pale, suffering, conscious of the nobility of his attitude, distinguished by the curious white headdress that dropped over one squinting eye like a miter awry.

She was conscious too of a suspicion of uncertainty in his voice, as if he had suddenly, since yesterday, grown a little afraid of her. It was on the tip of her tongue to say, "It may just as well have been Luigino who left the bottle on the step," but something held the words back.

Vacca sent her upstairs to her mother, who was sitting, her hands upon her stomach, leaning back in her chair. It was a tearful face drawn with pain that she turned towards Marietta. Her mother seemed so strange that Marietta was seized with a sudden fear, and, without a word, threw herself down by her side.

How long was it since one of her children had come to cry its eyes out by her side? She was like a ghost in the house, a pale, noiseless ghost who sometimes called very softly from upstairs, as if she were almost afraid. But Marietta sobbed her heart out by her side, clinging convulsively to her mother's knees, and letting her hot tears flow upon those weak, heavy, cool thighs. The pregnant woman ran her hand caressingly through the child's hair, stammering, "You too are my child, you too. Last night, I couldn't sleep because of you . . . But you shouldn't have done that."

Nana came upstairs and, impelled by an uncomfortable feeling she did not understand, put an end to this weak weeping between mother and child. "Go downstairs," she said sharply to Marietta. "You're upsetting your mother." Marietta, recalled to actuality, slipped downstairs. She tried to glide unnoticed into the kitchen, but Vacca caught sight of her, and called her to him to show her to newly arrived customers as an object of curiosity. He declared in her presence, as a matter of unmistakable fact, that she had left the bottle on the stair intentionally. "With such a mischievous imp, you have to be careful," he said with a grin.

Without realizing it, he was growing proud of her. He reveled in her youthful demonic quality, and in the perpetual danger in which he lived. When he was alone with her, he would sometimes look inquiringly at her with a surly grin. When they went downstairs together, he made her go in front of him. From that time, he punished her only with sarcasm. He never beat her again. When he was in a good mood, he allowed her to come into the taproom to amuse his customers with her marvelous talent for mimicry, which even brought Nana out of the kitchen. With her great, dangerous eyes, the child appeared to see both the ridiculous and the unusual in the people about her. She had a striking knack of imitating voices, even a man's heavy bass. Vacca could not help laughing — a hoarse, wheezing, unexpected laugh that split his mouth asunder like a frog's. He winked at the others; but he did not know how perfectly Marietta imitated that very laugh and wink when she was alone with Nana.

Vacca's fall in the cellar was thus something of a blessing for Marietta; and this blessing seemed to descend upon Vacca also, for two weeks later, when he had given up all hope, he was informed that the Council had decided to raise Marietta's allowance from fourteen to twenty lire. Even at the city hall, they must have heard something of the injury he had suffered and the blow he had received from his foster child.

On that day, he decided to replace the burnt wig by a new one — a particularly handsome one, chestnut brown with a natural wave, and with a queue such as gentlefolks wore. Rejuvenated and beautified, Vacca rose like the phoenix from the ashes.

But fate, always jealous, spoilt his pleasure: his wife gave birth to a stillborn child.

THE

LIVING

PREVAIL

I

THE BRASS BELL BOOMED SOLEMNLY OVER THE QUIET city. If the noise went on much longer, it seemed that even the dusty stones, the petrified walls of the houses must listen in the end. The deathly stillness of the streets was filled with metallic reverberations. A door slammed here and there, hasty footsteps resounded for a moment, and then again no sound remained but the booming of the bell, the booming of the bell.

Every shutter was closed, every doorway framed in black crape. Out of a solitary grimy chimney, a pale gray feather of smoke rose into the blue, sunny heavens that stretched, taut and wide, over the town and the green mountains.

Carlino, the thin sexton, was ringing the bell. His face drawn with grief, his eyes darkly ringed, he swayed at the end of the rope, first touching the ground with his downward pointing toes, then sagging at his limp knees, then dragged upward again by the weight of the massive bell. Carlino was like some soul longing to rise up to heaven, but too material to shake himself free from this world and compelled therefore to dance this macabre dance to the torrent of sound that fell from the brass bell.

Deep down in the cathedral, the organ sounded, sending a shiver of emotion through the citizens who, pressed body to body, filled the floor space so completely that there was no room left to kneel. From the sculptured benches of the choir, the rusty bass of the priests droned forth, re-echoed an octave higher from the cloister opposite, where a badly trained group of children were singing the Dies Irae in voices as pitiless as they were clear — voices that were all the more moving because of their lack of concern, as free from earthly grief as must be the voices of the angels in the heavenly choirs.

Monsignore was dead.

Opposite the high altar, surrounded by flickering wax candles in tarnished silver candelabra, lay the dead bishop on a bier in the full panoply of mourning. The pearls, rubies, and emeralds on his silver-stitched silk miter, on the chasuble and on the robe, glittered and sparkled. On his white hands, which lay in the attitude of prayer, an amethyst gleamed mysteriously, as though it were, like a star, its own source of light. From a distance, the bier seemed to be a treasure chest illumined by candles.

The sickly smell that was already rising from the dead body was becoming obscured by the incense that was wafted solemnly over the bier.

Among the singing children stood Marietta, now twelve years old, and already noticeable among the older girls who surrounded her. Like them, she was dressed in black, with a blue gauze veil over her head — only the youngest were dressed in white. Singing with the others, pleased at the sound of her own full clear voice, against which the voices of the others sounded shrill, she glanced through half-closed eyelids towards the dead bishop there below as towards something she could not yet understand. Then, hastily, she brought her gaze back to the choir benches where, in colorful ranks, sat the prelates who had traveled from Perugia, from Orvieto, and even from Rome, upon the news that the old bishop of Todi lay in the article of death. She was disturbed by the coarse remarks of the boys who, in the intervals of singing, were making fun of some of the strange priests. With satisfaction she heard a deacon reprimand these little wretches dressed in their first communion suits: this unusual day had gone to their heads. She could see very well that the second canon in the front row on the left had a curious big nose, and she had noticed the pale, thin creature who sat between two fat-necked companions; but to-day she felt no desire to laugh at these human oddities.

Oh, no: for Monsignore was dead.

Strange tidings indeed they seemed, impressive in their magnitude, and having a restraining influence even upon the children — that a being so other-worldly as a bishop could die suddenly like any ordinary mortal. The boys and girls were constrained as they thronged in front of Gabriele Buongiorno's little workshop, where he was busily hammering together the coffin of the deceased, running backwards and forwards in distraction as he measured and adjusted his work, hardly giving himself time to wipe his clammy forehead. Then came liberation with the preparations that had to be made for the ceremony. All the citizens were involved, and, in the excitement, it occurred to nobody to remember that good old Monsignore would never again cross the piazza at exactly half-past ten on his way to celebrate the second morning Mass. As he lay there solitary in his hollow, echoing, somber, closed palace, he was forgotten in the glory of the unwonted appearance of important ecclesiastics from Rome, in the gratification felt by all at the sudden significance this little forgotten hill city had assumed. Money flowed into the grasping hands of the mourning citizens: Monsignore's death was proving their gain, not their loss.

And there he lay, among his faithful penitents, and soon he would leave for all time his cathedral, his city, its inhabitants; and still he lay solitary among them, buried under the cold pride of the jewels whose glitter he had not sought while he lived. More important than the hour of his death itself, when only two or three had been by him, seemed now the glory of this burial service. To attend it, peasants living hours away had come jogging in their carts through the city gates at crack of dawn; while in response to the summons carried by express couriers costly coaches bearing coats of arms and cardinal's hats on their doors had come pounding along from baithouse to baithouse, changing their foam-covered horses at every stopping place in order to be sure to reach Todi in time.

And, in the middle of the long-drawn-out Mass, to one here and there came a vague realization that, in taking part in this imposing ceremony, they had entirely forgotten to take leave in silence of the man who now suddenly rose before them in his simplicity above all this pomp. Looking shyly towards the bier, those close by experienced the sensation that more impressive, more beautiful than all the array of jewelry was the old, wax-pale face of the bishop himself, transfixed in noble peace. Others who had passed the bier recalled the blue-gray eyes, sunk in their dark sockets, and overshadowed now by the rim of the miter, which had given to that face such a strange penetrating expression. Gradually a new tender emotion swept over the congregation, and in many hearts a secret wound opened, a silent grief was felt, that could find no assuagement in the glory of this day. Women whispered to one another that the bishop had just given them a glance that was no longer of this world. . . .

Marietta, waiting for the moment when the choir had to fall into the procession, began to be conscious of this wave of new emotion. Everything in her was tense and alive. She gazed at the weeping women and then again at the bier, and suddenly there came to her the expectation that a miracle would happen.

For a long time, she had been absorbed by a mystery that had segregated her from her former playfellows. Just when Luigino began to roam about the city with boys of his own age, indulging in coarse language and pulling little girls' hair, Marietta almost ceased to stir from the house. Every afternoon she sat upstairs with her mother, sewing and mending. Her mother was again expecting a baby — it seemed that that was why she was so swollen and ill, and Nana had had the awful foreboding that "it would again go wrong."

To Marietta had come an awakening, an impulse to know, to understand. She felt that she was surrounded by mystery — the mystery of life itself, the mystery of birth, of being, of dying. The grown-ups seemed to know all about it, even stupid Camilla, who came visiting at the inn, bringing little parcels containing baby clothes. Without a word, this twelve-year-old child was pricking up her ears, spying out Nana's and Camilla's glances, trying to get to the bottom of things.

There must be mysteries in this world, or else people would not behave so mysteriously. Why were they hidden, these mysteries? She hungered for revelation. The mystery of death here appeared to be bound up by invisible threads with the mystery of birth at home. For a moment, she had the feeling that perhaps everything was one, one great mystery. If she could fathom it, everything would suddenly become clear.

Towards the other little girls of her own age, who had recently come to greet her with surprise and suspicion when she walked across the piazza before vespers, she maintained a haughty reserve as if she herself already had to guard the all-comprehending mystery. Their whispered chatter about the grown-ups, their teasing, tittering demeanor towards each other did not arouse her curiosity. What can they know about it, she thought, when even I don't know? She carried her head proudly upon her long, supple neck. Her voice had grown deeper, and sometimes had the throaty unmistakable tone of womanhood, which made Vacca start and glance at her childish form and at the adolescent curves of her breast. Her eyes, catching his, were no longer wild and unbridled, although they had not lost their penetrating power; they could moreover express a quiet contempt that turned Vacca's bad temper into mute rage.

The funeral service had come to an end. Monsignore was about to be taken to his last resting place, the consecrated ground near the convent of Saint Clare.

The nuns who inhabited the convent were forbidden by their rule to take part in the stately procession. Two by two in their black hoods, they got up and walked quickly out behind their abbess. They were in a hurry, because they wanted to arrive in time to observe the ceremony from behind the barred windows of their cells.

Meanwhile, members of the Brotherhood of Christian Mercy gathered round the coffin to screw down the lid. A macabre stillness descended upon the church; the tolling of the bell continued, but apart from its booming there was no noise save the creaking and shuffling of the Brothers' shoes. The congregation stretched their necks: they wanted to see the golden bishop's staff and the other golden symbols of ecclesiastical power, taken from the dead and carefully carried, piece by piece, to the sacristy. Those costly vestments had merely been laid loosely over the body. The gray head was raised by respectful hands, and the miter was taken off. Then the old beloved bishop lay there in stainless lawn and gossamer lace, which, a testimony to the devout industry of the ladies of Todi, was to descend with him into the grave. No one could fail any longer to remember the good, simple man who had also been a venerated Prince of the Church. Women, weeping passionately, tried to press forward to kiss his feet that were swathed in white velvet.

Choirboys and deacons prepared to make a passage towards the main door, where Franciscan friars had already begun to form the procession. Right in front, a venerable old monk with a beard took his place, carrying a draped oak cross. Carlino hung sidewise at the bell rope as he rang, so that he could see that everything went off as it should. Behind the Franciscan friars followed the other orders, and then the musicians, the acolytes, the priests, the juvenile choir, and the Brothers of Christian Mercy, who had taken it upon themselves to carry the coffin alternately along the whole route. After them, the authorities, the people . . .

The Franciscans helped one another to light the candles they were to carry in their hands: one small flickering flame multiplied itself into a hundred small flickering flames. Before picking up the coffin on their shoulders, the Brothers of Mercy pulled over their heads their somber, black, pointed hoods with the ghostly eyeholes: they seemed to have come from the kingdom of death to fetch the bishop.

Shuffling over the marble pavement, the procession set itself in motion. The praying of the Franciscan friars billowed through the wide edifice, dying in the dusky passages behind the pillars. The children, again constrained, fell in, in orderly fashion, pushed into their places by nervous guiding hands. First the little toddlers in white, then the boys in their first communion suits, then the older girls, each carrying a burning candle in their hand, all muttering together between their teeth, all staring in front of them towards the door, which stood open and aglow with the sunlight above the darkly silhouetted procession. In the portico they came to a standstill. The children stood with their chins pressed against each other's shoulders, holding their candles on one side in order not to set fire to each other's clothes and staring with frightened eyes to the left, where Carlino could be seen being dragged up on high by the bell rope as he sobbed aloud — that same Carlino who chased them away on Saturdays from the cathedral steps.

The sunshine, the robust life outside dispelled the magic of the dark interior. Coaches came rolling up, and the important ladies who preferred to ride rather than to walk in the procession stepped into them. Suddenly, with a blaring of trumpets, the funeral music broke out. The horses of the rich Galli family began to rear, and a speckled stallion tore down a guild banner with its hooves. Old Signora Galli, in her tall wig, looked out of her coach window in fright, and promised at once that any damage should be made good; but money could not obliterate this ill omen.

The gray-bearded monk with the cross who led the procession had already stepped out of the city gate, while the end was still forming in front of the cathedral. Many of those who walked in it carried huge homemade wreaths decorated with ribbons bearing decorous inscriptions.

From the city to the convent was almost an hour's walk, and the way seemed long under the hot spring sun. Above the vineyards the air seemed to stand still. A few white clouds drifted slowly over the mountains.

In front, the funeral music continued, but with ever longer interruptions. Like a confidential, vague buzzing, the praying of the Franciscan brothers floated back to where Marietta was walking. Behind her, she could hear the doleful Miserere sung by the women. The children had already given up the singing that had been arranged for them, and chatted together, smothering their laughter and calling out. The boys, having hit on the unseemly joke of dropping out of the procession on the plea that "they could hold out no longer," stood at the side of the road with bowed heads, and faces red with suppressed chortles, like a row of little fountains. The older girls said to one another, "No, but look at those louts! How dare they! Look, Marietta!" Her head erect, Marietta breathed in deeply the country air mixed with dust and incense, and struggled with all that was confused, all that was unexplained in this day. Were the grown-ups right to cry? She could not believe so yet. Within her, she felt a continued tension, a strange rising expectation; the crying of the women did not convince her, but the vision of Carlino pursued her. How he had hung there at the end of the bell rope!

Round a bend, between dark cypresses and wild twisted pines, rose the calm white walls of the convent.

There was not room for everyone in the small cemetery, not by a long way. The children, however, were let in immediately after the coffin. They had to sing by the grave, so that Monsignore might hear at the very end the voices he had loved most. As she passed them, Marietta looked at the disturbed faces of the sobbing women. Something about this uncontrolled, unfeigned grief shocked her.

The children stood round the grave, waiting while the speeches were made, until it was their turn to sing. Signor Orlandi, the podesta, expressed the loss Todi had suffered in losing its old bishop, and in particular what he himself would miss in the way of counsel and support in the carrying out of his responsible duties. He feared that this task in future would fall very heavy upon him. Signor Orlandi had grown corpulent and short of breath. He had had one heart attack, and at a little distance from the grave people were whispering among themselves that this day might well cost them a second life, and that, after its bishop, Todi might well have to bury its mayor. Signor Galli, gray and dignified, head of the richest family in the city, spoke after the podesta, recalling all that the bishop had given to the poor from his own pocket — and that, as everybody knew, had been little compared with the sums the Galli family itself spent yearly in charity.

Then last of all, while a stillness as of death spread over the small churchyard, a celebrated Dominican from Rome spoke, first in Latin, then in Italian, so that everyone should understand him. He spoke in a musical, sustained voice about the beautiful hereafter to which nothing in this earthly life could compare. The women stared with wet eyes at this gifted orator, still young, with his strong and comely face, from whose impressive shoulders the robes of penance flowed majestically in heavy folds.

No one presumed to speak after him, and the coffin was lowered into the pit by cords while the children chanted. Now Marietta too was seized with grief — grief for the miracle that had not come to pass. Now she too sobbed, sobbed without reserve like the women, like Carlino. During the Mass she could not understand why Monsignore, loaded down with gems, had lain there motionless while the living, red- and purple-clad prelates from Rome received the honors of this day. She had been so confident that he would confound them with a miracle, that he would humiliate them all, that he would rise up to heaven while the organ swelled into a mighty drone. As she sang with all the power of her lungs, she had closed her eyes in the certain expectation that suddenly she would hear a cry of amazement drowning every other sound. That cry had not come, the Brothers of Mercy had screwed down the lid of the coffin, and now Monsignore was sinking into the depths of the earth and the gravediggers were standing ready with their spades.

Now Marietta knew that it had not been within his power to rise to heaven, because his body, its hands joined together in humility, was dead, because the eyes which had stared on high towards the oak roof-beams of the nave were dead, dead, dead. The living remained here above, and saw the blue spring sky like a wide inverted bowl over the violet mountains and the green vineyards. The dead descended forever into the dusty earth where worms lived. All that had been said about a bright hereafter was but empty phrases for the occasion, designed to give a little consolation for that frightful, black hole under God's gleaming heaven. Sobbing, she sang with the other children. Tears streamed down her cheeks. Sobbing, still sobbing, she raised her face, to feel the warmth of the sun upon it.

As the first handful of earth dropped with a thud upon the coffin, several women — some of them too far away to have heard this sound — fainted, and were carried into the convent near by. Marietta, making for the gate with the other children, suddenly felt a heavy hand laid on her arm. She looked round, and recognized Cesare's worried face. He took her on one side, and said in a muffled voice, "They've carried Camilla inside, and I can't get to her. She'll be frightened to death when she comes round and finds herself among strangers. Go and find her, will you? And tell her I'm waiting outside."

Marietta nodded, and followed Cesare who, happy and grateful as a child, shouldered a way for both of them through the crush that was surging out of the cemetery. They had now really seen the last of Monsignore, and everyone had become suddenly aware that it was long past the hour of the midday meal.

"Mind where you're pushing," shouted angry voices at Cesare. Women, their cheeks still wet with tears, snapped at him irritably. Cesare was oblivious. For him, the only thing that mattered was that Camilla would be terrified if she came to and found no husband at her side. As for Marietta, she was strangely consoled by his big presence. She forgot her despair, in the entrancement of moving unimpeded through the sweating, ill-tempered crowd. When they could move more freely, Cesare bent down towards her and remarked confidentially, "Would you believe it, she really can't get on without me, yet as ill luck would have it, she's married a carrier, who's away from home from early Monday to late on Saturday. She's got no sort of a life, she says. Always alone with the children. Every night she dreams something awful's happened. That's what she's like. As if people ever got murdered in Todi! Can *you* understand it?"

Marietta, wise for her years, nodded: she could well understand that Camilla was afraid when he was away.

"They took her in there," said Cesare, and pulled at the bell that hung by the back door of the convent. A young nun, her face glowing like a pink fruit in the white of her coif, opened the door. Instantly, Cesare pushed Marietta inside, muttering with a shy averted face, "Keep her calm if you can, Marietta."

The nun looked at her distrustfully.

But Marietta, filled with a sense of her responsibility towards Cesare, made good her undignified entrance by saying with great seriousness, "I've come to tell Camilla, the wife of the Rome carrier, that her husband is waiting outside for her."

There was a pause; then the nun led her into the convent. After the noisy confusion of the crowd outside, Marietta was agreeably impressed by the still, cool, stuccoed interior.

II

When the three of them set out for the city an hour later, Camilla was still very pale. She leant on her husband for support, and as she walked talked continuously in a sad, listless voice.

Cesare tried to calm her by saying in fatherly fashion, "Now, now, do be quiet. You're just like a baby bird opening and closing its beak. Isn't she just like a baby bird, Marietta? You'll be fainting again in a minute, and then I sha'n't know whether to carry you back to the convent or on to Todi."

Camilla gave an unreal laugh, and said, "Lord, is that true? Am I really talking so much?"

"Yes, that's what my little bird is doing."

"He's exaggerating again, Marietta. But I just have to talk, it gives me such relief. When I stop, I see Monsignore in front of me, as he lay there when they took away his staff and bishop's robe, all in white with his dead eyes. I simply couldn't look when they laid him in the grave." Camilla put her hands over her face and began to sob wildly. Then she raised her head again, and looked at her husband and Marietta, startled. "If only Susanna knew we were coming," she remarked, "she could put on the macaroni. Cesare always likes his food as soon as he gets home, you know, Marietta. He never gets enough to eat on the road. It tastes so nice at home, he says. Gracious me, what time is it? I'm quite out of my stride, with all these holidays in the middle of the week. I keep thinking it's Sunday, and then that it's Ladyday — but that's not till next week. When I think that he who is now laid in earth baptized her with his own hand . . . Susanna, I mean! Cesare often had to deliver parcels from Rome to him. I expect you've seen him do it, Marietta. I said to Cesare, 'Just ask him,' — for Cesare will never do anything on his own: you have to drive him to it, and then he's only half-willing, — and of course all was well. With his kind old hands, he baptized our first child, and blessed it."

Camilla took a deep breath and shuddered.

Cesare tried to divert her attention by asking Marietta how her mother was getting on; but Camilla cut him short. "Marietta, it's worrying me to death. Won't you run on and tell Susanna about the macaroni? Stop with her a bit yourself — she's only ten after all, though she is such a strapping girl — and see the little ones aren't getting into any mischief. Lord, I oughtn't to have gone out, but I did want to see him buried. I did want to see him laid in earth. I should have gone mad if I'd stayed at home listening to the tolling of the bells; and I had to bring Cesare because I knew I should faint. I'm not sorry I did, mind. I'm pleased I was able to faint, because he who is no doubt already in heaven was perhaps looking down upon us. . . . And don't forget I've already put salt in the water. I told Susanna, but perhaps she's forgotten!"

Marietta took in only Camilla's concrete request. Drawing her shawl round her, she hurried on ahead. At the bend of the road, she turned her head, to find both Cesare and Camilla nodding with grateful warmth towards her. She smiled back at them a little sadly.

She was glad to be alone. Camilla's chatter had aroused all her feelings of despair again. At this moment, life seemed to Marietta hectic, full of pain, hopeless. She was not yet thirteen years old, but she felt already the infinite sadness that lay hidden under the boasting and the laughter of men — in Vacca's inn, in the street, everywhere, everywhere.

As she took her lonely way, her eyes half-closed against the fierce glare of the white dust, all sorts of things went through her mind. She thought of home, of the baby that was expected; and with a strange restlessness she hastened her steps.

Would the baby come from her mother? If not, why was she so fat? Would she, Marietta, be allowed to see? Here, here, was surely a miracle.

If only Nana had not said that awful thing, that awful, awful thing! It had been at the midday meal. Her mother had been sitting upstairs. Marietta had felt her heart stop beating, and had looked at Vacca, wondering whether he would say something; but he had been silent, had gone on eating.

Oh, if only she were at home now, with her mother! And she had just promised Camilla that she would stay with little Susanna.

Marietta thought to herself that perhaps once upon a time her mother had talked as much as Camilla did. Nana had said that she liked to talk and laugh when she was a young girl. But after her marriage, for years she had done nothing but cry. Now that too was over — she rarely cried; but, sometimes, she broke into tears for no apparent reason, and then, if Vacca flared up at her, she dried her tears hastily and looked at him imploringly, like a beaten dog. At such moments, Marietta felt that her mother feared him so much that, if it came to the point, she would not dare to protect her child against him.

She could not understand how her mother could be so afraid of him. She herself was brave. She would not retreat before Vacca if he had a kitchen knife in his hand. She only waited for her mother's cry for help to defend her against him, but the cry was never uttered, and on the few occasions when Marietta and Vacca had come into conflict on her behalf, her mother had betrayed her by going to stand at Vacca's side, looking at her the while out of miserable, guilty eyes that were filled with entreaty for forgiveness for such cowardice. Marietta despised her mother for the weak soul that dwelt in her strong body. Trembling with indignation, she ran out of the inn, after such an encounter; but she always returned an hour later, because her pity and concern were greater than her contempt. And when, after one of these occurrences, Vacca, delighted to find where his power lay, reminded Marietta of her defeat by supercilious references to her mother, she blushed and, filled with blind rage, longed to confound him with the absurd assertion, "She is not my mother!"

She looked about her elsewhere for an ally. Nana still sat with Vacca in the kitchen, but Nana, with the years, seemed to have grown smaller, more insignificant. She was useless now as a protector for the little Marietta — she had allowed the spirit of rebellion to die out in her. Now she never went beyond abusive language. When Vacca was in one of his rages, she hurled the grossest insults at him from the kitchen, the least being that he was murdering his wife and rejoiced over the birth of every dead child because he would not have to feed it. Vacca had grown used to her vituperation. He prized Nana's cooking too highly to throw her into the street. Confident of her position, she did not mince her words. Sometimes, however, when her yapping was too much for him, he limped to the kitchen, belaboring with his fists the door she had hastily bolted. Nana, inside, stirring the hot soup savagely, shouted, "That's right! Bash the door in, you brute. Murder me, as you're murdering your wife! But first I shall have the pleasure of pouring this hot soup over your face," and when the wood cracked under the pressure of Vacca's fists, Nana seized the handle of the iron pan. . . .

Then there was Luigino, who would have fainted with terror had he found himself imprisoned with his father in a small closed room. He dared to be insolent enough, so long as he knew there was an open door behind him through which he could slip away on his quick feet when Vacca had had enough, to reappear an hour or two later, after quarreling with some friend whom he suspected of having played him a trick. He seldom saw his mother.

Sometimes, Marietta could not believe that she and Luigino really lived under the same roof — he was such a complete stranger to her. But they were all, all strangers to her. In her heart was a gnawing hunger that sometimes welled up to such a pitch that it sent her to the attic of the inn where, with an oppressed heart, she peered from the window into the blue distances round Todi, her eyes filled with tears. But what did she want? To get away from here? But where to?

Occasionally strangers spent the night at the inn. Marietta made up their beds, examined their luggage secretly, and watched them. Perhaps they were no different from the people of Todi, but behind them lay mysterious distances. They themselves were well aware of their difference, took advantage of it, and ordered Marietta up and downstairs. Sometimes, meaning well by her, they asked her this and that as they shaved. They pinched her little chin smilingly and remarked that she would be a handsome girl, when she grew up. At such times Marietta changed curiously: she grew proud and coquettish, with an unaccustomed gleam in her eye, and a flush of excitement on her cheeks. Then the travelers went their way. It was as though a door had been slammed. They left such a stillness behind them, and Marietta wandered about the house in greater uncertainty of mind than before.

She reached the city gate, and ran straight to Camilla's home — two or three rooms on an upper floor of an old dilapidated house. The two youngest children were playing on the dark staircase. Susanna was busy in the kitchen. She was a small, sharp little thing, already an efficient housekeeper. She listened to Marietta's message with annoyance — it humiliated her. "I've had the water on the boil an hour already. I'll put the macaroni in now. Everything else is ready. I say . . ." Susanna looked at Marietta attentively and then rapped out, "Haven't they told you anything yet: about your mother?"

"About my mother?"

"That she's not doing very well, I mean."

Marietta stared at her, shaking her head. Susanna discovered her greater knowledge with intense satisfaction. In a grown-up tone of concern, she went on: "I just heard about it, from Racioppi's wife and that queer girl of Brogi's. They were passing by, and I heard them say they were going to see her. A baby's on the way — or didn't you know that either?"

"Yes, of course I knew that," Marietta hastened to reply, embarrassed. "I'd better go at once. . . ."

"Yes, I should if I were you."

But Marietta had already gone. Dizzy, she ran down the stairs. Like a sleepwalker, she avoided the two little ones at play, caressing their dark curly heads as she passed with an impulse of tenderness. With a beating heart, she stood in the deserted entrance, and suddenly she knew that she could not go home, that she would rather fall down dead where she stood than go home. She fancied that she heard her mother screaming just as Zanetta's mother had screamed when her baby came, only more pitifully still. She fancied that the screaming could be heard through the whole city, reverberated in the mountains round about. The world was full of that awful screaming, and nowhere could she escape from it. She saw Nana, pale and nervous, rushing about, saw Vacca pouring his customers' wine with unwonted gravity, listening ever and anon with a shake of the head at the foot of the stairs. With amazing clearness, all this passed before her eyes, matured too soon.

After a moment's pause, she raised her head, shook her wild black curls, walked out into the sun, and turned towards the piazza. The streets were empty — everyone was eating; but it seemed that the whole city was dead. Fear rose up in her again, and refused to be moved by reason. She dared not take another step towards the piazza. Instead, she turned about with trembling knees and fled in the opposite direction, out of the city and into the country again.

III

In her room at The Three Popes, Vacca's wife was for the third time during her married life brought to bed with a dead child months before her time. As she struggled for life, Luigino was sent for a priest. Disturbed during the banquet to the visiting prelates, he made no attempt to conceal how highly inconvenient it was for him to fulfill his duty on such a day. Perfunctorily, he administered the sacrament for the dying, and in a few minutes had gone from the inn again, leaving behind him an acrid atmosphere of incense. Barberini, the barber-surgeon of the piazza, had not yet abandoned hope. He paused a moment in his labors to swallow the little glass of benedictine that Vacca brought him. Nana ran with cloths and basins from kitchen to bedroom and back, carrying out Barberini's instructions faithfully, but expressing by her silence and her every movement how completely superfluous she felt all this activity to be. Sometimes she cast a compassionate, inquiring glance towards the woman on the bed —

as though she sought to ascertain how long the sufferer could still last.

When at last, despite every effort of the surgeon, the patient, exhausted by loss of blood, reached the last stage, nothing would move Nana any longer to go downstairs again and prepare further compresses. In an unreasoning contempt for all science, she pushed him aside, knelt down by the dying woman, pressed her already cold hand to her cheek, and began to cry softly, calling her, for the first time in her life, by name. "Anna. . . . Annina. . . . Is it sweet to die? Can he do you no more harm? . . . No?"

As she lay upon her bed, Anna opened her eyes. It was years since she had heard her name. Neither Nana nor Camilla had ever called her anything but "padrona." She had had so little to do with anyone else for so long, and Vacca had never bothered to do more than call her from the stairs with an "I say, you!" When the innkeeper's wife recognized the kneeling, weeping Nana, she asked in a whisper, "Where are the children?"

"Marietta's not home yet. . . . She can't know anything yet . . . and Luigino doesn't care. He's like his father, whose name you gave him. Don't bother yourself, Annina. Let him be. Marietta and I, we will always think of you, poor soul. You can die peaceful about that."

Barberini, realizing that only professional etiquette, professional optimism, was keeping him now, put away his instruments, and went downstairs to warn Vacca that the end was near. Vacca gave a somber, tortured look at the few customers who remained in the inn awaiting the issue from a feeling of neighborliness. Several women who had just come in to inquire he sent away with a gesture at once pathetic and pretentious, as if there were some indiscretion in their inquiries. Then he stumbled up the stairs in front of Barberini, and suddenly it seemed to him that he was mounting an unfamiliar staircase with difficulty and for the first time.

His wife saw an indistinct shadow rise up behind the kneeling servant, and probably did not realize at first whether she saw a hallucination or her husband. Nana, feeling the glance of the dying passing beyond her, turned her head and, to her unspeakable annoyance, discovered Vacca, to whom she had to give way. She scrambled to her feet and in the face of Death itself was not big enough to spare the tormented woman one last sorrow by putting before her a cruel choice: "Him? Right. Then I go." Her eyes glowing with rage, she moved away and stood watching from the far side of the bed.

And for the last time Annina chose the side of her tormentor, once she was sure that it was he. For the last time she made a desperate effort to soften him, to melt his cold, sterile heart. Her eyes searched the flesh-colored haze that was his face until they had found his. Then she held them with her own imploringly. Gathering together her dying strength for this glance, she stretched out her hands, and, breathing with great difficulty, moaned the one word, "Luigi!"

Suddenly Vacca tasted again a bitterness on his tongue, he felt again the weak sensation that had come to him once or twice before in particularly painful situations. He was alarmed by her outstretched hand. He would have liked to go away quickly, away from here downstairs, and later on, when everything had grown calm again, to call up the stairs, "I say, you!" But that was over, for his wife was dying. There stood Barberini, who would be sending in his bill, and Nana, whom he would throw out when everything was over. Yes, but stronger than anything else around him were those eyes that stared at him from the bed. He wanted to say something, to speak soothingly. He knew that he was white as a sheet, and that the sweat . . . Without knowing what he was doing, he fell upon his knees with a heavy thud that was heard below in the taproom. Suddenly he realized that all was over with his wife. He began to gibber, pressing her hand to his forehead. He wept, and his tears tasted salt upon his tongue. Distraught, he looked about him miserably, as though others could still help, as though he had come too late to receive his wife's last words.

This was the moment that Nana had long hoped for. The helpless look he gave her as he knelt by the bed met in her eyes an expression like retribution itself. Then, putting all her hatred, her scorn, her contempt into one word, she said, "Fool!"

"Why, why?" asked the fool, stammering.

Meanwhile, Barberini saw that a new phase had begun. He approached discreetly, bent over his patient, listened for the heart that was now stilled, and closed the eyes of the dead. Science took control once more, and sought with words of restraint to awaken a sense of the necessity of all things, to stem the boundless grief that might overwhelm the hearts of those who remained.

Science was successful: after a few moments, Vacca got to his feet, and substituted for his almost ridiculous demonstration of grief a more decorous sorrow that could be exhibited to all and might be expected to elicit respect.

It was easier, now that those eyes from the bed no longer looked at him. He was confronted with a concrete fact that had no disturbing implications: he was a widower. He had been prepared for this, and privately had thrashed out for himself the attitude a widower should adopt at the deathbed of his wife. He now went up to Barberini, who also knew how to comport himself correctly in these sad circumstances. They shook hands, and in this handshake Barberini promised silently to forget that he had seen Vacca groveling at his wife's bedside. After listening to the surgeon's vague words of condolence, Vacca invited him downstairs and begged him to take a glass of wine from him. Picking up his instruments, the surgeon nodded assent. Then, while Nana remained by the bed moaning softly, the innkeeper stumped down the stairs, pale still and in tears, but with his dignity restored. "They will understand everything when I appear," he thought to himself, and began to imagine the entrance he would make. Oh, yes, they all understood — that heavy thud above had told them the news. But they wanted to hear it from his own lips. They had a greedy desire to hear his voice quiver.

"It's all over," said Vacca, as he reached the last step, and then he was dumb. His old customers, much moved, pressed his hand and slipped quietly out of the inn to leave him alone with his grief. Vacca closed the door behind them, and drew down the blinds — but he peered after them through a chink. Then fear of being left alone with Nana and the dead beset him. He wished that at least Marietta and Luigi, the lout, would come home. Their mother dies, and they roam about the streets. That's filial affection!

Those who had gone out from the inn scattered over the little city, instinctively separating in order that each one of them should be a main artery spreading on all sides the sensational news: —

Vacca's wife is dead. On the same day that the old bishop was laid in earth, Vacca's wife died in childbed.

IV

In the gloaming, Marietta dashed through the back door into the kitchen and stood, haggard, before Nana, who came up to her with a strange passionate cry and folded her in her arms. Marietta sank into them and whispered, her face pressed against Nana's neck, "Is he with her?"

Nana supposed that Marietta had heard everything, and with a sigh of relief said, "I don't know . . . He's bustling about all over the house. But where have you been, child?"

Marietta told her what little Susanna had said, and how she had fled into the country and had only now dared to return. The first person she had met had told her what had happened at home. Nana listened, and said sadly, "She asked for you. . . . Perhaps she had a message for you. Hush, he's coming."

Both held their breath. In the passage, Vacca's uneven step approached.

He opened the kitchen door and stood looking at Marietta. With what he hoped was a tone of reproach, he said, "Oh, so one of them *has* come home! I can hardly believe my eyes. Go upstairs, Marietta, and see what's happened to your mother."

Marietta clung tightly to Nana. Wild fear welled up in her, fear of Vacca, fear of the dead whom she must visit by his order. Nana took her hand protectingly and said, "Come with me."

Led by Nana, trusting herself blindly to her, Marietta crept along the passage and up the stairs, while Vacca stumped after them. She reached the deathbed — and immediately her obsession of terror subsided.

There lay her mother . . . beautiful, young, peaceful as Marietta had never seen her before. This, this was a miracle. About her mother's mouth was a restful, satisfied expression that was almost a smile. Her mother was smiling because Marietta had been afraid to come to her. Marietta had been wrong when she had visualized death as an end bereft of all consolation. Her mother must have seen a better world rise up before her.

An infinite tenderness came over Marietta. Suddenly, her heart was at rest. Human unkindness and human resentment seemed to have lost all seriousness as she looked on the wonderful triumph of goodness lying before her eyes. Involuntarily, half-questioningly, and with something like a reflection of the smile of the dead upon her face, she turned towards her father; but Vacca did not understand: perhaps he imagined that her gesture concealed a hidden reproach, for the eyes that met hers held only grim severity. She averted her eyes sadly, and looked down at the dead again, the tears streaming down her cheeks. Even Nana, who stood there unmoved, inimical because of Vacca's presence, did not understand her. Neither understood the smile on Mother's face. . . .

Downstairs in the passage, they heard Luigino's suppressed cough. Vacca muttered something and went below. Immediately there was an uproar on the staircase. Blows fell, and Luigino roared, "I won't! I won't do it! I won't go upstairs."

"You won't, you lout? We'll see if you won't. . . . What, can you bite too?" There was a sound of stamping and kicking. Then the struggle was transferred to the kitchen, and the sound that reached them upstairs was more subdued. Nana approached the bed and, as a pretext for caressing the dead woman's forehead, smoothed a stray lock of hair. She said to Marietta, speaking in the melancholy tone of a woman of the people, "I have done everything. I washed her . . . changed the bed linen . . . and then lit the candles. Doesn't she look beautiful? Perhaps it's better so. Just listen to the noise in the kitchen!"

Marietta listened because Nana told her to, but her thoughts had drifted far away, were directed towards one point. . . . She looked about her, all round the whole room, first slowly, then with rapidly rising anxiety; and her voice was shrill as she whispered, "Nana, and where is the baby now?"

Nana stared at her bewildered. Then, swallowing the truth, she prevaricated. "What are you talking about?"

"About the baby! The baby that was to come."

"But your mother is dead. How can you expect there to be a baby? Use your brain, Marietta."

But Marietta persisted passionately, "But there *was* a baby. It only had to be born. Camilla brought all the little clothes for it."

Nana was speechless. She would have liked to go on denying the truth obstinately. But Marietta looked at her in such a way that she could not find her words. She sat down and shook her head over this child.

"I can understand," continued Marietta imploringly. "Nana, I should so like to know."

At this open avowal, Nana did not know where to turn. Did that child really want to know, and from her mouth? Would it be a good thing, perhaps, just to tell her? She would experience it all herself one day, in her own being. Could it harm her to tell her everything, seriously, warningly? Nana drew Marietta close to her, bent over her, and spoke.

She spoke in comfortless words by the dim candlelight. She spoke of the lot of woman here on earth, revealed to Marietta the great mystery of conception and of birth, explaining it as a long process over which lurked pain and sickness and the ever-present fear of death. Marietta listened, trembling in suspense, marveling meanwhile that Nana's story taught her nothing new. That the child was conceived in its mother's body, grew there, and was born, she had already understood. What she waited for now was a word from Nana that would reveal to her the mysterious bliss that gave significance to all this suffering and raised it to a miracle. Staring towards the dead woman, who seemed silently to confirm all that Nana said and at the same time to smile over it, Marietta waited for the one word that never came, because Nana did not know it. For Nana eliminated the man's part entirely — in the first place, because she would have preferred instant death rather than to enlighten Marietta on that point (of that mystery, for it was a mystery to her also, she had no desire to know more — what she already knew was just enough to rouse her disgust); in the second place, because once a child was begotten the man had nothing more to do with its bearing: that was the woman's concern alone. Only as she came to the end did she break out into angry accusation, "And for whose sake, do you think? For whose sake was all this suffering?" And, with a wild and hostile gesture pointing downstairs, she added: "*They* will it so. *They* think only of their own pleasure."

This, however, try as she would, Marietta could not follow. She was prepared to believe any ugliness of Vacca; but what about Cesare, who was devoted to his wife? "But Cesare?" she asked.

"What, Cesare? You've chosen a fine example! Cesare. . . . Just look at Camilla, she's a bundle of nerves. He'd have had twelve children by now if he'd had his way — he said so himself. Oh, yes, and why not? Twelve! But for a poor thing like Camilla, four children are four too many. As soon as they were married, one was on the way. She sat here in the kitchen, crying her eyes out, so frightened she was. I had to console her. And when the first one came, she said, 'Never again!' I spoke to him about it, and that great hulking fool swore to me with tears in his eyes, 'Never again!'; and now there are four, and what's more, number five is on the way. But they daren't tell me."

But Nana might as well have been silent. She felt that Marietta did not believe her, that everything she said was spoken to the wind, and that when, in four or five years' time, the men came running after this child, she would be no wiser than all those who had gone before her; no wiser than Camilla, no wiser than the poor thing who lay on her bed and had paid her account with her life. . . .

When things were quiet downstairs, they descended and found Luigino, his head buried in his arms, sitting at the table, while Vacca, flushed with fury, was stirring the soup in the pot that stood over the fire. Nana snatched the spoon contemptuously from his hand, and set the plates upon the table.

They began to eat. Luigino continued to sit with his head upon his arms. Then the smell of the soup penetrated to him, and with a tragic expression on his face he lifted his head and drew his plate towards him.

"Oh, he can eat all right," sneered Vacca.

"So can you," retorted Luigino unabashed.

Vacca grinned angrily and continued his nagging: "But his lordship won't go to see his own dead mother. Even Marietta went up, and she after all might have said to herself — "

"Eat, man, eat, and don't burn your tongue!" snapped Nana ambiguously, and Vacca, put out of countenance, pensively watched the hot soup flow back out of his spoon.

But Marietta had pricked up her ears. She knew Nana too well to be deceived when she meant something different from what her words expressed. She knew quite well that something was being kept from her. She was not stupid. The insinuations of other children had already given her food for thought, and more than once Vacca had made allusions in her presence to her being "no child of his" — Nana had not always managed to close his mouth in time. Marietta, without bothering much about it, or trying to understand fully, had come to know that there was something; that Vacca was not really her father. That she had felt; but she had never dared question the justice of his fatherly authority so far. She had never been able to form any conception of what illegitimacy meant, and she had certainly never connected her mother with it. This evening, however, she felt herself shaken out of the childish dreamland in which she had lived so long. Why had she given so little thought to these insinuations? Why had she always turned away her head proudly when she had heard a group of little girls, pert and mysterious, whispering about her? Why had the taunts hurled at her in enmity failed to reach her mind, as though they had not concerned her? Now she felt dazed because she was sure of nothing. Why should Luigino go to their mother rather than she? Nana would tell her later on. She must know why Luigino stood nearer to their mother than herself.

Lord, what a day!

Things turned out differently, however. Instead of Nana, it was Camilla who, that same evening, brought her enlightenment.

After the meal, Vacca longed for visitors to condole with him and distract his mind. He did not know what to do with himself, now that he had closed his inn to avoid shocking his customers. Cesare and Camilla, who came knocking timidly at the back door, had never been so welcome before. Of course, he could not show what he felt. He received them stiffly, inhospitably, and led them sadly and in silence to his dead wife. Somberly he spoke of her last moments, fell silent again, coughed, and then asked them if by chance they would not care to come and sit a while downstairs.

Two or three others arrived — Cesare and Camilla had but inaugurated the evening. Five, six times Vacca stumped up the stairs, and indicated his wife, standing meanwhile by the door like a custodian.

While he was upstairs with one group of visitors, Camilla's nerves were overcome for the second time that day, and she gave vent to an uncontrolled stream of words that Cesare tried in vain to stop.

"Let me alone, Cesare. It is too much. Two dead in one day! First the bishop . . . With his own hand he baptized and blessed my little Susanna. And now my old padrona, whom I served faithfully for three years. For three long years I saw her suffer under that executioner of a husband of hers. He can hear what I say. Three years! That's too long. When he comes downstairs I shall tell him so."

Cesare, shifting uncomfortably upon his chair, said warningly: "You might at least remember that his child is sitting here, Camilla."

He had chosen the wrong word. "His child?" blurted out Camilla tartly. "His child? Come here, Marietta. Come here. I've known you since you were two months old . . ." Camilla stretched out her arms, but Marietta did not move. She remained sitting on her chair staring anxiously at Camilla, who hesitated and turned helplessly towards Nana.

"Camilla, don't let your tongue run away with you," said Nana sharply.

But Camilla could be restrained no longer. Undeterred, she went on, "She must hear about it some time or another. She's now twelve. . . . She'd better hear it to-day, from my mouth, for I was there at the time. Nana and I were there. God is my witness, I cannot be silent. It's just itching to come out. Marietta, she who lies dead upstairs — may heaven have mercy on the poor tormented soul — she was not your mother at all. Nobody but God knows your real mother, and where she is. She was a woman much to be pitied. She could not help herself. She could not have acted differently. She saw you starving at her empty breast. . . . But tell her, Nana, tell her that what I say is true. She left you behind, here under this very roof. She was wrong, but she had no choice. I should not tell you this, Marietta, if Cesare had not said that you are the child of that revolting creature. Be quiet, all of you. Your father was quite different. He gave a ten-lira tip to both Nana and me. That's why I'm sure he must have been your father, for the others gave only half a lira or even nothing at all. They were only poor players, anyhow. But he gave ten lire, and he meant to say by that: 'This is my child. Look after her, women!' "

Marietta continued to stare at her; her only feeling at that moment was hatred for the large, foolish creature who said all this in public. In her impotent desire for revenge, Marietta believed that she was wildly happy that Camilla, against her wish, was about to give her husband a fifth child. *"May there be twelve of them . . . twelve . . . twelve!"* As she expressed this impressive and mysterious curse within her, a shiver of satisfaction went through her.

"I can still see what he looked like," went on Camilla nervously, talking about the father, the father of the ten lire, the father who had left his child with Vacca — with Vacca, of all people. "He was tall and dark, worn with care, yes, full of care. With eyes that looked right into your soul. Perhaps he wasn't handsome, but you had to look at him, because of his eyes. I only need to look at you, Marietta, to remember what he looked like. For God's sake, Nana, say something."

Nana shrugged her shoulders contemptuously, and got up to pour out the wine. Everyone looked at Marietta, who sat pale and cowering upon her chair. Into the expectant silence fell her cool, collected voice with the surprising declaration, "I knew all about it already from Nana."

This, this was her revenge against Camilla, who had given her away so stupidly in public. Camilla paled, burst into sobs, and turned to her husband for consolation.

But Nana was too moved by Marietta's declaration to remember what she had got up for. She subsided into her chair again, saying, "Let's talk of something else . . ."

When Vacca came downstairs, he noticed something suspicious in the bearing of the company, and inquired somberly what was the matter now, and whether they hadn't had enough for one day. Camilla at once lashed out at him in a wild flood of accusations, pouring out the pent-up venom of years. Nana listened calmly, shaking her head for the most part, but every now and then nodding assent, because, after all, Camilla was only expressing the truth. Vacca had great difficulty in controlling himself, but he managed to sustain the part of tragic and long-suffering widower. At last, Cesare, making confused excuses to his host, managed with soothing words, and some physical force, to get the furious woman out of the door. The guests who remained sat silent and embarrassed.

Upstairs on the bed that had been made afresh by Nana the dead smiled a fixed, innocent smile in the light of the burning candles.

V

Although Marietta had little time to think things over during the next day or two, she felt nevertheless that Camilla's revelation had changed her existence. The link between her and the dead woman upstairs remained untouched; but it did her good to know that she had been justified in always looking upon Vacca as a stranger. The widening horizon that came with her knowledge of the truth had brought something mysterious and new into her life. Distances were opening before her. The sense of being stifled, which had sometimes seemed almost to choke her, had lifted. She raised her head no longer in proud defiance of the world's littleness, but in order to look about her and measure the newly discovered perspective. It seemed to her more honorable to have a father whose short sojourn in Todi and departure for Venice had woven a halo about her in the eyes of all, than to be the child of Vacca. She found herself fascinated by this magical, bright background, and Camilla's disclosures, once she had got over her initial annoyance, made her look upon this father of hers as a hero. Later, Nana too spoke to her about her parents, and her picture of them was even more flattering, in her desire to outdo Camilla. Nana sang their praises, piling on her adjectives to describe the noble presence of her father, losing herself in even greater commiseration over the mother: "Such a sweet little woman — I really ought to say lady, for she was certainly of noble descent. You had only to look at her small hands. To think of being a *contessa*, perhaps, and then to have to see your baby drinking itself drunk at another's breast while it refuses your own because it finds nothing there. . . . Yes, there she stood crying. Oh, yes, and we cried with her."

The lure of the wide distances now contained a promise. Her father, dark, tall, with eyes that looked into your soul . . . might come along one fine day and take her away . . . to Venice, to Rome. Magic had entered into her life, and perhaps one day it would dominate it completely, as it did the lives of those in the fairy tales Nana told her in the kitchen while Vacca served his customers in the taproom.

Camilla came repentantly on the following day to offer her excuses to Vacca. She was still unstrung, and it was with many words that she begged forgiveness for the state she had got into the day before. To her unspeakable relief, she found that she and her Cesare were to be spared the scandal of not being invited to the funeral feast that was to take place on the third day immediately after the service.

During this meal, which was eaten by candlelight behind closed shutters that obscured the broiling sun outside, Camilla tried in a hundred different ways to make peace with Marietta also. She expressed regret quite openly for the way in which she had let her tongue run away with her. In her desire for reconciliation she did not shrink from any self-humiliation. But Marietta, repelled again, could only reply with a faint smile that committed her to nothing. Camilla noticed Marietta's hostility. She flushed and repeated five or six times, "I'm oppressed by those closed shutters. I can't stand this twilight in broad day."

They spoke of the dead. Carlino, the sexton, who had been invited to the meal, spoke with uplifted glass in honor of her memory. When the glasses clinked, Vacca began to cry and said how hard it was for him to be deprived of a wife so suddenly. Like Carlino himself, he was slightly tipsy. Marietta, however, who had never seen him drunk, and did not at first understand what was wrong with him, sat looking at him shyly, astonished at his tears. She could make nothing of it. Anxiously she tried to catch Nana's eye.

A little later, Luigino shocked them all by showing unmistakable signs of drunkenness. He broke into such lewd talk that Marietta, already troubled by Vacca's incomprehensible tears, went up to her brother and gave him a box on the ear, which he ignored. Nana took his glass away in passing. Vacca, hazy as to what was happening, began to reprimand Marietta pompously for choosing such a day to quarrel with her brother. When she explained, "Luigino is drunk," Vacca thought she said, "Luigi, you are drunk." He buried his head in his arms and sighed or cried — it was not clear which; and Marietta, who up to then had remained perfectly calm, suddenly found herself struggling hard with tears.

At last the nightmare of this funeral feast came to an end. The guests departed. Having eaten their fill, they proceeded to do violence to their feelings by offering further words of condolence. Camilla had a last attack of garrulity; and Carlino, unsteady on his feet, began to preach tolerance with complete irrelevancy. When the taproom was empty, Marietta on her own authority threw open the shutters. Vacca did not hinder her. The gold of the setting sun chased away the unnatural dusk. Even the sun seemed unnatural, a senseless flood of blinding light. The stillness remained, the stillness that the guests had left behind them.

Marietta hung about the taproom instead of helping Nana wash up. She was alone with her father. She could not help looking at him as he stood, with head bent, against the counter, gazing with concern into an empty mug, sighing now and then, and muttering to himself. Finally she could stand it no longer. She felt herself move towards him, she heard herself say, "Father." She paused after the word, and waited, but the stillness was unbroken. Then she asked, "Can't we try in future to get on with each other?"

Nonplussed, he stared at her. Then a feeling of weakness welled up in him also. His unfailing suspiciousness warned him immediately that this weakness was due to his drunkenness; and he promptly wondered whether he could not reap some advantage from this moment of tenderness. Nana would burst with annoyance if he were successful in winning the affection of this child, who after all apparently had some feeling for him. It would, too, stand him in good stead in the whole city. As cunning was to him the one way of winning anybody over, he decided to play the stern father who concealed his feelings from a sense of duty. He laid his hand upon her forehead, withdrew it again, put it in his pocket, and sighed. He wanted to speak, but could find no words. He raised his eyes to the ceiling. Then he thought it right to feel his legs weaken under him, so he sank heavily on to a chair and shivered. All at once, he began to imagine that he was genuinely affected, and under this impression he gave an almost genuine shudder. He found himself in tears again, and thought to himself, "They all think I've no heart. I had almost come to believe it myself. Lord, Lord, what swine they are!" He drew Marietta to him, and pressed her hand to his wet eyes; but at that moment Nana appeared in the doorway and put an end to the emotional scene by remarking that there were still a number of plates to be taken to the kitchen. Marietta, deadly pale, felt suddenly liberated and wanted to run away — away from the taproom, away, away. Vacca, giving her a rapid look from under his bent brow, wondered whether his duplicity had been unmasked. He continued to play his comedy of misery and sat at the table buried in surly grief, pressing his hands against his temples, until Nana pulled the tablecloth irritably from under his elbows because he refused to pay attention to her urgent request to him to lift his arms.

VI

Or had his wife's death changed him? In the following weeks, he was silent, withdrawn into himself. Even the customers of the inn noticed it. Nobody had expected him to take his loss to heart. When he noticed he was being talked about, he provided them, heretic and blasphemer as he was, with a new surprise by faithfully attending early Mass for a time. Perhaps he found a secret satisfaction in thus puzzling them all. He ceased to swear, avoided coarse language, and by his whole bearing compelled his customers to maintain a certain decorum, to give a thought to the one who had died under his roof a few short weeks ago.

Marietta talked about him to Nana, asked her what she thought of him. Exasperated, Nana shrugged her shoulders. It was only pretense, of course.

"Did you know he's taken to drinking?" asked Marietta. "He used to drink a glass here and there with the others, but he doesn't do that any more. He waits till they're gone. Then, when he's alone, he drinks."

"Oh, that too will pass," said Nana. But Marietta noticed an uncertainty in her voice. Nana also felt herself confronted by a mystery. These days she served her master at table with more discrimination, asked him upon occasion whether the food was to his taste. The only one who remained unaffected was Luigino. He cursed and continued to use obscene words, answered Vacca's admonitions pat with arguments from the street. Nana said that she wondered why his father didn't thrash him to death.

But what, what was the matter with Vacca? On the Feast of the Assumption, which was Marietta's birthday — her thirteenth — he gave her a pair of small golden earrings and a chain with a little cross, and asked her to put them on in his presence. "They suit you well," he remarked, and asked, "Why are you trembling?"

Nana had never seen these earrings nor this chain. "I swear I never saw your mother wear them," she said, excited and intrigued. "I couldn't have failed to see them. She never hid anything from me. Let me look at the little box." That same afternoon she spoke to Simone, the goldsmith, and learned that Vacca had bought nothing from him. This gift was an additional mystery surrounding Vacca — it made Nana restless and fractious. She went nosing about the house, looking into every obscure corner. "But what are you looking for?" asked Vacca. "If there were anything I wanted to hide, I should do it so that you wouldn't find it, anyhow."

On Sundays he seemed to Marietta so lonely that she simply could not leave him by himself, even though she had not forgotten the awful feeling that came over her when she was alone with him on that day after the funeral feast. He noticed it, looked round at her shyly, and grinned at her in melancholy fashion. Then suddenly, with a sigh, he laid his hand upon her shoulders, and again that feeling of indescribable confusion came over her. She could not breathe. If only he would speak, say something; but he was silent, and she was conscious only of his hand, that heavy, dangerous hand she had always feared, and which by intuition she now also distrusted. She remembered that she had to help Nana, and fled.

One night something awful happened. Marietta, who normally slept uninterruptedly, woke with a start. An oppressive dream made her jump up with a suppressed cry, as she gathered her nightgown about her breast in the vague consciousness that she had felt a hand there.

A dark shadow loomed over her bed. Vacca's voice said, "Don't be frightened. It's me" — but his own voice sounded uncertain, and it seemed as if his body were swaying to and fro. "I just came to see," he said. "You were calling in your sleep."

Marietta found she had no control over her voice. She only stared at him, her eyes fixed in deadly anxiety.

"Why are you so restless to-night?" he asked. "Come and sleep near me."

She heard his teeth chattering. Still powerless to utter a word, she shook her head, and clung feverishly to the bedclothes.

Thereupon a wild passion seized him. "What's the matter? What sort of nonsense is this? Why won't you? When I tell you to — " His great hands seized her.

"Let me go! I'll shout. Nana!" She bent over his wrist, dug her teeth into it.

Piercing pain brought him to his senses. He let go of her. With a curse he wrapped the end of his shirt round the bleeding wrist, thereby uncovering his body. With a cry of horror, Marietta jumped from her bed and fled up the passage to Nana's room, heedless of the angry orders that pursued her from the now sobered wretch. She pulled back Nana's blankets, and crept in beside her.

Nana, awakened with a start, received her with stuttering questions. "What, what's the matter? Marietta, is that you? Did he try to do something to you? Tell me."

But no word came from her. Only when, a few minutes later, no Vacca had appeared, and Nana asked her at last if she had been dreaming about her mother's death, she stumbled over her words, saying hastily, "Yes, Nana, yes, yes, I've had an awful dream. I won't sleep there again, Nana. Not in that room. I want to stay with you, Nana, with you, with you."

For the first time since Marietta was a toddler and exposed defenseless to Vacca's fists, Nana took her protectingly in her arms. The following morning she waited to hear what Vacca would have to say of the night's happenings. She looked at him threateningly, ready for the fray once more. Indifferent, cleaning his nails with a knife, he allowed her to speak. He had noticed nothing last night. It was not until he got up that he observed the bird had flown. By the way, he had torn his wrist on the fastening of that accursed window that was always so hard to open. Yes, he had bandaged it himself. He didn't need help for a thing like that. . . .

That same day, during the midday meal, he seized Luigino unexpectedly by the scruff of the neck, dragged him to the taproom, and with a stick he had laid ready in advance began to thrash him for all his misdemeanors of the last few months. In the kitchen Nana held back Marietta, adjuring her not to be so foolish as to come between them. But Luigino's howls reached the piazza, and some peasants who were unyoking their oxen, in order to shelter them in the shadow of the Palazzo del Popolo, came into the taproom and liberated the victim from the hands of Vacca who, in his blind rage, was still thrashing him.

Thenceforward, Luigino limped like his father. Nana poulticed the leg, but it did not get better; after a month, nobody noticed it any longer. Vacca limped. Why shouldn't his son limp too? They resembled each other now in every way. Luigino was the living image of his father. Only a limp had been missing to make the resemblance complete.

VII

After that night, Marietta always slept with Nana. Vacca made no remark — he even ceased to put his arm round her shoulders. He paid little attention to her, and perhaps he did not notice that she always avoided being alone with him in the room.

It was autumn, and Nana insisted that Marietta must go to bed earlier again. At nine o'clock she took her little candle and went upstairs. She undressed, but she did not close her eyes until Nana joined her.

Nana usually sat downstairs for an hour or two, talking to Vacca after the customers had gone. Vacca felt a need to talk to her, to ask her advice: How was he to deal with that rascal of a boy of his?

"Well, he's your son," said Nana.

"I can't do more than be severe with him," sighed Vacca. "I have to deal with him alone. . . ."

Luigino happened to come in just then, slamming the front door behind him. He muttered something that was meant to be a greeting, and then, with his back to them, began to eat the food that Nana had put down for him by the smouldering charcoal fire. Silently, the two grown-ups watched him. When he had finished, he passed them with a challenging look, went down the passage, and up the stairs, where he flung himself down upon his bed with a thud. Vacca had followed him with his eyes. "What's the matter with his leg?" he asked drily, cynically.

Nana, sitting at the table, looked up at him speechless.

"Oh, is it still from that time?" asked Vacca, genuinely surprised. "Isn't that better? Why did the scoundrel make me so damned angry?"

"Perhaps you would have controlled yourself better if you'd had to deal with somebody as strong as yourself."

"Mayn't I teach my own children a lesson when they ask for it?" protested Vacca. He stuck his stiff leg out from under the table. "Look at that. My father was after me upstairs. I jumped out of the window on to the piazza, and got up on the wrong foot. That, and the inn, were my heritage, and they have accompanied me through my life. Perhaps it hasn't been all roses. . . ."

"Perhaps you have only yourself to thank for that."

"Perhaps. I certainly ought never to have married an ailing wife."

"It was you who made her ill."

"A lie! That's a lie! From the very first she was always hanging about upstairs. I should have liked a wife who showed herself in the inn. All my life I've had to stand alone. My temper was soured by the thought all day of what was over my head." His voice trembled with a disappointment so genuine that Nana looked up in astonishment. Instantly aware of her hesitation, he went on, self-pityingly: "I was a stout enough fellow once upon a time, even though I had that leg. But you've forgotten that."

"To tell you the truth, I've never paid any attention to you," she snapped out, feeling ill at ease.

"That's a pity."

"Why a pity, fool?"

"Because perhaps I should have had a better bargain in you."

Nana looked at him with infinite contempt. "I should have declined the honor with thanks."

"Don't give yourself airs. After all, I had the inn."

She moved uncomfortably on her chair. "Oh well, perhaps I should have been mad enough, but you wouldn't have been pleased. I should have dealt with you very differently from the poor wretch who now lies in the churchyard yonder through your fault."

He took no notice of her last malicious remark. He only asked her, with pressing curiosity, "Oh, really? So you would have polished me off, would you?"

"Wouldn't I?"

Vacca burst out laughing. He leaned back and, amused, looked at Nana, who turned away, sulky and embarrassed. Growing suddenly serious, he came and sat close to her. Then he hissed in her ear, "And supposing I had preferred that to the eternal Yes and Amen and tears every night before going to sleep?"

"Keep your hands off, please!" exclaimed Nana, pale with an aversion that he thought exaggerated and refused to notice.

"Steady, now, steady. I'm not going to murder you. Go upstairs, if you'd rather not be near me. Go to the devil! I'm not holding you back. I shall sit here alone. I've told you before, I'm used to it. . . ."

Nana struggled with herself. Then she got up and, tossing her head, left the kitchen. "Has he gone mad?" she muttered out loud to herself as she went up the stairs. And then, stopping halfway up to take breath, "Before I'd allow him to lay his hands on me . . . !" Her heart thumped heavily. "The man's stark, staring mad!"

She opened the door of her room soundlessly, and was startled to find Marietta lying still awake. "What's the good of my sending you to bed early?" she muttered.

"Why do you?"

"Why? Why? Because I have to talk to your father about this, that, and the other."

"What do you talk about?"

"About Luigino, for instance. What's to be done with him to make a reasonable being of him. Do you mind?"

Nana's tone had suddenly become wounding; and why did she talk about "your father"? Hitherto when she had talked to Marietta she had never found it necessary to allude to Vacca in any other way than as "he," with a nod towards the door. And now she was talking about "your father"; and a little later she said, while she buttoned up her nightgown in bed, "We shall see a thing or two yet. A man like that can't remain alone. Soon he'll get it into his head to marry again. But whom he will take is another question. You've got to know him at close quarters, as I've done, before you care to be under the same roof with him. Tales are going the rounds about him. It seems that that girl of Brogi's would take him — but then she'd have anybody, for the sake of being married. While your mother was still above ground, she turned up here once to see if a second servant was required, the innocent. Every child in Todi knows that, year in, year out, I do everything here, except when there happen to be too many guests."

Marietta said nothing. Her attention was directed to something strange in Nana's voice. Why was she so terribly excited over "that girl of Brogi's"? Marietta had heard the story from her before, but it seemed to be preying on her mind. That Vacca might marry again did not penetrate Marietta's brain at all.

That night, Nana lay tossing restlessly, keeping Marietta also from sleep. "Oh, are you awake?" asked Nana in the middle of the night, when she could no longer hold her tongue. "Did I wake you? I can't help it. I was dreaming that that girl had come into the house after all, and that I was saying to your father that in that case I would go."

"Nana, tell me — would you go away from here?" asked Marietta.

The strange calm, the desperate resolution that was in her voice, brought Nana to her senses. She realized suddenly that she had perhaps estranged herself from the child, who must have felt herself abandoned indeed, to rise to such heights of resignation. Nana transferred her hatred to Vacca. All her old rancor blazed up against him. "Don't be afraid, child," she said consolingly. "Nana will remain with you. Nana will never leave you. I'm here only for your sake. So far as I care, he can bring her into the house, marry her too . . . my dear. Then he'll be properly punished for the way he treated the padrona. But they'll keep their hands off you, both of them. That I shall see to, so long as I have the strength."

As dawn was breaking, Marietta woke up suddenly from a light sleep and heard Nana muttering into her pillow, "I don't care what he does. What have I to do with him? . . . with that creature? If only he makes up his mind soon, that Brogi girl . . . let him get on with it. . . . Then I shall know where I stand."

But they were all to no purpose, these midnight resolutions of the good faithful Nana. She was only floundering against the stream. She was no wiser than the others — she only thought she was, in her pride. Her mind was unsettled at the thought of being the new padrona, of having a man of her own, whatever he might be like, of proving that after all she had not been overlooked like some she knew — that girl of Brogi's, for instance. And then there was the response of her blood, that response she had never perceived because there had never been anyone to rouse it. But now this boor whom she despised, this gross creature, was devouring her with his eyes, because in his hunger anything was welcome to him. Suddenly she felt herself a woman like the others who had married and borne children. Trembling, she waited for him to stand behind her, to put his arms round her, to kiss her. She made up her mind to slap his face, she meant to defend herself. . . . Yes, but in that awful moment she could not be sure that her limbs would not suddenly give way, grow powerless. . . .

Inevitably, the time came when Nana averted her eyes from Marietta's, and a guilty silence hung between them, the same silence that had formerly been between Marietta and her dead mother. Vacca, invisible, stood between them.

These days he showed himself more and more in the kitchen, would inquire of Nana what was simmering in the pot, and when she refused to tell him would teasingly go nosing under the lid. He extolled his own cooking abilities, boasted that he could prepare macaroni in the famous Bologna manner. She ought to let him try. In the end she chased him out of the kitchen, but with a boisterous good humor that aroused the greatest surprise in Marietta, who happened to be present. He pushed his stiff leg in the door, and refused to go — until Nana promised that she would allow him to prepare for her *spaghetti alla Bolognese*. He was like an incorrigible naughty boy. . . .

One Sunday, Nana wore a dress that Marietta recognized at once as having belonged to her dead mother. It had always hung unworn in the cupboard. Nana had had it made over to fit herself, and she looked unrecognizably young in it. Or was it that the bloom of youth had come back to her?

That night in bed, Nana began to sob. Marietta entreated her for a long time to explain the reason for this sadness, and at last Nana asked whether Marietta could ever be angry with her, and whether she had taken it ill that Nana had had her mother's wedding dress refashioned for herself.

"But why did you do it?" asked Marietta. She had not known that it was her mother's wedding dress, and she was certainly unpleasantly surprised that Nana should have chosen just that frock to deck herself in.

"He insisted," complained Nana, and moaned. "I shall never put it on again, Marietta, never again. I'm mad. . . . I don't know myself what I'm doing. Why is he turning my head like this? Oh, Lord!"

Marietta could not speak. She was sure now that she would lose Nana. Nana was in league with the enemy — not without regret, certainly, but she appeared to be unable to withstand him. While Nana's guilty body lay tremblingly pressed against hers, Marietta realized dimly that Nana was weeping not for what she had done, but for what she was about to do. Powerless before the inevitable, Marietta was afraid she would humiliate Nana if she spoke. She was silent, casting about for some way of escape for herself, holding her head high in her solitude.

A week later, walking casually into the kitchen, she surprised the two larking together. Vacca disengaged himself. Nana, flushing scarlet, smoothed down her ruffled clothes, and stammered, "Oh, is it you? . . . We thought you . . . Listen, do you think it very terrible?"

Marietta shrank back. She closed the door immediately. Dizzy, she hurried through the taproom into the street. It was a chilly autumn evening. She shivered, but she did not feel the cold as she went through the streets without her shawl, staring in front of her like a sleepwalker.

Walking at random, shrinking into the shadow of the houses when she met anyone, she tried to collect her feverish thoughts. Away from here. Away from people: suddenly she could not bear people any more.

But where was she to go? Where?

There was a blankness, a stillness of which she had first become conscious on the day they had buried Monsignore, when she went to console Camilla. During the night, when she lay awake with open eyes and the life of grown-ups moved and eddied mysteriously before her, a new longing had grown up in her — a longing for seclusion, for the protection of thick consecrated walls from behind which the whole of human life could be seen only at a distance. . . .

The vesper bells were ringing, and the streets were filling with people on their way to church. The cathedral, in honor of the dead bishop, was closed for ordinary services until All Saints, and the faithful worshipers went instead to the smaller churches, to Santa Catarina and San Jacopo. Unable to decide what she wanted to do, Marietta hurried first in one direction, then in another, whither the alternating sound of bells called her. So light was she of step, it seemed as if the reverberation of the bells were carrying her. More and more she was losing the sense of reality.

Then suddenly inspiration came to her, swallowing up all her fears and hesitations. She could breathe again, now that everything had become simple and obvious to her. Turning neither to the right nor to the left, she made her way to the city gate. Now she was outside the city — and the road led straight to the convent. The sound of the bells seemed to press her forward, as the wind presses on a virgin sailing ship. Onward she went, between darkly undulating vineyards whose ragged foliage hung in wild fantastic silhouettes from gnarled and twisted stakes, onward between the maize fields, onward until she heard a new, high-pitched sound: the voice of the little convent bell that also rang at this hour.

When all these sounds were still, behind her in the city and before her in the convent, — when vespers had begun before and behind her, — Marietta, now calm and full of trust, walked on through the dusky autumn evening that was steeped in the strong perfume of grain and moist earth, of overripe fruit and rotting leaves.

After an hour, she stood before the bare, crumbling convent door, and when she pulled the rusty bell a startled bird flew out of the dark foliage of the surrounding tall cypresses. The fluttering of the bird and the jangling of the bell, which hesitated hysterically between two tones, re-awakened her disquiet. Wooden heels clattered in the corridor — it was as though they had to bridge a whole world before they reached the door. "They will get here sometime," Marietta said to herself, trying to drive away the terrifying illusion that under the curse of these clattering steps she would be fettered forever at this gate. . . .

They would get there sometime. Now to the patter of the feet was added the gentle jingling of a bunch of keys. . . . Or was it a metal rosary, such as old nuns were wont to wear?

In the old door, pale golden cracks appeared. The shutter of the judas was opened, and through the grating peered distrustfully the shriveled face of a nun, warmly lit by the flame of an oil lamp. It peered at Marietta and then vanished again. A bolt was drawn back, the opening door creaked. A dark apparition stood in the moonlight, and asked: "What are you doing here at this hour? Who are you?"

Marietta did not know what to reply. She stared at the old woman and was afraid. Suddenly she herself did not know how she had got there, and what she had hoped to find. Who was she? What was she doing here at this hour? She had not chosen the right moment. . . . In what sort of dream had she been living? Had she thought they would let her in without question? Give her a straw bed and a piece of bread? Just say, "Come in, creature of God?" And now she stood at the convent gate knowing nothing, feeling terribly tired. . . . She sank down by the old nun, and clung to her coarse gray dress.

The doorkeeper, growing more distrustful, stood stock-still, and plied Marietta with further questions — severe, but reasonable questions, to which no answer came. Then a star shot across the heavens, and this Sign was not lost on the devout soul, who vaguely recalled sacred stories of miraculous meetings with the Virgin, of visits late at night to convents whose inmates had gloriously withstood the test of Christian virtue, and had subsequently attained to high honor and fame. . . . She grew certain where there was uncertainty, and in her ready and receptive piety she accepted the possibility of a miracle. She bent over the small figure at her feet. With her work hardened hands she seized her under the armpits and, panting with the effort, lifted up the childish body that trembled like an aspen leaf. Now that she saw Marietta's face clearly, she thought she recognized it. This surely was the little girl of Vacca the innkeeper. She no longer believed that a miracle had happened; but she would leave a decision to others. As a lay sister, it was certainly not meet for her to decide.

"Pull yourself together," she said encouragingly. "The convent turns nobody from its doors, and you need not explain to me. I'm only the gatekeeper."

"Mother!" protested Marietta, recovering her voice.

But the old woman, drawing her inside the door and shooting home the bolt again, was too conscious of the glory of her humility to allow herself to be deprived of it. "No, no, not mother. You must talk to the abbess. She is the mistress of us all. We have only to serve her, and on her head rests the hand of God. Come!"

Muttering to herself, looking round inquiringly once or twice as she went, she preceded Marietta down the endless stone corridor. Her wooden soles clattered, echoing against the walls. The metal rosary (it *was* a rosary after all) clinked. Somewhere between two dusky worlds a lantern hung, and under it in a niche was a little image of Our Lady of Pain.

Looking round shyly, Marietta glided under the soft, suffused light of the lantern. Would everything turn out as she had dreamed it would? Was she under the protection of God's hand here, as the old woman had said? Would the abbess keep her here, or would she warn Vacca that he must come and fetch his foster child?

A short while back, lonely under the autumnal sky, walking rapidly in the night wind that swept down from the mountains, she had felt neither doubt nor anxiety. . . .

THE

NEW

BISHOP

I

AUTUMN PASSED, AND AFTER DEAD, DARK WINTER days came the boisterous storms of spring. But none of these changes changed the day-by-day routine that ruled in the old, low-built convent. While the spring drove the sap up from the earth, and under the full moon the nightingale warbled in the silvered luxuriance of the leaves like any lovesick troubadour, pious Aves and Te Deums continued to rise from the convent chapel.

Then came summer, glowing hot. The sun burned up the grass between the stones, the wells ran dry, and in the bed of the Tiber near Pontecutini only a little mud flowed slowly by. The nights brought no relief of coolness. Every morning the sun rose red behind the mountains . . . angrily red. . . . Animals fell dead in the fields, and a black swarm of flies buzzed over their carcasses. A pilgrimage was made to the convent, and the small miraculous Madonna over the back door listened to the supplicants: she sent rain in abundance, cloudbursts. Part of the bridge at Pontecutini was swept away by the flood. Then the summer was gone. A cruel summer, like so many. But its afflictions were forgotten in the joys of autumn, with its young wine and fragrant fruit, and a new glory of flowers in the bare, seared fields.

Yes, it was autumn again. Around the convent every evening a fine gray mist wreathed itself, growing thicker and thicker until in the early morning hours the low building was hidden by the blanket of moisture that drowned every noise of the outside world. But the clear, golden sun brought deliverance, precipitated the mist onto the tiles of the convent, onto the leaves and stones about it. The silken threads of thousands of spiderwebs sparkled with the crystal-clear color that quivered in the drops of water clinging to them, and the world rose up from the night again, renewed and rejuvenated.

In the vineyard, sheltered by carmine-red and ocher-yellow vine leaves, hung heavy bunches of grapes, several of which Sister Maddalena nipped off each morning for the midday meal. If a fine bunch hung too high for her to reach it, Marietta fetched the ladder, climbed rapidly up it, and plucked the somber glowing fruit while Sister Maddalena held the basket high.

Upon the shoulders of Sister Maddalena, who though only thirty years old was already the abbess's right hand, rested the entire housekeeping of the convent. Every day she inspected the long refectory, roofed with heavy oak rafters, the novices' dormitory, the washhouse. She ruled both the great tidy kitchens where, against the cool white of the plastered wall, hung the brightly burnished pots and pans of red copper. The old, wrinkled abbess with her prim, receding mouth and her shortsighted glance clung grimly to her last domain — the dark little chapel with the choir, where Sister Maddalena knelt meekly among the others.

Tall and full-breasted was Sister Maddalena. Upon her cheek was a peachlike bloom, and her eyes were kind. As she was always busy, she was always too warm, winter and summer alike. Beads of perspiration nearly always stood out upon her downy skin. She herself laughed as she wiped them away. She looked more like the mother of a large household of children than like a nun. If the rules had allowed it, she would have turned up her sleeves and joined the lay sisters at the washtub, demanding for herself the largest articles.

It was to the nervously mumbling, ever-protesting, spluttering abbess, that, on the evening of her arrival, Marietta had had to confess what had driven her to the convent; but it was Sister Maddalena who, the following day, went to the city to convince the podesta that it was better to board out a thirteen-year-old girl in a convent than in a widower's house.

From the podesta's she had gone straight to The Three Popes to demand Marietta's clothes. Observing Nana with a certain skepticism and distrust as she ran sobbing to and fro, she asked: "Now is this all put on? Or do you really care for the child?"

"Who could care for her more than I?" Nana had answered from the bottom of her indignant heart. "If I could die for her, that would be a good death to me."

"Oh, well, you can come and see her now and again."

But Nana shrank from this invitation. "No, no, I won't come. Not at present, at any rate. Perhaps she'll be able to forgive me more quickly if she does not see me for a bit. Here, give her this. Tell her that it's from me, and ask her if she still . . . No, better ask her nothing!" Nana rummaged in her bosom, scanty beside Sister Maddalena's buxom form, and extracted from it a little silver heart hung upon a thin chain.

Working under Sister Maddalena's supervision, Marietta learned something fresh every day. For instance, how to decorate a dinner table with field flowers in common earthenware jars. Nana had never had time for such niceties. Also, there was no cloth on the table in the convent, but the dark wood was polished to a gleaming brightness in which the tin spoons and forks that were scrubbed with sand, the water mugs and the white plates, were reflected; and Sister Maddalena was of opinion that the convent was no whit the poorer if a few variegated autumn leaves were laid under the fruit in the fruit bowl, or if a few wild cyclamen and marguerites were stuck between the fruit.

Marietta served at table, helped by Virginia, a young novice over whom hung the glamour of a romantic love affair with an unhappy ending. Sister Maddalena made Marietta help too in the washing up,—which took about an hour every midday,—with the scrubbing of the corridors, the baking of the bread. The lay sisters did all this; while the nuns, in the free hour left to them after they had finished their needlework and their devotions, tended the flower garden in the cloisters. Antonio Buongiorno, the son of the coffinmaker of Todi, came to dig and manure the vineyard. The sisters still called him Antonino, although he was tall and strong and already eighteen. He was so shy that while he worked he never dared to look up, and he always waited till he was alone before he blew his nose or wiped the sweat from the inside of his straw hat. He was the only outsider allowed to enter the convent day by day, except the uncommonly ugly and self-contained father confessor, who lived almost like a hermit half a mile from the convent and entered by the back door of the chapel, with his own key, in order to perform the service before the altar.

All the novices and younger nuns were a little enamored of the silent gardener, with his comely boy's face. Happily for him he had no idea that this was so. He turned pale as death when Virginia, on his Saint's name day, gave him a handkerchief embroidered by herself with an Antony of Padua preaching to the fishes, and warned him that the abbess must never hear a word about it.

Marietta had been a little jealous — she idolized Virginia, who was seventeen and the youngest novice, and who, besides, was admired by everyone for her high spirits and helpful disposition, and for her very great gifts. She made the prettiest fancywork that ever was seen, and she gave it away with a lavish hand. She could paint, too. She was a Venetian, and she had landed in this Umbrian convent only through the tyranny of her brother. From Venice her father sent her colors and paintbrushes, and engravings of Venice to paint from. She had been at the convent only a year, and already the ladies of Todi had learned to appreciate her art. A petition had even been sent to the abbess by these ladies, asking whether Virginia could not join their little circle once a week and give them lessons in fancy needlework. To Marietta's satisfaction, the abbess, who had received special orders to guard her young novice, decided to refuse this request.

In the evenings, after the long day's work, Virginia was still busy at her handiwork, and Marietta, pale with sleepiness, watched her. She was enthralled by it, just as she was enthralled by Virginia herself, by her friendly voice, which held a gentle irony, by her fair, transparent complexion, in which stood dark, velvety, thoughtful eyes that lit up unexpectedly and sparkled with mischief, as if determined to take nothing too seriously — neither the old convent with its venerable walls nor the abbess and the nuns, neither life, nor even herself. Nobody could quite fathom this smile. It made some of them feel ill at ease — for what was there to smile about? Marietta often watched her when she smiled. She herself always took everything seriously, plunged to the full into every sorrow, to recover afterwards, tired and wounded. But Virginia only smiled. She had been sent to the convent as a punishment, and she behaved as though she had taken up her abode there for her pleasure. Who could help admiring and loving her?

Every morning before sunrise Marietta attended early prayers, proud of the early hour and of mixing with the nuns and the novices. She followed Sister Maddalena through the dark corridor towards the lighted doorway at the end — the chapel. Each sister had her own place in the choir, the novices knelt in the chapel itself. Marietta contrived to arrange things so that she knelt beside Virginia on the back bench. She did not feel the hard wood under her knees. The organ music sounded fine in the dawn, while the body was still fasting, still half-stupefied with sleep — when the soul still seemed to wander helplessly in the infinite darkness of the night, and heard the summons thankfully that called it towards the light. She shivered slightly at the heavy droning of the deepest pipes. It was a glorious moment; and she could not forbear to look round at Virginia, who knelt beside her, her face buried devoutly in her hands. Surreptitiously she looked at the little red-gold curls, gleaming in the candlelight, that danced mysteriously from under Virginia's sober novice's coif. What wonderful hair it was! She wondered whether Virginia would let her see it, just once, in its full glory. For months she had wanted to ask her, but had not dared. Surely Virginia would not refuse. Did she not allow Marietta all sorts of little privileges? Didn't she ask her advice now and then as to the colors she should choose for her fancywork? Didn't she make her pose sometimes when she was painting her little views of Venice?

One day Marietta would dare to ask her. . . . But perhaps it was a grevious sin to think about this, just at that moment. Conscious of guilt, she turned away her head, and prayed fervently with the others . . .

In the convent she felt herself at peace. She wanted nothing different. She enjoyed her daily tasks. She liked scrubbing the floors with sand and water. She liked washing up plates and dishes, and ranging them in their dozens on the racks. She liked piling up the mugs in sixes in the cupboards, putting away the knives and forks, rinsing out the kitchen cloths, and hanging them to dry while garrulous Elisabetta, who did the cooking under Sister Maddalena's supervision, talked endlessly to Sister Martha, a younger lay sister, of all that she had just heard from old Catarina the doorkeeper, who went twice a week to market in Todi.

"Yes, the podesta is retiring and it looks now as though we should get a new podesta before we get a new bishop. Old Signor Galli wants his son, young Signor Galli, to be podesta. They'll get some votes, for they're the richest family in the city and can afford to splash it a bit. But the Gallis are from Siena, and the podesta's always chosen from a Todi family. So what does old Signor Galli do? He builds a magnificent vault in the churchyard here. Nobody can say now that Galli doesn't mean to remain in Todi. And what else does the old fox do? Upon the podesta's retirement, he summons him to a great banquet and invites the whole world to do him homage. And that's not enough — You needn't hang out that kitchen cloth, Marietta: it's going to the wash — No, that's not enough. He sends a donation to the committee for the celebration of church feasts, and to the fund for widows and orphans too, to the cathedral restoration fund, and the society for the care of the sick. Thank you very much, old Signor Galli. You can sleep in peace. Your son will certainly be podesta. . . . And do you know who is going to marry? Vacca the innkeeper. And his servant! They've just waited till the year is out, but not a moment longer . . ." Elisabetta, chattering gaily on, suddenly put her hand to her mouth and looked at Marietta; but she, flushing, merely said, in the silence, "What's that to do with me? He isn't my father."

"Oh, but if he had been I shouldn't have said anything, Marietta," Elisabetta assured her, relieved.

After a moment, Marietta realized that she hardly cared at all. How strange and far away the world outside the convent had become! Only now did she realize this fully. So they were going to marry? Instead of that girl of Brogi's, it was to be Nana herself.

Nana, who, since Marietta had come to the convent, had made no sign of life.

II

Yes, the world outside the convent still went on, even though Marietta had almost forgotten it; and in this world, the marriage of Vacca the inn-keeper roused mixed feelings, lightheartedly ignored by Nana. Now that her once sinful relationship to Vacca had received the consecration of the church she dared, for the first time, to appear before Marietta. As a peace offering, she brought with her a goose for the convent, and for Marietta a little box containing a few trinkets.

"You needn't thank me, my child — they've always belonged to you. Where did you think those earrings and that chain came from? It gave me no peace. I went on and on at Vacca until he showed me where he'd hidden the stuff. He told me your mother gave it him when she left you behind fourteen years ago. Take it, keep it, or give it to the abbess to take care of. And how are you, child? Here, here's something from me . . . for your last birthday. D'you know, I spent the whole day crying? I dared not come to see you. I should have set out a thousand times if I'd only been sure you'd forgiven me."

But on the very night of her arrival at the convent, Marietta had forgiven Nana everything; and afterwards she had longed for Nana to come so that she could say to her, "Nana, don't worry about me. I'm happy here. You be happy too. Take Mother's place with Vacca, if that is what you want." But the months had passed, and Nana had not come. And Marietta could no longer speak of that night. Now Nana was married to Vacca, and the words of forgiveness would not come to Marietta's lips. Nana had changed in that one year. They were completely estranged from one another.

Nana refused to understand this at first. Her old proudly maternal feelings for this quiet, precocious child came back to her. She was sure that everything would be as before between them. She came to the convent every Sunday, bringing with her some titbit or other for her little

Marietta; and each time she came she brought flowers and put them on the grave of her former padrona, without knowing exactly whether she did this out of respect for the dead or in the hope that Marietta would notice.

"But what's the matter? Aren't you going to kiss Nana any more? Is that too much to expect?" she asked sadly, sometimes, and gradually she came to think that she had the right to feel a little wounded. Her former humble, serving love was slowly but surely changing to a feeling of maternal authority. On her first visit she had shed a flood of sincere tears, and she now felt that it was only right that Marietta should forgive the past. That Marietta made no declaration of forgiveness began to irritate her, particularly as it consorted ill with her newly acquired self-esteem.

Since Vacca had raised her to the position of padrona, Nana had begun to bloom — an autumn rose. She had grown loquacious, and was inclined to ostentation. One day Virginia was with Marietta, and several inquisitive novices who had come to listen to Nana's lively tattle from behind the grating constituted a gratifying public for her. Nana's glory, that had come to her so late, had gone to her head, and she proceeded to tell these future nuns how to deal with a man like Vacca, once one had been caught in the toils of matrimony.

Nana had acquired very different views on men from those she had held in other days; and she was determined too that they should look at her with different eyes. She demanded admiration for her swelling charms. And things went as she wished. Vacca's customers called after her teasingly as they raised their glasses, and liked to smack her sturdy buttocks as she passed them with a challenging sweep of her skirts. Vacca looked on grinning, noted that his inn was becoming more and more popular, and that Gaetano, the toll-house keeper, who had a little café by the city gate, was losing his clients to him, all thanks to that devilish little wife of his. His takings went into her pocket, and he received weekly pocket money. But that was all right. She wouldn't throw his money down the drain. Besides, he was prepared to agree to everything — he was after all a lamb, though no one would have believed it. When he had reached out to her because she had happened to be near at hand, he had had no idea that she would turn out to be such a rogue. She had made another man of him — a man who could throw away a lira or two among his customers. Weekly pocket money indeed! It was enough for him to wink at her — she slipped her hand into her skirt and gave him something extra. He knew well enough how to play on her weakness. Madonna! she was like a withered plant that had only required attention to put forth leaves and blossoms.

Nana longed to make Marietta realize what had happened to her. But how could she? After all, Marietta was but a child. Still she did succeed in making it clear that Vacca was under her thumb.

"You should just see him! You wouldn't believe your eyes. I only have to whistle, and he comes running up and eats out of my hand." And in her proud elation she did whistle too, awkwardly as a woman does. She made the novices laugh, and then they turned round hurriedly in case any of the older nuns were about. Nana began to chuckle herself. Then she put her hand over her mouth in mock fright, as if she had been no older than these girls who listened to her greedily. "Heavens above! What am I talking to you about? I really ought to know better. No, really, I was forgetting I'm in a convent, but that man's so extraordinary!" she cried, then pulled herself together, and, wiping her forehead with her handkerchief, forced herself to a pretended seriousness that was broken immediately by little gurgles of laughter. "Lord, Lord! Well, I only wanted to make you understand that I'm keeping him well under. Child, if you wanted to, you could come back to us quite safely. Nothing would happen to you again. Oh yes, I made him tell me that, too, you know — about that night when you came to sleep with me because of your bad dream. Do you remember? I told him what I thought of him, and I didn't mince words either; but it's no good. They're all the same, those men. And they always manage to make you laugh! I said to him, 'I could tear your eyes out of your head for what you did' — and what does he say in reply? 'And what would I have left to look at you with, then?' What, are you angry, Marietta? Lord, she's running away. But what have I said? Marietta!"

With tears of laughter still on her cheeks, Nana stared in astonishment towards the door through which Marietta had vanished. She began to tremble, groped blindly for her basket and umbrella, and tried to get up. But at that moment she burst into sobs. She sat down again limply, and, turning to the novices, she said, weeping, "What have I done to her? Tell me — you saw. What have I done? I'm like a mother to her. Every Sunday I bring something for her, and she doesn't even say thank you. I'd go through fire for her — and she runs out of the room and lets me sit here like a fool. Everybody likes me these days, everybody. She's the only one who doesn't. And once upon a time everything went right between us . . . I shan't come back. Perhaps I'm out of place here. Maybe I said more than I should have done. I don't know. Lord, I'm only a human being. Say good-by to her for me. Tell her that Nana will come back when Nana is called for."

She staggered up, catching her breath, and, carrying her basket and umbrella, tottered towards the door.

Virginia, who had looked on in silent pity, got up and left the room by the other door; while the novices, half-ashamed and half-laughing, exchanged glances with one another.

No, Marietta was not to be persuaded, even by Virginia, to call Nana back. She could not bear her any more. Nana's tears, Nana's exuberant embraces and moist kisses, Nana's vociferous contrition, Nana's glorious present as padrona of The Three Popes. . . . Marietta had no wish to hear what Vacca had said, and that all men were alike.

Each of Nana's visits convinced her anew that she could no longer live in the city. She bathed her soul in the unruffled peace of the convent. She was satisfied and happy as she stood in the garden within the cloisters and watched a butterfly here and there hovering from flower to flower. She leaned against the high rim of the well, picked up the pail slowly, and let it drop into the depths, the chain jingling after it, listening to the glorious sound of meeting metal and water that rose in the undisturbed serenity of the clear morning. She looked up at the gray, weatherbeaten tower with its clock and its sundial. Oh, how good it all was, how good! In the cloisters Sisters Veronica and Teresa went by silently together, and nodded to her with quiet friendliness — during working hours, talking was not encouraged. Marietta poured the water from the pail into her pitcher, and returned to the kitchen.

Soon after her arrival at the convent, a new mother had been tacitly assigned to her. Every morning Sister Maddalena set her her daily task and gave her instructions in reading, writing, and reckoning, interrupting these lessons only to talk about the Miracles of the Saints. Nana too had told her about the saints, but with a certain predilection for the frightful temptations they had had to overcome. Nana had spoken of bloody self-castigation, of martyrdom and decapitation in heathen Alexandria, and of recent exorcisings of devils by a Pisan father confessor. But Sister Maddalena conjured up beautiful visions that struck deep into one's soul instead of rousing terror — visions of Saint Cecilia playing upon the organ of the unbelievers to the glory of God; of Catherine of Siena instructing the Pope at Avignon on his duty to return to Godless Rome; of Clare of Assisi overcoming her earthly love for Saint Francis; of Fina of San Gimignano visiting the plague house. Pictures of quiet and lowly heroism in young, tender maidens like Marietta herself.

Real life with its strife, its demons, its bitter grief was too remote from the convent to bind Sister Maddalena and Marietta together like an actual mother and her child. But they were also spared the daily suffering of the more intimate relationship. Sister Maddalena, not realizing herself the incompleteness of her motherhood, received from it a permanent quiet satisfaction and joy: for if she was deprived of the highest bliss, she was also spared the wormwood. Marietta, who had come into conflict with life too soon, found in the other's untroubled mothering something infinitely beneficent, and asked for no more.

Marietta slept in Sister Maddalena's cell. Sometimes she woke when Sister Maddalena got up carefully from her plank bed for midnight matins and opened the door leading into the corridor where the nuns were shuffling by. Marietta was not yet allowed to take part in this service. With open eyes she lay listening in the darkness. Now the footsteps had ceased to echo in the corridor, and the door of the chapel had been closed. There was only the stillness, which seemed to be creeping round the convent on felt soles. . . . Between intervals of silence she could hear the monotonous chanting of prayers. She remembered that once upon a time she had been afraid of the dark when Nana sent her to bed, and had never dared to go to sleep so long as she was alone. But here the darkness was good and concealed no danger. Here the night belonged to God — God's dark compassionate night.

It was at night that Marietta asked herself, "Couldn't I always remain here, near Sister Maddalena, near Virginia with her red-gold hair? I should like to become a novice too, and later take the vow. I never want to go away from here, never, never. . . ."

III

One morning Sister Maddalena said to her, "Do you know where you're going to-day after the midday meal, Marietta? To the city, with Signora Galli's fine linen."

Old Signora Galli of the piazza, the mother of the new podesta, sent her fine linen to be washed at the convent. Hitherto, Catarina had always delivered the washing on her way to market once a week; but the previous Saturday, fishwater had unaccountably found its way into the basket, and the next day Signora Galli had come round in her coach, given Catarina a piece of her mind when she opened the door, and afterwards in the library, which served as reception room, had reiterated her complaints to the abbess. Every word she said had been heard by the novices, who happened to be passing down the corridor. And now Catarina was relieved of her combined duty. She had only to go to market. Marietta was to deliver Signora Galli's washing in future.

Appalled by this duty, Marietta could only obey. The basket was hung over her arm. With bowed head she listened to the warnings and advice with which the abbess herself overwhelmed her, and with a heavy heart she set out. But as she followed the familiar way between the sunlit fields, in spite of herself a more lighthearted mood welled up in her. She had forgotten what it felt like to walk through the fields at the foot of the mountains. From behind the convent walls had she perhaps seen the world outside as something too dark, too dangerous?

"God's wide world," she suddenly heard herself murmuring, "God's wide world!" She ran faster and faster. She could have embraced every tree. Softly she began to sing to herself, "God's wide world," and looked round shyly to see if a peasant working in the field had perhaps heard her. She did not know what was the matter with her. But she was certainly very small and childish. She sat down by the side of the road and took off her sandals in order to walk barefoot as she used to do. She did not put them on again until she came to the city. A great joyous feeling rose in her when she reached the point of intersection of two glowing lines of hills whence she could see Todi, blooming, twinkling in the pure light of the blue autumnal sky. She knew every roof, and it was as if the towers greeted her. . . . Why had she remembered only the shadowy side — the old creaking stairs in Vacca's inn, the funeral feast behind closed shutters?

How could she have been so afraid of the city? As a child, she had roamed its every nook and cranny, carefree and innocent, threatened with no danger. Her fear had gone. Looking back, she had to smile at all the wisdom and advice with which the old abbess had just burdened her. Perhaps she was living in a dream, in a much too bright and joyous dream; perhaps disillusion would follow. But she could not help herself. She had been deprived of all this gladness too long — the blitheness of the bright red roofs of Todi, of its fine old towers. . . .

From a distance, she tried to make out who was talking to Gaetano by the city gate. She felt a burning desire for people, for people's faces. Soon she would see the piazza again, where the children played. She would pass by Vacca's inn quickly and unobserved.

She reached the gate. She greeted Gaetano, and looked at him half-mischievously. He recognized her at once. How surprised he was! She felt a strange attraction to Gaetano. He had never done her any harm, and now he was the first person she met as she entered the city.

" 'Morning, Gaetano" — and instantly she began to regret not having run past him with merely a nod, for he buttonholed her, insisted she should tell him everything about herself, whether she was remaining in the convent of her own free will, or because Vacca wished it, what truth there was in what people were saying, that one night she had just taken flight and gone

there. Marietta freed herself only with difficulty. "I'm in a hurry, Gaetano.
I must go. Some other time."

She realized that she must avoid people. They would, all of them, ask
her questions. She must curb her feelings of tenderness, make a show of
reserve though her heart stood open and weak. With bent head, flushed
with a strange shame, and daring to look neither to the right nor to the
left, without turning her head when she heard her name called after her,
she went straight to the piazza, on the other side of which stood the Gallis'
marble palace. She refused to see the inn; but of course she did see it.
Luigino happened to be standing outside and his face wore a look of
astonishment when he saw her.

She fled through the wide entrance of the Palazzo Galli into the courtyard within, and knocked at the kitchen door. Xenia and Rosalina, the
two youngest maids, nosed inquisitively into the linen basket. Rosalina laid
a flounce of lace over her wrist to see the effect, and said, "Now go upstairs at once before the visitors arrive."

Xenia and Rosalina asked no indiscreet questions — they thought themselves too important to be interested in Marietta's fate.

"Can't I just leave the basket here?" asked Marietta tentatively, intimidated by the luxury of the house.

"You don't know her very well. She likes to poke her nose into everything. It's just at the top of the staircase, on the left."

Old Signora Galli, sitting in state on a chair upholstered in Gobelin
tapestry, was waiting for her visitors, who were late. Marietta's appearance at the door filled her with satisfaction.

"Come in, come in! You've brought the washing? So you're to bring
it, in future, instead of that old know-all? Set the basket down on that chair
and bring it up to me."

Signora Galli was very large and very heavy, and her dress stood out
round her like a cloud so that it was impossible to bring the chair up as
close as she wanted, and Marietta had to hand up the garments one by one
for her inspection. Her dress made her unapproachable as a queen. Her
skin was covered with a thick layer of powder. No flower in all the world
was as scented as she. Her bosom was confined by a bodice and pressed
into a deceptive youthfulness whose glory was enhanced by a garland of
flowery lace and a monster heart-shaped locket. Her wig, half an ell high,
would have passed even in Venice or Naples for a masterpiece of the hairdresser's art. It had, however, been created by Barberini, the barber on the
piazza, and was the result of a series of sleepless nights. He had toned down
the conventionally dignified severity of the headdress by a coquettish and
cunning arrangement of ribbons and of little mirrors that reflected every-

thing in the room. This remarkable coiffure framed a face that, though withered, still retained something ingenuous and childlike. From head to foot, Signora Galli was laden with gold and jewels. The ornaments that hung from her small and dainty ears represented a fortune in diamonds. Her wrinkled wrists were completely concealed by rows of bracelets. At every moment, she glittered and jingled like an Oriental dancer.

While she passed the washing under review, carefully, piece by piece, she began to chatter confidentially to Marietta. "One moment, if you please. This neckband smelled so horribly of fish that I doubt whether my son will ever put it on again. That old Catarina of yours is a shameful liar. You can tell her so from me. She actually tried to deny that she'd taken the basket to market with her. The arrangement was that she was always to come to me first; but of course upon reaching the city gate she heard a rumor of some cheap fish and rushed straight off to the market. Yes, and the washing of old Signora Galli had to go with her. The whole room reeked of fish after she'd gone. The whole room testified to the truth, and still she denied it. Look here, just for the fun of the thing, smell this — Giacomo is terribly fastidious about his neckbands. My son, I mean."

Marietta dared not put her nose to the neckband held out to her. She shook her head nervously, embarrassed, to imply that she smelled nothing at all. Meanwhile Signora Galli peered at her through her lorgnette as inquisitively as she did at the washing. "What's your name?" she asked. "Marietta who? Oh, wait! You're surely the little girl I've heard about. I must have seen you playing on the piazza as a child that high. At least, I think so. But I can't see very well at a distance. It's different close to. Now tell me why you ran away. I've heard one thing and another, but I do like to know the truth. I'm an old woman. Or have they warned you against me?" she interjected suddenly, distrustfully. She seized a black ebony cane that lay within reach of her arm. Marietta, turning pale, stepped back involuntarily. "Here! I can hardly walk any more. Except with this stick. I can't get anywhere. . . . They like to keep me out of everything. . . . That's why I like to know everything. Guess how old I am."

Marietta was afraid to guess. She was also afraid to run away. There she stood, as if nailed to the carpet. Old Signora Galli peered at her through her lorgnette, and answered her own question herself, burning with curiosity as to the effect she hoped to read on Marietta's face. "Seventy-seven! What do you think of that? Have you heard of the family vault they built in the spring? The idea is that I should take possession first, for my husband is thirteen years younger than I. I told my son straight out: 'Giacomo, you're building a handsome house for me. Yes, but I've no intention of taking possession first. I want to see who will manage to last longer, your father or I.' In my family, we all live long, and I'm heading straight for ninety." For the third time she raised her lorgnette to look at Marietta, for it was of paramount interest to her to discover whether Marietta looked optimistic as to her successfully reaching ninety years of age.

Then Signora Galli subjected her to a severe cross-examination full of sly questions that sounded perfectly innocent: How old was Marietta, and which of the nuns were nicest to her; had she by any chance a special friend among the novices, and did she on occasion sleep in one bed with her, for the sake of companionship, when unobserved by the sisters, and was there perhaps one of the sisters who wanted her to go and sleep with her? And in the summer, when it was warm, did she sometimes take off her nightdress, although it was against the rules? Signora Galli herself always took hers off in the summer; but she always bolted the door, because she would not allow her husband to surprise her in that state. Yes . . . and did Marietta feel that confession was a great relief to her feelings? And the Franciscan friar who came for the purpose, did she always honestly confess everything to him? Or was she sometimes embarrassed? And if he were a handsome young brother, like so many these days, did she want to appear innocent in his eyes? It would really be better if the abbess could hear confessions, for novices, and even nuns, would sometimes confess to an attractive young Franciscan all sorts of sins they had never committed, in order to make him forget that he wore a consecrated cowl. It was against such temptations that the saints had fought successfully. But not every young, attractive Franciscan with dark piercing eyes and a handsome beard was a saint. Oh, not by a long way — too many tales went the rounds.

To all her sly questions, Signora Galli received replies that were at first stammering, unsatisfactory, and gradually even reluctant. As she dwelt on the wickedness of the world, she involuntarily recalled how she herself had once thought of taking the veil. That was forty years ago, after the death of her first husband. She showed Marietta the inside of the locket that hung on her bosom. Marietta, however, whose heart was sinking by this time, could not distinguish the features of the deceased — indeed, she could hardly bring herself to look at them; and Signora Galli put back her first life companion into his place of honor, and related how while traveling he had driven into the Arno, carriage and all, and been drowned. The horses had been startled by a team of oxen. The accident happened in Pisa — and she had always found it such a dull, unattractive town. Yes, yes. She had wept till her pillows were drenched, and she had really thought seriously of retiring to a convent. But God sent her a dream in which an angel with a flaming sword stood before a convent gate barring the way — and a month later the young and affluent Signor Galli had come and honored her with a proposal. Such was life. Looking back, she could laugh about it all; but she still wondered sometimes what it would have been like if she had really turned her back upon the vanities of this vale of tears in order to dedicate herself to God in solitude and austerity. Then she wouldn't have had a podesta for a son, and she would have been less useful in other ways too — for instance, her donations. The convent would get its usual Christmas present again; but Marietta was not to say a word about that to anybody. . . .

From downstairs could be heard the voices of Signora Rigogli, wife of the judge, and Signora Perosio, mother of the papal tax collector. Old Signora Galli raised her head to listen. Suddenly she lost all interest in Marietta, told her to put down the contents of the basket on the table in the back room, and then to get the soiled linen from the kitchen. Next Saturday she would expect her again.

As she went down the narrow back stair, Marietta could not remember whether she had curtsied. Sister Maddalena would be bound to ask her if she had; but in the end her nausea and abhorrence had got the better of her. Never, never would she come here again. They might punish her, do anything they liked to her. . . .

She had to cross the piazza again, then go through streets and past Gaetano before she would be in the open fields again. She would stop for nobody, speak to nobody. But as with bowed head she went swiftly past The Three Popes, a little woman shot out by the side door straight in front of her and barred the way.

Nana. Of course it could be only Nana. Their eyes met, and Marietta knew that she could not get through with an imploring word, an assurance that she was in a hurry. In Nana's glance, there was desperate resolution. The words she hissed out were full of bitterness. There was a strange hoarse ring in her voice. "No, that won't do. That just won't do. You're not going back to the convent without coming in to see me first." To make quite sure, she seized Marietta by the arm and led her towards the inn.

"You needn't see him," said Nana, recovering her voice now that Marietta was following her weakly. "I've told him not to come into the kitchen. Let's go through the side door."

Now they were sitting together in the old kitchen they both knew so well. It seemed to look down on them with surprise. After her display of forcefulness Nana relapsed, weak and downcast, with nothing more to say.

Here was Marietta inside the inn, sitting with her; and still they were like strangers to each other. At last Nana understood what she had not been able before to believe: that she no longer meant anything to Marietta. A deep sadness caught at her throat. With an attempt at ingenuous frankness, she said, "It's only for the sake of appearances. What must they think when you come to the city and don't visit your old home? Have I really deserved that?"

But was the child listening to her? There she sat, with great strange eyes, gazing slowly round the kitchen. Nana was silent now, following her glance. In that moment of unaccustomed lucidity, inspired by grief, did Nana realize that things were not so tidy here as in the convent? Did she feel something of the confusion that reigned here? Did she see how flyblown and cobwebbed the ceiling was? Did she perceive the slightly sickly odor of badly washed kitchen utensils, stale greens, soap, olive oil that had turned rancid? It was almost unbelievable that she could sense it — she had breathed this atmosphere all her life. After so many years, surely she did not notice that the little table at which Marietta sat was rickety: but then why did she lean against it, so that it stood firm?

Something inside her was saying, "This place is no longer good enough for the child, Nana. She is accustomed to order and cleanliness, and notices at once that the floor tiles are loose, and that your apron is dirty. And don't be mistaken: you yourself are no longer good enough for her. Her childish body and her soul are pure. . . . Do you still know what purity is? You who have crept into the bed of your dead padrona? What is the good of your leaning against the table so that it doesn't wobble? It isn't the table — it's you yourself, you yourself. . . ." With a heavy sigh of discouragement, she got up and prepared some chocolate. "You'll have a cup of chocolate with me?" she asked humbly. "You used to like it." With exaggerated care she cleaned two cups, remembering only when it was too late that she ought to have got a clean kitchen cloth out of the cupboard.

Grinning like an ape, Luigino appeared at the door. In her most menacing tones, Nana ordered him sharply to come and greet his sister from the convent. But he paid no heed to this show of authority — he simply continued to stare loutishly at the unaccustomed guest; and while he stood there, Nana explained that he was the greatest calamity she knew, that he had no fellow feeling for either man or beast, that through him she expected to go down to her grave early and with gray hairs, and that he himself would end his days behind bolts and bars. Oh, it seemed to her that the glamour had suddenly gone out of her life. Everything seemed poor and contemptible. Marietta would be quite right if she did not come back again.

Luigino went away, and in silence they sat opposite one another, swallowing their chocolate with difficulty.

But when Marietta was leaving, several people happened to be passing. They looked at her and at Nana with astonished interest. Nana suddenly brightened again, and as they parted said, "It was nice of you to drop in, child. But you needn't do it again. This once is enough. Thank you for coming."

For the first time Marietta looked at her attentively. Surely there was a new tone in Nana's voice? All the feeling that had seemed frozen within her began to thaw. Suddenly she understood that she could not go away like this. She wanted to be friendly with Nana; but the words stuck in her throat when she perceived Vacca and Luigino both grinning at her from two different grated windows of the inn: for a moment, she was almost paralyzed by their resemblance to one another in their ugliness.

Nana did not seem to want her to speak. She went back into the inn with a lighthearted farewell, as though to say, "All right, all right, you run along now."

Nana did not want her pity.

When Marietta had left the city again, and was going between the fields across which slid the still light of the setting sun, she knew that henceforth she would always go in and see Nana. She would walk past the grated windows in the front of the inn as though through a fire; but at the back in the old kitchen Nana would be waiting, and no one in the city would be able to say that Marietta had fled to the convent because of Nana.

And of course she would not refuse, either, to take old Signora Galli's washing. She was not so cowardly; now that she knew what she must expect there, she would no longer be drawn. She would counter cunning with cunning, and when next time she was overwhelmed with a flood of questions, she would pretend to be stupider than she was.

She reached the convent, and was received by old Catarina — who had allowed fish water to drip on to Signora Galli's fine linen, and now tried to read upon Marietta's face how the visit had gone off.

"God does not will that we should lie," preached Catarina, as if she had sensed the decision that Marietta had just taken. "But if that old vixen on the piazza should try to get to know things from you about the convent or anything else, you just lie to her. You have my permission for it." And she gave Marietta an example in devotion by bending her stiff knee and making the sign of the cross as she passed by Our Lady of Pain halfway down the long, dusky corridor.

IV

Winter set in early that year, and with uncommon severity. Heavy snow had fallen, and for a couple of days the convent was completely isolated, while outside roamed a pack of howling wolves, driven by hunger into inhabited regions. Special intercession services were held in the chapel for the speedy recovery of the bishop who had, meanwhile, been newly nominated in Rome and was prevented by sickness from taking up his duties. But just before Christmas, the disturbing news came that he had died a week ago — and further prayers were offered for his soul.

How long was Todi to be without a bishop? It was whispered in the city that a certain reluctance prevailed among the high prelates in the Vatican to accept appointment there. Did they then consider Todi too small and provincial? Hadn't it a fine cathedral? The people felt they were being unfairly done by. The newly deceased bishop in Rome had hesitated long before accepting his nomination: had God punished him for his sinful hesitation? It was wrong to say such a thing, but it was also difficult not to entertain a thought that concealed such secret satisfaction.

In the convent, the prayers were gradually assuming an almost desperate character. The abbess had decreed that twice a day prayers were to be said for the appointment of a new bishop, and were to be kept up until God answered them. When there continued to be no definite news from Rome, the abbess could no longer conceal from the elder nuns her displeasure at the sinful remissness of the high prelates in Rome. In her feverishly rising religious zeal she gave expression to her expectation that terrible punishments and curses awaited the world. She felt herself called to be the last of the righteous in Sodom and Gomorrah; she trusted in the power of prayer. What times were these, when young abbés sprinkled themselves with powder and perfumed water, when high ecclesiastics associated with worldly women, when nuns were brought to bed in their cells, and the stillborn fruit of their sin was buried in the convent garden! What dreadful reports came from Venice, Naples, Rome! In Todi, at any rate, the banner of true Christian piety still flew. Todi should not be left without a priestly shepherd so long as the abbess had a tongue to pray and a pair of knees upon which to fall in humility before God the Father.

The elder nuns passed on the abbess's holy indignation to the novices, reminding them of cases in which prayer had wrought wonders. In Lent a psychosis spread through the convent to which everybody fell a victim, even little Marietta. Sister Maddalena had ceased to be more than her religious instructor. Virginia, formerly so full of sunny irony, had begun to acquire a strange stare in the eye, and no longer made little jokes when she and Marietta fetched the dishes from the kitchen. Every feeling seemed to have given way to prayer, and they passed each other like strangers, without the usual nod. Only in the chapel did they form a unity with one voice, rising in a single wave of prayer. There was no alternative for Marietta except to surrender herself also to this painfully mysterious atmosphere that constituted the one remaining link between them. For a short time, she was consoled; but before long she was as unsatisfied and as unhappy as before. She could not keep it up, this living for nothing but prayer — some of the younger nuns had become so enamored of it that they implored the abbess to raise the daily services of intercession from two to three.

When Passion Week passed without bringing an answer, Marietta began to ask herself what they expected. Her healthy nature rebelled. Finally she found a refuge with Catarina, who still went twice a week to the city and could give her some understanding. Regular contact with reality had preserved Catarina from the delusions afflicting the others but, pious zealot that she was, even she prayed assiduously with the rest, and in her Marietta found no real consolation.

Then, one day, a report reached the convent that a new bishop had been chosen, and that the dean and chapter were about to set out for Rome to express to him Todi's delight and satisfaction.

A spasm of hysteria ran through the chapel when Catarina whispered the great news in her penetrating voice into the abbess's ear. She had just come back from the city, and, still out of breath with running, she knelt down among the others. Their prayers became a song of thanksgiving. All felt that a miracle had been vouchsafed to them.

On that day, a modest banquet was held in the convent. No one in the city need know that Todi owed its salvation to the persistent prayers offered by the nuns. No . . . but Catarina could not keep her mouth shut about it, and naturally it was impossible to prevent the citizens from marching spontaneously to the convent in thanksgiving. For several days, the younger nuns continued to break into unexpected fits of weeping. Elisabetta fell to the ground suddenly in the middle of the kitchen, laying about her with hands and feet and calling out that she saw Christ approach. Foam stood on her lips. The abbess was summoned, listened to her in a state of profound disturbance, and waited to hear what further revelations Sister Elisabetta would utter.

She was carried to her straw mattress, where she lay in a deep stupor until the following midday. The words she uttered during her unconsciousness were carefully taken down, and improved upon with flowery turns of speech. The resulting masterpiece was to be sent to the Holy

Father in Rome, signed by those who had been present in the kitchen. Elisabetta, awakening from her stupor, was given a glimpse of the document and its red ribbon fastening before it was dispatched; and as she could not read, it was read out to her. Her eyes opened wide in amazement, and she began to tremble all over. Fearing that she might faint again, they hastily rubbed her forehead and wrists with vinegar, and the abbess went to close and seal the missive. As she hastened through the dark corridor, she pressed it unconsciously to her agitated and beating heart. To nobody did she dare express the profound hope that was in her, that had been consuming her since the previous evening: the ambitious hope that her convent might be declared holy before she died.

The epistle was dispatched; but it was long before an answer was forthcoming, for correspondence of that nature could not be dealt with expeditiously.

Meanwhile, a fresh report came in that Monsignore would take up his office on the second Sunday after Whitsuntide. In the chapter hall, the abbess held a lengthy conference with the nuns. How was the convent to receive and do homage to the new bishop on his first visit? It was worrying to think of all the necessary preparations. To begin with, the nuns and novices must learn a song of welcome. Somewhere in the little library lay buried the song with which the previous bishop had been received in state thirty years before. It would serve again, since it had proved itself suitable. The whole convent must be spring-cleaned; the vineyard and the churchyard must be rendered immaculate — not a weed must be left where the episcopal eye might rest upon it.

For perhaps it was a stern eye that would suffer no weed, even in God's acre.

The entrance, the refectory, the chapel, and the library must be gaily decorated; and the abbess would naturally invite the bishop to share their meal. Fortunately there were still some very old wines in the cellar. But it was a pity that fruit was still scarce in June. It was to be a great, great day, a day of gladness and thanksgiving towards God.

For the sake of her sweet, pure voice, Marietta was to be allowed to join in the song of welcome. Indeed, a solo part was allotted to her. She was to be a child who asks innocent questions — Who is the Virgin? Who is Jesus? And who the Holy Ghost? A row of angels would answer her. And who was the devil, and how he was to be recognized? And what was the mission of the Church here on earth, and who were her first servants? And finally, she had to describe what a very special day this day seemed to her: why had God made the sun shine more beautifully than upon other days, why did the clouds in the heavens stand still like listening sheep, why did no leaf stir, no stream murmur? Why did no birds sing, and the whole world seem petrified in veneration and awe? Thereupon the row of angels would explain to her that all this was because of the solemn entry of Todi's new bishop, to whom might it please God to grant a long life, and to direct his actions with His wise understanding.

Marietta acquitted herself of her task with enthusiasm. Sister Maddalena, whose motherly feelings had been reawakened, could not conceal her proud joy. She was certain that the bishop would be pleased with this innocent voice that seemed weighted down by the exalted questions it had to put. The row of angels, however, were troublesome. Sister Veronica, pale and pockmarked, who played the organ, was in despair. It was very difficult to get them to come in at exactly the same time after Marietta had sung her question.

Another great surprise was planned: Virginia was told by the abbess to leave all the needlework and painted fans she was doing for the ladies of Todi, and was also exempted from all other work, in order that she might devote herself undisturbed to making an altar cloth that was to be the convent's gift to the bishop on the day he entered Todi.

Virginia was fully conscious of the distinction that had devolved upon her, and in her happy agitation she kissed the abbess's shriveled old hands. For a whole hour she conferred with Sister Maddalena over the kind of silk to be used for the background and the colored skeins for the embroidery, and that same afternoon Sister Maddalena went to the city to purchase all that was necessary. Until far into the night, she worked at the design. An old, faded, but very handsome altar cloth from the convent chapel was to serve as model. Only seven weeks remained in which to finish the work. Time was short.

So great were her exertions that she grew thin, and her eyes became sore. Regardless of the danger to her health, however, the others drove her on, knowing no fear but that the bishop upon his arrival might not find the cloth upon the cathedral altar. Virginia worked, worked — the whole day in the pale stillness of the convent, her face averted from the sunny garden; the whole evening by the bad light of a candle; sometimes grateful and happy when she had been successful with some difficult detail, sometimes struggling desperately because she could no longer see what she was doing. Then she had to give it up, but she could find no rest in bed. Her brain went on reckoning up the weeks, days, hours. . . . How many hours were left, if she worked, upon an average, fourteen hours a day?

Marietta watched her with concern. Ever since the days of concentrated prayer, Virginia had been different. Her naturally happy disposition, the smile that enthralled Marietta, had vanished. If only the new bishop would come!

Virginia talked about her work as if it had been a task imposed upon her by faith, a task in connection with which she must have no thought of herself. Evening after evening she worked till midnight. Then she went with the others, who had already slept, to midnight matins. In the chapel she sank upon her bench, unable to pray. She covered her burning, dark-rimmed eyes with hands that trembled from fatigue, and allowed the waves of sound from the organ to sweep over her.

Now there were only two more weeks to run. Every day in the convent was filled with scrubbing, scouring, polishing, brushing. Antonio had to weed and rake in the garden, although his father Buongiorno the coffin-maker was sick and could ill spare his help. The chapel received a thorough cleaning. The saints were taken from their niches, dusted, patched up with paint, and the broken bits replastered. A Saint Peter was endowed with a complete new forefinger: this masterpiece, to everybody's astonishment, was contrived by Catarina, whom nobody had suspected of such an accomplishment. Old Catarina was found to be equally skillful in making new little bouquets for the images of the Madonna. Out of a few pieces of silk and lawn, she cut them by the dozen — roses and marguerites. She filled the centers with sawdust and sprinkled them with scented water. Encouraged by everybody's unstinting praise, she ventured upon difficult flowers like lilies, and also upon mysterious flowers that nobody recognized, flowers that originated in Catarina's fancy, flowers of a sort that perhaps grow only in paradise. The old bouquets, faded, dusty, and fly-blown, were consigned to the dung heap as though they had once been living flowers.

On the Friday before the bishop's entry into the city, Virginia laid before the abbess a superb altar cloth. They all came to see, and were greatly impressed. Sister Maddalena held it up against the old cloth that had served as a model — and only then did everybody appreciate fully Virginia's wonderful talent. Every line had been closely followed, but rendered more delicately; and how radiant were the colors! Virginia of her own inspiration had introduced some little angels into her embroidery. From each corner charming *putti* on dove's wings fluttered down, witnesses to the center scene, which represented the birth of the Church. Signora Galli had graciously provided some real pearls ripped from an old dress to serve as an edging for the clouds. None of the nuns and novices had ever seen such a beautiful cloth. They said so in whispers. Virginia stood by, ashen pale. Her hands, her wrists had become transparent. There was something disquieting about the slight fixed smile round her drawn white lips. Now that the cloth was finished, they hardly dared look at her. These last weeks, Virginia had been supported by some mysterious power that had seemed to possess her, giving a radiance to her eyes and making her hold up her head with unconscious pride. Now, suddenly, it was as if the light in her eyes had been dimmed. Large and tired, they stood in her sunken face where only the little forced smile sought to belie her exhaustion.

Next day Virginia lay delirious in bed. She talked continually in her feverish dreams. No doctor, however, could be admitted to the convent and she was dependent upon the healing resources of the abbess, whose head these days seemed to be completely confused.

In the city, suspense had reached its acme on the Saturday. At eleven o'clock on the following morning, if the city's hopes were not falsified, the bishop would enter the gate. At sunrise a procession of the inhabitants was to leave the city carrying the banners of the guilds and the standards of the brotherhoods, in order to meet him at Pontecutini. The Tiber bridge was the proper setting for such a meeting. At the boundary post of the city domain, maidens would be waiting with baskets full of straw-flowers, and a deputation of the city dignitaries would hand over to him the holiest relics of the cathedral, together with a cushion stitched in gold on which would lie the keys of the great central gate that had been closed a year and a half. Monsignore was to be invited to celebrate High Mass and to address the congregation from the pulpit. Subsequently there would be a great banquet in his own palace. At nightfall he would go in solemn procession to inspect the illuminated triumphal arches erected in the various city wards and to receive the homage of choirs of songsters; after which, with the canons of the cathedral chapter and one or two city nota-bilities, he would rest in the Palazzo Galli after the fatigues of a full day. The program for the next day would be settled only after consultation with him. It would be filled with visits to the city churches, all of which were contending for the honor of being the first to welcome him within their walls, and with the reception of a series of deputations from all over the diocese. And after that, it would be difficult for him to evade the obligation of visiting the convent of Saint Clare.

The rules of the convent were not very clear in relation to the entry of a new bishop. Exceptionally, the nuns could be allowed to attend special ceremonial Masses in the cathedral or in the other churches of the city; but it seemed wiser to the abbess that they should wait until the bishop came to the convent, instead of appearing before his eyes in public. Such a mark of other-worldliness could not fail to make a good impression. Only little Marietta was granted permission to witness the festive entry — or, rather, she was sent. Thus it was that she set out on the Sunday morning, conducted as far as the convent gate by the younger nuns, and envied by all as she started on her way to the gaily beflagged city. A feeling of strangeness possessed her. Would she really be seeing the bishop himself soon? After all that had happened in the convent during these last months, it was difficult for her to imagine him as a creature of this earth.

From all the windows flags were flying. Over the window sills hung decorative cloths. The streets were festooned with Chinese lanterns that were to be lit in the evening. The figures of the saints that usually stood indoors had been brought out and arranged on some sort of wooden scaffolding adorned by leaves and flowers. Around his Madonna the florist Martini had created a miniature garden with real shells from the sea, and to the wrist of the little Jesus he had attached a string from which a captive thrush fluttered. All the citizens were dressed in their finest apparel. Impatiently the drums rolled, and the crowd was profoundly moved as peals of bells from all the spires announced the approach of the procession.

The half-dozen *sbirri* who represented the police force of Todi cleared the street. In their midst, high on his horse, was their captain Ferrucci, son-in-law of Falciai, the master baker, who just had time to shake hands with him. Then appeared standards, gleaming basshorns and cymbals, Franciscan brothers, Benedictines, Augustinians, Dominicans in their cream-colored cowls, papal horse guards from Rome who for purposes of protection had accompanied the expedition — huge fellows in steel cuirasses and yellow-and-white-striped trousers. Under their helmets, their dark bold eyes looked down cynically upon the astonished crowd. There were high ecclesiastics from foreign parts, notabilities, guild leaders. . . .

Standing upon her toes, Marietta witnessed the spectacle. There was the new bishop. Tall and powerfully built, he strode forward, serene and stately, under a canopy. There was something unflinching about his walk. One simply had to look. It would have been impossible to turn aside. Those who were carrying the canopy had difficulty in holding it up high enough before him. Little Signor Fiorini seemed on the point of breaking down. The bishop too was flushed with the heat after walking so far in his heavy ceremonial robes. In his hands he carried the sacred relics that had been handed over to his keeping. When the crowd tried to sink to its knees in unison, difficulties arose, for they had been standing pressed far too close to one another. The bishop turned his gaze in one direction and, impelled by his eyes, the crowd tried to kneel, stumbling over one another; but before they had succeeded he had turned his head away, and was striding on

to the accompaniment of the solemn music of the brass band, the odor of
incense and of pious sweat. It was only after he had passed that it was
possible to see clearly his powerful figure as it rose somberly above the
cassocks that gleamed duskily in the sun.

They stood up again. A dazed expression in their faces, the women
tried to catch each other's eyes. The men also looked at one another. Todi
had its leader. If they had closed the city gates against him, he would
have broken them down without a touch of his hand. If he was no saint,
he was a condottiere. Todi had its leader. One peasant who was standing
far behind remarked, "We shan't bury this one." Unpleasantly affected,
people looked round at him. "Bury?" Obstinate, the peasant stroked his
mouth, and stared with his old pale eyes across the heads of the onlookers.

Marietta attended Mass in the cathedral, which was filled to overflowing. But she could hardly see what was taking place before the altar, and
had no wish to press forward. She was no longer a child of the city. Halfway through the service the oppressive air made her feel faint. The droning of the organ seemed to die away in her ears. She felt the coolness of
the pillar against her cheek. Then she heard a deep voice speaking from
the pulpit. Stillness as of death reigned: it was as though a storm were
threatening. Sometimes the voice broke like thunder over the congregation.

She allowed herself to be pressed by the others to the door, caring for
nothing except to save herself from falling. Her lungs began to breathe
in the fresh air deeply — it was as though she had awakened from a dream.
Antonio the young gardener stood beside her. "Are you feeling better?"
he asked, "Shall I take you back to the convent?" "I'm all right again
now," said Marietta, steeling herself at once and, afraid to offer her his
escort a second time, he remained standing at her side, abashed and with
an embarrassed smile, until she nodded good-by to him and went her way.

In the convent they were waiting greedily for her, and she had seen
enough to give them a report. . . . But how was it that Antonio had suddenly been standing beside her? Was it he who had supported her when
she had nearly fallen on leaving the cathedral? Someone had seized her
under the elbows. She had looked round, but all the faces had seemed
sunk in a haze. She was not pleased that he should have been the one to
save her. Perhaps she ought to have thanked him. Yes, she certainly ought.
A stiff little acknowledgment. Then he would not be so ready to seize
her under the elbows again. How had he dared? She had thought that he
was so shy. Perhaps she was unfair to him. Perhaps. But she did not want
his help. What was it that had happened during the winter when wolves
had been seen in the neighborhood? The first Saturday at noon he had

rung the convent bell, and had asked whether it was known in the convent that the roads were unsafe. If Marietta had to go to the city all the same, he said he wanted to accompany her. Naturally, Catarina had told him that nobody was going out, that she herself was not going to market as the convent could make do with what provisions it had; and she asked him, "And what would you do to keep off the wolves?"

Thereupon Antonio had pointed to a pitchfork upon his shoulder, and had produced a rattle.

"And do you suppose, idiot, that hungry wolves could be frightened away with a rattle and a pitchfork?" Catarina had asked him mockingly. "You just get home quickly before dusk. You may be sure we shan't send Marietta out so long as it's dangerous."

Later on, she had told Marietta about this in secret and had said, "I shan't say a word of this to the abbess"; and when Marietta had vowed that she never saw Antonio in the city, old Catarina had only winked.

All that had happened this last winter. But what did he want with her?

At the convent she was besieged with excited questions that she could answer only in part. Yes, the bishop had been flushed with walking in the heat. . . . In the cathedral she had not been able to see the altar cloth, nor whether it had impressed the bishop. . . . She had hardly understood anything of what he said, but there had been complete silence among the congregation. A deep voice . . . He was tall and massive. The people had flung themselves down when they saw him.

While Marietta was in the library giving a separate report to the abbess and some of the older sisters, the novices and the younger nuns built up an ideal figure from the scanty materials at hand. Tall and massive he was, a godly man in the finest meaning of the word. A powerful protector of the faith. When would the convent be allowed to welcome him? When would he sit down to meat with them all? Pigeons and truffles were to be served, a turkey stewed in wine, and as dessert ginger and candied fruits.

A further conference was held in the library after Marietta's departure. It was strange that there was still no indication from the city as to when they could expect a visit. Surely it would be soon. But would the bishop arrive without announcing himself properly in advance? If that happened, the whole carefully prepared reception would miss fire. Could it be that he was averse to such a reception? Or was the convent simply to be forgotten as a reward for its seemly reserve? Surely the bishop must have heard how fervently they had prayed for his arrival?

Sister Maddalena was of opinion that this uncertainty was intolerable. Next morning she would go to the city herself and ask to speak with the bishop; but the abbess opposed this plan. No, that wouldn't do at all. She could find no plausible reason for her disapproval of Sister Maddalena's bold scheme; she just wouldn't have it, and that was the end of it. There was nothing to be done, therefore, but to accept her decision.

Nervous and restless, the abbess walked through the convent mumbling and muttering to herself, pursued by a mysterious fear. Monday came, and there was no news from the city; Tuesday, and still no news. The abbess refused to convene any further conferences, however. If the bishop wanted to come, he would come. The convent was not going to force him to it.

The abbess had now got it into her head that before the new bishop had left the Vatican the Holy Father had spoken slightingly of the convent — of the convent that prided itself on having had a miracle occur within its walls. Was it likely that God would reveal Himself through the mouth of a goose like Sister Elisabetta? Only yesterday, while she stood chattering in the corridor, she had allowed the food to burn. If only that letter had never been sent to Rome! Alone in the library, the abbess sat pondering over the copy. Those words, which at first had seemed to her so exalted and impressive, now seemed to be only pompous. They must have laughed at it at the Vatican. She could no longer sit at her table. She paced up and down, up and down, till far into the night; while the candle that shed a gold glimmer over the unfortunate epistle slowly burned itself out.

Wednesday came, and Catarina on her return from market reported that the bishop had visited all the churches, even the small and insignificant San Damiato, known only to the mendicant friars because they could spend the night there with the verger.

Sister Maddalena was unable to restrain her indignation over this undeserved slight. She conjured the abbess to allow her to go to town. "I shall tell him we are expecting him. I shall tell him how we prayed; and that he has been ill advised by those who let him visit the whole world, and only then ourselves." Breathing deeply, her eyes flashing, she confronted the abbess, who these days was more shriveled up than ever and, withdrawn under her coif, averted her glance, weak and irresolute, before the direct onslaught of the stronger woman.

At that moment, there was a ring at the gate, and Catarina, hastily answering the summons, was handed a courteously worded note in which the bishop announced his visit for the following day in the afternoon at four o'clock. Sister Maddalena could not forbear to remark tartly that they ought all to be pleased that he had chosen Thursday and not the next day, which was a fast day. But the abbess did not even hear her, as with long steps she sped towards the library, there to reread the letter by herself.

The nuns, who had sunk into apathy under the general feeling of disappointment, recovered as by magic. Immediately, they got to work making leafy festoons to be hung over the doors — to-morrow morning early, fresh flowers could be stuck into them. Had the nuns been worldly brides and had the following morning been their wedding day, they could not have been more agitated. Even at vespers, they could not find their way to a higher feast.

Catarina was sent back to the city at once to make the necessary purchases.

V

From three o'clock onwards, — half an hour before the episcopal coach left the city in a steady downpour to take the way through the fields, — the little convent bell tinkled restlessly; and behind the closed doors the abbess and the older nuns stood waiting, sighing over the bad weather. Shortly before four, however, it cleared up. Patches of blue broke through the clouds, and the rain abated. Just as, in Babylon of old, the augurs peered through the little roof windows of their priestly observatories, so the sisters now took turns peeping towards the sky through the little grated judas in the door. They talked of nothing but the weather, grateful to have a subject of conversation. Then suddenly, in the distance, could be heard the clattering of horses' hooves over the drenched soil. Old Catarina, breathing deeply, stepped forward. With trembling hands, she slipped the key into the rusty keyhole; with the entire weight of her gaunt body she pulled the oak door open, and then, immediately, leaned against it, for she knew well the propensity of that door to close again with a bang. Arms tightly crossed over their tightly laced bosoms, hands and wrists hidden in their wide black sleeves, the women stood there, their eyes flickering like those of owls in the sudden burst of sunshine that fell slantingly on them; and at first they had no notion at all of what to do or say.

The bishop's coachman, gleaming in his rain-drenched green satin livery, permitted himself an ironical glance as he drove up and reined in his four-in-hand. The groom had already jumped down to open the door for his master.

The bishop stepped out. As he rested one foot heavily on the footboard that groaned under his full weight, in the flicker of a second he took in the waiting company, not without a certain friendliness. Then he turned to his coachman, and in a gentle tone ordered him to drive the horses carefully home, to return precisely at nine o'clock, and on no account to drive furiously in such bad weather.

The abbess, vaguely conscious that Sister Maddalena had given her a soft push in her back, pattered forward towards the bishop. She was so tiny beside him that it seemed as though she were creeping up to him upon her knees, and when she knelt before him and kissed the ring on his purple-gloved hand, it was as though the earth had swallowed her up at his feet.

He helped her to rise, thanked her for her words of welcome, and side by side with her moved towards the waiting nuns, greeted them, asked their names, and also for the name of the doorkeeper who, overwhelmed with such attention, flung herself upon her knees in front of him for the second time, holding in her hands the while the surplice in a dust sheet that the groom had handed to her a moment before. Above her back, Monsignore looked out towards his horses that had now turned round and were trotting away. Then, looking somewhat impatiently in the direction of the dark corridor that lay beyond the open door, he suggested that they should go inside. The door closed behind them all, and the sound of trotting hooves no longer reached them.

He allowed himself to be led towards the library-reception room. It was soberly furnished to accord with the dignity of the thick folios, in the wall cupboard, that were seldom or never disturbed in their contemplative rest except on the one day in the year when all might borrow a book. Sitting bolt upright in his oak chair, leaning his elbows heavily upon its arms, he listened with becoming gravity to the abbess's story of the origin and past of the convent. He then inquired as to the precise ins and outs of the miracle that had been mentioned to him in Todi. Starting up, the abbess was at first unable to speak. Then, gathering all her courage, she told him, without listening to her own words, of the faithful prayers they had kept up so long and of the strange sentences that the lay sister Elisabetta had uttered. With raised eyebrows, listening in respectful silence to her small, shrill, nasal voice, which rose at times to an incredibly high flutelike pitch, he stretched out his hand thoughtfully towards the glass of Spanish wine and brought it discreetly to his lips while his eye wandered round the table, reviewing them quietly one by one. His eye rested longest on Sister Maddalena — she certainly pleased him more than any of the others. Yes, it occurred even to the others that the shadow of a smile played about his broad, firmly cut mouth — as if a secret understanding existed between the two. Sister Maddalena, burning with desire to take the story out of the abbess's mouth, amazed and disturbed at her poor and unconvincing account of the miracle that had taken place, suddenly was no longer sure whether she herself could have told it any better, and alternately flushed and grew pale.

Not one of the nuns was now listening to the abbess's story. They were all on tenterhooks, wondering whether the bishop would again look towards Sister Maddalena in that mysterious manner. They were wholly absorbed by his rugged commanding appearance. Whether they wished to or not, they could not prevent themselves from following with their eyes his every movement. His large, strong hand, that rested so still and self-conscious on the table, was to them at that moment something more miraculous than the miracle that the abbess was describing. There he sat among them, as large as life. Just as actors in the wings listen only for the cue that summons them to the footlights, so the nuns directed towards the abbess only enough attention to say in unison, "Yes, venerable mother," when, helpless and floundering on the stream of her own words, she appealed to them to save her from drowning by asking imploringly, "That's right, isn't it? That's how it happened?" They were delighted with the opportunity such agreement gave them of nodding towards the bishop.

The abbess's story came to an end. With infinite relief, she ceased to listen to her own voice, and wiped her face with her handkerchief.

Then Monsignore spoke.

First of all, the miracle: He had been greatly interested in the abbess's account of it, and also in the fact that a careful report had been sent to the Holy Father. He no doubt had failed to mention the matter to him when he took his leave only because of the great pressure of work and the many duties that fell daily to the lot of the Pope. It was a strange year. From many convents in the papal states miraculous occurrences had been reported. It was a year of prophecies and great events. He would like to have a word with the sister in question later on. The abbess could rest assured that the Holy Father would give his attention to this miracle too when his secretaries found an opportunity to place the document before him.

The altar cloth: It was the first thing that had met his eyes in the cathedral. Of course it had been mentioned to him beforehand. But this artistic product of convent industry would have struck him anywhere, even in St. Peter's at Rome. He liked everything that was beautiful, artistic, and rare. For instance, he possessed a small but very carefully selected collection of incunabula, and some hour-books and chronicles of the saints in manuscript, artistically illuminated.

Suddenly, Sister Maddalena started up from a sort of stupor that had descended upon her. Hour-books! Chronicles of saints! Surely he would not take it into his head to cast a look at the folios in the cupboard. The books in the library were the one thing that had been neglected in the great spring cleaning, primarily because she had been afraid that the lay sisters might turn over the pages in search of the illustrations and allow themselves to be diverted from their work. . . . She tried to find something to say to turn the conversation in a new direction, but could not. The movement she made as if about to speak, however, was enough to attract the attention of the bishop and the rest, who looked towards her as she sat there, tall, blooming, helpless.

He nodded to her encouragingly, and suddenly she found something to say: "A young novice made the cloth."

"From an original here in the chapel," said the others. "But it wasn't by any means a slavish imitation," interposed Sister Maddalena hastily. Words came flowing to her: she grudged everybody else the privilege of speaking to the bishop. She made bold to inform him that this young novice came from Venice, and not only did magnificent embroidery, but also had a great talent for painting on fans, on satin, and even in oil paints on little panels; and that in embroidering the altar cloth she had overtaxed her powers so much that she could not be among those who would welcome him in a moment.

He listened with obvious pleasure to Sister Maddalena's strangely excited voice. "From Venice? I spent years there as a young abbé." Then turning again towards the abbess, he asked her whether it would not be possible for them to pay a visit to the devout young novice as she lay on her bed of sickness.

That would be a very great, but certainly a well deserved distinction for the young girl, said the abbess. She was weak with gratitude that the bishop still respected her authority after her preposterous account of the miracle. That would certainly be excellent; and wouldn't he also like to inspect the convent?

Naturally — the convent also.

To herself, Sister Maddalena was saying that he might inspect everything, everything, the whole convent — if only he left the books in their places. She tried to catch the eyes of the others, to convey to them with a glance that everything had gone well up to now; but was it a coincidence that they all happened to be looking away? Bothered, suddenly uncertain again, she got up with them. "Wouldn't you like to see the garden first?" she asked, and she was unpleasantly aware that she had lost control of her voice. "It is quite a sight at the moment."

"Certainly, sister. You lead the way," he said in fatherly fashion.

The abbess, getting up from the table with difficulty, gave them both a side glance — she did not herself understand the strange feeling of ill humor and distrust that was beginning to sweep over her. Looking straight in front of her, she shuffled along with the rest, struggling against an oppressive feeling of inferiority, finding consolation ultimately in muttering inaudibly to herself, "He will be gone soon. He will be gone soon."

And so the bishop inspected the convent, found the necessary ingratiating words of admiration for the decorations over the cell doors, for the well-tended flower garden. When he reached the vineyard, which the nuns wanted to show him only in the frame provided by the doorway from the corridor, he stepped into the open. Sister Maddalena followed him — then came back at once, with a scared look, to where the others had gathered together, hesitatingly, in the doorway.

Antonio, who had been digging at the back of the garden, came running up, nervous and respectful, stammering replies to the string of rapid questions the bishop addressed to him about the state of the vineyard in relation to the vine cultivation of the district. When Antonio had answered to the best of his ability, Monsignore could not immediately make up his mind to return inside. He seemed to find it difficult to take his leave of the fresh air. He took a deep breath; he stared a moment into the dark green of the cypresses behind the western wall, where they rose up almost black against the yellow evening sky. At last, he appeared to recollect that the nuns were waiting for him. With a final glance, he turned towards them again and rejoined them.

They then approached Virginia's cell — for the sake of greater quiet, she had been relegated to a private cell away from the novices' common dormitory. Sister Maddalena rushed hastily on in front, to prepare her for the visit and to straighten the blankets.

With great, ecstatic eyes, Virginia saw her exalted guest enter. He had to bend his head to pass under the lintel. Sister Maddalena, who was herself overagitated, had tried in vain to enjoin calm upon Virginia, who was still not free from fever. She showed the bishop examples of her work. He recognized at once the pictures of Venice that adorned the fans, inspected them with eager satisfaction, mentioned their names: the Ponte della Paglia, with the Riva degli Schiavoni, the Grand Canal with the Pescheria. . . . Thirty years ago as a young abbé he had lived among these places, and he could still not forget the quiet, fair city of a thousand wonders, the gentle lapping of the waters against the steps and quays. To draw Virginia into conversation, he asked her questions about Venice; but when she tried to reply, tears came into her eyes. He nodded to her in a friendly way, found the right words to calm her and to loosen her tongue. Only these two might have been in the cell — the others were so quiet. Raising her thin face towards him, Virginia told him about her family. She was just about to point out to him where her father's palace stood, when the bishop pointed to it himself, and told her that long ago he had met her father. He could remember him very well.

While they were thus conversing, the nuns had eyes only for Virginia. What was happening to Virginia? It was not the red flush on her cheeks — that might be only excitement or fever; it was the curious line about her mouth, the smile that none of them had seen upon her face for months, and that they had almost forgotten. It was Virginia's old, irresistible smile. . . . What strange conversation was this between them, that simply eliminated the others? They said but a word, these two, and they at once understood one another. What mystery was there about this city of Venice, that seemed to be a link between them? Here in the convent it connoted only sin. The sisters, huddled together in the narrow cell, were dazed by what they saw and heard. Sister Ursula, taking advantage of a short silence, began hastily to speak of the altar cloth, to tell Virginia that the bishop had noticed it at once in the cathedral, and had thought it beautiful. The bishop confirmed this. Then he spoke of his collection of old hour-books, and promised to send some of the finest examples to the convent for Virginia to look at during her enforced rest. Instead of thanking him suitably for this great mark of favor, Virginia merely nodded her appreciation. Sister Ursula drew attention to her remissness, and she put it right, but the mysterious smile never left her face. Her smile was above formality — even the least sensitive among them felt that and it discomfited and annoyed them.

The abbess suggested that it was time to leave Virginia: in a moment the bell would ring for vespers, and no doubt Monsignore would like to retire first to the sacristy. As she was about to follow the others, Sister Maddalena felt a tug at her dress. Uncertain, she stayed behind and asked Virginia, "Is anything wrong?"

Virginia wanted to attend vespers. Sitting bolt upright in bed, she asserted that she was strong enough. The bishop's visit had cured her. Sister Maddalena, undecided, ran her hand over her burning temples. A moment ago, this child had seemed calm as a saint; he had hardly gone, and she seemed like one possessed. What sort of magic was it that this man had wrought?

"No! No question of it! You're ill."

"I'm not ill any more. Really not, really not, Sister Maddalena."

"Yes, you are. You only think you're cured. We've had enough miracles here. You'd break down halfway along the corridor." Her motherly instinct overcame every dangerous hesitation, provided her once more with the necessary ascendancy. "The bishop will come again soon. Get better as quickly as you can, then you can make something else nice for him. You'd like that, wouldn't you?"

Yes, Virginia would like that very much. She sank back again on her pillows, her eyes staring towards the beam in the ceiling. Sister Maddalena sat another moment beside her. Then, very gently, she disengaged her hand, gave the invalid a rapid caress on the forehead, and left the cell, remarking as she reached the door that she must be in the choir in time.

Robed in magnificent vestments and attended by two choirboys from the city, Monsignore celebrated vespers in the intimacy of the dark little chapel. As they knelt in the choir, the nuns riveted their eyes upon the bishop's quiet and forceful gestures, upon his almost matter-of-fact performance of the rites during the Magnificat, and their hearts beat faster in the firm expectation of some exceptional occurrence.

Was he himself conscious of the suspense that everything he did aroused? During all the years of his priesthood, had he learned to calculate his effects like a successful actor? Now it was coming. . . . He had exposed the monstrance almost casually, he had knelt during the Tantum Ergo, he had rested his forehead for a moment wearily against the side of the altar. . . . Then, as he gave the Benediction, turning his back towards them and holding up the gleaming monstrance for a moment in silence — then he revealed an unexpected emotion: with a great effort of self-control, he stared fixedly in front of him.

The nuns, the novices, and the lay sisters, only too willing to believe in him, understood him perfectly. They had understood his initial matter-of-factness: one who is seated so near the throne of God and has become so familiar with it cannot at all times be as acutely sensitive to its glory as the young priest who bows before it for the first time. But see! even the highest dignitary of the church is affected by the mighty symbol of Christ's flesh and blood; his emotion is even greater, perhaps, because it is so unexpected, bringing him to his knees, long unaccustomed to bend, despite himself. There he stood, portentous as a prophet. He raised the monstrance above their poor, sinful heads, and all shrank back within themselves, seared by God's eternal greatness, and not one of them now dared to look at him.

He continued the service, following the old familiar rites. The gold monstrance was returned to the tabernacle; but all had seen a miraculous light radiate from it — the light of God.

Never before had Sister Veronica played the organ as she played it that evening; and even the shrill tinkle of the bell seemed, that day, to derive from the music of the heavenly spheres.

The service was over. Novices and lay sisters, huddling together like obedient lambs, had left the chapel, followed by the nuns, and last of all by the abbess. The bishop pulled the alb over his head, and handed his stole and surplice to the choirboys, who folded them neatly for him and put them back into their cover. "You've behaved excellently, boys. Here are four soldi each for you; now away with you as quick as you can."

Left alone, he blew his nose vigorously, and produced his snuffbox. He then looked at his watch, fingered it caressingly, admired its pearl setting, sighed, and put it away again. Another two hours and a quarter before his carriage was due. Would Michele have dried the horses properly?

His horses, his superb team of four. He had always liked horses better than men. He would have liked to celebrate a funeral Mass for Moro, his faithful red roan that had been shot down in a riot just three years ago this month. The murderer he would have liked to consign to hell with the power of his episcopal malison.

Ah well! It was time he sauntered back to the library, where that old woman was waiting for him. . . .

He threw up his head and left the chapel with long, stately steps. The nuns heard his heavy tread in the corridor and felt in it the thundering power of God that was implicit in his whole being.

What a bishop!

Marietta was helping Elisabetta in the kitchen, which the bishop had not visited. But at intervals a lay sister who had seen him go by in one of the corridors came rushing in to describe him excitedly in highflown terms. Elisabetta, her nerves on edge as she waited for the moment to serve, accidentally dropped the onions into the tomato sauce. Loudly lamenting, she was just sieving them out again when a flushed Sister Maddalena came running in and said to Marietta that she must go at once to the refectory to take part in singing the song of welcome to the bishop.

"I should so like to have heard it," lamented Elisabetta as Marietta hastily undid her apron. "And now this happens to the tomato sauce."

"What's wrong with the tomato sauce?"

"Oh, nothing, nothing! I'll get them out again somehow."

Smiling patiently, throned in the seat of honor at the head of the table, the bishop accepted the song of homage he was never able to escape. He had come prepared for it. He consoled himself with the thought that nothing else could possibly separate him from a plate of hot, fragrant soup. He had learned by experience that the tastiest soups in the world were prepared in religious houses. Food in general, he had found, was good in religious houses. The matter had once come up in a discussion between him and the Pope, and His Holiness had mentioned with special favor the food at the Carthusian Monastery at Pavia. . . . Yes, a plate of hot soup would indeed be pleasant.

Then he forgot his anticipations of a good meal, struck by the moving purity and warmth of a child's voice. He looked at Marietta attentively, as she sang her part with complete absorption.

What kind of child was this? What was she doing in the convent? With astonishment, he took in her half-childish, half-womanly figure.

At the same time, he was conscious of being watched. He turned his head to the left, smiled at Sister Maddalena significantly, and then noted that she had merely been waiting for some such sign of appreciation. While the angels sang his praise in unison, he whispered to her, "Is she your pupil?" and deduced from her happy blush that this was precisely the question she had hoped he would put. She refused, however, to answer him at once. Shy and confused, she signed to him that he must pay attention because the little girl was on the point of singing again. Marietta sang so beautifully that Sister Maddalena had to close her eyes, in order not to miss one single intonation of her voice. As soon as the band of angels took up the song again, the bishop whispered to her behind his hand that later on she must tell him more about this attractive child. He was thinking that the singer had a real gift for acting, since she expressed her supposed emotions not only by her voice but also by the expression of her face and by her gestures.

When the song was over, he wanted to speak a special word of thanks to the little girl; but it seemed she had been called away. Perhaps to serve at table?

Suppertime. He had been quite right about the soup. He must write to the Holy Father in Rome about it; and he was not disappointed in what followed the soup, either. The pigeons had been splendidly prepared. He must ask for the recipe, to give to Immacolata, his old servant. Gradually, Monsignore fell into a great good humor, told little anecdotes of his life, drank to the prosperity of the convent. For the most part he conversed only with the older nuns, but now and again he addressed a question to those who sat farther away, thereby releasing them, or so they felt, from their customary silence during meals. The candle flames on the long table, covered in honor of the day with a pure white cloth, flickered gaily; the wine gleamed like dark blood in the nuns' crystal glasses. The novices drank only water, but their cheeks glowed none the less for that; and when a flower fell unexpectedly from the central ornament of the table into a large bowl of sauce, upon which it drifted like a water lily, they all burst into loud laughter.

The old plastered walls seemed to look down with surprised astonishment at such unwonted exuberance. The abbess, too, was far from comfortable. Queer thoughts had been flashing through her old head — even during vespers, which had moved all of them like an act of grace. Her distrust would not melt. Distrust, anxiety — an inexplicable uneasiness. With a vague hostility, she looked down the table, watching the course of events, and said nothing. Finding little encouragement on her side, the bishop turned to his left, towards Sister Maddalena, who told him about little Marietta, how easily she learned, how intelligent she was for her years, which did not yet number fifteen.

Marietta offered the sweet to the exalted guest. He looked up at her good-humoredly, asked her what wonderful dainty she was bringing him, and then, remembering what he had intended to do earlier, told her how much he had enjoyed her singing.

"Did you just learn singing by yourself?" he asked. "Would you like to have lessons?"

At his first word, the soft buzzing of voices down the long table was stilled. All craned their necks to look at Marietta, whose turn it now was to be honored by Monsignore. Marietta turned pale in the silence that had fallen. She did not know what to say in reply to the bishop's question. Would she like to have lessons? Helpless, she turned to the neglected abbess who, moving restlessly upon her chair, said sharply in her shrill old voice: "It is the same to God whether a voice is trained or not."

The nuns and novices were transfixed with fright at the reproof which the abbess presumed to direct to the bishop. The first thought that crossed the minds of all was that she had drunk too much: her wineglass stood empty in front of her. Just at that moment, perhaps merely to appear unconcerned, or perhaps from a sense of satisfaction, she stretched her arm towards the decanter. Then, as if conscious of the general suspicion, she changed her mind and fell back sulkily.

The bishop, unpleasantly surprised, turned towards the devout, ill-tempered old woman who had presumed to read him a lesson. But when he saw her sitting there so old and neglected, his annoyance immediately gave way to understanding, pity, and kindly amusement. He bit his lip, and without a trace of resentment expressed his regret for putting a question that seemed to displease the abbess. His delight at a pure and natural voice had made him feel that it would really be a pity to leave it untrained.

"For after all, why shouldn't one do honor to a beautiful voice, which is also a gift of God, by bringing it to the highest perfection?" he inquired. Then he added, mischievously: "It is true that God in his righteousness listens to all voices, to the bad as well as to the good; but that is no reason for denying Him all musical taste and judgment. The last Holy Father was in the habit of saying, 'Only angels' voices are good enough for God's ear.'" The bishop turned to Marietta again, and advised her always to listen to the pious advice of the abbess, who meant well by her — meant better than anyone else in the world.

And then he helped himself to pastry.

The old abbess heard his words with some embarrassment, made no rejoinder, and refrained from further painful participation in the conversation. Instead she stared, unhappy and dazed, at the festive board. She was no longer a restraining influence, and the spirits of the nuns rapidly rose again.

Even when, at the end of the meal, the bishop expressed a wish to see the lay sister who had so pleased his palate, and when Elisabetta, in utter confusion, appeared upon the threshold and, thinking he was about to question her concerning the miracle, began at once to assure him that she could remember no single word of anything she may have said during her convulsions — when, thereupon, the bishop replied that he would not presume to express an opinion about the miracle in anticipation of the Holy Father's verdict, but that all he had intended was to congratulate her upon the miracle of the meal — even then, the abbess betrayed by no single movement what was in her mind. The nuns were beginning to feel a little uncomfortable over her silence.

The fruit course had been served and Monsignore had enjoyed a second cup of fragrant black coffee, when Catarina came to announce that his coach was waiting. A quarter of an hour later, he was thanking the abbess in friendly terms for her really lavish reception. He rose; his cloak and hat were brought to him. Shivering in the cool of the evening, the nuns crowded into the doorway to watch him mount into his coach. They saw him nodding to them for the last time from the interior of the dimly lit vehicle. Then the horses drove off, carrying him away into the dark cloudy June night.

As they withdrew, the younger nuns talked to one another of his friendliness, and from such a high dignitary of the church too! How superbly he had celebrated vespers! With what kindliness he had reproved the abbess when she presumed to criticize him! He had not shown a moment's anger — he was too great a man to be offended even by an intentional affront. It was not merely on account of his episcopal title that he stood above ordinary mortals. . . . The older nuns followed in silence: they were realizing that it was time to resume normal discipline and order. Fortunately it would soon be time to seek the chapel again.

In the refectory, they found Marietta in quite a state. She had broken a large meat dish. Perhaps it was good for her to be upset for such a commonplace reason. With more than their normal kindliness, the nuns and novices consoled her, and Sister Maddalena released her at once from her customary task of helping in the washing up.

The abbess was still sitting at the decorated table, staring vacantly before her while it was cleared. The novices, all of whom were helping that evening, were very conscious of the awkwardness of the situation. Not one of them dared to remove the empty plate in front of her or to ask her to raise her arms so that the cloth could be folded away. As soon as they had done all they could, they withdrew, commenting in whispers to one another on the fact that the abbess, when the others had gone to see the bishop off, had quickly slipped into his chair — her chair, ordinarily — at the head of the table. The older nuns who remained with her after the novices had gone looked at one another hesitatingly. They threw questioning glances at Sister Maddalena, wondering whether it would not be better to leave her alone with the abbess. She nodded in reply, and quietly and discreetly they left the room.

The abbess looked round her. Slowly she turned her head but did not notice Sister Maddalena, who stood near the door, struggling to regain her composure. The old woman sighed. Her gray, death-shadowed face was illuminated by the candle flames. Her thin, prominent nose, across which the skin was stretched like parchment, cast a sharp shadow over her sunken mouth.

The clang of the convent bell roused her. It was as if, suddenly, she had begun to breathe again.

The old abbess felt a sudden resurgence of life within her. She prayed that God would give her the strength to reach the chapel; that He would grant her the strength to resume her sway over the convent. Had the reins dropped from her aged fingers a little while back? Had she been set at defiance? Or had she only imagined it? She could still hear the sound of laughter and illicit exuberance. Should sin enter the convent while she was the abbess?

She was supposed to have seen nothing, to have heard nothing. She had heard everything, seen everything. She had seen the way he looked at Sister Maddalena; she had seen how Sister Maddalena caught her breath. She had heard what he said to Elisabetta, that he would not presume to express an opinion about the miracle. That was to be left to the Holy Father in Rome — but the meal . . . ! Was that the way to talk of miracles? Was that how they spoke of them in Rome, on the steps of the papal throne? They had sent her the anti-Christ from Rome clothed in consecrated bishop's vestments. Yes, she was not afraid to express the truth to herself. Here he had sat in this very chair, in her chair, in the guise of a noble man of God. Thus had her prayer been answered. Or was this a trial from God? She would go to the chapel, she would fling herself down, she would pray with all the power that was left to her. Leaning wearily upon the table, she tried to get up, her almost toothless jaws set tightly. She felt herself lifted under the arms. With a start, she looked round and saw Sister Maddalena's face, now wonderfully composed and serene.

"Were you here? I thought . . . Leave me alone."

"Where are you going? You should rest."

"No, I am going to the chapel."

"Let me help you."

"But if the others come . . . I would rather they did not see . . ."

"They're all there already."

The old abbess nodded. She was grateful in spite of herself for the strong hands that helped her to stand. She was grateful for the calmness that Sister Maddalena had reassumed — a calmness that strengthened her too. She wanted to express something, to Sister Maddalena at least, of the frightful misgivings the new bishop had aroused within her. She glanced round, to make sure that they were really alone. Then she whispered, "The old bishop was very different. Don't you think so?"

Sister Maddalena averted her face, shrugged her shoulders. "I don't know," she said, hoarse and inimical. "Let us go."

A stillness hung over the convent. No sound came from the chapel. The candlelight streamed softly through the crack under the door. In the kitchen, working silently like one possessed, Elisabetta was clearing up. It had been a good day for her. In the presence of everyone, the bishop had declared that it was a miracle, the way she cooked.

Marietta — free for the evening, but lingering in the kitchen — she sent to bed in kindly, noisy fashion. "Off to bed now, and have a good cry on your own. That's what I always do when I feel like that, and the next day it's better. I can manage very well alone — work's a pleasure when it's appreciated. What a fright I had over the tomato sauce! And it turned out well after all. Run along now."

And Marietta went.

Virginia, lying awake and recognizing her step, called her in. It was against the rules for them to be together in one cell, but in Virginia's voice there was something strange and enticing. Besides, Marietta had lost her bearings, and felt the need of Virginia's consoling company. What extraordinary unrest had taken possession of the convent? What were the nuns concealing from one another? It was as if they had spoken with different voices at table — Marietta suddenly felt them to be strangers. She was lost in an unfamiliar convent where a mysterious, important guest had for her sake been at variance with the abbess, an unknown abbess, venomous, crooked with hate, a witch struggling against a more powerful magician.

Marietta went into Virginia's room, and lay down beside her.

And what did Virginia do? She carried her off to a distant white city with magnificent old marble palaces rising up sheer from the water so that one stepped out of the door straight into a gondola manned by two rowers, Vittorio and Marco. The lagoons . . . they were large lakes connected with the sea. In the evening one went boating there in gondolas with Chinese lanterns. There was music everywhere, for carnival had just begun; and lovesick youths in masks sang four-part songs that carried far over the still waters. "Venice!" said Virginia, and there was a catch in her voice, and a city arose with wide expanses of sky and water.

And Marietta gazed, gazed into the darkness. Was this Venice? The place towards which her parents had gone? Suddenly she realized that she had imagined all cities to be like Todi, only larger, infinitely larger. That was the way Cesare the carrier had described Rome. It was with difficulty that she shook off her surprise.

Virginia told her how, as a little girl, she used to go to market with old Zanetta, the cook. They crossed by the ferry, and on the canal gondolas and barges swarmed in the morning sun. Zanetta haggled over everything, no matter how cheap the things she wanted might be. She haggled, and the fishwives hurled insults at her; but with the money she saved Zanetta bought something for her little Virginia in the shops by the bridge.

As she described her childish memories, there was an infinite hunger in Virginia's voice. "Oh, Marietta, while I copied those prints, I thought to myself how beautiful Venice is; but now he says so too, the bishop. I haven't had much chance to think. I've been busy all the time, with the needlework and the rest, and all these days in bed my one thought has been whether the altar cloth is good enough. But he has been here himself now, and he said it's beautiful, and suddenly I don't care any more. I won't stop here. I won't spend my whole life here. If they won't let me go freely, I shall escape, even if I die on the way to Venice from want of food. I want to live there, among people. I don't want to be a nun. After all, they can't force me to be, even though I have become a novice. God, why did I do that?"

There were tears in her voice; Marietta was weeping already. They fell into one another's arms, and Virginia sobbed out, "First he makes me work so hard at that cloth that I fall ill, and then he comes and makes me sick with longing for home. When he came in here, Marietta — had he been God himself I couldn't have trembled more. That's what they've brought me to, the abbess and the sisters. And suddenly he speaks to me simply, as if he had been my father or an uncle, and tells me he was once an abbé in Venice. . . . And Marietta, I know so exactly what that means, to be an abbé in Venice. After all, I was abducted by a young abbé."

Virginia disengaged herself. Suddenly she could not help laughing through her tears, and she began to tell Marietta how she had been abducted and how she had reached the convent. Marietta trembled — she had scarcely dared to hope that Virginia would ever tell her, and now it had come. But instead of a sad, lovelorn tale, it proved to be a gay adventurous story. Virginia's face became a mask of mischief. She found the airiest words. She juggled with them in the lightest way. She broke off into suppressed laughter.

"I had a real little abbé, you know. He gave me lessons in French, and at the same time read his verses to me. My hair made him think of the gold of the setting sun, and he was prepared to become an officer in the Venetian service, if only he might marry me. But now I must tell you about my brother. To him, abbés and highway robbers were one and the same thing. He was always against those French lessons, because all abbés are set upon turning the heads of rich young girls, and then dropping their breviaries into the Lagoon so that they may marry into some old family. I believe mine was busy following exactly that recipe, for after a time he spoke of nothing but young girls who had allowed themselves to be abducted, to prove that they could choose for themselves. I couldn't decide whether to give him a chance or not. I thought it was perhaps rather weak to keep on saying no to someone who wanted to abduct me so much. Mariano was my little abbé's name. He had a sweet voice, you know, and he was as vain as a woman."

Virginia herself seemed to be amused by this description of her lover.

"What's the matter?" she asked when Marietta looked at her open-eyed and failed to join in her laughter. She seized her by the ears and excitedly drew her towards her. Marietta flushed. She was ashamed of her intense seriousness. A strange happiness chased away her initial amazement. Weakly, uncritically, she followed the mad adventure that Virginia related with sinful merriment. For the first time, a screen was removed and she saw the world as it was, a strange, infinitely mad world, a colored reeling world in the midst of which, without being aware of it, Todi and this convent lay wrapped in gray sleep. On Virginia's words she was borne, out of this darkness, into a bright world full of movement, of the wild pursuit of happiness, of ludicrous collapses into red, turbulent sorrow, which passed, however, in the fun of carnival.

Virginia told of a dark autumn night. It was windy and it was raining, as is seemly for an abduction. The branches of the trees in the garden brushed against the windows. She slipped out by the back door, taking with her some clothes and a few jewels she had been given on the day of her first Communion. At the last moment, a terrible fit of sentimentality suddenly overcame her. She wanted to cling to the doorpost. She said that she wanted at least to say good-by to old Zanetta. No, no question of that. Zanetta would bring the whole house down. Come, for God's sake. Everything was settled. A barque was waiting at Chioggia to take them to Ancona, and from there a letter would be sent to her father imploring him to receive them and give them his blessing — and asking for the blessing of that old vixen, too, if that was so very important. Virginia realized how good old Zanetta would have raised the alarm: Help! Wake up! Thieves, murderers! She could picture to herself the faithful Zanetta rushing downstairs in her nightgown, poker in hand, to give that ass a piece of her mind. But instead of warning Zanetta, Virginia allowed herself to be lifted into the gondola that lay waiting. She hid her face from the grinning gondolier. Mariano put his arm about her and whispered that this was the happiest hour of his life. Farewell, last chance of salvation! The gondola glided away over the dark waters.

The Grand Canal was black as the Styx itself — there was no need to go by back ways. They reached the Lagoon, where their boat danced on the waves. It was much windier than they had realized. The gondolier predicted heavy going to Chioggia. He would do it, but only because he had given his word. "Marietta, what a night! Soon the gondolier was fighting for our lives. It took hours. . . . I had given up hope of ever reaching Chioggia, and to return seemed equally impossible. The waves nearly capsized us. Long before we got there, I had ceased to notice anything, I was so seasick; and Mariano was worse. The gondolier implored him to help, but he couldn't; and then that rascal said that once we were safely landed he'd give him such a kick he'd fly after the prophet Elias. At once, by way of punishment, the awning of his gondola was swept overboard, and the rain beat down full upon us. Mariano prayed for his soul and mine, and in the intervals was sick. And that pagan of a gondolier swore every time he plunged his blade into the water. Never before had I heard such oaths, and, Marietta, it's terrible to say so, but it was the only thing that gave me a little confidence. If that gondolier had begun to pray too, I should have known we were lost."

Marietta and Virginia, lying there in a convent cell, felt at that moment the mysterious power that can emanate from swearing. If the little abbé had been a man, standing beside the gondolier, he would have defied the sea too, and steeled his muscles with the most awful blasphemies; and he would still have had time to pray if the oar had cracked in the middle under the pressure of their bodies, and had flung one of them overboard on either side of the gondola.

They reached Chioggia safely, however, at last. Had the Holy Virgin listened to the abbé's prayers, or had the devils of the Lagoon been vanquished by the gondolier's murderous oaths? Upon reaching the quay, the gondolier seized his knife and demanded three sequins above the agreed price because, by the special intercession of the Madonna of the Sinners' Refuge, he had been enabled to save the life of the abbé and of his lady. But Mariano did not possess three extra sequins, and Virginia gave him a jewel instead. Then they made a mad dash towards the barque. While the skipper made ready to weigh anchor, Mariano flung himself down before a harbor Madonna: the flame of her lamp had been blown out. A tile clattered to the ground at his side. He fled on board, and with one small sail set, they departed. From a barque that had just come in seeking refuge from the storm, a voice called to their skipper to ask him if he were crazy. But he shouted back that he was ready to sail in even worse weather for the sort of payment he was to receive for this journey.

"Marietta! *Gran Dio* — Marietta! For a day and a night we lay like the dead, each stretched on a bench, listening only to the creaking and the cracking of that old tub. Water was lapping in the hold. It made the rats come running on deck. They were as big as that . . ." With her hand she indicated not rats but cats, and both faces registered disgust.

Their arrival at Ancona was wild confusion. "We swept into the harbor — and the first person I saw standing on the quay was Piero, my brother, a horsewhip in his hand. It was as if I had seen a ghost, and my little abbé didn't know where to fly. The barque wasn't made fast when my brother

was already on board, clutching poor Mariano by the throat. 'I'll be
merciful to you, you dog — I challenge you to a duel.' Mariano adjured
him to remember that as a priest he was not allowed to touch weapons.
'As a priest, you should have thought earlier of what you should not do.'
I implored my brother not to murder him. The skipper put in a word
too, said that he'd put his hand into the fire if I wasn't just as I was when
I left my father's roof. Meantime, Mariano jumped overboard and was
picked up by a rowing boat that happened to be passing by. His savior
received on his head the heavy leather horsewhip my brother hurled down
in his fury. 'Come,' said Piero to me. 'It's a good thing you packed some
clothes to take with you.'"

There followed a wild drive towards the west. At every baiting place
they changed horses. Virginia found herself kidnaped like an Eastern
bride. Beside the coach galloped the cruel bridegroom, her brother.
She moaned in her anxiety. She knew nothing of the compass, but instinct
told her they were going farther and farther away from Venice.

"Where are we going?"

"You'll see."

"Not to Venice?"

"Venice lies behind you."

"Wretch! Where are you taking me? Turn round, I implore you, by
the memory of our dead mother!"

"Leave our mother out of it, you little fool!"

He gave her hardly any rest. Early next morning, they traveled on.
The road climbed higher and higher.

"What mountains are those ahead of us?"

"The Apennines."

"Must we cross them?"

"Yes. There is no alternative."

Virginia had heard of the Apennines. They were far from Venice.
She jumped out of the coach and fled in the opposite direction, into
the wilds. Immediately he overtook her, hoisted her up in front of him
in the saddle. "Don't behave like a lunatic, you little fool." She shed
bitter tears. But he only laughed, blunt and good-humored. He was no
longer angry. He held her in front of him in the saddle, not because he
feared she would escape, but because he liked to have her near him,
between his arms, as he held the reins. He loved her. She felt her power
over his narrow, true-hearted soul, and tried to persuade him to turn
back, with cunning and with gentleness. She promised him that she would
be a good girl. Although he was only one year older than she, he shook
his head like a father over her. At the same time he kissed her as though

she were his little love. He said, "I should like to take you back, but it won't do." His sense of honor was stronger than his tenderness, stronger than anything else in him. He had sworn to his father and to his friends that he would take her to that convent in Umbria, and now he must do it. This, of course, he would not admit. Instead he began to preach at her. "It is really better for you, dear little sister; I'm taking you there for your own good." She played her last card, threatened that she would do something desperate if she were left behind in a convent. "I have the same blood in my veins as you, Piero. I don't say a thing if I don't mean it." She despised him for his exaggerated laughter, for the pedantic seriousness that followed upon his laughter. "No, little sister. You won't do anything desperate. You'll cry a little when I've gone, and then you'll see it's better like this. I am your brother. I've always been proud of you, and I can't bear to see you snapped up by the first sponger that comes along. You'll do nothing desperate. If only for my sake, you won't." Thus he had dared to speak to her. He was bursting with pride, and did not know it himself. She couldn't help admiring him in her heart. He tyrannized over her, over the house, over the whole world; but she knew she was safe with him. She knew she cared for him more than for twenty Marianos. She was almost in love with him when she saw how, on the way, he made himself obeyed — how he dictated to those scoundrelly innkeepers, how he obtained the best post horses, leaving the lean ones for the rich old count who was expected later in the day and had reserved the best.

Thus they reached the convent, and her brother, who was possessed with a passionate hatred for all inmates of cloisters, of whatever degree, had conversed at length and courteously with the abbess. The nuns had been loud in their praise of him.

And then he had gone.

Back to Venice.

"Virginia," said Marietta suddenly, her eyes wide open, "he'll come and fetch you. He'll take you away from here, just as he brought you."

Virginia could not help laughing. She bent her head backwards and laughed. Still, perhaps Marietta was right. That had been the hope she had clung to in the beginning. One day he would feel regret. Perhaps one night he would be unable to sleep for wondering whether the singing of litanies in the convent wasn't boring his little Virginia very terribly. During the first months she had dreamed every night that he was at her side again; but that dream had gone, and she had found consolation in piety, had of her own free will become a novice without any pressure from the abbess or the nuns, without informing her father — and now suddenly Marietta had come and called forth the old dream again. . . . Virginia was so profoundly moved that she could not speak, could only smile in silence.

A strange, tender happiness came over Marietta too. What a brother, like a tornado before which one must bend. And what a world it was, a world but a moment ago new and mysterious, and already growing familiar with astonishing rapidity. She seemed to recognize it. How well she could imagine it, this traveling at breakneck speed on horseback, by carriage. The sleeping villages and towns on the way, the scenes at the post stations, and the greed of the innkeepers. Then farther afield next morning, over mountain and plain, the sun at one's back. What did the others know of this, here in the convent? But she and Virginia understood one another. They had never been so intimate before. She saw again the old smile on Virginia's face. She felt a stirring within her. Virginia and she, she and Virginia. She could well imagine that a young abbé would fall in love with Virginia, even if he wore the cloth a thousand times. Anybody would fall in love with her; and how could a brother be other than proud of a sister like that? How could he do other than, seething with vengefulness, rush after the wretch who had dared to elope with her? How could he do other than lock her up in a convent after her father's house had proved insufficiently safe?

But there was something Marietta wanted to ask Virginia, if only she could summon the courage. The question burned on her lips. It must be now or never.

"Virginia!" She tried to control her voice. "Let me see your hair!"

Virginia looked at her in surprise. A roguish smile lit up her whole face. She cast a quick glance towards the door. Then, without saying a word, with nimble fingers she unfastened her novice's coif — the coif that held in subjection a whole torrent of luxuriant, red-gold hair that she now spread before Marietta's eyes. She half-turned around, to give her a full view of its beauty and an opportunity to stroke it with her hand.

"Oh, how glorious!" stammered Marietta weakly. "It is like golden thread . . . every hair . . ."

Virginia took some of it in her hand too, and looked at it, with disdainful raised eyebrows. Oh, but she liked it well enough. "When I become a nun, it'll have to be cut off," she said, and tried to read in Marietta's eyes how terrible that would be.

Then a startled look came into her face. From the depths of the corridor footsteps were approaching: the nuns were returning from chapel.

Marietta jumped up. "Till to-morrow, Virginia!" and she was gone, light as a shadow.

Alone again, Virginia rapidly put away her golden hair under her novice's coif and listened. As they passed, the nuns were talking excitedly about the abbess, the bishop . . .

Now a heavy silence descended again upon the convent. Virginia, suddenly exhausted, sank into her pillow.

Yes, it was still, very still. She could hear only the beating of her heart. How weak she was. Formerly she was strong. When she was small she used to fight with her brother, and he could hardly master her. Now she felt her heart beat as if it were much too big for her body.

When her brother did come, it would be too late to take her away alive. Then he would have had his wish.

No, she would not die here. Not here. She wanted to see Venice again . . . Venice.

She shivered, closed her lips tightly. With the sleeve of her nightgown she wiped a large tear from her eyes.

How still it was! How terribly still! Piero, when would he come? When would he come, Piero? . . .

VI

God granted the abbess the strength for which she had prayed so fervently that evening. The reins of power had fallen into her old hands again, and she pulled them extra tight so that all should know it. The following morning she commanded that the decorations be torn down — nothing must be left to remind them of the previous day's festivities.

With the older nuns, she considered the daily routine. The activities of some of the lay sisters and novices must be looked to. Instead of working every minute of the day and being mindful of God, they wasted their time in idle chatter.

The abbess slipped on the large felt slippers that she normally wore only in winter. Her gout was troubling her, she said. Noiselessly she crept on felt soles through the convent, and listened to hear if any talk was going on in the course of work. Suddenly she swooped into the kitchen and inveighed against Elisabetta, against whom she had a special spite since the miracle that had led to that unfortunate letter to Rome. But Elisabetta was not the only victim — all suffered from her distrust. Sister Anna and Sister Beatrice, whose cells were contiguous, were soon separated by cells occupied by older nuns. Sister Veronica was so frightened one evening when the abbess appeared suddenly before her that she fell down with a shriek and lost consciousness. When she came to, she was given to understand by the abbess that it testified to an evil conscience to be thus startled by meeting one's own abbess unexpectedly; and the abbess added a general homily ending with the prophecy that the convent would be given over to the devil once she was dead, since the vanities of life still had such a hold upon them all. She was thinking, she said, of the banquet given in honor of Monsignore. She had been silent then, ashamed before God. She had been silent because of Monsignore's presence, and had tolerated what her old eyes and ears should have been spared. Once more she warned the novices, and even the nuns and lay sisters, not to raise any living being into an idol, not even the Holy Father himself. Honor and veneration were due to the bishop, yes; but at the same time they must not allow themselves to be influenced by his accidental human shape. God had poured his spirit into men hunchbacked and weak of limb and uglier to look upon than a leper, and it was said that the devil chose the comeliest human forms as his habitation.

The nuns listened in amazement. Surely by these last words the abbess could not have meant the bishop? But who shall say that the novices and lay sisters had understood her properly?

To avenge himself, the bishop sent a little note to the convent in which he coolly asked the abbess to hand Marietta over to him as a help for his old servant-housekeeper, whom he had brought with him from Rome and who would set an example to her in all the virtues. He had already come to an agreement with the podesta, her legal guardian. But he would, of course, abandon the plan if the child herself were reluctant.

The abbess shrank into herself again. Hysterically fearful of the bishop's designs, she discussed what was to be done with Sister Maddalena, who also grew pale upon reading the note. Quite at a loss, the two women faced one another, each tormented by her own misgivings, which neither dared to express.

"The note itself provides the only solution," said Sister Maddalena finally. "The child must be made to refuse."

The abbess heaved a sigh, and pattered up and down as though the ground beneath her feet were burning. She fumbled nervously with her rosary. "But how?" she gasped. "It would come back on our heads. No one would believe that a child like that would dare to refuse . . . or that we should allow her to refuse either. We must give her up, we must, we must." She stood still in front of Sister Maddalena, looked searchingly into her eyes. "Or would you dare to go to him and ask him to abandon his request?"

Sister Maddalena, flushing scarlet, shook her head negatively.

"Why not?" asked the abbess, her distrust flaring up. "You're not usually so afraid of going to the city and putting things right. You wanted to go to him before he came here, to tell him the convent would be grateful for the favor of a visit. Isn't that so? Didn't you want to?"

She stood looking at Sister Maddalena who, with averted eyes, merely said, "I'm not going to him."

"All right. In that case we can only give in," said the abbess, with spiteful resignation. She shrugged her narrow shoulders. Now the decisive word had been said, she felt relieved. Let them get on with it. The child was to be shown the door, and for the time being, so long as it was God's will, there would be peace in the convent.

Marietta was summoned. In icy tones the abbess told her how matters stood. Monsignore needed help in his kitchen. His old servant from Rome could not do all the work alone, and therefore the convent had decided to send Marietta to him.

Marietta stared from one to the other. This amazing news penetrated but slowly to her mind; but she was wounded by the cold disdain that rang in the abbess's voice, and most disquieting of all was the dreadful fact that Sister Maddalena averted her face. With trembling lips Marietta declared that she would obey.

The tone of her voice upset Sister Maddalena. "Come with me," she said. "I will help you get your clothes together. You must take a few things with you. Antonio can fetch the rest to-morrow."

Marietta followed her down the dark corridor, wondering dimly for what transgression she was being sent away from the convent. Listless with shame and grief, she looked on silently while Sister Maddalena folded up her clothes with practical hands.

Then a feeling of injury awoke in her. A gust of rebellion welled up within her. "What have I done?" she asked, crying softly.

Sister Maddalena interrupted her work. For a moment, she was on the point of telling Marietta the whole truth. . . . But she restrained herself, and resumed her packing. "What should you have done?" she asked in her turn. "You have done nothing . . . nothing. Did the abbess say you had?"

Marietta was silent. She bit her lip.

Sister Maddalena wanted to say something more. She refrained again. Then she lied. (Yes, as sure as fate it was a lie.) "It is a great honor for you, to go to Monsignore."

At the same time, she avoided looking at Marietta. Her presence seemed actually to annoy her — finally she sent her away. "Go and say good-by, while I get everything straight here. Go to the abbess first and thank her for everything."

There was a hard note in her voice, harder than was necessary. Marietta stumbled out of the door.

The abbess overburdened her with advice, reverting again and again to her main point: that she was never to hear a single complaint of her from the bishop. Marietta promised. She would have promised anything that was desired of her.

Outside, the novices were waiting for her. They had already heard something of what was happening and were very agitated as they said good-by. Several of them fell on her neck three or four times. One after the other, they repeated Sister Maddalena's lie, that it was a great honor to go to the bishop. In reality, it was something quite different — it must be something quite different that they were concealing behind their sanctimonious words. They looked at her strangely, as if there were something new about her that they had never noticed before. The nuns joined them in their farewells, but they showed a marked reserve in contrast to the novices' exuberance. They even appeared to hesitate about adding their own good advice and admonishments to the abbess's. They only said that they hoped to see Marietta from time to time.

Oh, yes, naturally, she would come often. Every Sunday, if the bishop would permit it.

That was settled.

She was sitting by Virginia, whom she had not been able to visit since that evening on account of the abbess's strictness. Virginia, to whom she had fled in despair, looked at her with large thoughtful eyes, and finally interrupted her with an inquisitorial, "Who has made you so terribly afraid of him?" Marietta raised her burning face. "You're trembling with anxiety. That's their contriving."

"No, they've said nothing, Virginia. They've said what a great honor . . ."

"They've made him into a bogey man, with their great honor. A bogey man. Because they're not chosen to go to him. Because they're imprisoned here, and see you going out by the gate."

"God, Virginia, yes, I am afraid," admitted Marietta, her teeth chattering.

"But think, Marietta. You've seen him too, just as they have. I tell you he spoke to me like a father. Be happy that you're going away from here — they've all taken leave of their senses. Be happy that you can live among people again. It is better to suffer there than to be safe here in a madhouse."

Marietta breathed deep, her confidence restored by these few words. She knew at once that Virginia was right. One must, one must live among people. So long as she had not noticed all that lay hidden under the surface here, she had been happy in the convent; now she could not breathe any more. Her foolish fear of the bishop had evaporated under Virginia's magical words, and she thought it would be very nice to go and live in the palace near the cathedral, and wait upon the bishop. This was surely a great honor. Of course it was. . . . How was it that this same declaration when made by the others had seemed a lie to her?

"But what about you, Virginia?" With a start she awoke from her self-centered thoughts.

A haughty line came over Virginia's mouth. "Don't worry about me." She wanted to reassure Marietta; but perhaps she feared that her words would not sound quite convincing. She confessed: "I dreamed again last night that he had come to fetch me unexpectedly . . . my brother. I have dreamed of it the whole week. If only I had desired it as strongly ever since I have been here, perhaps he would have come already. Wait! I hear somebody," she whispered hastily, pushing Marietta away from her.

Sister Maddalena had come to fetch Marietta. With a side glance, she observed the leave-taking of the two girls. The younger gave free rein to her tears, the elder was remarkably composed, smiled even, as Marietta reached the door. As they went out together, Sister Maddalena felt an urge to speak, but she waited until they were in her cell. Then, handing over to Marietta her little bundle, she said, tender and overcome, as if she wanted to put everything right, "If there should ever be anything the matter, child . . . come to me."

Marietta, still profoundly moved by her leave-taking from Virginia, recognized suddenly in Sister Maddalena's voice the old familiar sound. She threw her arms wildly round that broad womanly frame; but even at that moment a foolish prudery and fear of sin prevented Sister Maddalena from surrendering to her maternal feelings.

Just as the little bell was ringing for the midday service, Marietta, carrying a little bundle that contained only what was strictly necessary, left the convent to take up service with the bishop.

At the bend of the road behind the pine wood, she looked round for the last time, and nodded towards Sister Maddalena and old Catarina, who had seen her off and who now went indoors. The old convent door stared after her in surprise.

Marietta could not help marveling at herself, so little afraid did she feel. She had Virginia to thank for this great, wonderful peace, Virginia who was left behind in the convent.

But what could Sister Maddalena have meant when she said, "If there should ever be anything the matter . . ."?

What could happen to her that should make her want to flee to Sister Maddalena? What could happen to her in the palace of the bishop himself?

TWILIGHT IN

A PRIEST'S

LIFE

I

RUGGED AS ITS PRESENT INMATE, THE EPISCOPAL palace stood in the quiet blaze of the sunburnt piazza. The interior was curiously bare. Large, unwieldy pieces of furniture stood arbitrarily against the blank walls, sometimes connected by a cobweb to the brass chandelier that had not been dusted for months. The gently winding marble staircase was covered with a narrow worn carpet runner that continued on to the landing and then came to an abrupt end.

The bishop did not bother about such trifles as his heavy step reverberated through the hollow building. A valuable copy of a Donatello bronze, carelessly placed on one of the pillars of the banisters, was gradually displaced by the vibrations of his tread, and collapsed eventually, badly cracked and dented, into the entrance hall. When that same afternoon Monsignore, in searching for the *Confessions* of Saint Augustine that had fallen behind a chest, found himself wallowing in thick dust, and even then could not find the book, he suddenly realized that many things in his house might be different, and he was on the point of summoning his housekeeper to these Augean stables; but he feared her tears, her indignant reminders that she had served him faithfully for seventeen years. Besides, it was nearly time for his next meal; she would pay him out by serving it burnt. *Basta!* He would return to the matter at a more opportune moment.

Immacolata, the immaculate, was the name of the fearsome old woman in the kitchen. "Imma" the bishop called her, and sometimes when he was in a good humor he said to Marietta, "Where is the mustache?" Marietta had to bite her lip, but at the same time she looked round in concern lest Immacolata should hear. She would have been hurt, even though she was not vain enough to stand before the looking glass and pull out the disfiguring hairs from her upper lip, like more important ladies.

She was small and round, just half as tall as her master, and a twisted black bun of hair on top of her flat, gleaming skull did not mend this misfortune. Everything about her appeared to have been wantonly compressed. When she ran down the stairs, it was as though a ball were rolling down. As everything about her, everything she wanted to lay hands on, was as high as her breast or higher, the motions of her arms were always horizontal, as if she were swimming in invisible water. She seemed always to be in danger of drowning, to be imploring for God's help and pity.

Actually, however, there was more of rebellion than of humility in her soul. She found fault with the whole world for having been created an unnatural size. Whenever she rummaged in the top cupboards of the massive oak press, her every movement was an accusation.

In the house everything danced to her piping. If the smallest thing was undertaken that was not in her day's program, a storm broke out, and none was spared, not even her idol, the bishop himself. With shy amazement, Marietta saw how this little woman compelled her master (and what a master!) to submit to the rules he himself had once promulgated.

Sometimes Immacolata was out of humor without knowing why herself, and then she was at her most dangerous. Monsignore could elude her by retiring to his study. Sebastiano, the stableboy, who usually spent half the day in the kitchen, could go into the courtyard to curry the horses, whistling unconcernedly; but Marietta was doomed by her unlucky stars to remain in the vicinity of the irate Imma, to listen to her bitter comments on the world, the Church, and the tomato purée. The little woman did not rest until she had discovered some transgression committed by Marietta, and had said everything there was to be said about the matter. Only when Marietta stood before her drenched in tears did peace descend upon Imma's incensed soul, and for the rest of the day an almost celestial goodness radiated from her. By the evening she was nearly swooning with remorse; sighs, a slavish desire to serve could not liberate her. Shortly before she went to bed, she recalled that she had come into the world an orphan. . . .

Of the whole great building, the bishop inhabited only the front rooms of the first floor that looked out on the piazza. Immacolata and Marietta slept on the top floor. Downstairs, next to the coach house, was the kitchen.

Monsignore, who was not very particular, had taken over the furniture left by his predecessor. From Rome nothing had come except cases of books and a large black harpsichord that found a place in his study. The couch that had formerly stood there was removed, despite Immacolata's protests, to the room where the bishop was in the habit of hearing the confessions of the rich ladies of Todi. In this same rather more comfortably furnished room hung a series of paintings representing the master of the house at various periods of his ecclesiastical career. One of them, a pastel drawing dating back thirty years, showed him as a young abbé in daintily curled wig. Every one of these paintings bore witness to the bishop's impressive, manly appearance. Out of each of them he looked down with a severe self-conscious glance upon his devout lady visitors.

In the morning, on the stroke of six, he rose and as soon as Ercole his barber had done with him, he received the priests who had come to discuss current affairs with him. After they had gone, he paid a visit that lay infinitely nearer to his heart, to his horses downstairs in the stables. Each of the four was black with white stockings and a white star. They were called Mohammed, Mustapha, Bayazid, and Suleiman, after sultans of the Saracen kingdom. Michele his coachman saw to it that he too was present at that time, in order to exchange opinions with his master on the condition of the animals. When Sebastiano had finished currying and brushing them, and no speck was left on their gleaming trappings, Michele harnessed them and drove carefully out of the entrance to give the horses their daily run in the sunny morning, and to regale the citizens of Todi with a sight of Monsignore's magnificent team.

This operation Monsignore watched from the window of his study. He leaned out a little, resting his hands upon the window sill and taking pleasure in the magnificent bearing of the animals, in their gleaming black backs and powerful necks. The snorting and the stamping, the soft creaking of the leather harness, the harmless cracking of the whip (never was one of his horses actually touched with it) — all this was music to his ear, and unconsciously he took a deep breath and inhaled, like a connoisseur, the odor of horses and leather harness.

He watched his coach leave the piazza, listened to the tramp of hooves as they resounded in the main street, glanced up at the swallows circling high in the sunny sparkling air — and then, with a sigh, drew in his head from the window, to read his breviary until the eleven o'clock Mass, which he celebrated daily in the cathedral as his predecessor had done before him. The day's duties were upon him again.

The hours after the midday meal that might have been dedicated to meditation were largely taken up by a voluminous private correspondence with Rome and Venice, where many of his friends, and one or two aged patronesses, still lived.

From four o'clock onwards, he was ready to receive representatives from the religious houses and villages of the entire diocese. They brought him presents for his house-chapel and for his table, bored him with their all too transparent flattery and their simulated piety, exasperated him with their small-minded disputes, their complaints, their requests for special privileges, that, if granted, immediately aroused discontent in other villages or religious houses.

On Friday afternoon, the ladies of Todi came to confession. Not within human memory had they had so much to confess. The clarion voice of the new bishop shed peace upon their souls, a peace they had never found with the quiet, obliging, gently ironical old man now in his grave. The wife of Judge Rigogli — yes, even haughty young Signora Galli, wife of the podesta — did not shrink from waiting an hour long in the dimly lit, uncomfortable waiting room until the bishop could bend his ear to listen to them and sweep over them with his punishing words like a storm. Young and old alike among the ladies of Todi seemed to have a curious liking for hearing the unvarnished truth once a week from the bishop. They seemed to enjoy wetting their bepowdered cheeks by the half-hour with their tears, to enjoy wringing their bejeweled hands. During these Friday admonitions, the walls were not always so discreet as they should have been, and Immacolata downstairs in the kitchen shook her gray head over all she heard. "The world, the world," she said to Marietta with a sigh. "Be happy you don't understand anything about it yet."

It was true that Marietta understood but little yet. But she trembled under the heavy thunder that rattled above, and her soul too was purified when the bishop's wrath had blown away. It did not surprise her that these ladies should come for the special purpose of taking such a punishment.

The confession sometimes took another turn altogether. When young, attractive Signora Perosio, the twenty-year-old wife of the elderly papal tax collector, confessed her sins, it was uncommonly quiet upstairs. Immacolata leaned her head sideways to listen; but she could hear nothing. Exasperated, she clattered noisily among the pots and pans, and sighed audibly with relief when Anselmi, the bashful secretary, came rattling the door knocker at a quarter to six.

"Marietta, quick! Go upstairs and say . . . Don't bother to go in — just tell Monsignore from the landing that his secretary has arrived."

When a moment later the penitent came downstairs, Immacolata, small and impertinent, stood provokingly at the kitchen door, embarrassing by her deeply contemptuous stare the young lady who had just been absolved from her sins.

In spite of Imma's occasional tantrums, in spite of the friction that resulted from them between the old woman and the bishop, Marietta felt happy in this new home, and protected as she had done during the first days at the convent. She was living in the city again and through her position knew herself to be safe and unassailable. When she went marketing she was treated with respect. Everyone was obliging to her. Sometimes she began to believe that she had misjudged them all. There were moments when she would have liked to mix with them again. She felt her reserve, which she could not overcome, to be sinful pride that she ought to confess.

One day, as she passed Vacca's inn, she was an unwilling witness of how Coretti, swaying uncertainly on his legs, thrashed his wife, who had dared to peep in at him. She was thankful once more that she was allowed to live in the stillness of the great marble episcopal palace, aloof from the all too human odor, composed of sweat and tears, of unaired corners and stale washing, that came floating out to her from the houses of the poor.

On her own initiative she came to grips with the problem of dust. Imma left her to herself, pretending not to notice what was happening, though she rarely allowed anything to escape her. Monsignore himself looked on distrustfully when Marietta came too near his books; but he ceased to worry when he observed that Marietta respected his capricious and unaccountable arrangements.

And how could she do otherwise? She served her master with an infinite respect, with a blind, joyous devotion. Every day she enjoyed it as a renewed privilege when she brought him, as soon as he was back from Mass, a cup of fragrant, hot chocolate. She tried to read his wishes in his eyes, and was proud and happy over the meanest task he set her.

But best of all were the evenings. After the evening meal, when the bishop was not expecting visitors, he liked to sit at the harpsichord and improvise; and as soon as Marietta had finished her work in the kitchen, she would come to him and practise under his supervision some air from Pergolesi or Scarlatti: Monsignore had set himself the grateful task of developing her voice.

He was teaching her, too, to improve her writing and to reckon better. Her quick brain soon led him to extend his instruction to anything that came into his mind, and so it was that he wandered with her at ease into the regions of abstract thought, of philosophy, and of metaphysics, amusing himself with the subtle questions of this fifteen-year-old girl whose healthy feminine mind resisted any attempts to digress too far from the world of reality. Immersed in the pleasure of teaching her, he sometimes forgot the time until Imma came to say that it was ten o'clock, that she herself was going to bed, and that Marietta had certainly studied quite enough for one evening.

The old woman had received Marietta with severity and suspicion; but she had at once shielded her from Sebastiano's rather coarse jokes, and, after months of watchful caution, had at last decided to take "that child" to her heart — when Monsignore sprang it upon her that if there were no guests little Marietta was to sit with him at table.

Up to then, Imma had looked on passively while the bishop made a lady out of the girl assigned to her as a kitchen help. She had not protested when the child stood beside the harpsichord and sang to Monsignore's own accompaniment — she had even been honest enough to admit that the sound was not unpleasant, as she stood listening to it from the kitchen downstairs. But to sit together at table! That was the last straw. She must think about it. Staring sombrely in front of her, she returned to the kitchen. (Marietta, all unconscious, looked at her with concern.) Then suddenly Immacolata decided what she must do. She took off her apron and went upstairs again.

Only on very solemn occasions did Immacolata divest herself of her apron. When the bishop saw her reappear without it, he knew that she had come to give notice.

Listening patiently, he opened his snuffbox. When she had finished speaking, he asked her if she had ever counted the number of times she had come to give him a fright of this kind. "Imma, come to confession to-night, and go to bed early. To-morrow everything will be right again."

No, this time it was not as simple as that. She had been engaged to serve him. She made bold to think that she had done this to the best of her ability for seventeen years. If he had any complaints to make, he had only to say so. Then she would know what she had to do, and besides she knew what to do in any case, for she had no intention of serving two people.

Right: he took cognizance of that.

And what did he mean by that, Immacolata inquired suspiciously.

What else could he mean except that he *therefore* gave up his plan. He had no need to give that a moment's consideration. He would give up anything rather than lose her devoted services after all these years. And now, was everything all right?

Immacolata stared at him — she had to give some thought to the matter before she could decide whether everything was all right again or not. The position was changed at once by his reference to her devoted services, by his chivalrous admission of gratitude. If she could only understand why he had tried to affront her like that . . .

"Affront?" asked the bishop, astonished. He had never thought of such a possibility. But of course, on consideration, he quite understood. Either she would have been delighted by his plan or she would feel affronted by it. She chose to feel affronted. Well, that was quite in order. It would have pleased him to develop to the full the remarkable aptitude of that little girl, and to have had her at table with him would have helped to fit her to move in better circles . . . But now that that project had fallen through, he would not bother to persevere with the evening lessons either. Looking back, it was perhaps a pity that he had wasted so much time over them; but these evening lessons might also seem an affront to Immacolata: and affront her, he simply would not.

Imma observed that she had never said a word against the evening lessons; but all the same, she could not see why she should be delighted about them.

"Well, Imma, just in the same way as a mother rejoices when she helps her child to go further in the world than she herself has done. But there is no need to talk about it any more. Will you now be so kind as to leave me alone?"

Immacolata did not take this request very seriously. She could not believe that a matter involving her almost leaving the bishop after seventeen long years could possibly be disposed of in so few words. She was now just prepared to come to an amicable agreement, with a little give and take on both sides. She smiled unctuously as she stood by the door. Very good. As, according to him, she could not rejoice like a mother, she would also bear in mind that she herself had never known a mother; and just as she had always been a lonely orphan, she would now again be as she was before — eat alone at her little table downstairs in the kitchen. And this evening she would come to confession in accordance with his advice . . .

Suddenly he jumped up from behind his table, brought down his fist upon the top of it so that the wood cracked, and roared at her, "No, that you will not do this evening."

She rolled her eyes in dismay. Her mouth trembled as she tried to utter a protest; but she only succeeded in bursting into a sob as she went out slamming the door behind her.

Immacolata felt that she could not reappear in the kitchen looking as she did; instead she went upstairs to her room and had a good cry. Ten minutes later, as she was going to leave it, she burst into tears again. At last, Saint Anthony, her own particular saint, gave her, in response to a long prayer, the necessary peace and strength to go downstairs. To Marietta, who awaited her return with concern, she said, "We have been talking about you. You are to sit at table with Monsignore and learn manners."

Marietta looked at her speechless. Then she stammered, "Must I? Did he say that?"

"Yes, you must, and that's what he said. Or would you perhaps prefer me to teach you how ladies and gentlemen eat in the great world?" Imma was glad to see that Marietta herself was astonished at the plan. Perhaps the demon of pride had not yet possessed her. Gently she pushed the child, already half as big again as she was, towards the kitchen door. "Go upstairs, just as you are, and thank him. Go! Don't put on airs. Say I've told you, and that it's all right . . ."

II

Lent was over, and Marietta had been with the bishop a full year. She had long grown accustomed to sitting with him at table. She talked to him naturally, and she could hardly remember the time when he was a forbidding stranger in whose presence she felt she must wither in the consciousness of her own insignificance. She had learned many of his weaknesses, and in a number of small matters he made her his confidante. When Imma was in one of her bad moods, Marietta exchanged a quick, significant look with him. Little Marietta — she was a big girl now: she would be sixteen this summer.

Looking back, Imma realized that the bishop had been too clever for her, and that he had filched Marietta from her by a trick. She avenged herself by referring to Marietta as the Signorina when she talked with Sebastiano, who now took his midday meal with her. But oddly enough the mockery seemed gradually to go out of the word, even for Imma, and one fine day she caught herself saying to a lady who wanted to gain admission to the bishop, "The Signorina has gone to inquire if he is free"; and she even felt a pride in mentioning the Signorina.

Marietta did not cease to fulfill her part in their joint daily tasks; but, unobtrusively, Imma became the servant. She it was who asked Marietta what Monsignore would like to eat on Sunday, and what she should bring from the market.

Marietta herself was aware that something new was taking place within her, that the chains seemed to fall from her; and for the first time she breathed freely. Sometimes she was filled with astonishment to discover what an ascendancy she was obtaining, and over other people besides Imma. She no longer felt it necessary to go about the streets with the modest air of a nun in order to feel safe. It was a wonderful sensation, these first intimate contacts with life. The convent seemed far, far away — a pale, gray dream in the past.

With the pocket money that Monsignore had given her from the beginning, and which she had at first accumulated without purpose, she had had made for herself shortly before Advent some simple, tasteful clothes to replace the drab, formless garments she had grown out of. She had observed how the well-to-do young ladies of the city dressed when they went out, and now before she appeared at Monsignore's table she always changed and smoothed her rebellious, gleaming, curly black hair. The bishop noted this unexpected change in her appearance with obvious satisfaction, and expressed his pleasure. He was completely surprised by it, for, manlike, he had never realized the possibility of such a transformation.

During lessons, he was sometimes so exacting that she grew hot with anxiety and slept uneasily the whole night; but at table he let himself go, talking to her of his experiences, dwelling for preference upon his youth. Some of the memories awakened within him he stopped short of describing, shaking his head over them instead.

One day, when he was in one of these half melancholy, half joyful moods, he expressed his desire that henceforth when they were alone Marietta should call him "*Babbo*" as if he were her father — everybody called him "Monsignore." Old Imma was transfixed the first time she heard the familiar name coming from Marietta's lips, for up to now, it had been her privilege to be permitted in moments of great loyalty to call her master "*figlio mio*."

Babbo. Those who saw him daily in his home were inclined to forget what an exalted person he was, so great was his simplicity in all things. His horses were his only luxury, and unfortunately he could seldom give himself the pleasure of driving. With his meals, which needed only to be well prepared to meet with his approval, he drank for preference the ordinary wine of the district: he said that he found it tasted best because it retained the taste of God's good earth. He deemed it sinful pride to scorn the wine of one's own district in favor of expensive wines from afar. He soon learned to distinguish by their taste and color the wines of the various growers round Todi. When he took a fancy to some particular wine, he drove to see the peasant who had supplied it, went with him through his vineyard, amicably discussing methods of viticulture, quite at home and full of his own ideas, and as he left, ordered a cask, promising to sing the praises of this wine everywhere, gave the children half a lira each for their money boxes, promised the peasant's ailing wife to pray specially for her recovery, and thus left behind him a pair who looked back upon the day of his visit as the day of their lives. If that evening old Signor Galli or the papal tax collector Perosio with his charming young wife happened to be guests, Imma was told to produce that wine and no other, and it was defended fervently by the bishop against their friendly condescension.

The ladies of Todi, now that he had been there a year, would have liked to refurnish his palace in a manner more in keeping with his dignity; but when they sounded him cautiously on the subject, he disappointed them by declaring that his preference had always been for a few large pieces easy to keep in order — in fact, he liked things to be as he had found them in the house. Other proposals were likewise shipwrecked upon the bishop's discouraging satisfaction with everything he already possessed; but as the ladies insisted upon giving some tangible expression to their respect, they finally fell back upon their needlecraft. The house chapel of the episcopal palace became a veritable treasure house, while Marietta had to allot an entire shelf in Monsignore's wardrobe to the expensive kerchiefs presented to him by the ladies. Sometimes he found this devotion too much, and then Marietta was privileged to hear his sarcastic remarks on certain of these industrious ladies. This mark of distinction brought a flush to Marietta's cheek, and, in her secret joy and satisfaction, it never occurred to her that his mockery was directed exclusively towards the older and less attractive ladies of Todi.

The festivals that fell in Lent, Passion Week, and Easter itself, with all that followed, had taken up too much of Monsignore's time to leave much over for the evening lessons, and it was then that he conceived the plan of entrusting Marietta's voice to the good offices of Maestro Angelini. This Maestro Angelini, the subject of the most exaggerated rumors, had for some mysterious reason been obliged to leave Florence, where, according to his own report, he had been all the rage. After a short and secret interlude in Siena he had swooped down upon Todi one fine day, and there began to give lessons to various ladies, old and young, in the playing of the lute and the harp, in chorus and in solo singing. After being an inhabitant of the little city for three months, he still cut a strange figure in the street with his elaborately curled wig, the strong scent of violets he left behind, his unnecessary use of a monocle, and his pretentious wielding of a cane inlaid with diamonds that, according to him, had been a present from the Queen of Naples, for whom he was supposed to have played the lute.

When Maestro Angelini, recommended by the younger Signora Galli, came to pay his first visit to Monsignore, he was announced in tones of veneration by old Imma, who looked upon him as the eighth wonder of the world. But he nevertheless had an uneasy feeling that he was not being received with the seriousness and the attention he might have expected from his introduction, his gifts, and his outward address. He thought he had observed on Monsignore's face a faint amusement not accounted for by anything in their conversation. Maestro Angelini's thin mouth tightened. He grew silent and absent-minded, appeared unable to follow the bishop's ironical remarks. But when he took up his lute, which had been ceremoniously carried before him by one of the Galli servants, he revealed in his playing such a rare, almost diabolical virtuosity, such a genuine musical gift, that Monsignore was forced to conceal his embarrassment under a flood of genuine praise that was very like a confession of guilt. He told Imma to summon Marietta, and then chivalrously declared that he had allowed himself to be prejudiced, that he had conceived it impossible that a music master of such great gifts should have elected to dwell on so modest an Olympus as Todi.

"But if Todi is not beneath the contempt of a priest of great gifts . . ." retorted Maestro Angelini courteously.

Monsignore smiled subacidly, and reddened faintly. He had an uncomfortable feeling that he in his turn had been made to look foolish, and with some reason. While he still struggled against the strange feeling of weakness that had overcome him as he listened to the truly heavenly music made by that all too earthly seraph, Monsignore was irritated to find that the right word with which to parry the perfumed knave's dagger thrust simply refused to occur to him.

It was now Maestro Angelini's turn to smile delicately. Modestly he related how, driven by an inborn urge to wander, he had won his spurs not only in Florence, but also in Venice, Milan, Turin, Rome, Naples —

yes, literally in all the great cities of Italy; and now, before repairing to France to try his luck at the far-famed court of Louis XV, he had been seized with the impulse to visit some of the smaller places of his beloved fatherland, and he had been drawn in particular towards Todi for the sake of its local wine, whose reputation had recently spread throughout the entire Papal States . . .

From this pleasantry, Monsignore deduced that old Signor Galli and Perosio the tax collector had woven his predilection for the local wine into an anecdote that had not escaped the attention of the newly arrived music master. But at that moment he did not care: Marietta had just come in, and all he wanted was that she should receive lessons from Maestro Angelini.

As she entered, this favored son of the muses greeted her with a courtly bow that embarrassed her greatly, for Imma had not been at all clear as to the object of his visit. Monsignore poured out full-blown praises of Angelini's art in a stream of words that did not conceal from her a fundamental hesitation she had never noticed in him before.

She did not know what to say, but just stood waiting while it was settled that Maestro Angelini was to come every Saturday afternoon to nurse her musical talent, and by his genius bring it to fruition.

After a few lessons, she grew accustomed to the strong perfume of violets that, an hour after he had gone, still filled the room. She began to grow accustomed also to his affected voice, to his too well-tended, bejeweled hands, and would have begun gradually to derive profit from his lessons had it not been that Maestro Angelini, whose love of ease drove him to give way to every mood of his capricious nature, was far from being always in the frame of mind to give lessons.

Sometimes he decided to play her one of his own compositions, and filled in the remainder of lesson time with ridiculing some of the Todi ladies or with elaborate disquisitions on shoe buckles, and new dance steps, and the kind of lace neckbands that should or should not be worn. He took infinite pains to make her laugh, deplored her gravity, which affected him even after he had left her, and then suddenly asked her to look into his eyes because that night she had appeared in his dreams and he had imagined with great certainty that she had gray eyes like a pet cat of his early youth that had been almost more musical than anyone he had since met.

Monsignore, at work in the adjoining room with the communicating door open so that he also could enjoy the music, was sometimes exasperated beyond words when, for half an hour on end, instead of the music he was expecting, nothing but the sound of Maestro Angelini's voice penetrated to him. An unpleasant, shrill, challenging voice it was, always breaking off into high-pitched hoydenish gurgles and impotent little cries. By way of protest, Monsignore coughed ostentatiously, or shifted his chair noisily, but he did nothing further. The calm assurance that was so very much his own seemed to have deserted him in relation to Maestro Angelini. He seemed to entertain a mysterious awe bordering upon timidity for this foolish effeminate little cur of a musician whom he expected to work wonders on Marietta's vocal chords.

To distract his mind, he rang for Anselmi his secretary, who was busy in the little room on the other side of the landing dispatching correspondence, and dictated a serious letter to the Pope arraigning the prior of a monastery for having sent a petition direct to the Vatican instead of through him, the bishop. Intimidated by this loud dictation, Maestro Angelini began to whisper and to smother his tittering. This only increased Monsignore's exasperation, who as he dictated began to walk up and down his study with long steps, showing himself at the door every time he passed, with a menacing look that was answered by Marietta with one that was imploring and helpless.

Whereupon Maestro Angelini, getting up from his place, asked the bishop, with an irresistibly friendly smile, if he might be allowed to close the door in the interests of his lesson, and the unbelievable happened: Monsignore acceded to the request with a grim nod and an embarrassed side-glance. Now, on one side of the closed door Maestro Angelini's chatter continued undisturbed. On the other, an obstinate prior who, on the strength of old privileges dating back a thousand years, had thought he could prove that as head of his particular monastery he owed obedience only to the Holy Father in Rome, was described in a letter to the Pope as a rebel and a heretic who should forfeit his dignity on the spot and begin in another monastery a new life of humility and repentance as a mere lay brother.

When Maestro Angelini came back the following Saturday the communicating door had been lifted off its hinges and removed. As it happened, he was this time so much under the sway of his own inspiration that he did not even notice the absence of the door. Only when he was about to depart did he notice it, and then could only smile at the poor bishop who, in his own palace, had not the courage to say, "The door remains open."

There it is again, thought Maestro Angelini. I am not trusted. They prefer not to leave me alone in a room with a young girl. It was so in Rome, it was so in Venice, it has been so everywhere. It happened in

Florence and in Siena, and it was a fact that these suspicions had always been justified.

The following Saturday, the door was back on its hinges. Monsignore had a look at it, saying that it had been repaired; and he then asked Maestro Angelini whether he would prefer the door to remain open or closed.

Open, open of course. Then Monsignore could hear how his pupil had already progressed. Maestro Angelini was impressed by his own choice — virtue in person must have inspired him to it. He had been so tormented all the week by the vanished door that he had been put off his sleep. His self-esteem was shocked at the idea that a door need be closed before he could seduce a young girl. Till that moment he had scarcely noticed the little girl in question. Oh, she was well enough. He might have noticed her before had she not always been so serious, and if she had contributed something on her side — he was used to women meeting him halfway (or perhaps a little further — he was not quite sure); but it might be rather a piquant change to assume the rôle of the sly seducer for once. In his right coattail pocket he had secreted a small bottle of essence of roses, the gift of that little red-haired Countess in Turin who had wanted to be able to boast to her girl friends that she had weaned him from his predilection for "mille et une violettes" . . . Was it in Turin?

Yes, he had the little bottle with him, and now was the door to be closed? Not in a thousand years: it should remain open.

He began the lesson with gusto, and could not find sufficient words to praise his pupil. In his enthusiasm, he took her little hand and pressed it to his lips. As Marietta, confused, withdrew it, he took the opportunity of slipping the little flask into it. Then he smiled at her, exultant and innocent, making sure at the same time with an unobtrusive glance behind him that Monsignore was not observing them.

Marietta stood helpless, not daring to look at what lay in her hand, not daring to put down in front of him the cool, smooth object she held.

"Sing, sing! Where's your voice?" demanded Maestro Angelini in astonishment. "What has suddenly become of your marvelous voice? Listen to me . . ." He sang a couple of verses. He had a small, shrill voice, yet there was nothing ridiculous about him when he sang. He knew how to give it form and shape, to make it mysteriously moving. While he sang, very serious and rather melancholy, he looked at Marietta and with a friendly pressure opened her hand and showed her his gift. When he noticed that in spite of herself she smiled — a captivating, innocent smile — his joy and satisfaction went to his head. Without further thought, he put his arms about her, lowering his voice until he whispered into her ear the tenderly endearing conclusion of the song.

Marietta recovered herself, uttered a repressed cry, and shook off his embrace. Maestro Angelini, accepting his bad luck with philosophically raised eyebrows, stepped back discreetly, glancing round instinctively for his hat and his cane, the cane that had been the gift of the Queen of Naples.

When Monsignore appeared at the door, large and menacing, ready for instant action, Maestro Angelini was rolling his music sheets with a practised hand. He slipped them under his arm, like a long but harmless rapier, and, looking about unconcernedly, took his leave with the same sort of bow with which a few months before he had entered the palace, on the recommendation of young Signora Galli.

Monsignore stood on the threshold of the room, a prey to speechless, impotent rage that was mingled with concern for Marietta.

"What did he try to do?" he asked, speaking with difficulty.

Marietta did not answer. She only looked at him, still pale with disgust.

"Well, he has been here for the last time," announced Monsignore. When he saw the relief on Marietta's face, he said, full of self-reproach, "I ought to have been wiser. I knew all the time that it would turn out like this. Of course I knew. Yes, but I simply couldn't resist his playing."

Marietta pricked up her ears at the peculiar sound in his voice. Suddenly Maestro Angelini was a thousand miles away. What did he matter to her? There was something in Monsignore's unaccustomed helplessness that moved her profoundly; and unexpected and deep joy spread through her being in warm waves.

"*Babbo!*" she said.

Quickly he raised his head. Still distrustful, he noticed that the smile had returned to her lips. Then he came up to her with his heavy tread, took her face between his large hands.

"Is it all over?"

"But didn't you say he's not to come back?"

"That I promise you." Now they found nothing more to say to each other for a moment. They looked into each other's eyes. Marietta's happiness awakened a smile round his lips too. Then he said, filled with undiminished repentance and with great gravity, "Marietta, when you came to the house a year ago you were a child, and it did not occur to me that one day you would cease to be so."

Marietta flushed. There was something she wanted to say. She could not remain silent. "*Babbo*," she asked, "am I *your* child?"

He nodded to her, slowly, silently, and kissed her on her forehead.

Then he turned, went back to his study and closed the door behind him.

An hour later he summoned Imma and told her what had happened that afternoon. In dismay, Imma crossed herself; with long steps Monsignore strode up and down the room, saying, "You know why I took this child into the house, Imma." (No, Imma did not really know, but she was very interested to hear.) "I heard her singing with the others, and by accident my eye fell upon her. It suddenly crossed my mind that they would try to keep her in that convent for good. You know, Imma, if somebody of his own free will takes the vow, then after all it's his own affair. But such a child, who knows nothing of life and discovers too late all the things that lie outside a convent . . . ."

Yes, yes; Imma knew an example: but when she wanted to cite it, he seemed not to have the patience to listen to her.

"I couldn't help thinking of that child. Perhaps her beautiful voice had got hold of me, as that rascal's playing did. Perhaps it was the large, dark, childish eyes with which she looked at me . . . Do you know what I couldn't help thinking, Imma? If I had a daughter, she would have eyes just like that, and no other. Yes, and now she is with us, and this happens. That little girl counts upon our protecting her. A moment ago she asked me straight out, 'Am I your child?' "

Monsignore groped for his snuffbox, and watched Imma, who stood looking demurely before her.

"I sometimes think that a good father of a family has been wasted in me," he remarked humorously; and then, with emphasis, "you've often said it yourself, Imma." He paced up and down, lost in thought and speaking to himself. " 'Am I your child?' she asked me suddenly." He had to laugh. But at the same time this question made him think. "That child expects me to direct her, and now she has just reached that awkward age when you don't know what you can talk to her about, and what you should keep your mouth shut about. I can talk well enough to a young woman."

Oh, yes, Monsignore could do that very well. He sighed and thought to himself how mad he was to feel so unaccountably weak towards this child . . .

Imma kept her eyes fixed to the ground, brooding. Perhaps she was a little jealous because Marietta had asked him, "Am I your child?"

"Yes," she said, shaking her head, "the world, the world." If there was one man in the world she would have trusted, it was that respectable Maestro Angelini who, to all appearing, knew exactly what was what.

Well, she must return to her cooking, otherwise the food would burn.

III

Marietta soon forgot Maestro Angelini. When Imma called her to the window to watch him as he crossed the piazza, she stood and looked at him as at some stranger in outlandish attire, and she could not help smiling at the admiration that still rang in Imma's voice. Marietta could no longer conceive that he had actually been in the house and had given her lessons, so complete a stranger had Maestro Angelini remained to her.

The only difference his visits had made was that she could no longer stand the perfume of violets, and, as ill luck would have it, that was becoming the fashionable scent among the ladies.

Perhaps as a result of what had happened, she could not keep her mind off Virginia.

Virginia. . . .

During the first months of her life in the bishop's palace she had thought of her friend, left lonely behind, day and night. Why, in a whole year, had she never once been to the convent? When she took leave of the nuns, they had pressed her in unison to come and see them now and again. Had she not been very selfish when, feeling herself so happy and satisfied in this house, she had allowed her aversion to the convent to hold her back from visiting Virginia? Yes, she had been selfish and narrow-hearted.

One evening she could keep silent no longer, and for the first time spoke to Monsignore about Virginia. She told him, blushing and sometimes searching awkwardly for the right word, how Virginia had reached the convent and how homesickness for Venice was eating out her heart. The bishop listened rather absent-mindedly, sometimes even with a smile. When she had finished he said, "I can't be expected, Marietta, to release a young novice from a convent. If life does not please her there among the nuns, she must write to her family, and should the abbess open her correspondence and burn it — then she must find another way for her letters to reach their destination. I imagine the abbess would not be particularly grateful to me for even these few words, but I have incurred her displeasure in any case. I feel like saying, 'Just go yourself to the convent to-morrow and see how your friend is getting on . . .'"

That same evening, he indited a short note that Marietta was to deliver to the abbess and that would be the ostensible reason for her visit. While he was drying the wet ink with sand, he remarked in passing, "If only it isn't already too late."

"Too late?"

"Too late for it to be in the power of her family to liberate her from the convent."

Marietta breathed again. A sudden giddiness had come over her at the thought that she might have been about to hear some awful news of sickness or death. The other possibility adumbrated by Monsignore gave her no anxiety. "No, no, *Babbo*, she hasn't become a nun, and even if she has . . . You don't know her brother."

Thereupon, on rational grounds alone, Monsignore could only keep his counsel.

On her way, Marietta was able to make use of the coach, as the horses had to take their daily run. Sitting beside Michele on the box, she could not help recalling how she had taken this road every week with Signora Galli's fine linen in a basket on her arm. In those days she imagined herself a nun inclined inimically towards life. What would it be like, seeing them all again: Virginia, the abbess, old Catarina, Sister Maddalena — Sister Maddalena, who had been a mother to her in the beginning, and had behaved so strangely when she left?

When the convent came in sight, Marietta, embarrassed by this too stately arrival, asked Michele to stop. But teasingly he cracked the whip in the air, and the horses increased their pace. Thereupon she sprang from the fast-moving vehicle, stumbled and fell, and one of the iron back wheels grazed her. But she was up again, to Michele's relief. He capitulated and turned the coach. As he passed her, he tried to conceal behind a wink the fright he had had. For a second, a vision of Monsignore in the guise of an avenging God had flashed across his mind. Sebastiano, on the back seat, pursed his lips towards Marietta in the shape of a kiss — the monkey.

She walked on in the still summer morning. In cloistered peace, the convent lay sheltered behind the dusty gray of its surrounding woods.

The bell tinkled as before. The sound still hesitated between two notes, and after a minute's silence she could hear old Catarina's slouching approach. . . . It was all so familiar, and yet so long ago.

Catarina looked at her astonished, over her iron spectacles (they were new), as if in doubt as to who she was.

"Marietta?" she asked, and when Marietta bit her lip, confirming her identity with a smile, they embraced each other — both feeling a little unnatural, however.

They went down the long dark corridor together. "And how are things these days?" asked Marietta, when old Catarina continued to be silent.

"How are things? Oh, very well. Everything is just the same. How would it be otherwise? One gets older. I have to wear spectacles now. But you are changed. You are so changed that it's necessary to have a good look at you to be sure who you are . . ."

Catarina wanted perhaps to say more, and Marietta waited in suspense; but they had just arrived in front of Our Lady of Pain, halfway down the corridor, and when they had both knelt and crossed themselves, Catarina resumed her former silence. Assuming that Marietta had a message for the abbess herself, she took her to the library.

Marietta knocked three times, as was, she still remembered, the rule of the convent. Then she entered. With the abbess was Sister Maddalena, who stood up to take her in her arms. She seemed deeply affected at seeing her again; but the abbess remained distant. With a sour face, she opened the bishop's note. She would reply at once — Marietta could wait.

While the abbess sat at her desk, Sister Maddalena asked how she was getting on. But her question had none of the unrestrained warmth of a moment ago. Bitterness seemed to have welled up in her again, as on the day of their leave-taking. She had to struggle with herself as she listened with a little forced laugh to Marietta's talk about the bishop — how he was like a father to her, gave her lessons in French, in music . . . Marietta herself scarcely knew what she was saying, she was so put out by that forced little laugh, and the strange, almost hostile look with which Sister Maddalena dragged her statements from her as if she were looking for some hidden meaning behind each word. Marietta did not tell her that she sat at table with the bishop, and that he allowed her to call him "*Babbo.*" She did not speak of it, because it might lower him in a stranger's eyes — she did not want to exalt herself at his expense; though had she been alone with Sister Maddalena this too would have been extracted from her. Marietta was aware of this, and, oppressed by her awareness, became almost tongue-tied, until they stood together in silence, like strangers, waiting till the abbess had finished her letter. Her pen scratched and rasped in the silence of the room.

It was ready. Marietta could go. . . .

Outside, as on the day of her departure, the younger nuns and novices were waiting for her. Two of them were new. A childish curiosity consumed them all, making them ask questions that at another time would have made Marietta smile. But she still felt nervous owing to Sister Maddalena's curious demeanor, and she answered reluctantly, briefly. What curious ideas they must have about the bishop. Was it really necessary to ask such foolish questions? Was it really likely that he would eat and drink differently from any ordinary mortal? They went on asking questions blindly, rapidly, as if they were afraid they would forget something until Marietta had gone. They stumbled over their words with embarrassment, because they saw that she had become a different person, and that perhaps in her heart she despised them.

But they had to satisfy their curiosity — it was stronger than their embarrassment.

Marietta was infinitely relieved when Sister Maddalena, coming from the library, released her from this ordeal, and consented to her going to see Virginia, who was making a drawing of the convent garden that had been commissioned by old Signora Galli. As she turned away, she added, "Remember, it's Sister Virginia."

Marietta could find nothing to say in her bewilderment. Sister Virginia? With quick, silent steps, she hastened to the garden. Surely it was not possible that Virginia had taken the veil!

She found her friend in the black garb of a nun, sitting alone in a corner, a sketch book on her knees.

"Virginia!"

Without any show of surprise, she looked up on hearing her name. When Marietta, laughing through her tears, stood before her, Virginia did not laugh too, but looked at her with her old dreamy look, saying with calm gravity, "How pretty you have grown, Marietta!"

Marietta dropped down beside her, flung her arms nervously round her, and pressed her head against her shoulder. "Virginia, what is this? Say something! You didn't want to become a nun, Virginia."

Virginia looked down at her sketch book. "No. At first I didn't, but as they have forgotten me . . ."

"But how do you know they've forgotten you?" cried Marietta despairingly. "Now if your brother does come to fetch you, you can't go with him. Have you thought of that, Virginia?"

Virginia raised her eyebrows philosophically, and said gently, "Perhaps that's why I've done it."

"Why you've done it? What do you mean? To revenge yourself upon him? Oh, you should never have done that." In her despair, Marietta wrung her hands.

Virginia abandoned her unnatural restraint. Her far-away voice came nearer. Marietta heard life in it again. "Don't let's talk about it any more, Marietta. It's nice to have you here. I've thought of you often. I should have liked to know if you were happy in the city. That was the first thing I thought of when I saw you — and at once I was set at rest. Oh, yes, I've regretted you more than once. And now you're here, now you've come." She laid her hand on Marietta's.

"I've thought of you too, Virginia," Marietta assured her. "It often kept me awake at night. I wanted to write to your brother to come and fetch you, if only I had known his name, *your* name . . ."

"You? You wanted to write to him?" asked Virginia with a smile. "I could have written to him myself, but I am glad that I didn't. I should have written so that it would have appeared as if I were crawling back to him. Now I have been silent, and I should like to see his face if he comes here and hears from old Catarina that he is too late . . ."

She smiled mockingly, then continued more gently: "You know, I'm not angry with him. Venice is the city where one forgets everything, and it is certainly far away. The parcels of paints and brushes have become rarer too. Once in the month I write to my father to tell him I'm all right here; but when I miss a month he does not even notice it.

"You know, Marietta, you must not think I spend my days moping. Sometimes, perhaps. It may come over me at any hour of the day or night, and then for a moment it's as if I should die. But we all die in the end. Then it passes, and I get a little private amusement at the thought of what they would say in Venice if they heard I'd become a nun. For the rest, I do needlework, I paint. Look, this is for old Signora Galli. At least once in the week she comes to have a look at it, and she tries to drag everything out of me — more than there is to find. I always think out in advance what I shall make her believe." Virginia held the drawing in front of her: it represented a view of the garden between two Romanesque pillars, with the roof of the cloisters and the old clocktower in the background. "Just look at those hideous stone masks on the capitals. I've changed one of them a little, to make it look even more like old Signora Galli . . ."

Virginia had to point to the mask before her meaning penetrated to Marietta. Then, before her dismayed eyes, the face of old Signora Galli appeared with fascinating clearness. "Virginia!" she cried, catching her breath.

"She won't recognize herself, but her lady friends will," said Virginia quietly.

"And if they should tell her?"

"They won't do that, and even if they did . . . It's all one to me, Marietta. That's what makes me, sometimes, so happy. If I have to remain here, it's all the same to me. In my little corner I can laugh at the whole world. But why don't you laugh any more?" She looked at her with the old smile in her eyes. "By the way — I'm doing something for your bishop, too."

Marietta flushed and turned her head towards Virginia: it was as though Virginia had guessed everything — that she sat at table with him, that she called him "*Babbo*."

"What are you making for him?" asked Marietta, and tried to conceal the burning curiosity that suddenly overshadowed every other interest.

Her question increased Virginia's mirth. "Will you promise not to tell? I'm copying for him an old hour-book with miniatures that lies forgotten in the library here; but as I can only work at it an hour now and then, it may take ten years to finish. But tell me, do you think he'll really like to have a copy?"

"Oh, yes, certainly," said Marietta emphatically, and in her pleasure she did not remember that she had often wondered how Monsignore had come by the beautiful collection of hour-books and psalters, of which he was so proud, though he rarely looked at them.

But that was enough for Virginia. "Oh, well — perhaps, in that case, I'll hurry up with it. You remember when I was ill he lent me several beautiful books — I didn't think he'd remember them again, but the abbess soon took them away from me because reading and looking at pictures was supposed to be bad for my eyes. Do you understand . . . ? They were very worried about my eyes."

Virginia suddenly fell silent: Martha, the lay sister, who was a little sneak, had come into the cloisters with a message that Marietta was expected in the kitchen. Marietta nodded, but as she did not get up to follow her at once, Martha remained there too, looking down at Virginia's drawing, comparing what was on the paper with the reality to make sure that nothing had been left out. If she was hoping to overhear what they were talking about, she was disappointed.

"I must go now," said Marietta at last.

"Not a word!" said Virginia, finger on lips, as they parted, at which they both simulated great lightheartedness.

"Of course," promised Marietta, and then began to wonder whether Virginia meant the secret of the present she intended to give the bishop ten years hence. Sulky and crestfallen, the lay sister walked by her side. Elisabetta clasped her heartily in her arms the minute she appeared in the kitchen.

Elisabetta too wanted to hear about the bishop, and among other things whether he still sometimes mentioned the Convent meal that he had enjoyed so much. Did Marietta remember how all the onions had been dropped into the tomato sauce? What an evening it had been!

In the kitchen a basket of peaches from the garden was ready for her. Leaves had been placed among the delicate fragrant fruit to protect it from bruising: the arrangement of the basket was unmistakably the work of Sister Maddalena, but she did not appear again. Elisabetta, awkward but kindly, hung the basket over Marietta's arm, bidding her be careful of the fruit.

"Oh, yes . . . with the abbess's respectful greetings," she called after her.

Without any doubt, that also had been impressed upon her by Sister Maddalena.

But why had Sister Maddalena herself not given Marietta the basket?

Outside the convent Marietta saw Antonio, the young gardener — he had apparently been working in the churchyard. It was months since she had seen him; and then only once, in the market, when he had given her a shy glance but had not dared speak to her. He must have noticed her pass, from over the cemetery wall, and have waited for her return.

As he approached, struggling with his diffidence, Marietta wondered why she used to feel an aversion to him. Now she felt only compassion because, tall and broad and rather prepossessing in features, he was yet so terribly bashful in her presence. According to report his father was lying ill of an incurable disease, and Antonio had to work for his parents alone, without receiving even a soldo of pocket money from his tyrannical mother.

"Good morning, Antonio."

He was visibly surprised by the friendly tone of her voice, and had some difficulty in bringing out the question he had been preparing during the hour he had waited for her: Was she also going to the city, like himself?

Yes; where else should she be going?

"Oh!" said Antonio, changing color, and now, instead of offering her his escort, he walked by her side, gauche and silent.

Marietta gave him a side glance. Yes, he had become tall and broad. How old would he be? Twenty? She could not help remembering how, during that severe winter when wolves had been seen, he had come to the convent to protect her; and now he had put on, in her honor, the little coat that usually hung loosely over one shoulder.

"How is your father, Antonio?"

Antonio hastened to reassure her. "Father is still in bed, but he's no worse during these last weeks. Master Barberini agrees. If only he doesn't get worse, and if he can keep down the nourishing foods that Mother gives him . . ."

It was far from Antonio's intention that Marietta should worry over anything concerning him.

He now fell to brooding. Once or twice he tried to say something, but fortunately thought better of it in time. As they walked along, Marietta thought of one thing and another she might have said, but this walking together in silence pleased her. She could follow her own train of thought so peacefully.

What had Virginia said? What had been her first words? At the time, Marietta had not wanted to hear those words. They had embarrassed her; but she hadn't forgotten them. She had preserved them somewhere in a hidden corner of her mind from which she now drew them out. Virginia had said, "How pretty you have grown, Marietta!"

She had said it quietly and very gravely, as if she had wanted to convey, "You're no longer a child." Marietta could not put into words the significance that she felt this greeting held. She felt, suddenly, that a new period, to which she had never given a thought, was dawning for her. Hitherto everything had been but child's play; but now, something was beginning. A serious, important time was coming. . . .

Was she really pretty? No, pretty in the usual meaning of the word she was not. Had she been, she would have heard of it already. The daughter of Fiorini the wood merchant — everybody turned to look at her, in the street. The younger Signora Galli was pretty, too — with her little mouth, and her hands always overadorned with rings. No, pretty in that sense Marietta was not. Virginia could not have meant that. But there was something about her that made people say, "Just look at that Marietta!" Even the nuns and novices had looked at her — but they would all have gone to the stake rather than say anything to her.

Marietta had to admit to herself that it had been splendid to hear praise from Virginia's mouth. She had been completely confused at the time, but now that she had taken it in, it gave her a comfortable feeling, it made her rejoice more than ever over this world, over this sunny morning. Suddenly everything was rose-colored. She was ready to believe that the rumors about Antonio's father were exaggerated, that he would get better again if he could only digest the nourishing foods his wife gave him. She also felt more at rest about Virginia. Had not Virginia herself said that she could laugh about everything, that nothing could affect her any more? Marietta also found it really pleasant to have Antonio walking by her side. There was no need for him to speak — it was sufficient that he had waited for her after he had seen her enter the convent. . . .

How pretty you have grown, Marietta!

Meanwhile, Antonio was casting despairing glances at the basket of peaches on her arm. It had not occurred to him, at first, that the basket might be heavy — for him, it would have been nothing; but for her . . . ! And now he was struggling for courage to ask her if he might take it from her. Perhaps she was thinking him far from nice for not having offered to do so in the beginning. In his mind the basket became an intolerable burden to her arm, growing heavier and heavier. It gave him a feeling of oppression. He pulled his coarse handkerchief from his pocket, and wiped his neck with it. Oh, Madonna!

Marietta looked at him, and smiled. "Are you finding it so warm, Antonio?"

"Not I, but you surely must be — with that basket!"

Marietta read everything he was feeling in his glance. The day before she might not have understood so quickly, and it would not have come into her head to smile and hang the basket over the arm of the shy creature.

Antonio's whole face shone. Now everything, everything was right. He was carrying the basket for Marietta — and he hardly felt it upon his arm.

Suddenly his tongue was loosened, and he asked her boldly whether she would have to go to the convent more often for the bishop. It was a happy coincidence that he had met her to-day. He had been busy in the churchyard, in the convent itself. He could only go back to work there regularly after his father was completely cured . . .

At the city gate, where their ways parted, Marietta took back her basket and thanked him for his help. His gentle dark eyes looked at her hungrily, in a way that betrayed all his feelings for her, and it was Marietta's turn to feel shy. For a second she felt again something of her old irritation with him.

While Antonio went up the side street that led to his home, Marietta made for the piazza with quickening footsteps. She felt a sudden longing for the old palace with its few pieces of large furniture among which Monsignore moved quietly, massively. As she caught sight of it, she saw the Venetian courier just delivering the mail. She hastened her steps, and contrived to be in time to take the letters from Imma and to carry them upstairs to Monsignore while the old woman nosed inquisitively in the basket Marietta had brought from the convent.

As she went upstairs, Marietta raised the perfumed envelopes to her nose, wondering how many ladies of Venice had a soft spot in their hearts for the bishop. Then she knocked, and from the way he called, "Come in!" she knew that she was welcome.

Spontaneously he spread out his arms, but he did not put them about her. Instead he pushed up a chair in front of her. He took the letters from her hands, and without looking at them laid them down on his writing table. "Tell me first how you found the little sisters," he said, with a mischievous sparkle in his eye.

Marietta smiled at his twinkling glance, and began to tell the story of her visit. She did not realize that she was imitating the old abbess's voice, but the bishop, who was discovering for the first time her talent for mimicry, opened his eyes wide. "Where did you get that from?" he interrupted her; but then he nodded to her to go on. She came to Virginia. He listened, noting with surprise how much more lighthearted Marietta was now about her friend's captivity. He himself could not help feeling, from various suspicious remarks, that the new nun (for she had taken the veil, as he had half-feared) was perilously near complete despair. But so long as her despair did not upset Marietta's rosy-hued day, he also was content.

"So they saddled you with a heavy basket of peaches," he said, as he cast a hasty glance over the abbess's note.

Marietta told him that Antonio had helped her carry the basket. "Antonio who?" inquired the bishop, and then teased her for a moment over the coffinmaker's shy son. Marietta flushed, and, maintaining obstinately that with a boy like Antonio she could safely walk the same way even by moonlight, tried to conceal what a great and strange pleasure Monsignore's teasing gave her.

"Yes, I'm well aware of it. You're growing up," said the bishop, peeping among the leaves in the basket as Imma had done before him. "Who gave you the peaches? Is the abbess suddenly so well disposed towards me? Or was it one of the nuns? . . . That tall, blooming one, perhaps."

Marietta knew at once that he meant Sister Maddalena. "Yes, they come from her," she said, without considering that this was after all only a supposition on her part.

Monsignore smiled to himself. He was used to Marietta's presence again, and his thoughts wandered back to his correspondence. "Well, well, take them back to the kitchen," he ordered.

As Marietta left the room with the basket of peaches, she saw his hand reach out towards one of the small perfumed envelopes . . .

IV

During that autumn, Immacolata was afflicted by her old complaint, the gout. Sighing and groaning, resting one hand on her hip, she came upstairs to clear the plates and dishes. Marietta, who saw her suffering, told her to go to bed and leave the work to her. Imma refused, obstinately, until the bishop commanded her and gave her some gout pills, in whose healing power she believed because they came from his hands.

Marietta cleared the table and went downstairs. Monsignore, who had too much correspondence for the usual lessons, asked her to bring some needlework or a book and sit with him — he no longer cared to be alone.

She washed up quickly, set the coffee tray, took it upstairs, and opened the door carefully so as not to disturb Monsignore. In silence, she sat down with her embroidery frame on the other side of the table, so that she, too, could profit by the candlelight.

There was no sound in the room except Monsignore's deep breathing and the scratching of his pen. When Marietta put down her needlework to replace a dying candle by a new one, he looked up and followed the movements of her slender fingers.

"Look, just read this nonsense," he said suddenly, and pushed a letter towards her from an abbé, requesting protection on the grounds that he occupied the same room in Venice in which the present bishop of Todi had finished his studies thirty years ago.

Monsignore had never before shown her any of his correspondence. Shyly, reluctantly, Marietta picked up the letter.

"You can answer him for me, too," he said, giving her an encouraging, amused, but compelling look. Passively, she allowed him to hand her a blank sheet of paper and a quill. "Read the letter," pressed Monsignore, and then bent over some more important letters with ostentatious concentration.

Marietta, thus abandoned, studied the missive from the abbé who sought the bishop's protection. Not until she had read it twice over were his motives and intentions quite clear to her, and then they roused her righteous indignation. She cast a hesitating glance towards the bishop, who ignored it. Then she took her courage in both hands, dipped her pen in the ink, and in her flowing hand wrote:

My dear abbé, —
Do not ask me for protection, ask the walls of the room that saw me study hard to become what I now am.

Monsignore looked up inquiringly, drew the note towards him, read it with his tongue in his cheek, and with a serious face dictated the following continuation: —

Should my landlady, the faithful Margherita Leoni, still be alive, which God grant, give her my blessing.

And then, with a flourish, he signed it with his virile signature.

Later in the evening, he put his letter-writing on one side and began to talk with Marietta, asking her about her childhood in Todi. He listened gravely while she reviewed that very dark period, in which nothing but the comic muse of circumstance or the infinite suspiciousness of Vacca occasionally compelled a smile. Monsignore inquired more closely about Vacca, returned to him again and again, undermining her evasiveness with his leading questions. It was as if he already knew the whole truth, but wanted to compel her to tell him of the dreadful thing that had happened that night when she fled to Nana's room.

At last she could no longer evade the issue, and slowly, word by word, admitted that Vacca in his drunkenness had leaned over her bed, had wanted to compel her when she refused to sleep with him. She had tried to eradicate that night from her memory. . . . Only now did she feel herself liberated from it. Her cheeks glowed after the painful confession; but she was pleased that Monsignore knew everything, everything — even this thing that she had mentioned to nobody.

Her deep emotion gave her the courage to seize his large strong hand and lay it on her forehead. He caressed her curly hair lightly and asked, "Are you still afraid of him?"

"No, not any more, *Babbo*." In her relief she raised her head to show him that she was smiling again; but his own face was uncomfortable and embittered.

After a moment he said, "It's late, Marietta. You must go to bed."

She stood up obediently, and went to her room; but she felt she could not go to bed immediately. She blew out the candle and stood by the window. The moon was flooding the piazza with soft light. It gave mysterious life to the façade of the old cathedral. Purified by wind and rain, the saints stepped out of their niches, lustrous and unreal.

Vacca's inn loomed darkly on the other side. Marietta could now look in that direction without feeling an oppression rise up in her. What was Vacca to her? He and Luigino had become strangers whom she passed in the street without a word of greeting. Even with Nana she exchanged only a few hasty words of goodwill. On the first anniversary of her birthday that she had passed in the bishop's house, Nana had come on a visit. Nana and Imma had sat opposite one another, stiffly and inimically, in the kitchen. The visit had not been repeated.

Marietta's thoughts returned to the bishop. People always thought that a priest stood above everything and could not be moved by earthly sorrow. . . In that sense, the bishop was perhaps not everything he should have been. He did not stand above the sorrow of others. He was a human being, even though a bishop.

This gave her much food for thought. Somehow or other, she was reminded of Giuseppe Fiocchi, who on his twelfth birthday had been sent to the seminary in Rome because his parents were so proud of him they wanted to make him a priest. He was a brave lad who had dared to jump from one roof to another over a fairly wide alley. In Rome he would grow to manhood, and who could tell whether one fine day he might not like to have a wife and children? Perhaps, then, he would curse his parents who had thoughtlessly dedicated him to the exalted solitude of ecclesiastical life.

With a surprising certainty she became conscious that even Monsignore had not adapted himself entirely to his exalted loneliness. Was it this tormenting feeling of loneliness that had caused him to make her call him *"Babbo"*? She trembled with pride and joy at the thought that by her dependence she could help him to endure the chilly heights of episcopal dignity. Oh, she would love him always, with all the warmth of her soul.

In spite of herself, she could not think without a strange shame of the ladies who came to confess to the bishop, and who did embroidery and crochet work for him. Did they also want to console him in his loneliness? Marietta, feeling almost spiteful towards them, suspected them of self-interest.

A week or two before, Imma had refused to let in the young Signora Perosio, wife of the papal tax collector, although she had come to confess at her usual hour. Signora Perosio had departed in tears. Imma had said nothing to Monsignore; but an hour later he had asked whether a note or a message had come from Signora Perosio, and when Imma told him the truth, there had been an angry scene. Imma had let fall something about couches in confessionals: whereupon Monsignore had ordered her to join him upstairs, banged the door of his study behind them, and bolted it. For nearly an hour they were alone, and then Imma emerged, her eyes red with weeping.

Marietta had sensed rather than understood the ugliness of Imma's suspicions; but this couch, which had never before struck her, had now become an object of distaste to her.

Yes . . . Perhaps it would be pleasanter and quieter in the house if the ladies stayed away.

The coolness of the night made Marietta shiver under her thin clothing. She stepped into bed, where she lay awake a long time.

Next morning old Imma asked, "How late was it when you went to bed last night?"

Marietta told her the truth. Monsignore had sent her to bed at half-past ten, but she had not gone to sleep immediately — the moonlight had been so fine.

Imma made a grimace, because just at that moment a pang of the gout shot through her. She said nothing further, only muttered to herself.

From that evening, however, she began to spy on Marietta's doings. Sometimes she rushed into the room where Marietta and the bishop were at work and prowled about unnecessarily. Irritated, Monsignore asked, "Why do you disturb us, Imma?"

She was speechless with astonishment. What, disturb them? She had not said a word. In any case, she was glad to know, after eighteen years' faithful service, that she was a disturbing factor in the house. She had not realized that before; but if she really was, perhaps it would be better if she . . .

Monsignore tried to calm the rising storm by requesting her to remember that there was a time when she knocked decorously before coming into his room.

Knock? . . . Certainly, naturally. So far as she knew, she was still in the habit of knocking when there were visitors, or when he was alone in his room, but when Marietta was with him . . . Why in the world should she knock? He was silent, looking at her. She tried to conceal her rising discomfort under an impertinent, challenging look. Marietta, upset, bent over her writing and waited for Monsignore to flare up and order Imma from the room. Imma, however, left just in time, closing the door behind her with a bang.

One night she appeared unexpectedly in Marietta's room. She opened the door gently, but Marietta, who was restless, awoke with a start, and was a little scared to see a white nightcap gleaming in the darkness. Before she had a chance to say a word to the ghost, Imma snapped, "Aren't you asleep yet?"

"Yes, I was asleep."

"Really?" said Imma, and then, "Who did you think had come into the room?"

"I knew it must be you. Nobody else but you, do you hear?" broke out Marietta bitterly. "Because for weeks now you've come sneaking after me. If only I knew what you wanted to catch me at!"

Imma was silent. She came nearer and sank down on a chair, resting her hands upon her hips. The honest indignation in Marietta's voice had disarmed her. She panted with fatigue and nervousness, and seemed to be very near to tears. "Lord, Lord, why does she speak like that to me?" she said, pitying herself. "What could I catch you at? I don't know myself what's the matter with me. It must be the gout. I can't sleep, Marietta. When the pain gives me a breathing space, I lie wondering whether you are leaning out of the window instead of lying in bed as you should be. I know all that means, when a girl leans out of her window and looks at the moon . . ."

She turned her head and, biting her lips, stared herself into the moonlight that flowed over the roofs.

Then she looked at Marietta again. Coolly, consolingly, Marietta said, "Put your bed in here again, Imma, if that will make you sleep better — just as you did when I first came here."

But Imma rejected this humiliating offer. "No, certainly not. In any case, he wants you to have a room to yourself, like a young lady. I'm all right again now. You go to sleep."

Miserably, she leaned towards Marietta and offered her her cheek, upon which, so as not to hurt her, the girl pressed a kiss.

Then she went, leaving Marietta a prey to hours of nervous sleeplessness.

V

After a stormy, rain-sodden January and February, the spring set in among the Umbrian hills — and before anyone knew it, Lent was approaching again. Immacolata was so busy that she found no more time to think of her gout. By Easter, the whole house must be spring-cleaned, so that one could eat from the floor. There must be no spot on the curtains or the bed linen, no speck of dust on the furniture, when Monsignore blessed the house again for a whole year.

Everyone in the city was preparing for the annual blessing, and it would therefore not have been easy to obtain help, even if Imma would have accepted it. Once a year Imma was infected with a holy fury of cleaning. Like a purifying fire, it raged through her, leaving her exhausted and broken after Easter, incapable, for the rest of the year, of sweeping away a single cobweb. In the midst of her violent activities, she realized with astonishment that her gout had gone, leaving no trace, and that she could sleep again at night. Her spring depression had changed into an unexpected pleasure in living — and, most wonderful of all, Monsignore had predicted this very phenomenon at the beginning of Lent.

Having acquired a new lease of life, she attended High Mass in the cathedral with Marietta on the morning of the first day of Eastertide. The bishop was to perform for twelve old peasants the same service of love that Jesus had performed for his apostles — the washing of the feet.

Seated in a circle, the men who represented the apostles waited in their neat Sunday clothes. Their gray or silver-white beards had been carefully combed, their feet had been meticulously washed in advance. They concealed their awkwardness behind a solemn gravity, and seemed dazed by the booming of the organ and the uninterrupted ringing of the bell above their heads. They tried to pick out their friends and relations, but could not distinguish them easily among the many faces that devoured them. They had difficulty in grasping the fact that they, to whom normally no one paid the slightest attention, had for this one day become objects of curiosity. They could not quite follow why they themselves, who, in their daily lives, looked at each other with hostility, distrust, and aversion, now constituted, the twelve of them together, a transcendent unity — the living symbol of a miracle.

To-day was a great day, an impressive day. Preceded by boys carrying censers, and followed by acolytes carrying water, a towel, a basket of ring-shaped bread, and a bowl with lemons, the bishop strode forward, knelt down, and with a steady hand washed the blue-veined feet, emaciated with age, that the apostles-for-one-day thrust out to him. He dried one pair carefully, rapidly, then was already kneeling before the next. The acolytes pushed a loaf of bread under the arm of each man, when he had been washed, and thrust into his wrinkled hand a golden lemon — which each of them held as solemnly as a king's orb.

Marietta watched intently. Never had the bishop so impressed her before. His kneeling in humility before the poor people, the confident movements of his hands, that almost transformed the symbolical washing into a real ablution, conjured up as by magic the days when Christ himself walked upon earth. Marietta was more deeply moved by this ceremony than by the rites before the altar. He seemed to be indeed God's chosen servant.

He stood up. The light fell upon his magnificent chasuble and spread across his massive shoulders. He had the bearing and the voice of a patriarch. Like Moses, he could have led the people forty years through the wilderness, keeping their faith in the Holy Land alive within them. Like dwarfs, like creatures of a lower order, the acolytes followed him.

How sinful of Marietta to think that Monsignore could ever feel lonely upon his exalted pedestal! True, he was on this earth, but only as an envoy. He lived in another, higher world, the world of the great men of the church. She could hardly believe that she dwelt under the same roof with him.

She exchanged looks with Imma. They understood one another. Imma remembered with dreadful self-torture her habit of giving notice to such a master, and on their way back to the palace, overwhelmed with consciousness of guilt, she remarked to Marietta: "If only I die under his roof . . . if only I can do that."

VI

They certainly wanted to serve him in all humility, if only the bishop had not made it so difficult.

On Easter Monday, Monsignore dined with the podesta. Next evening, he himself received the members of the cathedral chapter and several priests from Rome who happened to be passing through Todi. They were regaled with a sucking pig. From early morning, Imma and Marietta were kept busy, to make a success of the meal; and Monsignore gave Imma her reward by begging her to come upstairs, and praising her in the presence of the guests. She returned to the kitchen radiant with satisfaction. Marietta served at table, playing the part of the lady of the house. When she went out of the room, the bishop could not forbear speaking of her innate distinction, her intelligence, and her beautiful voice. When she came in again to serve coffee, he said, "Marietta, these gentlemen would like you to sing the Sancta Mater we have been studying together."

Marietta looked up hesitatingly; but a glance at his eyes showed that he really meant what he said. Assuming a lighthearted tone, she said: "The gentlemen will repent of their wish, Monsignore."

But the guests, who were in the best of humor, thanks to the good wine and the spiced sucking pig, assured her in unison that they were prepared to take the risk.

"The venerable father with the long beard will accompany you," said the bishop, laughing.

The guest indicated put down his napkin immediately, stood up from the table, and led Marietta to the harpsichord with awkward, facetious courtliness. Sitting down before it, he began to strum the opening bars, clumsily, before silence had fallen. Marietta's first notes, however, brought him to order; and a threatening "Sst" from the bishop compelled immediate quiet: they realized that their host did not regard this as a moment for merriment. In her pure voice, well under control, Marietta sang the Sancta Mater to the end — when spontaneous applause broke out, and the guests, without concealing their genuine surprise, begged for another song.

But Marietta had already stepped off the footstool upon which she had stood, and, smiling happily, declined the honor of singing a second song. Instead, she gathered together the empty coffee cups and retired.

Imma, downstairs in the kitchen, was still open-mouthed at the sounds that had reached her from above, and could not make up her mind whether to be exasperated with, or proud of, Marietta.

"Did he tell you to sing?" she demanded. "In that case, I'll say nothing."

For days afterwards, Monsignore was in high spirits at the credit Marietta had done him. He told her the guests had advised him to send her to Venice or Naples to study under an experienced singing master. "But I shan't let you go yet," he said immediately, recoiling from the idea. "I might as well get a little more out of having taken you away from that convent. Then your voice would have been buried forever, and you aren't yet seventeen."

Monsignore was remarkably agitated, and strode up and down the room rapt in thought. "In a year's time I shall write a letter to a friendly old lady in Venice and ask her to take you under her wing and introduce you into society. I know several friendly old ladies who would do that for me."

And he turned to a subject he had never touched upon before. Actually, Maestro Angelini had been the first to put it into his mind, and his guests of Tuesday evening had said something too, so that he felt he must consider the matter seriously. He spoke of her marriage. No, it wasn't mad to be thinking about that already. His pride was involved in her making a *good* marriage, and for that purpose she must get away in time from Todi, where everybody knew the circumstances of her upbringing. He certainly must not keep her in Todi for more than another year. Many a girl married in her sixteenth year; but seventeen was quite soon enough, and he would like to meet anyone who would assert that a handsome, gifted girl could not make a good marriage even in her eighteenth year!

She must tell him truthfully if she had never thought about it herself.

"No, really not, *Babbo*."

"Now tell me, confess. You can tell me, Marietta. I only want to know because . . ." He could not find the end of his sentence. "You're not going to make me believe that you'd like to remain with me for the rest of your life. A young girl has ideas. After all, that's only natural."

A great tenderness welled up within him. He put his hand upon hers, and the look he gave her was strange and melancholy. Marietta could not bear it. Everything within her rebelled against the sacrifice he wanted to make, and against the sadness that was descending upon them as a result. Why must he talk about all this? Everything had been so right, and now he had let fall words that could not be unsaid. Silently, struggling with her tears, she looked straight in front of her.

Then Imma came in, and unobtrusively he withdrew his hand.

For the time being, Monsignore did not return to the subject of her going to Venice. Marietta was aware that he was deliberately evading the subject, and on her side she was only too anxious to do the same; but for this very reason it remained uppermost in their thoughts.

Although separation grew to seem less imminent, Marietta did not recover the quiet content of her first year with the bishop. The strange agitation within her refused to be quietened by the thought that a year was a long time. Perhaps that strange feeling had been there for months already, but deep down, so that it had given her no anxiety. Now suddenly it had come to the surface, and sometimes it seemed to grip her by the throat — she felt herself suddenly imprisoned by it.

At times a mysterious joy would spring up from deep within her and would sweep through her whole body — a great moving joy such as the sun had sometimes made her feel, or a cool downpour of rain on a broiling summer day — a joy that her very skin seemed to drink in, and that made her finger tips tingle. Everything about her acquired a new and deeper significance. Then, as abruptly as it had come, this joy departed, leaving her body listless and defenseless. She felt empty, empty; her own soul was a stranger to her. Beads of perspiration stood on her forehead, and she moved about the large house avoiding Imma and Monsignore.

And Monsignore? What was the matter with him? In the mornings, he looked as though he wanted to tell her something with his eyes that he could not utter with his lips. He took the cup of chocolate from her hands and said something to make her laugh . . . and she laughed. What he said was not always very funny, but she was too agitated to notice that. She heard only that peculiar tone in his voice, and a shiver went through her.

He could make her cry as easily. It scarcely mattered what it was that he said — by the vague intonation in his voice, he could compel her tears.

Sometimes he was somber and withdrawn into himself. He avoided looking at her, as though her presence were unwelcome. Then her heart was seized with fear — all the blood seemed to be drained out of her. Noiselessly she left the room, and when she reached the kitchen, Imma asked her what was the matter.

One night Marietta got it into her head that a chat with Virginia might give her peace. With whom else could she speak freely? If only she could have an hour with Virginia alone, without being disturbed by Sister Martha or anyone else. Perhaps Virginia would say the word that would end this mysterious sinking of her heart. Why hadn't she thought of her before?

She asked the bishop's permission to go to the convent again, and next morning set out upon the old familiar way. Passing the churchyard, she looked over the low wall and was relieved that Antonio was not working there: she preferred to return alone.

Old Catarina came trotting to the door with unaccustomed haste, and before she had opened it called breathlessly through the judas: "Have you any news?"

Marietta looked at her in amazement. "News? I want to see Sister Virginia — "

"Sister Virginia!" exclaimed Catarina, bending down to unfasten the bolt of the door. "Sister Virginia! . . . Merciful Lord! Didn't you meet Sister Maddalena?"

"No. Why?"

"Because she's gone to the bishop to tell him the dreadful news."

"Catarina! What's the matter with Sister Virginia?"

"She's gone, gone. A sister who has taken the vow! We tremble to think what the bishop will say. The abbess will die of it. It is a scandal for the convent, a scandal for us all . . . I was standing here at this door," wailed old Catarina, "this morning. Matins was just over. A man stood before me. A little way off there were two others on horseback, all three covered with mud from hard riding. I had a premonition, Marietta. Great God! He asks, 'Is there a Sister Virginia here?' 'Yes, at your service.' 'And do you know who I am? I am her brother, and I wish to speak to my sister this very minute.' 'I'll go and ask the abbess, sir.' 'What, the abbess? It's my sister I want to speak to.' 'Yes, I'll ask the abbess, sir.' 'Look here, old thing. Take this.' 'You can put it in the offertory in the waiting room, sir, if you wish to give something to the convent. Follow me now to the abbess.' 'Right, go ahead then. Take me to this abbess of yours.' "

Old Catarina raised her arms to heaven. "If only I had slammed the door in his face, the wretch! But I had that money on the brain. I wanted him to put it in the offertory. I let him come in. I let that wolf into the sheepfold. I locked the door behind us, and fastened the bolt. While I was praying before the Madonna in the corridor, the heretic said, 'I'll teach you to make a nun of my sister.' My ears refused to hear, Marietta. I preferred to be deaf. I preceded him, leading him on, but it was as if he was driving me before him with a whip; and lo and behold, just as we neared the library, the sisters were leaving the chapel. . . . I'm trembling, trembling. Here, feel my hand. . . . I knew a terrible misfortune was going to happen. I wanted to draw him away. I pulled at his sleeve, but I might as well have pulled at a rock as at that man. Sister Virginia almost fell down with fear when she saw her brother standing by me. In a moment he had seized her by the wrist. Her prayer book had fallen from her hand. It was as if I saw Christ's heart falling. But that wasn't all. He took out his knife, and came up to me. . . . O Holy Mother of God, St. Joseph and St. Clare, I thought to myself. . . . But he only cut the leather girdle that held my bunch of keys. The sisters rushed shrieking back to the chapel. Only Sister Maddalena had a mind to go after him; but the abbess fainted — and, as it happened, just in her arms. Who in the end was the only one to run after that robber with his shining knife, Marietta? It was me, on my old legs, as true as I'm standing here! Me alone. I called out, 'Stop!' and perjured myself with awful curses. On they ran! When I had reached the gate the keys were in the lock, and the horses had gone. I just saw them disappearing in a gallop behind the woods. I rang the bell like mad, Marietta. What more could I do? Only fall down on my knees, and say to myself: 'You've done your duty, Catarina!'"

With her sleeves, Catarina wiped the sweat from her gray face. She expected Marietta to break out into holy indignation at the action of the shameless intruder. But when Marietta continued to stare without uttering one word of censure, Catarina froze, ceased her excited and plastic account of the morning's happenings, and became reserved, even hostile. She remembered with a jerk that Marietta no longer belonged to them; that she would judge this frightful act of violence from the point of view of the sinful, godless world that was only amused by a convent's distress. Catarina recollected that the abbess was waiting for her. She went into the convent, closing the door behind her. Then, through the judas, she asked Marietta if she had any message for the abbess; after which, with a very cool nod, she closed that too, and it was only after hearing the bolt slip sharply into place that Marietta awoke as from a dream.

It was as if she had been listening to a fairy tale.

Everything about Virginia had been like a fairy tale. The reflection of it rode sparkling in her eyes. And now the prince in the fairy tale had come and brought her liberation. That morning he had appeared before the gate, vowing by heaven and earth to his friends that he would get her out of the convent, and chance had given him a helping hand, as is right in fairy tales. Marietta could almost see how it had happened; see the abbess swooning in Sister Maddalena's arms, see old Catarina losing her sandals in her flurry, pursuing the fugitives — an ineffectual avenger. It was as if it had happened to herself; as though *her* brother had come from Venice — a mad tyrant of a brother, who with one blow shattered every chain.

She was breathing heavily, restlessly. It was sinful for her to be envious, envious of Virginia, who need only place her fate in her brother's hands. She ought not to be envious of anybody in the world. Was not Monsignore there to look after her? Every hour of the day she would obey his orders blindly. Yes. . . . But why did he not give her orders? Why was he not a tyrant to her, as he was to Imma and to everyone else who came under his sway? Why did he consult with her, as if it really mattered what she thought?

At the bend of the way, she saw the figure of a nun approaching from the direction of Todi. If it had not been too late, Marietta would have hidden, so painful was this meeting with Sister Maddalena to her: Sister Maddalena, who answered her greeting with a vague, insincere little smile from the shadow of her coif, and did not detain her even for a moment.

Marietta hastened her footsteps, in a sudden desire to get home quickly. She regretted having left Monsignore's roof in search of rest elsewhere, rest she had not found. The world was punishing her by its cold hostility.

Later, when the city was in sight, she remembered that to-day was the first time Sister Maddalena had been to see the bishop. She must have found it very pleasant to go to him, even though she carried such grave news. Yes, Marietta was sure that Sister Maddalena had found it very pleasant. . . .

On getting back, she found Monsignore in particularly good humor, dictating a letter to Anselmi; and from Imma she heard the reason for his almost exuberant spirits. A letter from Venice, accompanied by a dozen bottles of Cyprus wine and a smoked tongue, had arrived to remind him that to-day was the twenty-ninth anniversary of his appointment as a young abbé in the diocese of His Grace the Patriarch of Venice.

"But this is not the day for the post from Venice," Marietta exclaimed in astonishment. "It must have come by a special messenger."

Imma shrugged her shoulders. "That's more than I know," she said.

"The fellow who's played this trick seems to be a scoundrel of the first water," remarked Monsignore at the midday meal, and his condemnatory tone was not without a touch of admiration. "I very much doubt if they'll catch him. The *sbirri* are hard upon his tracks — but neither he nor his friends seem to be bothering much about pursuit: they actually went out of their way to make a parcel of the nun's cowl and leave it at the prior's door. What do you say to that?"

Marietta said nothing. She could not pretend agreement with his pretended condemnation when she could hear from his every word that in his heart he was pleased with the success of the whole exploit. Why could he not lay his cards on the table? She was not Sister Maddalena.

When she remained silent, he demanded, "Or are you glad about it all?"

"Yes, *Babbo*. I *am* glad." She flushed as she made the admission vehemently.

In spite of himself, a smile curled the corners of his mouth. "I see," said he; then added mysteriously, "did Imma tell you about the wine from Venice?"

Marietta nodded, waiting to hear more.

"Did she tell you how it reached me?"

"No: how?"

"If I but knew . . ."

"But don't you know?"

"I haven't the faintest idea." Then, more excitedly, he added, "I found it lying here in my study. Here! It must have been left during the night. First thing this morning, it escaped my notice. Imma nearly fainted when she saw it. So you don't know anything about it either?"

Marietta, dumbfounded, only shook her head, and continued to look at him in the sure expectation that he would disclose something further that would explain the whole mystery. To her inquiring glance, he replied with a look just as penetrating; and then she felt that he was trying to provoke in her mind the same suspicion he himself nourished.

"Was it . . . Virginia's brother?" she stammered.

"Why not? It might have been committed to his charge," he answered drily. "He was the first person that crossed my mind, too. And if it was he, Marietta . . . Do you know whom your friend has to thank for being now on her way to Venice?"

A wave of gladness suffused her face. She flushed. "Was it you, *Babbo*? Really you?"

Alarmed at so much indiscretion, he hastily parried with, "*Sh!* In God's name, Marietta! I'm more astounded than anybody else. The world must never know. It must remain a secret between us." For a moment, he seemed vaguely troubled. "The Holy Father in Rome himself could not protect me from the avalanche that would sweep down upon me, even though I am innocent." Then, carried away by his secret delight, he lowered his voice and proceeded: "Some time ago, in writing to an old friend in Venice, I happened to ask her whether she knew a young Venetian who took shelter here in a neighboring convent a year or two ago, and had now taken the veil. That one word must have been sufficient. In Venice everybody knows everybody else, and now my old friend sends me this letter, brought here by I know not whom, and in it she asks me only whether I can still remember that nine-and-twenty years ago, on the thirteenth of May, Anno Domini 1708, I came to Venice as a young abbé; and with it was this consignment of twelve bottles of Cyprus wine, and the smoked tongue. And the rogue who happened to come here on this same thirteenth of May, to kidnap his sister from the convent, seems to have had the audacity to beard the lion in his own den by night, and leave these twelve bottles here in my study. And I? What must I do? Put the *sbirri* on his tracks — and pray God he won't be caught."

Monsignore's eyes were sparkling. His cheeks wore a deep flush. Marietta had never seen him like that before. "And then they go on asking me," he said in mock self-pity, "if I can remember the time when I came to Venice as a young abbé." Half-humorous, half-melancholy, he sighed, and passed his hand over his closed eyes.

"You must go to Venice," he said, brightening up, "you must be there while you're young to know what carefree happiness is. What can you learn of it here with me? I've had my share. In an auspicious moment, God permitted me to be in Venice when I was young; and now it is His wish that I should be a bishop in Todi, and in humility wait to see if He will let me die here . . ."

Marietta allowed him to pour out a glassful of wine for her. She hoped it would free her from the melancholy that had again descended like a mist upon her. She would have liked to join in Monsignore's gaiety, to escape the underlying melancholy that lay between them.

"Taste, taste this wine," he said pressing it upon her, looking at her face expectantly.

She raised her glass, "*Salute, Babbo!*"

"*Salute, figlia mia, salute, salute!*"

That afternoon, Marietta had to listen to Imma's indignation over the morning's happenings at the convent. Imma had known cases where God Himself had brought about the downfall of such fugitives by opening the earth at their feet so that they tumbled, living, into limbo, and became the prey of lustful devils. There were also authenticated cases of dogs that had never done anybody harm, but had suddenly attacked an escaped nun and torn her to pieces before the eyes of all. God did not hesitate, in the exercise of His Supreme Righteousness, to make use of miracles; as for instance in that case of the nun who saw the water evaporate in her hand before it reached her mouth. Imma was convinced that in this case, too, God would show His wrath. Perhaps He would change the fugitives' horses into swine . . .

But to Marietta's surprise Imma made no further reference to the mysterious consignment of wine. Could it be that Imma, too, had felt there was some vague connection between this wine and what had happened that morning in the convent? Did she realize, perhaps, that Monsignore would have been compelled to refuse this unexpected gift if there had really been a connection? And did she think that that would be a pity, for him and for herself too?

As they were washing up after the evening meal, Marietta noticed that Imma waved the plates about rather wildly, and once or twice knocked up against her. "What's the matter with you?" she asked, and Imma with a sigh collapsed on a chair, asking, "Look here, did you have some of that wine, too?"

"Yes, a little. And you?"

Imma shook her head. "I don't exactly know myself. A glass or so, perhaps."

"Go to bed, Imma, if you're so tired. I can get through this alone."

Imma was obstinately silent — she had to consider first whether Marietta had perhaps wished to affront her by saying that she could get on well enough alone.

"I'm not as tired as all that," she said. But then, while Marietta continued to work without speaking, she asked, "You won't forget to set the coffee?" — and added, "Then I think perhaps I will go to bed, soon."

And then, misinterpreting her own word "soon," she hoisted herself up from her chair and stumbled up the stairs.

A little later, as she carried the coffee upstairs, Marietta stood still half-way up and looked down at the tray in her hands. Should she too ask Monsignore's permission to go to bed? After all, she could tell him the truth, that she felt tired and rather depressed; but then he would ask her questions. No, she would not be so childish. This day was a sort of anniversary for Monsignore.

"Do you know Imma's gone to bed?" he asked her, laughing, as she came in. "I could have predicted that this morning as soon as I saw the Cyprus wine."

Now Marietta had to laugh too — she found she could do so more easily than she thought. She had a feeling that something agreeable was going to happen.

"No lessons this evening," he proclaimed. "We'll talk instead."

She nodded and went to fetch her embroidery frame. Something was going to happen this evening. . . . There was such a strange stillness within her. Although she did not look round, she felt that he was following her with his eyes.

She had hardly sat down opposite him, and was still picking over the strands of silk with her needle, not having yet decided what color she wanted, when he began to speak. It was Venice, even more than the dark fiery wine, that had gone to his head. Slumbering memories of the far past had wakened to-day. With arms crossed upon the table, or fists pressed against his temples, as he gazed at the embroidery frame, he held forth, conjuring up word pictures of the time that now seemed so wonderful, when he had lived in the city of the Doges and was young. One picture followed another — and there were many more for which he could not find words quickly enough. Besides, he could not tell everything. In that sinful, eternally merry city, the life of a priest differed little from that of an officer, a merchant, or a man of leisure. Besides successful sermons that made fair penitents faint at the thunderbolt of his words — besides passionate polemics with other ambitious young priests, which, printed and published, were the week's sensation in fashionable drawing-rooms — besides hours of bitter regret and pious contrition; other memories rose up in the bishop's brain: memories of worldly festivities in the palaces of the nobility or in their summer residences on the banks of the Brenta, where love and Bacchus tempted to pagan rites in the green shelter of arbor and grotto. And — oh, carnival time! When a mask covered everything! What cynical, what diabolic spirit first hit upon the idea of dispelling shame with a strip of black silk no larger than a hand?

There were balls in costume and mask in the public gardens. "Did I by any chance see you last Saturday in the pulpit, sweet Pierrot, preaching so movingly about the divine parables? Your voice seems very familiar!" "Certainly, loveliest of shepherdesses. You may even have seen me floating in the Grand Canal, ankles in the air, like a bottle upside down. . . . Just to make sure, look at the soles of my feet, to see if they, too, are familiar."

Expeditions in gondolas in the silver moonlight; masked rendezvous in the gaming rooms of the gayest of the gay beauties of Venice; reckless gambling in the Ridotto, where everybody with self-respect left a purse of gold behind him sometime or other. Pacts of friendship with other masks, that usually lasted for just one night, and ended at dawn in a blind scuffle during which, as a rule, some innocent passer-by was the only person to receive a serious dagger-thrust. . . .

Later, as he increased in years and rank, he had had to wear the mantle of decorum; but it had never ceased to oppress him.

He told Marietta of how the Bucentaur, the ceremonial barge that was like a water palace, put to sea every year with the Doge and all the notabilities of the Republic on board, for the symbolic marriage of Venice and the Adriatic Sea — the Doge personifying the city.

"Naturally, the sea has to be as smooth as a pond, or the beautiful mermaids on board would be sick; and besides, at the faintest ripple the barge would have capsized, and the admiral of the fleet would have lost his head if the Bucentaur did not return safe and sound."

Marietta nodded, waiting for more.

Marietta, what a city! Like a great, festive hall with artificial pools, of which the sea was one! Everybody felt himself a guest there — even the man whose forbears had for seven centuries owned a white marble palace on the Grand Canal. . . .

And then carnival time! It began in November and continued throughout the winter. In the evenings they went off gaily to the theaters — how many celebrated Pantaloons and Harlequins he had seen! Yes, and counted them among his intimate friends. Once, spurred on by a charming young Columbine who believed in his talent, he had attempted, in his youthful presumption, to write a comedy; and it would have been performed, too, if at the last moment he himself had not withdrawn it. His Grace the Patriarch of Venice had conveyed a warning to him, and his patronesses had united in conjuring him not to jeopardize his career. They had succeeded, at last, in bringing him to his senses; and then had subscribed to buy off the theater manager. He had had an even harder task to console Columbine, who wept and threatened suicide and insisted that her rôle in his comedy, "The Applecart of Thespis," was to be the success of her life. . . .

Later on, he had seen the comedies of the famous abbé Chiari; and, seeing what nonsense people were capable of applauding, he had been unable to help regretting that he had allowed himself to be persuaded. If only he had been independent, he would have let things take their course. He felt that he had been born to be a protector of the arts; but the fairy who distributes worldly goods had forgotten to leave the necessary wealth in his cradle. Poverty had forced him to burn his play, "The Applecart of Thespis," and become a bishop. . . .

He looked up expecting to see a smile on the face bent over the embroidery frame. As Marietta did not look up, his face became grave, and he asked, "Marietta . . . Tell me, you do like the idea of going to Venice?"

Her work fell from her hand. Her eyes rested uncertainly upon his. She had been unable to resist, altogether, the spell of his breathless anecdotes; perhaps that was why she had kept her face down when he had sought her eyes. The city he conjured up before her she could not possibly imagine as real. If he were summoned to Venice, thrilling with expectation she would follow him; but the thought of having to go there quite alone oppressed her indescribably. Or was it only that she would have to leave him?

"I don't know, *Babbo*. I think it fine when you tell me about it. . . . But I don't know that I want to go there myself. No, really not." And then suddenly with more conviction she continued: "Formerly, I wanted to get away from here. Formerly, yes. I sometimes wished for it day and night, — to get away from Todi, — but since I have been with you, that is over . . ."

A tender emotion passed over his face; he stretched his hand out towards her, drew her slowly to him. With a nervous laugh she gave way to his dumb entreaty. Now she was standing beside him. Monsignore leaned back in his chair, as if expecting her to sit down upon his knee. She was afraid, however, to understand his silent invitation. She merely leaned slightly against his knee, and said nervously, to say something, "With you, I am all right. With you I am happy, *Babbo*. . . . I don't want anything else."

"Yes, now. Now you feel happy here." His eyes looked up at her, and they seemed to draw her to him by a mysterious glow while his hands, feverish and warm, encircled her wrists hesitatingly. It was the fault of his eyes that Marietta seemed on the point of losing all control over herself, felt her knees grow weak. She had the sensation that his hands were drawing her down. Slowly she sank against him.

She felt herself a captive in his arms, and lifted gently but powerfully on to his knee. The dreadful consciousness of a great strange sin vanished as she buried herself in his broad chest. She could not think any more; she only felt her blood rising warm to her head, and a burning where his hands touched her. It was several moments before she heard his voice again, and knew at once that he was trying to set her and himself at rest.

"Marietta . . . why do you think I want you to go to Venice? Only because I am thinking of your future. The whole of Venice will take you for my daughter; but that is just the point. You, my daughter — my big daughter. . . . Almost a woman now, as I take you in my arms. Do you know that? I shall miss you, little one. The house will be too big when you are gone."

"*Babbo*, I'm not going away. I want to be with you, with nobody else but you, because I love only you, *Babbo*, only you, only you." She clung to him, passionate and distracted.

He waited for her voice to die away, and gazed down at her as he held her tightly enfolded in his arms. Why did she say that now, that she loved only him, only him, her *Babbo?* She should not have done that. She ought not to have awakened him from his madness. He himself had called her his child. It was a base, cowardly lie that, later on, when he had fought out this struggle with his accursed senses, would make him even more pitiable in his own eyes. What could she, in his arms, know of this deeply humiliating end? He knew, he knew; he saw it before his eyes as in a flash. He knew his guilt in its entirety — and found in that knowledge no strength.

Yet, did he desire her only as he had desired the others? Or was there something more? Something that would have made him laugh if it did not catch at his throat? Something that suddenly banished guilt and made it meaningless? Why was this moment not only infinitely sweet, but also full of a comfort such as he had never known? This was right, to remain as still as death, simply looking down at her — at her delicate white neck, the little shell of her ear under the soft, ruffled hair. He had called her his child, and while he kissed her forehead like a father, he had drunk in the perfume of her hair, drunk in the trembling virginal light in her large, bright eyes, caressed her awakening body with his glance when he thought she was not noticing. He had spun a web about her as a cunning spider does round a fly, the web of his secret and sinful desire, and . . .

His silence and immobility had disquieted her, and she half-turned her glowing eyes to his. He bent down helplessly towards her, covered her with kisses. His hands trembled as, in a mad rapture, they caressed her body that asked unconsciously for his cherishing.

But on the instant he came to his senses again. He groaned in angry self-reproach, and she looked up at him in deadly fear, not understanding. Then, vaguely sensing what was the matter, she threw her arms comfortingly round his head, wanting to press it against her. He disengaged himself forcibly. Shame and irrepressible rage overcame him. Shaking his head wildly, he said peremptorily, "Get up, Marietta."

Trembling, she obeyed.

Then slowly he himself got up, prey to a terrible disquietude. He took a step towards his writing table, stood still again, conscious perhaps of the senselessness of this movement. Marietta was so giddy that she could scarcely see the vague outline of his back that was turned towards her.

"*Babbo*," she asked, "have I done anything wrong?"

He turned round. A sudden fear possessed her that he was going to stoop to ask her forgiveness. Hastily, she began to speak again, "It was not so terrible as all that, was it, *Babbo*? It was my fault, *Babbo*, my fault. . . . Nobody shall ever know, nobody, nobody!" She sank down at his feet, seizing his hands and pressing them to her hot cheeks.

But he could not bear to see her on her knees. He raised her from the ground. "Get up, please, please," he said with an urgency that hurt, adding more softly, "Show that one of us at least can be sensible."

When he mocked at himself, what was there for her to do? His hands fell from her, and he began to pace up and down the room, making his usually heavy tread light — for fear, it seemed, of disturbing the stillness, the stillness of the old house that was like a great eavesdropping ear. He walked past Marietta, but did not look at her.

After a time, he stood still, saying, as he cast a restless glance over the papers on his writing table: "We must wait no longer. You must get away from here as soon as possible."

Marietta was afraid to reply. To her his decision seemed cruel, unnecessarily cruel. But he knew best. . . . She was too weary to think. Perhaps he had hoped she would say something — obviously, her silence distressed him. He went and stood behind his writing table, resting his hands on the high back of the chair, and asked, "Marietta — will you do something for me?"

"*Babbo!*"

He continued, deeply moved, "Listen, Marietta. Could you forget about this evening . . . if I asked you to?"

Marietta stared at him. . . . Hadn't she told him already that nobody would ever know anything about it? Was that not sufficient? No, that was not sufficient. Suddenly she knew that. He did not wish his secret to be in her keeping. Her knowledge was a stumbling block to her remaining in the house. That was why he wanted her to leave. That was why he put her this humiliating question, to which she could find no answer.

Perhaps he himself felt how unreasonable his request had been. He did not press it. Hesitating, he began to speak again . . . After a time she noticed that he had returned to the subject of Venice; but now it was no longer a fair, alluring, gay city. His words sounded unconvincing as he spoke of the new and happy world that would open out before her and eliminate Todi from her memory. Under her apparent torpor lay a strange watchfulness. She was not to be deceived: all his fine words conveyed to her only that he was trying to increase the distance between them. If intimacy was so painful to him, why had he not thought of that before? Then he need not so wound her now.

He was put out by her protracted silence. He glanced at her as she stood leaning against the table, looking down at the floor. She felt his eyes on her. . . . Was he still talking about Venice? She did not care. It was terrible that she no longer cared what he was saying; but she could not help that. Sadness over their separation had disappeared from his voice. Misery descended upon her. Now, now she began to feel the shame of what had happened this evening — the terrible shame that would never be overcome.

At last he remarked that she ought to go to bed. He asked her drily whether she would go to sleep or lie awake thinking. It was with difficulty that she brought herself to say she would sleep.

She went up to him in her normal way to wish him "good night." She bent her head, and with a strange obstinate pride waited for him to lay his hand upon it and press his lips to her forehead. He hesitated, then bent towards her. "Go, go!" he said unsteadily under her embittered look, and turned away.

Candle in hand, Marietta went up to her room. She closed the door behind her, placed the candlestick upon the table. Then, as she sank down slowly on the side of her bed, an unexpected clarity broke through the mist of her thoughts. She stared wide-eyed into the candle flame. In this still, solitary hour, it appeared to her that everything might have been simple and without pain. . . . If only he did not distrust her. There was no need for him to struggle with himself so terribly. After all, no one, no one would ever know, nobody in the whole world, not even old Imma. And he would be happy. His eyes would smile again as they did when he drew her towards him round the table. Perhaps this smile would astonish people; perhaps they would try to guess its meaning; but Marietta would allow them to read nothing on her face. . . . But he did not trust her.

He had not even trusted her when he held her in his arms — that was why he had groaned so that she had been frightened. There could be no other reason. He had not understood her when she had said that she loved him. That she loved nobody but him. . . .

The magical glamour that had enveloped her meditations vanished: the wick of her candle collapsed against the side of the candlestick. How long had she been sitting there?

She undressed and lay down, but she could not keep her promise to sleep. With short, drowsy intervals she lay awake till the new day stared her in the face. In the gray, flat light of morning, what had happened the previous evening became an oppressive, improbable, feverish dream, out of which the bishop rose immense and unassailable in full canonicals. At that dreary moment, she believed that she had at last awakened from the illusion that had held her for weeks, for months; and that her guilt was almost too great to be borne.

VII

Imma, who had slept herself sober, would have liked it to be forgotten that she had drunk too much wine at supper last night; and when Monsignore appeared half an hour later than usual, she seized the opportunity to charge him with intemperance. Tired and abstracted, he let the accusation pass.

Marietta waited with despair in her heart for the moment when she would have to enter his presence for the first time that day. When it arrived, he tried to ease the awkwardness of their greeting by chatting at length of various small matters that his morning's visitors had communicated to him. The previous evening, she would have thought such tactics humiliating. Now she was grateful to him.

At the midday meal, he could not keep it up any longer, and fell into a brooding silence. Marietta made desperate, vain efforts to eat. This eating together was a torment to both of them. She would have liked to beg him to let her go downstairs; but appearances had to be kept up.

Suddenly Monsignore surprised her by asking whether there was something that kept her in Todi.

She stared at him without grasping his meaning.

He grew embarrassed under her look, which showed him that the happenings of the previous evening lived in her mind no less than in his, and that it was senseless to go on talking round things. He told her then that he had written last night to the old lady of whom he had spoken. Tomorrow the post from Venice would come, the letter could then be sent off, and within ten days there might be an answer. Yes. . . . But he had gained an impression that she was not very keen to go. Perhaps she did not want to make use of his good offices any longer, perhaps she no longer believed he had her interests at heart.

Marietta, at the end of her tether, burst into sobs. Alarmed, he tried to soothe her. She must remember that Imma would be coming immediately with the dessert. Of course she had had a bad night, and a little later she must go out into the open air for a while, to pull herself together.

Obediently Marietta tried to control herself; but her tears would not listen to reason. She implored Monsignore not to be angry with her — she did not want to cry, she did not want to make an exhibition of herself. . . .

He said nothing, but took her hand and held it in his until he heard footsteps in the passage. Imma brought in the dessert and cast an astonished glance at Marietta, who sat biting her lip desperately. It was something new indeed, that Marietta should be sitting at table with the bishop and crying. She looked at her master questioningly, but he merely intimated coldly that she was to go.

When they were alone again, Marietta gradually recovered her self-possession. Something of warmth had returned to their relationship and she could speak again.

Monsignore could surely not believe that she would no longer be grateful for his kind offices; but she had become terribly afraid of Venice.

He looked at her in astonishment, saw the anxiety on her face. Had he made her afraid of Venice? That had not been his intention. On the contrary . . .

He forbore to inquire into the reason of her fear — even if he had, Marietta would have found it difficult to supply him with one. Last night she had grown afraid of that remote, wonderful city. Less perhaps on account of what he had told her than of what she had sensed that he had kept silence about . . .

"There'll come a time when you'll laugh about everything," was all he said, and then added, as though finding consolation in this sudden conviction, "Later on, you'll laugh about it all, my child. Even about things that now seem to you serious. You'll have a hearty laugh about life in general as mankind has organized it." For the first time, something of his old mocking smile played about his mouth again.

But when he observed how far she still was from laughing, he shrugged his shoulders uneasily and sighed.

He was extremely busy these days, or perhaps he was only pretending to be. Anselmi, who always arrived punctually to the minute, happened unluckily to be a quarter of an hour late that afternoon. He was sharply reprimanded. And pithily and loudly the bishop inveighed against the rebellious prior who, in spite of a reprimand from Rome, still persisted in writing him long documents proving his perfect right to owe obedience, not to the head of the diocese, but direct to the Pope himself. "If he is so keen upon obeying the Pope, let him hold his tongue when the Pope tells him to. Add that, Anselmi, add that! Just write, 'Most venerable father, In answer to yours of the so and so . . .'" And Monsignore went on with his dictation, freely interspersing it with general comments on the present universal lack of ecclesiastical discipline, and on the decline of the Church as a result of such slackness, ending with, "If I should ever become Pope, Anselmi . . ."

Downstairs in the kitchen, Imma nodded in silent rapture. That's how she liked to hear him, and, mind, eighteen years ago he had already been saying, "If I should ever become Pope, Imma." Lord, Lord!

Marietta did not see him again until the evening meal. The dictating of letters seemed to have brought him complete relief. Later, his exaggerated good humor made her suspicious. He inquired in light, ironical vein whether she had been very hard-pressed by the inquisitive questions Imma had doubtless showered upon her about her tears at midday. Then, suddenly and without transition, he began to speak about Antonio.

"I should like that boy to come round here sometime or other — it's really his father I want to speak to, but I'm told he's ill, and with sick people one can't discuss the cemetery. And it's about that I want to speak. What do you think — is his son enough of a man to be able to measure up for me very precisely what room is still available? I want to find out whether the report is true, that there'll soon be none left."

He looked at Marietta, waiting for her opinion. She replied that Antonio was certainly already a man. He could get Monsignore the information he required quite as well as his father, who could not leave his bed.

"If I am to believe Anselmi, the boy is very well thought of," said Monsignore; "but you don't seem to be much taken with him."

Oh, why not? He was terribly shy and modest. Apart from that, she knew little about him.

"But you two have sometimes been out together."

"Been out together?"

"That morning, when you went to the convent, and you let him carry your basket of peaches."

"Oh, then he was waiting for me. Yes."

"Did you find that boring? Shall I tell him next time he ought . . ."

She was startled by his hastiness. "But, *Babbo*, he's done nothing to me. He's a very good boy, and . . ." She got involved in her explanation, because Monsignore listened to it with such unwonted attention and looked at her so inquisitorially. Why did he suddenly take such an interest in Antonio?

He was only half-satisfied by the replies he received from her — but he did not wish that to be obvious. "All right, then," he said when she was silent. "Tell Sebastiano to go and say I want to see him."

Sebastiano had already gone home; but she suggested she herself should run along to Antonio's workshop.

"Won't you find that boring?"

Why should she find that boring? Monsignore need only tell her at what time he wanted to see Antonio.

"Oh, this evening sometime," he decided, gazing moodily before him.

Half an hour later Marietta was on her way to the home of Buongiorno the coffinmaker. She passed through the dark entrance and reached the courtyard — where children still played, and gossiping women nodded to her with some surprise. The open door of the lighted workshop was immediately opposite the entrance. Antonio was sitting painting, and looked round abstractedly when he heard one of the women call his name. Paintbrush in hand, he ran forward.

"Marietta!" He opened his eyes wide as if he could not believe them.

"Are you still at work?" she asked — and informed him that he must come to see the bishop, who wanted him to do something.

"My good suit . . ." stammered Antonio, casting a worried glance at his paint-smeared hands. Then, in the excitement of the moment, he boldly asked her, "Come upstairs with me, will you? . . . My mother would like to see you so much."

Hesitating, she nodded. While he was washing his brush, she peered past him into the workshop. Turning round, he caught her glance, smiled bashfully, and stood aside so that she could see clearly the few pieces of furniture and a row of children's coffins, made more or less for show, and covered with red velvet adorned, on the lid, with a cross of silver ribbon.

When he stood back like that, Marietta realized that he was still an innocent child: he loved his work and it did not cross his mind that it might repel her. These little waiting coffins, carefully carpentered and covered, had no sinister meaning for him. Here death had lost its sting. Even the children who played in the courtyard thought no evil of their big friend Antonio. They were accustomed to seeing him at work, and ran up to hear what "the bishop's Marietta" had come to speak to him about. Antonio stood up on end the half-painted coffin at which he had been busy, and Marietta found herself asking, without understanding why, "Who is dead?"

"Nobody," answered Antonio, anxious to correct her mistake. As he took the lantern from its hook and bolted the door, he added, "Nobody is dead. We always make the usual sizes for stock. Sometimes two or three are needed at once, and then we'd be in a fix."

The children listened to this simple wisdom, and looked at Marietta. What would she say in reply? She said nothing. Without knowing why, she suddenly found peace in his explanation: "We always work for stock."

"We." How long had his father been in bed?

"Up this staircase?"

"Yes, I'll light the way," and very carefully he suited the action to the word, warning her against all the dangers the old steep wooden stairs offered. He took her through the corridor to the rooms occupied by his parents, in this great house where many families lived, and he introduced her to his mother Lucia with ill-concealed pride. She was a small, nimble woman who led her guest immediately from the kitchen, where Antonio remained to rub the paint off his hands, to the front room, where stood images of saints upon the mantelpiece and little paper bouquets of flowers in vases. Above the door hung a softly cooing dove. Antonio's mother began a conversation with Marietta, in stilted phrases calculated to give a good impression of her, and of the general tone of the house. She told her that Antonio spoke of her continually, and she sang his praises as an exemplary son — attentive and obedient.

Marietta, abashed, changed the conversation by inquiring after the invalid. To her surprise, the little woman gave the same answer that Antonio had given her once before. "He is no worse these last weeks." As she spoke, she glanced irritably towards the farther end of the room.

Puzzled, Marietta turned her head, and through half-drawn curtains saw two dark eyes in a pale, emaciated face directed towards her. She had not noticed the alcove in the half-darkness of that corner, and Antonio's mother had not thought it necessary to draw her attention to it.

Marietta had to gather all her courage to get up and go towards the bed to greet old Buongiorno. She had shunned him as a child because of the great hungry eyes that stared from his pale, drawn face; now his face had so fallen away that she scarcely recognized him. He looked at her as she reluctantly approached. It was as if he were trying to read, upon her face, her secret thoughts at this meeting. But when no word came from her lips he began to speak himself, forming his sentences with difficulty.

"Marietta, the innkeeper Vacca's Marietta. I used often to see you play, as a child." He held her hand tightly, and seemed for a moment as if he were trying to raise himself by it. Then he sank back on his pillow again.

His wife stood up and, saying she wanted to make coffee, disappeared into the kitchen. Marietta, alone with the sick man, looked helplessly towards the door behind which Antonio and his mother were talking together. Old Buongiorno still clutched at her hand, as if afraid she might run away. His eyes sought hers until he found them again, and then he said with an attempt at emphasis: "You're not taken in, Marietta? I'm a dying man — you must see that." He waited a moment, and when she seemed unable to say anything, unexpectedly he begged, "Take him!"

She stared at him nonplussed.

"Don't you understand? Take my boy."

"Antonio?" She could not hear herself speak.

"Yes . . . Antonio." In his weary voice there was a moan of disappointment.

"Think it over," he said after a few moments. "Think it over, whether you can't care for him. He has a good heart, and you're the light of his eyes. If you don't have him, he will remain alone. He's not the sort that cares for one girl one day, and another the next. And his mother won't make it easy for him to marry. You're good enough for her, because you're connected with the bishop. And according to what people say, he's like a father to you . . . We're very simple folks. Take him, Marietta."

"But how can I . . . ?" she stammered. "I've never thought about it . . . I . . ."

"Do! Yes, do. Think it over. I can ask it of you, Marietta, because I'm a dying man. Perhaps I may live another month or two. I don't myself know why God tortures me so long. It's here, here . . ." He pointed to the region of the liver, and for a moment looked like a frightened child. "It's slow murder, this gradual dying, and no doctor can do anything. And they won't believe it, because I've been ill so often in my life and have always looked so bad . . ." He brought his lamentations to an end as his wife came into the room again. He let go of Marietta's hand at last; and she returned, slowly, to the table, where she sank down upon her chair again.

Lucia looked from the one to the other as she put the coffee tray upon the table. "Ah, well, now you've heard the worst," she said to Marietta, as if she had been present. "He's been singing that little song now for six months. He knows better than Maestro Barberini, who's already pulled him through twice."

"But he won't this time," was the helpless protest that rose from the bed. Impatiently, Lucia shrugged her shoulders, and then apologized to her guest by casting her eyes despairingly towards heaven. To change the subject, she asked Marietta how she liked living in the bishop's house, and without waiting for a reply, went on to say that everybody in the city knew how kind the bishop was to her . . .

Antonio appeared from the kitchen wearing his father's Sunday clothes. The mother was all proud attention to her son. She got up to adjust the coat, which sat rather tightly on his broad shoulders. "I sent it to the tailor to have it let out to fit him," she said, "but it's too skimpily cut." Smiling good-naturedly, Antonio looked at Marietta while his mother pulled at his clothes. He seemed to feel nothing terrible in the peaceful assumption that old Buongiorno would never need his best suit again. Marietta perceived in that moment how completely he was dominated by this small, strong-minded woman.

She felt infinite relief when she was able to leave the stifling atmosphere of that front parlor. Rapidly crossing the courtyard, where the women still huddled together and looked at them both curiously, she reached the street a step ahead of Antonio.

Proud to walk through the city at her side, excited by the unusual happenings of the evening, Antonio talked a great deal, for him. He asked her first covertly, and then openly, whether she had noticed what an exceptional mother he had. For fear that she might not immediately pour out the highest praises of her he hurriedly went on to say that one had to get to know her to appraise her at her real value.

Marietta's answers were brief. She had never given a thought to it before; but old Buongiorno's entreaty and his wife's hints had aroused her distrust and led her to a strange conjecture: she now believed that Monsignore's desire to speak to Antonio had a subsidiary motive. She recalled the way he had looked at her when he spoke of the matter, and his forced lightheartedness during their evening meal . . .

A little smile of contempt appeared round her small, pure mouth. Suddenly she had seen through Monsignore's intentions as with the ripened glance of maturity. He was playing a little game of which she was the stake, and at once she knew that she would not spoil his little game. Perhaps this was the best solution, even though she felt a clammy sweat upon her cheeks at her discovery. If only she could grow accustomed to the idea . . . Perhaps she ought to be grateful to Monsignore for his wise insight; and he in his turn should be grateful to old Buongiorno who, not even guessing the hidden significance of her visit, had of his own accord spoken words that in advance broke all resistance in her. She did not know whether she considered herself quite good enough for Antonio; but if he cared for her as much as his father said, she need not give that any further thought. His mother repelled her. She had rarely felt such an immediate aversion; and she shunned the bed of sickness in that clean but airless parlor. She shrank from death, which, dethroned, roamed through the workshop downstairs, and, with the mask of an assassin, through the living rooms upstairs too. But she wished to overcome her fear. Perhaps she could wipe out her terrible guilt by offering herself up as sacrifice . . . Yes, she would do that. It was no longer seemly that she should be overfastidious about herself.

She only wanted to be sure. When she found that Antonio stayed more than an hour with Monsignore, and when she heard from Imma that he had gone away excited and in tears, she knew enough.

VIII

He had hardly gone when Imma came to say that the bishop was waiting for her. Marietta nodded and went upstairs. On the landing, she stood still for a moment, took a deep breath.

Monsignore received her with deceptive gaiety, and, deciding to plunge straight away, said, "I have just been making a discovery. There is somebody here in Todi who cares for you more than for himself, and would gladly die for you if need be . . ."

Marietta stood in front of him, and looked at him.

"Can't you guess who?" he asked, and he had some difficulty in keeping his voice cheerful. She felt that he too suffered as he played out the comedy he had staged. She would have liked to help him, but she had not the strength to answer his question. She could not get Antonio's name over her lips.

When she remained silent, struggling in vain with her distress, suddenly he dropped his assumed cheerfulness. Brusquely he drew her to him. "Marietta . . . don't you understand that I'm looking for a way out? Do you refuse to understand? You cannot remain in this house — you must believe what I say. What am I to do? I speak to you about Venice. . . . You tell me that Venice frightens you. Can I just send you away? Can I do that? Why do you make me feel like your executioner when I only wish you well? If you tell me you don't care for that boy who was here a moment ago, that you would be unhappy with him, you won't hear another word from me on the subject. But don't leave me groping in the dark. Don't distrust my good intentions. Give me some support . . ."

"*Babbo*, I want to support you. I'll do anything, anything . . ."

"What sort of answer is that?" he complained excitedly, though with a certain relief. "I don't like to hear you say you'll do anything, as though you were a thief condemned to the gallows."

"I mean — I am willing to marry him."

Surprised by something in her voice, he turned his head towards her, and asked suspiciously, "Would you really prefer that to going to Venice?"

"Yes."

"Do you know what you're turning down? No, you don't. You could make a different sort of marriage in Venice — I've told you that already."

"But, *Babbo* . . . Isn't it your own wish that Antonio should . . . ?"

"Yes, all right. I do wish it." Then he added with a sigh, "It was my wish only because I could see no other way out. I understood that the boy cared for you. I heard nothing but good of him from Anselmi. . . . I thought that perhaps you yourself might prefer a simple marriage to . . ." He broke off, irritated, and looked at her dubiously, probing her deepest thoughts.

"Marietta, tell me one thing. It is all I want to know. If you have him

. . . do you do it for his own sake or only because you think perhaps I want it?"

Marietta looked down. She did not know immediately what to answer. As in a vision, she saw Antonio before her, his robust, well-grown figure, his boy's face with the soft brown eyes; she heard again old Buongiorno's entreaty, as he asked her, though not in so many words, to save his son from the self-seeking love of his mother. On the other side she saw that Monsignore, who, flattering himself that he was thinking only of her, in reality thought only of himself, was fighting for the peace of his soul. Slowly Marietta turned her eyes towards his again, and to his very significant question she gave the reply, "If I marry Antonio — it will be for himself."

Although this was as satisfactory an answer as he could have expected, there was something about it that shattered him. He tried to talk away his curious disappointment. Very well. He was reassured on that point. Why hadn't she said so immediately? Everything would have been so much easier. There were still one or two other things that had to be talked about, but they could wait now that he knew she thought she could be happy by this boy's side.

Yes . . . Antonio had just confessed the whole truth to him, that he had always been in love with her, ever since he had first seen her in the convent garden. It was really impossible not to feel friendly towards him, though he expressed himself clumsily. The workshop was doing quite well, though it would not bring in too much as long as two families had to live from it; but the boy deserved to be helped, and he should be.

Monsignore could find little more to say about it for that evening. He was happy that something had been provisionally arranged. He was tired and wanted to go to bed early. Marietta ought to do the same. In the morning, they could consider the matter afresh.

Then there came another moment of uncertainty and silence. Marietta was staring in front of her. Monsignore inquired if everything was all right, and whether he could go to sleep leaving her alone with the decision just reached. Hesitating for the right words, looking into the impenetrable future, she broke the silence, saying gently, tentatively, "I believe . . . I shall find it wonderful . . . to be able to make someone completely happy." She turned her head towards Monsignore questioningly. Involuntarily he raised his eyebrows. Then, feeling the need to conceal his uncertainty behind a gesture, he went to his writing table, took up the letter he had written to his old friend in Venice, and tore it in four. Marietta was hurt by his tearing of the letter before her eyes:

she felt it as an unexpressed reproach against her. But she could find no words to say, and bit her lip in silence.

IX

Once having her consent, Monsignore took the matter in hand with his usual energy. He felt that he was recovering his ascendancy and the sure touch through loss of which he had momentarily broken down. He was a born negotiator.

Next day, already possessed by a feverish need for haste, he summoned Antonio and his mother to the palace, had a long talk with them, and then called Marietta, who came into the room very pale, but quite composed. In her presence, the bishop repeated that Antonio had told him of his great inclination for her, and had come to-day, with his mother, to ask her hand. Monsignore felt that he had reason to believe that Marietta, who had also spoken to him about her feelings for Antonio, would entirely agree to his accepting this proposal as her guardian. He felt further called upon to say that he had the very best expectations that this union would mean a happy future. During the two years Marietta had been with him, he had discovered her to be a young girl anybody could only be congratulated upon possessing; and with a very little knowledge of human nature it was possible to see that Antonio was a good young man more than fit to provide for a wife and family of his own.

At this point Lucia gave her son a gentle push. Hesitatingly and with flushed face, he approached Marietta, who, with an impressive virginal gravity, laid her hand in his.

Monsignore got up, and gave them his blessing as they sank down on their knees before him.

Lucia began to cry. Immediately Antonio looked with concern in her direction and great tears gathered in his own brown eyes. "Kiss her, kiss your betrothed," said his mother, turning away.

Monsignore summoned Imma. She came dashing upstairs immediately, and, before she had been apprised of the facts, fell sobbing on Marietta's neck. "So suddenly too!" cried Imma, "and this summer only just seventeen." Antonio, too, she embraced greedily. What a bride God had given him! A real young lady, with a heart of gold. He ought to hold her in high honor! Did he know all the things she had learnt from Monsignore — French and . . . ?

The bishop, embarrassed, asked her to go and fetch wine, and while she hobbled downstairs in agitation, he told Marietta of the practical measures he had agreed upon with Antonio and his mother. They had

provisionally fixed the Feast of the Assumption for the wedding. Marietta
would be seventeen; and the city would be in festive humor. Sixteen
years ago the municipality had set aside a modest sum for her trousseau;
but he would like to provide the actual wedding outfit himself. It was a
privilege for a priest to be able to give himself for once such a fatherly
pleasure. He told the momentarily startled Marietta, too, that Antonio's
mother was entirely in agreement with him as to the advisability of leaving newly married couples to themselves. They would try to rent for them
a few rooms that happened to be standing empty in the same house, just
over the workshop.

Antonio testified by an uncontrollable outburst of grief that this separation from his parents had not been his desire or wish. His mother tried
to calm him by declaring, in a tone lacking in sincerity, that she herself
had pressed the point with Monsignore.

Imma brought salvation by appearing with the wine. They touched
glasses, and a general embracing followed — at which, however, Monsignore remained a spectator. Marietta did everything she ought to do.
With something of the stern devotion of a nun, she kissed her future
mother-in-law. Antonio looked on, deeply affected. Imma laughed and
cried at the same time, as she declared that she had foreseen it months
ago. Marietta could testify that Imma had spied upon her to get at the
whole truth, and now it had come out. What a day! She would never
have imagined it when she saw Marietta step into the house, a child, but
two years ago. Lord, Lord! She herself had come into the world an orphan,
an orphan, an orphan. . . .

Subsequently, however, it turned out that Imma, despite her statements
that she had been spying upon Marietta for months and had known everything in advance, was nevertheless very surprised at the betrothal. An
hour after Antonio and his mother had gone (Marietta went with them
to visit the sick father) Imma was still sitting on a chair in the kitchen
staring before her. What had really happened? How in God's name had
this been possible? If something had been brewing between Marietta and
this boy, she, Imma, could not have failed to notice it. Did she keep her
eyes in her pocket? Not so far as she knew! She had allowed herself
to be carried away by the unexpected solemnity of this visit, by the fact
that she had had to take wine upstairs . . . But was *this* the marriage
for which Marietta had had to be educated into young ladyhood? Was it
for this that she had learned French and eaten with the bishop at table?
All the humiliations Imma had had to endure over the education of this
child came into her mind and roused feelings of bitterness within her.

She was convinced that this betrothal was against the wishes of Monsignore. She understood now why the child had been crying at table yesterday. He had allowed himself to be moved by these tears, and she had got her own way. Imma condemned him for such weakness. If you gave way to young girls' fancies, what sort of marriages would come of it? Madonna! What could be behind all this? She must get to know more. She got up from her chair and looked round, wondering what she could find to do upstairs.

Wait: the wine glasses must be put back in the sideboard.

With half a glance she could see that the bishop was as out of humor and uneasy as herself over what had happened. He was very offhand, asked her what she was hanging about upstairs for, when she knew he was working, and with an ungracious word sent her back to the kitchen. In any other circumstances, Imma would have given him notice; but she spared him because she was really concerned for him, because she understood how bitterly disappointed he must be with Marietta's choice. A short while ago he had felt like a bride's father, was able to make amusing, friendly remarks; but now, like Imma herself, he was realizing things. No, she would not give him notice: it would soon be quiet enough in the house . . .

Lord, why had Marietta done this to him?

X

Was Marietta aware of what she had done? Did she live in a dream during the days and weeks that followed? Or was she the only one of the three who was fully conscious of what had happened?

On the first Sunday after the betrothal she shared the family meal at Antonio's house. Old Buongiorno wanted to sit at table too, even though he could not eat with the others. He was placed in an armchair, propped with cushions. Several uncles and aunts, whom she knew by name and by sight but had hardly seen for years, were there too. Everybody was friendly to her and complimented her upon her appearance and upon the fact that the bishop thought so much of her and wanted to conduct the wedding ceremony himself; and old Buongiorno tried to tell her with his eyes of his thankfulness and joy: he had an air of mysterious triumph that made the others look at him in wonder.

Antonio himself was full of attentiveness. His gentle humility moved her — he was never tempestuous or importunate in his love. Intuitively he was wise enough to wait patiently until her feelings for him had ripened. His kiss when they met and parted was tender and full of respect.

From time to time, he confessed that he could not himself understand how he had her as his promised wife — a confession that moved Marietta to great joy, for she felt that she could give him happiness, and give it safely without any danger of his becoming exacting and so depriving her of her pleasure in giving.

Her happiness increased from day to day. In the evenings he came round to fetch her, and they wandered about the streets or sat on the stone bench that surrounded three sides of the piazzetta behind the cathedral. They did not say much to each other. They sat quietly in the mellow spring evenings, listening to the fountain in the middle of the piazzetta, sometimes looking up at the soft blue sky with its bright golden stars. Children still played round the fountain, sailing their little ships in the basin, while their mothers, tired and melancholy, conversed among themselves about their household worries.

Antonio said occasionally, "How wonderful it will be later on, Marietta!" and ventured to lay his hand upon hers.

Marietta listened to the longing in his voice. It filled her with a vague fear. She nodded, so as not to disappoint him, but at the same time counted anxiously the few months that separated her from her wedding day. Everything was right as it was — could not things remain so? She was afraid of every change in the timeless present in which she had lost herself — but had she the right to be afraid?

She had feared people once, and had fled from them to the convent, and now she saw how mistaken she had been. At last she had broken down the wall that, invisible, had surrounded her even after she came to live at Monsignore's. She had descended from her solitary pedestal, and, instead of their turning their backs upon her as she deserved, those she had feared received her with open arms. Was it perhaps only for Antonio's sake that they were so friendly to her? That must be the reason. His goodness moved them, just as it moved her . . . She had still to deserve affection. The way to do so was by making Antonio happy. This she intended to do, with all her strength.

Both Imma and Monsignore observed her with increasing astonishment. She seemed to live in a world of her own, a quiet, peaceful world, the happiness of which was reflected in her eyes, in her whole being. Monsignore, trying to convince himself that under the given circumstances he could not have acted otherwise than he had done, was sometimes saddened by her apparently unintentional reserve, and was beginning to feel lonely before she had left his house. As she sat next to him at table with the same friendly, respectful attention as of old, he had the feeling that all her thoughts were already set upon the moment when that boy would take her away. It seemed easy for her to forget what had happened that one evening. Well . . . surely that was what he wanted. Hadn't he himself asked her to forget? What more did he want? He had asked something impossible of her, and she had agreed; more than that, she had almost succeeded in making him wonder, himself, whether anything had happened between them.

The only thing that still pointed to it was this betrothal, this insane betrothal that was his doing. Looking back, he made the painful discovery that he must have acted in complete confusion instead of in cold blood, as he had imagined. He must have taken leave of his senses, whereas she had kept her head. That was the humiliating distinction between them. She had accepted the rôle he had hastily allotted to her and with the histrionic talent that had often surprised him in women had so completely immersed herself in it that within a few days the lie had become the truth for her. But when she awakened — what would she think of him then? Of him who had first held out to her the prospect of a golden future, only to deprive her of it in a moment of cowardly perplexity? What had been the matter with him? Against a disinclination a thousand times as strong he should have persevered with his intention of sending her to Venice. One day's traveling through unknown villages and cities would have restored her to happiness, would have made her realize his wisdom, and would have awakened that gratitude in her without which he could not live, vain weakling that he was.

He had indeed brought things to a pretty pass. She herself did not know what awaited her, and it would not help her if he told her. He ought to have considered, sooner, that she was no longer suited to be the wife of a coffinmaker here in Todi. Naturally, he would give the boy money. That had been his intention all along. He would give him as much as he decently could — and perhaps that would do more harm than good. Would the women with whom she would now be compelled to mix ever be able to forgive her for having been the spoiled child of a bishop, and for having been brought up by him as a young lady? No, they would not — that they would not, those jackals in skirts!

In torment, he paced up and down his study, confounded by the enormity of his error. Was there nothing he could do? Should he speak to her again? Should he? He went and sat down, trying with all his willpower to compel himself to calmness.

Then he rang for Marietta.

When she entered, serene and expectant, his tongue grew paralyzed. What was it he had wanted to say to her? After his pitiable blunder, he could not find courage to interfere afresh with her life. He dared not disturb that magnificent quietude within her. Besides, how much power had he over her now? If he were to tell her to pack up her clothes and prepare to leave immediately for Venice, she would fly from his house to her Antonio, whom she had come to care for at his behest.

Oh, yes, she was waiting to know why he had called her upstairs. Well, something had just crossed his mind . . . Yes, it had been in his thoughts for days. He wanted to advise her from the beginning to be friendly but distant towards her mother-in-law. At first, Antonio's mother would no doubt be discreet, and Marietta should seize the chance to draw fences round her married life. Births and sickness brought the mother-in-law into the house, and once she was there, a sea of tears would not wash her away again. Although he himself had never had anything to do with mothers-in-law, life had taught him how dangerous they could be; and the one in question seemed to him to be anything but an exception to the rule. Old Buongiorno was a dying man. His death would bring a critical period into their young married life. "Antonio must never allow her to come and live with you, Marietta. His almost exaggerated love for her may make him weak on that point. She would destroy your marriage. She would rule you within your own walls. In the end you would seek desperately for some support . . . I hope you will come to me if you can no longer find it with your husband."

After this proffer of help he was silent, pale with emotion. Marietta smiled at him, innocent and unafraid. "Don't be afraid, *Babbo*. I intend to be happy with Antonio. I will it, *Babbo*."

To that there was nothing more to be said. He signified with his hand that it was all right, and that she could go. As she left the room he gazed at her from under half-closed eyelids, gazed at her young womanly form that had suddenly become strange to him and unattainable . . . Only when she was gone and he heard her step on the stairs did he move his gaze away from the door.

He was beaten, beaten, and he could not understand how. In his sudden deep depression, he fled with his thoughts towards the past, looking for something to fasten on. He thought of his days of triumph: distressingly colorless they rose now before his mind. Was everything vanity, then? He sat and sat and stared before him. He reviewed his existence. . . . He summed it up in a few bald sentences bereft of all self-illusion, as a chronicler might have done — impartial, mindful only of the chronological sequence of events. Strung up thus, they became pitilessly symbolical.

Since when had he become interested in the symbolical aspect of his life? He asked himself the question with a vague, bitter self-mockery.

With all the opportunities for meditation his priesthood had offered him, he himself had never seriously thought about the matter. Instead of looking back into the all too significant past, he had preferred to look forward into the future that had always seemed to him full of promise. Had something suddenly changed now? When he left Rome, the Pope had, unprompted, represented his somewhat discouraging exile to him as the hard row he must hoe before he could reap his harvest, in which would undoubtedly figure a cardinal's hat; since, he had corresponded regularly and amicably with the Pontiff, and he ought therefore to be full of courage. . . . Why did all this now seem to him hardly important?

From early youth he had always striven after the highest. His temperament had driven him on blindly, confidently. His best moments had been when his progress in life had assumed visible shape. And now suddenly he had the uneasy feeling that he had been tripped up. . . .

Was it because of his enforced seclusion in this little provincial hole that he found himself drawn into this dangerous brooding? Would it save him if he returned to Rome? Or was it his five-and-forty years that had brought him to this fateful crossroads? That surely was impossible; but he refused to believe, either, that this child had caused him to lose his bearings. He ran his hand over his forehead, and found that his skin was covered with beads of perspiration. He got up and went towards the open window. With his hands resting on the window sill, he breathed in the fresh air as, struggling to recover his normal calm, he gazed over the blocks of houses on the other side of the piazza toward the pastel red evening sky.

Gradually he had forgotten, here in this little city, who and what he was. He was leading the life of any parochial chaplain. He was growing countrified — country life was in his blood. He was bishop here, as his father had been master in the castle-farmstead in Friuli; but he needed the life of great cities. He needed to mix with other high ecclesiastics, men of ambition like himself, among whom he had to use his elbows, his sturdy peasant elbows. In such an atmosphere, an idyll might bloom unseen, but would never smother him in its multitudinous shoots. Standing still was dangerous to him. The provinces were dangerous to him. They turned him into a human being. He was not a human being, he must not be a human being. He was a priest.

He smiled to himself.

What would his life have been if he had not become a priest? As he walked up and down in the room that was growing dim, he felt an urge to ponder this question.

His mind went back to his childhood. It pleased him this evening to investigate how early his fate had found him. It had happened even before he was born. His mother, a pious provincial woman, dedicated her unborn child to God if, in His mercy, He would answer her nightly prayer: that after bearing five daughters she might be vouchsafed a son. His father, a nobleman turned peasant, more at home with the vine than with the dagger, and through his plebeian marriage erased from the golden book of the nobility, would not hear of his only son assuming the black coat. He saw him already as his successor, living proudly in the rustic castle-farmstead, or riding on a heavy stallion over the property. His fatherly eye rested with pleasure on the little Giambattista, who crept among the horses in the stable unafraid, clambered on their backs, and moved masterfully among the grooms, issuing his first orders that, after a moment's hesitation, were obeyed.

Then the day came when it was time for him to go to the seminary. His mother, growing gradually more bigoted, regaled him with holy legends full of heavenly consolation. She ran daily to her father confessor, and brought a Jesuit into the house, to remind his father of his duty; but before the preacher of hell-fire could say a word, he found himself put outside the gate followed by the threat that next time the dogs would tear his cowl from his body. Giambattista stood straddle-legged near his father. Later on, he shouted, stamped, and hammered, with his fists, Gemma the servant, because she said that he too would be a "paternoster mumbler." His mother cried the whole week until she had no tears left, and prayed day and night; and his father threatened that henceforth he would utter nothing but curses.

Then the warning finger of God manifested itself for the first time. Death came knocking at the house. First Teresa, his eighteen-year-old sister died; then next day Margherita and Lucrezia, the older two, followed. Two days later, his father was attacked. The Jesuit was recalled, and nobody set the dogs upon him—in any case, half of them had died. Head erect, the servant of the Lord came in and found the dying man cured of the sin of mockery. He wailed and bellowed his repentance; it reverberated through the hollow building, so that the menservants trembled and the maids crossed themselves; and later they learned that he had sanctioned his wife's vow to dedicate his only son to God.

Hardly had the plague departed, when the castle-farmstead burst into flames. The children were awakened in the dead of night by the red glow of the fire. The servants rushed about in confusion, shrieking aloud. Only his mother remained calm, and spoke of the trials of God. The cattle were lowing in their stalls; but when the twelve-year-old Giambattista and some of the agitated menservants tried to open the doors they found the crossbars were up. A hatchet that always stood behind the barn was nowhere to be found. . . .

Nothing was saved, nothing. This second warning was as clear as the first. . . . God wanted to spare the widow, faced with the cares of the farmstead, from the terrible temptation of calling in her only son's aid. Perhaps, too, He wanted to make his entry into the seminary less of a torment to the son, whose heart had been attached to the farmstead. However that might be, Giambattista learned at an early age that God's warnings were hard, and that it was as well to comply without delay.

Meanwhile, rumor of all these happenings had reached Venice, and several pious and noble ladies gathered together a sum of money to support the portionless widow and make it possible for her to pay her son's college fees.

At home, the little boy dedicated to God was spoiled by his sisters. They were eight and twelve years older than he, and had never married owing to their secluded life, their father's tyranny, and their own pride, which made them despise their mother's equals, though they, in fact, no longer belonged to the nobility. All their unclaimed love they lavished on the little brother, the son and heir — and consequently in later life he always accepted women's favors as a matter of course. All the time he was in the seminary, devout matrons sent him parcels of food, clothing, and sweets. Young married women caressed his curly head and wiped the oppressive sweat from his face with heavily perfumed lace handkerchiefs that they pulled from their corselets and afterwards slipped into his coat pocket, saying that he might keep them. In his sixteenth year he made his glorious entry as a young abbé into Venice, and within a week he had his first secret love affair with the plump little wife of a rich old shipowner who, spurred on by her, put in a good word for him with the mighty Patriarch of Venice. Finding that things did not move quickly enough, she went in person to His Grace and arranged with him for the young abbé to preach his first sermon. When, however, through an overconfident remark that escaped her, the young abbé realized the price she had paid for this favor, and how cheaply she esteemed it, in abhorrence he flung his contempt in her face, abandoned her, and, as the text for that first sermon, chose "The Adulterous Woman as the Downfall of the Younger Clergy." By its fierce passion and obvious appropriateness, the sermon made his name. His Grace the Patriarch himself complimented him in a fatherly letter that he had always kept as an example of exquisite hypocrisy. Recognition came from other quarters. A number of young married women felt the need to express their approval of this young apostle of morality: they gave him neckbands and gloves . . . Oh, what did they not give him! He had only to stretch out his hand. His manly figure was seen in their drawing-rooms, they filled the church where he preached, they spread abroad his marvelous story, the story of the mother's vow and of God's warning finger. They contributed to his advancement; and their reward was that he despised women from the bottom of his heart.

Women! He had never been able to get away from them. In moments of repentance, which somehow always seemed to synchronize with bodily exhaustion, he had forsworn them; but always he rediscovered that his vows were perjuries, and in the end he ceased to make them. As he rose in dignity, he had to be more careful of appearances, — an abbé is forgiven more than a prelate, — with the result that he had desecrated the confessional in the service of the goddess Venus. Fair sinners left him, consoled, forgetting that they had not received absolution. . . .

The higher he rose, the more dangerous his game became, and his contempt for women grew more bitter as he had more to fear from their betrayal. Knowing full well that he was in their power, he asserted the opposite, dangled before them the cool independence of his blood, so that, in their common fall, the woman felt herself to be alone guilty. Against his nature, he made them tremble with threats of his vengeance should the desire to speak ever steal upon them; and still he was not reassured; he knew them too well: Fear and consciousness of guilt made them silent to their husbands and to all the world — except their best woman friend. Her they must tell, were it only to put her nose out of joint by their revelations.

During recent years, there had been times when his contempt for women had developed into hatred. Women-haters he had always looked upon as contemptible fools, worthy of pity — and was he now one himself? Why did he hate women? Not because they exposed him to danger, and would one day put the halter round his neck, on the principle that the pitcher goes to the well once too often and comes home broken at last. No: if they had been worth going under for, he would have played the game with spirited passion and a light heart; but they themselves had destroyed the idol he had set up in his soul. How long ago was it since he had abandoned himself to dreams? The first woman he had met had begun to cure him of all dreams. She had convinced him that women were kneaded of earthly clay, and that God himself had forgotten to bestow on them the faintest recognition of higher things. She had inspired him to preach his first successful sermon; but a splinter had been left embedded in his heart, a splinter that had wounded him all his life. He had remained unsatisfied. They had satisfied his senses, these women, sometimes too little and sometimes too much; but his soul had remained hungry. His soul was hungrier than his senses had ever been.

Marietta took her place in this review of his life. Who had sent her to him? By some mysterious compulsion, he had freed her from the convent, and taken her to himself — a child. But when she had sunk down beside him, when she had said that she loved him, only him . . . was she still a child? She had come to save his soul. And what had compelled him to reject salvation at her hands? Was it the cloth? Was it the cloth that forced him to destroy her dream with his own? Then accursed be the cloth! A curse be upon the third and most terrible warning in his life!

He had flattered himself that he had wished to spare her anguish. Had she been grateful to him for that? Since she loved, perhaps she knew by intuition that Love and Sorrow are two sisters. He could no longer doubt it: she was prepared to sacrifice herself. She did not ask him for solicitude; in return for her sacrifice, she wanted only his counter-sacrifice, and he had not dared give it. Had he not been a little concerned for himself? That morality approved his action was cold comfort. Morality was always on the side of the faint-hearted. Faint-hearted he had been; and disappointed, proud in her lowliness, she had turned aside from him.

But still, it was impossible! It was impossible that she should suddenly love that boy, who had meant nothing to her before. She still loved him, but would not admit it to herself. Yes, and he would tell her so, now — when she brought in the candles. He would point out to her first the sort of life that awaited her here in Todi by the side of . . . No, that would be a further insincerity. He would tell her that he could not go out of her life, that she must save him by offering herself up to him. . . . He would tell her — that he loved her. Was that so mad? Would it sound like madness if he said that to her?

He shivered, and looked round the room. The furniture, in dim contour, took on strange shapes. Of course this was idle dreaming. His black satin robe was not suitable garb for a lover. He had to smile at himself. He dared not declare himself — if only through shame over his faint-heartedness.

He had played, and lost. A bitter jealousy cut through him: was it jealousy of the boy who would have her to wife, or was it jealousy of his other self to whom she had wished to give her love?

What was he to do now? Resume his old game? Retain the memory of his lost happiness pressed against his heart and brood over it like a religious over a relic? Or should he try abstinence at last? He had reached a suitable time in life to repent of his sins, after the pattern of Augustine, the only saint whom he read for pleasure. Should he play that trick upon the world, to cheat it as it had cheated him?

He might make a beginning by receiving no more ladies to confession for the time being. He might allege pressure of work; and should Satan again obtrude his cloven hoof, there was always little Signora Perosio, who really sighed too charmingly under her weekly sin, and told him how she always felt remorse afterwards when she thought of his priest's robe, and of the honor she owed her husband, — the tax-collector of His Holiness Clement the Twelfth, — who was alas no longer filled with youthful fire. . . .

Naturally, it was Imma who brought the candles upstairs, and not Marietta. He had not thought of that, that her Antonio might have come to fetch her by now. In the golden candlelight, Imma's face expressed the greatest surprise as she received her master's order to refuse admittance for the time being to the ladies who came to confession. After nineteen years' faithful service, she looked upon this as a miracle that needed only an order to remove the couch from the confession room to be complete. Unable to utter a word, she departed.

He bent automatically in the candlelight over his writing-table, and dipped his quill in the ink to initial a letter that Anselmi had laid there for him; but in the act he raised his head again. Why had old Imma looked at him in that queer way? Did she see through him? Was she secretly laughing at him? He could not prevent her from laughing over a . . . Harlequin.

XI

During the following weeks, realities slowly but surely pressed upon Marietta. There was the furnishing of their little home. They got rooms just above the workshop. Antonio himself made some chairs and a table. Monsignore summoned Antonio to him and pressed into his hands sufficient money to buy everything else they needed. But Antonio was not to mention this to Marietta. . . .

Imma helped with the sewing of the trousseau. She worked her fingers to the bone, and felt that she could now mother Marietta again as she had done in their early days together. From time to time she lamented not only that was she an orphan but that she had never had a dowry or a lover.

One evening, Marietta said unexpectedly to Antonio, "I love you." He was completely taken aback by the suddenness of this declaration, and began hastily to talk of other things. He remarked that she was well educated, that she was really a lady. "What's all that worth, Antonio?"

she asked, staring before her, and with something of contempt in her voice that disconcerted him more than ever.

Later, when she was alone, she gazed at the little ring on her hand that he had given her.

The nights were warmer. In the trees round the convent the nightingales sang.

And then came the day itself, on which the bells pealed in honor of Mary's ascension, and in honor of Marietta and Antonio, who, in the house chapel decorated by Imma, were joined in wedlock by Monsignore.

EVENING
MELODY

I

EVERY MORNING THE WOMEN BROUGHT THEIR
pitchers to the city well on the piazzetta behind the cathedral.
Patiently they waited their turn and patiently they returned to
the piazzetta again and again with empty pitchers. Only a few saved time
by bringing all their pails and pitchers at once, and these few were regarded by the others with something near to mockery: why be in such
desperate haste when there was always so much news to be gathered at
the well — enough food for thought for the remainder of the day?

There was no subject that was not discussed by the well. Three voices
always predominated, and they took the whole morning over these discussions. There was old Barberina, a blowsy vixen: her ugly mouth was
full of black teeth, her eyes glittered with insolence and cunning. Silvery
hair fell like cobwebs about her brown face, the skin of which was tanned
like wrinkled leather. On her forehead was a wart as large as a swallow's
egg. A monster she was, in frayed rags — a real Sybil, liberal and violent
in her taunts. Then there was Xenia, the barren, discontented wife of
Buonvino the undertaker's man, who was always drunk. Her husband
averred that she kept a stick ready for him behind the door, and implored
his friends to take him home and protect him. Xenia, however, did not
look as though she needed a stick to make life hard for her husband. And
then there was the third, Maria Testagrossa, still young and a widow, pale,
flabby, and slatternly in her clothes that hung upon her in such a way
as to attract the attention of the men. Perhaps she had the most viperish

tongue of the three; but that was not immediately noticeable, because she always spoke protectingly of her victims in a dull, impassive tone, and her biting cynicisms were accompanied by a melancholy laugh that seemed to say she was the first to grieve over the world's wickedness.

Every morning these three heard one another's reports and made their comments on current events. With open ears the rest of the women listened, putting shy naïve questions when they had missed the full meaning of something. Suppressed guffaws rose from the women by the well at every timely jest, and above the noise the shrill voice of old Barberina crowned the fun with an obscene word that pleasantly titivated the others.

The city well was their one daily diversion. These women, who drudged from early morning in homes full of children and could never find time to sit quietly for a moment, made of these necessary expeditions to the well a change and a rest. The sun felt good on their backs, already tired by many tasks. The water spouted with a refreshing gurgle from the dolphin mouth into earthen pitchers or metal pails. The women, enjoying the respite, were in no hurry to reach their turn — the free entertainment provided by the mischievous trio, Barberina, Xenia, and Maria, made them lose all count of time. For half an hour they were able to forget the lives of toil they lived in the dark buildings with sordid courtyards where flies swarmed. They listened shyly, respectfully, to the three loquacious sluts, who never stopped except for a moment when old Signora Galli passed in her caroche — or Signora Spinucci, wife of the town clerk, went by in her sedan chair on her way to visit her friend, the wife of the notary, with whom she was if possible on an even more intimate footing than she was with his wife — or when a coach drew up to set down travelers bound for Vacca's inn. Or when Maestro Angelini strutted past, treading the ground fastidiously as though he were squeamish of it, and casting vague, inquisitive glances through his monocle towards the handsomer women by the well. And then it occurred to the gossips that their children were at home alone and that some horrible accident might have befallen them.

For Marietta, these morning confabulations by the well were a new experience. Monsignore had forbidden Imma to send her to fetch water, and when she was a child it had never crossed her mind to join the little girls of twelve and thirteen who roamed about the well, hungrily snatching up titbits from the tittle-tattle that went on there.

Superficially unmoved by all this open and veiled backbiting, she stood among the other women, asking herself in astonishment, at times, whether any of them ever gave a thought to the fact that to each one of them would one day come her turn to be torn to shreds by the three chief furies. No, it did not occur to them. They were oblivious of the glance that Marietta gave them as they laughed heartily at Barberina's latest sally.

They all liked Marietta and tried to get friendly with her. They liked to confide in her the sad stories of their lives of drudgery. Full of compassion, painfully moved by so much sorrow so patiently borne in all those dark houses, Marietta tried to console them. But the women did not want consolation. They had given vent to their own misery, and they knew that nothing could be done about that. What they wanted was to hear in return about Marietta's troubles; that was the only consolation they would accept. Marietta, however, was disinclined to talk about herself. She evaded their questions. At most she spoke of her parents-in-law, of the incomprehensible slow wasting away of old Buongiorno, whose condition these last weeks had actually grown no worse.

The women sighed: "Yes, yes. Everything is still all right for you. Just married, and no children . . . A decent husband, a prosperous workshop. May things go on as they are!"

Marietta answered with a soft, hesitating smile, filled her pitcher, and departed with her thoughts, followed by stares of secret envy.

She walked on, a full pitcher on her left shoulder and another in her hand. In the rarefied morning air, the sun's warm rays caressed her cheeks and roused a feeling of happiness in her young, resilient body. She had been married some months, but it still seemed strange to her to go to her own little home above the workshop where her husband Antonio hammered and sawed. When would it become real to her?

The more she thought about it, the more incomprehensible everything seemed to her. When she looked back upon her life, — a strange and unreal life, that she was able to contemplate with astonishment as though it were not her own, — she could not understand what had led to her sudden marriage with Antonio. It had all happened so quickly, perhaps too quickly. And yet she knew that it had been her own wish. She had turned to Antonio for salvation; had found it, too; but her obstinate thoughts continued to wander.

She tried to keep them under control. She told herself a hundred times that she was now Antonio's wife, and still she could not believe it. She waited, waited impatiently for clearness to come out of this confusion. . . . At other moments, again, she wished only to go on living in this half-dream where everything, happiness as well as sorrow, remained vague and formless.

Was she unhappy? It was impossible for her to say. There was a smarting pain within her that she felt continually during the day and even at night in her sleep. Sometimes when she was alone it took her breath away. She could not remain seated on her chair, and yet did not know where to go. Antonio could not help her. On the contrary, she was glad that he was downstairs at his work. Nobody, nobody could help her. She did not want to speak about it, either. She kept it to herself.

She did not want to lose this pain, this secret pain that sometimes was so cruelly bitter-sweet. It was for her the only proof that she was still attached to life. It enabled her to look without shame into the eyes of the other women in the great house with its many inhabitants. It enabled her to listen quietly to their confessions, and to speak consolingly to them. It did her good that they brought their confessions to her, even though she was sometimes shocked by a revelation, offended by a chance word. It warmed her. She wanted to be accepted by these simple souls who carried their hearts on their sleeves.

Would Marietta's life ever become simple, clear, and tangible like the lives of all these others?

A longing for Antonio suddenly welled up within her. She walked more quickly in the shadow of the houses, and passed into the courtyard where children were playing: Cesarino, Paolino, Pepino, and little Teresina who always wanted to go with her when she went to market. She knew them all now, and the children knew her, and continued with their games undisturbed.

Antonio was on the lookout for her. He had had his eye on the courtyard ever since she went out, half an hour ago, but he pretended that he had just looked up from his work as she put her head into the workshop.

"Have you been to the piazzetta?" he asked, dissembling.

Marietta pointed to her pitchers in reply. He mustered up courage to give her a kiss. "What are you going to do now?" he asked.

"What should I be going to do? Cook for you."

He gave her a happy smile, and asked, "Whom have you seen?"

"Seen?"

"At the well, I mean."

"Oh, I don't know. Does it matter?"

"No, I just asked . . ."

And they went on talking idly, in their happiness to be together, to see each other, and to hear each other's voices. Antonio, however, had something else at the back of his mind; but no natural opening for its expression occurred, and he sounded a false note when he asked, as she was going, "Are you looking in to see Mother?"

This timid request was no new thing to Marietta. She might have expected it. Yet each time she allowed herself to be unpleasantly surprised by it. She knew quite well that she must try to create a bond between herself and Antonio's mother. She was striving to find the right approach, struggling to overcome her aversion to the older woman. But Antonio destroyed her inclination by his persistent pressure that was sometimes open, sometimes disguised.

"I was going in to her in any case — even if you hadn't asked me," she answered.

He was too grateful for her words to note their undertone of vague bitterness. "Father is always pleased to see you, too," he added hastily.

Marietta looked at the ground in silence. She knew that the sick father was only a pretext. Had he been well, she would still have had to go upstairs to Antonio's mother. In point of fact, his father might have been long dead, so little did he exist for Antonio. Lucia too spoke of him as of a dead person. But occasionally it was convenient to rouse "Father" from the dead, which was irritating. Perhaps his face did brighten up when Marietta came in, bringing a gleam of light into his dark loneliness — but it annoyed her that it had been noticed, and was taken advantage of by Antonio.

Naturally, she meant to pay her duty call that morning; but Antonio had stultified her own good intentions. With a somewhat forced smile, into which she tried to put the appearance of a happiness that had suddenly gone out of her, she left the workshop and climbed the stairs. Antonio looked after her dubiously; then flushed with unexpected shame, and returned, awkward and depressed, to his work.

Marietta put down her pitchers when she reached her rooms, and then went into the kitchen and parlor, looking for something that needed immediate attention. Finding nothing, she rearranged her hair and crossed the corridor to the old people's home.

To her surprise, Buongiorno was not in bed, but was sitting in an armchair in the dim light of the shuttered room. Perhaps he had recognized Marietta's step in the corridor, for his head was turned towards the door.

"He simply would get up," remarked his wife. "He insisted upon receiving you in his chair to-day." The old man looked at Marietta with an abashed smile, while his wife continued, "And six months ago, he was already talking of dying. He lay the whole day with his head turned to the wall, and wouldn't hear of getting better. And a man doesn't get better when he just lies looking at the wall, bent only upon helping himself towards the grave. But I'd better be quiet. He won't let me talk of his getting better, even now. And how are you two, Marietta? I had a glimpse of Antonio this morning — "

"When was that?" asked the old man, with vague jealousy.

"While you were asleep, my dear, if that's allowed."

"But you never told me —"

"Must I tell you every blessed thing? He's not in the least inquisitive: only wants to hear everything at once," said his wife, winking at Marietta. "You can thank your stars you haven't got a husband like this one."

He looked so helpless and hurt that Marietta could not refrain from nodding to him consolingly. She could not understand why he was sitting in a chair again: for six months his whole being had seemed to intimate the approaching end. There was something baffling about this unexpected getting-up. "I really do believe you look better than you did a month or two ago, Father," she said.

His wife took some coppers from a drawer and hung a basket over her arm. "Sh!" she warned Marietta humorously. "He doesn't like to hear that. Tell him that death is written all over his face. Then he's pleased. Can I leave you with him a moment? I want to run out."

With a look of astonishment and distrust, her husband turned to her. She was already standing at the door. "I shall be back in a quarter of an hour," she promised, and went.

Marietta and the old man sat opposite one another in the dim parlor, upon which a strange quiet had descended. Over their heads somebody was walking up and down: it was Pinzi, the hatmaker, who probably had a customer with him. Marietta wondered what Antonio's mother had gone to do. But old Buongiorno gave the matter no further thought. The one thing that mattered to him was that Marietta was sitting beside him alone. This unexpected intimacy moved him. He wanted to entertain her, but could find no words. He made an airy gesture to indicate that he was not the pessimist his wife affirmed. The gesture failed, however, for his hand fell lifeless and heavy on his knee. Convulsively his fingers clutched at his clothing. Marietta looked compassionately into his gray face, where pain uneasily borne had distorted features naturally kindly. Her commiseration helped him. He felt more at peace. His difficult speech momentarily lost its stammer.

"Do you know, Marietta," he said, trying to conceal what a great and mysterious pleasure it was to him to speak her name, "do you know, Marietta — what I can't stand is that they never believe me. It's taking a long time — but a day will come, and they won't have given it a thought until that moment. I'm not afraid of death now that I know Antonio has got you. But I should like to be able to talk about it quietly, sometimes, if they did not begin saying at once, 'You'll get better again.' I don't want to get better again, Marietta. I only want . . . I only want a little more warmth. I say to myself, 'If only they would realize that I'm going to die . . .' " He could not continue. With moist eyes, he gazed at the ceiling, biting his bloodless lips despairingly. After a moment, he went on: "Marietta — my wife knows right enough. She knows quite well I'm going to die, Marietta. That's the awful thing about it. She knows quite well." He grew excited, tried to sit bolt upright, fixing wide anxious eyes on Marietta's face. "And why won't she admit it? Why does she behave as if I wasn't so very bad? Because she doesn't want . . . Antonio to come to me, to talk to me, to be sorry about me. She torments me intentionally, Marietta. I sometimes think . . . that she must be a devil."

He looked anxiously towards the door; then, reassured and satisfied at the effect he saw his words had made on Marietta: "Yes, sometimes I think that."

And a shiver went through his whole body, distorting his face.

Marietta, carried away by sympathy into the demon world he conjured up, whispered without a moment's hesitation, "Tell him so yourself. Tell him how his mother is deluding him too."

Immediately he drew back in fear, tormented by remorse. "No, I can't tell him that. It would upset him too much. Perhaps I'm mean, Marietta. Perhaps my wife is right when she wishes Antonio to be kept in ignorance. Sometimes I'm pleased about it too. I should like to be able to think like that always; but my illness has made me so . . . ! After all, he's only a big innocent boy who doesn't pause to consider things unless you call his attention to them. No, let's leave things as they are. Lord! I sometimes don't know myself what I want."

He was silent for a while, in bitter conflict with himself. Marietta could not speak, either. During these minutes of silence, the thoughts of each went their own way, drifted so far apart that Marietta looked up at him, not understanding for a moment when he began to speak again. "It's doubtful whether it would penetrate to him. Sometimes he's with me in the room . . . I say something and he doesn't even hear it. But when his mother speaks he hears all right. Yes, he hears then. He and I are strangers to one another. We don't even know what to say to one another when his mother's out of the room. They're strangers to me, he and his mother, strangers. It's been so always; but I used to be pleased he cared so much for his mother. She had to wait for him a long time — we'd been married six years. I didn't grudge it, Marietta — that she had him to herself. I never thought of myself. It was enough for me that I was able to work for them. Only now, now that I'm ill . . . and know that I sha'n't get better . . . and have the whole day to think about it, only now I've begun to feel it. Only now I suffer about it. Yes, and now you've come, and I can tell you what I dare not tell my own son. Now I have you at least, Marietta, you, you . . ." He put out a trembling hand, but withdrew it again immediately, struggling desperately for composure because the door into the passage had opened, and he heard footsteps approaching through the kitchen.

A little out of breath, his wife came in: in the basket on her arm lay some magnificent grapes.

"Here I am again," she said. "Haven't I been quick?"

She took a dish from the cupboard and arranged the grapes on it, adding a few leaves to heighten the effect.

"Antonio wanted to keep me," she went on happily, "but I wouldn't let him. He was curious to know what was in the basket. I said, 'What's in the basket isn't your concern, my boy.'" She looked at the other two, who were so strangely silent, apparently hardly hearing what she said. Her husband's face struck her as suspicious. His usual fixed, tormented look had disappeared, washed away by some liberating emotion.

"What have you two been talking about?" she inquired.

"About Antonio," he said, turning towards her with something rebellious and defiant in his whole attitude.

The answer appeared to give her pleasure. While she arranged the last bunch of grapes upon the dish, a little contemptuous smile played about her lips. "Here, put this down in front of that Antonio of yours," she said good-humoredly to Marietta, pressing the dish into her hand.

Marietta, upon returning to her rooms, stood deep in thought, her hand resting upon the table.

What had he said, old Buongiorno? "Sometimes he's with me in the room . . . I say something and he doesn't even hear it."

Lucia grudged Antonio to her husband, too, then. She wanted him for herself alone.

Slowly Marietta looked about the little room. How strange it still seemed to her, and yet she had been living here for months. How was that? Downstairs she heard the scraping of a saw. She raised her head to listen.

His saw.

For him she had come here. She loved him for the goodness that illuminated his every word and act. She loved him for the expression in his eyes, for his simple, full mouth, for his hands calloused by his work. She loved his quiet walk, his smile, the passing smile he gave to a child, the way he had of coming to her in the kitchen to ask her where he could find this or that. He could make this very room familiar to her. He could even change as by magic the unreal and the impenetrable in her life into something comprehensible and obvious. She would have liked to rub her head against his shoulder, close her eyes peacefully, feel herself hidden, protected from the whole world . . . including his mother.

She sighed, and carried the bowl of grapes to the kitchen, looking down at the magnificent blue-black and opal-gold fruit with a certain displeasure. Perhaps she might have gone out herself to buy some . . . but now it wasn't necessary. They were particularly beautiful grapes. Yes, Antonio's mother always gave him of the best. Marietta herself would not have dared to buy such expensive ones. She knew where to buy well and cheaply. But then of course they weren't so big. But they were just as juicy and sweet, and she had to be careful with the household money. She foresaw herself being compelled by his mother to buy everything fine and beautiful — otherwise it would look as though she did not care for him sufficiently. And yet Antonio looked concerned when she spent a little too much money in the week. Only his mother was allowed to spring expensive surprises upon him day by day. He sang her praises to Marietta, not realizing that in the end it was he who paid for everything. His mother did not ask him for more money for this purpose — she may have saved it on her own food; she may have had a secret hoard that enabled her to mortify his wife.

Marietta felt bitterness creeping over her.

There was a knock at the door. Annina Cerio, the wife of Simone the stonemason, peered round the door, and with a diffident smile asked for a few onions — her two children were ill, and she had not been able to go to market that morning. Marietta, suspecting that perhaps she had no money in the house with which to go to market, gave her a whole string of onions, and was very much tempted to give her also the dish of grapes. She refrained, from prudence; but she allowed herself to lay the ripest and heaviest bunch in Annina's hands.

"And this afternoon I can look after the children for an hour or so," she said. "Are they getting on a little better now?"

"Yes; though Guido is still feverish. Come along, then, at dusk. I shall be ready by then to take home the washing. The Holy Virgin will . . ."

"All right, then. I will come." A faintly triumphant smile played about Marietta's lips when Annina had gone with her booty. She was in better spirits for having played this trick upon Antonio's mother. Was there no better means of getting her own back — a much better way? For instance, by taking Lucia's son away from her? After all, if she set her whole mind upon it, had she not also a little power over Antonio? Was he not in love with her, hopelessly in love?

Half-past eleven had already struck. She set the pan with water for the macaroni on the fire. Then she went to the window in the parlor, opened one of the shutters, and called, "Antonio!"

He came running out at once, a plane in his hand. Happy and full of expectation, he looked up. Her enticing tone had not escaped him. "What is it?" he asked.

Marietta leaned her elbows on the window sill and looked down at him with a mysterious, almost inviting smile. A glow came over his face. His eyes glittered in the shadow of the hand with which he screened them from the sun. He opened his mouth, uncovering his white teeth in a smile.

She asked him how he was. He was very well, and how was she? Very well too, fortunately. His dinner was on the fire, and there was a surprise for him later on. A surprise? He repeated the word, not understanding what she meant; looked up at her, struggling visibly against his desire to go upstairs; but his sense of duty got the upper hand.

"Wait a minute," commanded Marietta, and disappeared abruptly from the window. She returned with a lump of sugar, which she thrust through the trellis work of the dove's cage that hung outside the window in the sun. "Sweet Grigio! Grigino!"

This dove had been Antonio's since he was a boy. He had always looked after it himself. But now Marietta did that, and Grigio was as much hers as Antonio's. It had also been her idea to hang it outside during the day in the sun instead of over the door.

He returned to his workshop. Marietta closed the shutters against the sun. Against the prying glances, too, of Manuela Lascari, the cobbler's pale, slatternly wife, who saw everything that happened in the courtyard, including this little scene at the window.

Full of courage again, Marietta listened to Antonio's voice: he was making a coffin for Martini the flower grower — and he sang as he worked. Lascari, the cobbler on the other side of the courtyard, caught up the tune. His voice, shrill but penetrating, soon drowned the modest humming from the carpenter's workshop. His wife would shortly be singing quite a different tune: she never let his good spirits go unpunished.

When Antonio went upstairs for the midday meal, he could not find Marietta. She was not in the parlor, where the table was laid, and the kitchen seemed to be deserted too. This discovery disconcerted him: downstairs at his work, as he waited hungrily for the midday gun to go off, he had planned to take her in his arms the minute he got upstairs. Yes, that was what he had planned, and he had hurried upstairs so that

his courage should not ooze away before he met her. He had wanted to
fold her in his arms, to kiss her, and to utter some endearing phrase —
and now she was not there. Helpless, he stood in the kitchen, gazing at
the saucepan on the fire as though she might have hidden herself in it,
and would in a moment raise the lid and spring out of it. It had not occurred to him that Marietta might peep out at him from behind the door,
that she was at that very moment shaking her head over him, and, no
longer able to control her longing, was creeping up to him from behind on
tiptoe. She had nearly reached him when he did hear a sound, turned
round, and there she was, looking into his grave face that suddenly
brightened.

It was fine, it was moving to be together again. He had not caught a
glimpse of her since she leaned out of the window, and that was more
than half an hour ago: and then he had come home, and failed to find
her. He laid his head on her shoulder — of the tempestuous passion that
had stirred within him while he had been alone at work downstairs, only
a boyish desire for tenderness remained. It would hurt him to hear that
she had hidden purposely. Yes, but she wanted to hurt him — she had
planned to. She did not want to be a second mother to him — one was
enough.

"You should learn to look about you more," she said reprovingly.

He raised his head, a shade upset. She smiled coquettishly.

"What do you mean by that?" he asked.

She did not answer. She closed her eyes and surrendered to his embrace
with a passion that surprised herself. Despite a feeling of shame at this
passion, she was swept by a deep unsuspected bliss at being able to
forget herself so entirely in his strong arms. It crossed her mind that
it was astonishing how, up till now, she had always had to fight against
herself, anxious to maintain a last reserve. And now he seemed afraid.
Disappointed, she opened her eyes, and saw his hesitation and surprise.
Perhaps he didn't quite know what she expected of him. She smiled, freed
herself, and with a flushed face went towards the fire to take off the
saucepan.

He stood a moment perplexed, then slowly followed her, regretting that
he had let her escape so quickly. Confused and roused again to ardor, too
late, he said: "Marietta . . . sometimes I still can't believe it's true. At
times, I don't understand at all. . . ."

"Why not? You're a man . . . You ought to be able to understand,"
she answered airily without looking round. Was she shy? In any case,
she could not bear his standing like that behind her. She said in a tone of

command, "Now run along and sit down at table. I'll serve up the food."

Obediently, he did as he was told. She served him, pushed the carafe of wine towards him, then helped herself.

And then they ate.

Marietta, breaking the bread and dividing the portion between them, pretended not to see his imploring glances. Suddenly she remarked, "Oh, yes, your mother thought of you again to-day."

It did not escape her that at this piece of news his vague oppression entirely evaporated. She had made the remark purposely to test him, and the result made her bitter. He felt safe again under his mother's protection, safe from all troublesome complications with his wife. He wondered in what way his mother had thought of him again to-day, and tried to find out in roundabout fashion. That, surely, was the surprise of which she had spoken, he suggested in childish elation.

But Marietta was silent. It crossed his mind that she might have meant something else when she spoke of a surprise . . .

"How were things at home?" he asked.

"At home?" queried Marietta, challengingly. "Surely your home is here."

Antonio swallowed hard. "I mean, was everything all right at home . . . with the old people?"

"How can you ask, Antonio, whether everything is all right there when you yourself know how things are with your father?"

"Oh . . . Father, yes," he stammered, overwhelmed, and so helpless that Marietta suddenly found it impossible to go on being angry with him.

"Yes, you didn't think of that," she mocked. "Eat your food."

He bent over his plate; but all the joy had gone out of him.

"Did I vex you?" she asked, after a few moments.

He was struggling against tears, and could not reply.

"I only vexed you because you vexed me first," she insisted.

"I vexed you, Marietta?"

"Yes."

He made a gesture indicative of despair, covered his face with his hands.

"And you understand well enough . . . You simply refuse to understand."

"Tell me what you mean," he begged, crushed under a strange sense of guilt.

"No, you tell me something. Answer this question: on whose side would you be if there should ever be anything . . . between your mother and me?"

Startled, he raised his head. "Is there anything between you?"

His recovery after being downcast was so sudden that Marietta was almost tempted to laugh; but her voice sounded bitter, irritated, as she said: "*If* there were anything, I said. Keep calm, and admit that you would defend her against me — not me against her."

Unsettled though somewhat relieved, he prevaricated. "Why should there be anything between you two? . . . There mustn't be, Marietta, there mustn't be. You always think I love her more than you. But it's something quite different. She's my mother. She has never thought of herself, always only of me. For instance, it was quite a big thing for her to remain alone with Father. She did that for you — Monsignore asked her to. For you, she would do anything. She always inquires after you. It makes her sad that sometimes you don't want to go and see her . . . She notices at once, although she says nothing. I only want things to be all right between you, nothing more. That's all. Can't I ask that of you?" He had grown very agitated as he spoke, and could no longer restrain his tears.

Marietta listened to him, silent and pale.

"Of course you can ask that of me, Antonio, and I'd do it for you gladly. I'd put up with every humiliation: do you hear? If only I knew that you would be on my side supposing anything went wrong, if in spite of my good will there were disunity, after all, between her and me."

Antonio, ashamed of his tears, wiped them away with his sleeve, and stared before him with great moist eyes. "I don't know," he admitted in a toneless voice. "It's too awful to think of. It would be awful . . . awful."

Silence descended upon the room. Marietta struggled against the tender feelings that welled up in her. "All right," she said at last, grudgingly. "You can rely on me."

With a passionate gesture he seized her hand and rested his head against it. She looked down at him, stroking his soft dark hair.

"Eat what's left on your plate anyway," she said, and poured more wine into his glass. A painful frown on his forehead, he obeyed. When he had finished, she got up to fetch the dish of grapes.

"There. Your mother gave me this for you. A dishful; but the nicest bunch I gave to Annina Cerio for her sick children — you don't mind?"

He dared not look at her, listened anxiously for some trace of mockery in her words. She dispelled his distrust with her laugh that suddenly returned, and, while she chose an attractive bunch for him, held out her cheek for him to kiss.

II

Antonio had work that afternoon in the cemetery. Immediately after the meal, he departed, with his tools on a small handcart. Marietta washed up the plates, then sat down with some mending by the open window from which the sun had departed. Downstairs in the courtyard the children were romping, their clear voices resounding in the afternoon stillness. Sometimes she interrupted her work to look at them, a thoughtful smile about her lips.

Several times, these last weeks, she had wondered how it would be if she herself had a child. Her days were not very full . . . All that would change if she were expecting a baby. But there was no sign of anything yet.

She had a sudden longing for this mysterious germination in her own body. To become a mother must be a liberation, a victory over all destructive forces. Yes, she longed for such a victory. A child would engross her entirely; would leave her no time to feel lonely — neither would she be, any more, for she would possess her child. In this world where everything seemed to her so unreal and impalpable, she would have her child; and if Antonio wanted to share it with her, he must surrender himself entirely to her. And that he would do: he would be happy and proud, his child would turn him into a man. She and her child would have power over him; together they would be more powerful than his mother, who would have to step down from her proud height and strive for Marietta's favors. . . . That would be a sweet revenge!

But why didn't it come? They had been married fully three months already, and some knew after a month that they were to be mothers. Surely it would come. And it must be a boy, the first one, and look like Antonio, as one drop of water resembled another. He must be Antonio himself, but in miniature — the little head, the little body . . . only the eyes would be big from the beginning. His grandmother would say that it was just as if time had gone back twenty years, as if she saw Antonio himself again in babyhood. But why was it so long in coming? It was more than three months — it was nearly four months since they were married.

Antonio had not been gone an hour when she began to long for his return. It depressed her when there was silence downstairs in the workshop. She could hear the thud of his hammer above all the other noises in the great house.

How strange it was. When he was far away, she would dream of his proximity. When he was by her in the room, then she would notice that the fulfillment of her wish brought no relief. At night, in the warm shelter of their bed, when his breath stirred in her hair, and his hand rested shyly on her breast, sometimes suddenly she felt wonderfully safe by his side in the pitiless, wide, noisy world that was stilled for the time being; but with the first gray light of dawn, doubt stole into her heart again. Sometimes she feared the daylight. Sometimes she wished that the darkness would remain around them, around Antonio and her, and that he would go on sleeping peacefully beside her . . .

She had not been quite right in her reckoning of a moment ago. It was true that they had been married almost four months, but a month after their wedding day she had still been a virgin. She had not known it herself, neither had he. He had lived in innocence, in innocence had loved. His growing desire had made him approach her, but always fearfully. She, in instinctive anticipation but likewise groping uncertainly, had not dared to meet him halfway. Gradually their bodies had become familiar with one another, and suddenly, without their quite realizing how, they had lost themselves in one another . . . A short, sharp pain, a deep dizzy bliss. Antonio had been startled by her cry, more than she had been herself, and had wept in her arms while his powerful body still quivered. Since then, the magnificent gift of physical union had absorbed them. Every evening desire for it rose up in her afresh; and the mornings found her filled with a languor that gave a dreamlike undertone to her days.

But she wanted something more. She wanted a child. Surely she would notice if one were going to come. . . . She had only to ask the first person who came along — Annina Cerio or Camilla, the wife of Cesare the carrier, who lived just above them. Or anybody — all would hasten to give her good advice. Perhaps she was in need of advice. But she could never bring herself to give away her secret, their secret. She would sink into the ground for shame if she had to talk about these things.

Antonio might ask his mother — that was different. That, that now, his mother could tell him, and when they were alone together in the darkness he could tell her . . . But he would never dare broach the subject with his mother. If it came to the point, perhaps he would dare even less than Marietta. Worse still, because of their secret, he could not look into his mother's eyes. Marietta grew angry as she thought about it: Antonio's consciousness of guilt towards his mother. After all, he was married, and need no longer render account to her for what he did. But it seemed as though every day afresh he had to ask her for her consent to his marriage.

If only a child would come, then at least he would see to what purpose their sin had served. Then perhaps he would be ashamed that he had carried their love about with him as though it were a sin.

A plan was maturing within her — a plan that was really no plan at all, but only a figment of the mind: to-night . . . to-night the child should have its being within her. She would demand it of him: I don't want you to weep in my arms. I want a child of you. Why don't you give it me? You're a man. She gazed before her, unseeing — she was unaware that Manuela Lascari was watching her, trying to catch her eye in order to ask her where Antonio had gone . . .

At that moment, Marietta suddenly remembered an evening . . . when for the first time a man had bent over her. . . . A man by whom for a moment she had been completely dominated. . . . A man whose eyes had lit up with drunken ardor, who . . .

She got up, wandered aimlessly about the room, stood by the kitchen door, the handle in her hand. What in God's name was she running away from? There was nobody. Why was she suddenly out of breath? In a little while Antonio would be back, Antonio would be here again soon. She could not stand it, being alone in these rooms. Several times before, this invisible menace had assailed her, this vivid recollection of a terrible evening in Monsignore's house — that evening which, during her engagement to Antonio, had been completely blanked out of her thoughts.

When she thought she had recovered her calm again, she returned to the window, and resumed her mending mechanically. She was ashamed of herself for her stupid nervousness. She would have liked to cry. What was the matter with her? What could be the matter with her?

Since her marriage, she had been to see Monsignore only once, with Antonio. It was a mere duty call. Monsignore had been ostentatiously friendly, refused to allow Antonio to say a word of thanks, summoned Imma to join them. Wine had gone round, and in the conversation he skimmed over all the pitfalls that might have beset them.

As they had taken their leave, he had said they must come back . . . but something in his voice suggested to her that he did not mean it. But had she been mistaken? Once he had nodded when she had asked him, "Am I *your* child?"

After that visit, she had not known what she ought to do. Whenever Antonio suggested going again some Sunday afternoon, she cast about for reasons to put the visit off, and recently he had given up making the suggestion. Several times she had intended to go to see Imma — she would hear from her whether Monsignore still spoke about her. That had been her plan — but she had not done it. Imma must be thinking her ungrateful, even if Monsignore did not. And was she perhaps ungrateful? As a child, she had been accused of ingratitude by Vacca. But she was quite prepared to see herself through Vacca's contemptuous eyes and to tax herself with gross ingratitude to avoid having to admit to herself that she was afraid of going to the great house on the piazza, that she was afraid of Monsignore, afraid, unspeakably afraid. Had he deserved that of her? During her engagement to Antonio, she had continued living under his roof and had felt safe. What could have changed since then? Her trouble had driven her to the cathedral once or twice when he was celebrating Mass. She wanted to see him as other women saw him — other-worldly, unassailable in his consecrated surplice. By a glimpse of him like that, she wanted to overcome the menace of that one evening, that now in her marriage had risen up before her again; but as soon as she had left the church, the lustre of the priestly robe was dimmed, and she saw him again as he was when he returned home from Mass, and took a cup of chocolate from her hands . . . As he was when he stretched out his hand towards her that evening when he told her about Venice.

Surely Antonio ought to be able to liberate her from this foolish fear. Did he not see how restless she was sometimes, as though tormented? When would he open those eyes of his, into which his mother had thrown so much dust?

When dusk began to fall in the courtyard, and Lascari the cobbler came outside with his work to take advantage of what remained of the light, Marietta got up and made ready to go to Annina Cerio. Annina was standing in the low kitchen, still ironing, her back stiff with fatigue. She looked round gratefully.

"How nice of you to come, Marietta. I'm nearly ready. Only a few more shirts. Just look what I've got through."

"But why didn't you ask me to come and help you?" asked Marietta reproachfully, as she cast a glance at the pile of ironed linen.

"You help me so much already. Here, you might put this iron on the fire, and hand me the other." Annina put her hand against her side; but she smiled — she was always smiling, as though she were at a loss to understand why she had to work so hard and yet remain so dreadfully poor. The red glow from the charcoal fire lit up her womanly face that was furrowed with care.

"Sit down and let me finish," ordered Marietta. Annina obeyed without further protest. She dropped down on a chair, still supporting herself, with her hands on her back. As she ironed, Marietta looked at her. Something in Annina's way of sitting struck her.

Annina, fancying that her friend had guessed, came out with the truth herself. "Yes, I believe I'm that way again . . . I get tired so quickly these days."

Marietta continued to iron, her face bent down and turned away.

"You do it very well," said Annina, admiringly.

"Where's this washing got to go?" asked Marietta. "If what you think is true, it would harm you to carry anything too heavy."

Annina shrugged her shoulders. "The two previous times I carried round the washing up to the last day," she said, with a touch of pride. Then, continuing in a surprised tone: "But why do you ask? Do you want to do it?"

"Yes, why not?"

Annina thought a moment. "No, you mustn't. That isn't work for you."

"Why is it all right for you and not for me?" asked Marietta. "What are you laughing at?"

"Everybody would laugh if you ran round with such a basket, and delivered washing to the rich."

"I've done it myself before now."

"Oh, yes, I remember, when you were at the convent — a little basket of fine linen for Signora Galli; and every Saturday you dropped in to see Nana at The Three Popes. When she was expecting you, she locked the door between the kitchen and the taproom, and put on her best clothes for you!"

"Her best clothes?"

"Yes, and she said, 'It's just as if I were receiving a saint — anybody would be blessed who had such a child'; and when the others poked fun at her and said, 'But she isn't your child at all,' she used to get angry and say, 'She may not be my child, but that's the way we happen to feel, she and I!'" Annina suddenly became serious. "Yes, and now you live among us as though you were just like us."

Marietta went on working, restive and with a troubled mind. "Am I different from you others?"

"Of course you're different."

"What an idea!" exclaimed Marietta, and felt her blood rise to her cheeks in sudden despair. "You all know I was brought up here as a child. I'm not different from you — I'm not. I won't have it."

Annina was afraid that she had hurt Marietta unwittingly, and tried to laugh it off. "Well, in any case, you can't go taking that washing round for me, if only because people might want me to be there in case something were missing, or things had got mixed up. In this little kitchen, I can't always separate one lot of washing from another. Sometimes I get

mixed up altogether — that's happened twice. And last time, on my way
from the wash-house, I lost one piece, and that same day a chemise blew
off the line . . . that was gone, too. That was a day of misfortune, Marietta. We couldn't make it good, and I felt like a thief when I had to go
and tell them." In her bitterness, Annina said spitefully: "On my life, I
believe that Manuela could tell a tale about the chemise that blew away.
Who is there here would steal it? But it's just the sort of trick she might
play. And how can I prove it? I can't very well say, 'Take your clothes
off: I want to see your chemise.' Falcometti ought to know: he's seen her
in her chemise, and perhaps without it too."

Satisfied by her own sally, Annina changed the subject. "If you'll keep
an eye on the children, you'll be helping me enough."

"Are they asleep?"

"I think so, for I don't hear them. Giannino ate all right to-day, and
Guido isn't so feverish as yesterday. That's a load off my mind."

Annina got up slowly to pack the washing; but she still stood a moment in thought. "You know, Marietta, when they lie raving there beside
you in bed, the lambs, and you put your hand on their little heads and you
feel how it burns . . . And everything is so dark about you, and everything so quiet, and nobody can tell you if you will be able to keep them
. . . You may well be pleased you two are still without them. They give
you a lot of worry, you know. Simone and I, we console ourselves with
the thought that perhaps things will be easier for us later on when they're
grown up, if they don't forget us. For the rest, it's better not to think.
Just trust in God, and work with all your might and main: then at least
you have peace inside you. Yes . . . and soon we shall have three. We
can't do anything about it, Simone and I. Camilla and Cesare already
have seven, and when you see her, you know there's going to be a number eight."

All sorts of questions came into Marietta's mind, but she dared not
bring them out. She felt too ashamed. She put away the iron, and
helped Annina to pile the washing in a basket. Accustomed as she was
to it, Annina placed the basket on her head, and then slipped sideways
through the narrow door. Marietta, smarting with envy, acutely conscious
of her own inferiority, watched her cross the courtyard and disappear
through the entrance.

Then she went in to the children. Little Guido was panting in his
troubled sleep. Giannino, the elder, a toddler of four years, looked towards
the door as Marietta entered softly, shielding the light of the candle with
her hand.

"What? Aren't you asleep?"

"No. I'm better."

Marietta smiled. The small voice relieved her from depression. "Oh, and so you don't need to sleep?"

Instead of answering, the little one said: "I heard you talking with Mother in the kitchen. Where is she now?"

"She'll be back soon. You go to sleep. I'm staying here until she comes back."

"Has she gone to take the washing round?" asked Giannino importantly. Then, seizing the opportunity, he promised, "I'll go to sleep if you first tell me the story you told last time."

"Oh, about the miller and his donkey who went together to look for the golden witch-ball?"

"Yes, and when the robbers came out of the wood."

Marietta obediently told the story. When it was finished, she had to begin it afresh, but interrupted herself halfway through when she saw that Giannino had fallen asleep. His little brown head with its lanky hair lay peacefully on the pillow. Guido, in the other little bed, began to talk in his sleep. Marietta tucked him up again — he had thrown all the bedclothes off. It was quiet now, and Guido's breathing seemed easier.

Yes. It was quiet now. How strange, to be alone in this room with two children lying there asleep. If only they had been her own! If only she were watching her own children! The thought of it caught at her throat. She listened to the familiar sounds that penetrated to her from the great house inhabited by many families. She had learned much of the intimate relationships of these people; and what she had not observed for herself the tittle-tattle by the well had revealed to her. The few words that reached her from the half-open doors through the echoing corridors were sufficient to give her an idea of what was happening. There were Bartoldi and his wife Bettina: they led a cat-and-dog life. Every Saturday evening, when he was paid, they had a fight. Bettina went to her neighbors, even before he got home, imploring them for help. But if anybody happened to come between them, man and wife turned jointly upon the meddler; and on Sunday mornings, dressed in their best, they went together to Mass as if there never had been a harsh word between them. Just above the room in which she sat lived Falcometti — a bachelor, and a stonemason like Annina's husband. When after the long day he returned home in the evening, he went straight to his room and fetched his cornet. Then he sat in the courtyard playing his precious instrument with rough fingers. The children stood about him listening. He liked to explain to them the difficulties of the higher tones, with demonstrations. The plaintive, melancholy sound of the cornet crept in through all the open windows. He ate with Lascari the cobbler, whose wife every spring and autumn came with pail and broom to clean his room. The water dripped through the crevices of the floor into the bedroom below, but Annina bore up under this as she bore up under everything else. No one dared speak his mind to Manuela. Behind her back, though, it was whispered that Lascari, poor soul, allowed himself to be sent out to deliver shoes while she received Falcometti in the back room: his melodies had conquered her heart.

Then there was the haughty Signora Brunetti, who had a fruit and vegetable shop on the street side of the house. She thought so highly of herself that she sent all her three little girls to school, and made them wear shoes and stockings summer and winter; and she had a bead curtain hanging in front of her shop to prevent flies from settling on her grapes. Yes, and when she wanted to eat, she closed the shop for a whole hour; and there were people mad enough to buy from her, although everything cost at least a soldo more than it was worth, simply to be able to say that they bought in the shop where hung the bead curtain as a protection against the flies. Yes, and all this would perhaps have been forgiven her if it had not been that her eldest daughter was the image of the tailor Mariotti, who had made her husband's wedding suit so cheaply. Brunetti, poor fool, actually spread it abroad that he had only had to pay for the material for his wedding suit! That tailor Mariotti! The eleven-year-old girl who served in the hosiery shop kept by Brogi must also be his — he himself bragged that it was so, anyhow, and stood with his friends in front of the window nodding to the little one.

To each and all of the people in the great house belonged some mystery, fit subject for gossip. Dislike and lies, bitter mortification and pleasure at the pain of others . . . But all the same they poured out their hearts to one another, and in times of want and trouble, or in the presence of some cruel blow of fortune, a feeling of tenderness welled up between them that washed out everything they had done to one another and suffered at each other's hands. They knew then that they were dependent upon one another, children of one great household.

While Marietta sat listening in the candlelight, she knew she envied them all — envied their solidarity, their consciousness of unity, momentary though it was. What difference would it make to this house were she to go away? Would not everything remain just the same? Where did she belong, if she could not take her place here? She must belong somewhere. For a moment, it was as if the ground had slipped away from beneath her feet. Confused thoughts flashed through her brain, and her whole being was one great longing. She could not tell whither this longing was leading her. Even as a child, she had never felt at home. The convent where she had sought refuge had soon become too narrow for her . . . Later, Monsignore had spoken to her of Venice, but she did not want that. No, no. She still shuddered to-day at the thought of the remote and the unknown. Could she not at Antonio's side, serving, working with all her strength, and if need be a little more, as Annina had said — could she not become one with these others? Why was she rejected? They were pleasant to her. They were obliging, yes. But they would not accept her.

Downstairs in the courtyard, Falcometti was playing his cornet. The closing notes swelled up and died away. He himself was enamored of these sighs that made the dusk so infinitely sad. Marietta began to ask herself whether Antonio was perhaps already back. Why was he so long? If he came home and did not find her, surely he would remember that she had told him she was going to look after Annina's children — and surely then he would cross the corridor. What was it he had had to do? To put a railing round a grave. Or perhaps old Ruocco was busy digging the pit for Martini the flower grower: if so, he would certainly have asked Antonio to lend a hand, and Antonio was not one to say no.

Antonio's work had long since ceased to seem gruesome to Marietta. She watched him, quietly, gently carrying out his daily tasks on the borderline of life and death, and receiving payment for it. He approached all the confusion of death with a profound simplicity. To die was to take leave of the vanity of life, and then to be measured carefully by Antonio, coffined and brought to earth on the road to eternity . . .

It was growing quieter and quieter in the great house. They were all sitting at their evening meal. The youngest children were already in bed. Manuela's shrill voice had just sounded across the courtyard, and the sound of the cornet had died away in the middle of a long note.

The bells were ringing for vespers, and she was still sitting alone. Surely they must be working by lantern light, old Ruocco and he. But he must have guessed that as dusk set in, she would be on the lookout for him. Surely nothing could have happened to him. She felt this supposition to be foolish, and struggled to shake it off. Antonio . . . Why are you so long in coming? Why don't you come, Antonio?

He was everything to her — if she had not known it before, she knew it now. If he did not return, she would be lost. She would flee from this great house. . . . But where? Of course he would come back. She must not be frightened over nothing, over foolish fancies. He might even be sitting at home, waiting for her, simply because he had forgotten what she had said to him at mid-day when he left. That would be just like him. She would cross the corridor and make sure . . . Yes, she would do that;

then she would know. Softly she got up from her chair, casting a look at the sleeping little ones.

Then, suddenly, Simone appeared on the threshold. He did not notice how he startled her, and with undisguised disappointment in his voice, which he had difficulty in muffling, burst into the room with: "Oh, is Annina still out?"

"Yes, delivering the washing . . . Do you know by any chance if Antonio has come home?"

Simone thought a moment. "I do believe I saw a light burning in your place."

Marietta sighed with relief. "They're sleeping quietly, both of them," she said, while Simone approached the bed softly, looking down upon his children with a strange tenderness.

"Was Guido able to eat?" he inquired. She heard the concern in his voice, and was ashamed — he had so much more reason for anxiety than she. As she talked, holding the candle above little Guido, who was less feverish and flushed than he had been, she gave a side glance at Simone's tired, prematurely furrowed face that was hidden under a gray coating of fine dust, and for a moment this stranger's face became known and familiar to her, until suddenly it became Antonio's face bending over his children.

"Your food is ready in the kitchen," she said, awakening from her dream. "I will just take it off the fire."

"No, leave it. I would rather wait till Annina comes back. You'd better go home." Simone had sensed her longing. Blushing, grateful, Marietta left him, and rapidly crossed the corridor to her own home. Her heart beat with joy when she saw light through a crack under the door. He was home then, and waiting for her — the dear blockhead. But as she laid her hand on the doorknob, she heard voices inside, and a deep disappointment came over her: his mother was with him — she must have been waiting for him in the corridor; and he had forgotten to seek his wife. The beautiful happiness had disappeared from her face when she opened the door and went in, half embarrassed, half proudly conscious of her right.

There they were, standing together. Lucia seemed to be on the point of leaving. Somewhat absent-minded, as if they had been caught, they looked towards Marietta, who suddenly felt heavy at heart and full of bitterness that she had to enter her own home as a stranger.

Lucia smiled — sadly, faintly forgiving — and said, "Here's Marietta."

Her son started up from his stupor. He hurried towards Marietta and closed her in his arms, very gravely, painfully.

"What's the matter?" murmured Marietta, alarmed.

"Antonio will tell you," replied Lucia. She laid her hand upon her son's forehead — he was struggling with his tears — and gave him an encouraging look.

Then she went. "Good day, children," she said.

They were alone. Antonio stood by the door through which his mother had gone. He turned his pale face towards Marietta. No longer able to contain herself, she rushed up to him, and clinging to his breast, demanded, "What is the matter? Tell me, Antonio! What terrible news did she bring?"

He turned away his head. He could not speak at once. At last he brought out with difficulty, "Father . . . won't get any better."

His words sounded so amazingly foolish in her ears that at first she could not understand him. "Did she come here for that? To tell you that?" she asked tonelessly.

He nodded. Tears broke through his voice as he said, "She's known it a long time. Barberini told her. . . . She's kept it from me. She wanted to bear it alone."

Marietta suddenly disengaged herself from his arms and shrank back slowly. Helpless, scared, he looked up. Was she leaving him standing there, at that terrible moment?

"And why did she tell you now, if she wanted to bear it alone?" asked Marietta.

"Why? Because it cannot go on much longer, Marietta. Barberini said . . ." He could not finish his sentence — Marietta had disconcerted him. While he had been speaking she shook her head; she kept on shaking it.

"Barberini has said nothing. Barberini hasn't seen your father for months. She came to tell you this evening, because she didn't wish me to be first, because you were not to be allowed to hear it from anybody in the world but from her. That's why, that's why," said Marietta passionately.

He stared at her, not comprehending her accusation. All he understood was that Marietta knew already.

"But how did you know?" he asked.

In her indignation, Marietta could hardly find words. "How did I know? How do you think I knew? Perhaps I knew it because I'm not blind . . . like you. Everybody knew a year ago that this sickbed would be his deathbed. Everyone is amazed that he has lasted so long. Only you have never seen anything, only you, because your mother didn't wish you to see anything, because you never look at anybody but at your mother. That's why. This morning she saw that your father and I had spoken about it together. She did not hear a word we said, but she saw it — she hasn't kept her eyes in her pocket like you; and from fear lest I should tell you, she comes running along here this evening to tell you, so that you can at last see that your father is dying. She would like to swallow you whole in her love — so that there would be nothing left of you for anybody else." Marietta sank down upon a chair, bursting into sobs. Antonio, who up till now had stood in proud defiance at these accusations leveled at his mother, now suddenly grew weak, came hesitatingly towards her, in an impulse to console her.

Full of aversion, she held him off. "Leave me alone. Don't come near me. Go away. Go to your mother. Go! Then she'll have what she wants. Go to her, do, you fool!"

Antonio remained standing in front of her, very pale.

"Why do you say that to me?" he asked. "I want to understand, but I can't. Naturally, I ought to have known — if the whole city knows. But Mother always said he would get better again. Oughtn't I to have believed her, then? You may say what you like about me. You may think me ridiculous — I know now that I am — but what harm has my mother done? If she hid things from me, it was to spare me; and when she feared I should hear of them, all the same, she wished at least to tell me herself. . . . Is that so bad?"

Marietta could not control a bitter laugh. "Don't ever talk about it any more," she said, in a dull tone. "It's no use, anyhow. I don't know how I can make you understand."

She sat still a moment; then got up to fetch bread and wine from the cupboard. Mechanically, Antonio sat down at the table, concealing his face in his hands.

"Let us talk about it again to-morrow," he suggested. "Perhaps we shall understand one another better. My brain won't work now. While I'm talking, I keep thinking all the while that my father is going to die."

Marietta's anger had passed. Her grief was stilled. "Go to him," she advised, now without malice. "Perhaps you'll come back calmer."

"Now? This evening?" asked Antonio, surprised and full of doubt. "But he will know then that . . ."

"And what will he know then? That he's going to die? Then you thought he didn't know already? You really are funny! He has said so a hundred times, every time your mother allowed him to open his mouth."

"Yes, yes," stammered Antonio helplessly — "yes, he himself has always said it."

"And you didn't hear him say it. You weren't allowed to hear it — your mother wouldn't have it. You haven't looked into his eyes, where you could have read everything. You haven't seen how he stretched out his hands towards you. Your mother didn't wish you to see. Go to him, Antonio. Talk to him as man to man. Perhaps then you'll understand many things for the first time."

"All right. I'll go," said he, and shivered. He got up from his chair, and looked at Marietta as if begging for support, but she was standing with her back to him.

She was alone again. She felt as though she were always alone. She tried to eat, but could not swallow a morsel. Despair seized her wounded heart. A moment ago, she had dared to hope, faintly, that Antonio might become a man this evening, that his father would say to him, "Look here, Antonio, listen while there is time. You must open your eyes at last, for at present you're blind. Your mother is deceiving you. Your mother is robbing you. When you were a boy, your mother stole your friends. She has stolen your father from you. Now she wants to steal your wife . . ." No, that wouldn't happen. The mother would not leave them alone together, not this time. The father would be silent. He would run his hand over his son's hair, and tell him not to cry because everything would be all right. He had never wanted his son, his Antonio, to kneel down by his bed and cry, "Father, are you going to die?" He would not think of Marietta, alone in her room and a prey to despair because she would have to struggle against the mother by herself after his death.

How vigilant that mother of his was! One glance, that morning when she returned with the grapes, had been enough to show her the danger. And then she had decided to tell him the sad news herself, and if possible make capital out of it for herself. "I wanted to conceal it from you, for your sake, my boy. I wanted to bear it alone" — and he believed her. He did not hear the lie in her voice. Marietta had read her guilt in her first glance at her this evening, in the little smile she gave, so triumphant and so sad. His mother had not kissed her, as she usually did — she had been afraid to, because she knew that Marietta had seen through her. She had but one purpose: to keep her son for herself.

And he, Antonio, said with a somber face, "Father is going to die," and had no idea that his mother was making a fool of him. When his wife told him so, he did not understand; and if his father also told him, this evening, he would still not understand.

Marietta looked about her in despair. Was there anywhere she could find help? Yes. . . . From one quarter she could expect help. If she put on her shawl and went to the piazza and knocked at the door of the episcopal palace and said to Imma, "I want to speak to Monsignore," then Imma would forget all the evil she had thought about her staying away and would say, "Go upstairs — you know the way" — and Monsignore would be sitting at his harpsichord, or reading, or writing a letter, and would look round towards her, just as surprised as Imma; and with one look he would read everything in her eyes — why she had never come to see him, and why she had now been driven to him, and he would say, "Sit down . . . I knew you would come one day." Would he really say that? "I knew you would come one day . . ." But whatever he said, she would cry her heart out with him, and tell him everything, everything, until there was nothing more, and then peace would descend upon her.

Perhaps she would be consoled before he had spoken a word. Perhaps he would lay his heavy arm consolingly across her shoulders . . . Then she would forget everything — where she was actually living, and that she was married to Antonio, and that she was carrying on a bitter struggle with his mother. It would be as if she were living under Monsignore's roof again, and had never been away from it. . . . Again his child, safe under his protection. But then a moment would come when he would say, "I'll talk to him; go home now. Everything will come right." Yes, then she would have to go again; but it would be hard to make up her mind to do that. She could feel his look that would not let her go. It would become strangely still in the great room. She would hear only the sound of her own breathing. . . . She would realize, then, how heavily solitude had pressed upon him. Perhaps she would not be able to go away.

These thoughts confused her. She was no longer a child. She understood now — and therefore she understood also that she could on no account go to him.

Yes . . . But supposing she were to go all the same: what would Antonio say when he came back and found the room deserted? What would he do? First he would go to Simone and Annina to ask if she were there. No, she was not. Nor would she be with Cesare and Camilla. But where, then? Manuela Lascari, of the observant eyes, would perhaps come and tell him that she had seen Marietta leave the house. What would he do then? Look for her, all over the city, through the night, and — realizing that his mother was the cause of her distress — make a solemn vow to himself henceforth to live only for his wife?

Or would he just go to his mother and sob in her arms, and let himself be consoled by her: "She'll come back again, my boy. It's one of those women's tricks. Don't be upset. You're a man. She'll come back, all right. Every woman who runs away returns to her husband when she sees that her capers make no impression on him, and that no decent person will have anything to do with her. Come and sleep here to-night, my boy. That's the old-fashioned way." Would he do as she said? Would he allow himself to be consoled, make himself believe that she would come back to him again, once she had run away from him?

Suppose she were to run away this evening — just to see what he would do.

What queer thoughts were passing through her mind!

She sat on her chair, her arms on the table, lost in vague brooding. Memories rose up of how she used to sit working of an evening at Monsignore's, of his explanations of the right way to sing a song by Pergolesi — never sacrificing the melody for the sake of the words; tenderly and with restraint, the face slightly raised; listening, oneself, to the melody, the better to be able to bring it out . . .

She started up at the opening of the door behind her. It was a perceptible moment before she could bring herself back to where she was. Antonio loomed out of the darkness of the passage, his clear, dark eyes gleaming in the light of the lamp. His expression was calmer than it had been. She looked at him expectantly. Quietly he closed the door, came and sat by her, took her hand.

She could be silent no longer. "Did you speak to him?" she asked, weak with suspense.

He nodded. "Yes . . . I have spoken with Father."

She was startled by the solemnity of his tone. He only spoke like that when he was acting on instructions from his mother. She listened attentively as he went on, "I'm sorry, now, Marietta, that Mother didn't tell me everything sooner. It did Father good to be able to talk quietly about everything. I told him . . . how ashamed I am for having been so blind. He's forgiven me. It was fine, Marietta. I wish you had been there too. I did not dare to come and fetch you — I was afraid you might still be excited and would refuse to come. It would have done you good. I'm quite calm again now. Father then called Mother, and we spoke about it together . . ."

He hesitated, looked at Marietta with a vague shyness, and then, taking courage in the consciousness that he was fulfilling a duty, he ended, "We also talked of what is to happen to her when Father is dead . . .

"To Mother . . ." he added, gauchely, as Marietta continued silent.

She got up and stood before him. "Does she want to come here? Come to us in our home? Does your mother want that, Antonio?"

"She doesn't want it," he declared hastily. "She's the very one who doesn't. If you think that of her, it only proves that you don't know her . . ."

"Who does want it, then, if she doesn't?"

He made a gesture as if he were trying to make her see reason. "I begged her to — and she said she wouldn't. Now the question remains whether we're going to leave it at that. She wouldn't refuse if *you* asked her."

"I . . . ? I, Antonio?"

With flashing eyes she stood before him, all her pent-up hatred naked in her voice, a flaming determination to resist. He went an ashen color, but his eyes met hers steadily, and suddenly she knew that the wound she had inflicted on him had awakened the man in him. But this man was not going to stand by her: he was going to stand against her — with a bleeding heart perhaps, but hostile.

How strange his voice sounded as he said, struggling with grief and nervousness, "Yes, you."

Marietta laughed a bitter laugh. She turned away from him, went to the table, and looked down at her fingers as she drew them across the top of it. "Antonio . . ." she said. "If your mother comes here . . . I leave."

He stared at her. "You won't," he said, containing himself with difficulty.

"Yes, I will."

After a long hesitation, he asked weakly, "Where would you go?"

"If one of us two knows that, that's enough."

He sighed deeply, and repeated in a dull tone, "You won't — no, no." He shook his head. "You won't run away if my mother comes to us." Then with a great, sad gravity, "And if you did . . . I should know where my duty lay."

Concealing her sorrow, she jeered, "Thank goodness you do know. So much the better for you! You go and set up house with your mother, and listen to all the spiteful things she will say of me to console you."

"She has never said an unkind thing about you, Marietta."

"If only she had," burst out Marietta, throwing herself hysterically upon a chair. "If only she had! But she has been careful not to. She won't come into our home, do you hear? She sha'n't come into our home. I won't have it. If you bring her here, I run away. I shall just run away, and I don't care where I go. I won't live with her . . . I won't, I won't, I won't!"

He paced up and down the room nervously, opened the door leading into the passage, fearful of an eavesdropper.

"I don't understand you," he sighed, when she was a little calmer. "At Father's bedside everything seemed so beautiful. If only you had been there . . . I didn't know you hated my mother so. I never knew that. Perhaps you think me stupid again. . . . Well, laugh at me. I was hoping you would learn to know her better if she came to live with us, and that you would then see she was not imposing herself, and was only thinking of us, never of herself. Really, really, you're mistaken about her . . . How can that have come about? Has someone put you against her?"

She shook her head in despair.

He could get nothing more out of her. He was about to give up, when suddenly something crossed his mind that gave him fresh hope. He went and sat beside Marietta; timidly, intimately he laid his hand upon her wrist. She let him do it: perhaps in her grief she did not even notice.

"Marietta . . . do you know who else wanted to ask you to take Mother into our home?"

Slowly she raised her head, looked at him with tearful eyes. "Your father?" she muttered sullenly — "Your father wanted to ask me that?"

She had first to consider that. Then slowly a little smile appeared round her mouth. "You seem to have got him down, the two of you." And when she saw a dark flush of anger rise in Antonio's cheek, she added with hard cynicism, "I suppose your father was thinking that, in any case, he wouldn't be there."

Yes, anger flared up in Antonio. Suddenly regaining her composure, she was astonished to see that he also could be quick-tempered, that anger could flare up in his gentle, humble eyes. Was he going to hit her?

No, he did not. He only said, "Shame, Marietta!"

She nodded slowly to herself. Yes, she should feel ashamed. He was right to say that. She was ashamed, ashamed of what those two had done to the father who was pining away, ashamed of what they were doing to her here. Oh, she was terribly ashamed. . . .

III

Worn out in strife, they went to bed at last. What was the good of words, and more words, and passion, and tears, and the cold mockery with which they cut themselves to the heart when they could not convince one another? There came a moment when everything had been said, and a kindly fatigue enveloped their strife. Outside their room, filled with its soft light, there was darkness, night, an impalpable world. At last, after long pauses of spent silence, and the ever-deeper consciousness of the unprofitableness of all the grief they were bringing to each other, they began to feel one another's proximity as a consolation. Suddenly, they became aware that in spite of everything they loved and respected each other. In the night, as they lay peacefully side by side, the hope awakened in them that this silent tenderness would bridge their foolish difference.

But when day returned, the dreadful problem of the mother rose up again between them, inescapable. And they used their recovered strength to arm themselves afresh — the one, sacrificing his marriage to feelings which in genuine innocence he called duty; the other, realizing that she was struggling desperately on the edge of an abyss.

Meanwhile, life went on. Antonio went to his work as usual; Marietta prepared his food and kept his home in order. Every day Lucia brought some dainty for her son. Marietta said nothing about it. Antonio said nothing about it. Both were trying to avoid another clash. The day after their quarrel he hesitated long before paying his usual visit to his parents; and when he returned, very relieved, Marietta knew that his mother had elected to join in the little comedy.

Thus the three of them tried to evade their problem; while Death, which at any moment might spoil the game, held aloof.

Next evening, without any suggestion from Antonio, Marietta went to see his father, who was again in bed. Lucia, friendly and attentive as ever, with truly deceptive innocence, soon left them alone: she happened to have something to do in the kitchen. But the old man was unable to speak at first when he saw Marietta sitting there at his bedside. Should he speak? Did his wife and son expect that of him? He breathed uneasily, and dared not look at Marietta.

At last he said in an uncertain voice, "Yes . . . Antonio knows now. He knows, and I'm wondering whether it wouldn't have been better after all if he'd been told only at the very end. That time is drawing near. It's drawing near . . . Don't you think so too?"

Begging secretly for forgiveness, he raised his eyes to hers.

"He was sitting exactly where you're sitting, Marietta. It did me so much good. It was such a fine moment. If only I had died then! It can only become uglier now, only uglier. Why must I go on living? I've been asking myself that all day long. I'm in pain, in pain all the time." He sighed, gathered up all his courage. "Did he speak to you about his mother . . . About what is to be done with her?"

Marietta did not reply. She just looked at him. Like a guilty child, he turned his face towards the gray wall beside the bed where hung a crucifix and a holy water stoup, and moaned, "I was afraid of that, and now I see it. Yesterday it was different . . . Was it yesterday? . . . I saw things in too rosy a light. I don't know, myself, now, how I saw them. It was in quite a different light, as in a dream. While the two were sitting here crying, I thought that you yourself could not wish it otherwise but that his mother should come to you. I thought you would all live in peace, in peace, in peace. But now I understand that that is an impossibility. What must you be thinking of me?"

Before Marietta could say a word, he continued in self-reproach: "I have been cowardly. I wanted Antonio to know everything. Marietta . . . it is better to be brave and to bear grief in silence. Then you have nothing to reproach yourself with. Then you're not afraid of appearing before God. If you'd been here too that evening — then I should have seen your eyes. Then I couldn't have betrayed you. But I saw only my wife and my son . . . only my wife and my son . . . Can you understand?"

Marietta nodded — she could not speak. As she sat on the side of the bed, he lay panting with closed eyes under his guilt that weighed upon him no less for her silent forgiveness. Convulsively he clung to the hand she put out to him. "What is to happen then? . . . What is to happen when I'm dead?" he repeated at intervals. "It's all my fault. I asked you to take him. I hoped that you could save him. You won't be able to . . . You won't, either. His mother is stronger than you. His mother is stronger than all of us together. She will not rest until she has got the better of you. . . ."

He did not see Marietta look up at his last words, with raised eyebrows; and if he had noticed it, and had asked her whether she still hoped to be able to defy Lucia, she could not have answered him. But a strange anger awoke in her, coupled with an overwhelming determination. She felt it only for a moment, but long enough to know that it was there; and a great peace came over her.

Get the better of her. . . . No, not that.

An hour later, Marietta returned to her own rooms, completely withdrawn into herself. Antonio cast anxious glances at her as he sat opposite her at table. He did not dare to ask about her visit to his father. When at length he did say a word, he had to repeat it before she understood him, before she could reply.

During the next few days, she continued to be completely absentminded. Abstracted within herself, she seemed to have lost all interest in the world around her. Was she working out a plan in secret? In her reserve there was unintentional menace, which nobody about her could fail to notice. It drove Antonio to his parents, but he found no support in his mother. Behind her consoling words, he felt that she too hid a secret anxiety; and that only increased his own. It was beginning to affect his health: he was not looking at all well. When Lucia noticed that, she determined to go and speak to Marietta.

Marietta was standing in her little kitchen, preparing food, and she saw the indignant older woman come in, not without surprise.

From the threshold, Lucia started off: "Why does Antonio look these days as if he would be following his father?"

"Does he look so bad?" asked Marietta, and confessed innocently, "I hadn't noticed it."

"Oh, you hadn't noticed it? Don't you think you might take a little notice of how your husband is looking?"

"I thought — you did that very well."

"Yes, I do — that's why I'm here now."

"Perhaps he's worrying about his father," suggested Marietta, as she continued to prepare the vegetables. "Perhaps it would have been better if you had told him nothing of how matters stand with his father."

Lucia laughed scornfully, and left the kitchen again abruptly in impotent rage. She was no longer what she had been. She had lost her self-control. She never used to get excited, to show herself sharp or unfriendly. Perhaps she would grow calmer again when it was all over with her husband. God sent His trials to His children in many different ways. For Antonio too it was high time that this suspense should end.

Old Buongiorno did all he could to fulfill his tacit promise to die quickly. Each day brought him fresh pain. He lay in bed, his face stubbornly turned towards the wall. Why didn't death come? There was one thing of which he was glad: Antonio again came less frequently to his bedside. Buongiorno no longer had the courage to turn his head towards him. He pretended to be asleep, thankful when his son went back to his mother, and, in a tone that grew more level each time, inquired of her what kind of night his father had had. The boy had troubles of his own. Old Buongiorno did not need to turn round or to listen to his wife's angry complaints to know that Antonio was having trouble with his wife.

His fault . . .

One night a plan grew in him, so simple, so obvious that he was filled with amazement that he had not thought of it before. With a beating heart, he waited for his wife to come to his bedside and give him his medicine. He held down his wife's hand when she was about to uncork the little bottle. "Leave that alone — it doesn't help me any more."

Astonished, suspicious, she looked at him. "One must do what one can," she said curtly.

He shook his head. "I won't drink it any more. Ask Barberini to come again."

"What do you want with Barberini? If there were a better medicine to give you, he would have given it to you. And his visits cost money."

"I want to speak to him. He hasn't been here for months."

"You know best why he doesn't come any more."

"I want to ask him something else this time. It isn't anything about get-

ting better. It is only to still these frightful pains. I should like — an end
to be put to it."

She looked at him, and understood his secret entreaty. She had a moment's hesitation. For a moment, quick as lightning, she considered the
advantages that might accrue to her: the end of the suspense, under which
Antonio was breaking down, and herself with him . . . But already the
temptation was past. Her husband and Marietta might think that she was
a kind of she-devil, but she knew, fortunately, that that was not so. Even
though they were trying to make her one by wanting to take her son
away from her, her boy who was everything she possessed in the world.
No, no, she had not stooped to crime yet. A hard, proud line came over
her mouth when she noticed that her husband had seen her moment of
weakness and had built expectations upon it.

"Certainly not. Barberini is not coming here, not for that at any rate.
If you want to see him, all right; but I don't leave the room. You've lived
a Christian, Gabriele, and you'll die a Christian. Look and see Who is hanging on the wall."

He sank back in his pillows again and closed his eyes in defiance. He
refused to look at the wall at her command. He had looked at the wall
for so many months. Let her look herself — she who wanted him to go
on suffering, she who grudged him death.

"Here, take this," she said, lifting the spoon into which she had poured
the medicine. He refused, closing his thin, gray lips tight. She had to laugh
— a gall-bitter laugh, in which she tried to liberate herself from her own
grief, her own disappointment. "Be a man," she said, contemptuously. But
he did not want to be a man, he wanted to die.

When she had corked the little flask again and had gone away, she returned unexpectedly to the sickbed. "Gabriele," she said, threateningly,
"you won't ask Antonio, will you?"

That had not occurred to him; but she need not know that. With almost
devilish satisfaction, he heard the anxiety in her voice. He was silent: one
need not answer every question.

She was really amazed at him. This man had always been gentle as a
lamb. They had never had a quarrel, and now he was surprising her like
this. It would never have happened if that girl had not whispered things
in his ears, that girl whom she herself had brought into their lives because
she had got it into her head that her son, her Antonio, would be less
esteemed in the eyes of the world if he remained unmarried . . . Yes, and
she had been punished for her sinful pride. The foundling, brought up
by the kindness of the city and the Church, who should have been only
too happy to marry at all, wanted to rob her not only of her son but of

her husband. She could not even wait until her husband had passed away naturally. Lucia had to think a moment before she could find the right thing to say to him. Then she bent over him, looking close into his eyes: "Gabriele — you wouldn't make a murderer of your son, would you?"

Fortunately that produced an effect. That wicked girl had not brought him to such an extreme. He did not want to make a murderer of his son, not that.

Set at rest, she left him. She had prevailed again.

The old man, intentionally left to himself the whole day by his wife, wept until his pillow was wet with tears.

IV

It was not long before the women by the well were aware that Marietta, despite her expressionless face, was consumed by a secret grief. Antonio looked so depressed, too. There must be a reason. It could not be Buongiorno's slow decline — that was too old a story. Puzzled, the women tried to gain Marietta's confidence, spontaneously taking her side against Lucia. Some of them went to see her, sincerely admired the cleanliness of her home, and the furniture carpentered by Antonio himself. Full of sympathy, they inquired after her father-in-law, and came quite naturally to speak of her mother-in-law also. She must be delighted that her boy, her Antonio, had hit upon such a dear little wife, who kept the home so neat. But they did not succeed in extracting confidences from Marietta. She was friendly, hospitable, but she did not break the intentional silences of her visitors. . . . The sounds of Antonio's hammer and saw came from below, but they had lost their old happy rhythm.

When they left her, the inquisitive women crossed the corridor to visit the sick man; but none the wiser they left him also.

Upon one of those December days when darkness descends early, Nana dropped in. They had become almost strangers to one another; but a few days before, Nana had spoken to Marietta by the well, and now she had come to visit her. Marietta wondered why she had come: she was no inquisitive gossip; but why did she come visiting now, when so many others had shown an interest in Marietta and her household?

Nana answered her surprised but friendly look with a sad little smile. She sat down by the table, peered into the charcoal fire, and said, "I just came round to see how you are, Marietta." Then she was silent.

Marietta hesitated. It moved her to have old Nana here as her guest, and she would certainly have poured out her heart to her if she had not feared Nana's explosiveness. Nana would take her side and would go and give a piece of her mind to Antonio's mother, or whoever might be involved. Marietta wished to fight out her struggle alone. Who could help her with it? She wanted to maintain the tense resilience within her by maintaining silence.

She would not understand the purpose of Nana's visit. She talked of the past. Nana, at first disappointed and affronted, allowed herself to be put off — she was in reality only too happy to talk of old times.

If Marietta refused to make confidences, Nana had some to make to her — she was not proud like Marietta. Her pride had been broken long ago. Her brief glory had quickly tarnished; and who was the chief culprit? Luigino. It was he to whom she owed her gray hairs, he who was sending her to her grave. He stole money from the till. Indeed it was safe from him nowhere. He had always been trouble enough, but it had not been her concern until she married his father. She had a money-box of her own. She had started it fifteen years ago. She had hidden it under the beams of the roof and had left it there, even after she married — one never could tell what might happen in life; and recently when she had wanted to add something to it . . . it was gone! Luigino was gone too. After ten days he had returned. He had gone to the great city, to Bologna, to have a good time. They had all hoped he would never come back. Vacca could no longer beat him. She, she had beaten the lout when he returned. With a brutal laugh he had turned out his empty pockets, and — you would hardly credit it — had struck her back. She would rather sink into the ground than say a word about it to a living soul. Marietta could see — great bruises on her breast and on her legs. Bad language, and drinking himself stupid: those were his occupations all day and every day. It was wearing her out. She could no longer do the work she used to do. Last week, when there were a great many guests, Vacca had called in that girl of Brogi's to help; and to-day he had suggested they should take her on permanently in the spring, when they got busy. It didn't mean much more expense, because naturally she was prepared to come for board and the tips . . .

Yes, yes . . . Things took strange turns in life. There she sat now, beside Marietta, who was a married woman and lived just under Camilla. Nana simply couldn't understand it. She had been so sure that Marietta would rise higher and higher, and in the end perhaps leave Todi. Nana would have watched her go with tearful eyes, and would have remembered with pride that the child had come to her for protection and found it. She was profoundly disappointed and dissatisfied over this marriage with Antonio the coffinmaker. He was no doubt a good, well-conducted boy; but after all he was only Antonio the coffinmaker, son of old Buongiorno. And now everyone was saying, at the well, that Marietta was unhappy because her mother-in-law tyrannized over her, and had her son tied to her apron-strings, and naturally wanted to live with them as soon as the old man was dead. When Nana heard that, something had awakened in her which she thought had gone forever: she thought that one more opportunity had been granted her by God to protect Marietta. She had come here to-day to hear the truth. She might not be equal to standing up to a seventeen-year-old lout with rough, clumsy fists, but . . .

Marietta declined her offer. She did not believe that Nana could help her, and she did not want her intervention. On the contrary, she pitied her, and it certainly did Nana infinite good to talk about herself. . . . So much so that she almost forgot the purpose of her visit, and began to feel as though she had come to seek consolation and not to give it. She decided it was time to be getting back to Vacca, back to the old kitchen where Luigino now ruled, as he did everywhere in the inn. She could do nothing against him. Her strength was broken.

Nana's visit was not a bright one. Sometimes her words had not penetrated to Marietta — she heard only her voice, burdened with the sadness of life that came streaming out of all these great houses to meet her. She thought of how different it had seemed when she was engaged to Antonio and they sat together in the evenings upon the bench in the piazzetta, the spring sky above them.

When Falcometti the stonemason played his cornet in the evening, Marietta stood still to listen. Such an intense longing welled up within her that she felt her legs tremble under her. She remembered that she had experienced this same longing as a child in Vacca's inn — the longing, growing to desperation, to get away at once, away from everything.

After the evening meal, when Antonio and she were sitting silently together, she got up from her chair and opened the cupboard in which she kept her clothes. Antonio, a prey to a vague anxiety that had been haunting him for weeks, observed her kneel down and gather this and that together from the lower drawers, keeping out some things and putting back others.

"What are you looking for, Marietta?" he asked at length. She stared at him like a sleepwalker: had she thought herself alone in the room? She put everything back hastily and returned to the table. "I don't know, my-self," she admitted in confusion. She sat silent afterwards, wondering what she had been looking for. She had intended to find the little package that Nana had brought her when she was in the convent, the things that had come from her mother. . . . But as she had stood before the cupboard, she had begun to put things together. . . . Was she thinking at that mo-

ment of going away? Could she go away? Where? It was the very question that Antonio had asked her once, and she had found no answer.
Where?

Camilla, the wife of Cesare the carrier, was a regular visitor. She lived just above Marietta. She was pregnant again, and that gave her a feeling of importance. For a long time Camilla could not bring herself to take Marietta seriously. When Cesare was at home, she was inclined in any case to be rather truculent with the other inhabitants of the house, feeling herself above them for some unaccountable reason. But when her husband had gone upon his journey, early on Monday mornings, she discovered that she was lonely on her exalted pedestal; and towards the end of the week, as the moment of his homecoming approached, she felt faint-hearted and nervous, and cast about for something, someone to hold on to. Thus it was that she came sailing in to Marietta asking, "May I come in, child? It's so restful here with you. Susanna's looking after the children. She still has to put Carlo and Teresina to bed. I couldn't, really I couldn't do any more — just look at me." This was said in a tone of tragic accusation, and with a sigh. Camilla was as large and heavy as she had ever been. She was growing slatternly — she who had formerly prided herself upon her neatness. Her eyes were slightly bleared, and had a helpless look. "One shouldn't go on having children continually — it's a bad arrangement," she complained. "You've been married six months already, and there's nothing wrong with you yet. Am I right? I can see it at once. . . . Yes, but Cesare and I were only just married when I was already white about the nose every morning. He'll be back soon — he's a bit late to-day. I needn't even be afraid of him now, because the misfortune has happened again — and yet as soon as Friday comes round I begin to tremble. It's always been so. I've never been able to get accustomed to it, to a man who's been on the road a week!"

Camilla held her hands over the fire. She was cold through and through, from nervousness. She was talking intimately to Marietta. Cesare did not always get what he wanted. She often said she was tired, terribly tired — and besides she usually was, with such a family. Fortunately he was a good soul. But it never failed to happen. They would wake up together in the middle of the night, and then she was not very alert, because she came out of her sleep so warm. Yes, and then she would sit for weeks in terror until she was sure again. If only Cesare would at least go sensibly about it. . . . Some men were sensible about such things. She had heard that from other women, but wouldn't she just happen upon Cesare, who was about as sensible as a small child. This was the very last time — she had sworn it. Eight children were enough. If she had any more, she would go crazy. She had made Cesare swear it to her. A man must come to his senses some time or other. He would be fifty at Whitsuntide. At that time of life, a man should remember that he has had his share . . . Fancy Cesare having had his share!

Why should she conceal it any longer from Marietta? She had set up Antonio as an example to him. "Look at a boy like that, who already has more sense than you. He wants to live economically. He doesn't want to have a train of children behind him while he still has to work for his sick father . . . And no children come, either. You go to Antonio. Have a talk with him, and see what you can get out of him." But that would not do for Cesare — he was much too shy. He was not too shy to bring eight children into the world, but he was too shy for that.

Camilla was silent, waiting for Marietta to reply. A few weeks ago Camilla's story might have moved Marietta profoundly, filled her with shame and despair; but now it passed over her — it perplexed her a little, that was all. Her desire to have a child by Antonio was dead. There were moments when she despised him. He had felt it, and slunk away like a beaten dog. For Camilla, too, she had only contempt at the moment. She looked at her with a faintly mischievous smile. Camilla, who had not expected that, suddenly saw again, as in a vision, the child who, after the death of Vacca's first wife, had listened silently to her revelations about her origin.

"What are you looking at me for?" she asked, put out. Marietta reassumed a demure expression, and told her the truth — that she had longed for a child, but that it would not come.

Camilla breathed again. She must have misunderstood Marietta's look. "Yes, yes, that happens sometimes too. That is something different." She raised her eyebrows in thought. Unexpectedly she was consoled. That would never have occurred to her, with two young people, but of course . . . Yes: one person has too much of what another would like. Against her will, she felt a sudden pride in her fruitfulness.

And then Camilla rose from her chair and waddled away like a scared goose: Cesare's cart was rolling into the courtyard.

No, Marietta no longer desired a child by Antonio. She was even pleased that she was alone, that she had nobody, nobody at all.

Once upon a time she had been afraid of the abyss. Now she was cured of her fear. Indeed, the abyss drew rather than repelled her. This realization gave her a sudden liberation from the leaden weight that had seemed to take away her breath, and filled her with the mysterious joy she had known as a child, muffled within her for years. If Antonio preferred to live with his mother rather than with her, that was his own affair.

Downstairs in the courtyard, Falcometti was again playing his evening melody. Marietta's longing wandered away upon the sighs of his cornet. When she thought of distances, she no longer thought of Venice as Monsignore had conjured it up before her. Still less of Rome, which Cesare represented as an infinitely greater Todi. No, she thought of distances as she had imagined them in her childhood. She pictured nothing at all, simply an endless flight, as a dream is a flight from reality. While Falcometti played soulfully on his cornet, she simply refused to acknowledge that one can flee only from one reality to another. She was already fleeing now, as she sat there in that room gazing out in front of her — and this flight was the great, new, liberating thing in her that nobody could take away.

One evening — the very evening which was to be the prelude to the whole stupid affair of her marriage with Antonio, who though married to her did not belong to her, the prelude to her finding herself in surroundings where she did not in the least belong — that memorable evening, Monsignore had said to her: "One day you will laugh at all this, Marietta." Had she reached that day? Could she now laugh at everything? A week ago, she had faced the death of Antonio's father with despair. Now only a proud, even a faintly mocking, smile played about her lips.

But the most surprising visit of all was to come. Next day, which was Sunday, Imma stood at her door. When Marietta saw the little woman step inside, she was so surprised that she forgot for a moment to greet her.

Imma laughed somewhat grimly. "Yes, it's me!" she said. "Do you mind if I sit down?"

Marietta pushed forward a chair, and Imma flopped down on it with a sigh, loosening her shawl meanwhile. "I'm surprised, myself, to be sitting here," she admitted. "If anyone had predicted it to me a month ago I should have asked him, 'I? Visiting Marietta? And who can that be, Marietta?'"

"I have often wanted to come," said Marietta, uncertainly.

"I understand. You've forgotten the way," said Imma, as though to smooth things over with a dry cynicism. "Monsignore still lives on the piazza near the cathedral. You remember the piazza?"

"How . . . is Monsignore?"

"Oh, well, very well, thank heaven! Why shouldn't he be all right? Oh, of course — I forgot: because you no longer sit at table with him."

Marietta gave her a penetrating look, a look that astonished Imma. Her answering glance was at once hostile and sad.

After a long pause, Imma asked — and in this question there lay her first willingness to negotiate, "If you've been on the point of dropping in so often — why haven't you? Were you afraid we should eat you up? After all, we could have done that long ago, while you still lived in the house with us and Monsignore treated you as though he were your father."

"I will come," promised Marietta, nervously.

Imma nodded; but Marietta puzzled her. If Marietta had assured her that she had not dared, that she was terribly sorry, that she was ashamed . . . But no, she seemed to feel nothing of the kind. Imma had no longer any understanding of her. The child had outgrown her. But though Marietta uttered no word of remorse, and though Imma did not understand Marietta's reserve, she knew that she could rely upon her promise. That was a load off Imma's old heart, and took away the acidity from her voice. "It's nearly six months since you left the house," she said, still reproachfully. Then she looked round the room, and added, "So this is where you live?"

"Yes. We live here."

"And your husband's workshop is downstairs?"

"Imma . . . Is Monsignore sad because I haven't been to see him?"

Imma found this a perplexing question. "Sad because of you?" she exclaimed. Then, when Marietta continued to look at her with those penetrating, desperately earnest eyes of hers, Imma relented and, mixing confession with reproach, said, "How can you ask? Of course you have made him sad. After all, you know, yourself, that he looked upon you as his child. Heaven will forgive him that sin, if there are no worse ones! Every Sunday he expected you, although he would not admit it to me. How could you think he wouldn't be sad about you? What else would have brought me here to-day after I had sworn to myself a thousand times I would never, never come near you?"

"I'll come with you now, Imma."

"No, you won't," broke in Imma, flaring up again. "Do you want it to go the round of the whole city that the bishop sent for Marietta because she would not come of herself? I'm already ashamed at the thoughts of all the people who may have been standing in the courtyard and saw me come up here. I waited till it was dark before leaving the house . . . But of course I had to ask a hundred times before I could find you. Just wait another day or two. Now that you've waited five months, half a week is neither here nor there. Do you hear? You're not going to thrust yourself upon us at once . . ."

The door opened, and Antonio came in hastily. The little woman, jumping up from her chair in alarm, resumed her seat again with a demure expression. Antonio barely greeted her. Too agitated to notice any visitor, he hurried towards Marietta, and whispered, "Father is throwing up blood."

Slowly, Marietta turned her face towards him, trying to understand the news with which he had so suddenly interrupted her conversation with Imma. Imma, all attention, listened with bowed head.

"It happened twice during the night, too. Mother did not mention it to us this morning, but just now while I was sitting beside him . . ." Antonio was wide-eyed at the recollection of that dreadful moment. He was still deathly pale; sweat stood on his forehead.

"I'll go over," promised Marietta, strangely self-possessed.

"Yes, all right . . . Then I'll run along to the piazza for Barberini." He spoke more collectedly. A heavy load must have fallen from his heart. "Good. Go to him. Father was unconscious a moment ago. The end will come to-day."

He spoke these last words with unwonted gravity, looking her straight in the face; and, though she averted her own, she understood that he had wanted to convince her by voice and look of the tragic importance of this hour, to break down her resistance by its weight. . . . He was not even aware that he was attempting to intimidate her. No, during all these anxious weeks, it must have been his hope that grief at the hour of death would bring her to repentance at last, that her unnatural aversion to his mother would abate in the softening effects of death. Now the great moment had come, then. Now his father was about to die, and his death would at least bring triumph to those who mourned it. "All right. Go then, Marietta. I shall be seeing you again in a few moments."

"Yes — in a moment. I'll go in a moment."

He rushed away again, as he had rushed in; and Imma, getting up from her chair embarrassed, prepared to go. She still wanted to say something — a word of sympathy . . . But it had looked as if that boy were almost pleased that his father was dying.

"Can I do anything?" she asked. "But perhaps I'd better go now. Don't be angry if I've spoken harshly to you to-day. It would happen, just to-day; but how was I to know? I knew he was ill, but . . . Child, are you very sad?"

"I don't know," replied Marietta, while Imma bent over her in compassion. "We've waited for it so long, Imma. I shall go along to him now." She got up. "Tell Monsignore that I shall come soon. Tell him. Greet him from me."

Imma wrung her hands. "Lord, Lord, how can I tell him that? Surely you must understand he knows nothing of this? He's celebrating vespers in the cathedral. If he knew I was here! At the very most, I could say I'd met you — but then he's sure to see when I'm lying. No, I'll tell him nothing."

At the door, she still chattered on, holding Marietta's hands. "You know, he's been in an awful state. He paces up and down his room, up and down, up and down . . . till late into the night. I lie listening upstairs in my bed. I can't sleep for thinking, when will she come — then perhaps he'll grow calm again. That marriage of yours, he didn't like it at all, Marietta. He wanted to hold you back. He's told me at least a dozen times that he just could not understand how you could have wished it."

"Did he say that, Imma?"

"Does that surprise you? I've never been able to understand it either, that you should . . . with this boy . . . Ah well, his father's dying. But think of the plans the bishop had for you. You would have lived like a lady, if you'd left it to him. When you were gone he snapped my head off. He didn't want to have anything to do with anybody. No more ladies were to cross his threshold. They wanted to confess, did they? They could go elsewhere. And then these dark days . . . Candles burning already at four o'clock, and we alone in that great house; and he won't take any servants. He will never hear of servants since the first and the second cheated and robbed him. We've always been alone together. But in the old days I never felt it."

She groped under her skirts until she found her handkerchief. She dried a tear, and turned her cheek to Marietta for a kiss. "Ah well, if you want consolation, you just come. I know now at any rate that you're still the same. I go away feeling happier than when I came."

Imma went.

Marietta was alone. Now she was alone. Now she must go to old Buongiorno, who was dying. She had promised Antonio; she must go. But after a time, she was still sitting there, unable to make up her mind to fulfill her promise. Antonio had allowed it to escape him that the old man was unconscious . . . Surely she needn't go there for the sake of Lucia.

Nervously, she stood by the door, and rebellion rose in her. Why must she go to Buongiorno? Had he asked for her? She had sat by him and talked to him while the others passed by his bed. They had nothing more to say to one another, and certainly not when Antonio and his mother were about. She had already seen the old man dying. Already, that first time when she had visited him, and he had asked her to marry his son . . . Death lay on his features then, when she withdrew in fear from his entreaty. She had seen him dying in her dreams . . . Oh, how often! It had become a nightmare to her, this dying of an old, tormented man, and the comedy that his wife and son would enact in the face of death, to soften her and make her agree to their plan.

She was not going. Even if Antonio came to fetch her — she would not go.

Things would be easier for old Buongiorno in his last moments alone with his wife and his son. He would have forgotten her, as he had done that evening a few weeks before. She could no longer wait to go to the bishop. Everything was drawing her towards the old palace on the piazza. She could not wait, though Imma had ordered her to. Now that she knew Monsignore was suffering for her sake, she could no longer wait. Imma had conjured him up before her again, large, living, a sorrowful giant. His eyes were upon her, his sad, reproachful eyes. Whither could she flee from those eyes? There was no hiding place, not in this house, not in the whole world. She could only hurry to him and throw herself down beside him.

She felt already how warmly he would receive her . . . The world about her fell away. Her marriage with Antonio, this house where she had never belonged, fell away . . . There was nothing left but Monsignore and herself, Monsignore and herself!

It had been foolish pride in her to think that there was nothing for her to do in life but to smile at its bitterness. Life was great and powerful and full of a deep seriousness, now that Imma had told her Monsignore was waiting for her. The promise she had given to Antonio was small and of no importance. It was like something given to a beggar — half from compassion, and half to get rid of him.

She threw her woollen shawl round her, listened for a moment scarcely breathing — then hurried, feeling her way along the walls, through the dark corridor and down the stairs. She crossed the courtyard and went through the cold, draughty, deserted streets towards the piazza . . . It crossed her mind vaguely that a young married woman should not be going along the streets at that hour alone. She shivered and ran on, in her anxiety lest she be seen, spoken to — ran on faster and faster until she reached the piazza.

A biting wind was sweeping across the square. She did not notice it. She did not feel the cold. Strangely grand and gray, like a ghostly building, the episcopal palace reared itself up on the other side . . . The whole world was gray and ghostly. But what was the world to her? A ray of light streamed through a crack between the curtains on the first floor:

Monsignore was in his study. Perhaps he was busy writing letters. She hurried through the entrance and knocked at the kitchen door.

Imma, who had only just got back, looked out of the window in astonishment, and went hastily to open the door. "Didn't I tell you . . ." she began, but she did not finish her sentence. "Oh, well, all right. You're here now. Perhaps it's better so." She closed the door again; with unexpected tenderness she threw her arms around Marietta. "Didn't you go to see your father-in-law after all?" she asked hurriedly, and then continuing at once; "Here she comes, all by herself in the dark! Well now, go up at once, but not a word to him about my having been to you."

A moment ago, in the dusk of the street, Marietta had known no hesitation. Now she was suddenly uncertain. "Imma . . . You go and ask him first. I dare not go like this."

"I'm not going to ask him anything. I won't have anything to do with it. You just talk it out together. I'm not going upstairs. Don't be afraid that I shall come upstairs. Do you understand? I shall leave you alone . . ."

Imma put a strange emphasis on the assurance that she would not come upstairs, and that Marietta could rely upon being left undisturbed in her conversation with the bishop — and she gave her a look as she said it, lest Marietta had not understood her. But Marietta evaded her glance, and Imma was reassured. She opened the door, and, with the kitchen lamp in her hand, stood in the doorway to light Marietta up the stairs. In Imma's voice and demeanor, there was a peculiar theatrical gravity.

"Go now — I'll hold the light up until you're inside."

Marietta, beside herself with nervousness, obeyed. Her legs were trembling. . . . She was upstairs. A door opened and a large, dark silhouette loomed in front of her: Monsignore. Downstairs, the light moved stealthily away. Imma had withdrawn into the kitchen.

Perhaps Marietta would have collapsed if Monsignore had not supported her. But that gave her peace. She felt safe. She found herself sitting on the divan, and it crossed her mind suddenly that it had been moved from the confession room . . . Then slowly she raised her eyes towards the face she knew so well. She saw that his mouth was murmuring her name. .

"*Babbo*," she whispered back.

"Are you better now? Shall I get Imma to bring you something?"

She shook her head. She felt her hand resting in his. She looked down at their two hands, quickly, secretly. Then, as she sat on the divan with bent head, motionless and scarcely daring to breathe, the thought went rushing through her mind that perhaps she ought to ask his forgiveness for having remained away so long. She could not find words — did he expect them? When, hesitating and confused, she looked up a second time, she read only gladness in his face. She found she could not take her eyes from his. They were lost in each other's eyes. Then, slowly, the happiness of being together again brought a smile to both their mouths. It was unbelievable that they had not seen each other for six months . . . it seemed no longer than a day.

"*Babbo* . . . how are you?" she asked, and, her joy turning suddenly to boldness, with a half-childlike, half-womanly gesture, such as she had never attempted before, she ran her hand over his cheek.

He closed his eyes under her caress, and tried to smile. "I have missed you," he admitted, unasked. "I have wanted so much to see you here again."

That, fortunately, sounded quite natural. He was glad he had been able to say it like that, with fatherly feeling — he had been afraid for a moment that something mad might escape him. He seized her wrist, to make sure she did not caress his cheek again. Then, gradually daring to believe again in his own sedateness towards her, he put her questions, serious questions. She heard how serious they were, and answered them with equal seriousness. That a smile continued to hover about her lips did not in any way detract from the seriousness of her answers.

It was more than a relief to get everything off her mind. She spoke without reserve, she seldom hesitated, and then only over something that was not yet quite clear to her. She did not conceal her struggle with Lucia, or its exceeding bitterness at times. She told him clearly of her disappointments, of her despair. As she told her story, it was amazing that so much misery could spring from a mistake. Fortunately the misery was over now, and for the moment no longer affected her. It was as though it had happened in a strange and foreign land from which she had now safely returned home to the old familiar room.

No — she did not suffer any more. He was suffering. When she noticed how he suffered, she was alarmed. But she could not conceal the truth from him, for all that. He had asked for it, and perhaps it was a good thing he should hear it now — later on they could laugh about it together.

He ceased to ask her questions — just let her go on talking until she came to an end. He rested his head in his hands so that she could not see his eyes.

So she had come to him, not to console him a little in his miserable loneliness, as he had sometimes hoped she would in moments of vain weakness. No, she had come to him to place her fate in his guilty hands.

"*Babbo*, I have struggled with all my might. Now I can't do any more. You must help me" — and he knew that he could not, that with all his

power and influence he could not build up happiness where she had failed.
Even if he summoned that boy to him and took him in hand as he had
never taken anybody in hand before: Do you know what you're throwing away, you young lunatic? How old are you? Aren't you old enough
yet to be a man and to know that one must defend one's wife — and what
a wife — against a thousand selfish mothers? . . . And if the sinner did
go away with tears in his eyes and the most sacred promises to amend, *he*
would know how much those tears and promises would be worth. Besides, the boy could stand up to his mother even less than could Marietta.

He had realized the position already, when mother and son had visited
him for the first time, and when that Niobe, petrified with grief, had said,
"Kiss your betrothed." At a glance he had fathomed it, and still he had
not had the strength to . . . Ah well, he had reproached himself often
enough for that already, and now the train of unhappy events was accomplished. Before his pitiless imagination the whole drama of this struggle was re-enacted. It was with difficulty that he restrained his tears when
he thought of the humiliations and torments she must have suffered, the
responsibility for which lay with him.

A gust of grim rage swept over him. As she sat there beside him, he
would have liked to press her to his breast, to protect her against the world
he knew so well in its venomous harshness and its base cowardice . . .
Only God could tell whether she too longed for that without herself being aware of the longing. But all he could do was to use his influence as a
priest and as a father; and of its inadequacy he was only too convinced.

She had finished. Stillness descended upon the room. Downstairs Imma
was noisily rattling plates. Why did Imma do that? Oh . . . that he might
know she was not standing behind the door listening. Yes, Marietta was
waiting for him to speak. Suppose he were to begin by proving to her
that it was he she had to thank for her misfortune.

He felt her hands upon his — she was trying to draw them away from
his eyes. He moved away from her, his face burning with shame. Then
suddenly he heard her voice again, speaking with impatient, almost happy
commiseration.

"*Babbo* . . . Why do you do that? After all, I'm pleased that everything has turned out like this . . ." Perplexed, he raised his head.

"Pleased?"

"Don't you believe me?"

"How can I believe that?"

"It's quite true."

She shook her head slowly, even teasingly. There was a mysterious
sparkle in her eyes that he had never noticed there before. She added, "I

don't know, myself, why it should be; but it is so." Gradually a more serious, thoughtful tone crept into her voice. "I don't care any more about everything that has happened, because I cannot help thinking all the time that, had it not happened — perhaps I should not be sitting here beside you . . ."

His laugh was bitter. "All the same, Marietta, I think I should have preferred . . ."

But she was no longer listening to him. "And you actually wanted me to go away altogether, to Venice!" she cried, with genuine surprise. "Well, fortunately, I'm still here . . . And yet I've been so far away . . . Yes, isn't it as if I had been a very long way away? *Babbo* — what does it all mean? Why is it everything should be as it is, could not be anything else? What is it, *Babbo*, what is it?" A wild agitation, joy and grief rang together in her voice. She covered her face with her hands and, scarcely realizing what she was doing, sank against him.

His lips paled, as he laid his arm about her.

"Marietta! My child! I will help you, I shall help you," he promised, and in his despair he vaguely realized that perhaps she did not want him to promise that at all. No, he had been mistaken: it was not for that she had come to him. She really had come to bring him consolation in his loneliness. But had she no idea of the fight he had to make when she threw herself into his arms? Had she forgotten that other evening? Or had she perhaps come . . . because she had *not* forgotten that evening? At that moment, nothing of his priesthood remained but the somewhat foolish garb he wore. Yet he must save her: that was the last duty of his conscience towards her.

And he asked her one more question: "Marietta. Tell me one thing: do you . . . After everything that has happened between you — do you still love your husband?"

A little devil chortled in his ear at this ridiculous question: surely Marietta must hear the insincerity, the clumsy jealousy that lurked in it. He wanted — of course he wanted to hear her say again: "*Babbo*, I love you, nobody else but you, only you, *Babbo*, only you . . ."

She looked up at him, and he read her reply in her eyes. He kissed her thirsty, longing mouth: all their struggles were engulfed in the blaze of sin that encompassed them.

It was night — a timeless, eternal night in which worlds were born and passed away. A night of horizons shot with lightning, a windswept night redolent of magic herbs. Then a mysterious stillness descended upon it, and the deep wisdom of dreamland. Out of such a magical night, Monsignore awoke, and did not know whether this awakening by the light of two guttering candles was not merely a part of his dream. Memories of his youth rose up, long-forgotten memories. "Marietta . . . my love," he murmured as he saw her lying with closed eyes in his arms, and he hardly dared listen himself as he uttered that last word, that last sinful word.

As a boy, he had murmured it quietly to himself one night, thinking the while of a little girl in Piombino. What was that little girl's name? . . . It had been Marietta, and the coincidence almost made his heart burst with senseless joy, as it had threatened to burst in his boyhood.

"Marietta . . . my love." It was childish that such a mysterious shiver should go through him at the utterance of that word — a word he had not dared to use for thirty years. The common property of all men, for him it was new — "Marietta . . . my sweet little one . . . my love."

Everything was new in this wonderful awakening. His whole life, as the years had formed and transformed it, had slipped away from him. He was purified and rejuvenated — so young that for a moment he had the illusion that this life had still to be stormed and conquered. What a dream this was, the most wonderful dream of his life!

The last dream, he thought to himself, while a bitter melancholy pervaded his whole being.

The last dream.

He looked down upon Marietta as she lay there in his arms, a mysterious smile about her serene mouth. He still could not understand what had so stirred and overcome him.

This child of a year ago had become a woman able to give him sweetness and oblivion, able to desire him, to undo him, and then to take him under her protection. Once he had taken her under his: an insignificant accident, but a blessed one.

In silent contemplation, he marveled at the beauty of her young body. She herself had opened her dress in the simplicity of her surrender. Her skin was smooth and cool and, in the soft candlelight, radiant as a flower. Was this contemplation sin? Then sin was life itself, and the compensation of life.

Sin was worth a heavy atonement; and he was prepared to atone. But the moment of atonement had not yet arrived. This hour still belonged to both of them, this hour was still theirs alone.

Was she waking up? He did not move, no — he did not move, although he noticed that the arm on which her head was resting was numb. Could she see through her closed eyelids that he was engrossed by her gentle, heaving bosom, by the innocent seduction of her breast? She uncovered her small white gleaming teeth for a moment. How alluring. Was she laughing at him? She might: it did him good that she should. The smile slipped from her face: it became childishly pure and innocent.

Yes, this child had brought him the gift of sin, this child who was a woman, the woman whom he loved.

Yet another candle in the candelabrum went out . . . What time was it, he wondered? Wouldn't Imma be coming upstairs at last? And would she not be amazed to see them sitting here in the half-light? He smiled to himself. Marietta had whispered to him — and her eyes were large and confused and grave as she said it, "Imma won't come upstairs . . ."

And now it would seem that Imma really was not coming upstairs. It must be long past her bedtime. That was another mystery added to all the rest: how did Marietta know that she would not come upstairs? Imma must have told her. Oh, Imma! Imma who for twenty years had stood in his way with her troublesome watchfulness, defiantly reminding him of his priestly vows. . . .

Oh, Imma, Imma!

Marietta awoke. It was strange that they — two people in a world that for the moment had no significance — need no longer feel shame towards each other, that they could at last exchange the caresses and endearments of lovers unafraid.

It was striking midnight. Twelve strokes boomed from the deserted cathedral. He half sat up, listened, left the divan, looked outside through the velvet curtains at the moon riding a purple heaven.

Then, turning away from the window, he renewed the burned-out candles. He wanted light, abundant light. He wanted to look at Marietta, make his eyes drunk with her . . .

But when he returned to her, she was no longer what she had been. She was sitting up, resting on her hand, and seemed in a brooding, earnest mood. The night was still young, but she was thinking of the day that must break. He tried to deflect her thoughts. Why think of the day already? The day is cruel, Marietta. "Yes; but it must come, *Babbo*."

He felt skeptical of the future, almost indifferent. He was only too well aware that when this night was over he would have had his share of earthly bliss. He was prepared to be satisfied with it, for the rest of his life. No more then of the approaching day! It was still night. Nothing yet need stand in the way of their happiness.

But she could not reason like that — she was a woman. Surely it was not true that with the daylight their brief happiness must end? She could not believe it, she would not believe it. Despair transfixed her. "*Babbo* . . . But we shall see one another again." No one would think it wrong if she visited the episcopal palace more often — she had slept under it long enough. She made plans, barely conscious that she was doing so — clever plans, ingenious plans. He listened to her, to the agitated voice of an enamored woman, and at first a faint renewed hope awakened in him, too. (Renunciation would, perhaps, weigh more heavily upon him than he realized.) But then he was amazed at her: he could hardly follow her as, outrunning him by far, she brushed aside the qualms that made him still falter. She trampled down every objection, without giving it a moment's thought. She had but one purpose: to ensure the continuance of their love.

He laughed gently, caressingly at her insistence, and suddenly she realized his reluctance. She was shocked so deeply that she broke off in the middle of a phrase. He tried to soothe her; but she was oblivious to his arguments. She seemed scarcely to have appreciated the bearing and gravity of her words, words that had been spoken in a kind of intoxication from which she had been abruptly awakened by his laugh.

He fell silent. Something very near to bitterness welled up in him. Why must she think now of to-morrow? Her insistence was making their love almost commonplace. Could she not understand that it could never be an affair of every day? *He* wanted to renounce, he wanted this exquisite experience to remain unique, unassailable.

It had been all beauty, when she lay in his arms, smiling in her sleep . . . Then reality had seemed a dream, and a dream reality. Perhaps a woman should be asleep and smile in order to be perfect.

"Marietta," he said beseechingly, hoping she would understand that he had no wish to hurt her, that she was wasting the short night of their happiness. He took her in his arms again, entreatingly.

She did not resist, neither did she surrender. It was as if life had altogether departed from her. Her great eyes stood tired and expressionless in her face. When he looked at her, doubtfully, she turned her face away.

And then Imma came.

There she came, stamping upstairs. A fit of coughing seized her in the passage. She knocked at the door and said, while she was still outside, that it was only she, Imma; and then she came in. She did not glance at the divan, but turned immediately to the straight-backed chair behind the writing table where she might have expected to see Monsignore sitting, and announced that Antonio had come, and had asked her whether by any chance his wife was there, and that she had said she really didn't know, but she would go upstairs and inquire.

When she had finished, she waited expecting Monsignore to order the intruder to be shown the door.

It was a moment before Monsignore grasped the situation. Then he said: "Let him come up, Imma. How could you have come up first to ask whether . . . ? Let him come up at once."

As he spoke, Imma saw for herself that it was not possible to turn him away. . . . After all, he was within his rights. Naturally, she could also have let him come upstairs at once — Monsignore's remark was very true. As she departed again, she cast an innocent, investigating look in Marietta's direction.

A few seconds only remained to them. Monsignore looked at Marietta urgently, wanting to exchange with her some warm, parting word before her husband came upstairs. But she appeared not to see him — she only listened with wide eyes to the sounds that reached them from below.

Disturbed, he got up from his chair. He would not sit and act the priest when he received her husband this time.

It was over, over. Now it was over. He could have borne that if it had been only her husband who had come between them, if only she had remained his to this last moment. But what kind of parting was this? What had he done to her that she should abandon him when he was most in need of her understanding — if only to save appearances? God, how she sat there, on that divan! As a woman, could she not realize that she ought not to remain sitting on that divan when her husband was about to come in? Must he also tell her to brush away the hairs from her cheek? Her dress she had fortunately closed while he renewed the candles. . . .

"Yes . . . come in." He raised his voice, to convince himself that he was equal to the situation. Antonio stood on the threshold, shy and embarrassed, with Imma holding up the lamp from behind him, lighting him upstairs as though she were a gaoler and he a prisoner.

"Come in, Antonio," repeated Monsignore, stifling with difficulty a sudden warmth in his voice . . . In spite of himself, the mere sight of this boy awakened fatherly feelings in him that, under the circumstances, were ridiculous and brought a flush of shame to his cheeks.

Uncertainly, Antonio came forward. Had he but known how powerfully human right rose up behind him, he would perhaps not have bent his head so low. Monsignore looked at him penetratingly. It did not elude him that Antonio gave one glance at his wife, then lowered his eyes and colored. That had not been necessary. She might have spared her husband — and him also. He had thought that this once he would be secure from betrayal; but there was such a thing as betrayal without words. Must she, just she, commit it?

Antonio knelt before him, but Monsignore raised him brusquely from the ground, saying curtly, "Get up, get up."

Speaking quickly and clumsily, Antonio excused himself for coming at this late hour. "The doctor is with Father, Monsignore. We expect the end to-night. I have come to fetch Marietta. I thought she might perhaps be here — that she might have returned with . . ."

He looked round towards Imma, who, still carrying the lamp, had taken her place in front of the closed door, and now opened her eyes wide. "Returned with whom?"

Antonio, taken aback, looked from one to the other, not knowing how to proceed. Again he looked towards Imma, who stood there by the door as though barring the way to him. How strangely quiet it was in the room! He looked apprehensively at Marietta, hoping to read in her face whether he had fallen into an ambush, and was now standing as an accused before his judges.

"Yes. Marietta told me your father is dying," said Monsignore.

Antonio slowly turned his eyes away from Marietta, and then answered, "She knew it, Monsignore."

Marietta appeared to be slowly waking up. "Yes, I knew it," she said softly, repeating his words. His reproach was not displeasing to her. She had also noticed what he had said as he came in. He might have said, "I have come to fetch my wife," but instead he had chosen to say, "I have come to fetch Marietta."

Then Monsignore remarked, "It will be a heavy blow for you, Antonio — and a greater one for your mother."

Antonio shrank a little at this last word, and waited a moment before answering stiffly: "Yes, for Mother most of all, Monsignore."

And then there was renewed silence in the room.

The moment had arrived. Monsignore would tell him that he must not do this thing to his wife, must not bring his mother into their home. Marietta had realized, at Monsignore's question about the dying father, in what direction he was steering; and something rose up in rebellion within her. Why shouldn't Antonio bring his mother into his home? Why shouldn't he — if that was his will? She wondered how Antonio would answer him. He did not seem at all nervous; to-night he appeared to have grown older, more manly. If that were the case, — if to-night he had become a man, — would he allow himself to be dictated to by the bishop — or by his wife, as to what he should do in his own home?

Oh, Monsignore looked at her, asking her with his eyes for her authority to speak. And why should she give it him? He also was a man . . . He also should know what to do and what not to do. Perhaps he was thinking that this was, after all, an affair that concerned only herself; but he had better think of his own affairs. He had better consider whether, at this moment, he was not losing something, had perhaps already lost it — something that was precious to him, or so he had thought.

But Imma continued to wait for Monsignore to speak, Imma who still stood belligerently by the door. Yet her faith in her hero had been shaken. She had firmly counted upon his knowing better how to protect one he loved against this rascal, this jackanapes who had the temerity to intrude on him after midnight and make a scene about his wife. Instead of giving the intruder a piece of his mind, however, he was pacing up and down, up and down — pacing up and down and looking grim. Imma herself could have done as much.

And then the young bounder had the presumption to break in upon his meditations with, "Forgive me, Monsignore. We must go now. Otherwise we shall be too late."

Marietta got up from the divan. Monsignore observed her movement with a side glance, and said (yes, he did say something at last), "In that case, I must detain you no longer."

They stood up, all three of them. The moment of separation had come. There was still one last hope in Marietta — she did not herself know exactly what she was hoping. It was as if she had completely lost her will. If Antonio told her to follow him, she would do so. But if Monsignore said, Remain — and if then it pleased Antonio to leave the house without his wife — then she could not do otherwise than remain. Monsignore of course said nothing of the kind — how could he? Consequently she must go with Antonio, who had come to fetch her. She wondered whether Antonio was restraining himself only for the sake of Monsignore and Imma; whether perhaps he had sworn when he found that his wife had left their home . . . He never swore, but perhaps for once he had, and had vowed to himself that he would bring her back if he had to go and fetch her from the portals of hell.

Surely he must have seen what she had done to him that evening. Of course he had seen it — one look was enough; and if not, she would tell him, in a moment when they were together outside. Then he could decide whether he wanted her back.

He took leave of Monsignore, who wished him strength for the coming ordeal. But it was not Antonio who needed strength: it was Monsignore — the strength to be alone.

Marietta kissed his hand after her husband, and as she raised herself again, she read in his eyes a dumb, desperate question. What were his eyes asking her? If she would come back? And shortly? He had laughed when she had spoken of that. Or were his eyes only begging her to forgive him for having mortally wounded her heart and humiliated it? Oh . . . If that would please him — why not? She lowered her gaze and followed Antonio. Behind them came Imma with her lamp.

Silently they descended the stairs.

Imma said not a word as she let them out. For a moment Marietta was grieved: did Imma say nothing only because she knew that Marietta would never come back again?

Marietta seized her hand, but Imma did not respond. The expression on her old face was cold, dour, and set, and grew more so because Antonio happened to look round . . .

Across the piazza, lit by the moon, went Marietta and Antonio together. Her husband's broad frame protected Marietta a little from the wind. She expected that he would speak when they reached the narrower streets.

Why did he continue to be silent? Since Monsignore had let her go she had felt herself wavering . . . oh, even before Antonio had arrived. If only Antonio could take advantage of this moment of dreadful abandonment she would be grateful to him for the rest of her life; if only he would dare to be her master now, she would recognize his authority ever after — that she knew.

The thought of his first words made her tremble. She hungered for them, hoped for them, hoped that they would sweep over her, through her like a tornado, that he would beat her down with his contumely and dark rage, and when the storm had passed would raise her up again because his love was all the stronger. She waited, waited. Why was he in such a hurry? Oh, yes . . . his father was dying. But she could not walk so quickly. She could not, she could not. In a moment they would reach home, and not a word would have passed between them . . .

Then suddenly he did speak, and she knew that she had hoped in vain, that the storm she had waited for with longing terror would not break. Antonio was reproachful, not fierce. He asked her sadly, unable to overcome his wounded feelings, "Why did you do that, Marietta? I was coming back with Barberini . . ."

"I suddenly couldn't prevent myself from going to Monsignore," she excused herself lightly. "He had been expecting me a long time, Imma said."

Antonio was silent, perplexed, trying to understand her tone. "But you promised me," he said weakly.

"Yes, that is so."

He looked down at her. "Are you laughing at me, Marietta?"

"I don't know. I don't think so," she said, and then she laughed. "But did you go looking for me?" she asked, turning the conversation.

"Naturally I looked for you," he cried, an angry note in his voice. "At Cerio's, at Camilla's, although I knew you never went there. I asked after you everywhere in the house . . . and I was ashamed."

"And . . . then?"

"Then? Well, then it fortunately occurred to me that you might have gone along with that old servant."

"Why fortunately?"

"What's wrong with you, Marietta? I said fortunately because then I had an idea where you might be."

"Oh, yes."

"And then later on, an hour or so ago, Father recovered consciousness. The first thing he noticed was that you were not in the room."

"And then you came to fetch me."

"Yes . . . then I came to fetch you, because Father wanted to say something to you, Marietta."

"Because your father still wanted to say something to me, you came and fetched me?"

"Yes, that's why, and for a hundred other reasons too. Can't you see reason, Marietta? Why must you go to Monsignore's just this evening? Go and complain to him about Mother? Ask him to help you to prevent her from coming to us? I noticed well enough when I got there. But now she shall come, do you hear? She shall come. It is my will that she shall. It isn't she who wishes it, as you're always thinking, but I, I." His voice was growing husky, "And you yourself shall ask Mother."

Marietta did not reply, but went on looking in front of her with an almost amused expression. Antonio lost his assurance and added weakly, "Marietta, I shall go crazy if you behave like this. Lord, what an evening . . . what a night! I can't talk about it any more now. We can do that later on."

Marietta nodded to herself. Later on . . . He would talk about it again later on. He had not beaten her, though she might have deserved it. He had not even cursed her. He had just flared up against her, and then his anger had blown over again immediately, and he would talk about it again later on . . . But not about her having gone away from him for another man. He had not even noticed that. Ah well, he had certainly said to himself: A bishop. He's a bishop. But not every man would have been so easily reassured. And even before he knew for certain where she had gone, he had not been anxious . . . Not anxious enough to leave his father's deathbed. When he had returned at dusk and had not found her at home or with his parents or anywhere in the great house, he had said to himself, Probably she has gone with that old servant of the bishop's. Yes, that's what he had thought. And later on he would talk with her about his mother.

Oh, it was the old story . . . she knew it well enough already. And now she could not think any more. Without will, without thought she followed him towards their home, because she did not know what else to do. Perhaps something would occur to her later on, later while he was carrying out his intention of talking with her about his mother.

They had reached the courtyard of the house, to be greeted at the foot of the staircase by an almost ludicrous occurrence. Barberini and a father confessor — the fat father confessor from the priests' house of San Jacopo, well known for his readiness to grant absolution — were leaving the house together talking in muffled tones. The father confessor was still standing on the lowest stair, in one hand an oil lantern, the other hand resting on Barberini's shoulder, and he was telling a humorous story to which Barberini was listening with an incredulous expression. As Antonio appeared, the father confessor cut himself short in the middle of his story, transferred his hand from Barberini's shoulder to Antonio's, and said with a wonderful transition from jovial profanity to grave piety, "My son, fortify yourself. Your father is no more. But he has received extreme unction, and the prayers for the dying have been said over him . . ."

Antonio smothered a cry, and hurried past the two men up the dark stairs.

Whereupon the father confessor, whose hand had suddenly been left without support, wanted to replace it on Barberini's shoulder, and bring his story to an end. But at that moment he discovered Marietta, who had been standing on one side. He raised his lantern towards her face, and, recognizing her, he offered, not without a certain gallantry, to light her up the stairs and conduct her to the door of the death chamber. He was sincerely disappointed when, instead of accepting this offer, she hurried past him with bowed head. Astonished, his lantern still raised, he looked after her.

She stood before the room where old Buongiorno had just passed away — her hand was already resting on the handle. Then she hesitated, looked round cautiously into the passage. Was she afraid somebody would see her? But who, at that hour? Antonio's mother was not the sort of woman to summon her neighbors when her husband was about to die, and of their own accord they would not have gone up: for everybody in the great house, the old man had long been dead.

Nobody, nobody in the passage . . . Of course not. Carefully she let go of the handle again, and on tiptoe slipped away to her own rooms.

They were lit up by moonlight; there was no need for a lamp. Grigio, awakened with a shock by the unexpected opening of the door, jumped from the highest perch, on which he always went to sleep, down to the lowest perch, and cooed restlessly. All day Grigio had been agitated. He had lived so long among human beings that he was always aware when anything unusual was on foot. Marietta closed the door behind her, and looked round as though she could not quite believe that she had really returned there. Then she sat down at the table. She stared an unaccountable time into the moonlight; finally laid down her tired head upon her arms, and closed her eyes. A little later she began to cry.

Then suddenly she raised her head. Footsteps were creaking in the passage — Antonio's footsteps. He opened the door, looked into the room, came in.

"Do you still refuse to come?" he asked her gently in a tired voice. She shook her head, but perhaps he could not see that in the half-darkness.

"Are you angry because I left you standing there alone?" he asked. "I should not have done that. I'm sorry."

She did not stir.

"I was beside myself . . . You must be able to understand that," he complained.

There was silence. He tried to see her face. His own was drawn with grief. He tried again to bring her to speak. "Or are you perhaps just afraid to see Father — now that he's dead? It's just as if he were sleeping peacefully."

"I'm not afraid of seeing a dead person . . . I've already seen dead people more than once," she said.

He was grateful to hear her voice at last. "Well . . . Come then, Marietta."

Then she looked at him for the first time, and asked, "Did your mother send you?"

"No, that's not so," he said defensively, sad and embarrassed. Then, getting the better of himself, he came closer and bent over her. "Marietta, come. I've suffered so dreadfully to-day, and all these days. Let everything be right between us all, to-night at least. Mother is there crying . . ."

"And I'm here crying. Didn't you notice?" She tried to make the question sound harsh, but her voice was small and filled with a self-pity that made her feel ashamed.

"Of course I saw that . . . of course I did," he answered hastily. He was so glad at her seeming to relent a little, even if involuntarily. He was on the point of crying himself. He seized her hand and kissed it, although she tried to draw it away. He went and sat beside her at the table and began to cry with her, stammering her name, "Marietta . . ."

There was silence around them. Grigio in his cage had turned his little head sideways to listen and was peering down at them.

Once more that night a new shy hope burgeoned forth in Marietta's heart. It did her good to have him sitting by her, just sitting by her alone. She was content with so little that evening . . . just a little quiet intimacy.

Will he remain with me, thought Marietta. Will he remain with me? She hardly dared believe it yet. But he sat so still, crying, his head resting on his hand. He was tired, and was resting beside her. She looked down upon his head . . .

Her unreasoning hope grew and grew in the wide, formless dusk of the silent night. If only he would remain with her . . .

But no, he did not remain. Of course he did not remain. How could she have expected it? She noted the first indications of reawakening agitation. It had been but a momentary intoxication . . .

Of her own accord, she withdrew her hand from his.

As if to excuse himself, he moaned, "Mother is alone."

"She's not alone. Her husband is with her."

"Marietta! But Father is . . ."

"He's with her all the same. But where are you? You are not with me. You leave me alone. You just go now."

Beaten, he got up saying tonelessly, "If you won't come with me, I must go alone."

"Yes, do your duty."

"Marietta . . . Is it perhaps *not* my duty?"

"Perhaps it is. But that's not why you do it. Just go now, please."

"Tell me . . . why are you so cruel to me?"

"I'm not cruel. You are. Go now."

"I shall go, and then immediately come . . ."

"No, you need not come back. When you are with me, I'm still alone all the same. That's the awfulness of it. It's worse than if you were dead."

He stood desperate, hesitating by the door, and did not know himself why he brought forth a last argument, so weak that he himself immediately sensed its weakness.

"Marietta . . . Only think what people — what the whole house will say, about your not having been with us this evening."

"In any case, nobody will say anything about your leaving *me* this night . . . You needn't worry, so far as you're concerned."

He did not understand her immediately. Then, when her sarcasm had penetrated to him, he uttered a hoarse sound and staggered out.

Under half-closed eyelids, she watched him go, holding her head still to listen until his steps died away in the passage. Then she got up to close the door. In the middle of the room she paused deep in thought.

She looked round. Then she went to the alcove cupboard. Her movements, uncertain to begin with, rapidly grew purposeful and deliberate. She dragged some clothes from the cupboard, and laid them upon the bed; then she found the bits of jewelry she had recently been looking for. She took them to the window, and let the moonlight shine upon them. She gazed at them a long time, as if rapt in deep thought. Finally, when three o'clock struck from San Jacopo's, she looked up again, glanced round vaguely. She went towards the door, peered for a moment into the dark corridor, bolted the door from the inside. Then, realizing how foolish that was, she unbolted the door again.

She stood bending forward into the alcove, gathering things from the cupboard in sudden feverish haste, continually overlooking something that she wanted to put into the red bundle she was making ready. When she had finished, she took a deep breath and looked down at the bundle a moment, her hand resting on her hip. Then she felt its weight. She could lift it easily, and if need be carry it a long way. But she had something else in her mind, apart from walking — something else, something else.

She sat at the table. For an hour, she did nothing but listen to every sound in the great house. She was waiting and listening, and through a thick gray veil she sometimes saw dream pictures before her eyes which she stared at long and in astonishment. What were these pictures? There was a landscape she must have seen in the past. Oh, it was the landscape in the painting of the Madonna in the cathedral — a green landscape, with gentle hills and rustling cypresses against a golden heaven. A path meandered along the slopes, disappearing now and then behind a hill, and then emerging again somewhere else in the green landscape with the golden heaven behind the Madonna.

She looked up towards Grigio, who had not gone to sleep again, but was cooing gently in the cage, sometimes shaking his feathers and taking a careful little gulp of water. Marietta got up and went and stood on her toes before the cage with a lump of sugar dipped in coffee. "Grigio . . . will you take a little bit of sugar from the woman?"

"Coo . . . Coo."

The lump was too big to pass the wires; it would have to be put in through the little door. As Marietta opened it, she thought she heard something . . . Fumblingly, she closed it again, leaving the sugar where she had dropped it. But Antonio did not come back. She went and sat down again. She had not recovered from her fright; and meanwhile Grigio was without his little lump of sugar. Out of small, astonished, beady eyes he looked at the woman, who was not in the habit of teasing him so. Then, in an angry mood, he tried to help himself, wormed his beak through the wires, turned his flexible neck this way and that, and fished up the sugar.

This time it was a real sound she heard: a shuffling above the ceiling. Cesare the carrier had got up. A moment later, somebody else was stamping heavily about: Camilla.

Cesare was in the habit of leaving every Monday morning about five o'clock. He got up a quarter of an hour before. Marietta must have dozed off after all: she had not heard a clock strike since three o'clock. She was ready. She cast a glance at her bundle; but Cesare was still stumbling about unshod: it was better to wait a little longer.

It was as if she couldn't breathe any more here. It was still quite dark. The moon had gone down. It was cold and draughty. Her sleepy limbs shivered. But her head was awake, quite, quite awake.

It occurred to her that she had fled to Monsignore yesterday. Without realizing it, she had dreamed of doing that for months. Now it had happened. It was good; it was well that it had happened before she left Todi. Now everything was all right. Their leave-taking had been rather sad. But every leave-taking is sad. Even saying good-by to this house, where she had always been a stranger — even that would perhaps be sad. When Monsignore's grief at their separation was stilled a little, he would say to himself, "It was wonderful . . . It has been fine." In thought, she sent him a last greeting. "Good-by, *Babbo*."

With Antonio it was different. When confronted with the choice between her and his mother, Antonio had chosen his mother. If Antonio was going to be sad for any cause beside the death of his father, he had only himself to blame.

Bump! bump! Cesare had his boots on now. Marietta picked up her bundle. For the last time, anger against Antonio flared up in her at the thought that, warned by some premonition, he might try to stand in her way with force or with tears, and make of her secret flight a spectacle for the whole house. Noiselessly she opened the door. A board in the floor creaked . . . On tiptoe she crept through the dark corridor towards the staircase.

Upstairs a door opened. Cesare was murmuring good-by in a heavy tone, and several times she heard Susanna's name mentioned. Susanna was keeping company with a boy from Grassi's bakery — she would have to be watched. Yes, and perhaps Camilla's confinement would take place this week. There was a resounding kiss. "Well, Mother, here we go again. Now for a week . . . Everything will be all right, this time too . . ."

What would be all right? The journey, the confinement? Both, presumably.

Cesare came down the stairs. It was as if he wished to bring the house down. Did nobody waken, then? No, they were accustomed to hearing the staircase broken down at dawn on Monday mornings. He was heavily loaded with the parcels he preferred not to leave overnight in his cart.

Suddenly in the darkness Cesare saw Marietta rise up in front of him. He probably took her for a ghost until it penetrated to him that there must be a connection between Buongiorno's aggravated condition of yesterday evening and Marietta's presence now on the stairs.

"Oh, is it *you?* What's the matter? Is it all over with the old man? God bless my soul! I'll just go round . . ."

"No, Cesare! Stay here."

He stared at her. Then, noticing the bundle in her hand, asked hesitatingly, "What do you want?"

"Take me away in your cart. You helped me once before, Cesare . . . Do you remember?"

In spite of all his parcels, Cesare was trying to run his fingers through his hair.

"I take you with me? You want to get away from here? It's just as if I were still in bed and dreaming. Marietta, have you gone mad?"

"I shall go mad, Cesare, if I don't flee."

This was too sudden for Cesare. He requested Marietta to readjust a parcel that was slipping from under his arm; instead of which Marietta relieved him of it. Cesare observed this maneuver anxiously: was she trying to force his hand? Cesare was a father and a husband, and had a good name to lose. After all, the affairs of Antonio and Marietta were not his business. The only thing he knew was that at the end of the week he would be bumping up against Antonio here: wherefore Cesare signified to Marietta that she was to slip the parcel back where it had been.

"Aren't things all right between you, then?" he asked, trying to trap her.

"Perhaps they would be all right between us, Cesare, if his mother were not there."

"Yes, yes. His mother's a bad woman," admitted Cesare at once. "There now . . . Now I've got it fixed again, thank you. Do you know what, Marietta? Think it over first. Wait at least another week. Meanwhile you may change your mind."

Silently Marietta went and stood in front of him, and when he met the challenge of her eyes Cesare suddenly saw again the little girl who had stood before him once — years ago — and had with her great gleaming eyes subjected him to her will, uttering an insane threat which had afterwards made him laugh, "If I may not sleep here, I shall do something to myself," or something like that. Yes, she was extraordinary, even as a child.

She was one of those queer people who can command obedience, willing or not.

He sighed, "And if anyone ever comes to hear of it?" he asked.

"If you hold your tongue, two will be silent, Cesare."

He yielded. "In God's name, then," he said, "go downstairs, and slip into the cart while I harness the horse. If anyone sees you, I'm a lost man. If Gaetano of the toll-house happens to look in . . ."

"Does he ever look into your cart now? He's known you too long. He'll be sleepy."

"Yes, it's easy to talk," said Cesare, as he proceeded to bump downstairs.

She followed him. There was no need for her to walk on tiptoe — Cesare made noise enough for an army. The courtyard was still in darkness, and she slipped along the wall into the wagon shed without difficulty. She had just acted the carefree bag of mischief before Cesare — she knew how to take him. Tears and entreaties he knew already, from Camilla. Tears and entreaties would have had this effect: that he would have gone to the door of the room behind which Antonio and his mother were sitting together, and would have knocked loudly, showing just enough respect for the presence of the dead.

She noticed that he was already regretting he had not done this. In his resentment, he spoke gruffly: hitherto, ever since she had gone to tranquilize Camilla when she fainted at the funeral of the old bishop, he had always adopted an almost deferential tone towards her. He hurled a piece of canvas towards her. "Here — conceal yourself under that."

Then he went to harness his horse. He did it hastily, almost nervously. It would soon be light now — the dawn was beginning to break. He stacked up the parcels, drove the cart outside, then returned to the shed to extinguish the stall lanterns; he then hung them under the cart.

Now he was sitting on the box, and the hour of departure had come. When he looked round, and noticed how she had obediently crept under the canvas, his better nature regained the upper hand. He dragged the cushion from under his legs, and shoved it under Marietta's head. "Here — the cart springs are not of the best."

Grateful, suddenly humble, Marietta accepted his attention.

What a way she had of looking out from under the canvas, thought Cesare. He really did not know whether he had obeyed a woman's entreaty or a child's whim. It would seem that she was both — a woman and yet a child still. Oh well, provided nobody had seen anything . . . He pushed on.

It was a strange moment, this riding away in the morning. Even for Cesare, for whom horse and cart and a departure in the early morning hours were an everyday affair. They crossed the courtyard at a footpace. Under her canvas and under Cesare's protection, Marietta felt herself a child again. Had it been otherwise, she would have had a feeling of deep shame at leaving the house and the city like this. She shivered. Her teeth chattered in the chilly morning as she lay there under the canvas.

Cesare sat on the hard wood of his box in silence, staring ahead of him, and with unconscious pleasure he sniffed the warm stable smell of the horse he was driving.

As regards the cart springs, Cesare's information appeared to be reliable. The parcels danced round Marietta. Like gray misty wraiths, the familiar old houses passed before the opening at the back of the wagon.

Now they were at the city gate. Cesare pulled up, stepped off with a sigh, and shook the door of Gaetano's little house. After a while, Gaetano came outside with his keys. Cesare wished him good morning with patronizing boisterousness — rather overdoing it, indeed.

Keys rattled, the gate opened creakingly. The cart was set in motion again. Gaetano's cheerless voice said, "Well, a happy trip again . . . and my greetings to Clement the Twelfth."

"They shall be delivered," promised Cesare, brightly but without gusto. Gaetano's weekly joke could change only through the demise of the old, and the arrival of a new, Pope.

Outside on the country road, it was easier going, and Marietta was able to stretch out.

"Ah well, you've been lucky," said Cesare.

He meant that he had been lucky. He meant that it had been a clever piece of work on his part to have come safely out of the city gate with his clandestine freight. All danger seemed to be over, particularly as a little plan had just crossed his mind whereby everything could be cleared up . . . He was silent. It was a bit too early to talk — it was not good for the lungs. The low-lying vapors that crept from the field across the road were liable to be blown into one's inside. He preferred to think of his plan: he would persuade acquaintances in Rome to take Marietta in, and when he got there again, she would have come to her senses. He would bring her home, as he had taken her away; and Antonio would press his hand.

When he got back to Todi next time without Marietta, he would have to be careful. If anybody asked him, "Have you heard that Marietta Buongiorno has run away?" he would reply, "What? Antonio's Marietta? Has she run away?" and his face would have to register astonishment.

And on their way, should he be questioned, he would say she was his wife; and there was something in that that made Cesare laugh, because, after all, she was not in any way his wife. Yes — except at Giulio's in the inn at Narni: he could not say that there, because he had already told Giulio that Camilla was again in her ninth month.

What in God's name could he say to Giulio?

Marietta lay under her canvas, her eyes closed. She would fall asleep with fatigue in a moment, in spite of the jolts.

Perhaps a little later on she would understand better that she had fled from home. Perhaps a little later on she would understand that this journey with Cesare would come to an end, and that then . . . Yes, what was to happen then? But now she cared about nothing. She could not worry about anything at that moment. She still carried within her the recollection of sorrow; but that recollection was becoming ever dimmer. There was a joy within her, a mysterious hidden joy pressing back all her sorrow.

It was the joy of a deep and unexpected recognition. She seemed to have experienced all this before — traveling in a badly sprung cart in the dark; hearing in her sleep a pebble crunching under the wheels; sticking her head out at dawn, where a damp fresh mist rose up over the fields and the mountains loomed darkly against the light of the new day. . . .

When Cesare looked round and saw that she was sleeping, a smile played round her lips.

Cesare could not help looking at her, could not help shaking his head over her smile.

MELODY OF
DISTANT THINGS

BOOK TWO

MELODY OF
DISTANT THINGS

THE TRIBULATIONS

OF CESARE

THE CARRIER

I

I T WAS THE NEXT YEAR, AND CESARE THE CARRIER WAS returning to Todi after his weekly journey to Rome. For the hundredth time he was pondering a problem that weighed on him, and still he could not come to a decision. He raised his head that had been sunk deep in thought and, still troubled, breathed deep the cool afternoon air of early spring.

Without looking about him he knew that at the next turning Todi would come in sight — a deep rut in the road that had almost shaken him and his cart to pieces told him that.

Another hour to go.

He was late. Camilla would be in a state again. When on any Saturday he failed to come driving into the courtyard precisely at sundown, Camilla was always upset; and, properly considered, it was his own fault, for he prided himself on leaving Terni exactly in time to reach home at sundown. But that morning he had overslept a full hour: he had spent a large part of the night turning and twisting on his straw mattress at the *Vero Cristiano*, going over the whole business again and again, the whole accursed business in which he had become involved against his will.

Porco di . . . What a business!

The cart reached the turning of the road. The horse neighed. Pale in the soft blurred light of late afternoon, the dusty little city of Todi glimmered in the dusk among the gray mountains. A round, faint moon hung slantingly from the pallid blue heavens.

A shiver of well-being shook Cesare's powerful frame; Cesare had been on the road since Monday morning. For him the dull, gray, unreal, distant silhouette of the houses behind Boncini's vineyard had solid form and depth, and while he gazed at them broodingly from under his bushy gray eyebrows he experienced the comforting, intimate sensation of being between four walls. He saw his Camilla in her ample white nightgown — her glowing black hair, already threaded with silver, falling in heavy tresses down her back. He saw the curve of her buttocks as she preceded him to their bed. With his thumb he pressed down the burning wick of the candle into molten grease, and then glided deliciously away on the consoling warmth that came from Camilla's opulent body. The soft caress of the clean, rustling linen his wife was wont to wear on Saturday evenings signified for Cesare the peak of luxury that man could dream of on this earth.

Yes. . . . But conscience recalled him from his vision: before he could make it real, he had a duty to fulfill.

He must go to Antonio Buongiorno, the young coffinmaker. There was no getting away from that; and already he foresaw all the agitation that would flow from his visit. For life was such that people could never listen to serious news without being themselves upset, and upsetting others. Camilla too would want to hear all about the matter. . . . Oh, yes, life had taught Cesare that one unpleasantness always led to another. Camilla would overwhelm him with the bitterest reproaches for ever having got himself involved in so scandalous an affair. What could he have done? Had Camilla been in his place . . . ! Instead of trying to picture what she would have done in his place last year, Camilla would remind him that she was now once more eight months gone. She would start complaining that it was bad for her to get upset, and that he ought to go and sleep on the floor if he really cared for his wife as a man of fifty should. She would then ask him whether he had no vestige of shame before his elder children, who must have thoughts of their own about the punctual arrival of another little one every year. . . . Susanna had a way of looking down when she noticed how, on Saturday evenings, her father was after her mother at every step and kissed his wife in the neck in the middle of the kitchen at most inopportune moments, like any infatuated young ne'er-do-well.

Cesare sighed. This Saturday everything would go awry. He had no illusions about that. Never, never in his life should he have got mixed up in this affair.

When, on that winter morning over a year ago, Marietta had clung to him in the dark stairway imploring him to conceal her in his cart and to take her away to Rome — then, like Pharaoh in the land of the seven plagues, he should have hardened his heart and said: "It's no affair of mine, Marietta. I've a family, I've seven children, and an eighth almost here. I've my own troubles, and as a carrier I must think of my good name." Yes, that's what he ought to have said, and he ought to have knocked at the door behind which old Buongiorno lay dead.

Instead, he had been foolish enough to listen to her, and to think to himself, "Yes, it can't be much fun to live under the eyes of that cunning old Lucia." Oh, he had even thought he was being rather clever, planning to get Teresa Passano to put her up in Rome, and then to take Marietta back to her husband the following week when she had thought things over. . . .

That was how he had tried to lull his uneasy conscience that last time, when the thought that he might meet Antonio accidentally had made him tremble at his home-coming the following Saturday. His own wife, his Camilla, he had not then dared to look in the eye. That very week she had given him his eighth child. He had bent his head in silence when Camilla, with their youngest at her breast, had spoken evil of married women who run away from their husbands; he had been careful enough not to betray himself.

And now, everything had come out after all. Now, all his sly dissembling had been for nothing. Now Fate ordained that he must accuse himself, like the sinner who had met Saint Philip of Todi. When that story had been told from the pulpit the previous Sunday, Cesare had not had the remotest foreboding that he, too, would soon have to confess his guilt.

The whole story of that winter morning had almost gone from his mind. It was no longer talked about in Todi. The women by the well had long since exhausted their quiver of poisonous shafts. Antonio himself, who had grown even quieter, more self-sufficient, never referred to his wife's bad conduct, and seemed well satisfied to have his home run by his mother, who, that same day, while her husband still lay coffined in their dwelling, had taken up her abode with her boy.

Other happenings had distracted the general attention. Old Signor Galli, the podesta's father, had come to die, and thus after all had gone to abide in the marble mausoleum of the Gallis before his much older wife. What a funeral it had been! Who could waste a thought on Marietta, the runaway wife of Antonio Buongiorno the carpenter?

Meanwhile, she who had forgotten her duty, tortured by her conscience, had not stayed long in Teresa's house. On the third day she had gone farther afield, saying that she could earn a living in Naples.

Yes. . . . And now it had come to his ears, suddenly, that after a year she had returned to Rome without means of subsistence. Teresa thought she was ill too, and, not knowing whether Cesare would again be prepared to pay for her keep, had advised her to try to obtain shelter for herself and her child with the Merciful Sisters of Saint Clare.

For herself — and her child?

Knowing Teresa, having lodged with her overnight every week for twelve years, Cesare had at once feared the worst from her report. He had rushed to the Hospital for the Poor; and there he found Marietta, sick and emaciated, a creature to weep over — with the result that he had now no alternative but to go to Antonio and say, "Your wife is lying at death's door in Rome."

And the best of it was that she herself did not wish him to. That lifeless little soul had made him promise not to say a word to anyone in Todi: "Antonio must know nothing of this. Swear it to me, Cesare." When she was dead, Cesare might take the child to him.

What sort of child was this? God alone knew. Cesare had not dared look at it. . . . He found the presence of the old nun, and the entire surroundings, intimidating. He did not know what took possession of him as, having passed a number of beds, he suddenly recognized dark, fiery eyes that looked out at him from a face deadly pale, framed in curly black hair. From that moment, he saw everything as through a haze, and blindly promised all she asked.

Now, as he thought it over, he wondered what he could say to Antonio if he should ask whether the child was his. Marietta ought to have told Cesare. After all, he could not very well ask her.

Cold sweat stood out upon Cesare's forehead as he pondered the matter. Naturally, he would have to maintain to the last that he had heard about Marietta in Rome by accident, and that he had had nothing to do with her flight. But who would believe him?

And supposing he were to say nothing, after all? Supposing he did not go to Antonio? A hundred times upon this journey he had thought how much simpler that would be. A hundred times he had pointed out to himself emphatically that he would do far better to be silent: had he not given his oath that he would be? Yes, he had; and during the day it was quite clear to him that he ought not to break an oath. But at night, when he could not sleep for thinking of that movingly tragic young face — then the realization was borne in upon him that there was a higher Judge who could only smile over the use of the impressive word "perjury" in this connection — a Judge who demanded of him that he should sacrifice his own interest in order to save an unfortunate woman and her innocent child.

Could he hope that Camilla would understand and forgive his course of action? If he were to confess everything to her . . . But that was just the point: she would always believe there was something more that he was still hiding from her.

And suddenly Cesare realized that there was one thing, at any rate, which he must conceal from Camilla: if he were to avoid giving her an entirely false impression of the whole affair, he would have to tell her that Marietta had never stopped sobbing for a moment during their journey to Rome, and had already been repentant — for what would Camilla think if she heard the truth, that that journey to Rome had been like a childish frolic?

Those few days on the road came back vividly to his mind. They had perhaps been the most astonishing days in Cesare's existence: although Marietta had just carried out her terrible decision to leave her husband, although her undoing was therefore threatened on all sides, she had been as bright as a little bird on the way. Possibly she had felt that for her that gaiety could not last long. But what of Cesare himself? Had he been any more sensible than she? He had sung for her, unbelievable as it may sound. He, Cesare, who year in, year out was known as a man of few words, had sung for her, as though he had been an opera singer; and she had admired his voice — she had had no idea he could sing, and the power of his voice had made her gasp. She said he would certainly be asked to sing in the choir on Sundays if only people knew what a fine, powerful voice he had. "Yes, Marietta, and not a mortal soul knows that," he had said. "I only sing when I'm by myself on my cart, and there's nobody about. Then I sing. . . ."

She had sat beside him on the box. Sometimes he had felt as if she were his daughter. Yes; but he noticed that in the inns on the roadside the men looked from him to her and from her to him, and thought she was something quite different. And what's more, he had been foolish enough occasionally to leave the matter in doubt, with a view to confusing people. Sometimes he gave out that she was his daughter, sometimes his niece, and again his wife. He must have been mad, for it was not his way to make people believe the moon was made of green cheese, and he was bound to be punished for having done so. People would bring it up against him that he had dared to fool them; and as for her who was lying in Rome, they would set upon her — he knew it.

He would have to be careful not to lose his temper, not to cry out with flushed face as he hit the table with his rough fists: "What's the matter with you all? Do you imagine you're so very much better than that poor child who didn't run away from her husband for pleasure? Yes, she's half a child still. You can laugh if you like, but I know her better than you do. She's no flyaway like that Manuela of Lascari the cobbler. Life has been hard to her, and if you had seen her there in the hospital . . ." God forbid that he should let anything like that escape him!

How would it all turn out? Camilla would spend the nights in tears until he confessed that there had been a premeditated plan between him and Marietta, and that he had had secret dealings with her all that time in Rome. He might as well admit it — the whole city would believe it, in any case. And with his good name, he would very likely lose clients, too — just now, when the ordinary post was about to lower its charges.

II

When Cesare reached the tollhouse, Gaetano asked his regular question as to the welfare of Clement the Holy Father in Rome, and whether Cesare had conveyed Gaetano's special greetings to him. Cesare only grunted in reply, and, removing the canvas cover from his parcels, carried everything into the shed except what was destined for the secretariat and the authorities of Todi.

He drove right through the piazza, made his deliveries, and thanked Immacolata for the cup of coffee she offered him — which, however, he had to refuse, as Camilla had already been waiting an hour for him.

Cesare drove into the dark and deserted courtyard of the old *palazzo* where he lived. He looked about him in a depressed way while he unharnessed his horse and gave it fodder and drink in the stable, to which it found its way alone. Diamond, its companion, welcomed it with joyful neighing. On other Saturdays, when he reached home at his usual hour, children surrounded his cart, and he always stretched out his neck to see if Carlo was among them — Carlo, the apple of his eye, his eldest boy, who, though only ten, had already gone through so much illness. . . . Was he laid up again? But to-night there were no children to tell him in their clear little voices: they had all been summoned home to supper and bed. The large somber house with its dark entrance and blackened walls received him in hostile silence.

A light was gleaming through the half-closed door of Antonio's workshop. The scraping of a saw reached Cesare's ear. Vaguely he thought that it would be an opportune moment to speak to Antonio, while he was alone, and tell him the situation without old Lucia's presence. . . . Yes, but he must go and reassure Camilla first, and he was also a little worried because Carlo had not come downstairs when he heard him drive in. Yes, a little later on he would. . . . He picked up the new harness that he had bought in Rome two weeks before and did not care to leave in the cart, put it round his neck, and thumped up the creaking staircase in his heavy boots.

As he touched the doorknob of his dwelling, he heard squabbling inside. Susanna's shrill voice — she had been getting unpleasantly upon his nerves lately — rose above everything else.

"Of course, it would be Susanna again," he thought with exasperation, and forgot how little fitting it was for him to exert parental authority to-day. Angrily he opened the door and stood, silent and impressive, on the threshold. There was a hush. They all looked round.

Camilla, sitting majestically behind the table in ample motherhood, face flushed by her excited admonishments and black hair hanging down in slovenly disorder, looked at her husband with the drunken-seeming eyes that characterized her pregnancies and sighed, "Well, here's your father. He's arrived just at the right moment."

Cesare had not expected to hear that he had arrived just at the right moment. Large and lowering, he turned his eyes towards Susanna. "What's wrong with you now?" he asked.

Susanna burst into sobs, and her mother replied for her: "Carlo saw her a while ago walking with Luigino Vacca."

"That's a lie," shouted Susanna hysterically.

Carlo, with a grave little old man's face, looked at his father in silence. Wounded by Susanna's imputation, immediately convinced by the glance of his favorite, Cesare said with something tender, but at the same time menacing, in his voice, "Carlo doesn't lie."

"No, of course. Carlo doesn't lie. Carlo can never lie. You always believe everything he says."

Cesare stared at his eldest daughter, nodding involuntarily.

"So now it's Luigino Vacca," sighed the mother, heaping macaroni on the plates the little ones held up impatiently to her. "First it was that boy from the Grassi bakery — that wasn't so bad, although you might have waited a year or two. Then it was young Signorino Perosio — you probably thought he'd make a lady of you one fine day. When he went back to his studies in Bologna, you sat howling in the kitchen, and waited impatiently for a letter from him that you couldn't even have read. And now, just for a change, it's that seedy-looking ne'er-do-well of Vacca's. He went to Bologna once, too. Yes, but not to study. . . . He's a calamity. Every decent father gives him the cold shoulder, and even his own father throws him out on the street when he sees him coming into the inn."

"Yes, that's like his father, to be sure," broke in Susanna rebelliously.

"He beat his own child lame, and now Luigino has to go through life limping, and is no use for any decent work. You ought to know his father well: you used to slave for him."

"Hold your tongue," bawled Cesare, and Susanna was silent, satisfied.

"The things you dare say to your mother!" whimpered Camilla. "Don't you prick up your ears, Marianna — and hold your plate straight."

When the half-starved children had been satisfied, Camilla served her husband. She piled a mountain of macaroni on his plate, and then covered it with a thick, dark sauce. The sight calmed Cesare. It reminded him of the full comfort of home. He divested himself of his new harness and went towards the alcove to take off his outer clothes. His eye lingered with infinite tenderness on his youngest, who lay in bed sleeping peacefully, with his small fist in his mouth — until he caught sight of him, Cesare had for the moment forgotten his existence. Then he returned to the table, where spoons were clicking and greedy lips were smacking. He bent over his Camilla and gave her a discreet kiss, which she accepted passively, upbraiding little Pepino the while for making a mess with his food. She always responded like that, and Cesare had ceased to notice. He subsided behind his macaroni and began to demolish it.

They were all eating — no one spoke. Even Susanna's sobbing had ceased. Cesare looked at her again when his first hunger was stilled, and a new exasperation came over him when he saw her sitting there dressed up as though it were Sunday, her eyes swollen and red with weeping. She repelled him, now he knew she went about with boys: was it possible there could have been a time when she sat upon his knee and was his little caressing Susanna? She felt his disapproving glance, and looked at him inimically, with something of contempt. How dared she look at him like that? It completely nonplussed him. After all, she was his daughter. . . . She turned away her eyes, but her look had put him off his food. He was on the point of believing that Susanna must know something of the story through which her father's good name was at stake. "Idiot!" he finally said to himself.

He gulped down some wine to wash away his oppression.

In a moment he must think of a pretext for going to see Antonio. Upon other Saturday evenings he never set foot outside his door — Camilla would be astonished when she heard him say suddenly that he . . . Yes, what was he going to say?

The dishes were empty. Camilla helped little Pepino to dry his mouth with a piece of bread, and then, getting the better of her girth, got up to clear away. Cesare observed that during his week's absence she had grown heavier, and the fear that attended every pregnancy rose up in him again:

if only it were not twins. Of course, he could not help it even if it were, but Camilla would never be able to see that. Still searching for an excuse to go out, he followed her with his eyes. In spite of himself he cast a covetous look at her soft, full neck, at her opulent figure clothed in a full, pleated dress. . . . He would have liked to help her clear away — if the children had not been there. Their presence constrained him to do nothing except say to Susanna, "Get up and help your mother. Must she do everything herself?"

Then he got up, stood a moment hesitating, casting about for an opening, and at last began: "Ah well, I think I shall now — oh, just go and see . . ."

Astonished, his wife looked round at him. So did the children. He colored as he added, "I must just go downstairs."

"Oh, to attend to Diamond?"

"Yes." He nodded slowly, thanking his lucky star. "I shall be back in a moment," he said airily, and stepped out of the room. As he passed, still feeling guilty, he ran his hand over Carlo's black, lank hair.

III

On the stair, the feeling came over him that bad luck had set in for him. He had drunk more wine than usual. Being a sober drinker he felt the effects at once when, as this evening, he drank a whole bottle.

Downstairs in the courtyard he found Antonio busy closing the doors of his workshop. "Good evening," he muttered, and received from the shy Antonio as he looked up a somewhat vague greeting in return. Again, once again an opportunity was offered to Cesare to settle this ticklish business in the absence of old Lucia; but instead of making use of his good fortune, he allowed himself to be carried away by the ridiculous obsession that he must attend to Diamond at once, as he had told Camilla he was going to do. Blindly he drifted into the stable, stumbling about in the pitch dark and running his hand over the warm bodies of the two horses, trying to overcome his feelings of discomfort. When he left the stable he found Antonio about to go upstairs.

"Are you just going to your rooms?" asked Cesare with a sinking feeling; and even before the other had nodded assent, he went on, "Then I'll come with you. There's something I want to talk to you about."

Antonio glanced at him quickly. A tone in Cesare's voice had apparently struck him, made him ill at ease.

"What is it?"

Cesare coughed, pointing upstairs. "Better wait a moment . . . People might hear us here," he said. Did he after all really want old Lucia to be present at their interview? Clumsily, trying to gain the ascendancy over this boy who might have been his son, Cesare threw his arm round Antonio's shoulders, and, protectingly, with sudden commiseration, pressed him forward up the staircase. They entered the neat parlor, where Lucia queened it for her son, and sat down. She put down beside him a glass of wine, which he raised automatically to his lips, and waited. There was something malicious and inquiring in her eye, and a readiness to be on her guard. She was accustomed to regard everyone as a hidden enemy.

In the adjoining kitchen Antonio stood washing his hands, his back turned towards them. The communicating door was open. "How far is Camilla gone?" inquired Lucia. "She's getting near her time, isn't she?"

"Yes, yes, it won't be long now."

"It'll be your ninth, if I'm not mistaken. Yes, I always say they that have plenty of butter can lay it on thick."

Cesare hastened to assure her that things were none too well with him. The ordinary post had again lowered its charges, and for freight carriers that was the beginning of the end.

"Oh, so the end of your affluence is in sight?" asked Lucia, and laughed. Her laugh savored of satisfaction at another's woes; and Cesare, disagreeably affected, began to emphasize the good side of having many children. The girls could help in the home at an early age.

"Yes, and then they marry, and that doesn't take you very far."

Cesare looked towards Antonio anxiously, wondering how he was to introduce the subject that had brought him there. Meanwhile, he said, "That may be, but you'll have done your duty . . ."

"And thus we go, driving backwards and forwards from Todi to Rome and from Rome to Todi," said Lucia, laughing. "Why don't you drink? I shall think in a moment you don't like our wine."

Obediently Cesare brought the glass to his mouth. *"Salute!"*

Antonio came and sat at the table. It struck Cesare that there was a difference in his face that had come since the last time he had looked at him closely. How long ago was that? The dwellers in the great house called to each other across the courtyard without really observing one another. It was the same boyish face, but there were furrows drawn in it that would not disappear. Suddenly it occurred to him that Antonio, in his young life, had had more troubles to grapple with than had ever beset Cesare.

Silence hung over the room. The expectation in Antonio's strangely grave eyes made it impossible for Cesare to hold back the truth any longer. Lucia was also silent, waiting. One could almost hear the suspense in the little room. At last Cesare opened his mouth and said, as if replying to a question, "Oh, yes — I really came to say . . . Marietta is in Rome."

His words made an impression. Antonio turned a contorted face towards his mother. His lips moved almost imperceptibly as he said, "Marietta?"

Cesare nodded, holding his breath. Softly, with an artless allure, Grigio was cooing — Grigio the dove in its little wooden cage above the door.

"I thought I ought to tell you — " said Cesare again, gauche and ponderous.

And at that moment Lucia blurted out, "Really? You thought that, did you?" Her hatred and impotent rage sought an outlet in a flood of words. "What have we to do with that woman? Hasn't my boy suffered enough through her already? Haven't you seen how he has suffered? No? Was he to shout his grief from the house tops before you could hear it; and is it to begin all over again? Do you think *I* can go through all that a second time? It's more than a year since she has darkened our door. In the middle of the night she ran away, like a common slut. Nobody had shown her the door. She chose to go herself. What business is it of ours if she's in Rome or in the land of the pagans? I've prayed — I'm prepared to do penance, but I've no regrets, and I don't mind telling you — a hundred times I've prayed that she'd go where there is no return!"

Cesare, his huge body crumpling with embarrassment under the hot lava of Lucia's hatred, started up at this last confession of Lucia's, and stared at her with astonishment and aversion. Then slowly he turned his head towards Antonio, who asked: "What is the matter with Marietta? As you've begun about her, you might as well tell us everything, Cesare."

"She's lying in the Hospital for the Poor."

"And where else should she end?" cried Lucia with venomous satisfaction. "She asked for it herself."

Antonio's gray face assumed an infinitely grieved expression. "Have you seen her?" he inquired.

Cesare nodded, and began hesitatingly, looking only at Antonio, "She was almost unrecognizable . . . I could have cried, believe me — "

"Better if you had, you fool, and not come here to make my boy half-crazy again," said Lucia spitefully.

Cesare made an angry gesture. His shyness had given way to indignation. In Antonio he felt a strange silent ally, and dared to counter Lucia's odious interruption with, "I didn't know it would make Antonio half-crazy if I told him that perhaps he could still save his wife. No, I didn't know that. Otherwise I should have held my tongue, which was precisely what she asked me to do."

Lucia stared at him, then burst out into hysterical laughter. "Really?

She asked you that, did she? Come, come. No, then I withdraw every-thing. Really? That was what you had to promise her?"

"Yes. I had to promise her not to say a word to anybody about having found her there; not to you, either — you may as well know it."

"That's what she said, is it? To nobody in Todi, not even to that old vixen?" asked Lucia, nagging and malicious. Suddenly despair broke through her voice. "And that's the trap you fall into, that's the trap you men fall into; and my boy, whom all my life I've tried to protect because perhaps I care for him too much — whom I've consoled during this whole dreadful year for what his wife did to him — he also falls into it. What is there to be done when men are so hopelessly stupid and will never become wiser? What can I do against that? I can do what *she* has done — run away from here and leave him alone to his fate. Then at least there's a chance he'll run after me and implore me to come back to him. All right. Bring her back here again, for that pleasure she'll still give you, even though Cesare was to say nothing about it. Take her back. Give people matter for laughter. Nothing amusing has happened in this house for a long time. And then, when she gets it into her head to run away again, when you're the laughingstock of the whole city for the second time, then come back to your mother, if she can still stand on her old feet, and ask her to run your home for you. She'll come back to you, all right. Don't worry. Your mother comes when you call her, and she goes away when you chase her. You can't have things easier than that. . . ."

Aimlessly, still muttering indistinctly to herself, she made for the al-cove. Antonio, nervous and dazed, sprang up from his chair to follow her. Then he locked the door and put the key in his pocket.

When she saw that, she let herself fall against the side of the bed and began to laugh again. "You forget, my dear: there are windows too, if I really wanted to get out. . . . But I'm not in such a hurry. Perhaps Cesare has more to tell. It's pleasant to listen to him. . . ."

Reluctantly, trying to conceal his perplexity under a gruff manner, Cesare admitted: "Yes. There is something else."

"Didn't I tell you?"

Lucia's sprightly derision added to Cesare's confusion. If only he had said everything at once! What sort of dangerous old woman was this? She extracted the whole truth from him in a trice, and distorted it into improbable common lies.

"I forgot to say . . . there's a child, too," he brought out.

"A child?"

"And even now he doesn't understand," moaned the old woman from the side of the bed, sardonically. "No one is so blind as he who will not see. She runs away from her husband and plays the whore; and a year later, sure enough there's a child. But a father must be found for it. Fortunately, there's somebody in Todi stupid enough to — "

"It's Antonio's child," snapped Cesare, not knowing himself how he dared suddenly take the responsibility for that statement. The laughter in the alcove stopped. Lucia got from the bed and approached the table, upon which she placed her wrinkled, blue-veined fists. She looked at Cesare closely with an odious expression.

"Yes, that's likely."

Cesare returned her contemptuous look.

"How old is it?" she asked, uncertainly.

"I haven't seen the certificate of baptism."

"But you've seen the child!"

"Not well enough to be able to say . . ."

"Cesare, don't think you can fool an old woman with cock-and-bull stories. My son, perhaps, yes, even probably; but not me. Tell me, how old is the child?"

"Didn't you hear me say that I hardly gave it a glance?"

"For a man like you, a glance would be enough to know whether it's a newborn babe or six months old. You have eight yourself."

"That may be, and I would have looked at it if I hadn't . . . if I hadn't seen Marietta there — in that condition — "

"We're talking about the child now, aren't we? You can talk about her to Antonio as much as you like. I only want to hear about the child. I'm wondering how you can maintain it's Antonio's — when you admit yourself that it's a newly born brat."

"I don't admit that. The child must be six months old. Otherwise she wouldn't have dared tell me to bring it to Antonio in the event of her not recovering."

"Oh, Antonio would be only too pleased to take on somebody else's child, provided *she* asked him."

"Yes . . . But she knew you were here, too."

The old woman thought a moment. Finally she sighed deeply and said in a voice suddenly grown tired, "If it were really Antonio's child — if it were my son's child — then of course it could come here. Then I would even be grateful to you for your message. But why didn't you wait until you could bring it?"

"Shame, Lucia!" said Cesare.

She did not even hear him. She was nodding to herself in thought. "I could tell you there and then if the child were his. A false certificate of baptism wouldn't help either way." She had sunk down by the table, her head in her hands.

She spoke no further word.

All this time, Antonio had been regarding Cesare's face tensely, trying to read the truth from it. Antonio's glance had become so strange. Was he aware that it was Cesare who sat there at the other side of the table? Slowly, hesitatingly, he turned his head towards the old woman his mother, and gently laid his hand upon her shoulder.

"Mother . . . Don't be angry with me . . . I . . ."

A little convulsive laugh shook her.

Cesare felt that he was now in the way. He stood up and said, "Ah, well — I'd better be going. If you're coming to Rome with me, let me know in the morning."

The word "morning" appeared to alarm Antonio.

"No, I can't wait, Cesare," he said hastily. "Mother will understand. She only pretends not to, but she knows quite well that I can't do otherwise than — go to her — this very evening — to my wife."

Carried away by a happy warm impulse, Cesare seized Antonio's hands and almost crushed them in his fists. "God grant, Antonio, that you find her still alive — and that everything may come right again between you. I always liked her. I never joined in when people spoke ill of her. Your heart will break when you see her again — and you, Lucia, try to be sensible. When you reach Rome, ask for The Red Hat. The innkeeper's name is Passano, but it's his wife you must deal with. She's called Teresa. Tell her you come from me, and she mustn't charge too much . . . Once you're on the highroad, you'll be able to jump on at the back of some cart or other. The Holy Virgin will see you don't have to do the whole journey on foot."

Not for nothing had Cesare put his trust in the Virgin. He felt her proximity. He felt she was rewarding him for his Christian virtue: it had occurred neither to Antonio nor Lucia to ask how he had come to know that Marietta was lying ill in Rome in the Hospital for the Poor, and he was already deluding himself with the hope that nobody else would ever raise that question. Yes, he had done a good deed this evening. Lucia could stew in her own juice if she would be so intolerant as not to turn a hair when she heard that an unfortunate young woman — and her daughter-in-law at that — was lying at death's door in the Hospital for the Poor. He made a move to go: he could hear shouts and the stamping of feet in his own rooms, just above the one he was in: the quarrel of a little while back had broken out afresh.

IV

An hour later, the noise in Cesare's home had died away. His stentorian voice, thundering above the women's shrill bickering, had, like a passing storm, cleared the air.

On the whole great building the first stillness of night descended. Annina, wife of Simone the stonemason, always cheerful despite the pressure of poverty, stood in her low-ceilinged kitchen ironing the linen of the rich. From the alcove came the wail of a little girl six months old; and Annina was convinced that she was expecting again: she tired so quickly, this last fortnight. Yes. They could do nothing about it, Simone and she. It was nearly a year since that dreadful accident had happened to Guido. Simone tried to prevent her from thinking about it; but she could not help thinking about it, again and again. She saw the thing happen before her eyes. She would go on doing so, until God vouchsafed them another little boy instead of Guido. Her husband was not yet home — he worked so far from the city. But she was not alone: Giannino, her eldest, not yet six years old, wanted to wait up for his father, who went to work in the mornings before sunrise and saw his children only when they were asleep. Giannino was actually helping his mother already, handing her the hot iron and setting down the cool one on the charcoal fire so that she need not interrupt her ironing.

And there was Bettina Bartoldi, wife of the farrier, waiting for her husband, who was as usual on Saturday evenings playing cards at Vacca's inn, and who, when he came in drunk, would thrash her. She had just been appealing to her neighbors for protection again.

Pinzi the hatmaker still sat working by candlelight, waiting till his wife came home to prepare supper. She always got up late, went out, and stayed out. She did not care when the other women railed at her — all she answered was that her home was empty. As he bent over a beaver hat, trimming it with a costly ostrich feather that he had just curled by the fire, Pinzi thought that everything would change if only God would grant them a child. Then Brigida would have to stay at home. Then she could no longer say her home was empty. Then their marriage and everything else would cease to be meaningless. Why did he go on working till his eyes burned? Why was he saving a stocking full of silver? If his wife knew of its existence she would take the money and give it away, as thoughtlessly she gave away everything she came by, without experiencing any of the joy of giving, to women bowed down under the cares of a large family. She jeered at him over his concern for the future: for her it had no value. A barren woman was a visitation from God. She was wearing him out — she could not even let him sleep in peace, tired as he always was with his work. An unquenchable thirst scorched her body, had rendered her shameless — she who on her bridal night had been so shy and fearful. But their embraces brought her no relief. Unfruitful they were, and they left a bad taste and bitter disappointment. Unjustified revulsion drove her from him, out of the rooms where he had to spend the entire day seeking rest in his work that had formerly pleased him so. . . . He was always alone, always alone.

Downstairs, in the home of Lascari the cobbler, there was a party of four, playing cards convivially round a candle stuck in the neck of an empty wine bottle. A full bottle stood between them, helping to keep them in good spirits. Manuela's high-pitched voice broke out now and then in shrill laughter. She made up like ladies of the nobility and light women, and her neckerchief was loosely arranged: Mariotti the elegant tailor and Falcometti the stonemason, her boarder, took turns glancing into her corsage where her worn though still luxuriant charms lay but half-concealed. Lascari himself, an ugly little goblin, cunning for all his seeming oafishness, had eyes only for the cards. The others, whose attention was not sufficiently riveted to the game, were sometimes amazed at his quickness; but Lascari only winked triumphantly and seized the neck of the bottle with his dirty hand, reeking of cobbler's wax; the wine flowed with a clucking sound into his toothless mouth.

"Pass it to me," said Falcometti, good-natured and boisterous, wrenching the bottle from Lascari's lips in order to place it to his own; but when he wanted to pass it on to Manuela she shook her head with ill-concealed aversion, so that Mariotti burst out laughing. Coquettish and appealing, she looked up at him. Was Mariotti laughing at her? He was the only one here who understood her — he realized that she was too good to be the wife of an ill-smelling cobbler. She only knew herself through him. If there were not something fine about her — something ladylike — would Mariotti trouble to pay her attention, Mariotti the tailor who went into the houses of the well to do? And into the beds of decorous ladies too, it was whispered, nor did he contradict the rumor — only smiling when the question was put to him.

"Get on with the game," cried Lascari in his common, humorous voice. They continued to play. Beside each lay a little pile of coins — much-used coppers, and a few small pieces of silver; but beside Lascari lay two such piles. . . .

Antonio flung on his coat and took a small sum of money. As he was putting on the heavy boots he was accustomed to wear for work in the churchyard when it was raining, his mother came to him, bringing a thick scarf. She stood before him, looking up at him. Tenderness and terrible disappointment were mingled in the look she gave him in a last, hopeless, obstinate endeavor at passive resistance. She still hesitated to knot the scarf round his neck though he waited patiently for her to do so, her obedient boy once more after the terrible half-hour that lay behind them.

"And what about the business? What is to happen to the workshop?" She spoke as though that were the most important thing of all.

"I'm going to see Ercole behind San Jacopo's: he's not busy and will be glad to earn a little more."

Her question had not frightened him — he had thought of everything.

"Wait at least till to-morrow morning," she entreated weakly. "You can go better by daylight."

"By daylight I want to be at Terni."

"Perhaps you'd think better of your plans, after all, if you stayed here to-night."

Tormented, he shook his head. "Why must you start again, Mother? I can't . . . I cannot wait. Perhaps I shall find rest once I'm on my way. After all, I love her, Mother — I didn't know, myself, how much until Cesare came and told us this. I love her . . . I love her still."

Lucia nodded to herself. Wild jealousy shook her heart. "You love her; but you don't ask yourself whether she's worth it. You love her, and you give your mother her deathblow."

When she saw how he had to fight against tears, she hated herself for her childish sulking; but at the same time she felt bitter triumph that she could still cause him to grieve. Gently she pushed him away when he threw his arms about her in his helplessness. "Now, now, it's all right. I know you don't mean it, but that will not decrease her satisfaction."

"Why do you think that, Mother? Why have you always wanted to think only ill of her? If you hadn't done that . . . perhaps the tragedy would never have happened."

Lucia smiled contemptuously. "You call it a tragedy. I call it a piece of good fortune. It all depends how one looks at things. In either case, I've lost now — I can see that. And I want still to tell you this before you go: If the child really is yours — listen, Antonio — then in my old age I shall still be crazy enough to rejoice over what Cesare came and did here. Then I shall ask her to forget everything that has happened. . . . What else could I do, anyhow? And if it isn't yours — then I here in Todi shall laugh loudest of all at you."

"Mother!" he cried hoarsely, and laid his head upon her shoulder. She struggled desperately not to press it against her. They stood thus a moment, sharing their grief over their misunderstanding until Antonio looked up anxiously.

"Yes, go now. Don't waste your time here," she said at once. "When you come back here with her and her child, I shall be out of these rooms — It's a good thing nobody wanted to rent a place where a man had lain dying a year and a half. If you come back alone, or alone with the child — I shall know soon enough."

Gently she pushed him towards the door. "Don't think I'm sacrificing myself," she added, magnanimously. "I'm only giving way to the stronger. I had the choice between filling you with aversion for your mother — and making you cry for her. I chose the latter, and now I shall pray for you. May the Holy Virgin be with you . . ."

When he had gone and she heard his footsteps on the stairs and in the courtyard, her head fell upon the table and she gave free rein to her pent-up tears. She herself did not know how long she sat thus. Later, she stared in front of her with her old colorless eyes, trying to imagine what it would be like when She whose name she would not utter even to herself was back again. She could hear already what people would say about her, Lucia, who had thought that she was so comfortably settled with her son, and had after all to give way to her daughter-in-law. Oh, let them talk. She would have asked nothing more than that, in talking of her, people might forget to drag her boy through the mire; but that they would not do. . . .

She saw him, walking lonely along the moonlit road, consumed with anxiety for his wife. Love was only a thing of the imagination, but what a dangerous, treacherous thing! For a whole year, the fire might continue to smoulder under the ashes. It seemed to be finally extinguished — and then it flared up again under an unexpected gust. . . .

Would he think of his mother to-night? Yes, he would think: "Fortunately she herself has made way. I haven't forcibly to . . ."

For he would have done that — old Lucia had no longer any illusions about that. How he had inveighed against her a while back, after Cesare had gone! He had not realized his own bitterness. Love, anxiety, had made him mad. He had thought that his mother still wanted to oppose him. He had not seen that she had already capitulated. When she had heard of the child, and Cesare had insisted that it was Antonio's, then her resistance had been broken. She knew then that she had lost. From that moment, the only thought in her mind was, "And suppose it is Antonio's, after all?"

It was of that she was thinking, and she forgave his every cruel word. It wasn't he who was speaking — not he, not her boy.

Lucia felt tired and old. This evening she realized how much the last twelve months had aged her. If Antonio had looked at her well, he would not have asked her to make it up with that creature in Rome. In her heart nothing new could germinate beside her love for her boy, and through him for his child — if indeed it were his child. For the rest, there was room only for hatred — grim, relentless hatred of which she had long since ceased to be ashamed before God and men.

Ah, well. She had better begin to collect her belongings. Why should she move in broad daylight under the eyes of curious neighbors when she could do it just as well in the dark, with nobody to notice? She had brought only her clothes and a few knickknacks to Antonio's rooms — it was as though she had known that she would be chased away again. She had left her bits of furniture untouched in the dwelling where Gabriele her husband had died and had lain in his coffin unattended.

It suddenly occurred to her that throughout this year she had given him not a moment's thought. She was filled with astonishment at the realization. She had tended his grave faithfully, however — nobody in the city could say anything about that. Would his ghost be her only company in future? Lucia felt so tired that such a thought was almost welcome. If she could no longer look after her boy, and if she must listen to some other sound than that of her grandchild . . . Then it was better so.

She packed her few belongings, as though she were going upon a journey. Her hands had ceased to tremble. She had grown strangely quiet.

V

Cesare had gone upstairs to his own home full of anxiety lest his little Carlo had come to some harm in the scuffle he had heard from below. He arrived just in time to step between Susanna and her brother. Susanna, in her sinful rage, had picked up a basin . . . God forgive her. It just missed Carlo's head, and landed against the Madonna, who had shielded him. The small terra-cotta image, which stood between two bunches of flowers, had been shivered to fragments, while the votive lamp in front of it had been extinguished.

Camilla, pale as death, sank upon a chair. Cesare seized Susanna by the arm in an iron grip and thrust her into the back room, ordering her to pray before the image of St. Antony that stood there so long as she had strength to do so. Susanna, however, declared at once that she would go tc confession to-morrow morning early — she had recovered from her anger immediately, and her eyes stood out, wide with shock and fear.

When Cesare returned to the front room to relight the votive lamp, it moved him to see that Carlo was already busy about it. His brothers and sisters were huddled together, helpless as sheep in a thunderstorm. Cesarina had carefully separated the fragments of the basin from those of the Madonna. The children were all sent to bed, and then Cesare sat down beside his wife and laid his soothing hand upon her fleshy wrist, rubbing and caressing it gently, as he pieced together the fragments of the Madonna and announced his intention of gluing it next day, so that it would scarcely be noticed where it had been broken.

Later, when Susanna had gone to her bed to cry herself to sleep, he said, "Camilla . . . if this misfortune should bring Susanna to better thoughts, it will not have happened in vain, and we shall have to be grateful to God that He has manifested Himself to her."

And very privately, without really admitting it even to himself, he thought that God had manifested Himself in another way that evening: owing to the uproar in her own home, Camilla had noticed nothing of what had occurred below. Naturally, he would tell her about it; but it would wait till next day. Next day he could say, "I didn't want to upset you even more yesterday evening. That's why I kept silent about it."

He comforted Camilla, and she liked to be comforted by him. After what had happened to the little holy image, she would not have known where to turn if her Cesare had not been there to arrange everything for her. He created order with his iron fist, and to-morrow he would carefully mend the Madonna.

Camilla rested her head upon her husband's shoulder. She turned her face towards his, looked into his eyes and smiled at him. She felt a tenderness that had not come over her for years — she could hardly remember how many. Perhaps she would long more often for her husband's love if every Saturday he could create such tenderness, instead of making her anxious with his clumsy silence as he followed her about and kissed her in the neck, under Susanna's very nose.

Outside, ten o'clock was slowly striking. They listened, and knew from the short, damp reverberations that it had started to rain. For a moment Cesare's thoughts went out to Antonio: had he already started upon his great expedition?

Cesare soon forgot Antonio again. Like a great and beautiful miracle, the moment he had dreamed of during the whole week was dawning: that soft magical moment when Camilla, in her full white nightdress, stepped forward in front of him towards their bed.

THE WONDER

OF THE

SAINTS

I

FOR AN HOUR, A THICK CLOUD OF DUST HAD STOOD
up against the southern horizon. Antonio, dragging himself along
in the stark midday sun over the crumbling volcanic surface of
the torrid road, saw that it grew larger and larger every time he raised
his head. Straight in front of him it hung over this inhospitable, comfortless land, through which — muddy, tawny, and slow — the Tiber flowed
barrenly.

At length the puzzle of this mysterious dust cloud was solved: sheep
appeared through it, and soon the whole flock was swarming about Antonio — gray, heaving, woolly bodies, bleating themselves hoarse. Then,
as if risen from the earth, the shepherd stood before him, making one
with the flock and the landscape in his fleece and his colorless undergar-
ments. His face was heavily lined and as gray as his beard. Dust covered
him completely, even to his eyebrows and the lashes of his dark, unexpectedly tender eyes.

"I don't understand. How far is it still to Rome? Oh, a long way. Rome
is still far away. Wait until you can ride behind a cart." The old shepherd
looked inquisitively at the youth before him, who, above the turmoil of
the animals, pierced the thick wall of dust with fixed burning eyes, and
said insistently, "But surely you have an idea how far it is?"

"Not by an hour. You had better wait for a cart. It's safer after dark.
For us the Campagna is safe; but then we belong here."

The flock seemed to echo his words with their bleating.

"They would steal your money," said the shepherd thoughtfully. "How long have you been walking?"

Antonio had to think. His excessive fatigue had made him powerless to answer any word that verged upon friendliness. He hesitated to say that he had been under way since the evening before last, and . . .

"Tell me, at least, if I can reach Rome before to-morrow morning," he implored.

"Before to-morrow morning? Yes, of course," said the shepherd consolingly, and then paused. "I think so, at least. How can I say for sure? Even when you see the dome it's still a long way."

To one who had grown old roaming over the gray expanse of the Roman Campagna — guarding his flock sometimes for weeks within sight of the city without ever touching the boundary where the first houses began and the animals could find no more food — to him, Rome appeared a long way off.

Antonio tore himself away from the futile encounter. They were wasting time staring in silence towards the south. Desperate, he pushed his way through the rear of the flock until he had freed himself from the pressure of their bodies: the oppressive atmosphere of dust and animal exhalations made him dizzy; and then he strode on once more in the glaring light of the day.

Yes, Rome was far, very far. The shepherd was right. Antonio had not imagined it to be so far. Neither had he thought that such exhaustion would come over him. So far, his young body had always easily fulfilled what he had demanded of it; but the year of dull despair that lay behind him had weakened him.

His eyes could no longer bear the glare of the sun; he kept closing them. When would the twilight fall? When would he feel the beneficent coolness of dusk upon his burning eyelids? He would have liked to go down to the river to cool his wrists in the water and to drink — the dust scorched his throat so.

Would he reach Rome in time? Surely Marietta would not die just as he was on his way to her after that terrible year of separation. Everything in the world was possible, but only if God allowed it, only if God allowed it. . . . And once he had seen Marietta again with his own eyes — and she had promised to return with him — then he could rely upon the Virgin, who knew how to soften God in His inexorable resolves, and whose tender heart was always moved by genuine grief if only one burned candles to Her, many, many candles! And the saints — there were also the good saints. In two double rows they stood, old and dignified and gray on the golden steps of the heavenly throne, like a merciful choir.

Antonio had not always thought sufficiently upon these matters. He had often neglected Mass because he felt it no longer gave him consolation. His sin would be forgiven him, for the sake of the great faith that now welled up in him.

He would find Marietta alive. And when she saw her terrible troubles fly away, surely that alone would half-cure her. Why, why had she elected to carry cares like millstones round her neck? If it had been hard for her to fight against his mother, why had she not thought how much harder it would be to suffer hunger and cold, and to have no roof above her head? His strong feet were already tired after a night and a day, and, after a few hours of feverish sleep, yet another day. Yes, they were tired, and the seams of his heavy shoes cut him cruelly. . . . But how describe the weariness that had driven Marietta to the Hospital for the Poor?

Surely she had repented of her flight. Surely she had longed, if only for a moment, to be back beside her husband, and to know herself cared for. She had forbidden Cesare to say that he had found her. . . . Oh, Antonio knew her pride well enough. Poverty and privation could prevail over her body only. But when she saw him approach her bed — would she not rejoice? After all, she had loved him once — before he had lost her love through his guilty weakness. She had loved him once — she had told him so herself, and dissemble she could not. . . .

And even if she could not rejoice for her own sake — then there was still the child, he said to himself, and breathed deeply. He had up to now put the child out of his mind whenever he tried to bring Marietta before his eyes. He had sought excuses for its existence. "She was defenseless, she had to look for support somewhere. She must have cared honorably for the wretch who subsequently left her to her fate." Oh, why should Antonio deny that a deep grudge was eating into him? But he would no longer torment himself so terribly. It was probably thanks to this child that he would see Marietta again, and for that alone he would take the child to his heart. . . . There was nothing in that about which he ought to be ashamed. O God, once she was with him again he would listen to nothing, not a word, not a word — if only things came right between them again.

Had everything they had both suffered during this year been mysteriously necessary? Had it been necessary for each of them to take the way of the Cross in order that they might find one another again at last? Would their separate griefs become one common grief that would accompany them like moving, beautiful music, raising a glad smile about their lips? How strange, how strange and how exalted was life! How difficult to fathom it; how rash ever to pass judgment!

A wave of hungry expectation rose up warm within him, bringing tears to his eyes. This whole year Marietta's image had remained vague and remote. Now suddenly he saw her close. She was regarding him with her fine, pure glance. She was opening her mouth to call him. She was stretching out her hand to him — her slender hand that distinguished her from all the other women in the building. He no longer felt his fatigue. He walked faster and faster. Before to-morrow morning he would be in Rome, before to-morrow morning . . .

II

Suddenly he stumbled and fell. The sun began to turn in the heavens like some great golden firework and then poured down upon him, singeing him through and through with light, light. . . . He felt a dull pain, and then nothing until consciousness slowly returned to him. "I am lying here on the ground; I'll get up in a moment, and go on — just in a moment!" he thought. He got up, and tottered on.

Then the cracking of a whip seemed to echo through his blood. The ground beneath him had been shaking for some time. He subsided on a large stone by the wayside, and was able to discern the luster of lacquered coachwork: yes, even the grin of the coachman on the box. A coach passed him by.

It was going to Rome. If only he had been offered a place beside the coachman . . . But Antonio did not think of that for very long; fortunately he knew his place, and that the Virgin watched over all, but that the rich had no care for the poor. He would get there just as well as those people in their coach — only a few hours later. What were hours, what was even a whole day when one thought of God? Antonio thought of God, he thought of the Virgin, and knew himself to be under the protection of both as he sat there upon his stone, resting a little longer. . . .

Slowly he returned from these other worldly thoughts to the world that surrounded him. What sort of world was this? It was almost a wilderness. Every human being appeared to have fled from it, probably towards the mountains that rose in the vacant distance gray above the horizon. Far or near, there was no house to be seen. Not a single farm, not a field. Yonder stood a bare tree over a swamp. . . . A little farther a rugged ruin of grandiose proportions: unaccountable scattered clumps of bricks with a broken marble pillar. . . . Had men lived here once? What curse had driven them away?

He drew up his feet to convince himself that he could no longer feel them. As he bent over to loosen the laces of his boots, he discovered, at the farthest end of the stone on which he had sunk down, a small beetlelike creature, crawling up it. When at work in the convent garden, he had often seen scorpions — but he had never shared the same stone with one quietly and without hostility. The little creature with its threatening sting and its dull black armor seemed only desirous of welcoming him: it was a worthy envoy of this barren land. Antonio stared long at it, losing all sense of proportion, and every idea of time. Eternity itself seemed no longer than a moment — a moment of longing for Marietta; and that longing appeared to him sufficient.

Then suddenly the scorpion scuttled away down the stone, and into the seared grass. At the same moment Antonio stood up, trembling in his whole body, struggling against a feeling of dizziness.

He must get on.

He did not notice that blood had coagulated on the hand he passed over his forehead. He did not notice that the shoe laces he had untied were hanging down about his feet. . . .

III

An owl hooted over the evening landscape. In the slowly gathering mist the dark low hills lay like islands. A bullock cart approached, creaking and grinding miserably. The milk-white hides of the draught animals gleamed unnaturally in the moonlight, their powerfully horned heads swayed slowly backwards and forwards, the bells about their heavy folded necks jingled meaninglessly. The driver lay back, as if felled, in his cart. Suddenly he started up and pulled on the reins.

"Hey! Hey! *Sacrilegi* . . . What did you say?"

"How far is it still to Rome?"

"To Rome? Better wait till you can ride behind a wagon."

"A while back three came one after the other. They didn't pick me up."

"Traveling coaches! But you can ride on the wine carts. They'll be coming along soon."

The carter looked with astonishment after the solitary figure that had already started walking again, tottering as it moved. An owl skimmed noiselessly over his wagon. "Bad luck, bad luck," thought the carter, and tugged angrily at the reins. The oxen threw their powerful bodies forward against the old creaking leather harness, the badly greased axles renewed their melody of squeaking and grinding. It was some time before the sound of the cart was lost once more in the stillness of the evening.

The moon lit up a strange ruin. A high, ghostly endless bridge it seemed, that had crumbled away here and there. . . . Through the mist, it looked like a gigantic antediluvian centipede that was marching upon Rome.

Antonio hastened his steps. Anxiety alone drove him on — anxiety for Marietta, who was lost if he did not reach Rome in good health, and in time. Since darkness set in, he had been pursued by the nightmare that God might pass judgment this very night, before the Virgin had received his candle and learned of the good work that awaited Her, before the good saints had been able to raise their voices all together for Marietta and Antonio and the child that was to be their child.

Why had he not lit a candle to the Madonna before leaving Todi? He ought to have realized that that was even more necessary than going to Ercole the carpenter to ask him to take charge of his business. Why had he not slipped into one of the village churches he had passed on the road? He had given himself no time. He had intended to go to St. Peter's in Rome. A voice from the church of the Pope himself must surely reach God's ear first, he had thought. But what could the church of the Pope avail him now, if Marietta was already resting in eternal sleep? He seemed to see her features, wax-pale and gleaming damply through the mist. Even in death she smiled at him. . . .

He fell down beside her upon his knees and covered her hand with kisses. He kissed her forehead and her transparent cheeks that were already cold. Her eyes were staring at him wide open — nobody had closed them. . . .

He looked behind him, realizing suddenly that he had heard it for some time — this drone of a song that was coming nearer and nearer, accompanied by the trotting of a horse and the rumbling of wheels: the first wine cart.

The horse was white as the mist through which it lifted its knees rhythmically. Half in the moonlight, half in the shadow of the movable hood, sat the driver — a brown and portly man, who interrupted his song when he perceived by the wayside a silent, tired figure.

"You must always keep a sharp lookout here before you take anyone on your wagon," he said later, after he had hoisted Antonio onto his cart in a wave of commiseration. No man was safe until he was under the walls of the city, and even within the walls there were more thieves and murderers than Christians — though he admitted that he was thinking in particular of the wholesale wine merchants.

When he learned that Antonio was bound for the Hospital for the Poor, he began to wonder whether it lay in the Trastevere region. He himself knew Rome only by night: he delivered his wine, received his money, and then loaded his empty vats again. Yes, he had been to St. Peter's, of course, and he had crawled up the Scala Santa on his bare knees. As to the Hospital for the Poor, he related various stories of beggars who had stumbled in there, sick and half-starved, and had been lovingly cared for until death; and then, when they were to be buried at the expense of the city, the merciful Sisters had found a dozen golden ducats sewn into their rags. He had stories to tell about the pious nuns, too; and he related that the great door in the front of the building was called the *"Bocca della Morte,"* because the dead were carried out through it, but no one ever went in that way. Those who wanted to go in preferred to knock at the side door. . . .

He glanced round at Antonio, who sat leaning back, his eyes closed, his lips tightly set. "Let's talk of something else," suggested the driver, groping under the box with his free hand. "Here, the wine bottle! Wash away your worries if you happen to have any. Trust in the Madonna. Look, I carry her on my bare chest!" He kissed a medallion that hung by a string round his fleshy, sunburned neck and let it slip back again under his shirt.

Trust in the Madonna . . . *Bocca della Morte* they called the front door of the Hospital for the Poor . . .

"Drink! Why don't you drink?" asked the driver, offended. "You must be very careful when you taste the wine of Gasparo Vicco, who is coming along behind us (and better not taste it at all); but you're quite safe in drinking Angelo Stefani's wine. As safe as drinking mother's milk. It'll make you feel gayer. You want your friends, you want your wife. . . . Do you know what the innkeepers in Rome call it? '*Fa-figliuoli*': they call it '*Fa-figliuoli.*'" Relishing his own joke, he burst out laughing. "Drink! Drink, my boy! Wait, we'll put the bottle between us, we'll empty it. Move up closer so that it doesn't fall. *Chk! Chk! Bianco, cuore mio! . . .*"

While the shimmering moon seemed about to drown in the softly swirling waters of the Tiber, the carter continued talking in an intoxication of self-sufficiency — about his wine, his Madonna, his family. Nine children, he had. And he was hardly five-and-thirty. *Fa-figliuoli! Fa-figliuoli! Salute!* And six of them were already working in his vineyard. There would have been seven if one had not died the previous year — but that made a dozen hands anyhow. Early in the trade . . . He himself had had to help pick the grapes before he was four, and during the busy period there was never much talk of going to bed, either.

Then he suddenly broke off, pointing in front of him with his whip. Above the bank of dust gleamed a small gray patch that — slowly — formed itself into the shape of a dome. A little later, through the overarching crowns of the old gnarled pine trees that lined both sides of the road, a pale phantom of towers, domes, houses, rose up upon a hilly base. Rome. . . . Rome.

IV

At an inn where the driver had to deliver his wine Antonio sat waiting, his head buried in his arms. Only a feverish shiver betrayed that there was still life in him. While they were busy reckoning, the other two men cast an occasional glance of commiseration at him. He stood up at last, listened in silence to the innkeeper's renewed warnings that it was unwise to go into the streets at that hour, at any rate in his exhausted condition — and, armed with directions, went his way after all.

Very soon he had lost himself. He was looking for a square with a fountain composed of large fishes and tortoises, and it simply would not appear. He found other squares, where water murmured in the stillness of the night, large squares overlooked by a church and some few great palaces. He found, too, a ruin here and there that had never been tidied up, some grandiose marble Colossus leaning perilously. He crossed the Tiber, and reached the quarters of the city where reigned squalor and abject poverty. . . . Was this Rome too, the great city where the Holy Father lived? Relentlessly driven forward, he wandered on aching feet deeper and deeper into those dark quarters of human misery. He believed that only there would he find Marietta.

He asked the way of the first passers-by: they were beggars chased from their lodgings, women on their way to the city wells, the exhalations of sleep still in their rank clothing. The air was full of the sound of bells ringing for early Mass as he was directed through meandering slums, where green-black ditchwater lay in muddy holes in which pigs rooted. Then he came to squares again, where in the first light of the morning carts were being harnessed and market stalls set up. The streets were growing busier. Carts rattled and bumped over the uneven pavements, and through the air floated the sound of cracking whips, the first crude curse of the newly born day. And there he saw a small party of *sbirri* driving a prisoner before them.

It was a jeering street urchin who put him right at last. "The Hospital for the Poor? It's straight in front of you. They're on the lookout for you!"

Over Antonio came the strange sensation that he had seen all this before: the great square still in the shadow of night, the *sbirri* driving on the captive thief who moaned loudly to indicate to his captors how cruelly they had kicked him, and in the background, against the gold of the rising sun, sleepy and patient, a broad gray stone building: the *Casa di Carità.*

He stared at it, and dared not approach nearer. Then the first rays of the sun struck the side of the roof, and it glowed, a warm rust-red. At the same time, the shrill sound of a bell reached him. The sharp voice came from the Hospital for the Poor, as if to testify that it still harbored life after a night sustained with difficulty. . . . But what a weak, sick life it was.

Antonio's eyes were fixed upon the front door . . . It was high, impressive, of dark wood. Whoever let fall the heavy bronze knocker would hear a hollow echo from the depths of the building. . . . Those who had died this night would rise up in fear, and, their emaciated fingers clinging round the grating of the judas window, would peep out with sunken eyes. With a stifled cry Antonio rushed forward and began to run up and down the length of the building, looking up at all the windows — Marietta might be lying behind any one of them. Then he ran round the corner, along the wing of the building into a narrow lane.

He stopped before a small, low doorway in which stood a broken wooden door. He pressed his face to a chink, through which he could see a little garden, and a refuse tub. He leaned against the door, he began to beat upon it with all his force, so that a chicken scratching round the refuse tub ran away cackling.

"I want to see my wife — my wife and child!" shouted Antonio, turning to a woman who was leaning out of a window on the other side of the little lane. He ran round another corner, and came to a long, blind, convent wall at the end of which a group of beggars was surging round a short flight of steps. Pressed tightly against the closed door, a pregnant woman, still young, with a child upon her arm, was crying out indignantly that she was being crushed. The beggars were undeterred, however. Unanimously they looked at Antonio, hostile, surprised, contemptuous.

"Is this the entrance?" he stammered, in response to this crossfire of hungry, bestial eyes.

Not one of the beggars answered. The young woman, however, in order to revenge herself upon them, cried out breathlessly, "Yes, this is the entrance. You just push a little, too. If a helpless brat gets crushed to death, that's no concern of theirs, the cowards, the murderers."

"When does the door open?"

"At sunrise."

"But the sun is up already."

"Not in the opinion of those inside."

This sarcastic reply had a crushing effect upon Antonio. In dumb

despair, he paced up and down the little lane, unaware that he was provoking derision and amusement among the beggars. He was struggling
with the dreadful thought that Marietta had had to stand in that place
among such outcasts as these in order to gain the protection held out to
them.

He stood still, and wiped the clammy sweat from his face. The child!
He had forgotten the child. What Marietta would never have done for
herself, she had had to do for the child. Unconscious of the pushing beggars, he took his place behind them in the noisome stench of their sick,
soiled bodies, their clothes drenched with sweat. The child sanctified
her flight into this retreat, sanctified everything that might have happened.

The little girl on the arm of the woman in front of the door began to
cry loudly in fear. The little judas window was opened and an old nun's
irate face peered through. Among the beggars rose a murmuring — a lament of human misery diversified by pious praise of the all-merciful Virgin. The old woman did not hear it. Her eyes, grown fixed and hard in
the service of this Virgin, did not see human beings — only a number.
"Eighteen," her lips muttered, and the little opening closed with a snap.
Silently the beggars waited, looking at each other in resentful resignation. There were eighteen of them to-day — they had not counted themselves. Indeed, some of them could not count. Eighteen! Yesterday there
had been room for seven. . . .

"Mother!" Antonio shouted, but too late: the judas was closed.

They waited and waited. At last the judas was opened again. "No pushing, please! You'll all be examined. He who is most in need will be received . . . What, you here again? There's nothing wrong with you."

"Yes, there is, I swear it by the Virgin. I have had to drag myself to get
here. I'm writhing with pain, but nothing can be seen from the outside.
Give me something to eat at least!" answered the cadaverous creature she
addressed, and there were tears in his voice.

Then the door opened. The woman with the child was shouting already in her fear of the wild rush that she foresaw. She fell, but was rescued
by an alert little brother, and taken protectingly on one side, her bitter
accusations unheeded. The old nun bolted the door behind the last suppliant, and signed to the pregnant woman to follow her.

Antonio barred her way. "Mother: I have come to look for my wife."

The nun looked at him, struck by his appearance, and exchanged a rapid
glance with the brother who was about to lead his sheep away.

"When did your wife arrive here?"

"I think — perhaps a week ago, but I only heard of it on Saturday evening. I come from Todi." In the hollow silence that surrounded him, Antonio listened to the echo of his own words. He hardly dared to breathe as he looked at the old woman; it seemed that but one answer could come from her mouth — "Dead!"

"What was your wife's name?" asked the old nun, unconsciously using the past tense.

"Marietta — Marietta Buongiorno."

"Marietta Buongiorno . . ." The nun considered, then asked the brother, "What was she called, the one who was lying upstairs and who yesterday evening . . . ?"

"That wasn't her name," replied the little brother with decision; Antonio listened as it was being debated whether his Marietta was still alive or already dead. Then suddenly a light appeared in the fast gathering gloom.

"Has your wife a child with her, by any chance?"

"Yes, yes, Mother."

"A little boy of six months?"

"Yes, yes."

"And is she still young herself? Younger even than you?"

"Yes. You're talking about her now, Mother. I'm certain you're talking about my wife. She's alive still, isn't she?"

• "Come and see for yourself if it's she," said the old woman, with some hesitation. The little brother, however, with a deeper faith in God's hidden ways, nodded reassuringly to Antonio.

"Well, now — are you coming?" he said, brightly, to the waiting beggars who, motionless, had been looking on. In his frayed cowl, he preceded them in one direction while Antonio blindly followed the old nun in the other. Patiently he waited in a little room with the woman and her child. He dropped down next to them upon a bench that stood against a wall. There was just enough room for him. He looked at the little girl. Within him was a great stillness. He caressed the little one's cheek and asked her mother what she was called. Oh . . . Carla? In the city where he lived he knew another little girl whose name was Carla. . . .

Then the old nun returned with a younger nun who looked at him inquisitively: there was a hidden struggle between the two as to which of them should accompany the pregnant woman and her child to the doctor, and which should conduct Antonio to his wife.

"This is the tenth day she's been here. I know quite well where she's lying," said the younger nun zealously. "She came from Naples. Someone has been to visit her before. . . ."

"From Todi," said Antonio hastily. "That was Cesare, the carrier."

By the side of the old nun he went down a long corridor, giving way before other sisters who, prayer books pressed against their straitlaced bosoms, were leaving the chapel, dark silhouettes against the golden candlelight.

"This isn't really the visitors' hour," said the old woman as she opened a door on one side of the corridor: she wanted to make him realize that he was being specially favored.

From the cool, deathly stillness of the dim corridor, he was ushered into a scene of fierce and colorful animation. A quarrel had broken out among the women — thin, withered creatures of every age, some sitting bolt upright against their pillows, some lying down. Their shrieks and shouts abated, however, as soon as the old nun, followed by a grave and embarrassed man, entered the ward. The women fixed their eyes upon him mockingly. One of them said something in a dialect he could not understand. The old nun looked round her severely, and beckoned to Antonio to keep close to her as she proceeded between the rows of beds. The momentary stillness was suddenly broken by hysterical screams lower down the ward: a nun, hurrying forward to cover up the unfortunate patient who in her agony had thrown off her blankets, looked at Antonio angrily from under her coif: he had no business to be there at this unusual hour. Some of the sick women lay stretched out quietly on their backs staring into space. Others followed the old nun with their faded, melan-• choly, hungry eyes, and whined: "Mother Cecilia — are you coming to me to-day? You promised — I want to tell you something." In a corner there were whispers. Two nuns pushed an empty bed forward, to fill a vacant space. On the wall hung a holy water stoup. One of the nuns took it down and handed it to another, who carried it away, hiding it in her wide sleeves.

The old nun stood still and looked towards Antonio. He turned his eyes, still confused by the quiet, mysterious happenings there in the corner, towards the bed on which she had laid her gnarled old hand. Stumbling forward, he approached and stared at the face of the girl on the pillow. . . . The face of a young mother, her eyes closed in deep sleep — sheltering under her chin an infant's round, brown head.

His knees gave way under him. He had to catch hold of the side of the bed, but he had the presence of mind to remain quiet as death, almost to stop breathing. . . . He glanced round at the old nun, over whose features a smile was playing that completely transformed her. He nodded to her affirmatively, grew pale, and then turned his eyes again towards his wife, towards his Marietta whose magnificent long curls had been shorn.

The first thing he noticed was her pallor. The transparent delicacy of

her face made it even more childlike than it had been a year ago. She
looked almost as she did in the days when he had watched her in the convent garden, from under the broad brim of his straw hat. . . . An insane
happiness, a pious gratitude sprang up in him as he saw her lying there
so helpless. He wanted to laugh and cry at the same time. He felt suddenly so deeply and simply that this was his wife, his Marietta whom he
was about to take under his protection again, together with the innocent
little creature who had so far breathed only in the shelter of her love. How
peacefully it lay there, one thumb in its greedy little mouth, its eyes
closed, its tiny round gleaming head covered with silken black hair, its
nostrils moving up and down with its short, sharp breaths. . . .

Antonio, standing motionless at the foot of the bed, was not himself
aware of his complete absorption in this little world that appeared to him
infinite. He forgot the ward in which he stood, he had no realization that
he was being watched with curiosity and some malice by the eyes in the
surrounding beds. He did not notice that the old nun, roused to anger by
the quarrel that had flared up again at the other end of the ward, had
shuffled away to the soft clinking of rosary and keys. . . . His glance
moved from the child to the mother again, and suddenly for the first time
he doubted whether his protection could still save her. In growing anguish,
he noted how blue were her temples, how thin her lips, how weak her
breathing. The smile about his broad mouth disappeared, giving place to
an expression of infinite anxiety. . . .

The little brown boy, startled by one knows not what, moved his head,
lost his thumb, opened two large, brilliant, brown eyes, only to close them
immediately again, and broke the stillness around Antonio with a wailing
cry. The mother instinctively passed her thin hand over her child. Soothed,
he found his thumb again, and began to suck with gusto. For a moment,
Marietta seemed about to doze off once more. Instead, she opened her eyes
— and became aware of Antonio.

At first she did not understand. The pupils of her eyes widened farther
and farther. Without daring to move, he met her glance, murmuring her
name. He felt that his fate stood in the balance. Her head seemed to sink
deeper into her pillow; her eyes reflected fear and aversion — the memory
of a thousand torments. With difficulty, she turned her face away from
him.

Oblivious of the whole ward, aware only of the fact that he must win
or lose everything now, he flung himself down beside her, pressing his
forehead against the cool hand she attempted to withdraw. Her name came
repeatedly to his lips as he stammered: "Marietta — I've come from Todi.
I can't do without you, Marietta. Cesare said . . . And now I'm here.

You didn't come to me when you were hungry and in want, not to me. You didn't come to me — Marietta."

He tottered towards the other side of the bed so that he could see her face. It was quite close to his. Her mouth began to tremble, and she looked at him through a shimmer of tears. He was emboldened to kiss her very softly, while happiness welled up in his throat. He tried to reassure her: "Marietta, you'll get strong and well again. I've come to fetch you and the child. Everything will be all right again. . . ."

He was interrupted by the child's crying, and this time it would not allow itself to be quieted. It raised a pitiless wail. The crying stopped a moment as its solicitous father bent over it, but the little mouth opened wider again immediately, drowning all tenderness with its cries. The old nun hastened forward and picked it up. Observed by the mother, anxiously followed by the dazed father, she laid it crying on the broad window sill and nodded to it encouragingly, saying, "What, crying? Just as your father sees you for the first time? *Ta-ta-ta-ta!* Yes, it's a drink you want."

She changed its napkins with her old, smooth hands — and then unexpectedly passed the little bundle to Antonio. He looked down upon the child in his arms and tried to feel akin to it. His glance wandered helplessly in Marietta's direction, but her eyes did not reassure him: there was something puzzling and tormented about them. . . . Suddenly he became aware that he was being watched by the others in the ward. From all the beds women smiled at him encouragingly, and, as if by agreement among themselves, cried out together, "How can a child resemble its father so? The boy is the very image of you!"

Flushing, Antonio looked at the women.

Meanwhile, helped by the old nun, Marietta had raised herself a little. With a gesture of the arms, she asked silently for the child. The old nun went off, pushing a chair towards Antonio, and said that he might remain just a little longer, and then return at the visiting hour. Meekly he sat down upon the chair, and with bowed head and a fixed stare looked at the child as it snatched eagerly and pitilessly at Marietta's transparent white breast. She too looked down upon the child through the veil of her long lashes, and rubbed away some drops of sweat that stood on the round, downy forehead of the little one from the effort of drinking.

The women in the beds near by, delighted at the morning's unexpected diversion, anticipated a conversation between the reunited husband and wife. They had had no idea that Marietta was married. They all liked her, and they had just given another proof of this; but they were disappointed that Marietta had not told them. They had always thought she had been seduced by some rogue or other, and deserted.

But there was little for them to overhear. Antonio had nothing to say to his wife. As through a mist, he watched the child feeding. Thoughts wandered through his brain: "I shall bring her fruit and ask her if she doesn't need something. . . . The child is drinking so greedily from her . . . If she won't go back with me to Todi, I shan't return either. I don't know what is to happen then. I shall remain with her. . . . After all, she won't chase me away if I insist upon looking after her. I'll just look after her — her and the child. . . ."

He cleared his throat and asked, "What is his name?"

"Benedetto," she answered softly, without looking up. It was the first word she had spoken to him, and it cut through him. Her voice was thin and expressionless, and strange as her voice was the sound of the name in his ears. Benedetto . . . Why Benedetto? After whom had she called him that? Oh, he had not the right to be displeased . . . An oppressive sense of his own inferiority weighed upon his shoulders. He almost collapsed under it. He felt himself rejected and terribly deserted, there in the presence of his wife and child. And why had all those women mocked him so cruelly by saying that the child was like him? He bowed his head lower still. He no longer cared to look at the child.

Then she appeared to have an inkling of what was torturing him. "The priest in Naples who baptized him gave him that name, because I had not thought of one myself," she said.

The explanation relieved him absurdly. Suddenly he found the courage to speak, glibly, passionately; and the women in the beds near by pricked up their ears.

"Marietta — I've never forgotten you — never. Only afterwards did I understand how guilty I was. All the time I've been with Mother I've thought only of you, Marietta — only of you. I used to lie in bed thinking of you, and wondering if I should ever see you again. I have prayed . . ." He broke off because he could not bring himself to tell his great entreating prayer.

She looked at him and whispered — but only to console him, "I also have thought of you, Antonio . . . and whether your mother would go to live with you, and if then you had found peace . . ."

"Not peace . . . It's you, it's you I want, Marietta," he brought out, and she moaned in despair.

"Why did Cesare speak? He didn't know what he was doing. What did your mother say?"

"Mother made room for you immediately. . . . She has gone back to her own rooms. She doesn't want to meddle in our home any more."

Slowly, full of aversion and deadly fear, Marietta shook her head backwards and forwards. "No, I'm not going back with you," she whispered hoarsely.

"But I want to look after you — you and the . . . Oh, God, Marietta, don't say no. It will be different now. What must I do, if you won't go back with me? I have nobody but you. If you want to know, if she hadn't I would have . . . You said once, 'You must choose between your mother and me — You must choose . . .'"

His voice was hoarse, his words confused, his large eyes helpless, filled with a desperate anguish.

Then an unfriendly young nun came to say that he had been there long enough, and that he could come back at the visiting hour.

"When — when is that?"

"A half-hour before sunset," came the information from different beds.

He still hoped for a glance from Marietta as he went, but she dared not look up at him lest he should read a silent promise in her pity.

V

He was outside the hospital again. He hurried past a few beggars who had been turned away and were hobbling ahead of him down the little alley. He knew where he was going. "St. Peter's — where is St. Peter's?" he asked, and people looked into his tired feverish eyes with involuntary compassion and pointed to the great dome that showed between the houses. He followed the direction, and soon there opened out before him the broad square with the two fountains glistening in the gold of the sun, and the circular colonnades that seemed like the wide embracing arms of the church that rose, overwhelming, from its broad and magnificent flight of steps.

With contracted heart, drained of everything except his faith in the all-merciful Virgin, Antonio mounted the massive white marble steps on which fell the grotesque shadows of beggars. From a dirty old blind woman he bought a large candle, the largest she had. His heart full of gratitude, he heard her call down a blessing upon him as, crossing himself, he entered one of the side doors.

The mightiest church in Christendom received him into its spacious stillness and marble cool. He lost himself among the great gleaming pillars that seemed to pierce the heavens. Between tombstones with angels stretching wide their shining gold wings and sculptured saints larger than life, overawed by the high altar, under the canopy supported by its spiraled copper pillars, he roamed along the aisles, where cold pomp stared haughtily back at him. . . . Perhaps this church was only for the rich. Surely the halting prayer of one unfortunate man hoping to win back his wife with the help of the Madonna would not be heard there at all. Was it not pride that had made him want to pray here? Would he not have acted better in the eyes of the Virgin if he had cried out his great need to Her in a more modest place? Evading an official, he slipped into a darker part of the church. This, this was what he was looking for, a smaller chapel less impressively decorated than the others. It contained an old, battered painting of the Madonna, surrounded by votive offerings as by the gleaming, living voices of the grateful whose prayers had been heard.

Here he placed his candle, and felt hope rising within him when he saw that his light made the chapel a little brighter, and raised a glow of gold in the background behind the Madonna. It was a lovable, childish Madonna, a little oppressed perhaps by the weight of Her jeweled crown. He sank down before Her and lost himself in fervid, incoherent prayer. He implored Her to continue Her protection of Marietta and to persuade her to follow her husband to Todi with her child, to their safe home in the old house where his workshop was, so that he could earn the daily bread of all three of them. Mother of God, was that too much to ask?

As he prayed, the first soft notes of the organ began to sound like an answering voice from heaven, and when, full of faith in the Virgin, he got up and kissed the glass that protected the old painting, the murmur of pious voices reached him from another chapel. He made his way to it and joined in the prayers for the soul of a dead man whose family, clad in deep mourning, were listening to the reading of the funeral service. Then he left the cathedral and fled from the great wide square upon which the sun was burning.

VI

A heavy cart was groaning over the stone bridge as Antonio woke. After breaking his fast at a small sordid inn, he had found his way to the Tiber: in this vast, distant city it was a consolation and a reassurance to him, for the water that here flowed in slow eddies brown with mud under the bridges was the same that danced pure and frolicsome among the stones at Pontecutini a bare mile from Todi. His head was so dizzy, his limbs so heavy, that he had sunk down upon a bench, staring at the bustling market women, the maidservants, the men in livery, postilions, beggars, monks, and horsemen, ladies in their lacquered sedans with crests upon the doors . . . until he saw only shifting color before him and heard but vaguely the tramp of horses and the cracking of whips.

He was wide awake again. He got up, crossed the bridge. It was too early to go to the Hospital for the Poor — the sun still shone high above the houses. The hour of the siesta was drawing to an end, but the bridge, which this morning had been thronged with people, lay deserted in the heat of the broiling afternoon. A feeling of faintness came over him. He went and drank from a fountain, and freshened his forehead and wrists.

He bought some oranges for Marietta, and a little later, without being himself aware of what he wanted, he stood glued before a shop window spread with costly stuffs, trimmed hats, ivory fans, embroidery frames, all sorts of embroidery, artificial flowers — and about a dozen dolls, ranged neatly in a row and dressed in wide skirts with lace frills and bows, such as great ladies wore. He stood looking at these dolls as if he could not make up his mind between them, — and indeed he could not, — until an assistant came out, a young girl who brought with her a cloud of perfume and was no less painted than the dolls that smiled as she did. Guessing Antonio's inclination, she mentioned the prices of the dolls — and he no longer dared to look at any but the two smallest of the row, which had wooden heads instead of porcelain. One was dressed in pink and the other in pale blue. Suddenly, behind the little panes of the window, he noticed amused faces. He flushed darkly. The little blue doll had a garland of flowers round its straw hat. The pink one had a little bow. That was the difference.

"Take the pink one; the pink one is the prettier," decided the young assistant suddenly, for him, as somebody tapped on the window and she noticed with a rapid side glance that a caroche with coachman and groom had come rolling up. Instantly, Antonio knew that his presence, clad as he was in provincial workmen's clothes and heavy soiled boots, was unwelcome. In his confusion he accepted the pink one and paid for it. The expeditious assistant put the doll into the satin lined box that belonged to it and slipped it under his arm. The caroche stopped. The shop door was opened wide. The radiant proprietress appeared at the entrance, and three attendants hastened forward to kiss respectfully the hand of an ample matron arrayed in purple who had some difficulty in squeezing herself through the little door of the caroche. . . . A fourth assistant rushed up to her carrying a sunshade to protect her from the Roman afternoon sun, so inimical to complexions, for the few steps that separated the caroche from the door.

Antonio went on his way. Dimly he realized that this first toy for the child had eaten up a considerable part of his travel money; but at the moment there was little room in his heart for anxiety: he felt himself too rich in the possession of the beautiful doll that he hoped would surprise Marietta even more than the little one.

VII

He found her with her face turned towards the entrance to the ward. Was she looking for him? She tried to raise herself a little when she noticed the freight of oranges he carried, and she could not restrain a certain childish happy pride in the glance she cast at the other women, who had also observed with satisfaction the appearance of the heavily burdened Antonio.

She told him at once to go round the beds near her with his oranges. Flushed and anxious, he acceded to her wish. He met with no refusals, though some of them did say, "But you've really brought them for your wife." But all the same they began at once to dig their teeth greedily into the bitter rind of the fruit.

The little that was left over he laid beside Marietta with an imploring look. Then he unpacked the doll. Marietta fell silent with astonishment: she might herself have been still small and receiving her first doll. How much he must have spent on it! Real lace trimmed the small skirt, the buckles on the shoes were of silver, the miniature fan that hung from the little arm opened and closed. It was far too pretty and costly for the infant. He might look at it, but on no account must he lay hands upon it. . . .

The women in the other beds wanted to see it. They wiped the juice from their fingers on their bedclothes before they took the little doll one from the other and gave vent to unfeigned admiration. They looked at Antonio with closer attention: he had enough money to buy such a thing as that, then — and their intuition told them that he had come by the doll honestly. Surely there was nothing money could not buy! Even the underclothing was of lace — had Antonio noticed that? The women showed it him, laughing, and, as they had expected, he blushed. Madonna! there were still men in the world like that! And there were also others. . . .

At last the doll was put where the baby could see it from his cradle. He gazed at it for a time; then lost interest in it, and peered once more on high towards the window, sucking his fingers contentedly.

The attention of the other women in the ward was attracted to a visitor to one of their number. A miserable old woman this visitor was, and she was accompanied by an unwashed, uncombed little girl who had brought food and sweets in a red handkerchief. They all listened eagerly to this garrulous old woman's comments on the world, and answered her with opinions on things and people of which they knew nothing. They had lost interest in Antonio and Marietta, who could have spoken freely to one another at last had they been so minded.

But Marietta only asked him general questions. How had he come from Todi to Rome — surely not on foot? Her question conjured up visions of scorching sunlight before his eyes, and his throat grew dry and parched . . . Oh, but he would not think about that any more. He was not going to be carried away by self-pity. He prepared to tell her about his business in Todi, and how it had prospered during the year she had been away. . . . Ercole, the carpenter behind San Jacopo's, rather envied him. . . . As for himself, he had not cared much either way, as he no longer knew for whom he was working. . . . Because, despite his good earnings, he had been unable to prevent his wife from suffering want in distant parts.

Marietta hastened to reassure him. In the beginning she had not suffered any want. At first in Naples she had earned good money. It was only later, after the birth of the child, that things had grown difficult. Yes, then . . .

He looked at her with infinite compassion as she broke off and stared before her with tired eyes. But he was afraid that if he asked her questions he would appear to be luring her into confessions that she did not want to make. . . . And he feared that she was growing overtired with all this talk, and the recalling to her mind of the recent past. He laid his hand upon her forehead to compel her to be silent. She closed her eyes obediently, and her head, which she had raised with difficulty, sank back into the pillow.

"Better be quiet," he said. "You must get well quickly. Nothing else matters."

About her mouth appeared a line of grief that filled him with fear.

"Marietta," he whispered.

She shrugged her shoulders despondently.

"Marietta, why shouldn't you get better? You will, you will. I'll bring you everything needed to strengthen you. . . . Tell me what you fancy. Are you eating enough? You will eat, won't you? After all, you must feed your child. If you don't care any more about yourself or about me . . . Think at least of the child — of our child, Marietta."

She looked up quickly and gave him a penetrating glance. He could not bear that glance, and began to sputter, not knowing himself what he was saying. "It is our child, isn't it? Marietta, I ask only because . . . Oh God, don't be angry with me. So much has gone through my mind since that evening when Cesare told us . . . Ah well, don't say anything at all.

. . . Mother asked Cesare how old the child was, but you need not say. If it comes with us to Todi, it will be our child. Then it'll be indeed our child." Filled with shame and grief, he buried his head in the blankets.

"It is five months old," said Marietta tonelessly.

Perhaps she wanted to say more, but the words would not come as, full of pity, she looked at Antonio's boyish head with its thick, dark, gleaming hair.

Gently she ran her hand over his head.

That gesture did Antonio good. Everything, everything was suddenly right. If only he could continue to sit thus and cease to think!

The child was five months old. He could say that to everybody in Todi. The child was five months old. Besides, by instinct he had just found a formula that satisfied him completely: "If the child comes with us to Todi, then it'll be indeed our child."

He did not raise his head. He remained quite still, accepting consolation. He had missed it so long: so many wounds were smarting within him.

He did not notice that Marietta was staring above her, her mouth tightly closed in repressed pain.

Only when the bell sounded for the end of the visiting hour and he got upon his feet, still dizzy and weak, did he observe how shattered Marietta was. He bent over her and kissed her. He tried to console her by saying, "I shall come back again to-morrow. Don't think about anything. Everything will come right. Have faith in the Virgin. . . . I offered a candle to Her to-day."

In his voice was an infinite, childish trust. She looked after him as he went, talking to Mother Cecilia. At the door, he turned to say, "Till to-morrow."

When she had closed her eyes again, his image continued to play upon her retina. She saw him standing at the door, young and strong and healthy, in spite of the fatigue of the exhausting journey he had undertaken for her sake. To-morrow he would come back, rested after a night of trustful sleep, and he would press his suit more vigorously, try to dominate her. He knew what he wanted. Probably the moment Cesare had broken his promise, Antonio had known what he wanted. Already he understood a great deal — everything, indeed, that lay within his understanding. He had understood and counted the cost, so that no subsequent surprise could deflect him from his purpose. . . . That was the dangerous side to his insistence. When she had said to him, "The child is five months old," that was an answer to his mother, an answer to all the venomous tongues in Todi. It was not the answer she intended to give Antonio himself: when he asked her on his own behalf, she would tell him the whole truth.

But so long as she did not go back with him to Todi, she could spare him by silence. Go back to Todi . . . !

But if she really did get well . . . Could she resist his will? Might not his will be even strong enough to compel her to get well? No, fortunately it was too late for that. Her exhaustion was too deep for her to struggle back to life. She had no strength left . . . no strength at all . . . She did not want to see the outside world again. Dark shadows glided before her eyes. She was already familiar with them. . . . Thicker and thicker they would grow, these shadows of death.

Her child was safe! She could afford to give way, to conjure up these dark shadows — the light had tired her so; and who was he that he should force himself into her own cherished little world where he was a stranger, and compel her to struggle once more?

He had appealed to her — on account of the child. *He* appealed . . . and for the child.

Later it occurred to her that when he went away he had forgotten to take leave of the child. She felt regretful — she was foolish, so foolish . . .

The moonlight fell upon the cradle. Soon Mother Cecilia would come to attend to the baby, and to give him to her for the night.

And suppose she did grow strong again . . . strong enough to face life . . . What crazy notions were passing through her poor, tormented head — away, away with them!

VIII

It was already getting dark as Antonio emerged into the street. In the slowly gathering dusk of Rome, in the shadow of the somber palaces and the fantastic stone masses from the far past, he found his way back to the little inn that Cesare had recommended to him. Teresa Passano, a rather surly youngish woman, had given him a small room under the roof. He sat on the side of his straw bed, eating a piece of bread, and listening to fighting tomcats and to the rats that played above his head. Then the bells of Rome began to ring — unknown voices that seemed to come to him from the moonlight itself, dark, warning, consoling voices. . . . Listening to them, he fell asleep, and in his dreams he returned with Marietta and the child to Todi. He was downstairs at his work, and she was preparing a meal upstairs, and the child lay peacefully asleep in the cradle he had carpentered for it.

Early the following morning, renewed restlessness drove him into the street. Not until he stood before the Madonna in St. Peter's did he begin to feel calmer. She seemed more familiar to him than on the previous day. She looked at him gently, full of loving-kindness and sweet pity. His candle had burned down to the socket: he stuck a new one in the same place, so that She should be in no doubt that this, the first candle to be lit to Her to-day, was offered by the same hopeful suppliant as had approached Her yesterday. Then he knelt down and implored for strength in the struggle that lay before him.

He got up, feeling at peace once more, and set about putting into effect a plan that had been in his mind. He was going to look for work. He needed money for Marietta. . . .

Refusals that brought the flush of shame to his cheek (would anybody have been treated so in Todi?) aroused a bitter obstinacy instead of discouragement in him; and in the end he was taken on by a small master-carpenter needing a man to replace one who had been seriously hurt the previous day by a ripping-chisel. Gratefully, Antonio allowed a plane to be pressed into his hand and set about the rough work he was required to do. His temporary master watched him with a side glance, and before the day was over he was put to more difficult jobs. Antonio, thinking of his own tools in Todi, regarded those with which he now had to work despairingly; and as he worked he wondered whether Ercole was being sufficiently careful . . . But he really could feel safe about that.

As he sawed and hammered, his self-confidence and his belief in a fortunate turn of events revived. . . . "What will Marietta say when she hears that I have already found work in this great new city?" He thought perhaps she would not have believed him capable of that.

As he hurried in the late afternoon towards the Hospital for the Poor, he remembered for the first time that Cesare would arrive in Rome that day, and to his great and happy surprise saw him waiting in the little alley. As Antonio appeared Cesare went up to him, an anxious question in his eyes.

"And . . . ?"

"I'm just going to her."

"Thank God! I've been growing more anxious all the way. How long have you been here?"

Antonio did not listen. He drew Cesare on one side: "I say, what has Mother done?"

"That same night your mother went back to her own rooms. That's quite all right."

Antonio stared before him. "It isn't all right yet. . . . But it will be," he said with a strange forcefulness in his voice, "once she has seen the child."

"Of course, of course."

"Cesare, if she speaks to you about it tell her it is five months old."

"Good, excellent! I'll tell her. Besides, I shall see it myself in a moment. But in any case . . . Good! I'm glad. It's better so, isn't it? Didn't I tell you?"

The door opened, and the two men joined the queue of visitors. Cesare tugged at Antonio's arm. "I say, I'm not in the way? Wouldn't you rather be with her alone?"

"No, no, she'll be so pleased," urged Antonio excitedly, dragging his neighbor along with him. He could hardly endure his longing to see Marietta again. He was longing for the child too. Again and again during the day he had tried to bring the little one's features before his eyes . . .

Marietta started up on seeing her two visitors. She feared the other women might cease to approve of her, they who had been so well disposed towards her and had even made clothes for her child. . . . Luckily, Antonio had brought more fruit. . . . How kind he was to her! And Cesare carried a parcel too.

Cesare greeted Marietta a little awkwardly — it seemed almost unbelievable that he had ever sung to her as though he had been an opera singer. He looked at the sleeping child sheepishly and expressed astonishment at the increase in its powers of observation in a single week . . .

Antonio, in an exaggeratedly lighthearted tone, told how he had already found work in Rome: this very first day he had earned enough to buy oranges, eggs, a flask of wine.

Cesare remarked on Antonio's good sense, saying that such an idea would never have occurred to him so quickly. It just showed what a stout fellow Antonio was. He patted Antonio on the shoulder with the protecting joviality of an uncle, and decided that this was the propitious moment to ask Marietta whether she was angry with him for having broken his promise. He had found he simply could not keep silent — even Camilla, who was usually rigid, agreed that that promise was one to be broken. . . .

He stopped, for Marietta admitted that she was pleased Antonio had come; he was good to her, much too good — she had not deserved such goodness. . . . Antonio, overcome by emotion, seized her hand and covered it with kisses, and Cesare felt about the occasion a beautiful solemnity such as he had thought belonged only to deaths and marriages. He too became emotional, and congratulated himself heartily upon having brought them together again. . . .

Cesare was infinitely relieved. He felt that he had atoned to Antonio for the past, that he could carry his head high again. As he looked round the ward, he was inclined, in his great satisfaction over the turn of events, to take a rosy view even of the human misery collected there. He thought he detected a certain involuntary admiration and approval of himself — a healthy-looking man, well set up in his clothes — in the eyes of the women in the surrounding beds. . . . Luckily, he had no need to look for a woman in the Hospital for the Poor.

He forgot them, and turned his gaze on the child. Suspicious old Lucia! The boy was six months old — he could see that at a glance. Where had his eyes been on his previous visit? Yes, it was a six months' old child. Oddly enough, he realized that he himself had not thought it was . . . He too must have been suspicious. Shame, Cesare! He looked more carefully at the infant, and began to see something of a likeness to Antonio: not the nose — the eyes, perhaps? The eyes were Marietta's . . .

Cesare remarked that he ought to be getting along now. He had only wanted to find out how things were going, and now he was satisfied. He urged Marietta to get strong again quickly; and when the time came for her to be moved, his cart was at her disposal — there was plenty of room inside for Marietta and the little man, and Antonio could ride beside him on the box.

Instead of falling in with his liberal offer, they both began to protest vigorously against his leaving them so soon. Cesare gave in; but all his comfortable feelings of relief evaporated: why did they press him so urgently to stay? Were they afraid of being alone together? Was there still something wrong between them, after all?

He began to feel indignant: he had brought these two children together again (they might both be his children), and still there was something wrong. He wanted to know more, and abruptly asked Marietta whether she was not glad to be going back with her husband to the old house. Everything was as she had left it a year ago — Antonio's mother had altered nothing, and had returned to her own rooms as soon as Antonio set out to fetch his wife back. Besides — Antonio was no longer the callow boy he had been. In Cesare's opinion, he used to let his mother do as she liked, but that was over. With his own astonished ears, Cesare had heard Antonio say to his mother curtly and plainly, "Look here, Mother, in all love and friendship, when my wife comes back she must find her home is her own, and you're not to interfere . . ."

Cesare was a little annoyed because Antonio, flushed and confused, merely stood by Marietta's bedside, and seemed by his demeanor to deny the truth of Cesare's account of the situation. *Was* it a true account? Had he perhaps not overawed old Lucia, thought Cesare, suddenly becoming less sure.

Marietta was watching Cesare doubtfully, trying to read on his face how much of truth and how much of lies his words contained.

"Cesare," she asked, "did people laugh when they heard why Antonio had gone to Rome?"

"Of course they laughed," retorted Cesare, angry and bitter. "Do people hold anything sacred? They'll laugh a great deal more when you come back together. Is that a reason for sending him back alone? Is that what you want? Then I'm disappointed in you — and I'd like you to know it."

Fascinated, Marietta stared into his honest face that was flushed with indignation. Then her glance traveled towards Antonio, who was sitting, pale as death, upon his chair. "I don't know," she stammered, terribly tormented. "I don't want to give Antonio more pain, after all the sorrow I've already caused him . . . But why does he want me to go back with him? Back to Todi? Don't you see that I . . . I dare not, no, I dare not," she moaned softly.

As for daring . . . Cesare insisted that it was not a case of daring to, even less of wanting to, but of having to. "We seem to have forgotten the child: how is the poor lamb to grow up? I suppose you haven't thought about that?"

"The child . . . the child. How often haven't I thought of the child?" moaned Marietta. "Perhaps you're right, Cesare. Perhaps I ought to . . . And not only for the sake of the child. But I'm a coward — these last months have made me a coward. I thought I ought to take it with me — in the grave. I've longed for it — for death. The child came between . . . How easy it would be to do just what Antonio wishes — not to have to think for myself any more. He has been kind to me. He is good — I had almost forgotten how good he has always been. But there's so much — I can't speak about it all. I'm too tired, Cesare. And he wouldn't understand, either." Weeping, she turned her head to look at the cradle, stretching out a trembling uncertain hand towards it.

But Cesare was not to be put off. "That's all moonshine," he said gruffly. "You'll forget all that as soon as you're well. Does a sick person think straight? Now take Camilla. The notions she gets into her head when her nerves are bothering her! There are times when she wants to run away from me; and has Antonio told you our number nine is on the way? Life just goes on. You'll see — once you two have a couple or so."

He felt suddenly that he was on dangerous ground, and stopped: for all his good intentions, he seemed to keep striking upon sensitive spots.

In the stillness that fell between them, whispers from other beds came floating to them. The women were talking about a patient farther down the ward for whom the priest had been summoned. Half a dozen nuns were standing round her. It was the pregnant woman who had been brought in the day before yesterday. They were all agreed that she could not last much longer.

Cesare did not hear the whispering, did not hear the death rattle, nor the innocent little bell of the acolyte carrying the consecrated oil. While he waited for his words to take effect, he let his eyes rest upon the child: it had awakened and was listening open-eyed to the clear tinkle of the bell. Cesare wagged his finger at the little man — an impressive, brown index finger with a thick black rim to the nail. The child stared at it with astonishment.

Marietta found it difficult to collect her thoughts and answer Cesare. She lay with her head sideways and peered between the two men into the middle of the ward. The priest was departing, and the bed was rolled squeaking after him. As it passed, the women crossed themselves anxiously. Some of them concealed their faces under the blankets — hiding from death, the cruel, the pitiful.

Suddenly a shiver went through Marietta. For the first time a hungry longing thrilled in her voice, a readiness to believe. "Cesare, is it possible that I might get better again?"

"Get better again?" Cesare opened his eyes wide. "Were you born a weakling? I can still see you as you were, a little rascal that high . . . The naughtiest boys in the city were no match for you. All you want is the will to get better. Then you'll be all right."

"If I hadn't been so strong — ten days ago I should have . . ." she admitted hesitatingly.

"Ten days ago? Ten years ago, more likely, when Vacca gave you more blows than food, when you came flying to me and Camilla for protection because if you hadn't Vacca would have beaten you to death."

Marietta stared before her. Life came back into her eyes. Where were her thoughts roaming? After a pause, she asked: "Antonio . . . is Grigio still there?"

Antonio nodded, unable to speak. Infinite bliss welled up in him. He found he simply could not express his gratitude towards life, towards his child, towards Grigio in his wooden cage above the door, towards the nuns who had received Marietta when she knocked, above all towards Cesare who had won Marietta back for him. He felt the full blessing flow over him, the blessing of the small battered Madonna in mighty St. Peter's. In the light of the setting sun that shone through the windows, he saw her standing by the bed, smiling sweetly. Behind her stood a double row of angels with rustling golden wings. The saints were there too, and the largest, the most broad-shouldered of them all, whom he at first took to be Paul or Mark, turned out upon closer inspection to be none other than Cesare the carrier. Out of the light of the sun itself, God the Father and the Son watched this miracle.

A CHILD

CRIES

IN THE NIGHT

I

ASHABBY HIRED CALASH DREW UP BEFORE THE
great central door of the Hospital for the Poor — that door before
which the only vehicles to stop were usually either a hearse or
the gleaming caroche of some rich old contessa devoting her last years
to works of charity.

Inside in the ward Antonio lifted Marietta in his arms. One Sister picked
up the child, another the parcel containing his little clothes. A week's
regular work had restored Antonio's strength — he could if necessary
have picked up and carried the ample Mother Superior. As for Marietta,
she was like a doll in his arms. Her lightness frightened him.

Laughter and tears accompanied Marietta's good-bys. All eyes in the
great ward followed the little procession as it moved between the rows of
beds. All drank in the magic of the smiles on Marietta's thin face and on
the brown, virile features of her young husband.

The driver of the hired calash smiled too as he stepped off his box. He
placed the bundle of clothes so that Marietta's feet could rest upon it.
She took the child upon her lap, and Antonio put his arms round the two
of them protectingly. The driver spoke persuasively to his horse, and the
wheels of the calash danced away over the cobblestones of Rome. In the
golden light of the afternoon sun, the nuns nodded and waved as long as
the vehicle remained in sight. . . .

In the calash Marietta babbled excitedly: —

"Rosa the cat came and slept last night at my feet. It's no good trying to entice her. If she wants to come, she does, and she goes when she wants to too. She'll never stay near anyone who is going to die — she knows, before the sisters or even the Mother Superior."

Marietta shivered. She peered out from under the hood of the vehicle. "Where are we?" she asked. "Do you know where we are, Antonio? I never thought I should . . ."

"You be quiet now," he said, huskily, folding her closer. She leaned against him, silent, and stared at the child. Her eyes grew larger and more absent, took on an expression of regret and melancholy. She sighed and bit her lip.

When the calash drew up before The Red Hat inn, Teresa Passano was looking through the window. Mariano her husband ran out and took the child and the bundle, and soon Marietta was lying in the alcove of the up-stairs front room. "Should she have something to eat at once?" asked Teresa, in her anxiety to be of service. Antonio, closing the blinds, merely put his finger to his lips: Marietta had dozed off already.

Teresa and Mariano went downstairs, and Antonio remained standing uncertainly in the darkened room. It was still strange to him, this great victory. He could not believe it yet, could not give himself over to his happiness.

The regular man of the master-carpenter he had been serving had re-turned to work, and Antonio had to look for work elsewhere. Perhaps he ought to try that very afternoon. He had laid his last earned lira in the hands of the Mother Superior at the Hospital for the Poor, and he was beginning to regret that he had not asked Cesare for a small loan — his mother would have repaid the debt when Cesare got back to Todi. It would not have been easy to say to Cesare, "When you're in Todi go to my mother and . . ." No, but it would not be pleasant, either, to be un-able to pay Teresa's weekly bill the day after to-morrow. . . .

Teresa's shrill voice penetrated to him from downstairs. He looked at his wife and child with concern and left the room on tiptoe.

"Of course you needn't remain in the house. I'll look after her," said Teresa, reassuringly. "I saw at once I should have some work with her. You and your friend Cesare just wouldn't believe it when we talked about the charge."

II

At dusk Antonio returned, agitated and downcast. He found Marietta feeding her child. He sat down beside her on the bed and laid down some fruit that he had bought on credit. Then he inquired how she had fared under Teresa's care. "Oh, well enough," she said with some hesitation. "She's a bit rough. But so long as she doesn't pick up the child while I'm asleep . . . I think I should wake up, though."

"Marietta — you mustn't get up, yourself."

"I don't believe I could," she answered despairingly.

"Why did I bring her here?" he asked himself accusingly. He had talked about it yesterday with Cesare, wondering whether there was not some other simple inn in Rome; but Cesare, having boarded for twenty years with Teresa, knew of no other.

Mariano brought in the evening meal and a fresh candle, and hung about, looking at the child, insisting on his likeness to his father, inquiring after Marietta's health and about the Hospital for the Poor, until Teresa called up to him from below.

Marietta did her best to eat, but could not. Antonio's appetite seemed to have failed too. Teresa, removing the almost untouched dishes, inquired if they had not been to their liking.

Antonio helped to make the child comfortable. Then he and Marietta sat together in the light of the candle.

"If only I could be my own master again, and didn't have to ask for work . . ." he said with a sigh, unable to keep his counsel any longer. Marietta heard the longing in his voice. She felt guilty, and tried to share his longing. But she was too tired. "It was better in the Hospital for the Poor," she thought.

Antonio slept on a sack of straw by the window. Once or twice he got up in the night to attend to the child and to Marietta, who was breathing restlessly.

In the early morning he went out again in search of work.

It was as if it could be seen on his face that he had been turned away everywhere. The tone of his voice was proud and defensive, as though he anticipated another refusal. They looked him up and down, and shook their heads: no, no work there. . . .

In the end he no longer shrank from returning to workshops where a few days earlier he had been refused work. He found himself treated even more ungraciously than before.

More and more, his thoughts dwelt in his own workshop in Todi. He could even feel his own plane in his hand, and he could hear the children playing in the courtyard, their clear voices floating in through his open door.

When he returned to the inn in the cool of the evening after roaming about all day, Marietta noticed his exhaustion, and looked at him inquiringly as she asked, "Where have you been to-day?"

By way of reply he made a wide, vague gesture.

She sat up, and her voice sounded firmer than it had been since he got to Rome. "But it's not so bad, Antonio. I'll ask Cesare if he can pay Teresa what we owe her. After all, we can easily pay him back in Todi."

He nodded; he did not dare to speak lest he should burst into sobs. At length he said, "But I want to go on trying to get work here."

"All right. Try. But tell me this, Antonio. After the year that lies behind us, what can still happen? And on Thursday we're going back with Cesare."

Astonished, he gave her a quick glance. "On Thursday?"

"By Thursday I shall be strong enough to undertake the journey."

The following midday, he was accosted by a hulking fellow. "I say, have you time to spare?"

Antonio stared at the man.

"Can you hammer packing cases together?"

"I'm a carpenter."

A moment later, Antonio was bending over a wooden bench, sawing planks with a saw from which several teeth were missing. At other benches were other men picked up like himself from the street. The noise in the workshop was infernal. Several of the young men were roaring at the top of their voices, and children prowled near the entrance trying to pilfer bits of wood to make into toy boats.

The hulking fellow, who was the master, came and stood by Antonio and explained to him that he never had settled work. They were working now on a sudden order for packing cases that had to be ready that same day. "Your work is too careful," he said. "The cases aren't destined for eternity. You ought to be able to make two in the time it takes you to make one. Of course they fall to pieces immediately — but that's to my advantage."

Time passed. Dusk crept into the workshop. The master lit two oil lamps that shed an inadequate light.

The children had gone. Most of the young men demanded their wages so that they could go and drink and play cards in a near-by inn. When the bells began to ring for vespers only two remained in the shed — Antonio and the master. Antonio took one of the lamps and hung it above the bench where he was working.

He had lost all conception of time. When at last he left the workshop everything was quiet in the streets. A light still burned in an inn here and there, from which came the sound of drunken voices. He met a dungcart drawn by oxen. Behind it, in the noisome air, followed a sedan with swearing lackeys waving torches. He hastened his steps. Marietta would be getting anxious.

Mariano was speeding his last guests. Teresa, behind the counter, called out to Antonio in an incensed tone, "Oh, you've come back after all! If you had money to spend, you might have spent it here." But he had gone.

Marietta was asleep, but she woke as he entered the room on stockinged feet. Half-sad, half-ironical, she asked him, "And have you found work?"

He had kept his hand on the money in his pocket as he walked through the dark streets. "I had to go on working so late . . . Were you anxious?"

"No, but I was sorry for you. Have you had any food?"

"Tell me if you've had any."

"I had to. You know what I said about Thursday. Go downstairs and see if Teresa has kept something on the fire for you."

Antonio felt no hunger. He would eat to-morrow. To-morrow was Sunday. He pretended, however, to obey.

Downstairs he asked Teresa for the bill, which he could pay only in part. To his surprise, Teresa took this news calmly. "I'm agreeably surprised that you haven't spent everything on fruit for your wife and toys for your child."

And she told him that Cesare had pledged himself to pay, supposing Antonio could not do so.

That Sunday morning, Antonio went and lit a candle before the Madonna under whose protection he felt his life to be. Marietta had urged him also to attend High Mass. He remained, and returned to the inn pale with emotion: he had seen the Holy Father, the Pope himself. He tried to describe that unforgettable hour to Marietta, and something of the pride and pomp of a pontifical Mass, something of the Sunday glory of Roman wealth and fashion, radiated in the room of that poor, inhospitable inn. Little Benedetto lay beside his mother in bed watching Antonio attentively and acutely out of his dark eyes. Suddenly Antonio noticed his strange, wise glance. Softly, as though it were already advisable to whisper, he said to his wife, "Do you see how he's looking at me? Do you think he already understands something? That he understands who I am?" He flushed as he put the question, which sprang from a natural pride.

Marietta turned towards the child, but did not reply. Antonio picked Benedetto up carefully, solemnly, with infinite love, and set him upon his knee.

He played with the child. The father played with his child.

At their evening meal, Marietta drank a full glass of wine. It produced a strange frame of mind in her. For the first time, she asked about people in Todi. She wanted to hear about Annina Cerio: she had been expecting . . . Had it been a little girl? Yes? So now they had three children.

No, they had not got three children; but it was unnecessary for Marietta to know yet awhile what had happened to the three-year-old Guido whom she had looked after when he had had fever. For the moment, Antonio's thoughts were filled with other things, too — an unexpected hope had welled up within him.

"Would you like . . . Would you like us also later on . . . ?" he dared to ask her.

She laughed a little shrilly, and inquired after Nana. "Does she still have trouble with that lout of a Luigino? And does Falcometti still play on his cornet every evening? I'm quite longing to hear him again. He used to blow with so much feeling! And is Ruocco the gravedigger still alive? I wonder how he will like somebody else digging his own grave and scooping up the money for it. And does young Signora Galli still go to confess to the bishop? And is the bishop himself still in Todi?"

Silence fell between them. "Yes," said Antonio. "Monsignore is still in Todi."

"And Imma? She'll come running to see me as soon as I'm back . . ." Antonio stared before him. The recollection of one evening filled his mind.

Marietta should not have mentioned the bishop's servant at the end of a day that had been full of fine moments. Nor the bishop — to whom she had once fled from her husband.

III

Next morning, Antonio wandered the streets of Rome again, picking up a few hours' work here and there. He felt humiliation in these odd jobs that could have been done by anybody; but in the end he succumbed to Marietta's lightheartedness, and his own mood brightened. As fate would have it, the very day before Cesare's arrival he was offered a month's work!

Cesare had his evening meal with them. He helped himself generously to the wine, and tried to be gay, since Marietta had got up for the first time in his honor. But he could not overcome his inner depression. When he reached Todi, he had found Camilla less large-hearted than on that Saturday when Susanna had smashed the image of the Madonna. Perhaps he should not have told her that he had offered to bring Antonio and his wife and child back to Todi with him in his cart. . . . No, he should never have told her that. Camilla had been thinking things over, as she called it, in his absence, and she had asked him how he came to know that Marietta was lying in the Hospital for the Poor. . . .

Marietta inquired after Camilla, and he became evasive, embarrassed. Her confinement had not occurred so soon as she had expected, and the delay was making her fretful about everything. . . . "But don't let's talk about that."

His half-confession depressed all three of them.

In the sullen dawn of the following morning, Antonio carried his wife downstairs. Cesare took the child, holding it as lovingly as though it were one of his own.

In the bottom of the cart had been laid a straw mattress for Marietta and the child. Antonio took his seat beside Cesare on the box; and the journey began.

It was a strange journey for Cesare, and for the horse too, which pricked up its ears upon hearing the crying of a child behind it. They left behind the uneven paving of the Roman streets, and entered on the age-long holes and ruts of the Via Flaminia. Beyond the arches of an aqueduct rose the sun, casting vague, endless shadows over the awakening Campagna. Skylarks, fluttering up from the coarse grass, ascended into the heavens.

By midday Cesare had overcome his depression of the previous evening, and burst into song. His stentorian voice astonished not only Antonio, but also the little Benedetto. Only to the horse was it familiar. Cesare sang from the fullness of his heart. In the villages along his route, he had picked up fragments of songs and these he strung freely together. They had all sprung from the same source — from the hidden, carefree desire for beauty of an unlettered people. Cesare winked at Marietta. She smiled back, and immediately he recognized in her eyes the glance of long ago. . . . And he felt again that he had done a good work.

Quite irrelevantly, Cesare sang the song of the maiden who, bending over the brook to see her reflection in the water, spied the ugly face of the devil behind her: —

> *Oh, perchè fu tanto vanitosa?*
> *Credendosi più bella d'una rosa?*
> *O ragazze, mettete giudizio . . .*

and then he lost the thread, but ingeniously rhymed it on to the beginning of the song about the bell ringer of Orvieto: —

> *Sulla torre, maestro Maurizio,*
> *Fa suonare bello, bello*
> *Il suo vecchio campanello . . .*

In the first inn at which they alighted a difficulty arose: Cesare could no longer remember whether he had introduced Marietta there as his daughter, his niece, or his wife. He broke into a sweat as he made mysterious signs to the innkeeper: from which the innkeeper gathered that the suckling child on its mother's lap was Cesare's but that the young husband must not be allowed to know that . . .

Grateful for the innkeeper's quickness in pretending not to recognize Marietta, Cesare drank a glass of wine, and he looked benevolently on the picture before him: the happily reunited parents with their child sitting at table in the sunny loggia of his friend Pepoli's inn. Pepoli himself served the thick, fragrant *zuppa in brodo*. "Here, that's good for your little belly, too," said Cesare to the infant. "Just take a little spoonful from your uncle Cesare, *pancino d'amore*."

Grinning broadly, the innkeeper turned away. That scamp of a Cesare! He'd put him through it next week!

They spent the night in a small village. Cesare slept on his usual couch. For the sake of cheapness, Antonio and Marietta slept with their child in the warm barn, where the cart was housed, and where there was an abundance of straw. Behind them they could hear the horse eating from the rack, grinding the dry hay between its teeth. A thin drizzle of rain pattered on the roof.

Next day it continued to rain at intervals; but this did not affect their spirits. A day in the open air had already done Marietta good. She slept a little in spite of the jolting of the cart. Then she wanted to see the country, and Antonio got down from the box. As he ran beside the cart, it was with proud joy that he saw Marietta sitting beside Cesare. Her face was glowing from the wind, the rain, and the sun. Her eyes had a sort of intoxication in them. Her hair streamed about her ears. She smiled at him as though she were a child.

In the evening they reached Terni, their last halting place. Cesare sat up late with the innkeeper — with the result that he overslept. Before he was ready the horse had neighed impatiently several times: after to-day's heavy pull, it would rest a full week in its familiar stable while Brownie dragged the cart to Rome and back. Cesare, still loitering, refused to admit that there was any hurry. It was less than a day's journey to Todi, he explained to Antonio as he was harnessing.

And if it were a full day's journey — need they drive into Todi in the full light of day? The foolish horse seemed to think so: the old reins creaked under his violent pulling.

Cesare did not sing that day. Antonio, lost in thought, was trying to imagine how the people in Todi would receive Marietta. He clenched his fists with an anger such as he had never felt before. Did Marietta sense his thoughts? Suddenly she leaned against his back, and when he felt her near him things looked a little less dark.

In the gloaming, they reached familiar ground. Marietta looked about her as if she recognized the landmarks of a dream in the far past. . . . Behind the dark cypresses stood the still, white convent. It was strange to think that Sister Elisabetta was at this moment washing up the dishes in the great kitchen. Which of them all inside could guess that Marietta was driving by with her child? Could she understand it herself?

They reached the last bend in the road. The horse whinnied for joy. Antonio, feeling behind him, found a slender hand that he held in a firm grasp. . . .

Gaetano the tollkeeper hoisted himself, coughing, onto the wheel of the cart, to convince himself with his own eyes that Marietta was really sitting there with her child. Speechless, he jumped down again. "And here they were saying she'd received a pauper's burial," he whispered to Cesare, who answered proudly, "It's always best not to listen to gossip, Gaetano."

Through the dusky streets, they reached the deserted courtyard of the house unobserved. Cesare stepped off the box to open the stable. He pretended not to see Carlino, who stood in silence in the doorway observing, with his solemn child's eyes, all those who stepped down from his father's cart that evening.

When Antonio pressed Cesare's hand gratefully, he discovered that it was trembling. Upset, he returned to the cart, and took the child from Marietta, who declared herself strong enough to walk up the stairs without help.

She was the first to pass the silent little figure in the doorway. She lifted his chin to look into his eyes. "Is that you, Carlino?"

Carlino returned her look without answering, and Marietta went on, stricken by a sudden unreasoning grief.

Antonio broke out angrily against the little fellow: "What are you doing here? Go and welcome your father — see whether you can't help him."

What sort of child was this? Would Cesare put up with such behavior?

Yes, Cesare put up with it. He stabled his horse in haste and then, like a repentant sinner, went up to Carlino. Embarrassed, he laid his large hand upon the little boy's narrow shoulders and asked, as he tried gently to push his severe little judge up the stairs before him: "Why are you still out here? Haven't you had your supper yet? Does Mother think it right for you —"

"Mother's in bed."

"Has it happened, then?" asked Cesare with a start.

"The day you went away."

"And is everything all right? Mother, too?"

Carlo nodded, like a little old man. Life had already taught him not to take too seriously his mother's illness on the arrival of a new brother or sister. His interest was elsewhere, and he added, "I wanted to see if it was true, what Mother said."

"What did she say?"

"That you wouldn't be coming back alone to-day."

Cesare breathed deeply. It was absurd that he should be brought to book by his ten-year-old son; but his mounting annoyance subsided under the profound gravity of this child of his who already seemed possessed by an urge to dispense justice. He heard sadness in Carlino's voice, sadness at such a father.

Almost entreatingly, he flung his arm about the boy, sighed, and asked like a craven, "What, exactly, did Mother say?"

"Better ask her yourself, Father."

Burdened with his undelivered packages, Cesare almost stumbled up the stairs he had climbed so often in the same darkness. Carlino was right: it was better that he should ask her himself; he didn't want to turn his Carlino into a sneak.

"A little brother, did you say?" he asked, his hand on the knob of the door.

"A little sister," answered Carlino, and was deeply disappointed because his father had not relieved him from the oppression with which his child's soul had been filled by his mother's complaints.

IV

Upstairs on the landing, Marietta felt somebody glide by her.

"Good evening," she said softly; but her greeting was not returned — the figure did not wish to be recognized. Antonio broke out into bitter, contemptuous language that must have wounded the other: was that like Antonio, to insult an unknown person in the dark?

He opened the door of his dwelling, and went in. With an uncertain hand he lighted the lamp. Marietta was still standing on the threshold holding her child, whom she had taken from his arms. She stared into the room conjured up by the light. She stared at the table, at the chairs. She took a step forward. Antonio, tense and silent, closed the door quietly behind her.

"It's a bit stuffy — it hasn't been lived in for so long," he said, listening to his own voice in the silence. "I'll make a fire."

In the kitchen, he found some wood. "Come in here, Marietta. It'll soon be warm," he entreated. "Wait! Let me carry the little one — like this. I'll bring the lamp, too. You go and sit down. If only we could put on something to eat at once! There won't be much in the larder. Mother had no idea we should be home this evening. . . . Oh, here's some wine. It will be sour — Do you know what? I'll just go and ask Cesare and Camilla . . ." He broke off: at that precise moment a woman overhead burst out in hysteria.

Not knowing where to turn, he fanned the fire, put on more charcoal, and ran to the cupboard. "There's macaroni. I must try and get some water. You won't mind remaining alone a moment, Marietta? Only a moment. As soon as we have something to eat, it will be different. Can you feel the warmth already?" She nodded, and Antonio decided to go at once. "I'll be back immediately."

Marietta sat alone upon her chair, her child pressed against her, listening with large eyes to the noises overhead. Slowly she looked about her, stood up noiselessly, peered into the living room.

At the door Antonio ran into someone who tried hurriedly to disappear. He recognized him: perhaps by the smell of cobbler's wax. "Lascari! Did your wife send you to spy on us? I didn't think you'd do that," he called after the fugitive, and without any definite purpose, he hurried towards an old familiar door at which he knocked with beating heart. A moment elapsed before he heard shuffling steps inside. "Why is she so slow?" he thought. The door opened, and his mother stood before him. She seemed to have grown smaller, her face more furrowed; but perhaps that was because it was lit sideways by the candle she held on high.

She contrived to conceal her emotion. "Oh, you back already?" she asked in a hard tone. "When Cesare said you were waiting for her, I reckoned it would be at least another month. Come inside. People can hear us here."

She preceded him, her gray hair glittering metallically in the light. Antonio followed her. He wanted some water to be able to put on macaroni for Marietta. . . . Perhaps it would have been better if he had gone to Annina, and only to-morrow . . .

"So she's here with her child?" said his mother, turning towards him, and taking in his ravaged face and the dilapidated condition of his clothing.

He roused himself, saying acridly, "Why do you say *her* child, Mother? Come and see it."

She closed her eyes for a moment and asked, "Did she send you?"

"She doesn't even know I'm with you, Mother. But come along with me to her. Perhaps this is just the right moment. Perhaps this evening everything can be put right. It's terrible — nobody waiting for us here. Cesare has already been getting it from his wife for having brought us. Mother, it would be fine if, this evening, you . . ."

Yes, that was what he had hoped. Every time his conscience had brought his mother before his eyes in Rome, his mother who had entrenched herself in her solitary dwelling in Todi, he had thought, "The child will break the ban that she has pronounced on herself." Benedetto — "the blessed." That's what the priest in Naples had baptized him.

Only with the greatest effort did she withstand the entreaty in his voice. These last three weeks had cost her a great deal of her strength.

"There'll be time yet to see the child. It's been in the world quite a while already."

"Mother, why are you so hard?"

"You wait till you're as old as I am, and you've heard people laughing about your child."

"If you really loved me, Mother, you would — "

"Yes, let us suppose for a moment that I loved you." She laughed, and he did not know what more to say. A haze came over his mind. Water — he must have water for the macaroni. Marietta. . . .

"Have you two got something to eat?" she asked. "Take what you need from the kitchen — the child no doubt still receives the breast."

He nodded, turning his face away. . . . Had she been able to feed it all that time?

"In the hospital, another woman helped her to feed it."

She sneered, "Oh?" Then she asked carelessly, "Is it healthy?"

He nodded in silence. He did not notice how strange she was; his anxiety over Marietta was growing. Would he never again be able to leave his home without carrying the fear in his heart that his wife might run away from him?

"Ah well, I shall hear the rest later on," said Lucia abruptly, and went with him into the kitchen. She handed him a pitcher of water and a bunch of onions. "There; and here's some wine. Hurry up, or you may be too late," she said mockingly, standing motionless and stiff as he kissed her.

Antonio hurried, as she had advised him, and found Marietta still upon the chair where he had left her.

"Here, I've got everything. Mother's given me some wine, too."

Full of confidence, he poured the water into the saucepan and shook the macaroni into it. "Stay where you are. I'll do everything," he said, as he bustled about looking for a knife to peel the onions.

Somebody knocked on the door. Antonio turned pale as he interrupted his work: had his mother come to look at the child after all? He put down the knife and hurried to the door.

It was only Annina, the wife of Simone the stonemason. She nodded to him nervously. "Am I intruding? Marietta's back, isn't she?" At the same time she hurried past him and flung her arms about Marietta. "Madonna! Here she is! I've thought of you so often. We've talked so much about you always, Simone and I, and even Giannino. . . . When Giannino heard you were back he said, 'I want to come too, to Aunt Marietta' . . . Oh gracious me, and there's your child. He's asleep. No, he's awake, he's watching. Your eyes, Marietta; but it's his father's nose."

Annina's caressing hands took the child from his mother. She went on talking, talking.

"I can't believe it yet, that you're sitting here again. This whole year I haven't been quite myself. In the beginning not a day went by as I was busy ironing but I thought, 'Where can Marietta be at this moment? God knows! Perhaps she's in the greatest misery, and I can't stand by her as she stood by me when I had difficult days,' and Simone said, 'Don't worry yourself, Annina,' said he — for he could see that I had been crying again. Yes, and then we had that sad business with our little Guido . . ." Her last words came out in a whisper. Instinctively, she handed back the baby in her arms to his mother, asking with sad astonishment: "Hasn't Antonio told you about that? Guido wanted to pick up an iron. He had seen his elder brother do that so often. He wanted to help his mother at her work too. I was standing close by, Marietta, and saw him stand on his little toes to reach the kitchen fire. I wanted to catch hold of him, but he had already seized it. Oh Lord, with both his little hands he remained cl . . ." Annina threw her own hands in front of her face, and shivered in her whole body.

Marietta raised her eyes to Annina. Then she stood up and folded her former friend in her arms. "Tell me — is he dead? Antonio didn't dare tell me, that's what it was. Now, just tell me," she implored. "You do want to tell me, don't you? Is poor little Guido dead?"

Annina nodded, bathed in tears. "His little hands were burned. You don't know how terrible such an iron is; you don't know, Marietta."

Antonio stood looking on with concern. He was afraid Marietta would be too much upset by Annina's pitiful recital.

Annina recovered herself a little as soon as she had passed on her great grief to Marietta. All she wanted now was to give vent to an accusation that had been put into her head by other women, and had given her no rest. "Yet there was no reason for Guido to die, Marietta. It was the doctor's fault — we couldn't pay as much as the others." She tried to read in

Marietta's face what she thought. She tried to convince Marietta by the same words that had convinced her. "Isn't that true? Others lose their arms or legs completely, and still live, because the doctor sees to it that there is no gangrene. . . ."

Her little one had gone from her in fearful pain; but the Mother of God was standing at the gate of heaven to receive him, and all the angels sang and the old saints looked up smiling — that, that was Annina's consolation. Annina was still crying. The picture of Guido's arrival in heaven was too beautiful to leave her eyes dry. With quiet thankfulness, she told how Simone and she had received a little sister in place of Guido — yes; but before the year was out, perhaps they would have another little Guido as well.

Oh, and Antonio had made such a pretty little coffin, and had refused to take any money for it. If only they had been able to support him too in his sorrow. But they had never been able to talk with him, because his mother had always been there — and rather than sit beside him and be silent about what lay so heavy on his heart, they had preferred to remain away altogether. "What must you have thought of us, Antonio — Oh Lord, look at the man cutting up onions."

Annina sprang up and took the knife from him. She was able to laugh again: it surely was a joke to see Antonio wanting to prepare macaroni with two women in the kitchen. "Do you know what you can do? You can set the table in the living room."

He was about to hurry out of the kitchen, but Marietta clung to him. "Not in that room! Let's remain here."

Surprised at her vehemence, he looked at her.

"It will be too chilly there, Antonio," said Annina, shivering. "Let's remain here by the fire. We can take our plates in our hands." She blinked her eyes that were smarting from the onions. "I've had my supper, but perhaps I'll just have a bite with you. It's a pity Simone can't be here too. Others leave their children alone, but we should have no rest. You always used to say, Marietta, that I was afraid of the evil eye. Now you've a child yourself. Now you'll be on the lookout, too. Let me look at him again, Antonio, but don't come too near me, or he'll get onion juice in his eyes. . . . No, but look, he's laughing at me. Yes, yes, the little man is laughing at Auntie Annina. Such a little lamb, too. And he's already seen Rome and the world."

"He was born in Naples," said Antonio, and suddenly he could not repress a ridiculous pride in the travels of his son.

"*Gran Dio!* And do Christians live there? He was christened at once, wasn't he?"

"He's called Benedetto," Antonio reassured her; and when Annina cried out, "What a nice name!" Antonio said with a thrill in his voice, "He's already justified his name, by bringing us together, Marietta and me."

"But how did anything ever go wrong between you two?" sighed Annina. "Would you believe it, we've never had a word, Simone and I. We buried our child together — how could we quarrel after that? That's what we've said so often to each other, Simone and I. What can people find to quarrel about? I just want to say this, you'll have reason to be ashamed of yourselves if such a thing ever happens again. Not on my account — but on account of your child. I believe Giannino would throw himself from the window with grief if Simone and I ever had words. Oh Lord, words with Simone!" Annina shook her head a little sadly. Antonio flushed a deep red, and dared not look at Marietta, who stood silent and brooding.

They began to eat. Annina tried to get Marietta to talk by asking her a rather forced question about the twelve months she had spent in foreign parts — and immediately she regretted her question, because the subject could not fail to be painful to Antonio. Marietta, however, seemed grateful to her for rousing her from her faraway mood.

At first there was hesitation in her voice, but gradually life and color came into it. It was so strange, so strange, what she was telling. In Rome she had heard that in Naples women also acted on the stage. She had gone to Naples. She spoke of a happy coincidence that had led on to other things. At first she had earned only just enough to live. She had played lady's-maid parts — lady's maids with ready wits who stole jewelry from their mistresses' cupboards, and besprinkled themselves secretly with stolen perfumes, and ogled their masters. She had had to impersonate young abbés, she had laced herself up until she had really been mistaken for a boy. When her pregnancy began to be obvious, she was allotted the part of a grand lady in a wide dress with a high wig on her head. Oh, *Dio!* And the audience applauded when she plied her parrot with lumps of sugar and held long conversations with him; she had made her voice so shrill that it was difficult to discern whether she was speaking, or the parrot. From that evening she had begun to earn more . . . But in the autumn, when she was expecting her child at any moment, the company had had to go to Venice for the carnival, and she was left behind. She had worn out her strength, for every night had been a late night — one day a Neapolitan grandee and another an English lord as rich as Croesus wanted the whole company to attend his garden party after the performance. A month after Benedetto's birth, she was still not fit to travel and rejoin the company. The money she had saved went sooner than she had anticipated. . . . Oh, Annina knew all about that too, and also that charity was difficult to bear. . . . In midwinter, she had hit upon the desperate plan of going to Venice on foot. But she had got no farther than Rome. . . .

Annina could scarcely contain her excitement over the experiences Marietta had been telling. But Marietta only went on more quietly, "Yes, it all seems very strange, from here. But being here feels strange, too. I felt it on the stairs when Carlino refused to say good day to me. He used to be so pleased to come and get a sweet from me. And in the other room I knew at once — that Grigio was dead, when I didn't hear him call." Then, breaking out in uncontrolled grief: "Your mother let him die of hunger. Your mother let him die here in loneliness, because she thinks only of herself, only of herself. Because in her heart there's no place for any creature. And then — what was it then? Then you told me about Guido. . . . This last week I have thought of him continually, wondering how big he was grown. But the things one hopes for do not come to pass."

She buried her head in her hands.

Antonio hurried into the living room, and returned, the cage in his hands. Annina, her eyes red with tears, went to look at Grigio, who lay, a bundle of soft feathers, on the bottom of the cage. It was only a dove, a dead dove; nothing more. Annina approached Grigio with bated breath, much as her neighbors had approached the little bed on which Guido in his innocence had been laid out.

"Poor thing!" she sighed, and at the same time broke out against Camilla: "If I had been living just above . . ."

Antonio took the cage away.

"Annina," whispered Marietta, looking about her fearfully, "she didn't forget Grigio . . . his mother. She remembered him well enough — she remembered I always liked to look after him."

"Yes, yes, that's so," Annina broke in eagerly. "She wanted to pay you out, for the last time. But she'll receive her punishment, like the doctor on the piazza. . . . God is righteous. She herself will know hunger and thirst — and it need not be through lack of food and drink."

Marietta nodded hesitatingly. "For the last time, did you say? Do you really think it's the last time that she — "

At this moment Antonio returned without the cage. His eyes were swimming, the hands which he rested upon Marietta's chair were trembling. "I have told her. I went to her with Grigio. . . . I told her she murdered him only to give you grief, and that she is never to cross this threshold again. That it's all finished, finished; that she needn't see the child, our child. That's what I told her."

Marietta looked up at him in deep wonder, incredulous still.

Long after Annina had returned to her husband and children, Antonio and Marietta remained sitting together in their kitchen. Marietta rested her head upon her hand. Perhaps she was asleep. The charcoal flames were licking noiselessly in the stove.

Suddenly the child began to cry — he had been laid to sleep in the alcove. A strange feeling came over Antonio as he listened to this innocent wailing in the night. Surely this little wailing voice must also move the others in the house if they should awaken. Surely it must move anyone who heard it. Surely it must thaw the hostility that surrounded them.

Marietta raised her face towards him. "I'll go to him," she said. Everything between them was good; had he to thank his recent terrible encounter with his mother for that? He preferred not to think about it. He could not think any more this evening, anyhow.

Marietta got up, stiff with sleep, and went towards the little Benedetto. Contentedly he pulled at her breast, while Antonio, silhouetted against the lamplight in the kitchen, stood looking on from the doorway.

Her face held a look of mystery, and she was smiling.

She laid the little one down again and said, "Let us go to sleep, too."

On their way from Rome they had lain by night, half dressed, on the straw. In Rome she had been an invalid whom he had had to tend. But this evening — what did she conceal this evening in her voice? Her simple words roused a strange confusion within him. He had to turn away to hide his emotion.

Slowly he undressed; slowly he unlaced his high boots. Of what was he thinking? A moment before he had been completely ingenuous. Heavens! If she suspected. At the back of the room stood the straw couch that he had occupied during the year his mother had lived with him. Yes, if he only knew whether Marietta expected him as a matter of course to . . .

"Antonio!"

She called him. Whispering because the child had fallen asleep, he approached, not daring to look at her. She stood close to him in her thin nightgown. "Antonio! . . . I am your wife again."

As if to protect her against herself, he threw his arm round her shoulders, pressed her brusquely to him. "You're weak, Marietta. . . . You must rest."

"I want to rest beside you. Whom else have I but you?"

"Whom have I but you?" — that was the finest thing she had ever said to him, even though some deception lay concealed in it . . . a deception that did not entirely elude Antonio's acutely listening ear. This evening she wanted to conquer death with him. After a year of grief and terrible loneliness, she wanted to forget in his arms . . . Perhaps certain other things too, of which he knew nothing, of which he had better never know anything.

She drew him to her. If there still remained a last resistance in him — the bitter remnant of pride — then she scorched it up in the glow that blazed from her young, revivified body; the tremor in her soft, lonely, longing voice stilled his hidden wounds as she said, "Antonio — Come. I believe I — want you again."

SUNDAY

VISITING

NEXT MORNING, JUST AS ANTONIO WAS DRESSED,
and Marietta, still in bed, was feeding the child, Annina came
knocking at the door. She peered into the room, asking with a
smile whether it was convenient, and then stepped inside with the six-year-
old Giannino clinging to her hand. She inquired whether Marietta had had
a good rest, looking at the same time with a vague inquisitive glance into
Antonio's face that was suffused with happiness. Yes, Giannino would
give her no peace. He insisted on seeing Marietta and the child — probably
he thought he could already play with it.

"Look, there it is, Giannino. And Auntie Marietta — Do you remember
her? Oh, he knows you all right, but he never says much. Just like his
father. Simone sent me. You must both come and eat with us. I've been
to market already . . . Yes, we're grand these days! We ask people to eat
with us. What would you say to a little brother like that, Giannino? Perhaps your father and mother will give you one, one of these days, instead
of Guido who is in heaven. . . ."

While Annina went chattering on, Antonio thought he ought to go and
see Ercole the carpenter, if Annina could remain a while with Marietta.
He must go and thank Ercole and . . .

"Yes, you go, you go," said Annina, rather pressing in her desire to be
alone with Marietta — two women had a hundred things to talk about that
did not concern men; Giannino's presence scarcely counted.

"I'll be back inside an hour," said Antonio, from the door. In the passage other thoughts preoccupied him. Life had to go on . . .

He compelled himself to pass his mother's door unmoved. Downstairs
in the courtyard children were playing — they paid no heed to him.
Should he just . . . ? He entered his workshop, and his first glance reassured him. His tools were properly put away; there were no shavings in

the corners. Although it was Sunday, the floor had been swept. He took up a plane and ran his thumb across the blade — how he had longed for this moment! He felt safe again. For a moment he saw himself back in Rome — a fierce, cruel vision. That strange, faraway city where long ago, a thousand years ago, he had run from master to master looking for work. . . . Now he could laugh about it; but not without pain. He would have liked to start work at once, on Sunday, even against God's ordinance.

He laid down the plane and left the workshop, closing the door carefully behind him. It was a good hour to go out: few people were about, for High Mass was being celebrated. Here and there, he answered an astonished greeting stiffly. Ercole was notorious as a poor churchgoer, and Antonio found him at home as he had anticipated.

A fifteen-year-old boy with one little brother on his arm, and another hanging onto his hand, opened the door: it was Andrea, Ercole's eldest. "I'll tell Father," he said, conducting Antonio inside in friendly fashion.

Ercole appeared in his shirtsleeves: but he at once pulled on his coat that was hanging over a chair. Antonio was surprised by the solemnity of this action. Andrea was about to leave them alone, but his father said, "Take the children to their mother, and then come back," and turning to Antonio added, "He deserves to be here, because without his help I shouldn't have been able to manage."

"They were not bad weeks for me," he went on, bringing wine and offering Antonio a chair on the other side of the table. "I made good use of them! The wife flat on her bed these five months. You don't need to thank me, I liked doing it. I shall let you know everything exactly — how much wood and material I needed, and how much money has come in. Andrea has kept a precise account. There's something in that boy, more than in his father, who only knows about carpentering." Ercole sighed good-humoredly. He looked old and tired.

He spoke like a subordinate to Antonio, like a man to his master. He was loud in his praise of Antonio's business. "And what tools you have! You mustn't mind my saying so — Andrea has kept everything in order very nicely. Have you noticed?"

Antonio made an airy gesture as if he had not yet taken the trouble to go to his workshop. At the same time he blushed.

"You've not been there yet, but to-morrow you'll see for yourself," said Ercole. "Yes, yes — I'm jealous of your chisels, not to speak of anything else."

Antonio was beginning to feel a little uncomfortable.

"Now, now," he said consolingly. "Things won't be so bad with you, either. I know of workshops where there's less to do."

"Yes, that's so. But all the same, I should like Andrea to earn outside the home. By the time I cannot cope with the work here alone, I shall have Silvio and Giuseppe on my hands. I've wanted to ask you before — whether you might not be able to make use of him? At first, of course, for his food only. Just keep an eye on him for a bit. We've known each other so long, you needn't beat about the bush with me. But if there wasn't something in the boy, I shouldn't try to foist him on to you. Surely I may say that."

Ercole swallowed. In his nervous voice trembled the pride of the humble.

Antonio felt at once that it was going to be difficult to refuse his fatherly entreaty; Ercole had chosen so very favorable a moment for it. Uncertainly, he turned his eye on the boy, who looked down abashed.

"Don't look down as if you couldn't look people in the face," rapped out his father, and immediately Andrea raised his head, so that Antonio was suddenly moved to pity.

Certainly he would take the boy; and at that moment Antonio remembered how he had been looked up and down to see if he would be of any use. . . .

"Up to now I've always been able to do the work alone easily — but recently there has been more and more to do," he admitted, and Ercole hastened to increase his hopes with: "You don't need to tell me that, that you're getting more and more work. I've seen that for a long time."

There was silence. Then Antonio said, "All right — but you mustn't count upon his settling down with me for life," and heard himself adding: "I have a son now, too. . . ."

Without daring to breathe, he looked up into Ercole's face, to see if there were any trace of mockery there. No, Ercole was not laughing. He only nodded, saying gravely, "Yes, Cesare told me so."

Relieved, Antonio suddenly saw everything in a rosy light. "Well, that's settled then. Send him to me to-morrow."

"Thank your master, Andrea."

Andrea stood up, put out his hand to Antonio. It was a broad, powerful hand for such a gentle boy who mothered his little brothers. They clinked glasses. Ercole hung his jacket over the chair again — it got in his way.

Somewhat heated by the wine and by his unexpected decision to take an apprentice, Antonio left Ercole's modest home. Was it thoughtlessness that made him return by way of the piazza just as High Mass was over and the people were streaming down the cathedral steps and over the whole sunny square? Here and there he was met by mocking or compassionate glances, others looked as though they no longer knew him, and he regretted his challenge to his neighbors, since he was now compelled to join the throng of people in order to reach his home. Suddenly, in the haze of faces, he distinguished one that was familiar.

"Cesare!" he called with hollow good humor, and only then discovered that Camilla was walking next to Cesare, holding Carlo's hand. Cesare seemed startled, and asked, as he looked round about him to see whether their meeting had been noticed, "So, have you come from Mass?"

Antonio said, somewhat excitedly for him, that he had just come from Ercole the carpenter. "He wants me to take his eldest boy Andrea into the workshop: you know him, don't you . . . ? Oh — morning, Camilla."

Camilla, her confinement but five days passed, looked ill and tired. She nodded stiffly. "You two just walk on ahead of us if you've something to talk about."

Cesare had already stepped forward, and Antonio followed, asking himself what he had to talk about with Cesare.

Feeling the eyes of his wife and child piercing his back, Cesare began under difficulties. "You must understand . . . it's only because . . . there'll be sufficient talk as it is, and I'm a carrier . . . We've had words about it already, Camilla and I . . . But you needn't worry about that, you know Camilla . . . But perhaps it would have been better if, in front of all those people, we hadn't . . ."

Cesare could not finish his sentences — but Antonio understood him well enough. Seizing the opportunity as old Signora Galli's caroche passed, he slipped away. Cesare tried to hold him back, but Antonio, in danger of his life, dodged in front of the frightened horses, and did not look back as he ran, quickly, quickly, with bowed head, a guilty man among the righteous, until he reached home and, out of breath, entered the room where Annina and Marietta were still sitting together.

"There's that man back again," cried Annina. "Let's go to Simone. Then I'll get the food ready."

"How is Ercole?" inquired Marietta, looking at Antonio intently.

"Very well."

"Did you speak to anyone else?"

"No, only Cesare. He was coming from Mass with Camilla."

"Can Camilla go out already?" inquired Annina, astonished.

When he continued silent, Marietta asked no more questions. In a suddenly happy and carefree voice, she said, "Will you take the child, Antonio?"

In the corridor, unnoticed by Annina, she turned towards him and whispered, "You're lucky not to be Cesare — he's perhaps even worse off, with Camilla."

He pressed against her passionately. Then they went inside the door which Annina opened wide for them.

Simone the stonemason, a quiet and modest man, slow of thought, engrossed almost completely by his wife and children, listened with courteous interest to Antonio's talk of his apprentice Andrea. During the first hour, he avoided looking at Marietta at all, after he had offered her his hard stonemason's hand in welcome. He kept looking round towards his wife, who was busy cooking in the kitchen: he could just see her through the open door. Giannino, spurred on by Annina, was exhibiting a toy his father had made for him. It was the stable of Bethlehem, with Jesus in His little crib, the Virgin Mary, the ass, and everything. Much patient pottering and gluing had gone to its making. Antonio and Marietta looked at the work with genuine admiration, but Annina could not resist running in with a saucepan in her hands to draw their attention to the peculiar anatomy of the ass. Behind her mockery, however, was concealed infinite pride in a husband who could make such beautiful toys for her children.

"Yes, the ass is not very lifelike," Simone admitted at once.

"And you should have seen the table," continued Annina. "There were at least a hundred asses altogether. It looked like the eighth day of creation. I had to sweep away a whole basketful, and I said to Simone, 'I believe I shall sweep you away too, as the biggest ass of all!'"

Marietta, however, declared that she had seen at once that it was an ass. She had recognized it by the long ears.

"Simone, I suppose you mean," burst out Annina from the kitchen.

"I should like to see whether Antonio could have done any better," persisted Marietta, obstinately.

Antonio, coloring under her challenge, declared that he would carpenter a little cart for Giannino. . . .

The meal was over, and the babies had been laid to rest for their siesta. Benedetto was sleeping peacefully in the same bed as little Teresina. Their parents sat round the table, and Giannino was allowed to sit up, too, because he would soon be six years old. Simone got up again to make sure that the babies could not fall out of the bed. Annina shook her head over him. "But I placed a chair to protect them! That man can't remain comfortably seated."

Slightly ashamed, Simone came back and sat down again, waiting for Marietta and Antonio to tell the story of their travels. They had both been far away; they had been welcomed and entertained. They would have something interesting to relate. Nothing of interest had happened to him and Annina, except that Guido had died, and that the visitors knew already. . . .

Outside everything was still. It was Sunday afternoon. Through the chinks of the closed shutters the warm spring sun quivered. The first bluebottle buzzed along the ceiling. Giannino, half-hidden behind his father, stared at the guests, expecting to hear something unusual from their mouths. Suddenly Annina began to feel nervous.

"Yes — Simone would like you to tell him about things, Marietta. She was invited out in Naples to the houses of counts and I don't know what. I told you, didn't I, Simone?"

"But what's that to Simone, Annina?" protested Marietta, confused.

"Oh, Simone would like to hear about it. What has he seen in his life? I at least do get into the houses of the rich folk for whom I do washing. Signora Galli's and Signora Rigogli's, and . . ."

If this muster of resounding Todi names was meant to be a challenge, it missed fire. Upon Marietta's face appeared a contemptuous, irritated expression.

"Those aren't rich people, Annina. I used to think they were — but those people, with all their money, don't know what wealth is. What do people here know? All they can do is lay down the law!"

All Annina's grudges against the rich families of the piazza came to the surface: the rich who lived in state in their marble palaces and gave out their washing at a miserable wage and had never even got to know what had happened to little Guido. . . . She had never dared say anything, so anxious was she lest the washing might go elsewhere. . . . But now she listened with a greedy sense of relief and a consciousness of guilt to Marietta's comments on those rich folk, and thirstily she waited for more.

But no more came. Marietta's lips folded themselves again into the haughty, mocking, almost gay little smile with which she seemed to defy the people round her — not her faithful friends Annina and Simone, but everyone else in that pretentious, gray, dusty little city: those hypocritically pious churchgoers who that morning, as they came from the house of God, had so wounded Antonio that he came running home like a hunted thief.

Instead of tirades against the rich of Todi, Marietta began to tell of her experiences.

She spoke of a magnificent bay drenched in moonlight, and of darkly shaded gardens that looked out on it; of music that blended with the surg-

ing of the waves upon the beach; of happy company, careless of the morrow; and of singers from the people, who delighted aristocratic damsels
by their magnificent voices and were rewarded with silver — even gold —
coins, thrown into their caps. . . . Of pleasure trips in great sailing vessels, and banquets with cool wines and freshly caught *frutta di mare*. The
wide bay was without a ripple. At sunrise, the light morning breeze wafted
them homewards again.

Marietta told of amateur theatricals, in which countesses clad in silken
rags deliberately torn, and patched with costly brocades, went round
with collecting bowls pretending to be beggarwomen. It was mad, mad
and sinful, that mockery of poverty; mad and apparently purposeless, that
whole idle life. But the possession of money in itself was perhaps a sin that
would send one to perdition.

Annina nodded to herself. She had not followed all that Marietta had
said, but the main point she understood: To have so much money when
others suffered hunger — that must be a grievous sin. Luckily, Simone and
she were poor. They would get to heaven, where Guido was waiting for
them; but the rich of the piazza must wait in purgatory until they had
done penance for their sinful lives. Perhaps it was because they themselves
realized this that the rich ladies ran to confess to the bishop, and old Signora Galli, with one foot in the grave already, gave yet further sums of
money to the convent. But would that help? It was not enough, not
enough. Later, at the gate of heaven, they would be asked whether they
knew how Guido's little hands had been burned. . . .

Antonio too listened with amazement to Marietta's account of those
remote parts where perfect earthly happiness seemed to have been vouchsafed to mankind. He had not realized that she carried that kind of
memory of a time which to him had been a long, dark nightmare. Anxiety
welled up in him, a new terrible anxiety. He thought of the child. Yes,
there was the child, and for the sake of the child she would . . . But he
was no longer completely sure even of the hold the child had over her.
Nor, after last night, would it, perhaps, be altogether sufficient for him
if she stayed only for the sake of the child. . . .

Marietta's wonderful experiences seemed to make her unapproachable
by those who would pass judgment upon her. Annina sighed. "If only the
others knew about all this!" she exclaimed. "If only the others knew of all
you have seen and gone through!"

"Nobody knows — nobody knows what she has gone through," said
Antonio, wiping his clammy forehead. He continued to feel doubt and
anxiety. Would Marietta be able to appreciate safety in Todi, safety from

the terrible misery that lay concealed behind the beautiful, smiling mask of the life she had lived in Naples? It disquieted him that she spoke of misery and of happiness in the same tone, as if she could no longer distinguish between them.

WOMEN

BEND

OVER THE CHILD

I

THAT FIRST SUNDAY, THE PEOPLE OF TODI AS THEY left the cathedral in a body had certainly presented a united hostility to Antonio that had made him feel what they thought about his taking his wife back. On working days, however, such unanimity was impossible. Daily life did not lend itself to such common symbolic action.

When on Monday morning Marietta went to market, the vendors, wanting her custom, showed a friendly face, and expressed pleasant surprise at seeing her again. Other marketers, hoping to hear something interesting, pressed round the same stalls that Marietta visited. But though they examined the greens and the fruit very carefully and pricked up their ears to catch any titbit that might fall from her mouth, it was to no purpose: Marietta talked only of prices and goods. Indeed, she spoke very little, and was quickly satisfied, since the vendors chose the best for her, — anything for the sake of custom, renewed custom, — and even added an orange.

"For your baby, Marietta. They say you've got a baby?"

"Bring it along some time," said another flatteringly, nodding to her encouragingly.

Marietta smiled, and went on to the next stall. A little dazed, she walked through the bustle of the market. A hush fell where she passed. From various sides, she heard greetings: they were prepared to be friendly, if only she on her side would . . . Marietta nodded back, but often had difficulty in remembering who it was that was greeting her. She recognized the faces, but as if they had appeared to her long ago in a dream. There was nothing she did not recognize. The houses round the little market square . . . She had played among them as a child, and every broken windowpane was broken still. The one strange and incomprehensible thing was that she should be moving amongst it all again, that she had a child at home entrusted for the moment to Annina's care, and that Antonio in his workshop was sawing and hammering for them. . . .

Just as she was about to leave the market, Nana stood before her. Nana was so deeply affected that she could not speak at once. Instead of greeting Marietta, she mumbled something that sounded like "I'm coming along with you," and then walked by her side awkwardly and in silence.

They crossed the little square near the market, where women were filling their pitchers from the city well. Barberina, and Xenia, wife of the eternally drunk undertaker's man, and Maria Testagrossa had just met together for their morning gossip.

"Am I to believe my old eyes?" screeched Barberina, opening wide her toothless mouth. "Is that Antonio's Marietta going by again? Marietta, let's have a look at you! Are you in such a hurry? Nana, ask her if she's forgotten us."

Nana turned round furiously, but the chorus of women drowned her answer by bursting into a loud shout of derision.

When they had got round the corner, outside the field of vision of the hyenas, Nana snorted: "Now they know it, at any rate. Now they've seen with their own eyes that you're back, and that I'm walking with you. Do they bother you? As soon as we're in, I want to hear everything about you, and I want to see your child."

Marietta did not answer at once. As they reached the entrance of the house, Marietta noticed an old woman in the courtyard — Antonio's mother. Lucia had just descended the stairs, unmistakably with the intention of going to her son's workshop; but now she hesitated, blinked her eyes in the fierce sun, and turned round again. Nana, full of contempt, noticed this maneuver, and hastened her steps, dragging Marietta along with her. Nana climbed the stairs immediately behind the old woman, who hurried as much as she could. Just at the moment when, groaning with the effort, Lucia had reached her own door, Nana, still clutching Marietta's arm, steered past her with a flourish of flowing skirts.

"She's another who knows now what I think of her," said Nana triumphantly, complaining at the same time, "I've got palpitations of the heart with this rushing upstairs so quickly."

Then she insisted that Marietta should fetch her child from Annina's.

Nana took Benedetto from her and carried him to the window to have a good look at him.

The most divergent expressions chased one another across her face. The child was like his mother: Nana remembered an autumn morning eighteen years ago when she had held in her arms a little thing barely ten weeks old. It was a girl, and it was called Marietta. . . . But Nana looked in vain for another resemblance that she had been determined to find at all costs; and as though the baby could read her hidden thoughts and was amused by them, he returned her anxious look with his dark gleaming eyes. She was quite put out by it, and handed the bundle back to his mother, asking, "And his name?"

Marietta told her, but Nana was no wiser. Suddenly, she came close to her and whispered, flushing deeply with excitement and shame, "Marietta, is Antonio his father?"

Marietta gazed at the child. It was difficult to say whether Nana's question had affronted her. She shrugged her shoulders and turned away.

"Marietta, does that mean you don't know yourself?"

"What's that to you?" asked Marietta in a strained voice.

"What's that to me? You ask me that? Me? It would not concern *me*, if you, away there in Rome . . . ?"

With difficulty, reluctantly, Marietta compelled herself to make the reassuring declaration, "When I was there, I knew no man. The child is six months old."

Nana sighed deeply. "And why couldn't you tell me that at once?" she asked reprovingly, sad and not understanding. "Don't you want me to give them their answer when they're tittle-tattling about it here? Give me a cup of coffee — I'm not over my palpitations yet. And let me take the child."

Marietta went to put water on the fire.

When she returned, Nana said: "It's his father's nose. Now I can see it. . . . Can you sit up yet, little man?" asked Nana, growing more enamored every moment of the pretty doll.

"He may call me 'Granny,' " she decided, suddenly.

"You're still a bit young for that."

Nana turned round in lively protest. "I might have been your mother. And suppose he hasn't got a granny? No, you haven't got a granny, little man, or it would be Nana. Ta-ta-ta. Look, Marietta, he's catching at my hair." And sadly she added, "There's enough gray in it for a granny."

Now that the tension in her was broken, she relaxed more and more into sadness. "If only I'd had a baby like that — perhaps I shouldn't have turned so gray, and my face wouldn't have been so full of wrinkles. Then I should have had something to cling to. And do you know, I was expecting, once. Ah well! If it had come, perhaps it would have been stillborn — that happened to his first wife three times in succession. Or it might have been a calamity, like Luigino."

"Have you many troubles, Nana?"

"Oh, not I alone. Have they told you that Vacca did bring that girl of Brogi's into the house after all, when I couldn't get through all the work? I let him do it, even though I knew he'd sleep with her. There was a time, Marietta, when I was only too pleased to be in my bed by myself and have a good cry. But now you must listen: in the old days, that girl was always after Vacca — he couldn't guess that she'd find herself better accommodated by his son! That's the sort of mistake people make; and now those two are living under our roof, and we can't get rid of them, for Luigino stands up to his father, and I'm tired, Marietta . . . That girl's the boss. She's in charge of the till now, and I stand in the kitchen again, and cook with money I'm given, just as I did when the good padrona was still alive; and at midday we sit, the four of us, together at table. Oh, a fine time! Yes, and with all that I've got Vacca back again. Now he seeks consolation with Nana's gray hairs, and sometimes we are together as we were before. And sometimes I think that, after all, it's thanks to this girl that things are better again between us — although that wasn't her intention. Yes, these things you know nothing about yet, little man. You'll give your mother some worry yet — I can see it in your eyes. Lord! they're your very eyes, Marietta; I've never seen anything like it. Vacca ought to see this too. In the old days, you used to make him wild with those eyes of yours — he would have liked to burn them out with a red-hot poker. Yes; but he's become much calmer now. You ought to come and see us one day with the child, Marietta, just to please me. After all, he's Nana's old man, and life has punished him enough."

Thus Nana prattled on, while she dandled Benedetto on her knee, and the sadder the things she talked about, the brighter grew her mood. She could not forbear to smile even when she spoke of Luigino, who was after every skirt, so that that girl of Brogi's had her worries and annoyances.

Then suddenly Nana decided that she was wasting her time scandalously. She swallowed her coffee hastily, handed the child to Marietta, and fled.

II

But Nana was not the only visitor that day. Others also wanted to see the child, so that they could chatter about it at the city well.

"And the funniest thing of all is, that dear old Nana insists he's like his father. He probably does look like his father, too. . . . The only question is, who is the father? If he has anybody's nose, then it's Cesare's. In any case, Cesare certainly helped her out of the city in his cart, and if you use your common sense, you can imagine what happened on the way. . . . Yes; what Antonio couldn't bring off in a whole year, Cesare makes a success of between here and Rome. But he's a dark horse, is Cesare. Every Sunday he goes quietly to Mass with Camilla, but the mischief he gets into during the week! They say he has half a dozen running about in Rome. One thing I know, if I should ever want to do anything with another man (but I've only too much with my own), then I shall sleep on it seven times before I let myself in with a man like Cesare. He can't look at you but what you're already three months gone . . . And Antonio, the innocent, hasn't the least suspicion; but as for old Lucia . . ."

Thus the women rattled on among themselves, trying to drown each other's voices. When, however, they knocked at Marietta's door, they felt a sudden twinge of shame as they entered her room, and grew a little less talkative. They stammered out confused words of genuine interest, as Marietta showed them the little one sleeping peacefully, still ignorant of scandal. And they went away again sooner than they had intended. They were hardly beyond the reach of Marietta's eye or ear, however, when they burst into guffaws, and outvied each other in concealing their kindly human feelings, of which they thought they ought to feel ashamed.

That same day, when some later visitors were bending over him, the little Benedetto woke and looked up at them in surprise; but he did not smile as in the morning he had smiled at Nana, although the women tried all the usual devices.

"It's a serious child," they said. And the curious feeling came over them that it was on purpose that Benedetto would not laugh at them, as though with precocious discernment he had realized their perfidy. But no, he was only an innocent baby. He must have those eyes by nature. After all, he had certainly come not from God but from the Devil, born as he was in sin.

"I'm glad he's not my child," they said when they left.

When they had gone, Marietta bolted the door. She had had enough for one day. Anyone who came knocking now would receive no answer and could just go away again. As she hung her shawl over the back of a chair and with slow fingers loosened her bodice in order to feed the child, she also looked attentively at the small creature who, in the space of one day, had brought her into renewed contact with the women of Todi.

How he had looked at them out of his fine bright eyes that she sometimes could not resist kissing passionately, because there lay such understanding in them that it was surely a miracle from God! He closed them again. Everything about him was safe and well as he lay at his mother's breast and sucked the sweet milk into him.

It had become very still in the room, lately so filled with dissembling chatter. Not even Grigio's gentle cooing, which had been a consolation and a reassurance to her in her dark hours, sounded there — for Grigio was dead. . . . Drink, drink, my tender little man. Drink your belly full. Grow big and strong — a big, strong man. Perhaps Todi will become too narrow for you one day, and then you'll set out into the great world and leave me sitting here behind . . . But that's a long time ahead. We needn't think of that yet. . . . Drink; drink, little man. Take from your mother what she can give you. Drink until it hurts me. . . .

Downstairs Antonio was hammering at a coffin for the wine merchant Boncini, who had died that night. In the old days his hammering had sometimes got on her nerves so badly that she had gone running up and down in this same room. Grigio from his cage had watched her, concerned. Now she was thankful for the familiar sound. Antonio was working for the child. . . . What did it matter to her if it happened to be at a coffin for the old wine merchant Boncini? Her child was alive and flushed with health.

The women had said it resembled Antonio. They lied. But she would like to give him a child, a child that would resemble him so that all the world could see. This one — this one was hers; hers and nobody else's.

His mouth fell, satisfied, from her breast. She pressed him to her, then laid him to sleep. She wandered about the room, not knowing herself for what she was searching. A feeling of immeasurable wealth was almost bursting her heart. She ended by returning to the tiny sleeping fellow, and staring at him through a mist of tears.

III

The women called on Antonio in the workshop to wish him luck in his child. He scarcely listened to them while he wondered anxiously how Marietta had responded to all these visitors; and her almost exuberant greeting was an immense relief to him when later on he went upstairs. She told him she was no longer afraid to go to the city well in the morning to fill her pitchers.

Surely it was a miracle, that his life had suddenly become filled with reality; and to whom did he owe it, if not to the little man there on the bed?

Andrea took his evening meal with them; and he seemed to think it good manners to stay on even after Marietta had cleared the table, watching Antonio's tinkering at the little cart for Simone's Giannino. Antonio, who had been well pleased with the first day's work of his young apprentice, unbent a little towards him, and showed him how to construct such a toy cart.

Marietta was taken with Andrea too; he had a gentle friendliness, and something manly and serious about him. But after supper she would have liked to be alone with her husband, and when nine o'clock struck outside, she suggested to Andrea that he ought to be getting home — he must have enough sleep when he worked so hard.

Andrea got up immediately, without mentioning that he always went to bed at the same time as his father.

Antonio could not quite make up his mind whether to see his apprentice to the door. He decided to remain seated, and made a little joke to cover his uncertainty: "Just tell your father I'm not at all pleased with you, and that you must therefore come back again to-morrow."

Andrea smiled, wished them good night, and went away — after peeping at the bed where the little one was sleeping. Did he feel himself accepted as one of their household, and did he consider Benedetto a little brother? Or was he only flattering them to gain their favor? If that were his intention, he had succeeded so far as Antonio was concerned, for he began to sing Andrea's praises as soon as he had gone.

Marietta, sunk in thought, sat watching the making of the toy cart; until Antonio looked up, surprised because he received no reply to a question. Then she raised her head, too; and the desire in her eyes and about her mouth made him suddenly lose all interest both in Andrea and in his work.

"Marietta — " he murmured; and he felt almost afraid at the beautiful thing life, so long a stepmother to him, had become.

On the table lay the little cart unfinished, and beside it an open knife. . . .

IV

Antonio, rapidly overcoming the hesitations that were his by nature, drank deep in the full strength of his confident young manhood of the intoxicating sensations that filled their days and nights. His self-assurance towards other men increased. At every hour of the day, something served to remind him that Marietta was at home, and that her thoughts and long-ings went out to him — the wonderful, urgent longings that had been pent up in her during that year of separation. She infected him with them. Together, they succumbed to the bright light of their senses, and forgot the whole world outside.

They needed to say little in order to understand one another. Andrea was puzzled at the way in which they teased one another all the time with half-sentences and jokes that never hurt — it was like a persistent game between them. They played with the child too. Their room was a little world shut off in which there was no place for a stranger, not even Andrea — although he had as good a time with them as could befall any young apprentice.

Meanwhile, Antonio had renewed his habit of visiting his mother for a moment every morning, perhaps because there was no longer any room in his heart for resentment. On her side, Lucia had been pondering over her defeat. Before her son, she still tried to hold her head up. Safe in her room, she felt strong, and she could not forbear to try to wound him, either. Her onslaughts, however, seemed impotent to hurt him. Perhaps it was out of pity for his mother, now so lonely and joyless, that he would not fight against her. But sometimes Lucia thought she noticed that even his pity was not very deep. His thoughts were always with his wife and child. Everyone in the city seemed to have seen this child, ex-cept her. She did not want to see it, either. It was only an outsider. Yes; but why would she not be honest and admit to herself that she drank in every word that fell from his lips about this child, that she hungered to hear him speak of this child, this child that was making him ridiculous and had been the cause of her defeat?

Antonio brought her a daily report, as though there had been a secret agreement between them — she never had to inquire about the baby. He reported wonders about the child; and some day she would no doubt be-lieve in those wonders. On that day, grown childish, she would say to her-self, "But can't a man make a child his own with the power of his love?" The thought still gave her nausea. She still recoiled from the weakness to which old age was bringing her.

Upon one occasion Antonio said, "Perhaps Benedetto will have a little brother one day . . . Then people will see for themselves that Marietta doesn't need to go away from me to . . . ."

Lucia held her breath. She wanted wildly to know whether Antonio's expectation was fond imagining, or whether his wife had said something to him. Fortunately, she could keep her own counsel: she could afford to wait. But when she was alone again, his half-assertion became an obsession: if that happened, it would offer her an escape from her terrible predicament — perhaps she could transfer her foolish feelings to her second grandchild.

Next morning Antonio came and told her that little Benedetto was feverish; and at once Lucia lost all interest in grandchildren yet to be born.

In intolerable suspense, she waited that evening for Antonio to bring her news, and when he appeared she overwhelmed him with questions, advice, and household remedies.

Benedetto's fever lasted a day or two. Lucia could not sleep for worrying. She must be going off her head in her old age. Then she heard that the fever was gone. The little fellow no longer lay in bed hot as a stove, but enjoyed his pap again. A day or two later, Antonio did what she had so fervently hoped he would: he brought the child to her in his arms.

"Does your wife know?" she inquired in an uncertain voice from the half-light behind the door.

"Marietta handed him to me herself."

This confused Lucia even more. What a world of mistrust haunted her gray head! She felt herself the victim of cunning calculation. For a moment she thought she would collapse as she preceded Antonio towards the light where she could see the child. She stared at him with her old eyes. He was quite, quite different from what she had imagined. Suddenly she realized that she had grown accustomed to the idea that in some mysterious way the baby would resemble her son, after all. In her dreams recently she had seen an infant that was Antonio in small, as he was when she carried him in her arms. Chilled to the marrow, hostile, she saw only his mother in Benedetto. It was almost revolting, how he resembled that woman . . . Lucia could not think any more: it was as though Marietta were looking at her out of those childish eyes, penetrating into the innermost depths of her mind.

"Take him back now," she panted. "He's only just recovered from a fever. Did anybody see you bring him here?"

Her teeth chattered. She got mixed up in her words. Tall and broad-shouldered, the little fellow on his arm, unhurt in his quiet pride, Antonio went away.

That night, as Lucia conjured up in her mind the little Benedetto, again and again, she began to believe that after all there was a resemblance here and there. . . .

V

The illness of their child had restrained the passion of Antonio and Marietta, and now that he was well again their intoxication did not return. The strange, burning hunger that had driven them into each other's arms had passed.

It was in these days that Marietta realized she could not yet hope for another pregnancy. Why could she not give Antonio a child? She wept about it in her sleep. When she awoke the traces of tears still marked her cheek.

Antonio felt oppressed by a strange guilt. He grew quieter again, and humbler, and did his work as if he, like Andrea, were serving a master.

Lucia was astonished sometimes at what she noticed about her son. Sometimes she thought she could have regained her ascendancy over him if she had set her mind to it; but her heart was not in that desire any more. All she wanted was that he should bring the child to her again. She forgot to think of the second one that might come one day. She sewed a little suit for Benedetto. Antonio took him to her so that she could see how he looked in it. From that moment, Lucia had not enough spare time to suit her. There was always some mending to do. Antonio told her what was needed. Fortunately, Lucia had always been quick with the needle.

If only other people did not come to know about it . . . That was her great anxiety.

As if anything could remain hidden!

THE FEAST

OF THE

ASSUMPTION

I

ONE EVENING IMMA, THE BISHOP'S OLD SERVANT, was sitting with Marietta and her husband: she had descended upon them out of the blue.

As she looked with anxious fixed eyes at the little tub of a woman who sat there so complacently, Marietta turned pale and wondered how she had dared go every morning to market without a thought that she might meet Imma there at any moment. In what complete oblivion had she been living all these weeks? And now Imma had come again, bringing confusion into her life, as she had done once before on a certain dark winter afternoon. . . . And yet, for a moment, she was not sure that a certain gladness had not sprung up in her at Imma's belated appearance. No, she had not wanted her to come — she wanted peace, nothing but peace, if only for the sake of her husband, to whom she was so deeply indebted.

Had not Monsignore understood? He knew why she had fled from Todi. He must also have guessed what had moved her to come back. Was it possible that he did not know of Imma's visit to her? Marietta wondered, as she waited in silence, on the defensive.

Imma sighed and breathed heavily in her efforts to recover from climbing the stairs. But she did not complain. Nor did she seem concerned as to whether anybody had observed her coming. Imma was too absorbed by the purpose of her visit to give a thought to such incidentals. Moreover, she had an uneasy conscience, though she told herself over and over again that her master was denying the voice of his own heart when he had given her strict orders not to go and see Marietta upon her return.

Despite which, here she was sitting in Marietta's house after all, her back to the dusky light of the spring evening so that the expression on her face was difficult to distinguish. "Yes — I just dropped in. They told me you'd come back," she said with haughty bluntness, and lifted her eyes to Marietta as though she still had a great deal to say if only she had an opportunity.

"Lord, Lord!" she sighed, and irritably turned away her round head that sat upon her shoulders almost without a neck.

Marietta saw that Imma felt helpless and ill at ease despite her misleading assumption of boldness, and understood that she had not come as the bishop's ambassador, but on the contrary had defied his authority. She lost her disquiet, and smiled at her visitor, suddenly recovering her old ascendancy over Imma — an ascendancy the old woman had been reluctantly compelled to acknowledge from the time when Marietta was only fifteen. She got up, went to the little bed Antonio had carpentered, and picked up her child; for it was in the first place to see the child that, like all the others, Imma had come — though she may have had special reasons of her own as well. As she carried him to Imma, the certainty suddenly filled Marietta that through this child she had prevailed not only over the women in Todi, including Imma, but also over the bishop. . . . But *he* did not know that yet.

"You'd like to see my child, wouldn't you, Imma?" she asked, with an almost diabolical elation.

Imma nodded, flushing, and stared at the child. Her sharp, round little eyes opened wide. So did her mouth.

At that moment, Antonio said, "I'm just going out for a moment, Marietta — I promised Mother . . ."

Alarmed, imploring, Marietta turned towards him: "Antonio!"

"I'll be back in no time," he promised vaguely, and went. She bit her lip. Had she forgotten that he too was in the room?

Imma did not observe this exchange between them. Marietta laid Benedetto down again. Imma waddled after her, and stood looking at him from the foot of the bed. Some moments elapsed before she noticed that Marietta had returned to the table. Abashed, she rejoined her; and then suddenly a desperate urge gained the upper hand in her. She looked at Marietta compellingly and whispered hoarsely, "You must bring him to Monsignore. Do you understand?"

Marietta's eyes wandered over the table.

"Marietta!"

Oh, Marietta heard the entreaty well enough. Supposing this demand came from the bishop himself? Imma had no right to order her about.

Perspiration stood on Imma's forehead. "Why don't you say something? You just let me go on. If you still have a heart, Marietta, you must understand me."

"Did Monsignore send you?"

Venom flickered up in Imma's eyes. "No — I wasn't sent. No doubt you'd like to think I was — but you don't count in this at all," she said, viciously. "He has the right to see the child, and you know that well enough, too."

Marietta thought a moment. "Why don't I count in this at all?" she asked, with something childish, sad, and sulky in her voice that exasperated Imma. "The child is mine," she went on obstinately — and then asked in despair: "Didn't you notice how Antonio ran out of the room a moment ago? Monsignore didn't send you here, because he thought of me — of me. I'll see about it. I don't know, myself, yet — I'm not strong enough, either, to carry the child any distance."

"Your husband can carry it."

Marietta gave a bitter, amused little laugh.

"I, I'll carry it for you," snapped Imma.

Marietta felt a sudden repulsion to such insolent tyranny. She did not succeed in smothering the disgust in her voice as she said, "If I want to take him to Monsignore, then I'll carry him myself. Go now, please. Go. Leave me alone." She glanced towards the door, as though she had a mind to escape, herself, if Imma refused to go.

But Imma had something more she wanted to say: her eyes were almost bulging out of their sockets. And then she went, after all.

She hastened through the dark streets back to the piazza, a dwarfish woman striding with long masculine steps in the shadow of the unnaturally tall houses. At the corner, she stood still for a moment and pressed her hands against the stormily beating heart that lay concealed somewhere within her.

When Antonio re-entered his house with bowed head, as though he were expecting a blow, Marietta had regained her calm.

"She's gone," was all Marietta said; but there was something in her tone that made him breathe more easily: it sounded like "And for the time being she won't come back again, either. . . . Don't worry."

II

No, Imma did not come back.

It was early summer. Marietta carried her boy on her arm when she went to market. He could stand, and even take a few steps when his mother held his little hands. The market women lifted him up over their fruits and greens and pressed him to their hearts. "Come here, *putto, carino!*" Imma, hidden behind a stall, witnessed such scenes and her heart melted. On such a day she could never find anything good enough anywhere in the market. Contemptuously, she hurled back all that was offered her. "You godless creatures! To dare to sell such rubbish for Monsignore's table!"

Meanwhile little Benedetto trustingly allowed fruit to be put into his mouth. Everything he was given tasted fine. The vendors kissed his dear little face, smeared with fruit juice. Disarmed, his mother looked on as they spoiled him. It could not be unpleasant in her ears to hear the women cry out, "I shall eat you right up one of these days, *porcellino d'amore!* Marietta, how did you come by such a darling of a child?"

When she returned home with him, a basket with her purchases on her free arm, she ran in to Antonio before preparing the food. He picked up the child and kissed him tenderly, reverently. Andrea did not interrupt his work: that was what his master expected of him; but he hoped all the same that Marietta would go over to him for a moment — and fortunately she never forgot. Andrea pressed his lips on one of the tiny fists and made funny animal sounds. Marietta had to laugh. "But where did you learn that, Andrea? To imitate animals so perfectly?"

By way of reply, Andrea spat like a couple of snarling, scratching tom-cats. Then he too laughed at his own lifelike imitation, and bent once more over his work. Benedetto was astonished. He looked up at his mother with wonder in his eyes.

When Marietta left the workshop it often chanced that she met Antonio's mother coming down the stairs to go to market. The two women did not look at each other; they both devoted their whole attention to the child.

The old one did not lay a finger upon him. She just looked at him and asked, "Did he cry again last night?"

"Yes, his teeth are coming through."

"Antonio had four in his first year, but he was forward in every way."

Lucia inquired as to whether this and that little garment still fitted. "Good. And if not, Antonio will tell me."

"Say, 'Good day, Grandmother!' "

This was too much to ask of Benedetto — he could not speak yet.

"Ba!" said he, looking at his grandmother, and stamping with his little feet to indicate that he wanted to go home, where he could play with Mizio, the black kitten Andrea had brought for him.

III

It was high summer. In the noon hour, the courtyard was deserted: the children who played there all day long had been summoned to the midday meal. In the narrow strip of shadow on the shady side, Lascari the cobbler's chickens panted with open beaks as they waited for Manuela to call to them and feed them. In the gutter, sparrows bathed and drank. A ginger tomcat, invisible as a flame in the glow of the sun, came slinking up on satin paws, his murderer's eyes shining like tiny yellow lamps. Every shutter was closed against the heat and the flies. The whole house was silent, except for the buzzing of the flies and the sound of intermittent hammering that came from Antonio's workshop.

Todi exhibited human activity only in the morning hours, when the market was on and the women filled their pitchers at the city well, and in the evenings, when the women, with sleepy children on their knees, sat together in the dusky squares lit up by stars and moon and talked of the coming Feast of the Assumption, — of the newest scandals, the latest theft, — and of the wicked people who, as always just before the harvest, roamed outside the city gate and robbed the vineyards. The *sbirri* had been sent out after the rogues, to bring them to justice.

Marietta said to Antonio that she wanted to attend High Mass on the great day. Since her return, she had not been to the cathedral; she and Antonio had taken part in the spring feasts of the Church in the small church of Saint Clare where she had gone to confession as a child. The Madonna of that church had loved her fervently in those days; and recently she had lighted a candle before Her, now and again, taking Benedetto with her to kiss the altar. There had been a time when Marietta had given but scant thought to her faith; but her wonderful return to life seemed to have strengthened her sense of religion, and she wanted Benedetto to know and love the Madonna of Saint Clare's, who might one day protect him in danger.

Yes, and now she wanted him to attend the service in the cathedral to celebrate the Feast of the Assumption; and as she gave expression to her intention, an agitation came into her voice that made Antonio look up at her stealthily. Very well, if she wanted to go . . . He had not been to the cathedral either, for a long time. Not since before the year he had spent alone. It would be very crowded.

"We'll stand at the back — then we can always get out if we wish."

Marietta made Benedetto a bright red suit. She ironed Antonio's dark suit, carefully removing every stain from it. For herself she made a simple, tasteful summer dress, and as the Feast of the Assumption happened also to be her birthday, she wanted to invite Simone and Annina with their children at midday, and regale them with homemade cakes.

When the day came, Antonio and Marietta and their child made their way to High Mass through the sunny, decorated streets that were filled with gaily dressed churchgoers. Antonio, in his wedding suit with silver buckles on his shoes, noticed how the men surreptitiously eyed Marietta in her light and flowery summer dress. And little Benedetto, his curls combed up with water, seemed well pleased with himself as he glanced down at the new red suit that glowed in the sunshine.

In front of them walked Cesare and Camilla with some of their off-spring. They did not look round. Camilla had no wish to cast a glance at Marietta's child; for even though Cesare had sworn, with his hand on his little Carlo's head, that he had had nothing to do with Marietta, people believed he had, and that was just as bad. Supposing the frightful new scandal about Susanna should come out, this last punishment from heaven, the punishment for the breaking of the Madonna to fragments . . . ! God had seen the fragments, just as he had seen Susanna raise her sinful hand. God was not to be misled by the most careful piecing together of the bits. He could see cracks that eluded the human eye, and even though Carlo had immediately lighted the votive lamp again, it had been ex-tinguished for a moment. God, who counted all the votive lights here on earth, had seen one grow dim, and his wrath had been roused. To-day Susanna had been left at home to look after the youngest because her mother no longer dared show herself with her on the street. And still such a child, and so often warned by her mother! Cesare ought to have given her the stick while there was yet time; but that was Cesare all over. He was a bad example, too. He set the example.

And now? What now? When he got home the evening before, she had made him go at once to Vacca, for matters could not be delayed. Vacca had referred Cesare to Luigino himself; and then that girl of Brogi's had made Cesare believe that she too was as far gone as Susanna, and that Luigino had promised to marry *her;* and that fool of a Cesare had not known what else to say, although he ought to have known very well that that girl was lying — if she had had any aptitude for childbearing, she would have had a dozen already, and by twelve different fathers. Must Camilla go herself? She would burst into sobs upon confronting the girl, instead of saying what ought to be said, and all through her nerves. If Cesare had only been as clever as he was big and strong, a rascal like Luigino would have thought twice before getting Susanna into trouble.

But the only thing Cesare was clever at was getting another child, and when his wife told him she could no longer make do with the weekly money, because there were so many mouths to fill, all he could say to comfort her was that the post was going to lower its charges, and that meant the beginning of the end for freight carriers. The beginning of the end . . . Yes, that's what it was. Camilla felt it.

Marietta cast a side glance towards the windows of the episcopal palace . . . "He will be making ready for Mass; he'll have left his study," she thought. Perhaps that was why she dared to look up. It was not the first time she had crossed the piazza with little Benedetto on her arm. One morning a few weeks ago, when the market women had again outvied one another in singing her child's praises, she had suddenly taken the direction of the piazza, and she had crossed it in a strange, dazed agitation — as though she intended to pay a visit to The Three Popes. Nana had appeared at the door, and with impetuous greetings had dragged her in calling to Vacca, who came limping into the kitchen, looking inquisitively at the child and examining his mother impertinently. Nana, exuberant and jovial, brought out cakes from the cupboard, and plied the child with them until he could eat no more.

Since then, Marietta had crossed the piazza several times, the child on her arm; and now she was bringing him in his bright red suit to the cathedral where Monsignore was officiating at High Mass in honor of the Assumption of Our Lady.

They stood near the entrance, Antonio behind his wife and child. He looked round thoughtfully, perhaps a little astonished to notice how small the cathedral of Todi was compared with St. Peter's at Rome.

"Look, look!" whispered Marietta to Benedetto, and pointed to the choir benches, into which a number of priests were filing, all robed in white in honor of the Virgin's glorious ascent to heaven. The great central altar itself had been superbly decorated by the children of Our Blessed Lady.

Then came the moment when the bishop entered, dispensing his blessing as he strode down the center aisle. In the shimmering light of many candles, his features were difficult to distinguish: Marietta, breathing deeply, could see only his figure — motionless, impressive in the magnificent, consecrated robes. After a few moments, she began to feel more at rest. Fixing her gaze upon him, she ceased to look for the man. He was comely and exalted as he fulfilled the rites before the altar, and he seemed infinitely remote. Her presence, and that of her child in the congregation, had little significance. She averted her gaze, drew Benedetto's attention to the rows of stately candles that stood up round the altar like proud watchers. . . .

He had already noticed them, those golden, flickering little flames. With wide-open eyes, he stared towards them where they formed an open gateway of light. He was no less grave than the bishop over there, carrying out his high function. And why should the gravity of a child be a lesser thing?

Benedetto listened to the gentle clanking of the chains by which the censers were swung backwards and forwards. He started at the sudden tinkle of the silver bell. When his eyes grew tired with staring into the distance, he leaned his little head against his mother's shoulder and looked sleepily at another child . . . And then suddenly he raised himself again and listened astonished: the organ had begun to sound. He took his thumb out of his mouth and raised his small hand on high as he looked at the people around. They nudged one another. One kindly woman pinched his small thigh lovingly, and whispered to him, "Yes . . . that sounds nice, eh?"

Marietta, flushed with emotion, turned towards her husband. "Did you see that, Antonio?"

Antonio, proud, but remembering in time that it was not seemly for him to express admiration of his own child in public, only nodded.

Then a stillness fell upon the congregation, because the bishop had risen from his seat and was moving towards the altar.

IV

In the afternoon, Marietta told Annina and Simone how Benedetto, with as solemn a gravity as if he had been a little John the Baptist, had raised his hand when he heard the organ music. She was still excited about it, and tried to entice Antonio out of his silence. She asked him to tell them something about the High Mass in St. Peter's at Rome, celebrated by the Holy Father himself. And then, when Antonio began reluctantly to speak, she interrupted him, disappointed: she thought he had given her a more colorful account at the time. While Giannino listened to the grown-ups, the two little ones sat on the ground pulling at Mizio, who arched his back and spat as though he were already a real tomcat. Annina was very much bothered lest Teresina should dirty herself. She wanted to take her to see the procession that was to leave the cathedral at sunset, in which Giannino was to carry a candle. Teresina was wearing a white satin dress, much too expensive and fine for a child of Annina and Simone. Annina was, indeed, rather shy about it; but she was confident that every right-thinking person would understand that the handsome frock could only be one cast off by little Beata Ricci — Annina had done the Ricci washing from time immemorial. "Teresina, Teresina, will you leave that alone?" The little girl, who could not speak a word yet, immediately went and sat down, her small hands folded in her lap.

Andrea paid his usual Sunday afternoon visit. Did he regard this as a duty of politeness, or was he already so much attached to this room and to the people who lived in it that he could not remain away for a single day? After greeting the grown-ups, he sat down by the children on the floor, and Giannino ceased to listen to Antonio's story of the pontifical Mass in Rome. Andrea contrived to rivet the attention of even the tiny ones in a remarkable way. In an almost colorless voice, he told them long stories of a fight between a tomato and an onion. Mizio, too, played a part in Andrea's tales. He had to lie on his back, his paws folded, and purr; or he was the mount of a proud knight that Andrea produced — a knight with a wooden head and a red cloak about his neck; the knight was particularly mobile because there was no body in his cloak. He could hide himself anywhere, and could even disappear altogether inside Andrea's hand. He was called Orlando, and he had no mercy on robbers and other rabble. He lived in Andrea's pocket, and as a companion he usually had a fantastically shaped carrot that did service as a monster.

Even the grown-ups listened. Where did the boy get such stories from? After a while, however, their attention was diverted by the noise of a quarrel on the floor above. Cesare's words were drowned by Camilla's angry and excited shouting at Susanna, who broke out into pitiful sobs.

Annina looked at Marietta significantly. "Haven't you heard yet — about Susanna? Everyone's been talking about it, but her mother only noticed this week! I do believe the lamb doesn't realize what has happened to her. She had her dress all ready to join in the maidens' procession this evening. Didn't you notice any quarreling above your heads yesterday evening?"

"Yes but I didn't know . . . It happens so often," whispered Marietta.

Annina nodded compassionately. "She's a month further gone than I am. Of course it's Luigino Vacca's — she was keeping company with him."

"Luigino Vacca?"

"You may well think she could have chosen somebody better! Cesare went round there last night, but that girl of Brogi's won't release him."

Marietta was silent. Then there appeared upon her face an expression of contempt that Annina had seen there before. It made her regret that she had spoken about the matter to Marietta.

"Ah well, it's not our business," she said, trying to change the subject. A little later, Marietta stood up. "I'll soon be back," she said to her husband reassuringly, and left the room. Those who remained behind looked at one another. Andrea's peculiar monotonous voice droned on.

V

That disdainful little smile was still playing about Marietta's lips when later that afternoon she set out to go to the bishop. She was confident of catching him alone at that hour — she still remembered the hours he reserved for himself on feast days. Yes, now she was going to him, carrying her child in her arms, as Imma had asked her to do.

Why should she not smile? Camilla, who for months had not given her a look, would have kissed her hands a moment ago if she had not prevented it; and all because Marietta was going to talk to Monsignore with a view to arranging a marriage between Susanna and Luigino. Only the week before, so it was reported, this selfsame Luigino had shown an indignant Camilla to the door. She had described him to Susanna as a low, contemptible creature. Now suddenly she saw salvation in a union between her daughter and that unworthy being. Was the contempt of people over a bastard heavier to bear, then, than a loveless marriage? It would seem so. If Camilla had not regarded Susanna's future as rosier and more promising after Marietta's promise to use her influence with the bishop, would Camilla have flung herself on Cesare's neck for sheer joy?

Cesare, softened, paid attention at last to Susanna's entreaty to be allowed to take part in the procession after all. He gave his consent, and the child hastened to put on her virginal robe, and when she came to show herself in it, truth to tell, she looked no less innocent than the other little girls. Cesare said as much.

It was a relief to Cesare, who had listened for months to his wife's slanders about Marietta without finding the courage to contradict her, to be able once more to give free rein to his repressed feelings of friendliness towards her.

As for Marietta, with her disdainful little smile — had her offer of help been as disinterested as it appeared? Perhaps she had been unable to bear Susanna's shrieks any longer, when she had gone upstairs to pacify those foolish, childish people with her promise; but later, as she came downstairs again, she thought that she could say to Antonio: "I must go to Monsignore — about Susanna."

And as she was going, she might just as well let Monsignore see her child at the same time; he was bound to ask after him.

She wanted no more: she only wanted him to see Benedetto once. She could swear it, yes. And perhaps she wanted him to see her herself just once again too, so that he could observe how upon her distant travels she had learned to distinguish reality from mirage. Perhaps that would free him from a doubt that had not ceased to torment him — for though he had smiled at the comedy of life while she had still been nonplussed by it, he had not escaped untouched, either, in the comedy in which they had been the two chief figures.

She ought to have gone to him earlier. Had she refrained from doing so for Antonio's sake? Yes. . . . Since it was in the certainty that she was going to bring gladness to Monsignore that she trembled in her whole body, it must certainly have been for the sake of Antonio, who had guessed more than he had wished to show as she went out of the door.

If he *had* guessed something of the truth, perhaps the whole truth, then he must surely understand, too, that she had to pay this visit, some day if not that day. And surely he must also know that she would return to him, and remain at his side for the rest of her life, since she had followed him with her child. . . .

The streets were still scattered with flowers from the procession. There were still a few candles burning upon the altars. The small Madonnas smiled at her in the glow of these little lights as she passed.

VI

Imma, the child in her arms, stood listening by the kitchen door. Marietta, too, heard footsteps on the stair — steps of departing guests.

"They're gone. Now he's alone," said Imma. Still carrying Benedetto, she preceded Marietta up the stairs. On the landing she paused, handed the child back to his mother, knocked, went in first herself, and said, "The child is here."

Behind his writing table sat Monsignore. He did not move at once. He looked at Marietta, and at the child on her arm. Perhaps he could not see them very well, because the candlelight was in his eyes. His large, pale, priest's hand groped towards the candelabrum. He picked it up, and approached Marietta.

Marietta saw only his eyes. She saw that he suffered because he did not yet know how to interpret her unexpected visit. . . . Perhaps Imma was playing a trick on him: she remained standing by the door, not understanding that she ought to go away. He had to fight hard to retain his composure. His mouth took a hard line as he raised the candelabrum to look at the child that was being presented to him in such ridiculous fashion.

Marietta could not find the right phrase to liberate him from his embarrassment. She was stupefied by a sudden awareness of heavy guilt: how could she have been in Todi all these months without taking her child to him? By comparison, the guilt she had felt a short while ago towards Antonio seemed small and insignificant. She had imagined herself strong in the possession of the child that she had thought belonged to her alone — to her alone. Now, as Monsignore bent over it, she realized that this had been dreadful pride. Full of a deep remorse, she meekly raised her child higher in her arms so that the bishop could look at him better.

He glanced at her quickly, saw upon her face the dumb ecstasy of giving. The hard line about his mouth relaxed. He handed the candelabrum to Imma and took the child from her.

"Come and sit beside me, Marietta."

His voice came with difficulty, as if he had been silent long and often.

They sat on the broad divan. Behind her back, Marietta ran her hidden hand over it a moment. . . . It was the same couch. Between them, on sturdy brown legs, stood Benedetto, supported under his little arms by the bishop, whose hands enfolded his small body almost completely.

Imma came closer with the light. Tears were streaming down her cheeks. "Lord, Lord!" she said, and was on the point of saying more when her master said, "Bring something for him, Imma."

Imma had difficulty in making up her mind to go, and when she did, she took the light away with her by mistake. She brought it back, and placed it irritably on the writing table. The bishop listened until he could hear her shuffling down the stairs. Then he said, "I must thank you for this, Marietta."

She only looked at him, struggling with tears.

"What you must have been through," he said, after looking into her eyes for a perceptible space of time.

"How are you, *Babbo?*"

"I? I've no news. Life has gone on. Sometimes I heard that you were coming back from Rome, that you had crossed the piazza with the child. Once I caught sight of you, myself — I should have liked to know then what I know now — that there is no more ill will in you."

He was ashamed of himself for saying this, ashamed that his voice went hoarse with grief. He closed his eyes, passed his hand over his face. Marietta stared at him — she realized how nervous he had grown during this year. Suddenly, she knew more about him — perhaps because in Naples she had met many high ecclesiastics who had joined in every worldly pleasure and sin. It was so easy for her, now, to see the man through the priest's cloth. Nothing but the man . . . To see this wonderful, untamed, almost peasant creature in front of her who, with his natural gifts, had seemed predestined to shoulder his way through the throng to the Vatican — and was now in exile in Todi, a living being among dead ruins that hung about him like ill-fitting clothes. Life had done him an injustice, an injustice. She too had done him an injustice once. A feeling of motherly tenderness sprang up in her. Also a great and perhaps foolish happiness at this renewed contact. . . . It was impossible for her to be sad any longer.

"*Babbo* . . . Why didn't I come to you at once?"

Astonished by the new sound in her voice, not understanding, he looked up. "Does your husband know you are here?" he asked, with a certain hesitation. "Does he suspect perhaps . . . In general, something?"

"Antonio?" She had to consider a moment. "Antonio will forget, if he does suspect. He wants things to remain as they are now."

"And you? . . . Tell me, Marietta. Will you be able to hold out this time?"

She nodded. He could not understand the lack of gravity in her face.

"This time? Yes, *Babbo*," she said, and smiled. Gently, confidingly, she added, "I need only to think of the child . . ."

A silence fell between them. He ended it abruptly with, "It is good that you should be here again, Marietta. Where else should you be?" In his voice there was a weakness, a longing for her agreement. "How are things now between you and your mother-in-law?" he asked.

"Oh, very well . . . When we meet we talk about the child. She makes his clothes."

"Always, always the child," cried Monsignore. And suddenly he was as Marietta wanted to have him . . . An intoxicating feeling of joy came over him too. Again and again as they talked, he looked at the child that clambered on his knees. He thought he could already see how some lines in the little face would form themselves. He thought he could see a certain resemblance . . .

Then, when he wanted to speak, a treacherous tenderness welled up in him, so that his lips trembled, and it was with difficulty that he brought out, "Can you understand, Marietta, what this means for me?"

She paled. "I shall come again with the child," she promised.

He seized her hand gratefully, and in agitation insisted, "Marietta — tell Antonio that if he ever wants help . . . Tell him I have the greatest regard for him . . . Oh God, if it didn't sound so ridiculous! Tell him I'm lonely, Marietta . . . After all, he was lonely himself once."

Imma's footsteps were approaching along the corridor. "Here come the little cakes," continued Monsignore, turning to the tiny boy on his knees, and then to Imma: "What have you brought for him, Imma? What do you think of the child? His eyes alone are enough to make you want to hug him. Say something, Imma."

But all Imma could do was to offer Benedetto a little cake, opening her eyes wide to attract his attention.

"He doesn't want it. Isn't there anything else in the house? You can see he doesn't want it," protested the bishop.

"Take it, *cuore*, Imma baked it herself," ordered Imma. "There now!" she said triumphantly when she had succeeded in pressing some into his mouth.

"Would you believe it, first to make a face and then to take it after all!" cried Monsignore.

The victorious Imma looked at her master, as he sat with a child on his lap, younger and brighter than she had seen him during the whole previous year. *Dio*, what a year it had been!

"But why did you call your child Benedetto?" she asked Marietta, with contempt and hostility in her voice.

And Marietta told the story of the Neapolitan priest, and Monsignore listened with rising enthusiasm. Could Marietta remember his name? Monsignore would be able to find out . . . And even though, alas! he was no longer in such continued personal correspondence with the Pope as formerly (one loses touch with everything in such a provincial hole as Todi) he would see whether his influence in the Vatican could not help a young and deserving priest . . .

Later, as she was about to go, Marietta suddenly remembered the real purpose of her visit. Holding the restless Benedetto upon his knee, Monsignore listened with half an ear to the story of Luigino and Susanna.

"I'll see if I can put it right. It's a foolish world. One can always add a little to its foolishness. Does she care for him? Oh, well — that's only a secondary consideration. Look, the little fellow takes my cross for a toy!"

VII

The whole city was talking about it, about Marietta's influence with the bishop. It was not to be believed, after her scandalous behavior. But the fact could not be denied. She had only to run to the bishop, and he summoned Luigino and that girl of Brogi's, and actually — a thing never seen before — that girl left the palace in tears, and immediately crossed the piazza to collect her belongings from The Three Popes. . . . Furthermore, Luigino and Susanna swore eternal troth to one another before the altar, and Susanna, sanctified by holy matrimony, was serving in the inn;

and within a week Luigino was out of the house again after other women.
. . . Such was the way of the world.

But whatever could be said about the result, it remained astonishing
that Marietta had brought it about. Antonio ought to be proud of his
wife, and so he was. And in this pride vanished a faint suspicion that had
tormented him. Marietta had kissed him so passionately the evening she
had returned from Monsignore's that she had kissed away all his foolish,
sinful notions. But what had these been? He no longer knew himself. Why
should he go on probing for things so vague and dark that he himself
hardly knew how to give them a name? Antonio did not want to see
ghosts unless they thrust themselves upon him. It brought him a deep
satisfaction that the whole city recognized Marietta's influence with the
bishop — and was currying favor with her.

"Monsignore was very taken with the child," said Marietta. "He thought
him so intelligent for his age." Ah well, perhaps later on that might be
very useful. Marietta had arranged that very well. She was far wiser than
Antonio. She had a care for her child, and had given an early thought to
his future. All Antonio need do was to avoid standing in her way, to go
downstairs into his workshop. . . .

From time to time, Marietta took their child on her arm and went with
him to the episcopal palace. Monsignore ordered from Rome a magnificent
toy, a real caroche with four painted wooden horses and a coachman in
livery on the box. It was a marvelous toy, such as had never been seen
before in Todi. Benedetto's eyes opened wide when Marietta made the
little coach move in front of him. Other children came to look at it — and
a number of grown-ups, too, who could hardly believe their eyes.

Antonio himself went to the bishop, to thank him. The hearty reception he received embarrassed him deeply. Monsignore praised him for his
carpentering, his industry, and his courage in leaving for the great, unknown city of Rome the very night he had heard that his wife was lying
there in the Hospital for the Poor. In doing that, he had allowed himself
to be led by the voice of his love, had conquered his wounded pride,
thinking only of the misery into which his wife had fallen; and he had
been rewarded by recovering his happiness. Antonio nodded — his happiness prevented him from speaking. He was sitting with his son upon his
knee. Imma brought in cake and wine. Who else in the city had ever been
received in that way by the bishop?

Imma went to see them from time to time. She always brought some
trifle for the child, whom she delighted to take upon her knee. She paid

her visits at times when Antonio was at work. She said, "It's striking how like his father he is; I've never seen anything like it" — and it was very clear that she had not Antonio in mind. But she was exasperated beyond measure by the fact that Marietta refused to understand her. Imma deduced from this reserve that Marietta did not trust her, and considered this not only unjust, but also ridiculous, since to Imma the whole situation had been perfectly clear from the moment she set eyes on the child. If she did not speak out openly and nakedly, it was because she had the good taste to let Marietta say the first word. How much longer would she have to wait? Imma hungered for confidences, for whispered conversations; she wanted to hear all, all the details so that she could shake her head afterwards and say to her master: "Ah well, you're lucky old Imma can hold her tongue!" But Marietta would simply not say the first word; and out of revenge Imma talked of nothing but of the father, whom she made into a figure of mystery. Marietta grew irritable and nervous over her talk, and on one occasion, when she dared to conjure up this fascinating, legendary figure in Antonio's presence, Marietta abruptly showed her the door, with the intimation that she did not appear to be quite in her right mind.

Imma's wrinkled old face sank away between her shoulders. In her eyes was a treacherous glitter as she dashed on her old quick legs towards her master. She intended to tell him the truth for once. She refused to live any longer in the midst of such shameless hypocrisy. But she had hardly opened her mouth when she shrank back before his violence. She had never seen him so terrible before. She was possessed with the fear of death, and she fled in tears to her room, where she knew herself to be closer to heaven. It was very clear to Imma that she was the last righteous one in a lost world, in a Sodom and Gomorrah in which people wallowed like swine, even the very ministers of God. Imma was but a lowly daughter of God, and she too had sinned by allowing herself to become involved in a course of events that must raise His wrath. But at least she felt genuine repentance for her error, and therefore she dared to turn to Him and beg that the chief culprits might be mercilessly punished according to their deserts, and that no exception might be made for her master, even though she did care for him more than for herself.

But as she thought it over, she found that, after all, she did not wish to be the one to betray to the All Highest Judge this man, whom she had once taken to her heart as though he were her own son. She would try to influence Him to feelings of forgiveness. But to reach Him with this entreaty, she thought it safer to take a roundabout way: she turned to the

Madonna, and to Anthony, her special saint, who in the desert had been cested by grievous temptations.

An hour later, purified, she descended the stairs, glowing with an almost celestial magnanimity. She was invulnerable to the angry, ill-humored words of her master, who, unlike herself, had not yet reached a better state of feeling.

\nd a week later, she scrambled up Marietta's stairs again, to show that she was not one of those who misconstrue a word spoken in anger. She again took little Benedetto on her knees, and — was it because she had remained away longer than usual? — the tiny tot looked up at her in surprise, saying unmistakably, "Im-ma!"

She pressed him to her heart, almost crushing him as her tears fell. "Imma," he had said to her — and to his father and his mother he had so far said nothing. She had to go home at once and tell the bishop.

Many things were coming right of themselves. The only person still harboring bitterness in her heart was old Lucia, who looked askance at Imma's constant visits, after Antonio, excited and happy, went and told her that Benedetto had uttered his first word.

Of course it was none of her business, and she did not care one way or the other — only the child might really begin to imagine that that ungainly servant of the bishop's, that Imma created by God so small in order to induce her to modesty, was his grandmother!

A

MOTHER'S

ANXIETY

I

WHILE MARIETTA AND HER HUSBAND, IN THE quiet sufficiency of their home, withdrew if possible even more from the society of their fellow men, little Benedetto, to the great satisfaction of Mizio the cat, was beginning to investigate the outer world.

For a year now he had been able to scramble by himself up and down the stairs that led to the courtyard, where the children continued to play (how many were there in the great house?). His father and Andrea were busy carpentering their cupboards and coffins; and Zampieri, the dyer, his chest bare, bent over his tubs stirring his blues and reds. There was Lascari the cobbler too, who talked jestingly to a pair of old leather slippers with turned-up points before he set to work on them. A quarrel broke out between two women, and Benedetto was not the only interested spectator: just at that moment women leaned out of every window to take in the washing that hung across the courtyard. Sometimes a beggar came in, a rag over one eye, and wearing a large hat. He stood in the middle of the courtyard, opened his mouth wide, and proclaimed that he had led an evil life, had been a rogue and a ne'er-do-well, but that an old Franciscan had brought him to repentance, and henceforth he wanted to lead an honorable existence, receiving alms from pious Christians to the greater glory of God. He then spat on the ground, and took off his hat to receive in it the coppers that were thrown to him. He rarely missed one, neither did he count what he had received. He bent his head, and set his hat upon it with the money inside. And if by any chance he did miss a coin, Benedetto and his playmates had to pick it up for him and lay it in the hat, because he had sworn never again to touch money. When he wanted a glass of wine, the innkeeper had to take a copper from the hat.

And every Friday came Paolino, old and weakminded, with his coat turned inside-out, playing on his musical box. He sang of murder and of unhappy love, of war, and of the recent death of the Holy Father in Rome. Benedetto stood by enthralled.

Marietta was always reluctant to see her boy go out of the door; but she could not keep him at home when all the other children were allowed to play in the courtyard. She was happy when she took him with her to market. Then he clung to her skirt, in expectation of the dainties that came his way. He liked also to go with her to the city well. There he could sail the little boat his father had made for him.

When they got back home, however, she had no alternative but to leave him behind her in the courtyard with the other children. She was upset herself at her constant and causeless anxiety over her child. She simply could not work quietly when Benedetto was out of the room. She went to the window on the slightest provocation, and when she saw him below, playing quietly with the other tiny tots, she was set at rest again for a while. And then it began all over again. . . .

But what could happen to him? she asked herself, in order to prove to herself how foolish her anxiety was. Antonio and Andrea were also downstairs in the workshop. Yet anything might happen: Antonio and Andrea were always busy, and in a moment, when they were not looking, Benedetto might run out into the street. Perhaps he had heard the tramp of horses' hoofs outside. And the next thing would be that he would be lying under old Signora Galli's coach. Or he might climb onto some piled-up barrels because he had seen the bigger boys do it; or a half-rotten shutter might collapse on his head. At the very thought, Marietta closed her eyes in anguish. And boys liked to throw stones at one another. . . .

Sometimes she was ashamed when she considered how other women, trusting in the goodness of God, allowed their children to play for hours in the street. She tried to conceal her weak fears from Benedetto; but she betrayed herself in the passionate kisses with which she covered him when he came upstairs for his meals. Did her love weary him, or only leave him indifferent? While she held him close in her arms, his eyes were already on the table, where the food was waiting.

He ate quickly (much too quickly, Marietta thought: that was one of the things that roused her anxiety — in spite of all the good food he ate, he was so thin; whereas as a baby he had been a fat, round little fellow).

Then he turned upon his chair, to get away again. She told him he must remain seated until everybody had finished; he obeyed, and with a strange, unmoved look stared beyond them all, — beyond his mother, too, — until Marietta found she could not eat, and sent him away, after all, although Antonio expressed the opinion that she ought not to give way to him in everything.

An hour later that very afternoon she leaned out of the window, and Benedetto was nowhere to be seen in the courtyard. Her heart stood still.

"Antonio!"

Antonio ran out of his workshop — her voice had told him everything. Anxiously he looked about him.

"He was here only a moment ago."

"Tell Andrea to look in the street."

Andrea dashed out of the workshop; to show his good will he ran as fast as he could. Yes, perhaps he did make himself believe that he was really anxious about the little devil, although he was certain that he must be sitting indoors somewhere, eating somebody's offering of cake.

Marietta hurried down the corridor, leaving her dishes. He was not with Annina. Neither was he with his grandmother, nor with Pinzi the hatmaker. Perhaps he was with Signora Brunetti, the greengrocer's wife on the corner. As a last resort, she peeped into Lascari's and . . . Yes, Manuela had lured him into her back room. There they were sitting opposite each other at the table, a jug of lemonade between them! Marietta, after her first relief, was extremely annoyed at finding her boy in that particular spot and she could not contain her anger. "But you must surely see that I get anxious when I can't see the child anywhere . . . At least let me know when you call him in."

Manuela looked at her in astonishment. "Anxious when you don't see him? The whole city would bring him back to you if he ran away! Well, well, all right. I won't call him in any more. But let him drink his lemonade first — he likes it so much."

Marietta hesitated, ashamed, saddened. She feared to make herself ridiculous in the eyes of her boy. "He can get lemonade at home too," she said awkwardly. Little Benedetto looked up at her from his chair, suddenly pushed his mug on one side, and came and stood by his mother, who, helpless with happy astonishment, laid her hand against his cheek and pressed him to her. Manuela laughed. Then they left together, and went to put Antonio and Andrea at rest.

Next day, Benedetto told Manuela to her face that he did not want to go into her home. Manuela stood with her arms akimbo. "Such a manly little fellow! Knows already what he wants and what he doesn't. Just says to Aunt Manuela, 'I'm not coming to see you any more. You can drink your lemonade alone.' "

Confused, infinitely flattered by her admiration, drunk with triumph, he turned his back on her. A day or two later, however, he succumbed once more to the temptation of the attractions she offered him. She gave him wine to drink, with sugar in it; she sprinkled his hair with perfumed water. She gave these visits an atmosphere that he found irresistible. She said this and that to him, on condition that he did not repeat a word of it to anyone else. That there appeared to be no reason whatsoever for silence did not detract from the mystery at all. She took him on her lap. On the other side of the table sat Mariotti the tailor, declaring that he could no longer bear it, the way she was always kissing Benedetto. Benedetto himself was not very keen about it, either; but she went on, simply to tease Mariotti. Then she said, "Poor Aunt Manuela has no child of her own," and, putting him down, she fled round the table before Mariotti, who tried to catch hold of her. But Benedetto had had enough of this and ran away, out of humor.

In the corridor lurked his grandmother. She seized him and conducted him, a prisoner, into her room. "Oh, so you've come at last to see your granny too," she said reproachfully, hoisting him onto a chair. "Do you know who used to sit on that chair? Your father, when he was no bigger than you. And in that chair, your grandfather used to sit. Would you like a lump of sugar?" She had large, brown lumps of sugar and one of them lasted Benedetto for at least half an hour. It filled his mouth so full that he had difficulty in replying to her questions.

"Is he a good boy? Is he always a good boy? When your father was as small as you are, he never said ugly words. Who were those dirty boys you were playing with? I saw it. Granny sees everything. When your father tells you to do something, do you always do it at once? Whom do you like better, your father or your mother?"

"My mother," Benedetto succeeded in saying after some desperate swallowing, and his grandmother looked at him, jarred; was he perhaps deliberately tormenting her?

The silences into which she fell were even worse than the threats and reproaches. She broke off in the middle of a word, mumbled something, and looked at her grandson distrustfully. Benedetto, unaware of anything odd or remarkable in himself, found himself suddenly pushed towards the door. "Go! Go back and play with those dirty children," she said, and in her voice was deep contempt. The only thing he understood was that, for a few days to come, he could pass her door in safety. Carefree by nature, he might have forgotten altogether that he had a grandmother in the world; but one fine day she came bursting out again, like a spider on an innocent fly, seized him, piloted him inside, and regaled him with a lump of sugar while she administered reproofs in the interests of his proper upbringing, lest his parents alone should prove unequal to the task.

II

Before long Benedetto extended his domain. When no one was watching him he slipped out of the courtyard and went to pay a visit to Nana on the piazza. He had been there several times with his mother, and he remembered the hearty reception he had received — and the profusion of little cakes. Nana jumped when she saw him appear in her kitchen. She had been sitting crying; perhaps she was bathing the bruise on her forehead. At sight of him, however, she brightened up. "Good heavens! Look at the little chap who comes along all by himself to visit Aunt Nana. Does your mother know? Vacca!"

A halting gait was heard in the corridor. Benedetto looked up, smiling faintly — why need she call that ugly, limping creature?

"Oh, so it's you," said the creature. He grinned, and Nana inquired of her little guest, "What would you like? Something to drink?"

"At Manuela's I get wine with sugar," answered Benedetto.

"Wine with sugar? Do you hear that, Vacca?"

He grinned again, stumped out of the kitchen, and returned with a beaker of wine.

"He may have only a little," Nana warned him. "You must be mad, Luigi: a whole pot full! Here you are — with just a little water. Now you have a real glass of wine, like a big man. Did you hear that, Luigi? At Manuela's . . . Yes, with her, he's certainly in good hands!"

Benedetto sat at the table, his little hands clasped round the large mug. Nana and her husband stood opposite him, watching him admiringly. Another woman came in: it was Susanna, Cesare's daughter. On her arm she carried a little girl. Vacca said that she ought to come, too, and watch the small boy drink. But she passed on, turning up her lip contemptuously, — "You two give a child like that wine, do you?" — a reproof not without effect on Nana. She was half annoyed and half ashamed, because Susanna had made her feel guilty towards Marietta. True, wine was not good for a little tot like that; but he had asked for it, and he got it at Manuela's . . .

Benedetto put down the mug again, a little contemptuous of all the grown-ups in the inn. He wiped his mouth, slipped off his chair, and said he wanted to go home again.

"Aunt Nana will take you home," said Nana; but her husband held her back. "He found his way here alone. Let him go. He knows his way well enough."

Benedetto nodded his emphatic assent, which amused Nana. "All right, then . . ." she said, still hesitating, but also rather amazed at the small boy's unmistakable rejection of her offer to accompany him.

She watched him as he left, all by himself, as he had come. She was thoughtful a moment, and then said: "I say — do you remember his mother when she was just as small and . . ."

But Vacca was already limping down the corridor.

Quite by accident, Imma saw the little fellow come out of the side door of the inn. She stood still, amazed, in the middle of the piazza. Then she came pattering towards him. "Is that you? Your mother knows nothing about it, I suppose. And she there" — with a gesture towards the inn — "doesn't even see you home." She seized Benedetto by the hand. He, expecting that Imma would merely do what Nana had neglected, was agreeably surprised to find that he was being led to the episcopal palace instead. He liked going there.

As they went along together, Imma inquired what he had received at Nana's. "Little cakes? You could have had those from me — you needn't have gone to the inn for that," she said, disapprovingly.

Monsignore looked down upon Benedetto, who was himself impressed by the thrilling account Imma gave of his doings. Laying his hands upon the small boy's curly head, the bishop said: "You young gallows-bird! Fancy leaving your mother to her anxiety while you go eating little cakes! Take him home, Imma."

"Why, of course! That's what I intended."

"You intended that? And you bring him here instead."

This perplexed Imma, for she had brought the child to the palace on the bishop's account, and no one else's; and he was pretending not to be glad. If a week passed without Marietta's bringing Benedetto to him, he sat twisting upon his chair with anxiety and longing, so mad was he about the boy. But of course he would not admit that to old Imma. Such were the thanks she received for her many years' faithful service. If only old Imma had her eyes in her pocket, everything would be much easier.

She muttered something scornful under her breath, and dragged the unsuspecting Benedetto away with her. And while her master, really put out and annoyed, was considering upstairs in his room how he could bring Imma to have some motherly feelings for that child, she dived quickly into the provision cupboard and filled the hands of her angel, her treasure, her grandson Benedetto, with good things — to make up for her hardheart-edness of a moment ago, which had been directed only towards that hypocrite upstairs. . . .

Marietta found she had to get used to such escapades: the little devil gave her no choice. Sometimes she kept him at home by way of punish-ment. He did not cry or kick, as other children would have done. He seemed completely reconciled to his lot. Sweetly he played in a corner with Mizio, now grown into a respectable tomcat. Then suddenly he had had enough of that. He wandered about his home silently, something burn-ing in his eyes. He ran after his mother, turning round her in a way that unsettled Marietta herself. The sense of being confined, under which he seemed to suffer terribly, communicated itself to her too. Suddenly she realized that she was treating him unfairly. She hoped that he would say to her pleadingly, "I've been a good boy all the morning, Mother — may I go out now?" In that case she could have held out the prospect of a short hour in the courtyard after dinner; but he asked for nothing. He pre-ferred to wait until she was busy by the kitchen fire and then take free-dom on his own authority — even if it meant further punishment later on. Did it surprise him, perhaps, to find the key in the door when he had seen her take it out of the lock and hide it in her pocket?

Was she afraid that he might try to escape through the window? She herself did not know. In such sudden fear, she opened the door for him once, snapping out at him, half-angry, half-sad: "Go then, go! If you want your mother to have no peace." He had stayed with her. "But I don't want to go," he had said with a strange obstinacy, and had stood there behind her, struggling against tears, a tiny boy needing consolation.

Once he had stayed at home a whole day, as if he had felt she needed that in order to be able to breathe. But next morning he was away, up the street again, and returned home too late for the midday meal without even remembering what he had been doing.

She could no longer be angry with him.

III

The seasons changed. Little happened in Todi. Upon hot summers there followed cooling autumns, with driving clouds in the pure washed heaven. The autumn rains gave new bloom to the surrounding mountains and to the dusty gray stone of the houses. Into the very streets of the city were wafted strong, live odors of ripening fruit and autumn flowers; and from the dark cellars exuded the sour odor that came from the pressing of grapes. In the market, fruit was spread in luxuriant profusion. Behind the cathedral pigs were slaughtered, while lambs bleated and lamented.

The stormy wind and the screeching weathercock already foretold approaching winter.

Grim and unfriendly was the winter in Todi. During the day, it was possible to sit in the sun; but in the late afternoon everyone fled home — where, however, the meager fires were insufficient to combat the chill that rose from the stone floors. Long, long were the nights. Blankets were scarce in Todi, and its inhabitants went to bed in everything they possessed in the way of underclothing. Rising again in the glimmering of dawn, while the night vapors still hung about the streets, they wrapped themselves in woolen shawls; they bound their shoes with warm rags, and drank hot spiced wine. But in spite of all this, there was much sneezing and coughing. And then suddenly the wind turned. An almost forgotten mildness was in the air. *Grazie alla Madonna*, the winter had passed. Spring had come again. It was as though unkind winter had never been. The last solemn reminder of it came with the burial of the old, who were carried through the already soft green fields to the little churchyard behind the convent of Saint Clare.

The seasons changed, bringing with them as steadfast immovable milestones the feasts of the Church. Marietta attended them with her husband and child. Monsignore officiated at them, and then returned again to his great, empty palace where he lived alone except for Imma, a coachman, a stableboy, and a secretary. He received the delegates of the diocese, who honored him with presents and bored him with petty complaints. Ecclesiastics from the city zealously defended each his own church and privileges. He received rich ladies to confession, listened courteously to their sins, granted them absolution. He talked with his barber of the great problems of this city and of mankind in general; graciously accepted the magnificent basket of fruit that Sister Maddalena, now a tall, blooming woman of forty, brought him from the convent of Saint Clare with the abbess's compliments, at a time when Imma had gone to market. . . .

He dictated a few letters to Anselmi. New life had come into the Vatican with the election of the Bolognese Pope. Business was conducted more rapidly, more forcefully. He ate alone, reading a news sheet the while, which was still sent to him by an old patroness in Venice. The soft candlelight shone in his glass of red wine. In the evenings he sometimes played for an hour on the harpsichord . . . Why should he not improvise a little when there was nobody to hear except Imma in her kitchen? He could let his thoughts wander the while. It gave him pleasure, and no connoisseur was present to laugh at him. His harpsichord — that was a genuine need. His collection of incunabula and old breviaries with miniatures — that was something of a pose. Not that he never turned their leaves with proper attention and respect. But his main object had been attained when connoisseurs bent jealously over his folios; and when they said in Rome, "If you want to give Giambattista pleasure, give him an illuminated breviary" . . . And his horses? He had always loved fine horses; but after all, what were fine horses if one was never seen riding in a caroche drawn by them? There was no proper place for driving in Todi, and no one to watch one drive by, either. Besides, the purchase and upkeep of a handsome team of four was an expensive hobby. In the old days, his horses had all been gifts — from the ladies of Venice, of Rome. His ceremonial arrival in Todi had been the last occasion when his horses had done good service. He still had two, less valuable than he used to have — and in order to buy them, he had had to send one of his rarest manuscripts to Rome, to be disposed of without revealing its origin. But when it fell under the eyes of old Vivaldi, he would undoubtedly remember to whom it had once belonged. What did it matter, anyhow!

Here he sat in Todi, growing older, no longer sure himself whether he still wanted to get away . . . This week Marietta had not brought the boy. Oh, he was not the only priest in Italy with such emotional ties. In Rome, in Naples, in Venice . . . *Dio!* Perhaps it was ridiculous; but he could not laugh about it, now that he himself was in the same plight. It seemed too big a thing, too moving. Perhaps in Todi he had come to lose a real sense of values. But perhaps also he had found it: who could say?

"Is that you, Imma?" He was playing, and had not heard her come in. She was carrying a charcoal brazier. "What have you got there? I don't feel cold. Really . . . Is it as cold as that in the corridor? All right, put it down then."

No, he was not cold. The cold was not troubling him: his temples were flushed and warm.

"Imma, if you happen to see Marietta to-morrow in the market, ask her to come and look us up again."

Imma nodded; she was almost sure she would happen to fall in with Marietta in the morning. Quietly, pleased with the slightly more confidential manner of her master that evening, she carried the brazier from the music room to the study, where the bishop sank into his chair behind the writing table, and automatically spread some sheets of paper before him.

IV

Benedetto was six years old. He was still slim. His delicate wrists supported slender hands with wonderfully mobile fingers. His large, delicately chiseled head stood on a slender neck that turned quickly when he was interested in something behind him. He spoke little, and had a detached bearing when among other boys, whom he seemed to look upon with a certain disdain. Although introspective as a rule, he could in emergency make up his mind to a particular course of action in the fraction of a second.

With a troop of little boys, all somewhat older than himself, he roamed about the city from morning till night. They stood and gaped at the coaches that drew up before The Three Popes, and climbed upon one another's backs in order to peep in through the windows and watch the strangers sitting there at table, eating fried eggs. They visited the jail and looked at the vagabonds, caught by the *sbirri*, peering through the grating. They took the prisoners fruit and corncobs, and in exchange demanded to be told stories of their disreputable doings. Chased away from there by the *bargello*, they went to watch Gaetano, of the tollhouse by the city gate, weighing the goods the peasants carried into the city on their carts. They pinched the piglets to make them squeal, and pricked the mules in their haunches until they kicked up their heels and reduced the driver's seat to splinters. There was always something to pilfer at the tollhouse; the peasants had to choose between rushing after their little tormentors (who were too quick for them, in any case) and leaving Gaetano alone with their carts.

In the summer and autumn, the young rascals roamed outside the city, paying visits to the vinegrowers, who preferred seeing them go to seeing them come. They caught trout between the stones of the fast-flowing waters of the Tiber, they bathed, they rode naked on the grazing horses. Peasants who were anxious to teach them a lesson received a hail of well-aimed stones for their pains. In the cooler periods of the year, the troop gathered on the steps of the cathedral. After chasing away the little girls playing hopscotch, the boys played peacefully at dice against the consecrated wall. The sexton was less scandalized by that than by the hopscotch and the skipping of the girls. When he was in a good humor, he even looked on for a moment, with interest, as he passed.

Once one Monday morning Marietta was going to market. She took the market money from the cupboard where it was always kept, and as she went, knotted it in a cloth in order not to lose it. Halfway down the stairs, she discovered that several soldi were missing, and, assuming that she had left them in the cupboard, she returned. But they were not there. Slowly she let her hand sink to her side. She undid the cloth, and counted the money out upon the table once more. She ran her eyes along the floor. Then, for the sake of certainty, she lit a candle and carefully examined the dark landing and the stairs. Nothing. And she had heard nothing fall, either.

She put away the candle, and went out lingeringly, strangely undecided. A moment before, Benedetto had been alone in the room. Suddenly in her rising anxiety she felt helpless — a further cause for anxiety. She would have liked to summon Antonio upstairs so as not to be alone at that moment, but she restrained herself, tried to convince herself that her fears were exaggerated. What child did not take a few soldi occasionally if it was led into temptation? Or did the disappearance of the money affect her so much because he had stolen from his mother? If he must steal, surely it were better that he should steal from her.

That evening, as she put down the market money as usual on the cupboard, she looked almost involuntarily in the direction of her boy, and saw him casually avert his eyes. Now she was sure, and she was cut to the heart.

Next morning, significantly, he remained dawdling at home until his father had gone to his workshop. When she was alone with him she laid her hand under his chin and looked into his eyes. He immediately averted them. But if he knew himself trapped — why had he stayed? Any other child would have tried to get away.

"Did you take money from the cupboard yesterday?"

"Yes."

She was infinitely relieved at his ready confession: he had not lied to her. He did not lie to his mother. She threw her arms about him, and told him how ugly it was to take money, that people went to prison for it. If he wanted to buy sweets, he should ask her for a soldo, and she would give it him. Then he would not have to avert his eyes when she looked at him.

"Now go and play — mother's boy." From that day, she could leave her money everywhere. He never touched it. How could she have made herself so anxious?

And he still did not come and ask her for a soldo to buy sweets. He was too ashamed after what had happened. She decided to give him pocket money — a soldo every Sunday.

She wanted to surprise him: to put a soldo into his pocket so that when in the morning he thrust his hand in he would find it there. He was sleeping peacefully when she took his small breeches from the chair over which he arranged his clothes neatly every evening. As she examined them, she found everything that belonged to a boy's pocket: marbles, rusty nails, string, fishhooks, fruit pips; and underneath everything else she found a little roll of copper soldi bound together to prevent them from jingling. She felt herself grow pale as she let the little roll slip back into his pocket, and with her one soldo returned to the room where Antonio and Andrea were sitting together.

Benedetto did not need her pocket money.

It struck Antonio that she was very quiet and remote that evening. When Andrea had gone, he asked whether anything was wrong; but she would not admit that she was any different from usual: she had decided to say nothing to Antonio. He would not understand. He had always been the pattern of a well-behaved boy. He would never have done anything like that, and would be sad perhaps that Benedetto . . .

Was it Antonio she wanted to spare, or her son?

Next day, she pressed Benedetto to tell her where the money had come from.

"If you've stolen it somewhere, tell me, for God's sake."

"I didn't steal it. It was given to me."

"Given to you?"

He hesitated a moment. "By Aunt Manuela."

Marietta was struck as by lightning at the thought that that slut of a Manuela was giving her boy money. Perhaps also Marietta was none too pleased that he should be receiving from another what he had had to steal at home.

"But didn't I tell you to come and ask for a soldo when you wanted to buy sweets?" she lamented.

"It's not to buy sweets."

"What is it for, then?"

"To play dice."

She stared at him, not understanding at once. It seemed ridiculous. He was still so very small, and the expression sounded so very grown-up. She almost wanted to laugh. But suddenly it came to her mind how in her childhood boys had played at dice on the steps of the cathedral, fighting bitterly for a lost soldo, almost like grown-up men — egged on the while with coarse words by the other boys who stood round.

"Whom do you play dice with?" she asked, in a weary voice filled with revulsion.

"With the boys."

She might have known he would mention no names. She made him promise to give up the ugly pastime. "You surely can do something else?" she said sadly, feeling her powerlessness.

In the days that followed, she felt herself continually driven towards the piazza, and at last she could resist the impulse no longer. She could get no rest until she had seen him playing dice, until she had convinced herself that he had broken his word to her. Yes, there he was, just bending to pick up from the ground a piece of money he had won. She had seen what she had wanted to see.

Why had she extracted a promise from him that he could not keep? If his friends played at dice, he could not very well refuse. Dissatisfied with herself, she returned homewards. That same day, she saw Andrea surreptitiously press a soldo into Benedetto's hand. She was deeply upset, and as soon as she was alone with Andrea she upbraided him. Andrea laughed good-naturedly. "He was cleaned out," he said.

"But I won't have it, Andrea. You work hard for the money you earn. I thought you were saving, so as to have a workshop of your own later on."

"I do save, Donna Marietta. But a soldo — they all have money in their pockets, the imps."

"And do you know what they do with it?"

"Yes, they play for a soldo or something," said Andrea, understanding and conciliatory, so that Marietta had nothing more to say.

So Andrea gave him money, as well as Manuela. And one day she heard old Lucia ask, "Have you already spent that soldo I gave you yesterday?"

And who else did the same? The bishop.

And when he forgot, there was Imma. Marietta heard so from Imma's own mouth when she made a cautious inquiry there. The bishop must have seen the dice-playing from his window. He evidently did not think it so terrible, then.

Nobody, nobody thought it terrible. Boys played at dice for a soldo or two. . . .

Why was it that it awakened in her, in relation to Benedetto, such a wild, boundless anxiety?

V

When spring came round again, Monsignore discussed with Marietta a matter that, in his opinion, was becoming urgent. Something ought gradually to be done about the boy's education. Had she herself considered the matter? Tense with excitement, Marietta nodded slowly. Yes — he himself had spoken to her about it before. It would be a good thing to put an end to this roaming about the streets all day long, and a little learning would not be wasted upon him either. During the last winter he had had to stay in bed for a week, and she had tried her hand with him. He learned his letters rapidly; but the minute he was well again he had slipped from between her fingers. He had given her a strange look, as though he knew that she did not know much more than he.

Marietta heaved a sigh. Everything, everything that Monsignore had taught her with so much devotion, she had forgotten. Life had washed it away. Sometimes she wished she could begin afresh.

Monsignore only smiled, and returned to the subject of the boy. That was what interested him now. "No, he's certainly not stupid, the pickle," he admitted with satisfaction. "I discovered recently that he can count a little too. The street has taught him something, after all." Yes, he had a pair of devilishly sharp eyes in his head, and was never at a loss for an apt reply. Monsignore allowed his thoughts to wander further, wondering whether it might not really be the right thing to send the little devil to Padua or Bologna, where the best education in Italy was to be had — a thing that could hardly be said of the little school kept by Master Sabbatini in Todi. But of course she could not bear to be without the young rogue yet, and in a year or two her husband would probably take him into his workshop.

Marietta looked at him speechless. What did he want? To send Benedetto to Bologna, to Padua? Was he trying to pretend to her that he himself could do without the boy whose hurried, irregular visits were the joy of his life? Did he make such a suggestion only because his pride could ill bear it that Benedetto should learn less than the sons of the well-to-do citizens of Todi? She would not let him go, never, never. She would not surrender her child to his ambition. Cold sweat stood on her forehead.

In an uncertain voice she said, "Yes, Antonio wants to take him into the workshop."

"Good! I thought that would be the case." Monsignore was unexpectedly accommodating. It seemed almost a relief to him to have to give up his idea. "In that case it wouldn't even be good for the boy if he saw too much of the world first. It must be Master Sabbatini after all, then. And I'll get him here for an hour or so from time to time. He might as well learn as much as he has the head for; your husband won't mind, will he, if I just do . . ."

Marietta nodded, hesitating, ashamed, still fearful and suspicious. It all sounded so innocent — Master Sabbatini's little school . . . If only she did not feel so clearly that even this was the first decisive step towards a danger that was perhaps unavoidable. God, what was passing through her mind again? Ought she not to be happy, and to accept Monsignore's offer gratefully? Every other mother would envy her. The whole neighborhood would start scandalmongering again, since envy must find an outlet somewhere. Suddenly a flaming satisfaction flared up in her.

"Oh yes, *Babbo!* . . . Antonio thinks it's all right. If he really likes to learn, nobody wants to keep him back. But we can surely see about that later on, when he is twelve or thirteen. Perhaps then he himself will prefer to go into the workshop. That's a long time ahead . . . I needn't think so far in advance, not so far as that."

She fell silent. A breathtaking, light-extinguishing sadness overcame her. Monsignore, who was observing her carefully, got up from his chair, and strode slowly up and down the room, fighting something within himself.

VI

Antonio listened gravely to his wife. He had learned nothing outside his trade. When he had been little older than Benedetto, he had joined his father in the workshop. He had few ideas, therefore, on the subject of learning. He only realized that he would have occasion to be proud of his son as he had been of his wife when he married her. The one objection he saw to the plan was that people would accuse him of pride, since he, a simple carpenter, allowed his son to go to school. Yes, and that the boy himself might get ideas. But Antonio hastened to add that he had no wish to stand in the way of his child's happiness. Benedetto must put on his best suit, and go with him to thank Monsignore. He too would put on his best things for this visit.

Subsequently, while they were eating, he was thoughtful. It struck Marietta that he had not said a word about the project to Andrea, although Andrea must be thinking it strange that his master and Benedetto were about to go out in their best clothes. What was in Antonio's mind? But she did not inquire into that: she was too tired. If Benedetto's going to school did not suit Antonio, he had only to refuse: she had no will left in the business.

While she waited for their return, Marietta sat with Andrea. She spoke little, and Andrea rarely said more than was absolutely necessary. He was now twenty. Down had grown on his cheeks and his upper lip. He was a man. But his mind was still that of a boy. He was as gentle and bashful as on the first day he had come to the workshop. But he had grown strong and broad on the healthy food with which Marietta served him. Perhaps her own boy would never be so well set up. Andrea's presence had never irked either her or her husband. He had a natural wisdom that expressed itself in his quiet friendliness, in his patience with children and animals. He had a soothing effect upon Marietta when she sat waiting anxiously for her boy. She liked to hear him say, "But what could happen to a boy like that?"

Antonio and her boy remained away longer than she had expected, and at last Marietta broke the silence, and, in sudden expansiveness, told him that Benedetto was to go to Master Sabbatini's school. Perhaps she only wanted to see the impression this would make upon Andrea.

He opened his eyes wide. "Oh, but he'll become quite a scholar then! Much too learned to want to be an ordinary carpenter."

Andrea said this without the remotest evil intent. He had not considered that, in that case, he himself might be able to remain for good in Antonio's workshop. But by his very ingenuousness he brought the truth clearly before Marietta.

And she had said nothing to Andrea of the bishop's ambition — of Padua and Bologna.

Perhaps it was premature to allow such things to go through her mind, but Marietta could not help it. As in a feverish vision, she saw Andrea there upon his chair and Antonio in his. Two men, and she. Around them was the evening, dusk, quiet, as now; and Antonio was speaking of Benedetto, who was far away, beyond reach. . . .

Suddenly she could not bear Andrea's presence any longer. She could not bear it, that he should be sitting there, looking straight in front of him, and slowly coming to the realization that perhaps he would work in the workshop always, if Benedetto really . . .

She told him to go home. The master might be delayed. Andrea, flushing, stood up and departed, a slight guiltiness in his bearing, but with his usual quiet farewell.

VII

Marietta was busy with her needle, making Benedetto clothes in which he could go decently to school, where he would sit among children of a better class. Fortunately she was a clever needlewoman, and she managed with only a little help from Mariotti the tailor.

She knew that her boy liked to look neat: she had noticed it the first time he was allowed to take part in a procession: he had been so clearly anxious to avoid getting spots of candle grease on his suit. (As fate would have it, however, later in the afternoon he had become involved in a fight, and had returned home with a large rent in his trousers.) He followed her activities with interest, and stayed at home sometimes for hours, watching to see what she was making for him. He was burning with desire to be fitted. He wanted to go into the streets at once in his new clothes: he would not fight nor climb over walls.

She would have liked to fall in with his wishes; she found it difficult to refuse him anything. The urgency of his desire infected her; she enjoyed seeing him attired like a little prince. She made him try on the new garments, more often perhaps than was strictly necessary.

"Good. Take it off again now. You may wear it when you go to school."

When he went to school. A happy smile appeared on his face. What did he imagine school would be like? He thought of the going there in his nice suit, and of having his earlier playmates stare after him.

Then suddenly he had had enough of trying on and watching his mother, and he slipped away in his old clothes. In the hot summer months that still separated him from school, he seemed bent upon enjoying to the full the last of his free, untrammeled life. From early morning till late at night he was out in the streets, returning home heated, sometimes pale and with many bruises. Marietta asked him if he intended to use his school clothes in the same way.

She ought to have pretended to be angry with him — but she was always so happy at seeing him safe and sound again.

She wondered whether Antonio would not take it into his head to interfere; she was aware of his growing anger.

Antonio had changed in the last few years, but so gradually that she had not been clearly aware of it. Now, suddenly, she was able to look at him as at a stranger, but a stranger who could exert an influence on her and on her boy. What had caused this change in him? The struggle with his mother had been fought out. His struggle for possession of his wife had also been concluded. Things that at one time had been paramount in his life had sunk out of sight again. When Marietta saw him talking to other men — to Simone, to Cesare — it seemed to her that in growing older he had grown more like them. He had lost his former boyishness. Sometimes when speaking about him to others she alluded to him by his surname.

Had they drifted so far apart? There had been a time, soon after her return, when he had stood very near to her. It came back to her now. But she thought that all recollection of that time had been extinguished in him.

Had some bitterness, some concealed grief been gnawing at him all these years, finally hardening him? It struck her very clearly that he listened to her with less attention when she spoke to him, and that he no longer seemed to wish to be alone with her. When in the evenings Andrea wanted to go, he tried to keep him. Andrea was close to him: they understood one another.

Yes, he loved Andrea as a son. Whereas Benedetto irritated him more from day to day. Sometimes she wished he would speak out. His silent dissatisfaction oppressed and worried her. In a strange way, she felt responsible for Benedetto's pranks, for his very nature — which Antonio could never understand. Rather than that he should turn away from the boy, she would have preferred him to make his authority felt. In the days when he had taken the child upon his knee and told him stories, he had idolized him. Now he no longer insisted even that Benedetto should wish him good night.

She hoped more and more fervently for an outburst that might perhaps draw father and son nearer to one another again.

Meanwhile, other mothers came to her with complaints that Benedetto was fighting with their children, and hurting them. The indignant women would not be pacified when she remarked that boys would be boys. They made spiteful and wounding suggestions as to the unlikelihood of Benedetto's ever coming to any good, until Marietta showed them the door in anger. Benedetto observed all this, saw the tears in Marietta's eyes — and stuck his hands indifferently in his pockets. At mealtimes he was so unmannerly that his father knit his brows over his conduct.

Then, in the gloaming of the summer evenings, he took his revenge for the pain his mother had suffered.

There were a thousand possibilities of tormenting the devoted housewives who had hurt his mother. From the deserted market stalls, he picked up rotten fruit and hurled it at the washing that hung from their windows: fruit stains were difficult to remove. From some dungheap, he picked up a carcass with such a stench that he himself almost fainted as he stood waiting with it after having knocked hard at a door. When the door was opened, he threw the carcass into the face that appeared — and vanished unrecognized under cover of the darkness.

Some of the women, moreover, had a deep, ingrained terror of ghosts and devilish apparitions. White attire and a black mask — and then all that was necessary, on an evening of thunder and lightning, was quickness and a readiness to make a breakneck jump in the dark.

Pale with terror and anger, a woman came and complained. She could not even give a clear account of what had happened to her. She predicted the gallows for Benedetto. She burst into sobs and wanted to lay hands on the sinner, who sat quietly on a chair by the table, completely at peace and unafraid.

Antonio kept the furious woman in check as he asked his son: "Did you do this? The truth, please!"

"If only I could understand what she's talking about," answered Benedetto coolly.

Doubts came into Antonio's mind. He looked from Andrea to Marietta. "But has he been out all the evening?"

"Early this evening I looked in at Manuela's," answered the accused himself.

"Yes — just for a moment," declared Andrea, who seldom interfered in anything that did not concern him.

The woman burst into hysterical laughter at this conspiracy and spat venom until Antonio seized her by the arm and pushed her out of the door.

"May it fall upon your own head!" she yelled through the keyhole, as she departed, filling the whole house with her uproar.

Once she was out of the room, Antonio subjected his son to a severe cross-examination. Marietta glanced with almost a secret anxiety towards her boy, who bent his head to scratch the cat that was purring by the leg of the table.

Benedetto answered with a counterquestion: how could he have done all that was alleged in so short a time?

"I don't ask you how you could have done it. I ask you if you did it."

"Just go and ask Manuela where I was this evening."

Antonio got up from the table. Antonio, usually appalled at the thought of laying bare his family life before others, got up and went to Manuela's to ask her the truth. He simply had to know where he stood with Benedetto.

He found Lascari and his wife playing cards with Falcometti the stonemason and Mariotti the tailor.

Manuela looked up in astonishment. "Antonio! Come in. Here, quick, a chair for Antonio!"

Embarrassed by her gushing reception, he shook his head, and suddenly wondered which was preferable: that his son should be performing the worst sort of mischief all over the city, or that he should produce these surroundings as an alibi.

"I only want to know whether Benedetto has been here this evening," he said curtly.

Manuela nodded, continuing to look at him with curiosity, wondering what was coming next. Mechanically, the others confirmed that Benedetto had been there that evening.

"For about how long?"

"For how long?" repeated Manuela, thoughtfully. "He stood looking on . . . It made me lose a game. I always lose when people look over my shoulder — why do you want to know?"

Antonio would have preferred not to say, but he had no alternative. Manuela's eyes began to gleam with mischievous delight.

"That it should have happened to that Pelliccia, of all people! She's got what she deserves! Who could have played that trick upon her? Not Benedetto — he would have told me. Besides, he only left us a moment ago. Isn't that so, men?"

Antonio looked round the circle dubiously and with ill-concealed aversion. "Very well, then: I'm reassured," he said, trying in vain to feel it. "He can't have been in two places at once."

"Or he would be the Devil himself!" said Manuela, with a laugh.

When Antonio, after expressing his thanks, had gone, the four looked at one another with wide-open eyes.

"*Salute!*" burst out Manuela, raising her glass.

"He didn't do it," said Antonio, coming home, in a decided voice, as if to convince not only his wife but himself. Benedetto only nodded to himself, and lifted Mizio onto his knees.

VIII

Meanwhile, the complaints were piling up. The tormenting spirit who was at work in the city seemed determined to make life bitter for his fellows. Was it possible that Benedetto had all this mischief on his conscience? He never failed to produce an alibi, and to explain plausibly why he had no interest in carrying out such a prank. But in the end, it became clear to Antonio that there was something wrong with these alibis. When one woman came pouring out her grievances for the hundredth time, and then left threatening to report that gallows-bird to the *bargello*, Antonio suddenly became speechless. Pale, he got up from the table and went over to Benedetto who, under lowered eyelids, had seen the approaching danger, and stood up hastily.

"Come here!" ordered Antonio in a voice throbbing with anger, aware that he would not be able to overtake the boy.

Marietta stood between them.

"Do you want to beat him?" she asked. Antonio looked at her in a strangely penetrating way, trying by a glance to make it clear to her that she must give him a free hand in the interests of the upbringing of their child. This, this, was the moment Marietta had been waiting for for months. Often she had hoped that it would come. Yes; and now that it had come, she knew that she could never allow Antonio to take her boy firmly in hand, however much he might deserve it.

"Wait at least until they can prove to you that he really has done it," she said, averting her face from Antonio. She refused to understand his glance. She was hard and pitiless to her husband, who suddenly felt all his anger evaporate and, beaten and humiliated, returned to his chair.

A stillness fell upon the room. Antonio sat by the table, resting his forehead in his hands; for the first time he made Marietta think of his father. Benedetto was waiting, halfway towards the door. The tension had gone out of his bearing. He stood there, casual and unmoved.

"Go to bed, Benedetto," said Marietta in a tired voice. "You should have been asleep long ago — now you see how you plague your father and me."

"I don't plague you; the others do that," he said quickly, and was silent again; and then, after a further hesitation, he went obediently to the back room. Marietta looked after him. What had he said — "I don't plague you; the others do that"?

When she was alone with her husband, she avoided any discussion of what had passed. She merely consoled Antonio with the reminder that the time was rapidly approaching when Benedetto would be going to school. There, he would inevitably grow more sensible.

Antonio nodded absent-mindedly. "Yes, yes, school . . . perhaps . . ."

This boy, to whom once Antonio had thought he owed his reunion with his wife, and whom a priest in Naples had baptized Benedetto, the blessed, was splitting their marriage pitilessly asunder as he grew up between them.

IX

Marietta had little time to think of the increasing estrangement between her and her husband: she was exclusively filled with anxiety over her child.

Her child. After all, he did belong to nobody but her; what did the others know of him? Even Monsignore, who, shaking his head and concealing a smile as if he knew all about it, listened to her recital of the mischievous pranks. Benedetto was reserved by nature. There was something mysterious in his reserve. Only when they were alone together, mother and son, did he talk. Excited, uncontrolled, he let her share his feelings, thoughts — the world of his imagination that was more real to him than reality. He told her of his pranks, and from the ugly things they seemed in the tales brought by her neighbors, they were raised into glorious exploits. Of his fights he told her — always with boys bigger than he. He fought always from the noblest motives — he was no stranger to nobility. He liked to be a hero and to accomplish great deeds. But the streets did not offer him the best opportunities.

From his stories, Marietta discovered that her neighbors lied no less than he, and perhaps on less excusable grounds. It moved her deeply when, as soon as he was alone with her, he abandoned all the lies that, a moment before, had served as proof of his innocence. He did not even think it worth while to excuse them or to brag about them. They came so easily to him. Without its ever having been said between them, he knew that she understood the compelling necessity of his adventures, of his revenges; and his certainty of this eliminated all capacity for judgment in her. She could only listen and, deep in her heart, admire and venerate him. Sometimes he laughed as he told her of some adventure, and at once upon her lips came the reflection of his laughter. What could she do about it?

What could she do about it? This wonderful, trusting intimacy between them far outweighed all his sins. "How does he know?" she asked herself again and again. "How does he know I shall not betray him? That I like to hear him talk of his scandalous exploits? He tells me everything, never hesitates . . ."

Sometimes, also, when she was alone waiting anxiously for Benedetto's return from some exploit that would raise another hornets' nest about his ears, she said to herself: "And what does it matter if he does torment them? What didn't they do to me when I was a child? And how they spurned me and libeled me later without trying to understand!"

Yes, that was the miraculous thing about her boy: that in a higher sense he was her avenger. And the amazing thing, the royal thing, about his revenge was that he himself did not suffer when he made others suffer. That, in spite of herself, seemed to her superb. That, she had never been able to achieve. What a wonderful gift this of his, to have a heart — but that heart exclusively his mother's!

Who could understand what was between them? Nobody. It was the deep hidden secret between her and her boy. That he also was aware of it sometimes made her tremble.

Or was it only anxiety, anxiety, anxiety that made her tremble? Where would his overweening confidence, his uncontrolled imagination lead him one day? Would he not to-day or to-morrow come by some accident as the unavoidable consequence of his daredevil venturesomeness and contempt for danger? Or was fate giving him a free hand in order to strike him down more cruelly later on? Was he playing with life, or was life, invisible behind the wings, playing with him?

THE

LITTLE SCHOOL

OF MASTER SABBATINI

I

THE DAY BEFORE HE WAS TO GO TO SCHOOL MARIetta sent Benedetto alone to call on the bishop. Imma, startled at the small apparition, unfamiliar in his new clothes, felt that for the first time she saw him as he really was.

"Here we come! Here comes the son of a *nobile!*" mocked Imma. But she could not muffle the respect in her voice. She pattered off, and then called from the top of the stairs that he was to come up. She went back to her kitchen: Monsignore wanted to give the young imp a talking to.

She had often wanted to do the same: but when she came face to face with him, she could no longer be angry with him.

In the light from an antique bronze candelabrum, the bishop and Marietta's son talked together. Monsignore sat in his large Florentine armchair, Benedetto on a little stool at the other side of the broad writing table. At first it was the bishop who spoke: of the rumors that were circulating — rumors that appeared to be only too well founded, and that mentioned Benedetto as the leader of a band of ne'er-do-wells who by their misdeeds were making the whole city unsafe. The bishop expressed his disapproval of this hooliganism, and asked Benedetto in a somber tone whether he proposed to continue further along the same path. Perhaps he preferred to bring the contempt of his fellow men upon his head rather than to outgrow his companions of the moment and become a man whose knowledge and counsel would be valued.

The bishop paused and looked at Benedetto expectantly. The boy assumed that it was now his turn to hold the floor. He did not raise his voice. He did not evince pained surprise. He spoke softly, modestly, fluently — yes, especially fluently, for he had infinitely more to say than had the bishop.

First of all he spoke of his good intentions. For the future, he intended to devote his time to study, and to give occasion for the greatest satisfaction both to Monsignore and to his parents. He had already broken with his former companions, after discovering that they were all traitors and liars who, whenever any misdeed came to light, put the blame on him. For the future, he had decided to consort exclusively with boys of a better kind: the kind of boys he would meet at school. Federigo, Judge Rigogli's son, for instance, and Amadore Galli, son of the podesta, to mention only two. As he would probably learn more quickly than they, he would be able to prompt them. Master Sabbatini himself he intended to treat with the strictest obedience and respect, so that perhaps he would one day be set before the whole school as an example.

And then perhaps the stories that circulated about him would come to an end. Always it was he who had done every misdeed, every one. Sometimes a woman came to his father and mother to accuse him of having done this or that, and it turned out that, at the precise time she mentioned, he had been sitting innocently upon a chair somewhere or other; or two people came from opposite ends of the city and alleged that he had been in both places at once. Happily, he knew who had played him that last trick. He would not mention his name; he knew the boy, that was enough, and with him he meant to settle accounts — not, of course, in his new school clothes. Perhaps that maypole of a boy thought he was safe because he happened to be a head taller . . . Benedetto had refused to play dice with him, and was only waiting for the moment when he was asked to take part in the game again. Then he would hurl the whole truth into his face before all the others, and when that sneak grew pale and said "Prove it," then he would turn his back upon him contemptuously, as one turns one's back on what is too nauseating even to give a name to. But he would be careful lest that fellow come up behind to kick him. For such a contingency, Benedetto had a knife in his pocket — they would all know soon enough whether it was possible to kick him from behind with impunity.

The bishop sat on the other side of the table and listened with rising interest. The rogue was holding forth without the least constraint, without hesitating for a word in the expression of his feelings. Under his soft, even tone there lurked unbridled passion, a punctilious sense of honor, and boundless fantasy. His quick mind enabled him to use his histrionic talent astutely, gave him the ability to conceal his calculations behind a mask of austere righteousness. He thought he could take in the virile, graying man before him as, apparently, he had taken in his parents and the whole world — anyone who was prepared to listen to his talk. When he spoke of the boy who was a head taller than he and was a traitor and a cheat, he impersonated him for a moment, his coal black eyes glowing like dark, mysterious jewels in his pale, thin face, with sharply outlined cheekbones: a small, easily provoked beast of prey that would shrink from nothing.

The threat as to the knife ought to have disquieted Monsignore; but did he even hear it? He was staring at the boy, and was not himself aware whither his thoughts were carrying him.

"Faustina!" he thought. "My sister Faustina!" And at the same time his memory conjured up a scene from the past: In the front room of the castle-farmstead sat the newly rich grain merchant Riccoboni, who had taken it into his head to ask for the slender Faustina with the proud, thoughtful eyes as his wife. He thought he was in a position to declare himself her suitor: he had, after all, enough money to buy up a dozen such castle-farmsteads as she inhabited. Besides, by marrying beneath him, her father had forfeited his nobility. And the lady Faustina, then in her twenty-fifth year, had passed the age when a girl of any standing married. Yes, there sat Riccoboni the grain merchant, turning his hat in his hands, and not daring to look up when Faustina was summoned to the room. But the little Giambattista had seen her eyes glow in her sallow, drawn face — the eyes of Benedetto a moment ago when he spoke of his enemy.

And Monsignore was reminded of something else. In that same room, too large to be properly heated in winter, had hung a small painting of his grandfather. He knew that he himself was rudely built, almost a peasant in appearance. But his father had had something noble about his head. Even he, however, represented a falling-off from the painted portrait that had hung over the fireplace in the large front room where they had sat in the evenings away from the servants. Was it possible — was it really possible that the boy in front of him, with his delicately chiseled face, with that noble line of brow above those eyes like black coals — was it possible that Marietta's son conjured up before him the memory of that portrait? He would have liked to summon Imma and ask her: "What does he remind you of? Don't you recall something, when you look at him?" But he remembered in time that she had never seen the portrait in question. Oh God! if only Faustina, now living a lonely old maid somewhere in

Friuli, could see the boy! He would not have needed to say a word to her. But would he ever see her again, the little Faustina, who had never forgiven her father his misalliance? Faustina, who allowed her virgin body to pine away, preferring to guard the ruins of their nobility in uttermost poverty rather than go down safely among the nameless?

These thoughts, and many more, flashed through Monsignore's mind as, half-absently, he watched the well-bred, controlled gestures of the boy. He recalled stories of his grandfather that had been related of an evening in the family circle ten, a hundred times, life offering so little that was fresh: of his grandfather who, in the fleet of the Venetian Republic, had accomplished deeds of such conspicuous valor that he was rewarded by a grateful city with lands in Friuli. To discharge his gambling debts, he had been compelled to sell them all again, even before he had seen them, with the exception of the one strip whereon, long after his death, his grandson Giambattista was to be born.

Benedetto could not know that such distant memories were passing through the bishop's mind as he listened to the recital of the boy's good intentions. When, however, Monsignore continued silent, looking at him in that strange, staring way, Benedetto began to ask himself whether in his zeal he had not perhaps said things better left unsaid. He broke off and looked innocently into the face of the prelate. The smile he received set him at ease again.

He was less pleased, however, when the bishop suddenly returned to something Benedetto had said earlier, something that Benedetto had thought half-forgotten, and asked for his knife.

"The knife, Monsignore?"

Dubiously he plunged his hand into his breeches pocket, and laid it down between them on the table. It was a small knife that could be fastened in such a way that it became a dagger. The bishop looked at it attentively, and then put it away in the drawer of his table.

"You're still a bit small for a toy like that," he said.

Benedetto controlled his disappointment. He raised his eyebrows slightly, and to himself had already vowed that it would profit no one that his knife was now lying in Monsignore's writing-table drawer.

Conversation began to drag. Benedetto had no mind to talk further. He was beginning really to regret the loss of his knife. There came a bored tone into his voice. Perhaps Imma would see that he got it back. He was only waiting for the moment when the bishop would slip some money into his hand, as he did at every visit. This time, he was even particularly well treated: it was anything but Monsignore's intention that the other boys at school should have pocket money and that Benedetto should have none.

Then Imma came upstairs, and presented him with a slate, a sponge box, and a pencil that she had bought with her own money.

II

Some twenty boys attended Master Sabbatini's little school. Instruction was given in a large, bare room, from which everything even remotely ornamental had been eliminated. Behind the master's desk hung an impressive document recording that Master Sabbatini was authorized to teach; and immediately below it, before and after teaching hours, hung the ferule: Master Sabbatini's first solemn act upon entering the classroom was to remove the ferule from its nail and with it enumerate his pupils as they gathered for the opening prayers. A pliable Spanish cane lay ready on the desk, to deal with such offenses as would have been inadequately punished by the ferule: in the course of years it had become worn and black through application to the breeches of many pupils, but it had lost nothing of its resilience.

Master Sabbatini wore a wig that had once been white, and a brown taffeta coat, much worn in the back and at the elbows. His frill and ruffles hung limp and frayed. His stained breeches, once black, showed patches of green and purple when a ray of sun fell on them. Through great holes in his much darned white thread stockings peeped a pair of dingy heels; while his feet were covered in cracked patent shoes adorned with imposing silver buckles. In spite, however, of his sartorial misfortunes, Master Sabbatini made a stately impression. His dignity was second to nobody's. With long measured steps he strode about the room, his hands clasped together behind the shining expanse of his breeches. He had a way of flapping up his flowered satin-lined coattails from time to time that put one in mind of a peacock displaying. He carried the ferule under his arm, and not one of the boys sitting on the long low benches over which his imperious, ever-suspicious eye ranged could foresee the moment when, with a lightning movement, he would seize that weapon and bring it down upon a head whose reactions were wrong or too slow.

Of the two teachers whom the little city had lured within its walls, Master Sabbatini was the greater martinet. His punishments were so severe and pitiless that the upright citizens of Todi infinitely preferred him to his rival, who had been among them much longer, and who now eked out a care-laden existence behind the cathedral teaching the sons of some dozen of the less affluent members of the community.

The very parents who would have summarily dismissed any servant, however old and trusted, for daring to give a well-deserved box on the ear to the growing *signorino* regarded with satisfaction the bruises inflicted by Master Sabbatini's ferule: they were consecrated wounds received in the struggle for knowledge.

In a small adjoining room, one or two older scholars did Latin exercises or sums, while in the main classroom a bevy of new disciples grappled with the difficulties of the A B C. Master Sabbatini called out a letter haphazard, and if he pointed his ferule towards the right they had to continue in the usual order of the alphabet; if towards the left, then the class had to groan the letters backwards: *p, o, n, m, l* . . .

> *A è Adamo — viveva di frutta;*
> *B è il babbuino, colla faccia brutta;*
> *C è il cuor' nostro, che non batte eterno;*
> *D è il Diavol', rè dell'inferno* . . .

resounded monotonously through the hollow emptiness of the room. As the midday hour approached, a drowsiness crept over them against which they struggled in vain. Only Master Sabbatini remained awake, and he never failed to notice that at the line about the baboon some one of his pupils invariably mimicked a baboon's face in order to make his companions laugh. With apparent carelessness, Master Sabbatini approached the little jester — and the ferule accomplished its edifying work. During the prayer that closed the lesson, his watchful eyes roamed about observing whether any one of the boys was collecting his books while he should have been sunk in pious contemplation. At the "Amen" he was standing by the culprit, whose intoning of the consecrated word was cut short by a squeak of pain.

When their teacher considered them to be well grounded in the A B C, both forwards and backwards, they passed on to writing and reading. As a beginning, Master Sabbatini stood before the blackboard and drew on it a gigantic letter. Then he pointed to a pupil, whose duty it was to read the letter aloud. He was given time to think while the master counted three. At "two," Master Sabbatini laid his hand upon the ferule and slowly moved towards his victim, a deceptively encouraging smile upon his mouth.

In front of Benedetto sat Amadore Galli, who could never distinguish between *p* and *q*. For him also *b* and *d* and *m* and *w* treacherously resembled each other. The fact that his father was podesta afforded him no protection against Master Sabbatini's methods. On the contrary, the master felt compelled to show an exemplary severity on account of the important position held by Amadore's father.

Amadore bore all the blows he received patiently, smiling a little inanely.

Benedetto, jumping backwards so as not to be included in the castigation, saw before him only the round, broad back of the heavily built Amadore, and could not understand such slowness. Once he whispered the letter to him; but Amadore distrusted his help. Perhaps, also, he thought his position did not permit him to make use of it. With impressive indifference, he remained silent as Master Sabbatini approached. Benedetto's rejected aid had, however, been observed; and it was on his head that the well-deserved castigation descended. A moment later, Benedetto's pity again got the upper hand — or perhaps it simply was that he could not endure such stupidity. But when Amadore still ignored his help, he decided to leave him to his fate.

Amadore was mocked and teased by all the others, and he bore their treatment with the same good-natured little smile with which he accepted Master Sabbatini's correction. He had more pocket money than the others: his grandmother Signora Galli gave him anything he wanted. Every day he brought sweets to school, though he did not want them himself because he had already eaten too many at home. He wore a signet ring and carried a costly watch. An equally valuable watch he had already staked at dice. Federigo Rigogli won it from him, and flaunted it about until the transaction came to the ears of his father, Judge Rigogli, who, ashamed, had returned it to the podesta. Signor Galli, however, refused to take back the watch, since it had been gambled away; and Federigo announced that he was to receive it once more when he went to the university at Pavia.

Amadore was undoubtedly the stupidest one in the class; but Benedetto had no high opinion of the others, either. Oh, no: he had not been mistaken when he foresaw that he would turn out to be infinitely brighter than they. He told the bishop, who made inquiries. Master Sabbatini, after careful consideration as to whether Federigo Rigogli or Benedetto Buongiorno was his best pupil, decided in the end in Benedetto's favor; and, having become aware of Benedetto's pre-eminence, he placed him on the front bench and made of him a show pupil.

III

Before long, the report of Benedetto's exemplary progress at school spread through the city. His parents' neighbors received it with disdain and unbelief. Other mothers looked on speechless and disapproving when that scapegrace who never left any decent person in peace began to attend school as though he were destined to be a notability of the city. Master Sabbatini's school, too, where only boys from the best families went! The women stood in the street and jeered as the neatly dressed good-for-nothing passed by, and at the well the bishop's strange predilection was discussed and re-discussed.

But in spite of all the gossip and the backbiting, his going to school continued to shed an exasperating glory over his family that almost completely overshadowed another event: the fact that Carlo, Cesare the carrier's boy, had, after a year as a junior in the police, attracted the special attention of the *bargello* and had every prospect of one day becoming captain of the local *sbirri*. They watched the well-set-up, eighteen-year-old Carlo, too, as he left the house in his green uniform. In his eye already lay the austere gravity of a man; and when in the late summer a vine grower was set upon and robbed outside the city, Carlo upon his own authority pursued the villains as far as Perugia, where he seized them and brought them back prisoners to Todi. They were now lying under lock and key, with leisure to repent of their misjudgment as to how far the arm of the law could reach.

Yes, all that was very fine and meritorious, and no one grudged his mother Carlo's success: she was, after all, saddled with thirteen children, and with a husband who carried on with other women. And there was nothing to be said against Carlo himself either. Even as a child, he had been serious by nature, and had not hesitated to call his erring father to account. Besides, it was decidedly restful to be able to rely upon the police. Yes, Camilla certainly deserved some reward from her eldest son — Susanna had provided her with enough grief. But to what was Marietta indebted for *her* good luck?

Perhaps even Annina asked herself that question, good Annina who continued to work as hard as ever in order to keep her head above water. No new little boy had been born to her in the place of Guido. After her third little daughter, it was God's wish that she should have no more children. Perhaps he thought things were difficult enough for her and Simone; and that was true, too. But the void had remained, somewhere in her heart — or was it in the room? She did not know exactly.

Giannino had become barber's boy at the new hairdresser's on the piazza: she had no wish for him to choose his father's poverty-stricken calling. Barber's apprentice — that offered some prospect to a boy who could give satisfaction to people (and Giannino knew how to do that very well). He came into contact with the rich, too. To-day or to-morrow, someone who wished him well might know of some better post for him. But she was wounded that nobody considered these prospects sufficiently important to talk about them as they talked of the school-going of Benedetto.

Perhaps Annina would have accepted with gladness the prospect of

Marietta's only son becoming a learned and influential man if Marietta could have brought herself to express the view that the calling of barber's boy might also lead to fortune, and that Giannino deserved to attend school no less than Benedetto. But that Marietta did not say. She did not even inquire after Giannino, or after the girls; she never talked any more about Guido, although she ought to have known that Annina could talk better about her little lost boy to Marietta than to anyone else. Marietta's thoughts always seemed to be far away. She did not even seem to realize, any longer, how difficult things were sometimes for Annina during the winter months. Annina could scarcely point this out: after all, there had been a time when there was no need of such explanations.

No, the way Marietta behaved nowadays, Annina preferred to leave her alone. She tried to talk about it with Simone, but he was not the man to find the phrase that would set her mind at rest. He said that possibly Benedetto was particularly gifted: he had heard that the boy was the best scholar in the school. Simone was a good man, but he did not know how to stand up for his children. Oh Lord, she could only go trudging on. Life was so hard for some; others had everything thrown into their laps. Falcometti earned more than Simone, although he had no family to keep and could squander all his earnings with that whore Manuela. Was that fair? Oh, Annina did not want to throw doubt on God's righteousness. Those whom He loved He visited with earthly sorrow. . . . And who knows? Perhaps Marietta had her sorrows too, secret worries of which she could not speak.

Perhaps there was no need at all to envy Marietta.

IV

The first word that the children in the class were allowed to scratch upon their slates was "ferule." Sentences were built up round the word: "Our master has a ferule." "Why has our master a ferule?" "The ferule hangs near the blackboard." Later, they themselves were allowed to try and write down sentences relevant to this instructive subject. Benedetto, in an inspired moment, pieced together a few sentences that, though they contained one or two spelling errors, had the merit of rhyming. When Master Sabbatini saw this Ode to the Ferule, he experienced one of the greatest moments of his career as a teacher. He read the poem aloud to the class, which listened with suitable respect. Then he got Gian Porcello, one of the older boys, noted for his good hand, to make a fair copy of it, and it was hung on the bare wall as a worthy pendant to the municipal certificate. A new punishment was instituted: the writing out of this poem ten, fifty, a hundred times. In a short while it came to be heartily hated.

Benedetto had acquired a place of honor inside the classroom; but outside it, his fellow pupils tried to ignore him. Most of the boys had known one another before they met on the school benches. From early childhood, they had visited one another's homes. Not so Benedetto. But it was not only for that that he was kept at arm's length. They were all far too well aware of their superior status not to feel shocked at his having crept into their midst. They might have heard it said at home, too, that Master Sabbatini had taken this pupil only under pressure from Monsignore, and that it was also only for Monsignore's sake that their parents accepted the situation patiently. Some of the boys would readily have forgotten Benedetto's humble origin in daily contact with him, had not others, such as the thin, freckled Federigo Rigogli, made a point of remembering. These, when they stood waiting in front of the school and saw Benedetto approach in his neat clothes, ostentatiously turned the conversation upon coffins.

They made arrangements to see one another at home on their free afternoon, but they forgot Benedetto. He did not let them see that this wounded him. At home, he boasted of his ability to learn better than all of them put together, they were such dunces, and he told how Amadore Galli had again had to write out the verse hanging on the wall, five-and-twenty times — his verse. Sometimes, when Federigo Rigogli answered correctly and without hesitation Master Sabbatini's string of questions, hatred lit up Benedetto's thoughtful eyes as he looked at him.

With his earlier companions, he had had nothing more to do since he started going to school. When he had occasion to speak to them, he did so condescendingly. Was he afraid they might see the humiliation of his new position?

He grew lonely. He went his own way. In the afternoons, he often had a private lesson from the bishop. He was also allowed to practise on the harpsichord when no visitors were expected. This proved an unexpected consolation to Benedetto: to play on that large, fine instrument opened up a new world full of hidden enchantment, and of great significance to him in his loneliness. Monsignore noted his rapid progress with astonishment. And then he was surprised that for weeks on end Benedetto did not look at the harpsichord, and that when he was receiving a lesson in French or some other subject his thoughts were absent, and he was in haste to get away. What was his object?

In the long summer vacation, Benedetto roamed aimlessly through the streets, pursued by a strange restlessness. His home seemed a prison. He entertained a secret contempt for it, since he knew that the boys at school despised him for it. It did not surprise him that they were contemptuous of his father's calling. He himself never gave a glance to the workshop. Yes; but had they also the right to despise his mother? Was there anything to justify Federigo Rigogli in turning up his nose at his mother?

With these and other thoughts he wandered about. Federigo he would see again only when school reassembled — he had gone on a visit to Spoleto with the rest of the judge's family. A dark and stormy mood swept over Benedetto. His comrades of earlier days avoided him instinctively. Only behind his back did they dare to speak ill of him. To think that he imagined he was above them because he went to school! After all, his mother was only a . . .

His ears seemed to be like those of some nocturnal animal: he heard the word whispered by lanky Tito Brogi. Suddenly he sprang upon him sideways, so that they both fell heavily to the ground. He drew out his pocket knife and demanded, "What is she? Say it again, what is she? So . . . Now again. Three times. Four times. Five times . . ." The unfortunate Tito, who was panting in deadly anxiety, was compelled to repeat the low word a dozen times. The boys who stood round stopped laughing. Tito himself afterwards found the word bitter on his tongue. In his dreams he had to go on repeating it because Benedetto was still sitting on him brandishing his knife. . . .

But Benedetto was not satisfied. He still had a gnawing sense of inferiority. Why had he not settled his account with Federigo, too? At the moment there was no opportunity. But what had held him back before?

Meanwhile, friendly and unafraid, the little girls who played on the piazza smiled at the somber, self-absorbed boy. He had always attracted them. They bore it when he teasingly pulled their hair, while they snubbed the other boys in exasperation. The other boys were jealous, and said among themselves that it was only because Benedetto wore fine clothes all the week that the foolish girls ran after him. No: it was not only because of that. They rushed up to Benedetto to tell him indignantly that Gino, Silvio, and Pepino had taken away their skipping rope. The robbers stood on the other side of the piazza, petrified in their laughter. Benedetto looked listlessly towards Gino, who had the stolen rope in his hands. Then he went up to the boys, who stood their ground — all except Gino, who took flight, throwing away the rope with a flourish. Benedetto picked out a little fellow, and made him take it back to the girls. The small boy did it at once, honored by being chosen. When Benedetto resumed his lonely walk, the other boys plucked up the courage to taunt the one who had returned the rope.

"Well, he made you give it back, didn't he?" said the little girls scornfully, as they received their rope.

"Yes, we nearly wetted our breeches for fear," cried the boys. Little Pepino, however, in an exaggeratedly somber tone, only said to the girls, "He might murder somebody sometime."

V

Some of the little girls already had ten-year-old knights at their command, whose appearance brought the flush of love to their cheeks. They teased one another about Benedetto, though he had no special friend among the small girls who competed for his favor.

Margherita, the daughter of Taruffi the wigmaker, had never thought of love until the teasing accusations of her companions that she must be Benedetto's sweetheart so confused her that she herself began to believe they were speaking the truth, and one day she took advantage of an accidental meeting with Benedetto at dusk in the quiet little square behind the cathedral to throw her arms round his neck, much to Benedetto's astonishment. To his surprised questions she answered only with sobs. It was with some difficulty that he freed himself from her desperate embrace, and, under the pretext that they could be seen, got away.

When he had gone a short way, he was in two minds whether to go back to her or not. He had left her in tears. Perhaps she was sitting somewhere crying her heart out. Suddenly he felt again her little soft arms pressed entreatingly about his neck. A strange shiver went through him. He hurried on. He avoided her during the following days, but he could not help noticing how pale and listless she stood among the others. It gave him a soft pang that was new to him: he could make her suffer. He decided largeheartedly to be kind. At an opportune moment, he would whisper to her: "Forgive me, little Margherita; I did not realize how pretty you are — the prettiest of them all." Just as he had gathered up courage to speak such words to her, she proudly turned away her head from him; rebuffed, he shrank back, changing color. For a second he imagined himself in despair, thought he ought to throw himself upon the ground before her, to make himself for her sake the butt of everybody's jeers. But then he found he could continue on his way, relieved by the wonderful discovery that he had ceased to care for her since she was no longer prepared to suffer for him. He also said to himself that he was by no means sure that she was the prettiest of them all. Armellina, daughter of Mattei the baker, was a good deal prettier; and there were others besides.

He was shy with them, terribly shy. Nevertheless, when they all came together and surrounded him, he stood among them with complete super-ficial calm, listening to their complaints detachedly. In his eyes that wan-dered beyond them all lay something far away, indefinable, and it was just that that fascinated the little girls.

VI

Sometimes his boredom drove him to the home of Lascari the cobbler. Manuela, honored by his visit, gave up her place at the card table to him in the middle of the game. She pulled up a chair to sit behind him and watch how he won. Lascari wore a worried look. He knew he had lost his chance for the evening. They played only for soldi; but Lascari's in-come could also be counted only in soldi. He was in the habit of losing the first games every evening, amidst loud self-lamentation. Later, when the others were a little flushed with wine, he won game after game — much, it appeared, to his own astonishment. But his luck seemed to turn as soon as Benedetto took his place at the table.

As a mere tot of five or six years, Benedetto had been struck by Lascari's almost supernatural ability to regulate the luck of the game. In his over-weening confidence, the cobbler was in the habit of announcing how many games he would win in succession, and used to nod towards the little Benedetto as he did so. The precocious youngster had given his undivided attention to discovering how Lascari carried out his prophecy.

It was out of sheer perversity that Benedetto now won soldi from him. Falcometti and Zampieri the dyer, who had taken Mariotti the tailor's place at Manuela's card table, shook their sides with laughter at the cob-bler's sour face. They nudged each other and drank to the health of Lascari their host. Even Manuela seemed unmoved by his ill-luck. And then suddenly Benedetto had had enough of it, threw down his cards, and got up from the table. Manuela escorted him to the door. In a voice that she tried to make casual, but in which there was something humble and submissive, she asked him why he had to go away so suddenly and whether he could not come back.

When she returned to the others, her manner was absentminded. She was out of humor and not prepared to continue the game in Benedetto's stead, although Lascari, desperate and bitter, pressed her to do so. Un-abashed, she explained that she had no further desire, for that evening, to sit at a table with three such people. She yawned and shuddered with sleepiness. She wanted to go upstairs. Falcometti tried to catch her eye; but, suddenly disdainful, she refused to notice him.

"All right. Let's go to bed then," said Zampieri. "The city gun has gone off."

Without a farewell, Manuela left the room, after snatching the bottle from the table and putting it away in the cupboard.

VII

Under the spell of the oppressive, languorous August weather, Antonio and Andrea remained sitting over the midday meal. Benedetto followed their slow conversation until the idea crossed his mind that he would like to go and play on Monsignore's harpsichord. He stood up, and went almost unobserved. Just as he was about to cross the deserted courtyard that was stifling in the sun, he heard himself called by Manuela. Through the cracks of the shutter above Lascari's shop he could just see her. There was something mysteriously intimate in her voice. What did she want with him? He looked about him hesitatingly, still in doubt, sauntered towards the shop, bent his head under the low door. The cobbler was not at his worktable.

"Wait in the back room. I'll be with you in a moment," called Manuela from upstairs.

With feelings of constraint, he entered the darkened room, which was lighted only by the glass in the partition that divided it from the shop. On the table stood a carafe of red wine and two glasses. The stairs creaked. Lightly dressed for the hour of the siesta, Manuela flitted downstairs, throwing a strong, sweet perfume about her. Benedetto thought it all very strange, and, not knowing quite what to make of it, resorted to his usual device when in difficulties: silence, and a barely perceptible smile of disdain.

"Come and sit by me a moment," said Manuela invitingly, with a shrill little laugh. With fussy movements, she pushed forward a chair for him and filled a glass, her tongue clattering meanwhile.

"I thought I'd like you to come here. I said to myself, 'I'll ask him one day without those fellows whom he . . .' Or do you despise me too, perhaps? One never knows with you. Empty your glass, and I'll pour you out another. What I wanted to know was, do you like school? They say that you're so quick. What have you got hidden behind that?" Shy in spite of herself, she stroked his forehead. He did not stir; and, grateful, relieved, she went on: "But why won't they go about with you at that school? Do they think you're not good enough, perhaps? Just laugh at them! You're not one to have many friends. A person like you goes his own way. Lord,

I'm also alone. That's why I understand so well. Later you'll understand me, too. Oh yes, you will, better than the others. They may look down on me if they like. Yes, but as for caring about that . . ."

Manuela emptied her glass at one gulp, sighed, and poured herself out another with a hand that trembled. "*Salute*, little one! I should like you to tell me something. Be silent with the others, and I won't say you're wrong. But me you can trust. Tell me about the little girls — they're already mad about you. I've noticed it, right enough. How many do you kiss in the week? You're not afraid of them, are you? If you were, I should have to laugh. You can really tell me more than you tell the others," she added, poutingly. "How often haven't I helped you, by saying you were sitting here watching us play cards?"

She looked up with renewed hope, but was disappointed. Instead of opening his mouth, he answered her with silence and a glance of cold, proud mockery. Only a red patch on his cheeks betrayed his emotion.

"Why do you look at me like that?" she asked, humiliated. "Am I your dog or a piece of dirt, perhaps?" And, suddenly losing control, she exploded helplessly: "Be careful, little fellow, that you don't land yourself in gaol some time or other for cheating."

He momentarily lost his composure. Then immediately he countered with: "Your own husband cheats."

She could not help laughing. She rocked with inextinguishable mirth till she was hoarse. "Yes, he does. There you're right again, and if he should ever be put under lock and key for it, *I* shan't fetch him out. But you're so young to begin . . . How will it end? Sometimes I almost think you're a man already. I say to Lascari, 'That boy's already more of a man than you will ever be in your whole life.'"

She broke off: Benedetto was no longer sitting opposite her at the table. She stared after him with a pained smile on her painted lips. When she heard him bang the outer door, she hastened upstairs to catch another glimpse of him through the chinks of the shutters; but he had already left the courtyard.

As she felt sure no one had witnessed his flight, she gave herself up like a young girl to her disappointment, and threw herself down on her bed to mope. What in the name of fortune had passed through her mind when she sent Lascari out to deliver his shoes in that hot midday hour, when she got the carafe and glasses from the cupboard, and went upstairs to make herself attractive for that boy? She had wanted to draw him out. She could not bear his disdain. She was curious to know the secret he carried about with him. But had it been merely curiosity that had made her lie in wait for him behind the shutter, her heart beating as though she had been his own age? Was she, she wondered, going quite mad, at her time of life?

Actually, Manuela was not so very old: in the dim light of her bedroom, shot with patches of sun, and helped by a little paint and powder, she might have been no more than thirty. And that was the point. When she looked at herself in the glass, she felt she could turn the heads of other people besides that lump of a Falcometti, who always waited so patiently for her to come back to him. Or that unsavory dyer, Zampieri. And why had Mariotti abandoned her? Mariotti the tailor had manners, he knew how to behave. It was said that even quite important ladies in Todi could refuse him nothing. But she had never taunted him with that; rather, she had been proud of it. Had he perhaps been repelled by the evening card parties? He came only to see her. Only now was she becoming aware of what he really meant to her . . . Everything, she would forgive everything if he would only come back to her.

She was not angry with Benedetto because he had treated her like a dog and run away without a word. When she met him again, she nodded to him in friendly fashion, even though he refused to see her. Was it because of her persevering friendliness that he dropped in one evening after all? Delight caught at her throat. With devilish satisfaction she observed him win game after game — without being able to discover what he was doing.

"I knew that you'd come again," she whispered to him at the door. She could not help teasing him. She wanted to make him feel her power. Her power? The power of the card table, of the whole atmosphere of wine, fun, candles, and jingling coins.

Manuela watched him glide away into the darkness. He was cursing her at that moment for laughing at him. But he would return. She was quite sure of that.

Perhaps Manuela alone realized his terrible loneliness.

VIII

No, there was someone else who knew his loneliness, and she was oppressed by it even more cruelly than he. It was only from a sense of guilt that Marietta kept silent when she saw her boy flee from the house, up the street; and that brought him no relief either. Perhaps she had had a premonition of the loneliness that awaited him when the bishop had thought only of satisfying his ambition. And yet she had not opposed his decision, feeling helpless to prevent what seemed inevitable.

If he had not gone to school, where the boys turned their backs on him, would he have found other companions? Did he belong anywhere in

Todi? Perhaps that was what he was trying to discover, and could not. Could she tell him, perhaps? This, this was her guilt; and, as if he knew it, he avoided her. If only Marietta had had the courage to say to him: "It is my fault. I ought never to have brought you here. I ought never to have followed your father. And if I did that for your sake, I ought to have left him again for your sake, as soon as I was strong enough to make the journey to Venice or wherever some performing company would have provided us with bread. I ought to have been able to face the enmity of the people here and, worse, your father's curses. Even if we had had to endure hunger, we should have breathed free air. You would have been the son of an actress. What are you now? Perhaps, too, I pitied your father. I ought not to have allowed myself that pity: it has been your undoing. I see you suffer — and I could not be more terribly punished. And this is only the beginning . . ."

Even had Marietta been able to say these things to her son, how would it have helped? It was too late — too late. She could only wait, her sense of guilt growing deeper and deeper the while, and rely blindly on the bishop, the strong protector of her child. Perhaps he would once again advise that step which would deprive her of the courage to live.

One afternoon she was driven irresistibly towards the piazza, although she was by no means sure that she could pour out her great trouble to the bishop; but she was detained by Imma in the kitchen — Monsignore had an important visitor. An old friend of his, a cardinal traveling incognito to Rome, had paid a surprise visit. While they waited, Imma took the opportunity to talk about Benedetto and his marvelous musical gifts.

"I sit here in the kitchen and, nowadays, I can't tell who's playing the harpsichord over my head, the bishop or that bad boy. I used to know the difference; but now it's impossible, even if you were to burn me at the stake for it. Lord, Lord! And now they're going to play together. While I peel my onions here in the kitchen they'll be giving me a concert in my old age!"

Imma grew melancholy at the mention of her age. "Do you remember how you used to sing while he played? It seems like yesterday; but it's a good while ago now. It makes me feel how long I've been here. Yes; and what did he say when we left Rome? 'Imma,' said he, 'we shall be there five years — and perhaps, then, a diocese in Friuli. Then you'll see Venice again. Five years here, and then a step higher.' I could read his thoughts as he looked out of his window over the piazza — we know every stone of it now. Perhaps he had ceased to be like that when you knew him, Marietta — he used just to come out with everything that crossed his mind. 'Five years, but no longer, Imma.' And here we're still sitting, after twelve years! The best-laid schemes . . . But he's partly to blame, too. He used to send fat letters to the Pope regularly, and he got quite a number back, too, with the Pope's seal. But these days he does nothing but scribble about ordinary ecclesiastical matters that take Anselmi an hour to write — the sort of letters the Pope gets from all his bishops. You know, Marietta, when a man is stranded far away, and doesn't take care to be talked about in Rome, there are plenty of others actually at the Vatican who get in first when there's a good post going. Besides, he knows that, knows it much better than I do. But for a long time now he hasn't seemed to care.

"He prefers to listen to dissatisfied abbés from the diocese, and to give lessons to that boy of yours. Yes, and if he does sit down at his table to write a letter to Rome, it's to order a fiddle for that young rascal so that they can play together. Ah well, it's all the same to me. I've given up all thought now of brushing a cardinal's red hat. If he doesn't care, why should I? I'm getting older too, Marietta, and we shouldn't make a move for my pleasure. Besides, we manage all right here. We have a woman in every day to help with the work, and Sebastiano helps me too, now that there's less to do in the stables. He's been worrying Monsignore for a livery, and now he's got one, and that's how we came to have a liveried servant to open the door to His Eminence a moment ago. Nobody need know that he also washes up the plates and dishes. Yes, and we ought never to have been without a liveried servant. I've told him often enough, but he'd never hear of it before, even in Rome. 'I don't want hangers-on and thieves in my house,' he used to say."

Imma heaved a sigh. Even though Marietta had always kept her secrets to herself, Imma could not repay her in the same coin. She could not store up things forever in her heart. She had to confess that her master had disappointed her in her great expectations. But Marietta did not even understand — otherwise she would not have looked at her so strangely. She could think only of her boy, and of what would happen to him if Monsignore were called back to Rome. Yes, but what did that matter to Imma, seeing she was not even allowed to know the truth about the boy? It was not altogether Imma's fault if all her thoughts and feelings were concentrated on one human being, her master. Recently, he had been looking as he used to in the old days, full of magnificent pride and an impatient consciousness of triumph. There was one phrase Imma had heard him use that she could never forget. Now, of course, she could laugh about it; but twenty years ago she had not laughed. She had gone hot and cold all over when one day he had said to her, "When I become Pope, Imma . . ."

That was what he had said, and oh God, she had believed in him. She had believed in him, and she wished he had gone on to fulfill his ambition. But what could she do? All she could do was to look on while he received visits from a friend of his youth, who had attended the seminary with him, and who now wore the red robe and was already so bored with it that he chose to travel incognito.

Was Imma crying? Her eyes were gleaming and moist as she got up from her chair to go upstairs to answer her master's summons.

Imma had noticed at once that Marietta was thinking only of her son, and that the mere possibility that the bishop might be called back to the Vatican had made her shiver.

"Oh, he won't go! He won't go! He won't go!" thought Marietta, as she left the palace. He would not abandon her boy to his fate. He set too much store by the boy's proximity, and wanted too much to help him further. He had not lost his ambition, as Imma thought, but had transferred it to Benedetto. There were things too deep, too big for expression. To put them into words would have been to shrink back from the dreadful, sinful sound of them; although the reality of them had grown so familiar that for years they had not crossed Marietta's mind. Never had Benedetto's possible parentage been explicitly referred to between her and the bishop: the truth had risen up between them without a word. She had known it the moment she set eyes on her child — no, earlier. And perhaps he had known it too, the moment he had heard that she was a mother.

And if that were so, would he desire anything in the whole world more than to remain here and be a father to his son?

But, growing weary, she could find no more words to convince herself, and in the emptiness that took the place of her hurrying thoughts a question came into her mind: Had Monsignore perhaps really lost more in Todi than he had gained? And did he himself, perhaps, at moments feel that?

Must she then bear the burden of this heavy guilt also? Was Imma right? Had Todi been the downfall of her master — not the sleepy, dead, little city itself, but the city through her, Marietta?

And why not through the ladies who came to confession? Or through Sister Maddalena, who brought him fruit every week at a time when Imma had gone to market?

Had any of them loved him more purely than she?

In the evening Marietta threw her shawl round her, and summoned the Madonna in the little church of Saint Clare to her aid. Every day she lit a candle on the altar, and she herself did not know whether she still had the strength to believe.

The long summer vacation over, Benedetto sat once more on the school bench. He continued to distinguish himself in class — and to be excluded from his companions' little gatherings. Federigo, evidently, thought he had nothing to fear from Benedetto, for he carelessly turned his back upon him after openly insulting him in the coarsest manner. Now and again Federigo behaved a little less ungenerously towards him; and immediately the foolish and cowardly hope sprang up in Benedetto that Federigo would perhaps accept him, and thus increase his standing with the others.

Master Sabbatini was drawing the outline of Italy on the blackboard. He marked points to indicate where Rome and Perugia, Siena and Florence, lay; and with thin, meandering lines he conjured up the Tiber, the Po, and the Arno. The Tiber flowed past Todi and past Rome. The Apennines were a chain of mountains stretching from north to south through the whole of Italy; and around the country was the sea everywhere, except where high mountains lay, behind which lived foreigners who came to Italy to see the Pope and all the other things to be found only in that land.

Benedetto looked at the lines on the blackboard attentively. When Master Sabbatini spoke of cities, seas, and lakes, he saw everything before him as though he had already been there himself. In Venice the houses rose sheer from the water. As one went walking here, so one went in gondolas there. And near to Naples was a mountain that sometimes suddenly broke out into flames that came flowing down the mountainside. Fleeing men and animals, houses crashing down, downpour of ashes, dark night . . . Only the red glow of the approaching fire . . . The churches full of praying people, who thought the Day of Judgment had come . . . His mother had been in Naples, and had heard these tales from people who had gone through it all. And he had been born in Naples, so he could talk about it, too. Master Sabbatini looked up, surprised at all he knew. All the boys turned round in astonishment. He flushed with pride. And then suddenly Federigo Rigogli began to grin. Benedetto, about to tell of a fight between golden-winged angels and green devils in the glare of the erupting volcano, went very pale as he glanced towards the scoffer. Immediately the other boys laughed too. Master Sabbatini tapped for order, and spoke of the important fisheries in Naples, explaining that Neapolitan stockfish was eaten all over Italy, although much of it came also from Genoa . . .

Silently Benedetto looked straight in front of him. Instead of the fight between angels and devils in the crater of Vesuvius, he was seeing another fight. He had got Federigo by the throat and was pressing him down and squeezing, squeezing until everything went red before his eyes.

Yes. . . . But when school was over, he let Federigo go home untouched.

After talking for weeks and months about Italy's cities, mountains, and rivers, Master Sabbatini investigated to find out how much of all this information they had retained. He asked Federigo Rigogli what came to his mind when the Tiber was mentioned. Federigo replied that the Tiber flowed past Todi and Rome, and at Spezia entered the sea, as was the way with rivers. Master Sabbatini asked Benedetto whether by any chance he had ever heard of Vesuvius, and, amid the sniggers of the class, Benedetto replied quietly that Vesuvius was a fire-spitting mountain near Naples. Master Sabbatini inquired of Amadore Galli what was found in the Carrara Mountains. Instead of replying Carrara marble, Amadore astonished the class by the ridiculous reply, "Stockfish." Although strictly speaking that was perhaps not entirely untrue, there was general laughter, and even Master Sabbatini opened his eyes wide in amusement, as he descended slowly from his desk.

Benedetto had seen Amadore chastised a hundred times, and, like the rest of the class, had grown used to the sight. Nor did he feel much pity for the fat, good-natured son of the mayor who had nothing particularly likable about him. It was therefore nothing but curiosity that made Benedetto look round. Then suddenly, behind Amadore, he saw Federigo Rigogli's hypocritical face — and immediately he knew what had happened: Amadore had allowed himself to be prompted by Federigo, after sullenly and proudly refusing a similar service from Benedetto, and Federigo had betrayed him.

At that moment, Master Sabbatini was moving slowly past Benedetto, the ferule still innocently under his arm. Suddenly Benedetto had no desire to see a castigation; he himself did not know what swift revulsion came over him as his eyes fell upon the ferule so close to him. It was just like any other piece of smooth wood; and look, it could be pulled away from under Master Sabbatini's arm without the smallest difficulty.

A breathless cry swept through the class, and simultaneously Benedetto himself felt it was utterly impossible that he should really have the ferule in his hand. As he stood up, his eyes reflected the same amazement that was in Master Sabbatini's.

Nobody could understand what had happened. It seemed as simple as it was unbelievable. Then suddenly the veins stood out on Master Sabbatini's temples. His eyes rolled forwards, filled with a strange glitter.

He clenched his yellow jaw convulsively. He was about to speak — his lips muttered something incomprehensible. Did he want Benedetto to hand the ferule back to him, or could that be done only after some involved formal ritual? Benedetto solved all the difficulties unexpectedly — did he think that would settle the matter? — by airily, abruptly, throwing the piece of wood over his shoulder.

"Pick it up!" muttered Master Sabbatini hoarsely: he had decided what must be done. Crawling upon his knees, the boy must bring it back to him, receive a hundred strokes with it, and leave the school for good.

Obediently Benedetto left his bench. Only then did a strange elation come over him. Conscious of the heroism of his action, which had appeared so small a thing to begin with and had been quite unpremeditated, but which must now be filling the class with boundless admiration, a little roguish smile of triumph played about his mouth.

With his eyes he searched the ground until he discovered the ferule: it happened to have landed just at Federigo's feet. He was about to bend to pick it up. Helpfully, Federigo pushed it a little towards him with the point of his shoe. And then Benedetto did something that had not crossed his mind a second before: in a sudden blind fury he threw himself upon the judge's son, and together they collapsed over the bench.

He felt a greedy joy as his hands convulsively closed upon something, the satisfaction of a hunger that had long been gnawing at him. There was light. All around him was light, and shimmering colors. Voices bawled, hollow-sounding, in the room. . . . Hands tore at his clothes, but could get no hold on him. . . . All he saw was a face in front of him transfixed in deadly terror. A hated mouth uttered disconnected sounds. Two accursed eyes were turned towards the window. They were pulling at his legs too. Somebody was hammering at his head. As he half looked up, he noticed that it was Amadore Galli. Behind him, full of tragic discomposure at what was happening in his class and under his eyes, loomed the disarmed Master Sabbatini; but it was really the look in Amadore's eyes that suddenly softened Benedetto, and made him think "It has been enough." His hands loosened, he shook off a boy who was clinging to his neck like a burr, and then got up — erect, supremely relieved, as if some burden that had long oppressed him had fallen away. He did not prevent Federigo, who had now begun to retch, from getting up. He glanced at his clothes, and then smiled ingenuously again, because he had expected to find them torn to shreds.

Federigo sat down again upon his bench, flopping backwards like a sack of sand. His eyes rolled weakly, his lips muttered a request for water. Amadore dashed away to fetch some, and, happening to see the ferule as it lay, picked it up and handed it to Master Sabbatini who, still dumb-founded, took it from him — realizing as he did so, however, that this was a false move on his part.

Meanwhile Benedetto recognized that there was nothing more for him to do there. He left the school, chose without hesitation the direction of the piazza, and made straight for the palace of the bishop.

X

As Monsignore was engaged (old Signora Galli's caroche was standing waiting outside), Benedetto had to console himself at first with Imma's company. She nearly fainted when she saw his clothes. But he had no wish to tell her anything: he did not think old Imma good enough to take into his confidence. He behaved as though he were in his own kitchen instead of in hers. Grandly, he inquired whether old Signora Galli was in the habit of making prolonged calls. He strode up and down, as the bishop had done in his younger days; the world seemed too small for his tempes-tuous need of space. Then suddenly he forced himself to be still, flung himself upon a chair, and began strumming an unnerving tattoo upon the table, declaring meekly that he would wait.

He did not deserve it, but Imma decided nevertheless to go upstairs and inquire whether anything was wanted, and at the same time drop a word about Benedetto's sensational visit. She was angry with Benedetto, but also, and principally, she was seriously worried — and very curious, too, to know what his business was with the bishop.

A moment later, she told Benedetto that he could go upstairs. Up he jumped and shot past her . . . He was already upstairs knocking at the door. It was as if for him the stairs did not exist: whereas for old Imma the house was becoming more and more like a mountain the scaling of which grew increasingly difficult.

Upstairs Benedetto found not only the bishop and old Signora Galli, but also Maestro Angelini the music master, who still lived in the podesta's palace and was in the habit of accompanying the old lady on her daily drives. In the half-light of the caroche, beside the powdered, painted, tall-wigged Signora Galli, still impressive though a human ruin, bobbed up and down the sharp, delicate profile of spindle-shanked, discreet Maestro Angelini, who was always dressed with elegant simplicity.

For these expeditions, Signora Galli had to be carried downstairs by two strong menservants, chair and all. She had recently resumed them, after the burial of her husband — at which she had insisted upon being present in order to hear the funeral orations. The fact that she had been allowed to outlive her much younger spouse had endowed her with new courage and life.

Now she was sitting half-buried in the cushions on the bishop's divan. In the sunlight that came through the shutters she glittered with jewels. Her bodice was pressed high, as if she still expected people to compliment her upon her bosom, and she had impregnated the whole room with a suffocating, oversweet perfume. She turned her head towards Benedetto, observing him carefully through her lorgnette, which magnified her eyes into cow's eyes, infinitely sad and expressionless in their loose red rims.

Expressionless in another way, Maestro Angelini sat on a chair, his long legs crossed, and paid little attention to the new arrival. Perhaps his thoughts were elsewhere: for instance, at the court of the French king, Louis XV, where he had once wished to try his luck before finding it in the Galli palace.

The bishop, in his large chair behind the writing table, noted with inward delight how satisfactorily Benedetto acquitted himself in the intricate ceremonies of introduction and greeting; he then inquired what had brought him to the palace, and how his clothes had got into such a state. After a moment of slight hesitation, Benedetto said that he expected to be expelled from school for seizing the ferule from under the master's arm in order to save Amadore Galli. Turning to old Signora Galli, he explained how the master was always specially set against Amadore, and asked him questions that nobody in the world could answer — simply to have an excuse for plying him with the ferule. Benedetto was convinced that Amadore was such a bad scholar only because the master spent his time hammering with the ferule upon his head. Besides, that was the opinion of all the boys. Yes. But they preferred to say nothing about it, because they themselves were too afraid of the ferule — especially that sneak of a Federigo Rigogli, who was always playing into the master's hands. When the master asked how much two soldi plus three soldi made, Amadore would reply five crab apples, because that was what Federigo had prompted him to say. To-day Benedetto had been seized with pity for poor Amadore, and when the master came striding up with the ferule he had taken it away from him and flung it across the class, and as he realized that he would have to leave the school in any case after that, he had thought he might as well settle accounts with Federigo at the same time . . .

Signora Galli watched him with uncommon interest as he rattled off his story nimbly, dramatically, with many a circumstantial detail. From time to time she also gave her attention to the bishop. At last Benedetto had finished. He fell silent and his eyes, which had roamed absentmindedly over Signora Galli's bejeweled figure all the time he was speaking, came to rest upon a magnificent solitaire that glowed on her right hand, radiating all the colors of the rainbow.

With a suddenness that made him start, the owner of the ring broke the silence with: "No, it's not because of the blows — he has it from his father . . . couldn't learn either. It isn't serious. Later on . . . Podesta all the same." She spoke in a hoarse voice. Her every sentence ended in an incomprehensible murmur. She tried to repeat the last word, but gave up the attempt halfway, and her mouth remained hanging half-open.

The bishop hastened to reassure her as to Amadore's prospects of assuming the mayoralty of Todi later on.

Then she asked, "Why doesn't he — ever come and play with Amadore? It's the first time — I've seen him. It is really the first time — that I've . . ." She tried to go on, turning towards Monsignore a look at once obtuse and shrewd. He smiled at her ingratiatingly, and asked her if he might count upon her support should Benedetto's expulsion from school be insisted upon: it would be a sin to deprive the boy of the opportunity of learning more. He was not as foolish as he looked. It was purely for his own pleasure that the bishop had interested himself in his education and had given him the opportunity of practising upon the harpsichord.

"Perhaps the Signora would like to hear you play something," he said, and while she nodded mechanically, Benedetto slipped away and sat down behind the instrument in the adjoining room. His movements had been too quick for Signora Galli, who was still looking for him with her lorgnette. In the end she directed her gaze hopefully towards the door, through which he must have disappeared, and waited as though music were something perceptible to the eyes, which she would see coming round the corner in a moment.

Benedetto opened with a rapid dance movement that Monsignore had just taught him. He followed that with a more serious piece. Then he paused, his hands still resting on the keys, expecting Monsignore to call out to him to go on playing. Nothing happened, however. He got up from the instrument. As he returned to the room where the others were, he noticed tall, gaunt Maestro Angelini rise from his chair and then sit down again, wearing a look of embarrassment at having got up without cause. The bishop said nothing, in the expectation that his guests were about to express their satisfaction.

With a trembling, groping hand, old Signora Galli put down the cup of chocolate she had been sipping on the little table that Imma had pushed up beside her, and with a sigh she said: "I've promised — Amadore a pony — if only he will learn to play . . . No brains required for that, I said to him."

The bishop began to tell them how he had written to a friend in Rome for a violin for Benedetto, and how he thought this friend would probably be able to get him a good instrument — when suddenly, breaking all the rules of politeness, Maestro Angelini interrupted him. "Send him along to me sometime, when he has his violin," he said.

Recovering immediately from his surprise, Monsignore hastened to express his sincere delight at Maestro Angelini's offer, and went on to confess that it was not without an ulterior motive that he had got the boy to play before this select audience.

It was a white lie. The bishop had almost forgotten how this same Maestro Angelini had once dumbfounded him by his wonderful playing of the lute that was carried solemnly before him by a servant of the house of Galli. He had, like everybody else in Todi, grown accustomed to considering Maestro Angelini as nothing but the ridiculous appendage of a ridiculous old woman. Only now did he remember that he had before him a gifted artist who had failed through weakness of character but who contained within himself treasures that might enrich a world, and that for Benedetto it would be an immeasurable privilege to have access to this secret treasure-chamber.

"Thank Signor Angelini for his offer, Benedetto — you'll soon learn its value," he said excitedly, trying by the warm regard in his voice to make up for his long lack of appreciation. Maestro Angelini was alive to this sudden change of front, which, however, he waved aside casually and with some bitterness.

"Let us go," muttered the moody and petulant Signora Galli in the awkward silence that had arisen between the two men. Maestro Angelini stood up, went into the corridor, and clapped his hands; whereupon two lackeys came upstairs, and without further ado, picked up the old woman. She sighed and moaned and mumbled angry complaints, and from that moment had no attention for anything except herself, so that there was little formality about her farewells. With bowed head, Maestro Angelini followed her. On the landing he directed the descent, asking Imma why she had chosen just that moment to mount the stairs.

Benedetto hastened to the window to watch Signora Galli hoisted into her caroche. It was a difficult business, and Maestro Angelini, watching it, inquired why a sedan chair had not been brought, and why the horses had not been put back into the stable, seeing that the Signora's daily drive was over. The lackeys protested, fierce and quarrelsome. How were they to know that the Signora wanted to go straight home? Their faces full of anger, they interrupted their pushing and hoisting to turn to Maestro Angelini, so that Signora Galli, still floating between heaven and earth, snapped out to the music master to stop interfering.

In silence Maestro Angelini swallowed the reprimand administered in the presence of the lackeys. The children playing on the piazza had come running up to see the free performance. They had enjoyed it often enough before, but it never failed to be exciting; because after all it might happen that Signora Galli, halfway through the caroche door, would be able to go neither forward nor backward, or, being pushed too heartily, would fly out again through the other door. The children were sufficiently impressed by the wealth and power of the Gallis to feel no amusement; it was a lively interest and a genuine suspense that made them watch. On the other hand, they considered that curious, spare man whom they had dubbed Signor Morto-vivo ("Mr. Dead-alive") highly ridiculous. As he crossed the piazza on foot behind the vehicle, in which Signora Galli had at last been safely installed, the children caught one another's eyes, and a suppressed giggle went up among them.

Then one of the lackeys reappeared at Monsignore's. He was the bearer of an invitation for Benedetto from old Signora Galli: would he come and play with Amadore on Sunday afternoon?

When the lackey had gone, Monsignore laid his heavy hands upon Benedetto's shoulders, and said, unable to suppress the great joy in his voice, "And through Signora Galli's house, the way lies open to all the other houses. Go to your mother. Let her see your torn clothes, and tell her that I'm expecting her — No, wait a bit. We are alone now. Tell me exactly what happened to Master Sabbatini's ferule. The pretty trimmings you added for Signora Galli you can leave out this time."

A wonderful intimacy irradiated from Monsignore that afternoon. When, in the course of his story, Benedetto glanced at the attentively listening bishop, he looked into the eyes of an older friend who still remembered his own mischievous pranks. It was an older friend, too, who said to him later: "The way lies open for you now in Todi. But you are the sort of little fellow who may lightheartedly destroy what has been slowly built up. Do you understand yourself? Perhaps I shall take you severely in hand again, and put you right when I see that you're going astray — my boy."

"My boy," Monsignore had said. The undertone of tenderness that lay in the words reverberated strangely in Benedetto's ears, and made him immediately look down.

The bishop spoke to him of his own youth, how he had come from the land and had been brought up like a peasant, and for that reason had first been mocked at in the seminary; but how, later on, he had left them all behind . . . Now no longer, perhaps; because he cared less than formerly.

As he hastened home, Benedetto cast a side glance at the *palazzo* where he was to be a guest on Sunday. At home he overwhelmed his mother with the great news, betraying as he did so all the things that had made him suffer in secret. Marietta forgot to admonish him for his torn clothes — he gave her no time, in any case. He made it appear that, for the sake of his future, it had been necessary for him to plunge into that ruinous fight. As a reward, he had already been invited by the Gallis, and was to receive music lessons from the celebrated Maestro Angelini; and she must get ready to go to Monsignore's at once.

Marietta nodded, and dressed hurriedly. She was filled with joy, and at the same time with an undefined concern.

Surprised at Marietta's unexpected departure, Antonio went upstairs half an hour later. When he saw Benedetto there in his ruined clothes, resting his head upon his hands at the table, and heard from his mouth the proud declaration that he had been forced to give Federigo Rigogli a thrashing in class, the simple coffinmaker was silent. He wanted to be severe, to remind his son of his lack of respect for those above him in station, to warn him of the consequences of his act. But it would have been like water on a duck's back! At this moment Antonio felt that, more strongly than ever. It would be hopeless to attempt to bend this child to his will, to attempt to direct him. He would go his own way, and he would not let his father prescribe one to him. Now that Marietta was not there, Antonio felt even more powerless towards the boy. He said nothing, and returned downstairs. He talked to Andrea about it afterwards. Andrea was a good boy. For a long time now, it would have been impossible for Antonio to picture himself planing and hammering with anybody except Andrea.

XI

Thanks to the bishop and to old Signora Galli, Benedetto remained at school. Monsignore had spoken personally to the indignant judge and to the deeply affronted Master Sabbatini.

After what had happened, Master Sabbatini seemed no longer able to wield the ferule with the same case as of old. Sometimes the whole class expected a blow to fall — and then the master passed on.

He was also careful not to go too close to Benedetto.

No, Master Sabbatini was no longer what he had been; and the reason could only be the desecration of his ferule. Since it had been ignominiously trampled upon by a troop of fighting boys, it was no longer infallible, inescapable.

Master Sabbatini was no longer Master Sabbatini, just as Samson was no longer Samson after his hair had been shorn. It was whispered in the city that some of the well to do were proposing to send their sons to the other master behind the cathedral.

Master Sabbatini had foreseen that, and bore adversity as one might expect a fallen sovereign to do. When he observed that Benedetto was trying to make good for his unfortunate offense by doing even better than before, he discovered that he had forgiven the boy, did not even bear him ill will in his heart. Master Sabbatini had become gentler under the shattering blow that had made him dependent upon the mercy and clemency of the well-to-do citizens of Todi.

Amadore Galli, commissioned to do so by his parents, personally invited Benedetto to his home . . . Federigo happened to be standing by; overhearing the invitation, he made a face, as if he felt a pain shoot through him again. Barberini the barber-surgeon had adorned his cheek with a large plaster, and his right eye was still swollen. He was not a pretty sight.

At home, Marietta was busy mending Benedetto's torn clothes. She had also bought material for a new suit in which he could go visiting. Monsignore had given her the money for it.

NIGHT

SCENE

I

BENEDETTO WAS RAPIDLY APPROACHING FOURTEEN.
He wore satin coats and ruffles of Venetian lace and silver buckles
on his shoes, just like the sons of the well to do. True, he had
not, like Amadore Galli, his own servant, but he wore an enameled gold
watch that in costliness was hardly surpassed by Amadore's. It had been
a surprise present from Monsignore on his last birthday; and Babetta, a
little niece of the Gallis who had come from Siena to stay with them
that summer, had given him a miniature Madonna to hang on his watch
chain. His mother had given him a Saint Francis, and these two trinkets
tinkled gently against one another as he walked.

The little girls who used to play in the street had become young ladies,
with a proper pride in themselves. They gave him hasty, veiled glances
from under their lashes, and blushed when he acknowledged them with
a bow. He took little notice of them; perhaps his head was full of the rich
girls he met in the house of the Gallis.

He always walked rapidly, as though Todi were a great city with long
distances to cover.

He slipped in and out of his parents' home with slightly bent head,
to avoid seeing anyone. At home he was silent. He ate rapidly, with the
manners of the well to do — manners which, in that house, only Marietta
knew. Over his end of the table was spread a napkin, and by his place
stood a finger bowl such as he saw on the table at the Gallis'. In provid-
ing this, Marietta had defied Antonio's disapproval. During meals, Antonio now spoke only to Andrea. He took no notice of his son, who,
after all, seemed indifferent to him and to the workshop and received
from the bishop more pocket money in one week than a respectable man
could earn by hard work.

Without quite realizing it themselves, the other inhabitants of the great house had grown to look upon Benedetto as an aristocrat who had somehow strayed among them. Very slowly the voice of disapproval was dying down. They no longer harbored the delusion that Cesare was his father — more probably it was someone in Rome or Naples. Naturally it could not be Antonio, though old Lucia now tried to make everybody believe that it was. Oh, that Lucia! In the street sometimes she seized her grandson, as he passed her dressed like a prince. He freed himself from the grasp of her old hand, and left her standing, the mockery of passers-by, so that she called after him with curses and tears in her voice.

Andrea, on whose knee the little Benedetto had once ridden, who had protected him against the anger of his father and the fury of the neighbors — Andrea addressed him as "Signorino." This had drawn an unpleasant laugh from Antonio, who was rarely sharp or harsh. With eyebrows raised sarcastically, he asked Andrea to whom he was speaking.

Benedetto had no desire to be spoken to with deference at home. He was pleased if they left him alone, since they could not understand that he happened to be different. To humiliate his father, he sometimes joined in his conversation with Andrea. He filled in the gaps in Antonio's knowledge, and put him out of countenance by all the information he could produce casually on any subject that happened to be mentioned. Antonio's disapproval gave way to a feeling of shame. A sense of guilt awakened in Antonio, for not having seen the inner brilliance of his son through the exterior of his dandified clothes — his son who, in well-chosen words, was developing a train of acute thought. He regretted that he had restricted himself to conversing with Andrea. . . . Yes, that was easy for him, since Andrea always agreed with him. Depressed, he tried to get nearer to his son, and so fell into the trap that had been laid for him. Benedetto met the tentative gropings of his father's affection with cold indifference.

Marietta saw all this. It hurt her, and gave her satisfaction at the same time. Why had Antonio misjudged the boy?

From the bishop she heard of Benedetto's astonishingly rapid progress on the violin, but she herself had never heard him play. He would not bring his violin to the house. He played, however, in the podesta's *palazzo* before old Signora Galli, of whom she still thought with aversion, remembering the days when she had carried home her fine linen from the convent. He also played before the bishop; must she go to the bishop's, then, to hear him? He did not wish the people in the house where he lived to hear him play. He did not wish his father and Andrea to listen. But perhaps they would all be suddenly conquered by it. Perhaps they would forgive him on the spot for his better clothes and his school-going.

Perhaps they would fold him to their hearts again, instead of surrounding him with their terrible enmity.

Or was Benedetto wiser in this respect than his mother? Had he a juster perception: that people were not capable of understanding, that people did not wish to understand, because they were afraid to admit their own pettiness?

His whole outward appearance should have been enough to convince people of his superiority. She herself could not forbear to watch him continually, in secret. He was irresistible with his smile, with his proud silences; irresistible in his ruthless passion and the foolhardy savagery that brought a glow into his eyes. And the people who railed at his fine clothes: did they not see how well he wore them? Let other boys in that house put on the same clothes, and then try to move in them.

Sometimes he looked at her while she was entirely absorbed in him. She knew herself to be betrayed at once. Her innermost feelings were laid bare before him as she colored under his glance, defenseless as a young girl. He was puzzled by her behavior. His eyes registered astonishment. Then he smiled, a quick, imperceptible smile. . . . He had better go out again: she was almost afraid of being left alone with him. He must not know how confused he had made her. Go now — go now, my dangerous boy.

And he did go — after drawing her to him with uncontrolled tenderness.

"*Addio,* you'll see me again soon," he said, leaving the house a conqueror.

II

A somewhat musty smell permeated the vast *palazzo* of the Gallis. A smell of Gobelin tapestry, silk wall hangings, damask-covered furniture and worm-eaten oak. Into at least half a dozen rooms in the large building no one ever went. In the others, the inhabitants moved about more or less independently of each other. There was old Signora Galli, who lived for herself; the podesta, who always pretended to have so much to do; his pretty, drooping young wife; the very retiring Maestro Angelini; Amadore, always receiving visits from his young friends who haunted the house and the courtyard; and lastly, the lackeys and the maidservants.

Benedetto was the only one of the boys frequenting the house who had any contact with its inhabitants other than Amadore. It was a settled rule that before going to the music room he went to pay his respects to old Signora Galli. She recognized his voice, his footsteps on the stairs, and if he did not at once come to her, she grew impatient and sent Giambattista, who had grown gray in the service of the Gallis and whose special province it was to serve the troublesome old lady, to fetch him.

Signora Galli was pursued by a mysterious notion that had got firmly rooted in her ninety-year-old head. As soon as the impatiently awaited visitor arrived she sent Giambattista out of the room, and then instructed Benedetto, with winks and many significant gestures, to pull open the door again hastily to see if by any chance Giambattista was standing listening behind it. If all was found to be well, she looked at her protégé with an expression at once profound and drowsy, and inquired: "What does Monsignore speak about to you — when he is alone with you? Has he at any time — said anything to you? He is very taken — with you. With your mother — he was also very taken. Does your mother — go to him often? You can — tell me. I — am silent as the grave."

Benedetto seemed to take a cruel delight in putting her on a false track. She caught him in contradictions, and covered him with bitter reproaches. She sighed and groaned, she quickly grew tired and could no longer think clearly. She stammered something incomprehensible, and then began to cry because he told her such awful lies. Relieved by her tears, she recovered, and set a trap for him. "Last time — you said . . ." and then would follow something he had never said at all. When he failed to fall into her trap she sank for that day into the melancholy of one who had striven in vain, and asked him whether later on he would come and play to her. Sometimes she heard such beautiful music within herself. When she thought of the death of her first husband (and she felt as she spoke for the locket with his miniature that she carried on her breast), then she heard such beautiful music . . . Perhaps it was the music of heaven already opening before her . . . She had thousands of scudi lying ready for Masses for her soul; they could not be touched, nor could her jewels.

She asked Benedetto to take a key from the pocket under her skirts, and with it to open the secret drawer in her *prie-dieu*, in which she kept the jewels she did not wear. He first had to bolt the door, as she distrusted everybody else, in particular that shameless old thief of a Giambattista. With her veined hand, misshapen by gout, she scrabbled excitedly, aimlessly, in the little iron casket — imagining, always, that something had been stolen. She called down curses on Giambattista; but she never failed to find what she thought she had lost.

She gazed fixedly at the jewels until her lorgnette began to shake so much in her trembling hand that she could no longer see. Meanwhile she abused her daughter-in-law for selling some very costly bracelets her

husband the podesta had given her, so that she could make donations to
the convent out of her own pocket. When old Signora Galli heard of
that, she made her son Giacomo swear by the Madonna that he would
bury her with all her jewels. But who knew whether he might not listen
to the devilish prompting of his wife, who would sell her own soul in
order to carry the proceeds to the convent. She was not quite sure that
they would leave her the jewels she always carried on her. She had
asked Giacomo point-blank: "Would you care to pull the earrings from
your mother's ears, the rings from her fingers, when she lies dead before
you?"

She looked up into Benedetto's face, trying to read in it whether he
would trust Giacomo in a matter like that. And when with some difficulty he withdrew his eyes from the little casket, a devilish grin came
over her wrinkled face. "Here — put it away again," she said, her voice
filled with a mysterious pleasure.

"I'll give you something at Christmas; I've thought of something for
your watch chain," she promised lavishly. "Go now — but give me back
my key first."

Maestro Angelini occupied a room, right at the top of the Galli palace,
which was not much better than the rooms of the servants, with whom
he came into continual conflict because they tried to treat him as an
equal. The trouble began in the early morning. Maestro Angelini was
always the last to go to bed, and in the morning he liked to sleep late.
The servants, however, effectually prevented that by the intentional noise
they made on the upper stairs. They were satisfied when his tired sallow
face, with the white nightcap above it, appeared round his door and he
bawled angry curses at them, calling them swine, camels, murderers, a
godforsaken rabble. Although he was paid for his attendance on old
Signora Galli, although he shared with the servants in the monthly per
quisites derived from the selling of candle-ends, Maestro Angelini was
of an inaccessible hauteur. He was, moreover, equally contemptuous of
the masters of the house; and one of his ways of showing this was to
carry out his duties with ostentatious punctuality, despite the years he
had spent under that roof. On the stroke of eleven, he paid his morning
respects to the old lady, and complained at the same time that Rosalina
had again kept him waiting in his room with untrimmed hair.

When they set out for their daily drive, he was all attention lest the
old woman should be thrown downstairs through the clumsy carelessness
of the lackeys.

He shared the midday meal with the rest of the household; and it was difficult to understand his extreme thinness, so copious was the fare.

After the meal, he gave Amadore, last scion of this branch of the Galli family, an hour's lesson on the harpsichord: a hopeless task, which, however, Maestro Angelini executed with the same painful care. Not the most excruciating false notes brought the slightest trace of emotion to his face.

Young Signora Galli was present at these lessons. Prematurely fading, she still showed signs of uncommon beauty. In the subdued light that came through the shutters, she worked at her embroidery frame. Sometimes she had to close her eyes, they were so tired with much use. She herself could not have explained why she was always embroidering; it had become the sole occupation of her life.

She embroidered for the church, for charity, for her husband, for her son, for distant relatives. She had recently embroidered a silk neckcloth for Piero: it was thirty years since he entered the service of the Galli family as a coachman. And still there was so much to be done; she had long since given up hope of reaching the end of it. On Sunday afternoons, she drove to the convent beyond the city gate to look at the embroidery done by the nuns, whom she provided with silks. She also showed them what she had done during the week. Except for this weekly visit to the convent and attendance at special church services, she never went out. She just sat at home and embroidered. But she never complained of the heaviness of her lot.

She never asked Maestro Angelini to play to her; but she spent the whole day near the harpsichord: there was always the chance that he might sit down to it and play, either alone or with the mysteriously gifted pupil Monsignore had passed on to him. At the first sound of the keys, she dropped her embroidery, inclined her head a little, and stared in front of her at a faded red rose in the carpet.

Her husband the mayor paid little attention to her. He carried out his civic duties with inextinguishable zeal, and felt himself poorly requited. Certain members of the Council were actually opposing him! He meant to see whether his money was powerful enough to eject them from their seats, since they did not know how to comport themselves. He was often out of humor these days. His wife wished his behavior towards her were as tactful and respectful as that of Maestro Angelini.

In the evenings they frequently had guests, and then they played faro. Old Signora Galli liked to hold the bank. Giambattista leant over the back of her chair and whispered to her which cards had fallen, and sometimes told her what cards he had seen in the hand of a guest. During her moments of drowsiness, he played in her stead. Obstinately, she tried to prevent him from pulling the cards from her fingers; and if she lost, she dismissed him angrily, only to summon him a moment later because she needed his help. If Giambattista were not by, she sometimes asked one of the other servants, as he carried round refreshments, how to distinguish clubs from spades, and suggested that, as he happened to be standing there, he might advise her also which suit to play.

Dizzy with fatigue, young Signora Galli moved among her guests. Fortunately, Maestro Angelini was never far from her, and watched to see when the buffet needed replenishing — a duty her husband should have undertaken; but *he* was entirely lost in the game. At a sign from her, Maestro Angelini went to fetch her embroidery, which the guests had asked to see. He returned immediately and handed it to her with the respect of a trusted courtier towards his sovereign. She did not thank him, but her colorless cheeks flushed.

III

Every Saturday morning little Maestro Spinucci came to give dancing lessons. Then young Signora Galli retired to her boudoir and Maestro Angelini to the library, where rows of dusty books looked down upon him with astonishment, unaccustomed as they were to the presence of human beings. The old lady, on the other hand, witnessed the lesson from her wheeled chair; and of the twenty boys and girls gathered in the room, Benedetto was the one on whom her lorgnette remained fixed. "Look at him!" she advised her grandson Amadore. "Just do everything — precisely as he does."

Little, sprightly Maestro Spinucci danced as he played his fiddle before his pupils. Sometimes he laid aside his instrument and threw himself down with a thump behind the harpsichord, in order to put more force into his teaching. "One, two, one, two," he cried, strumming pitilessly on the keyboard. He was on the alert to see whether the boys adapted their steps properly to the measured dignity of the dance, and whether the girls smiled sweetly all the time, and bent their heads gracefully upon their necks, as he had instructed them. When they curtseyed it was of extreme importance that their skirts should be raised just so high — they might show the instep, or at most, at very most, the curve of the calf. "I see a knee! I see a knee!" shrieked Maestro Spinucci hysterically across the harpsichord. He stood up, and continued to strum standing, his eyes full of horror. Immediately old Signora Galli turned her lorgnette upon the forbidden spectacle.

New figures were danced by Maestro Spinucci first, while Benedetto sat at the harpsichord. Perfection of style and control banished all that was ridiculous in this aging, spindle-shanked dancing master. A smile, half-foolish, half-entranced, came over his seedy-looking, tired face — a mask he threw off again as soon as he had concluded his demonstration and grimly resumed his place behind the harpsichord. After each lesson, Maestro Angelini examined the instrument. Always he found it out of tune, and he wasted a whole evening with Benedetto putting it right again.

On New Year's Eve, there was a party to which the parents were invited, so that they could see for themselves what progress their children had made. The grown-ups sat in an adjoining room, to which Maestro Spinucci was summoned in order to receive their compliments. Meanwhile, in the music room a hired quartet played while servants dispensed cooling drinks. Little attention was paid to the children, and any boy who had a secret sweetheart among the girls tried to find a seat in her neighborhood.

Benedetto did not join in this rivalry. Nor did he dare to go and fetch a cool drink for Serafina Rigogli, the younger sister of Federigo, although he had thought of her day and night ever since the previous autumn, when she had begun to attend the dancing lessons. She seemed to him a princess, delicate and exalted.

She bore a strong resemblance to her brother, but everything that repelled him in Federigo attracted him in Serafina, in whom the same features reappeared, but magically refined. Like Federigo, she had red hair, but hers seemed like spun gold on which the evening glow was falling. Her face, too, was covered with freckles, but hers were very pale and as fine as pin points, and they gave a tender pinkish tint to her very white skin. She was altogether delicate in every way: the sedan chair was always sent for before the end of the lesson and she was carried away.

Last summer he had kissed Babetta Galli, from Siena, behind the door. He had whispered soft, foolish words into her ear and, a self-satisfied smile on his lips, had allowed the other boys to tease him about his success first with Rosalina Campioni and then with Babetta. But they found that it was dangerous to venture upon indiscreet allusions, to play with the sacred feelings that Serafina had awakened in him.

Only on rare occasions, and with a beating heart, had he dared ask her to dance. As she followed him to the dance floor, her face wore an expressionless look: she appeared to be gazing beyond him, over his head, just as Federigo her brother had looked past him. She did not show whether his invitation was pleasant or unwelcome, and her cool indifference humbled him.

On the evening of the New Year's party, she sat with a faintly sad expression on her face: no cavalier had come up to her for several dances. Benedetto, roaming in her proximity, pale with emotion, keeping her in his eye all the time, was aware that something threatening about him was preventing the other boys from asking Serafina to dance; and while he reveled feverishly in his power to isolate her, he felt that he ought to free her from her isolation.

Suddenly he stood before her and bowed. She got up without speaking, and without looking at him laid her cool hand lightly upon his, which was warm and trembling. They moved together under the great chandelier, the golden light descended upon her, enveloped her, radiated from her small head. As they danced, Benedetto could distinguish nothing about him. He was only dimly aware that he was alive. Vague and confused voices and the music of stringed instruments blended in his ear.

When the dance was over, he escorted Serafina back to her place and thanked her correctly. She made a formal response in her weak, elfin voice. Then he left her, but he did not know where to go. He exchanged a few meaningless words with someone.

And then he encircled her again with his power of isolation. Alessandro Campioni hovered about her, then thought better of it and, passing behind her, bowed to Agata Tadini. Serafina stretched out her little foot wonderingly and stared at it. When she raised her head, Benedetto stood in front of her again, and requested her for a second dance. She hesitated a moment before complying.

When in the course of this dance he tried to engage her for a third, she said she was tired and wanted to rest. Whereupon he declared that he would dance with nobody but her and, unbidden, remained with her. Should he bring her a cold drink? No, thank you. She was not allowed to drink much when she was heated. She cast an imploring glance at her brother, who passed by with a faintly mocking smile on his lips. Benedetto noticed the smile. Flushing scarlet in the consciousness of his inability to entertain her agreeably, he came out with an obtuse question. Oh, did the doctor forbid that? Did it make her ill? He recognized a boy who was passing near them, and addressed him boisterously. "Oh, you here too? Why weren't you at school yesterday?" The boy, filled with other interests, merely nodded, and bowed before Agata Tadini. Thus abandoned to his fate, Benedetto desperately began to relate a story about Amadore at school: he had been asked to name the Popes from 1012 and onwards, but he always forgot some of them: and the master had demanded whether he did not think it disrespectful to jump casually over these Holy Fathers.

But Serafina did not smile. She did not seem even to have heard. Had she disliked his story? She was not so very pious. Did she go often to Mass? No, but his tone had shocked her: he had not treated her with the respect that was her due. He shivered — perhaps she found it unpleasant merely to have him standing beside her.

At this moment the old servant who always fetched Serafina from the lesson came in. A dull despair seized him. Serafina noticed her at once, as though she had been on the lookout for her. She gave Benedetto an insincere little smile, bade good-by to her hostess, and then left obediently. The old servant threw a warm shawl around her.

Benedetto moved about aimlessly, waiting until midnight should relieve him of the obligation to stay longer. He tried to speak to Federigo Rigogli, wanted to ask his forgiveness for what had once happened at school. Federigo, however, turned away at that moment in order to offer a sweetmeat to a girl.

At midnight Benedetto took his leave.

In the darkness, while the bells were ringing in the New Year, he wandered about the dwelling of his idol, drawing back into the shadows when a vehicle passed or when revelers came swaying by from Vacca's inn. He kept muttering a name— "Serafina." She was as a star in the firmament: radiant, undefiled, infinitely remote. He had wounded her deeply, thrust himself shamelessly upon her; but perhaps she would forgive him if she knew that he was prepared to die for her. Perhaps she would die herself soon, her health was so frail. The bells would ring as now, and he himself would go to the grave with her. Would Federigo try to prevent his being joined with Serafina in one grave? In that case Benedetto would be obliged to kill Federigo before killing himself. He would do this with regret, however, as he no longer bore Federigo ill will.

A light appeared above: was it in her room? His heart almost stopped beating. No — she would not be sleeping so high up. It must be Innocenta, the old servant, retiring to bed.

A star shot across the sky. What was the mysterious meaning of that? Was it beckoning towards Eternity, which he had called up? He was ready. In the winter night he opened wide his cloak, under which his warm body was throbbing.

In the gray of dawn, fearing to be seen, he tottered home.

At midday Federigo announced that Serafina would no longer attend the dancing lesson. She had not enjoyed herself at all recently, and she had tired herself too much.

Although Federigo had not addressed this announcement especially to him, Benedetto understood that it was meant for him. He grew pale, and drew apart. Serafina had repulsed him through her brother's mouth, and Federigo had seen to it that all were witnesses of Benedetto's humiliation. A door had been slammed in his face. Nothing remained to him but his pride.

Next Saturday, he tried to make it clear to all that for Federigo's sister there were ten other girls in the dancing class. He began to turn Maria Perosio's head; and the fact that Federigo had set his mind on her was no deterrent.

Then came the reaction: a deep and general aversion to life. And about this time his grandmother died. As he followed her to her grave he was filled with the desire to become a monk in some monastery far from Todi, far from the world, there to await his time in meditation and study.

His father had carpentered the coffin for her himself, shedding quiet tears the while. Benedetto had not known that his father still loved her so much. Indeed, he knew little of his father. He only knew that his mother had never cared for the old woman who lived on the same corridor; and yet it had been his mother who had insisted that she should come and live with them when she could no longer fend for herself. Lucia had rejected the suggestion at first; but in the end she had come. For a fortnight she had sat by the window with a wry face, refusing all the delicacies that were brought to her — from which Benedetto had deduced, with satisfaction, that she was set upon dying. She did not sit with them at table; but as she sat in her corner not one of his movements escaped her, and afterwards she spoke ill of him to his father.

Her moaning kept them awake at night. When people came to see her, all she said was that she longed for her deceased husband, whom she had left alone as he lay dead. And in the end she had died herself. When Benedetto came home he had noticed how attentively his mother watched him, to see whether he was upset by the presence of a dead person in the room, and that person his grandmother. He had approached the bed, surprised at his own indifference; and then he had been even more amazed to see the peacefulness of the face that in life had been so ill-natured. Perhaps he would have loved her if she had looked like that when she was alive.

Later, the room was filled with people. Many of them he had never seen before. Old gray Cesare was there; and Camilla — large, fat, and nervous, still the mother of ten children although she had lost her three youngest from measles; and Manuela, who, with a mysterious little laugh, gave him to understand how well she understood what his feelings must be here among these people of a lower order. And there were so-and-so and so-and-so — the whole neighborhood, in fact. The room was so crowded that Zampieri the dyer, suddenly pushed against the bed, almost fell on it. Falcometti subsequently teased him, saying that he had wanted to give old Lucia a parting kiss.

Then she was carried out, and Benedetto her grandson had to hold one of the funeral ribbons that hung from the coffin. He had first of all protested, and then had given in for the sake of his mother. But when he followed in the procession, under the solemn tolling of the bells, a long burning candle in his free hand, he was impressed by the glory of the trappings of death. If he had entertained no respect for his grandmother living, he felt respect for her dead; and in the glance he gave the people standing at the street corners, bending their knees and crossing themselves, he gave expression to that respect. He was impressed with the majesty of death.

Antonio was hammering again at his coffins. He seemed to have forgotten that, among others, he had also made one for his mother. Marietta, however, remained under the impression for days, perhaps because after the funeral meal — for which they had been short of chairs — it had grown so quiet again in her home. For her sake, Benedetto refrained from going out for several evenings, and he noticed at once that this cheered her.

"Has it always been so, Mother? Have people never come to see you much?" he asked.

Surprised, she looked up at him, then shrugged her shoulders. "Why should they come here? Your father isn't one to encourage visitors." "Your father," she had said. The word "father" had never meant anything to Benedetto.

"It isn't because of Father," he said, slowly. "People don't come here because of you — because you're different. You don't fit in, in this house. Any more than I do," he added quickly.

She went over to the cupboard.

He looked after her, satisfied with the effect of his words. Well, now he had told her. You and I . . . We are strangers in these surroundings. Father is at home here. But you and I . . . He would have liked to run after her and throw his arms about her. Then she would have burst into tears, and perhaps would have betrayed things she would prefer to say nothing about. But that was not necessary. It was enough that she should know that he had guessed a great deal. What was she doing there in the cupboard? She was trying to avoid answering him, just as she had done the evening before. All right, if that was what she wanted . . . He threw himself into the armchair that had been moved into their house when his grandmother came. He knew he was giving her pleasure just by sitting in the most comfortable chair in the room. She liked to have him there; it did not happen very often.

She stood before him, watching him as he sat with the air of a prince in the chair against whose high back an ailing old woman had been accustomed to sit huddled up, guilty and stubborn. She watched the gesture with which he brought his wineglass to his lips and crumbled a cake on his plate. Perhaps she was dimly aware, herself, that he was acting a part to gladden his mother's eye. Perhaps, if for no other reason, she would have loved him for playing that little comedy. What had he just said that had caught at her throat? . . . You and I are strangers here.

Then, unexpectedly, Antonio came in. He had been to his mother's empty home. Benedetto got up as if he were about to go out. Antonio hung up his coat in silence. Benedetto knew his father's feelings at seeing him sitting there in his grandmother's chair while his mother treated him to cakes and wine.

The happy, tender, dreamy expression on Marietta's face vanished. It grew tired and dull again as she listened to what her husband was saying about the sale of the old woman's furniture. He wanted her to go and look at it herself, before he took the things to his workshop to be offered for sale, in case there might be something they themselves could use.

Oh, at the very most the crockery and the kitchen utensils, she thought. They had enough furniture as it was. It would only crowd their rooms. Antonio listened with bent head. She knew that every word she uttered gave him pain; but she simply could not live among that furniture to which he was attached. The large chair — yes, they would keep that.

Benedetto stood hesitating by the door until he was quite sure his mother had returned, from the distant regions where they had loitered together a moment, to reality and the world of his father. Then he went out.

Suddenly, feverishly, he plunged into music, infecting Maestro Angelini with his hunger. They played together in a common intoxication day after day for hours on end. They understood one another better than they had ever done before. Never had their instruments blended as they did now. Young Signora Galli sat with them, gazing absentmindedly at her embroidery. The whole world would go its way, toiling and moiling for its daily bread, quarreling, and going to church; in the music room of the Galli Palace, the wings of eternity beat to music.

Benedetto had sensed what lay between his music master and young Signora Galli. They loved each other without ever having admitted it to one another, without ever having given shape to their love. It was enough for them to be together and to know that they lived for each other. Maestro Angelini played and Signora Galli embroidered, and between them rose the high wall of worldly prejudice. They could perhaps have razed that wall to the ground. Yes — if they had had less respect for themselves and for one another, and if they had not both been too tired and too filled with the consciousness of the futility of this transient existence.

In the highly susceptible condition in which Benedetto then was, this unreal, other-worldly love seemed to him the one thing worth while on earth: it actually inspired him to compose.

One evening he took a sheet of music paper and wrote down a melody that, together with appropriate words, had been welling up in him. In the feverish joy of creation, he worked it out into a song with violin and harpsichord accompaniment. The human voice wailed with worldly longing and grief, the violin answered with the consolation of eternity. With a trembling hand, he wrote the dedication upon it: "To the Unattainable One," and hurried with it to young Signora Galli, who seemed the only person to whom he could show it. She read the song with silent admiration, and asked him to play it to her, overlooking the difficulty that it had been written for two instruments. He dared not summon Maestro Angelini. In the end, she suggested that she might try to play the harpsichord accompaniment. It was a long time since she had sat at the harpsichord — not since Maestro Angelini came into the house.

Next morning, while Maestro Angelini was out driving with the old lady, they practised in the music room. Young Signora Galli sat behind the harpsichord, girlishly excited and shy, her shortsighted eyes bent close upon the manuscript. It was with some difficulty that she played the notes of his composition; but when she had nearly mastered it, and could sing the words in a small but harmonious voice, Benedetto picked up his violin; and then suddenly it was borne in upon him that when he had dedicated it "To the Unattainable One," he had actually been thinking of the beloved of his music master. The discovery moved him so deeply that he could hardly play it through. When the song was at an end, he flung himself at her feet, burying his head in her satin skirt. He expected her to calm him with maternal kisses. He already seemed to feel the sweetness of her mouth. Instead of which, she caressed his head nervously, and begged him to control himself. She was not angry, but he must be brave and overcome his love. To prove to him that she meant well by him, she would accept his composition and keep it.

Benedetto nodded, fighting against tears. He got up, biting his lip bravely, but a little disappointed in spite of himself. At this difficult moment, they heard the sound of the returning caroche, and young Signora Galli hastily hid the composition dedicated to her under her embroidery box.

Once he had begun, Benedetto found he could not stop. He wrote canzonettas, short pieces for various instruments, tried his hand at a cantata and at a light opera in the manner of the seventeenth century masters. His muse and protectress was young Signora Galli, to whom he brought the results of his labors every morning, and in whom he confided grandiose plans for a requiem. Gradually, however, his creative urge weakened. He left one unfinished composition after another in order to throw himself desperately into new and more ambitious plans. In his general discouragement, he grew careless of his compositions, and so it happened that one morning Maestro Angelini asked him venomously on what sort of music he was at present wasting his violin and his talent. Benedetto hurried to the harpsichord, and, flushing with shame, snatched from it a sheet of paper he had, with unforgivable thoughtlessness, left standing there.

He was completely disillusioned. The insincerity and pomposity of the few bars that caught his eyes as he tore up the sheet suddenly stood out before him, and he wondered how he could ever have written them down and, even more, how he had found them beautiful.

Maestro Angelini gave him a troubled look. Then, while the pupil listened with bowed head, the master explained that there were two sorts of musicians: those who made music and those who wrote down music for them. Naturally, pride of place belonged to the first; for what were all the written notes in the world to mankind if no virtuoso had been born to quicken them into living sound? Benedetto belonged to those privileged to bring the miracle of music to other men, and consequently he should not trouble himself with the writing down of notes. Improvise, yes; but to put down on paper the divine inspiration of a moment was contemptible, unworthy of a performer. The very instant one took pen in hand, vanity came into play and made of beauty a lie.

Benedetto, stirred to the heart, drank in his master's wisdom, and felt the truth of his every word. It was vanity, nothing but vanity that had induced him to set down page after page of notes, as if Scarlatti, Corelli, Pergolese had never been.

Young Signora Galli shyly inquired why Benedetto had suddenly ceased to show her any more work. He rewarded her warm interest, henceforth, with secret contempt.

In the spring Babetta Galli of Siena came to stay again, accompanied this time by her somewhat older sister Lucrezia. Their arrival carried Benedetto's interest back to the dancing class which, since his grandmother's death, he had neglected. Young Signora Galli tried vainly to understand this sudden change of front in the strange, gifted boy who had once dared to make her a declaration of love.

IV

Babetta had now turned thirteen. She was as good-natured and smiling as she had been the year before, but her figure, then somewhat short and thickset, had grown taller and had assumed almost womanly lines. She was delighted to see Benedetto again. Her eyes smiled, teasing and satisfied, because he still wore on his watch chain her little gold Madonna. She tried to catch his eye, in the hope that he too was anxious to have a word with her alone. After half an hour, disappointment overcame her. He refused to understand her, pretended to be absentminded; and she knew him sufficiently to distrust his absentmindedness. Who was his sweetheart now, in the dancing class?

Lucrezia, her sister, was engaged to a young lawyer in Siena. When the girls tried to talk to her, she assumed a solemn air and talked of her betrothed, Conte Rizzi. Next year, when she would be sixteen, the marriage was to be celebrated. Lucrezia was uncommonly pretty, and knew it. Possibly, indeed, she cared more for herself than for her betrothed.

There was a concealed rivalry among the boys, who all wanted to dance with the girls from Siena. Some of them did not dare to approach Lucrezia. But four or five at a time they bore down upon Babetta. She could not help laughing as, half in triumph, half in sadness, she looked towards Benedetto; he, in order not to do what everybody was doing, bowed before the young girls of Todi who were receiving but scant attention. He danced with Maria Perosio who had been deserted by Federigo, with Agata Tadini who never could learn the figures of the minuet, with Serafina Rigogli who had unexpectedly reappeared at the dancing lesson, and who must have been secretly grateful to him for asking her to dance with him when he was requested by Maestro Spinucci to demonstrate a new measure before the rest of the class.

"So that is she," thought Babetta Galli, eyeing Serafina with a certain hostility, surprised that Benedetto should have preferred this frail little creature to herself.

During the pause for refreshments several of the Todi girls showed their disgust at the pretentious and haughty behavior of the Sienese sisters by adopting a very stiff attitude. To their infinite satisfaction, Benedetto devoted himself exclusively to them, conversing with them gallantly, and whispering amusing nothings to them so that they had to bite their handkerchiefs to prevent themselves from laughing aloud. Behind the little group reverberated Federigo's self-opinionated voice. He had conceived the audacious plan of making a conquest of Lucrezia. He was telling her that next autumn he was going to the university of Bologna to study law. Lucrezia showed great interest, and agreed with him that Bologna was the best university in Italy. Her betrothed, Conte Rizzi, had studied there. Bored and impatient, Babetta looked longingly towards the little circle round Benedetto. There, everyone was laughing; while around her and her sister reigned a dull politeness made heavier by the concealed annoyance and simmering ill will of the rest of the boys, who failed to shine against Federigo.

Maestro Spinucci, more agitated than usual, demonstrated a figure from the very latest dance: the description of it had just reached him from Venice. To the dancing master's astonishment it appeared still to be unknown in Siena, for neither of the young ladies from that city had ever heard of it. Benedetto accompanied him on the harpsichord. Lucrezia gave him a hasty glance as he sat there reading the music with casual ease and at the same time followed the movements of the dancing master. Federigo, noticing her glance, informed her that Benedetto was the son of an artisan, and that his mother had been brought up at the expense of the city. With a contemptuous expression on her red lips, Lucrezia cast a final glance at him over the superb curve of her shoulder.

"But who was that thin little thing he was dancing with a moment ago?" she asked him later.

Federigo, flushing scarlet, had to confess that it was his sister. "He has the audacity to ask her again and again, and yet she's made it perfectly clear to him that she's not keen — "

"But she has a brother to protect her, hasn't she?" asked Lucrezia in surprise, and not without a certain irony.

"I shall have to speak to him," declared Federigo bravely in his shame and annoyance.

V

A trip was arranged to Pontecutini, where the cool waters of the Tiber flowed glittering over round pebbles, and a field, richly shadowed with poplars, invited to a day in the open air. The boys and girls of the dancing class were to travel thither in three vehicles under the escort of Maestro Angelini and young Signora Galli.

In the calash in which the two guests had come from Siena sat Babetta and Lucrezia with Federigo Rigogli — and Amadore Galli, whom he had selected as a not very dangerous rival. Next came young Signora Galli's caroche, containing the Signora and Maestro Angelini. The last conveyance — a large traveling coach, unearthed and freed from dust and cobwebs for the purpose, carried eight others.

Against the legs of Benedetto, who was perched on high as on a throne, sat Agata Tadini and the pale, delicate Serafina. The night before Serafina had had a violent scene with her brother, who had almost persuaded her father the judge to prevent her from going — a scene that no one had expected of her. With many tears, she had attained her purpose — and already she was beginning to regret it. Her pretty dress had been crumpled in the crush. She was tormented by a slight headache that prevented her from joining in the gaiety of the others. She was doing her best, but the little smile on her bloodless lips was not very convincing.

Benedetto's voice behind her back disturbed her. It sounded insincere, as though he, too, were only playing at gaiety. He too — she had not expected that. Where, in truth, were his thoughts? Not with her certainly; and fortunately she set no store by that either.

The scattered peasants gazed in astonishment at the last vehicle, piled with boxes and baskets full of food, and crowded with frolicsome young people. The high-pitched voices of the girls resounded in the summer morning, and whenever the old coach sank into a deep rut they uttered alarmed little cries. The coachman, listening to the chatter inside, wore a grin on his pockmarked face. The groom of the middle vehicle looked round with disapproval.

A band of children in rags came streaming over the bridge across the Tiber. A sunburned woman stood at the door of a miserable farmstead, suckling a child at her breast. Chickens scurried away cackling. House dogs barked furiously. The young people in the last vehicle waved and nodded. Some of the young ladies had never before been outside the city gate, and were impressed by the pleasantness of life on the banks of the river. But they pitied the children because of the rags on their backs. They threw sweets and packets of confetti to them, and watched open-eyed at the desperation with which the children fought for these gifts.

Agata Tadini proposed that they should sew clothes for the children: a proposal that was greeted with instant approval. Rosalina Campioni went one better, and suggested that they should all come and live here together in a little house, look after the children, and teach the peasants manners.

Beyond the old stone bridge, a halt was called. The coachmen and grooms unharnessed the horses. The lackeys carried baskets and boxes to an open space under the trees. From the high bridge, the youth of the village watched these men in their handsome liveries spread cloths over the grass and lay out costly china; watched the young gentlemen careering across the field, some measuring their strength against an old he-goat which showed no fight, while three of them together jumped onto a tied-up donkey, so frightening the poor brute that it brayed for help.

The young ladies plucked flowers to decorate the cloth. The Gallis' cook, who had ridden on the box of the old coach, got a couple of fires going with wood and dried thistle that he had made the village urchins collect. He rewarded them with a box on the ears when, having finished their work, they lingered on. Peacefully the pale blue smoke rose up among the trees, attracting a bevy of inquisitive geese that were immediately seized by the servants and decapitated. A boy rushed away from the bridge. A fisherman returning homewards with a netful of trout was held up and compelled to surrender his catch. His protests were met with the name of "Galli." Meanwhile the weeping owner of the geese, warned by the small boy, was likewise paid with the name of Galli, as though it had been ready money. She was a widow, was she? The geese were her only possession? All right, then: she had only to go to the piazza and ask for old Signora Galli. She also was a widow and would understand. The servants grinned. Feathers flew in all directions. Franzo, the cook, stood ready to seize them by the drumsticks and turn them sizzling in the flames. A good half-hour later the youthful company was summoned to table.

Benedetto sat between Serafina and Babetta. He prepared a salad for them, and as he did so demonstrated to the others exactly how it should be done. The rest copied him more or less successfully. Babetta was proud of him, and told him so. Serafina, however, appeared if anything to be depressed by his success. With haughty contempt, she observed Babetta's clever maneuvering to sit next to Benedetto. Serafina could no longer conceal from herself that it had been for his sake that she had persisted in joining the expedition. It had been unwise of her: she realized that. And here she was, sitting next him, everything in her welling up towards him, seeking an escape with him. She wished he would be quiet and restrained, like Maestro Angelini, whose eyes wandered absent-mindedly over the boisterous company, though he was all attention to the wishes of young Signora Galli. She would have liked things to be between Benedetto and her as they were between those two. By her silence and her quiet smile, she tried to lure him into an atmosphere of gentle intimacy. He did not even notice her desire. He treated her with almost open indifference, and turned towards Babetta. Serafina did not enjoy the food — nor was she accustomed to sitting on the ground. At home she ate special dishes ordered by the doctor.

She cast a hostile glance towards her brother who, on the other side of the cloth, was preening himself before Lucrezia Galli. She would have liked to be able to blame him for her own presence there. Her former contempt for Benedetto returned, mixed now with shame and bitterness.

They clinked glasses and drank. As though they were already men, the boys all drank too much wine. There was much irresponsible laughter, as funny stories that went beyond seemliness were whispered from one to the other. Agata Tadini jumped up suddenly with a shrill cry, because she had imagined that something was moving under her — a frog or a serpent or something worse. To the delight of the boys, she raised her skirt far higher than would have met with Maestro Spinucci's approval. Young Signora Galli, faintly disapproving, looked at the blushing girl but said nothing.

An infinite quantity of liqueurs, sweets and tarts, and crystallized fruits was consumed. Coffee was served; and then one of the girls suggested that they should go and wash their hands by the river, and all dashed off. The boys started a competition to see who could reach the other side of the Tiber by jumping from stone to stone, and during the game Filippino Perosio, affected by the wine, slipped into the cool mountain water. His misadventure served as the excuse for assuming the fancy dresses they had brought with them. With much jubilation, these were unpacked and apportioned. Each boy took the costume thrown at him; while the girls, withdrawing behind the screen of poplars, bickered as to who should take which dress.

They were still busy when a Harlequin, a Pantaloon, a Doctor, an Abbé, and a Faun surprised them. These indiscreet strangers, peering through the trees, caught sight of a Columbine, a Diana, a market woman, and a fortuneteller, who dashed away with shrieks while each hastily secured the last band or ribbon of her dress. It did not prove difficult to recognize them behind their little satin masks. Benedetto, dressed as a donkey, galloped behind a little flower seller who had Babetta's contours. With his front paw on his heart, he knelt before her, and begged her for a flower. Amidst shouts of laughter, she stuck a thistle in his mouth.

On the deserted open space, only Signora Galli and her cavalier remained. She sat on the grass against a tree. He had brought her a cushion for her back, and now he stood by her side, leaning against the trunk, looking down at her. They were silent. . . . Perhaps Signora Galli was thinking of her embroidery which she had left behind in order to spare her tired eyes in the harsh light outdoors. They exchanged an occasional word, but not about this marvelous summer day, not about their being alone together for the first time in the green country. No! They talked of Signor Galli, and his excitement over the council meetings, of Amadore, and his going to college — perhaps trusty old Giambattista ought to be sent with him. It was all a question of choosing the right moment to approach the old lady on the subject. . . . By the riverside, the servants were washing the plates and dishes and packing them up again, drinking the wine from the half-empty bottles and eating what remained of the poultry.

Pontecutini lay sweltering in the midday sun. The whole world was sunk in languorous sleep.

"I say, isn't it time to go yet?" inquired Babetta, raising her flushed face from the cool grass where she lay next to Benedetto, whose ass's head had fallen back limply behind his shoulders.

He looked up at her smiling, and Babetta, who did not take her own question very seriously, could not forbear to smile back. "They'll never, never find us here," she said, reassuring herself with her own statement.

"And Lucrezia won't miss you. She'll be only too pleased to-day if too much notice is not taken of her."

"Yes, Lucrezia has her student who is not yet a student. Why are you always talking about her?"

"Because you're so anxious about her."

"Or is it because you're in love with her?"

"I thought I was so very much in love with that little girl of Judge Rigogli's! With whom am I in love now?"

"With you, who could tell?" sighed Babetta. "You're just as likely to be thinking of somebody else while you're running after me."

"If I'm thinking of anybody to-day, it is of Conte Rizzi in Siena."

"What is Conte Rizzi to you? Perhaps you want to let him know what Lucrezia is up to here?"

Benedetto shrugged his shoulders.

"She'll have nothing to do with you. Don't give yourself any trouble over her," pouted Babetta.

"Do I trouble about her?"

"How can I tell whether you're troubled about her? I did not know this morning that you still felt something for me; and now suddenly you talk of nothing but Lucrezia. But I'm used to it, used to seeing everyone going after her. I can see how pretty she is, although I'm her sister."

Moved, he drew her towards him; and in a sudden foreboding of danger that she wanted still to escape after having brought it upon herself, Babetta struggled laughingly to free herself, turned her head away from him, and closed her eyes under the burning kiss she felt behind her ear.

And then the danger passed of itself. She had been anxious about nothing. She saw that at once as, a little disappointed, she turned towards him again. What a strange boy he was! Was he only making fun of her? Babetta's little heart was still beating wildly: Lucrezia had told her that much about love, Lucrezia who knew its mysteries. It was all exciting, and terribly dangerous. If the accident happened, the shame and the scandal were so great that one could only die. And yet — when it came, it was inevitable. Babetta would be able to do nothing against it; she knew that already. She had longed to see Benedetto again, though she had been rather afraid; and then at once she had felt again the mysterious power he had over her — she could have denied him nothing he might ask. In the warm and languorous afternoon, the grass was fragrant, and it had been sweet when he kissed her. It could be much sweeter still. . . . Did he not know that? Why did it not come now, that of which Lucrezia had spoken? Did he want to spare her? She did not wish to be spared. She wanted to die, if necessary. Only she did not want him to laugh at her.

She looked at him distrustfully, with something almost hostile in her eyes. Changing her attitude, she smoothed down her dress with a prim gesture and asked, "How many girls have you kissed?"

He gave her a dubious look. When, in spite of herself, she laughed again, he begged her to bend towards him, and then he whispered the inevitable lie in her ear.

"Yes, that's very likely," she railed. "That's what you say to all of them, of course."

"And you? How many boys have *you* kissed?"

She gave him a withering look. "What are you thinking about? Do you imagine we go about so freely with boys in Siena? If Papa and Mamma knew about this . . . !"

"I'm not asking you whether you're allowed to go about with boys. I'm asking you how many you've kissed."

Instead of answering, she suddenly threw herself upon his mouth and kissed him madly. With closed eyes, he withstood her desperate onslaught; and, while her face was bending over his, while she looked at him with eyes drunk with confusion, he asked her: "And Lucrezia? How many has Lucrezia kissed?"

Without a word she slipped away from him and lay down upon her back in the grass, shadowing her eyes with her hands. Thus she lay without stirring, without speaking. Had he spoken, she might not even have heard.

An acrid smile, half of self-mockery and half of pain, played about Benedetto's lips. He looked at her broodingly. Under the ragged satin costume of a flower seller, her young breast rose and fell. Did he himself understand how it had been possible to withstand her allurement? Only an insane pride had kept him back: *She is not the one I desire.* . . . Suddenly he jumped up, frightening Babetta. "We're being called," he said, making a trumpet of his hands and returning the echo. Then he pulled her up and kissed away her tears. Pale, absentminded, she let him do it.

As they returned hastily along the riverbank, where they had to bend their heads again and again to avoid overhanging branches, Babetta stumbled and fell. Benedetto picked her up and carried her through the shallow water near the bank. Desire sprang up in him, and he began to kiss her again. As he laid her down, he had the temerity to request: "Babetta — help me with Lucrezia."

She gazed at him open-eyed. Then slowly turned away her face.

When they reached the open space, they were received with teasing hand-claps. Regaining control of herself with amazing quickness, Babetta played the part of one who is not averse to being under suspicion. Benedetto gave a long and serious report of their adventure, not calculated to inspire belief. Lucrezia, standing back with Federigo, gave her younger sister an inquisitorial look. She was not quite satisfied with the way Babetta met it.

The sun was already sinking behind the bridge. In a moment twilight fell. They dawdled so long over changing their clothes that the servants had to light the lanterns of the waiting vehicles. The moon rose over the mountains, casting its pale light upon the water where the shadow of the bridge stretched.

When all the others had taken their places, Maestro Angelini handed young Signora Galli to her seat. Silently he followed her. Nobody paid any attention to them: had they continued to talk of the desirability of sending old Giambattista to the university with Amadore? Surely that was not a subject to fill a whole afternoon, while the sun shone warm through the greenery and the little fish jumped out of the water after dragonflies — between two people who loved each other without ever having dared to confess it . . .

Slowly the vehicles rolled towards the hills. In the old coach, the young ladies were singing a little French song they had learned. On the box, in the green silver moonlight, the coachmen were yawning.

Serafina paid no further attention to Benedetto after his late return with Babetta, and his contemptible lying story. She had turned conciliatingly to Amadore, who was still put out by the way in which she had used him when he had tried to kiss her in the little wood. Sitting there in the last vehicle, she struggled with her headache. She had asked to be allowed to sit right in the corner, for the sake of the fresh air. She stared at the little farmsteads of the winegrowers: what was all the noise and chatter in the coach to her? She longed for home, to be alone in her room. . . .

Benedetto gave her a rapid glance from time to time when he was able to catch a glimpse of her delicate profile. He did not wish her to suffer over him, nor Babetta either, and yet that was what had happened. While he laughed and cracked his jokes, the prime instigator of all the fun in the coach, there was within him a melancholy and a mad pity for those whom he had made sorrowful, for all those whom he would yet make sorrowful . . . He had a foreboding that there would be many. And in the midst of his melancholy, pride blazed up in him over all that he would squander in the wild, luxuriant life that was opening before him. Mixed with all these thoughts was an undercurrent of restless wondering: how he could humiliate Lucrezia and bring her under his sway, how Federigo, who had been hovering round her in triumph, could be brought low.

They entered the city. The people in the streets looked up with curiosity as they passed. In the middle vehicle, they caught a glimpse of the austere, birdlike face of Signor Morto-vivo: they were astonished to see him sitting not by the side of the elder Signora Galli, but by that of the younger, whose eyes were large and dazed. . . .

VI

Shortly before the dancing class began, Babetta rushed past Benedetto into the music room and in passing pressed a folded note into his hand. Behind a curtain, he glanced first at the signature, then at the name of the person to whom it was addressed, and finally ran his eyes over the contents.

My dear little (?) Student: —
I have remained in my room to-day, alleging a headache — but actually to disarm all suspicion.
While dancing with you, Babetta will hand you this note. If you should be so unmannerly as not to ask my sister for a dance, you will not receive my missive. Perhaps that would cause you regret?
But no doubt you will ask her for a dance, in the hope of hearing from

her that you still occupy my thoughts. Were this not so, you would be unworthy of the invitation you are about to read.

Invitation: Will you come to our room this evening for a cold supper? We will provide everything, including the wine. You need only undertake to replenish the candles when ours have burned out.

You can easily bring some with you.

Amadore will invite you, and one or two others, this evening. After taking your leave, hide in the closet under the stairs. Everything hangs upon your having the courage to do this, and upon your being able to keep quiet until you see through the chinks the light of a candle, upstairs on the landing.

This letter is the greatest piece of imprudence I have ever committed. I can only rely upon a future student's being already able to comport himself as a man of honor — sometimes one must know how to take risks, or one would have no fun at all.

Thus speaks your

LUCREZIA

P.S. You will surely not boast subsequently of an adventure for which you have to thank only my weakness for you. Conte Rizzi, my betrothed, would kill me! You will also know how to keep yourself within bounds. And you must not be angry again, but must think of the presence of my younger sister, who has been entrusted to my care.

P.S. Will you also remember to bring with you the students' songs you were talking about?

P.S. It goes without saying that you will have to leave the house again before the servants are up. How will you manage that? Be discreet, for the Virgin's sake, and *burn this communication*. My life is in your hands.

Till this evening,

LUCREZIA

Benedetto slowly raised his head. Babetta was standing beside him again, stretching out her hand towards the letter. He put it behind him.

She remained standing with outstretched hand. "I won't give it to Federigo, if you forbid it. . . . But now I want the letter back."

"In a moment."

"What do you want to do with it? God will punish you for your wickedness if Conte Rizzi ever gets it under his eye."

Contemptuously, he shrugged his shoulders. He read the letter through again. She observed him, then sighed, and with a proud grief in her voice said: "You can do what you like. It's all the same to me. I didn't know I should ever turn traitor. It's not the first letter Lucrezia has entrusted to me; but it's the first time I've betrayed her."

She turned away and was about to enter the music room when, as she reached the door, she heard him call her back. She herself did not know in what foolish, hopeful expectation she turned round again. Perhaps he was going to thank her for having laid that letter in his hands; if so, she would fling her contempt in his face.

No, he was thinking of other things. She was almost startled at his power of concentration, his readiness to act boldly and quickly. She waited, a passive tool in his hands.

"Babetta, does Federigo know her handwriting?"

"How should he know it?" she replied, after a moment's thought.

"In that case, you must hand him the letter I shall give you."

She nodded, and, as he hurried away, she rejoined the others.

After the hot August day the calm of night descended heavily on the massive home of the Gallis. The faithful Giambattista had wheeled the old lady to her bedroom, and now before helping Rosalina to carry her to bed he was making his rounds through the corridors and rooms, as he had done every evening these last twenty years. He locked doors, snuffed out the last candles, slowly drank a few mouthfuls from a forgotten wine bottle, wearily recapitulating in his mind all that would have to be done again to-morrow morning. . . .

The podesta had retired to bed early that evening, wearied by his nerve-wracking troubles. His wife was then still sitting in the music room with Maestro Angelini. Her fine eyes were swollen with tears when she finally slipped over her arm the little basket, in which she had long since folded away her embroidery, and got up from her chair. Immediately Maestro Angelini got up also, and pressed a long kiss upon the hand she offered him at parting.

She closed her eyes. "Give me time. . . . Let me decide to-morrow. I still want to think it over. To-morrow I shall . . ." she murmured.

Silently he bowed his head. When she had gone, he sank back again into his chair. A long shadow glided in noiselessly. With a start, Maestro Angelini turned his head: it was Giambattista.

"What are you doing here?" the music master demanded. "Extinguishing the candles? You scamp! Can't you see I'm still here?"

Giambattista did not deign to reply. Moving away with a shrug of the shoulders, he stayed near the door long enough to take a pinch of snuff.

Maestro Angelini, roused from his reverie, extinguished the candles himself, all except one which he took to light his way up the stairs.

On the second floor, Amadore heard him go by, and hastily slipped behind his bed the portfolio of erotic prints he had secretly taken from the library. The dancing lesson had greatly excited him again. Amadore did not dare to be so free with the girls as were the other boys. He was not sure, either, whether he was in love with any of them. He was afraid to look at them closely. But when he was alone, afterwards, he conjured them up before his mind one after the other, and tried to imagine them undressed. . . .

Now all in the great house were asleep.

Giambattista was dreaming his pet dream: that old Signora Galli had died and left him an annuity of a hundred scudi.

Meanwhile, the prospective donor of the annuity lay panting in a nightmare. She saw herself lying dead upon her bed, her Siena relatives standing around her, the dead as well as the living. Even her first husband was present: he relit a candle that had been blown out by the draught — he was always attentive. Yes; and then they departed. She could still hear their distant voices. She was lying alone waiting to be coffined. But actually she was not dead yet. Otherwise, she could not have heard what they were saying round her in the room. One of them came back on tiptoe as if afraid she might hear him, so noiselessly did he slip up to her. She noticed his entry only by the flicker of the candles. Now he was bending over her. She could see nothing through her closed eyelids; but it was her son. It could be only Giacomo. He had come at the instigation of his wife, to rob her of her jewels. He hesitated a moment, then he quickly set to work. Carefully he slipped the bracelets from her wrists, unfastened a neck chain . . . He was not quick enough for his liking. Afraid of being trapped, he tore the earrings from her ears. Her rings stuck behind her knuckles that were swollen with gout, and he seized the knife that his wife had handed to him for the purpose — Oh, the pain! the pain! She noticed how bewildered he was as he stared at the blood from her ears and her mutilated hands. "Giacomo! My son!" Giacomo did not hear her muffled cry. A soothing sleep had at last liberated him from his official preoccupations.

His wife lay awake in the adjoining room, staring with wide-open eyes at the canopy of her bed. Would she be able to see to embroider tomorrow? But she was used to lying awake, crying. Every night she lay thus, quite still, so as not to waken her husband by the creaking of her bedstead. Her husband: a stranger, who on rare occasions slipped into her room in the middle of the night and, without a tender word or so much as a request, without ever respecting her weariness, thrust upon her the love he withheld during the day. Next day, he seemed to have no recollection that anything had happened. Perhaps he felt ashamed: to the outside world, he always tried to give the impression that he lived quite apart from his wife. She herself did not understand how she could bear the ignominy of their life together. She had never dared lock her door against him; moreover, she knew she would never have the courage to follow that other man who possessed her heart forever. She was mortally afraid of a decision, an act, and the commotion that would result from it. She felt a deep aversion to scenes, reproaches, and scandal. She belonged to the regions of quietness, to slow, dragging grief overshadowed by the dream of an unattainable happiness. She would choose to go on living here, and to die when her love killed her. Oh, she knew exactly what she must do — so long as *he* was not in the room and speaking to her. She was so terribly afraid of his words. Why had he not remained silent? If she had any grievance against him, it was that. Was it not enough that he should feel his power over her poor heart?

Maestro Angelini stripped his silk hose from his thin, hairy calves and hung his clothes, with his usual care, over two chairs. For sixteen years, Maestro Angelini had reproached himself before going to bed — for sitting here in Todi instead of at the French court; because his courage had failed him, because he had always refrained from declaring himself to the woman who was only waiting for him to speak the word. . . . Now, he had spoken. She had not said either "yea" or "nay"; but her hesitation, her lack of confidence in him, was sufficient to convince him that he was not the man to turn his words into deeds. He did not think the less of himself for that. Action came easily to the puny and the simpleminded. To dream had always been the hallmark of the great. While Signora Galli was still considering what she must do, Maestro Angelini made the consoling discovery that the longing for happiness must always be finer than happiness itself. Music, all music, was only a longing; and what was he if not the embodiment of music? It was predestined that the woman he loved should have bound him to Todi. Maestro Angelini had ceased to be unhappy. He knew that she, Leonilda, was thinking of him at that moment. For sixteen years he had been jealous of her husband, to whom her body belonged; but what was the body when the soul had fled? Maestro Angelini heard a melody and a countermelody. His violin was lying downstairs in the music room. To-morrow he would . . .

As his thoughts wandered to the next morning, he thought that of course Rosalina would be late again in coming to do his hair. That accursed staff, and that villain of a Giambattista who wanted to snuff the candles while he was still sitting in the room! Giambattista thought he knew something — otherwise he would not have behaved in such scoundrelly fashion. Giambattista thought he had got down to the truth — the coarse, gross truth of a lackey. . . .

A time would come, however, when things here would be too much for Maestro Angelini. A time would come when the old courage for adventure would rise up in him again; and anyone who was not prepared to follow him would have to look on from a distance and see Maestro Angelini — the greatest musician of his time, buried for years in a provincial Italian hole — giving concerts at the court of the king of France. As in a vision, he saw the platform in one of the state rooms: breathless silence — gleaming glances from superbly arrayed women — all the nobles of the court — light, light from a thousand candles. Or was it, perhaps, the other light for which he sometimes longed, the light of approaching death? If that were so — then it would be well, also. Perhaps dying, dying longingly, was really to hear the finest music of all. Would purgatory, heaven, and hell open without music?

With a childishly happy smile about his thin lips, Maestro Angelini dozed off.

There was a creaking in the old palace. It might have been rats in the loft, or one of the oak beams. . . . But no, there was a creaking again, and slowly a door opened. The light of a candle gleamed in the corridor. Suddenly a girl in night attire hurried towards the stairs, laid down a candlestick, and fled again on felt slippers. The door closed behind her, but in the corridor the light of the candle she had left behind continued burning. The draught that blew continually up the well of the staircase brushed the flame. Shadows flickered against the wall.

In the bedroom of the two young nieces from Siena, two white figures were moving stealthily. The taller was hastily setting the little table.

"Babetta — the wine! You're just running backwards and forwards. The chicken is still under the bed — Oh no, it's here!"

But she was still a little addleheaded herself, was Lucrezia, and rendered more so by her desire to show her younger sister how one took command of an adventure like this.

At that moment, Benedetto swooped down upon the candlestick and slipped down the stairs with it. At the same moment, a closet door below was hastily shut, and instantly the key was turned in the lock.

Silence.

A slight noise in the closet betrayed a nervous movement inside. Then a muffled voice: "Who's turned the key? Open! Is that you, Babetta? Lucrezia?"

Benedetto unfolded a sheet of paper, and holding it at the height of the keyhole allowed the light of the candle to shine upon it. "Read!"

Somebody was panting in the closet. Glancing coolly into the dark well of the staircase, Benedetto waited pitilessly on the outer side of the closet door, until he heard the stammering words: "But I burned the letter!"

"You burned the copy!"

With a coarse oath, Federigo tried to rise above the situation, mocking himself and his fate. "Convey my thanks to Babetta for what she has done," he begged; and then, "Are you going to leave me here the whole night?"

"If you keep quiet, I'll free you before daylight."

"What is there to prevent my shouting? I didn't write that letter."

"Shout, if you like — and be the laughingstock of the servants when they find you."

Benedetto waited a moment longer, until Federigo sank down apathetically on the floor of the closet. Only then did he take a deep breath and venture to go to knock at the door of the girls' room. Babetta opened, and he entered.

Lucrezia, behind the table that was laid ready, went as white as a sheet.

An insane satisfaction filled Benedetto when he saw Lucrezia's face transfixed with anxiety. Wild triumph in his dark, gleaming eyes, he met her glance — and then observed how anger and indignation took the place of anxiety. Her mouth showed decision: she went up to him and showed him the door, tried to overawe him with her pride. But he flashed out her letter, and spread it open above his head. She had not expected that. She uttered a muffled cry, and tried to seize the letter — but he hid it behind his back.

Lucrezia gave up the struggle, and turned in despair towards Babetta. "But you said you'd given the letter to . . ."

Babetta, staring towards Benedetto, nodded slowly.

"Then Federigo has allowed himself to be tricked out of it," declared Lucrezia, bursting into suppressed, sarcastic laughter. "Oh God! what have I done? How could I have been so mad? I who am engaged — who was to marry next year. It was only for the fun of it that I was letting him come here. He would have been allowed to have supper with us, and then we should have had a good laugh at him. The coxcomb, imagining himself a student already! Surely I can amuse myself so long as it's innocent? But who's going to believe that if they read that letter?"

She threw herself on the bed, and burst into sobs, burying her face in the pillows. When self-reproach broke through her voice, Benedetto lost his self-assurance. Hesitating, humble, he followed her with his eyes, which remained riveted on the figure outstretched on the bed in thin night attire.

She felt his glance, and reached for a coat that hung over a chair. "All right. There'll be time enough to cry," she said proudly, drying her tears. "It's just a farce. I invite a bit of a boy here, and in his place comes another, and I can't even show him the door, because he has my letter in his hands. Such scoundrels! The monkeys! But where's the other monkey? Is he coming, too?"

Benedetto shook his head. Lucrezia took her powder box and worked strenuously to restore her tearful little face.

There was silence. Mute admiration for Benedetto gave place to motherly tenderness in Babetta's heart, as he stood by the door almost ridiculously downcast after his proud entry. She went up to him and said, "Benedetto, give me the letter."

Startled, he turned his gaze upon her. Then suddenly Lucrezia put down her powder box, looking on speechless. He complied with Babetta's request. She rapidly read the letter, as she walked with it to the candelabrum. Then she slowly watched it burn in the candle flame.

"Now he's my guest," she said; and a proud, happy smile played about her lips. She looked round at Benedetto, who moved slowly from the door towards them and rested both hands on the back of the chair.

"Come and join us, Lucrezia," said Babetta coaxingly. "Now all is well."

Lucrezia sat on the side of the bed, balancing one of her little red mules on her foot. She contented herself with looking on, trying to understand the situation.

"Babetta, ask him why Federigo hasn't come — if Federigo won't give it all away."

Benedetto produced a key from his pocket and laid it down in front of him on the table. "Federigo is still in the closet. I've locked him up."

As if bitten by an adder, Lucrezia jumped up. "Locked up in the closet? And suppose he begins to shout, the ass?"

"He won't shout — and he won't say a word afterwards, either. He would make himself ridiculous."

Babetta nodded, pouring vinegar over the salad. "Come along too, Lucrezia. He's settled everything all right. He's not the naughty boy you thought him."

When Lucrezia neither moved nor answered, Babetta pushed the key towards her. "Here you are. Let Federigo out if you like, and let him come too."

A little mocking laughter was Lucrezia's only reply. Suddenly she jumped up from the side of the bed and sat down at the table. Babetta, well satisfied, poured out the wine.

Babetta played hostess. Her tongue was not still a moment. "Lucrezia, be a little sociable too. If you want to be angry with somebody, be angry with me, for it was I who let Benedetto see the letter. Yes: call me a traitor if you like. I didn't want to do it at all, Lucrezia — I swear. I intended to give the letter to Federigo, just as you told me. And then suddenly I gave it all the same to . . . I couldn't help myself. I'm so in love with him, Lucrezia. He won't have anything to do with me. There's someone else in his head. It doesn't matter. . . . To-night I don't care, any more. He gave the letter back to *me*, anyhow, when I asked him. Oh, Lucrezia — if you only knew how things are. This whole year I'd been thinking of him, in Siena. . . . He can do what he likes with me, even kill me if he wishes. I'm not afraid of him, as you are of Conte Rizzi. You don't even love Conte Rizzi — nor Federigo, either. Otherwise you'd have got him out of the closet. And you wouldn't have noticed how ridiculous he is. . . . You wouldn't have allowed yourself to be locked up in the closet, Benedetto. If necessary, you would have come upstairs, closet and all. Wouldn't you?"

She laid her little head upon Benedetto's shoulder, trembling in her whole body. Shyly he looked at her, and, hesitating, pitying, laid his arm about her. Lucrezia laughed. Quickly he turned towards her, let go of Babetta again, groped for his glass of wine, and emptied it at one gulp.

Babetta poured him out another.

"You're getting on, I do believe," mocked Lucrezia, amazed. "Only a year ago you were playing with dolls!"

"Oh, a year ago!" cried Babetta, lightheartedly. "A year ago I used to cry at what you said about Baldassare." And she whispered to Benedetto the story of her pet doll, a chocolate-brown Moor, whom she always took to bed with her. "And then Lucrezia said, 'When you're grown up, you'll get nothing but little Moors for children.'"

Vague and restless, Babetta caressed her white downy forearm. Then she laughed. She drank out of Benedetto's glass, and then handed it back to him. Dazed, he brought it to his lips, his eyes riveted upon Lucrezia, who at last rewarded his hungry gaze with playful coquettishness.

Babetta suddenly remembered something, and began to tap Benedetto's pockets. "The candles! Have you brought the candles?"

"He's deliberately forgotten them," suggested Lucrezia.

"Why deliberately?" inquired Babetta, childishly.

Benedetto flushed, and promised: "I'll bring them."

"Where? From the rooms downstairs?"

"Federigo has candles on him," said Benedetto, thinking out loud; and Lucrezia, immediately encouraging, said, "Yes, ask him for them."

"No — you stay here," cried Babetta, excitedly. "I won't have you going to him. When the candles are burned out, we'll let in the moon to light us."

"We could do that, you little fool — if the moon hadn't set long ago."

"I'm not a 'little fool.' When the candles are burned out, and it's dark — then I know a little game." Excitedly Babetta clapped her hands, and laughed.

Lucrezia said nothing more. Benedetto gave her a quick, shy look: it was difficult to know what was in her mind. He could eat nothing — could only drink wine. Lucrezia, visibly unmoved by Federigo's imprisonment there under the stair, began to dismember her chicken with quiet bejeweled fingers.

She said no more about fetching candles. A moment ago, she had been pleased at the idea that he should go and ask Federigo for his — he had noticed that. Babetta was talking — oh, he did not know what about; he was not listening. In almost unbearable suspense, he was waiting for what would happen when the candles had burned out.

He laid down his watch on the table. He heard himself saying that he wanted to know, for the fun of the thing, how long the candles would still burn. Did Lucrezia notice what a handsome watch he had? Suddenly, when Babetta could not see, with unbelievable temerity he pressed Lucrezia's hand, thus disturbing her as she was eating with provoking composure. Silently she freed her hand, looking at him with astonishment and mockery. At the same time, she was pleased to give him a happy, high-spirited look that conveyed a promise. Oh, Lucrezia knew precisely the effect of that glance of hers. She had recently practised it several times before the looking glass.

The whole room began to turn round Benedetto. He began to tell a foolish story of which he himself did not know the end. It made Babetta laugh gently. Lucrezia looked up, matter-of-fact and amused. Benedetto gave her a burning glance.

The first candle guttered in its socket. Then the struggling flame died away. Babetta uttered a faint little cry.

Did she utter a sound? Perhaps her mouth was only open with fright. There was a bellowing below. It was the wild, anxious bellowing of one whose nerves had given way. Benedetto got up, very pale. Superficially calm, he picked up his watch and put it away. Then he made a passionate movement towards Lucrezia, who evaded him. Babetta flung herself upon his neck, but he did not notice her. As he stared at Lucrezia, his eyes filled with tears. Then he freed himself, and left the room.

"Benedetto!" cried Babetta, plaintively, after him.

As soon as he had gone, Lucrezia flew to the door and bolted it. "Quick!

everything from the table! Out with the candles!" Babetta picked up a dish obediently, and ran about aimlessly with it, crying the while, until Lucrezia took it from her and pushed it under the bed.

In the passage Benedetto fell over old Giambattista, and, before he could be recognized, dashed the candle from his hands.

"Thieves! Murderers!" cried Giambattista, while dull roars continued to come from the closet.

The stately mansion started up from its heavy slumbers. While the podesta, jumping out of bed, leaned desperately from his bedroom window trying to raise the alarm throughout the city, Maestro Angelini, his night-cap over his spectrally thin face and a long rusty sword in his hand, set forth to meet the danger — and delivered his first attack upon Giambattista, whom he would have transfixed if that faithful old servant had not still been crawling about the ground in search of the candle that had rolled away.

"*Sangue di Pancrazio* — is that you, Giambattista?"

"At your service, Signore," moaned Giambattista, submissively polite.

Shrieking maidservants, cursing menservants, candles everywhere. The danger crumbled before so much light, and was finally localized in the closet under the stairs, where somebody appeared to have been locked up. They gathered near it and consulted together until Maestro Angelini cleared the way for himself and turned the key that stuck in the lock. Somebody fell forward into the arms of his liberator. . . . "Madonna! It's Signor Federigo!"

Yes, it was Federigo, deadly pale and covered with feverish sweat. His eyes rolled, as if he were on the point of death. He could remember nothing, not even how he had come to be in the closet. They laid him upon Amadore's bed, and bathed his face with water. Amadore himself disappeared hastily, carrying a large portfolio, in the direction of the library. The podesta, valiant once more, dispatched a messenger to Judge Rigogli's house to allay any anxiety there. As he hurried away, the messenger was informed by his fellow servants — armed with iron staves, they were searching the entire house by the light of torches — that Rosalina had fainted. Infinitely upset by this report, since he had the tenderest feelings for Rosalina, he yet dared not defy his master's order. But so great was his misery that subsequently he was quite unable to recollect whether the outer door opened of itself, or whether he had had to remove the crossbar first and unbolt it.

Yes, Rosalina had fainted. She was prone to faint when unexpected circumstances occurred. Xenia, who slept with her, advised them not to make too much fuss about her, just to let her lie. It was the best way of bringing her round quickly, and she did not suffer such a fright then from seeing so many people about her.

Xenia also had the bright thought of going to look at old Signora Galli — whom, strange to say, nobody had heard ring. And there Xenia found her, apparently stone dead, hanging with one limp hand on the bell cord. It was Xenia's turn to faint — but not before she had called attention to this new calamity by a scream so tragic that Rosalina herself could hardly have improved upon it.

That was the end of sleep for everyone. A priest came. Maestro Barberini of the piazza came. And together they contrived to bring back just enough life into old Signora Galli to enable her to receive Extreme Unction.

From dawn onwards pessimistic Pompeati, the undertaker, stood behind the door of her room, his hat under his arm, waiting discreetly for the gray bird of death to swoop down upon the roof. As, according to the provisional diagnosis of the barber surgeon, the old lady might well last the whole day, Signor Pompeati gave orders to his wife to send him some sustenance at the midday hour.

The whole house was in an uproar. Even the podesta appeared no longer to have his head upon his shoulders. The only person who remained calm was young Signora Galli. She even found time to talk with Federigo Rigogli, who had recovered his lost memory. As a result she wrote a short note to the family in Siena in which she confirmed the sad news that the express messenger must have already brought to them. She added that she preferred Lucrezia and Babetta to leave the atmosphere of a house of death, and was therefore sending them home at once, in the hope of having them as visitors again later on. She went upstairs to show the two girls, who had not dared leave their room, what she had written. The horses were harnessed while Xenia helped them pack. With tearful faces, the sisters departed — after making Xenia swear that she would never betray what she had found under the bed.

Young Signora Galli said little more after she had settled these affairs. She seemed more withdrawn into herself than ever. Was she perhaps establishing a mysterious connection between the fact that God had laid his finger upon her house on the very night when she was struggling desperately to decide whether she should follow the man she loved? She put aside her embroidery, and devoted all her time and attention to her dying mother-in-law, although the old woman had never had a good word to say for her. As a punishment for herself she refused to favor her beloved even with a look, nor would she make use of the services he offered her silently, despairingly. The one request she made, with averted face, was that he would refrain from touching a musical instrument until the old lady had died.

That evening, old Signora Galli was still alive, and next morning she was breathing a little more regularly. It would have been premature, however, to deduce from that that she would still regain consciousness. This lingering of death rather increased the suggestion of its inevitable arrival. The servants tiptoed through the corridors, and in the kitchen there was less rattling of crockery than usual. Rosalina and Xenia talked in whispers about a rumor concerning a box of jewels that was supposed to lie in the *prie-dieu* of the dying lady. It was really a good idea of that cunning old vixen to have hidden them just there, for who would dare desecrate a *prie-dieu* by stretching out a dishonest hand towards it?

Behind the bedroom door, in the dusky, draughty corridor, Signor Pompeati, hoarse and suffering from the gout, coughed discreetly, greeting young Signora Galli obsequiously as she passed, although she did not notice. Signor Pompeati had more hold on the podesta, who, when he paid his occasional enforced visits to the chamber of the dying, was made ill at ease by the mysterious link between this unbidden guest and death.

Signor Galli swore he would show the fellow the door; but he did not do so, hardly daring even to look up when Signor Pompeati addressed him with a respectful smile and recalled the day when he had enjoyed the sad privilege of burying old Signor Galli. It had been a funeral about which there had been only one opinion in the whole city; and this time again it would be no easy matter to fulfill all the expectations that had been raised. But perhaps Signor Pompeati would succeed — there would be a few extra expenses, of course, but that could be no serious objection to Signor Galli. First of all, the horses needed new cloths: the old ones were barely good enough for the burial of Signor Balsamo, the newly-rich wine merchant. The inside coffin could be ordered in the city; but for the show coffin, Signor Pompeati knew of a reliable address in Orvieto. It would, however, have to be ordered in good time. Signor Galli agreed, reluctantly. His self-assurance returned as he heard himself speak. Of course — but still one had to wait until . . .

"Oh, but that stands to reason, Signor Podesta. Patience is the first prerequisite of our calling. Something like this may last . . . Besides, God grant that the old lady recovers after all, provided I know that you won't . . . If in spite of all . . . Besides, who could serve you better, here in Todi? I have been here forty hours — but that's nothing, absolutely nothing, Signor Podesta. Yes, I should indeed much appreciate a chair, if that is not asking too much. . . ."

And the podesta personally ordered one of the servants to bring a chair for Signor Pompeati. A little later the undertaker's presence exasperated him again unspeakably: after all, the fellow could have remained away until he was summoned. Because he happened to have buried your father, he thought he had a right to the whole family including children and grandchildren. "What, he's asking for coffee? Is he mad? Giving orders in my house! Oh, well, take him some. Let's hope it won't last long now."

On the third day, old Signora Galli recovered consciousness. Maestro Barberini, putting down his twelfth visit, noted the fact with amazement.

It was quiet, quiet in the house. The old lady, who of them all would perhaps most have liked to talk, had lost her speech. Contorting her face hopelessly, she uttered only incomprehensible sounds. Enraged, she shed tears large as pearls. She was so repulsively ugly without her towering wig that Giacomo her son looked another way when he visited the sickbed for two minutes. Secretly, he admired his wife for holding out near this horror the whole day long.

Signor Pompeati had now provided himself with a large armchair. He ate what the podesta ate, but without appetite. He no longer jumped up whenever some member of the Galli family passed: he pretended instead to have dozed off.

On the fifth night Signor Pompeati was assailed by a nightmare. Old Signora Galli, bursting with health, stood before him — yes, and she had even grown younger. She was a blooming young woman with the features of Flora Balsamo, the widow whose husband he had recently buried. Roguishly, she flicked his nose with her fan as Flora was wont to do. With a stifled cry, he jumped up.

He could not fall asleep again. Deadly tired, he hungered for the soft bed of his beloved, rich in consolation: Signor Pompeati had a secret love, and he had Death to thank for it.

Everything, he had everything to thank Death for. But this time, he saw himself defrauded by his friend and breadgiver. The servants began to treat him half-mockingly, half-pityingly. Nor, when he asked for coffee, did they bring it to him with their former haste and respect. The podesta was emboldened to ask him whether he himself had not thought of consulting a doctor — he was coughing so, everybody in the house was anxious about him.

The relatives who had been summoned from Siena took their leave again. As their carriages rolled away, Signor Pompeati overheard a first halting word coming from old Signora Galli's lips. He rose from his chair and left the house, dizzy and blinded by the fierce glare of the sun outside.

For days afterwards, the armchair remained behind the door. They had all become too accustomed to it to think of removing it. When, however, old Signora Galli left her bedroom for the first time, wheeled along by her faithful Giambattista, the piece of furniture struck her eye. She spluttered and muttered something before she succeeded in bringing out the few intelligible words that constituted the order with which she opened her new era of authority in the Galli palace: —

"What's that — ch-air doing there? Take it away."

A BAT

FLUTTERS THROUGH

THE DUSK

I

OLD SIGNORA GALLI SAT LIMP AND CROOKED IN HER wheeled chair, her chin sunk on her bosom. With infinite sadness, she looked up at Benedetto, who refused to understand her.

"Now just tell me — 'twas you who locked Fe-derigo in the closet. No? Lord, what lies you can — tell." She caught her breath, and before she could continue to speak she had to free her thick, powerless tongue. Her right eye drooped permanently, with the result that Benedetto could never tell whether she was looking at his face or at the ornaments on his watch chain. "J-ust guess what was — found under the bed — of the girls. A dish with f-owl. I had it from Xenia. F-owl and wine, and more. You had your f-ill of that too, I suppose."

Benedetto looked up with ingenuous astonishment. Chicken? Wine? If Signora Galli really insisted that he had locked Federigo in the closet, he was prepared to admit the *possibility* that, as he was leaving that night, he might have found the closet half-opened and then have closed it thoughtlessly and turned the key. . . . He really could not remember. How was he to know that Federigo was hiding in the closet?

Old Signora Galli shook her head sadly. He was telling her lies, he was telling her lies. She was old, and the world lied to her, deceived her in a cowardly way. Her daughter-in-law Leonilda had looked after her as only a Sister of Charity could have done — just to find out where she had hidden her most precious jewels. Since her recovery old Signora Galli had put on all her jewels: that gave her the greatest feeling of security.

She contorted her face convulsively; tears poured down her cheeks. "Through your fault, I might have been lying in the grave! Giving me a fright like that — that night, you wretch!"

Did her reproach upset Benedetto? His eyes were fixed on her earrings — ancient, magnificent jewels he had never seen her wear before. Above her bracelets of brilliants, she had slipped others of emeralds set off with pearls. She was bejeweled like a miraculous Madonna.

Signora Galli waited for his expressions of regret; she thought she had a right to them. When she realized, however, why they were not forthcoming, a weak and happy mood came over her, and she fell suddenly silent, so as not to disturb him in his contemplation of her glittering person. Oh yes, she did not mind: she had a weakness for this boy who had almost been her death and whom she preferred a thousand times to that bumpkin of an Amadore, her grandson. The rich citizen's widow, Signora Galli, had a deep and mysterious regard for this boy who had sprung from the people. Sometimes he filled her with agitation — a beneficent, glorious agitation that sent shivers down her spine. She would still live to be a hundred, if only to be able to continue protecting him. Besides, she was inquisitive, and was afraid of missing anything. Once she was dead, she could never ferret out anything more. The most exciting things might be happening in the world, and she would not hear of them.

She laughed at him to show that she saw through him — at least, she wanted to laugh, but her mouth refused to curve and remained hanging open sadly; she saw quite well that he did not catch her meaning.

"Here — the k-ey! Bring out — the box once more," she ordered, bitterly. "Two gold little m-onkeys to hang on your watch chain. Two little m-onkeys, because you're such a — m-onkey yourself."

Even the bishop suspected him of having had a hand in the locking-up of Federigo, and when Benedetto went to visit him upon some other business, Monsignore tried to glean more precise particulars about that dreadful night in the Galli's house. It was impossible, however, for Benedetto to enlighten him further, as he himself could only speak from report. He gave it out as a supposition of his own that the little nieces from Siena had quite possibly locked the closet themselves. Perhaps they were well aware who was hidden inside.

There was little one could allege against this new and astonishing presumption. Monsignore had difficulty in curbing his smile. He could not help it if, instead of trouncing the young scamp as he probably deserved, he was a shade proud to show him off to the prelate who sat by the window, apparently reading his breviary. It was a friend of his youth, Alessandro Grioni, who had risen to be a cardinal and who, traveling through from Rome to Bologna, was spending twenty-four hours under his roof for the second time.

Well . . . Now about the matter on which he had summoned Benedetto. Monsignore had been under the impression, for some time, that Master Sabbatini's school had fulfilled its main purpose. Consequently, he had had a word with Signor Castagnoli, the old chief clerk of the municipality . . . Just incidentally, of course . . . However, he had been successful in obtaining for Benedetto the offer of a post in the secretariat, if he had any inclination that way. What did Benedetto think of that? He could thus start at once upon the serious business of life, and it might be the beginning of a brilliant career.

He looked at Benedetto. Monsignore was more excited than he was prepared to show. There was a graver tone in his voice than he had intended.

The secretariat . . . Benedetto pricked up his ears. The serious business of life . . . In his mind's eye he saw old Signor Castagnoli disappear from the stage, dead or alive. In his chair sat a still youthful clerk of the municipality, making the whole city, with its petitions and requests, dance to his piping. Benedetto nodded, all attention. Why, yes, Monsignore: Federigo, Amadore, and others of his age had already said good-by to Master Sabbatini's school. They were continuing their studies elsewhere; but Benedetto certainly thought it more attractive to distinguish himself by his zeal and industry in the Todi secretariat and thus earn Signor Castagnoli's highest praises.

Well: they could talk about it again later. That was all Monsignore wanted to know for the moment. "Tell them at home, and ask your parents what they think. Perhaps I can have a word with one of them to-morrow."

"Without a doubt, Monsignore."

After Benedetto had gone, he became the topic of conversation of the two ecclesiastics. Why should the bishop not pour out his heart to an old friend of his youth?

"Alessandro, forty years ago you were already a judge of men; what do you think of the boy? I shall not conceal from you that I have a weakness for him. I took his education in hand — circumstances led me to do so. But why should I trouble you about that? Taken all in all, I haven't regretted it yet. That he's a young devil, you've seen. But at the same time, there's a native nobility about him. You can see that, can't you?"

The other prelate merely gave his former fellow student an inquiring look, while the bishop, carried away on the stream of his own words, no longer troubled to conceal his passionate interest in Benedetto.

"Alessandro — I sent him to school. I've given him lessons myself. It's a pity I did not make him play to you, for he has music in his blood, the rogue. You should hear him play a church organ — that's his latest. How did he acquire it? I gave him some instruction on the harpsichord, so far as I was able, and later he fell into the hands of a stray musician who plays the lute and other stringed instruments like a master; but a lute is not a church organ."

"And for all these reasons you're getting him placed on the secretariat?"

Monsignore looked up. "Yes. What am I to do? What do you think of Todi? Is there room here for a musician? The churches take a brother or a friar to play the organ, to save an organist's wages. And then by accident this came from the secretariat. It's perhaps the best that Todi has to offer him. If he doesn't throw away his own chances, he can succeed the old clerk; then he'll be one of the bigwigs here. You saw how he jumped at it; and in his spare time he can still . . ."

There was a moment's silence. The other there by the window appeared nonplussed by his friend's hesitation.

"Giambattista," he said, "if the boy is as you describe him, and as his penetrating eyes suggest he is — then you're doing him an injustice."

"I? Doing him an injustice?"

"And you know it. Or have you forgotten the world outside Todi? Send him to Rome, to Venice, to a university town, to a musical academy — anywhere where he can spread his wings. What can you expect from the secretariat of Todi?"

The bishop looked worried. "I tell you I myself am not satisfied with this solution, but I don't know of a better one. I can't send him away . . . You may take it that I have already made an attempt in that direction. It's as well, too, that the boy should not entirely escape my supervision for the moment."

"Was it under your supervision that he carried out his prank in the Galli palace?" inquired the cardinal.

At any other time, Monsignore would have smiled at this question, but he was not in the right mood to-day. Somewhat irritably, he said: "Don't let's talk about it any more, Alessandro. I'll think it over again . . . There are difficulties." And then, with more fire, "I shall see what can be done, because you're quite right, of course."

The prelate by the window nodded his intellectual head gently, and continued to observe the bishop with a vague concern and a touch of irony.

"When you have the opportunity, write and tell me what you decide, Giambattista. If you should think of sending the boy to Rome or to

Bologna, you can rely upon my keeping an eye on him. Yes, naturally I can't do that as well as you. But, seriously, there's something in the young devil that attracts me. He puts me in mind of you, in the days when we drove the old Jesuit fathers of the seminary to despair." Gliding lightly over this insinuation, he continued: "Yes, and here you are — stuck; you for whom we all predicted the red robe. How is it possible? I hope His Holiness will keep his promise, and won't forget you altogether. The best thing would be, of course, if you came in person and showed yourself — you're a man after Lambertini's heart. You're of the same stamp. Only he was more on the *qui vive*, and got as far as the Holy See. I say, Giambattista — when are you going to ride again with your four-in-hand through the Porta Flaminia? What has happened to your horses — you once cared more for them than for your best friends. Wait! You must guess who has the finest four-in-hand in Rome these days."

"Who?" inquired Monsignore, raising his head as from a dream.

"Guess, I said. He's no friend of yours."

"What, not Boiardi?"

"Yes, Cardinal Boiardi!"

"*Per Bacco!*"

The other could not help laughing. "Well, I'm pleased that can still exasperate you. I hadn't dared count upon that any longer. Giambattista — just tell an old school friend: what has happened to you?"

II

From Siena, Benedetto received a perfumed pink epistle and a blue. The one was an unrestrained little letter from a despairing Babetta, who sent at the same time a richly embroidered handkerchief. The writer scoffed at her aunt, young Signora Galli; scoffed at the members of the family, who were full of annoyance at having made a fruitless journey for a funeral that had not taken place. She scoffed at herself and at him, for whose absence her heart was bleeding, and who she foresaw would pass over her passionate scribble to devote himself to Lucrezia's communication. This proved to be the letter of a well-brought-up young lady to a gentleman, very reserved and amusing, and adorned with many names from Greek mythology.

He decided to reply to Lucrezia at the secret address she had given him, and to allude in passing to the important position he had just come to occupy on the Todi secretariat. School lay far behind him. To demonstrate to Lucrezia how little the university could have taught him, he decided in his reply to include the names of all the mythological gods and demigods she had omitted. As he was maturing this plan, he slowly became aware of the fact that for the last few days tender feelings had awakened in him for Beatrice, the young daughter of Balsamo the deceased wine-merchant. As he reread Lucrezia's letter it suddenly seemed empty and futile compared with the soulful look in Beatrice's eyes. Lucrezia's invitation to Federigo Rigogli came back to his mind: it had been couched in the same style. She was growing dim in his memory. He could hardly imagine her to be more beautiful and desirable than Beatrice Balsamo. She could marry her aristocratic lawyer there in Siena in peace; Benedetto would not make things difficult for her. He bore Babetta no ill will. On second thoughts, he decided that Babetta's letter was perhaps the nicer: a pity he had torn it up. Ah well, he still had her handkerchief.

Beatrice Balsamo was a quiet, modest girl of thirteen. Her heavy mourning intensified her comely young gravity. She attended Mass faithfully, and Benedetto did the same. By the entrance of the cathedral, he waited for her, to hand her the holy water — a Christian service she could not very well refuse. In her turn she handed it on to her heavily veiled mother, Balsamo's youthful widow. During Mass he sat close behind her, so as to keep her in sight. Why was he not one of the young priests sitting there in the choir? It was said that girls and women looked favorably upon Bordoni, the young priest with the pale face . . . Benedetto glanced at him sharply. He trusted nobody, nobody — not even the priest in the confessional.

For some time he had been allowed to play the organ between the services in the church of San Jacopo. He experienced profound satisfaction in learning to subject this new instrument and to hear its heavy drone rolling through the arched roof. He often practised in the afternoons, until the bells rang for vespers, when he had to hand over his place to Geronimo, the lay brother, who was none too pleased at all the talk in the city about the young volunteer organist. . . .

Yes, they all came to San Jacopo's, all came to hear him play. Or so thought Benedetto. All except her, the one whose form moved before his eyes as his hand ran over the keys. She was not among the congregation in the little church. Neither did she show him, in any other way, that she had observed his homage and was honored and affected by it. For a week he had followed her wherever he could, always hoping that the heavily veiled figure of the widow would move away for a moment so that he could ask Beatrice whether it was her wish that he should be consumed with fruitless love. At last, one morning in the cathedral, she allowed her mother to precede her by a few steps, and when he slipped up to her side, immediately she pressed a note into his hand, and with her innocent

anxious eyes implored him to go away. He obeyed, more dead than alive.
Behind a massive pillar he read: —

Why do you always follow me everywhere? Mother will not believe
that I am not partly to blame. Why do you make me unhappy? Remember I am still in mourning.

Your

B. B.

"Why do you make me unhappy? Remember I'm still in mourning" —
He thought he would never cease to reproach himself. How was he to
reassure her? He had a comforting thought: he would make her a present
of the little golden cross Rosalina Campioni had given him to hang on his
watch chain. That would be more eloquent than words. He looked for
something to wrap it in . . . Unfortunately the only piece of paper he
could find in his pockets was the draft of his reply to Lucrezia. Ah well,
he would slip the little cross into her hand just as it was. He waited at the
exit of the cathedral for the service to end . . . Now the organist had begun the Agnus Dei . . . A moment later, the congregation rose and began
to stream outside. Beatrice was approaching, but dared not look at him.
Had her mother reprimanded her for lingering behind her as they entered?
  Benedetto cast a desperate, challenging look at the young widow.
Astonished, disturbed, she raised her veil slightly, and looked at her little
daughter's importunate courtier. He shrank back; he forgot the little cross
in his hand, he forgot Beatrice. He hurried out through one of the side
doors, and walked on blindly until he knew himself to be unobserved.
Here he tried to recover himself. He had never paid much attention to
Signora Balsamo. He was accustomed to seeing her pass with demure,
downcast eyes under her veil. For the first time he had met her glance.
Whatever there was of comeliness and nobility in Beatrice's little face she
had inherited from her mother; and she was small and insignificant compared to that comely, melancholy victim of adversity.
  The day went by as in a dream. He cogitated vague plans in his confused mind, one more audacious than the next. He thought of writing,
"Signora! Pardon this respectful missive from one who, brought to insanity by your beauty, breaks in upon the seclusion prescribed by your
mourning . . ."
  In the evening, he stood, deadly pale, near the entrance to the cathedral,
waiting for vespers to end. Behind his back he held a note for Signora
Balsamo: it had moved even himself to tears.
  The young widow was aware of his presence only at the last moment.
His whole appearance and the expression of his eyes made her feel ill at

ease. What! He had dared approach her! In sheer confusion, she took the paper he slipped into her hand. . . . Immediately afterwards, in her indignant agitation, she let it drop. Oh God! What had she done now? Her name was in it, perhaps — her unsullied name. She tried to go back, but she was pressed forward from behind: it was too late.

Benedetto had seen what happened. He had seen how she tried to retrace her steps . . . She had therefore only let the letter drop through confusion. He stood waiting. He was very calm. He knew where the letter had fallen. The throng lessened, and he saw the slip of paper lying there, soiled and trampled. He moved towards it. At that very moment, someone else noticed it and picked it up, looking round teasingly as he did so towards Benedetto; but the smile was petrified on his face, and he handed the note over without a word.

Benedetto overtook Signora Balsamo and Beatrice just before they had reached their house. They were at the moment acknowledging the courtly greeting with which Pompeati the undertaker was honoring the surviving relatives of his client. Benedetto brushed past them, engrossed as he went in reading the recaptured letter, which he then tore into fragments and scattered in the wind. He was sure that Signora Balsamo would breathe more restfully under her thick veil.

In order not to sadden his mother, he went home for the evening meal — at least, he sat with the others at table. Then, when darkness had descended over the city, he roamed through the street where the late Signor Balsamo had built himself a roomy, impressive dwelling. On the top floor a light was burning.

But were these still the stones of Todi? It was as if he were wandering through a strange city where he had never been. The city of the loved one. In a moment she would notice him pacing up and down, and appear at the window to call him in. Indoors, she would not wear a veil. She would shine in white beauty. Perhaps she would ask him to recite to her by heart the letter that, in her fear, she had let drop unread. He would see the contents reflected in her incomparably fine eyes. They would smile at him, now. Only in the street she had to cast them down demurely. She would draw him to her. . . . Already he felt the piquancy of their radiant bliss against the gloomy background of her mourning.

He continued to pace up and down before her dwelling. The street grew deserted. How much longer would he have to wait? Naturally, she could not call him to her until little Beatrice was in bed. Surely it was time she was? In many houses, all the lights had gone out.

In a moment of despair, he discovered on the other side of the street a little image of the Madonna. He knew that there was an image of the

Madonna at this place in Todi; but in the enchanted city in which he was wandering that evening, he had not noticed it before. He sank down in front of it and prayed. . . . Did he know, himself, what he was saying?

He got up again. How long had he been kneeling there? Was dawn far off? His knees had grown stiff. Shivering, looking fixedly up at the lighted window, he paced the little street up and down, up and down. Why had the light up there become so faint suddenly? Had it been like that for some time? Had she fallen asleep? Was it possible she had not noticed him?

He bent down and picked up a stone. He threw it against the lighted window. Immediately the candle was extinguished.

He hurried to the front door, laid his ear against the wood. Nothing, nothing, except the beating of his heart. Wait . . . Footsteps. He turned round, fell down again before the little image of the Madonna — he could see over his shoulder if the door were opened.

It remained closed. A few moments later, very gently, a side door opened. There was a whispered word. A figure in a wide dark cloak peered round the door, and then fled. The bolt was shot back into place.

Slowly Benedetto rose to his feet. For a moment he remained motionless, unable to understand. The figure slipped round a corner, but at the next corner Benedetto caught up to him: Signor Pompeati was no longer fleet of foot. His patient waiting in draughty corridors had given him gout, which had settled in his legs, and warming them in the beds of widows did not help. Benedetto followed close on his heels. The undertaker dared not look round, dared not return to his house — ran past it. Benedetto broke into a laugh. The fugitive bowed under it as under the lash of a whip; then he recovered himself, turned round, passed his pursuer with head erect, and groped for the lock on his door. After missing his aim several times, he found the keyhole and entered his dwelling, ridiculous and haughty.

Benedetto sauntered on aimlessly. A giddy feeling came over him. He would go home too. What was he doing out in the street?

Something flared up in him, and without his being quite aware of what he was doing, his feet carried him back to Signora Balsamo's house. To-morrow she could console herself again with her lover, if the atmosphere of burials did not put her off. . . . To-morrow Benedetto would despise her too much to look at her again; but to-night she should pay for the wound she had inflicted on his heart.

Again a stone tapped against the windowpane, behind which there was only darkness now. Oh, a light would very soon be struck. Otherwise he would bang at the front door, gently to begin with. She would not wait until the servants woke.

After the second little stone, a curtain was drawn on one side. Yes,

Signora Balsamo. Your humble servant is standing below. You will be compelled to let him in, for the sake of the good of your soul, and of your good pious name in the city.

The curtain fell again. No doubt she was slipping on some article of clothing. He tottered towards the door; he could hear soft, quick steps on the stairs . . . His triumph was even easier than he had thought. This, then, was the end of his dream. The strange realm about him was rent asunder. He was standing in Todi again, in the Vicolo dei Tre Leoni, where Balsamo the winemerchant had built a house. Balsamo's base-hearted widow was coming downstairs, panicstricken, ready — after many tears, heartbreaking entreaties, flaming reproaches — to pay for her unsullied name the price of the sweet body she had already given once that evening for nothing.

Addio, little Signora. Go back to bed and sleep without further anxiety. When you open the door, your terrible nightmare will turn out to have been a hallucination. Outside you will find only the dark, autumnal night, in which the votive lamp before the little image of the Madonna is shining peacefully.

III

It was early summer again. At the secretariat, the heat was already oppressive, even though all the shutters were closed on the sunny side, and all the windows open towards the courtyard. Flies buzzed about blindly. Benedetto felt drowsy. He took out an embroidered silk handkerchief and fanned himself with it. He seemed to have an endless supply of them: handkerchiefs with heavy lace borders, handkerchiefs finely embroidered with doves, flower baskets, and fruits, with emblems representing eternal troth and love.

For weeks Benedetto had arrived at the secretariat with the deliberate unpunctuality of a protégé, and he rarely stayed there longer than an hour: it was really too warm. In the autumn, when the summer had gone, he would, with an energy that nobody but himself would have suspected, work through the steadily growing pile of papers which lay ready to be copied, and which would have worried almost any other person — but Benedetto was as carefree as the swallows that built their nests under the dusty balconies of the city hall.

The old clerks, Cesarotti and Stefani, had children and worries. In their spare time, they copied such documents of his portion as were urgently required. Benedetto read through their work, punctiliously made the necessary corrections with pen knife and eraser, and paid them for their labors. He exacted, however, a certain ceremonial in the transaction. As he sat in his chair they brought him what they had done the previous night. Pale and tired, they stood waiting while he read through the documents and expressed approval or the contrary. They swallowed their exasperation at his boundless presumption: their interest compelled them to, just as it compelled them to maintain silence towards the chief clerk of the municipality who, during the summer, appeared at the secretariat with little more predictability than Benedetto himself, so that he rarely noticed the absence of the young copyist the bishop had thrust upon him with a hint that he should be rapidly promoted. Besides, little Matteo, the messenger, always ran like a hare to warn Benedetto whenever danger threatened, and Benedetto, repairing at once to the piazza, knocked at the chief clerk's door to get from him the latest documents.

Signor Castagnoli had a tendency to high blood pressure, and was inclined to be irritable and excited even in small matters. He complained that he had been waiting for Benedetto a whole hour. As he paced up and down the floor, he held his watch under Benedetto's nose, and asked him to read the time. He went on to say that he had not before been aware that work at the secretariat began at half-past ten. If Benedetto wanted to introduce innovations, he ought to occupy the chief clerk's chair at once. For the time being, however, it was still occupied by Signor Castagnoli, who had never cared much for patronage. If Benedetto had had more schooling than the other young copyists, he ought also to have learned how to carry out his duties in a seemly manner.

When he had said this, and a great deal more, he asked Benedetto what he had to say for himself. Benedetto drew attention to the fact that for the copying of these particular documents exceptional concentration was necessary, and he found he could work at them more easily in the library of the Galli palace than at the secretariat, where there was more talk than work, especially as Signor Castagnoli himself was not always present. There followed a silence while Signor Castagnoli read through the documents Benedetto had placed before him. When he had finished, he remarked that the originals dated back six months. Benedetto bent down and read without a qualm: " 'November 22d, 1756.' You're right: the feast day of Saint Cecelia."

Everyone in Todi knew that the still-lusty Signor Castagnoli entertained tender feelings that were by no means exclusively fatherly for Cecilia Sammaritani, an orphan niece of his whom his wife had taken into their home from pity. It was also known that he had refused her permission to attend the dancing lessons in the Palazzo Galli.

"November 22d — " repeated Signor Castagnoli, flushing scarlet. "Then it is not for nothing that complaints come pouring in. How many more documents have you lying waiting to be attended to?"

This question was less easy to answer. To begin with, Benedetto felt it necessary to point out, very modestly, the amount of care he had to bestow upon every page that he delivered. This was the more to be appreciated as in his spare time he had his musical studies; while in the evenings the podesta liked him to take a hand at his card table. Would Signor Castagnoli allow him also to submit a perhaps somewhat personal view? It seemed to him desirable that so important and exalted an institution as the City Council should not function too rapidly. The public would lose all respect for it, and would tend to run at once to the secretariat over every trifle — whereas now, fortunately, they thought twice before venturing upon such a step . . .

But Signor Castagnoli had ceased to listen to him. What had the young rascal meant when he said, "November 22d — the feast day of Saint Cecilia"? Every word he spoke had a purpose. The chief clerk, who was of somewhat portly build, broke out into a sweat, and that not only because of the heat.

Barely an hour later, earlier even than Signor Castagnoli, Benedetto turned his back upon the secretariat. He loitered a moment on the steps of the building, resting his eyes quietly on the piazza: those within must not be allowed to get it into their heads that he was going off by stealth . . .

Then he descended the steps, listening complacently in the still summer morning to the discreet jingling of the new ornaments on his coat. He bowed to a young lady who was passing by on the other side of the piazza. She did not return his greeting. She tried to look primly before her, as he had expected she would. She was still angry with him, Mattei the baker's little Armalina. *Disgraziata!* If in the overcrowded church she had not chosen to faint just into *his* arms, there would never have been anything between them. He had not remained faithful to her, but she should have been consoled by the fact that he had remained no more faithful to Giacomina. Oh, he still had a feeling for Giacomina — and she deserved it: for his sake she had ignored the sermons of her father-confessor, and even refused the Holy Communion, although she was pious as a nun. If he should ever fall upon evil days, perhaps he would seek consolation with her sooner than with Brigida, the new queen of his heart. Brigida could be allowed to see him only triumphant. Brigida! To her he could remain faithful to the end of his days, for she was the prettiest, shrewdest, most frolicsome girl in Todi. She should have the ring of which she had dreamed. He would like to array her in all the jewels of old Signora Galli. She ought to glimmer like the starry heavens. A ring such as she desired cost fifty scudi — he had inquired at the goldsmith's. Old Signora Galli would have to give him the money. Brigida could get anything, anything out of him. Fortunately, she liked receiving presents. If she had not, he would still have thrust jewels upon her. If only he could hang that old vixen's magnificent earrings on Brigida's ears . . .

He entered the shop of Maestro Pallanza, the new barber. It was on the shady side of the piazza, and, with the help of the boy who waved a fan, its atmosphere was just tolerable. Coffee and chocolate could be had, and people met there to exchange gossip. At his own express wish, Pallanza himself always curled Benedetto's hair. Pallanza had to renew the permit of his barber's shop every year, as it was next door to the city hall, and there was talk at times of building a new record office. Benedetto saw to it that this question of a permit received prompt attention — hence Maestro Pallanza's pleasure at seeing him enter. Nor would he ever accept payment, since a person of Benedetto's presence and importance was an advertisement for his business.

Giannino, the son of Simone and Annina Cerio, brought forward a chair for him. He sat down, and, while the master was still busy with Bordoni the cloth merchant, he let his eyes wander over the piazza, observing the girls hurrying to Mass.

It was a long time since, at that hour, he had stood with a trembling heart near the holy water stoup, waiting for little Beatrice Balsamo and her mother, the mourning widow. That lady had given him more than one imploring look, begging him not to betray her — poor thing.

What! Who was that with Marianna Gentili? But what did it matter? Benedetto had finished with her. She was dead for him. He wished her well of her new conquest.

The full moon of Maestro Pallanza's face, wearing his usual entranced smile, bent over him.

"At your service, Signorino Benedetto."

Benedetto returned the smile, and surrendered with serene closed eyes to Maestro Pallanza's loving and clever treatment.

Since he had joined the secretariat, his lessons with Monsignore had been neglected. It was partly Benedetto's fault: he had discovered that he already knew enough to intimidate everyone he met. And partly it was the fault of Monsignore, whose time was taken up more and more by renewed correspondence with the Vatican and with former friends in Rome by whom he had thought himself forgotten.

On one occasion, looking at him dubiously and a little mysteriously, the bishop suddenly asked Benedetto whether he was satisfied. Benedetto glanced up, astonished and all attention, waiting for what was to come. Monsignore, with concealed agitation in his voice, asked him whether he ever felt a desire to pursue his studies, like most of his comrades at school, and whether he would not like to have a good look at the wide world outside of Todi?

The bishop's words awakened a strange echo in Benedetto. Involuntarily, his thoughts flew to his mother. The wide world outside of Todi? For a moment his own world seemed shattered: the glory in which he felt himself enveloped threatened to grow dim — the glory of going to the secretariat, of having his head curled by Maestro Pallanza, of playing the organ in San Jacopo's, of making Brigida a present of a ring worth fifty scudi . . . Fear of losing all this, and perhaps another and vaguer fear to which he could give no name, made him recover himself quickly, and, to Monsignore's almost painful surprise, express doubts as to whether he could easily meet with such good opportunities elsewhere — he felt he was already on the high road to achieve rank and consideration, and thus to fulfill Monsignore's expectations for him. . . .

He also played less with Maestro Angelini, and, as it happened, this was not entirely his fault either. Ever since that night of misfortune when old Signora Galli had nearly died, Maestro Angelini had been strangely abstracted; and there was a strange oppressiveness over the whole Galli house now that Amadore had departed to college and it was no longer visited by girls and boys. Young Signora Galli did not appear in the music room, on the rare occasions when master and pupil played together, nor was she there during all the hours that Maestro Angelini stood alone playing his violin. She had withdrawn to her boudoir, and spent her days in prayer and the writing of letters. Letter after letter went from the house to the abbess of Saint Clare; and very promptly a nun came back with a reply. . . . It was whispered in the city that young Signora Galli was bent upon retiring to the convent in order to work and pray with the sisters. Her husband was supposed to have given his consent already. What a blow for the podesta! The rich also had their troubles.

Benedetto met her but seldom. Nor did he dare to intrude on Maestro Angelini when, through the half-open door of the music room, he caught sight of his long thin silhouette, violin under chin. He stood in silence in the corridor, listening to the soft languorous playing, until he was disturbed by the approaching footsteps of the podesta. Signor Galli, ever since he had been unsuccessful in bringing about the resignations of some of the obstinate members of the Council, had stayed away from the city hall as a protest and, like a soul in pain, wandered about his own house, where the playing of the music master whom Leonilda had once engaged for the instruction of their son vouchsafed him an occasional moment of oblivion. Benedetto got out of his way in time. He only wanted to speak to the old lady, who must give him a hundred scudi for a gold chain and pendant. . . . Oh, she would not refuse him. She would only want to know on what he thought of spending the money. Any lie would be good enough, provided it were connected with a woman or girl. She turned up her nose contemptuously at any other explanation. With self-mockery, suppressing all the feelings of unpleasantness that ever and again came over him on such occasions, he invented a string of fantastic lies for her benefit, in which he described himself as having become involved in gallant adventures with notable ladies of Todi. She believed him greedily. Alas! She had barely heard his tales when they were already forgotten. Then she wanted to hear them all over again. She was like a barrel without a bottom: Benedetto could throw into it anything he liked, and she was prepared to pay him in return fifty scudi, a hundred scudi. She had ceased to go out of the house, and she was getting more and more fantastic ideas about the world outside. It was unbelievable that she should still be alive; but she was, and she made very intimate confessions to Benedetto. She wanted to graft on to him her worldly experience and philosophy, the fruits of a long sojourn upon earth. Before everything else, she wanted to convince him of the universal corruption of women: there was not one who might not be willing at any time to deceive her lawful spouse with a rascal like himself. He had only to go straight to the point, without any foolish misgivings, without a misplaced respect that irritated her merely to hear of it; and above all, he must come at once and tell everything to old Signora Galli. . . .

Day and night she wore her finest gems, which were to go with her to the grave. Death, after all, might overtake her in her sleep. She was now reconciled to his coming, on the understanding that he would first let her reach a hundred. She wanted to be a hundred. That was her goal. She had ceased to have any clear idea of her age. Sometimes she imagined that she was still only eighty or even seventy. Then her son had to come to her bed in the middle of the night and talk to her a long while before she was prepared to believe, on his honor, that she was nine-and-ninety. Nine-and-ninety! That was the watchword of the house. The servants had to tell her that she was ninety-nine, and would be a hundred next week, and that then there would be festivities — fireworks — a food distribution to the poor.

"A hundred — years. I always told — my husband, in our family we all —

reach a hundred. How — old am I then? T-ell me — you I'll believe. The others tell me — lies. They resent my — becoming a hundred. Next week, they say. Next week — they're always saying . . ."

Maestro Angelini emerged into the corridor and threw his long, skimpy arm round Benedetto, who was about to leave the house.

"Come along with me. I want to tell you something."

They went together into the music room. Nobody could hear them there.

Maestro Angelini looked round once more; and then said, unable to control his agitation: "I'm leaving here — Do you know that?" He looked at Benedetto to enjoy the expression on his face. "Yes, it had to come, some time or other. How long haven't I wanted to! I must see again the cities where I celebrated my triumphs. Go to Florence, Milan, Naples, Rome, Turin, Genoa, and ask who is Romano Angelini!"

He stared before him, perhaps wondering, himself, whether in all those cities, after nearly twenty years . . . "Just ask for the fun of the thing," he added, less certainly. Then, overcoming his hesitation, his eyes brightening up again: "I want to go farther this time, Benedetto — away over the frontiers of Italy, like Tartini, of whom they still make such a fuss and whom I would never even listen to. First I want them to set eyes on me again here in Italy, and then yonder where no mortal has ever heard of Romano Angelini. To emerge from the unknown, from the outer darkness — and then to stand in the center, in the light. . . . Do you understand what I am saying? To stand in a blaze of light. . . . No; how could you understand? Nobody knows that here, nobody. They snared me when I came here. They made life too easy for me. I was accustomed to sleeping in a carriage between one city and another. I was used to wayside inns. And here, I lived as well as the master of the house — in the early days. And later, I couldn't get away for another reason. If you have a heart, you will understand. But note this: on the very day that she goes to the convent . . ."

He shuddered. He let his head sink into his hands. Benedetto looked at him with a vague, hesitating compassion.

"Then I won't remain here either," muttered Maestro Angelini several times. "I'm still the same. I've forgotten nothing. I'm a musician by the grace of God." His voice sounded solemn. It breathed a childlike faith. "Benedetto: there is no one on the face of this earth who can play a lute, a violin as I can. You will never learn to play like that. *I* may be allowed to tell you that. Sometimes I've wished you might surpass me — in the days when I had given up the idea of leaving Todi. I was mistaken in you.

You're gifted, you attain everything you want with playful ease, but you have no *love*, and therefore no instrument will give you what it gives me. There was a time when you took to writing music because your instrument wasn't enough, and now I'm told that day after day you play the organ in San Jacopo's. You did not dare to tell me that. It's all the same to you. You would blow upon a whistle if you could give people pleasure by that. That's the way of a musical charlatan. That's how a charlatan conquers the world: by playing with what is holiest in man. I wanted to tell you that. That is my last word."

Benedetto had difficulty in speaking. He was strangely moved. Was it because of the leavetaking? That grieved him, vaguely. But he had been more deeply moved by those words about conquering the world. Yes: that was what Benedetto wanted, to conquer the world. For that purpose, was he then to make no use of his gifts? Oh, fortunately his music master was thinking of another world. . . . What was that to Benedetto? The world he wanted to conquer, by no matter what means, that world was here in Todi, where once upon a time he had been barely tolerated. Did Maestro Angelini consider *that* world so joyless and narrow?

It was indeed true that Benedetto had tried to conceal from Maestro Angelini that he played the organ in San Jacopo's. His master loved restrained chamber music for stringed instruments. Benedetto dreamed of the great organ in the cathedral, the somber booming of its lower register, the mighty blend of sounds and melodies. His desire for it was sometimes so poignant that it robbed him of sleep.

He dreamed of the cathedral, filled with the citizens of Todi, who, overcome by his playing, sank helpless upon their knees. . . .

IV

Immediately after the evening meal, he left the parental dwelling, the dark, stuffy house whose inhabitants he now scarcely knew even by sight — their names he had mostly forgotten. His mother gave him a searching look: she guessed, perhaps, what he was after. She knew him — only she. The others, who thought they knew him, — even the bishop and Maestro Angelini, — they saw him only as he wished to be seen. He could make them believe what he liked. Where his inner being was concerned, they could only grope in the dark. He barely knew himself — and that was why it was sometimes a relief that his mother knew him and appeared to wish him no different from what he was.

He knew that everything he did was a game, nothing but a game. For his own ends he played with people and their feelings as he played upon his instruments, and it pleased him when the response he drew forth was a throbbing sound of grief. In his childhood, already hate and contempt had been mingled in him. Women came to taunt his mother, and at the same time caressed his curly head; and, although he restrained himself with difficulty from biting their caressing hands, he appeared the charming little fellow they wished to see in him. They had allowed themselves to be misled, and it had dawned upon him how wonderfully ingenuous and of what good faith people were, evil as they might be.

Oh yes, with his mother he felt he had a bond. But why did she live in a house like this? Why was she the wife of a coffinmaker? He would have liked so much to show her off. He would have liked to see her richly attired, decked out in jewels. Only then would people realize how pretty she was. She was prettier than the Widow Balsamo. She was still young too. All that was needed was that someone should come along, reach out a hand to her, free her from her surroundings.

As he paced the street, he thought again about his latest game, in which he believed as every player does. He was madly in love with Brigida Molinari. He would give her his life just as readily as he would give her the gold chain worth a hundred scudi. A chain with a dying topaz in it . . .

To-morrow was the feast day of Saint Philip of Todi. But to-night already fireworks were being lit, and in the little squares lighted with lanterns music resounded. Around groups of girls sauntered the boys who had formerly been Benedetto's companions — now, like him, grown almost to manhood. As he walked rapidly by, they looked after him, half-amused, half-mocking. To-night their looking round at him irritated him; he wished he had several *sbirri* following him, blindly subject to his will, who would have seized the dozen louts he pointed out and dragged them to gaol. He wished he carried a weapon. The sword was the privilege of the nobility. A sword he could never wear . . .

His eye wandered over the girls — they had red cheeks and eyes glittering with the fun of this summer evening. Yes, they dared to laugh at him, too, now that they knew themselves to be all safe together and could rely upon his passing on and not meddling with them.

He roamed through the city. It was too early — still much too early. The streets were full of people. On the piazza, where fireworks were spluttering up above the roofs, breaking out into many-colored cascades, he discovered Beatrice Balsamo among the throng. Amadore Galli, returned from Padua for the vacation, was her escort. Amadore was more thickset than ever. His eyes had a drunken look. Foolish and complacent, he greeted Benedetto after the manner of students, and was so innocent as to call to him. Benedetto nodded airily.

A little farther on he slipped his arm through that of a young girl standing alone — Margherita, daughter of the goldsmith, whom he had met that day in her father's shop. She looked round quickly in confusion. He bent over her and whispered a piece of nonsense in her ear. While she was still looking helplessly into his eyes, a boisterous band of girls approached, followed by half a dozen boys. Benedetto, thus trapped, bore up with smiling complacency, and annoyed the oncoming cavaliers and deprived Margherita of her just-raised hopes by fluttering from one girl to another. Then, suddenly, he disappeared. The girls looked about them in surprise: he had taken none of them with him. They teased Margherita, who, with bowed head, hurried home in tears.

The streets had grown still. Smoke from the fireworks was still drifting over the city. Only in the inns jollity continued in honor of Saint Philip of Todi.

Bats hovered in the air.

From the shadow of a small court a figure emerged, stood a moment in the moonlight with raised head. From a balcony fluttered a flower. The figure bent down, kissed the flower, put it away, then hastily and noiselessly ascended the trellis supporting the vine that grew against the house of Molinari the flower merchant. A mouldering piece of wood creaked for a second . . . Already the nocturnal intruder had slipped over the side of the balcony into the tepid dusk of a room.

A girl's anxious, laughing, satisfied, excited, whispering voice — "Benedetto!"

In the eyes of Maestro Angelini, Todi might be joyless and narrow — a forgotten eerie in the Umbrian mountains. Wide are the starry heavens that span it.

V

Marietta, deadly pale, raised her head and looked penetratingly at Monsignore. Then she bowed it again, and closed her eyes to recover herself. That was why he had summoned her this evening, then. Oh, she had known that he would revert to it. She had known it nine years ago, when Master Sabbatini's little school had scarcely been mentioned. She tried to consider the words with which he had tried to console her: there were holidays, he would come home in the vacations.

"Don't think of yourself. Think of the boy, Marietta," he had said.

But he ought not to have said that. She always thought of the boy, only of him. He was the very heart that beat within her. Night after night she lay awake, waiting for him. She could not fall asleep until she heard him come in; but she concealed her anxiety from him because she did not want to disturb him in his pleasures. She was ready for every sacrifice for the good of her boy. That she could swear before God. Provided only that she could see him, to convince herself that he was healthy and cheerful and not suffering. . . .

She must answer. Monsignore was waiting. He was pale with suspense. She might have answered that it was just because she thought of her boy she did not dare to let him go. Some misfortune might befall him so easily in strange parts. Haughty and proud as he was, he would get involved in duels. Yes, that was what Marietta answered. In the colleges of the university towns there were duels among the boys. The bishop himself had told her that, once when he spoke of his own youth. If Benedetto should cast an eye upon a girl he would if necessary abduct her under the very eyes of her betrothed . . . Furthermore, he was fond of gambling . . . Oh, there were so many valid reasons behind which she could conceal the only real one: that she could not live without her boy — could not live.

Repressing his embarrassment, Monsignore interrupted her with, "Marietta — you haven't understood me. I have told you that he would be under my protection."

She stared at him. Oh, had he said that? Under his protection? In Padua — under his protection?

Monsignore's eyes wandered over the writing table. Was he afraid to look at her? With abhorrence and despair, vainly seeking consolation and salvation in the black night that was about to surround her, she followed him with her eyes: he picked up a letter. . . . Did he want to show it to her? What had she to do with his letters? She listened intently to the sound in his voice. "Marietta, I'm telling you this before anybody else has heard of it — even before I have made up my mind what I shall do. I have received a confidential communication from Rome. It depends upon me whether I am allotted a diocese in Friuli."

What was she to say to that? He himself must know what he wanted. She felt it only as a great betrayal against which she knew herself to be helpless. This was the end . . . This was the end, she thought. Suddenly she was so weak that she had not the strength to free her hand when he laid his upon it. Another moment, and her bitterness would turn to hate, because he was destroying her and because at the same time there lay in his voice a vague hunger for her admiration, admiration that it depended only upon him whether a diocese in Friuli was allotted to him. Friuli — that was Padua. Oh, yes: he would not mind that. To live half a day's journey from Venice, and at the same time take away her boy. He had contrived it very well. So well that perhaps she would not even be able to refuse him.

Monsignore felt her quick suspicion. It roused a protest in him. "It is the land of my birth," he conceded, softly, humbly. "I spent my youth there. You know, Marietta, how I have always longed to go back there. But if that should really happen now, it is not because it was of my own doing — it hasn't been a plot, as you seem to think. I was quite taken by surprise, myself — and then I thought of Padua University, and of Tartini the famous music master who gathers about him in Padua pupils from every country . . . Oh, God — what didn't go through my head! It also occurred to me that one day the boy will find himself cramped, here in Todi. Sometimes I've a fear that the whole world will be barely large enough for him; and that's why, when I received this letter, I saw in it almost the finger of destiny. Padua is a great city — he will find air there to breathe, and I should be able to keep an eye on him for a bit, and guard him from the consequences of thoughtless pranks. Marietta — can't you see God's hand in this?"

It was all so dark to Marietta's eyes, so terribly, impenetrably dark; and now he dared talk of the hand of God. No, it could not be God's will that her boy should go away from her. She could set her face against that without sinning. She would not let him go, she would not renounce him. He was still content with her here in Todi. Had he not spoken to her of his fine and glorious future in the secretariat?

But his future here would be more in jeopardy, — might even come to nothing, — once the bishop, his powerful protector, had gone. Did Monsignore not know that? Did he not know how much concealed hostility was averted from Benedetto's carefree head by his hand alone? He knew it as well as she did. But he might compel himself to forget, if she refused to surrender her boy. Stronger than everything else, in the end, would be the longing for the land of his birth that had consumed him these twenty years, stronger his desire to return to life again after his long incarceration in Todi. She felt it. All his slumbering powers had reawakened and were urging him forward. Perhaps he realized all that, himself. It was not for nothing that he was fighting, fighting to retain the boy, while the effort to control his passionate emotions made him pale and confused. If only he had had a little pity for her, she could almost have pitied him.

Had he forgotten altogether what there had been between them? Did nothing exist for him now except the child? Had he never understood that since her return she had been able to endure life only because, even when she woke up in the middle of the night and saw the world at its darkest, she still knew that among the people of Todi *he*, with whom in her uttermost need she could find a refuge, still lived? If he went away — and if his prediction came true, and Todi one day became too narrow for her boy — what then? Oh, perhaps it was not so very important, that her life should come to an end. If it came to that, probably she could find peace by thinking that only so could the life of her boy begin. She could have reassured the man opposite her on this point, if only she had felt in him just a little concern for her. But there was nothing of that — nothing. Benedetto alone was in his mind. Perhaps at that very moment Monsignore was consoling himself with the thought that in any case the boy would one day come to him in those foreign parts. If not to-day, then to-morrow.

What bitter suspicions were haunting Marietta's whirling brain? She did not express them. She was only thinking, revengeful and mean, "He shan't have Benedetto — not so long as I can prevent it."

Her long, shattering silence roused his anxiety. He tried to read her thoughts. Flushed, excited, he broke out at last with, "Do you know, Marietta, what a frightful decision you place before me? Do you realize what I'm throwing away if I don't take the opportunity that has been offered me? I've neglected my future. This is perhaps my last chance."

Nervously he shrugged his shoulders, jumped up from his chair, paced up and down, stood by the window breathing deeply.

"No, you don't understand. How could you understand?" he muttered to himself.

"You must know what weighs heaviest with you," said Marietta gently.

He was silent, did not turn round. Had he heard her? Suddenly he replied, speaking with difficulty: "What weighs with me — is — the boy."

"Isn't it the same with me?" moaned Marietta, suddenly more hopeful.

"Why yes, of course. We're agreed on that point, Marietta — that he needs protection. Not only elsewhere, but also here in Todi. Can you provide him with that?"

Open-eyed, she stared at his back. "With the help of the Holy Virgin, I should — do my best."

Hesitating, ashamed, he turned round. He was shocked by the expression on her face, came closer to her — hesitated, however, to touch her. He sat down beside her. Suddenly he bent forward, saying hoarsely, "I shall see if I . . . I shall have to think it over . . . It is not a matter that I can suddenly . . . But perhaps I'll stay, all the same."

Silently they sat together. A profound weakness overcame Marietta.

She had to fight against collapse, so strong was the reaction upon her of victory in the struggle. Suddenly she felt small and powerless again beside this tall, heavy man whose authority was supreme in Todi.

When she began to cry, he flung his arm around her. Passively she leaned against him. She felt his kiss upon her hair. It was the first moment of great tenderness between them for long years — since that moment when he had bent over the child she had come to show him.

"He is our boy, after all," she whispered.

It was the first time she had admitted it. Such a simple phrase — how mightily it gripped them both, giving them at the same time a strange peace, a release that was pure joy. He went on kissing her. She raised her face towards him. Her eyes stood full of tears. What an infinite relief was his tenderness to her! How many years was it that she had missed it, without ever daring to admit as much to herself?

"Marietta — you have always belonged to me. Only you — whatever may have happened otherwise. Why is life like this? Why can't I take you away with me? Everything would be so simple."

She turned away. The passion in his voice bred a frightful confusion in her. Away from here, from Todi — away, away! No longer to see those faces that had become repellent masks to her — masks of dislike, masks of hate, and foolish contempt, and incomprehension. No longer to have to persevere with the lie, the eternal, gnawing lie, towards her husband — the lie that he knew to be a lie, although he refused to admit it to himself, the lie that stood between her and Antonio like an unscalable wall, the lie he had willed and that had to go on, because it had become the one thing of value in his life, everything he possessed. He was too lonely. She could never leave him. First his mother had isolated him; then his wife had done the same, without wishing to. Now he leaned upon her, like a lame man upon his crutch. Were she to take away the crutch, the living body would fall. No, no — it would pursue her forever, the nightmare of that falling body from which the crutch had been taken away. She had no need to consider. She had only to imagine the terrified, helpless look of that man who had become superficially so quiet and self-possessed, who fulfilled his duties faithfully, and laid upon the table the money he earned for his wife.

"Come and see me often, Marietta," a voice meanwhile was singing in her ears. "When I see you, I always know what I want. My restlessness will go — everything that consumes and pursues me, sometimes. How pretty you are, still! I haven't always noticed."

Melancholy, ashamed, she brushed the hairs from her forehead. Oh, she was no longer a girl of sixteen, as in the days when she had lived in his house. Her features had grown harder. They bore traces of anxiety and worry, pain and despair. She was now three-and-thirty. In her still-black hair, autumn had begun to spin the first gray threads.

Did he still want her to smile at him? She could even laugh, if he really wanted her to. She smiled at him and teasingly took between her hands his heavy head with the dark, guilty eyes filled suddenly with desire — even though it was certainly not without danger.

"*Babbo:* won't Imma . . . ?"

"Imma won't come upstairs. She had to go out. God, Marietta, what are you doing to me to-day?"

VI

Evening after evening they sat, the three of them, by the light of the lamp — Marietta, Antonio, and Andrea. Marietta was at her needlework. From time to time, the two men talked to one another. When Andrea got up to go, Antonio accompanied him to the courtyard, although it was perhaps unusual for a master to bow his man from his door. Master and man? They were father and son. Father and son — thus life had determined.

Marietta gathered her needlework together and stood listening for a moment, while the clock in the tower struck ten. Then Antonio came back and began to undress in the alcove. Not a word did he say of their boy — why should he? They were both used to Benedetto's being out still at that hour.

The neighbors had found a nickname for him: *il pipistrello.* "The bat" — noiseless in his unaccountable flight at dusk.

No, Antonio did not ask about him. Perhaps he did not want to irritate her. More probably he simply did not give him a thought. It was as she had always known: apart from the bishop and her, his mother, Benedetto had nobody.

She prepared to go to bed. Slowly she undressed in an accustomed intimacy that, for her, never came to be entirely without a certain strangeness. Fortunately her husband fell asleep the moment he lay on his pillow. Slowly desire had grown dim in him these last years. She was silently thankful for that. Lying quite still, she could wait with open eyes until she heard first a gentle creaking on the stairs, and then the quiet opening of the door. Her husband was asleep: that was as it should be. He needed his night's rest after his long day's work. She was content with little sleep. In the mornings she got up even earlier than Antonio, to open the shutters and fetch water . . .

A bat was fluttering through the night. Sometimes it was as though she heard the flapping of its wings close to her — No, it was another sound.

The night belonged to her boy. The day belonged to the others.

If only he had been in the company of friends. But he was alone, always alone. He was alone, just as his mother had always been alone. His silent shadow was his sole escort, quick and noiseless as himself.

No, he had no friends, only enemies. If he should ever be in peril far away from Todi, perhaps only the women would be able to save him.

The girls and the women were on his side. She knew that, although he never spoke about it to her. She felt it when his eye rested on her for a moment. For his sake, she dressed better than she would otherwise have done, dressed better than the other women in the house — another reason for slander. She did not care, provided she knew that his eye rested upon her with pleasure, and that he had no reason to feel ashamed for his mother.

For his sake, she also wore the blood-red earrings of coral that Nana had once brought to her in the convent as a memento of her mother. She used to leave them lying in the cupboard. She would have worn more jewelry, all she had ever had — if she had not sold everything else in the days when she was feeding her child in Naples.

Who was his sweetheart to-day? By the time she thought she had guessed who it was, he had found a new one. Other boys ran after a girl in the street. On Sunday afternoons for hours on end they followed the girl of their choice about the piazza, up and down, up and down. The whole world knew of it, even before they had kissed. Benedetto arranged things differently.

He laughed on the piazza with Nina and Gina, but it was Bettina he kissed in some deserted, dark doorway, though he did not glance at her when he had met her with her little friends — and heaven alone knew how he made his rendezvous with her. He worked with his quick dark eyes; he whispered disturbing, irresistible words into their ears. Sometimes his clothes were ill-used: he had caught them on a nail somewhere. White chalk — paint from a newly painted window sill . . .

It amazed her sometimes. How old was he? How many girls had already given everything to his seventeen years? Perhaps, too, she was a trifle jealous, as mothers can be.

But stronger than everything was her pride.

Her pride was stronger even than her anxiety. She had boundless confidence in him, in his quick-wittedness, his rapid and infallible decision, his prudence. But rivals could be cunning and cruel in their suspicion and hatred. They might snatch away a ladder standing under a balcony. He might break a leg. A girl might betray him from spite, or in the confusion that comes from the first great joy.

What was Marietta to do? Could she restrain him? Did she want to? Were she to attempt it, he would circumvent her, as he circumvented the whole world. No, no: let him think that she suspected nothing, or that she thought all was well. She *did* think all was well: everything was right, everything he did. He dominated her, as he dominated his sweethearts. She was powerless against him; she could only serve him.

But a day would come when the scales would change. The world would plot against him — the slow, cumbersome world that allows itself to be tormented so long, and then raises itself with a roar. Then Monsignore would have to stand in the breach.

She stared into the darkness. Looking back, her heart beat as she thought of the cruel choice she had dared to place before Monsignore. But would it have been right for him to abandon her? Were they not bound together in the one way that can bind people to one another? They had a son . . . Having dared to utter the phrase, she repeated it again and again. It soothed her to say it. There had been a time when it had been too awful, too terrible with human sin. But, in their common concern for Benedetto, the truth had been uttered once, and it had liberated both of them. A wound within her that had been bleeding deep down for years had suddenly healed. Goodness and gentleness had prevailed: was that God's forgiveness? Two human beings, they stood suddenly before God and felt His mercy.

But there would be days when he would reproach her. Then she would crumple under the consciousness of her guilt, for in her had flowed all the guilt of all the others. That had been her fate. How strange and unfathomable was life . . .

But there he was — her boy. She knew his step on the stairs. A few long strides. The floor creaked by the door, which opened without a sound. He was crossing the room. Would he salute the Virgin? He had already reached the recess where he slept. He was undressing. He made short work of that, although he was in the habit of hanging each garment carefully over a chair. He stretched himself upon his bed — and within half a minute, he had fallen asleep.

She dozed off, herself. She had a few hours still to rest. She was at peace. She knew that danger threatened; always, always danger threatened; but for the time he was under her protection. He was near her, near her. He had come fluttering home again, her bat — *pipistrello mio* . . .

THE MELODY

OF

DISTANT THINGS

I

A SMALL COACH LEFT THE CITY GOING IN THE DIREC-
tion of the convent of Saint Clare. The coachman and groom
wore the Galli livery — gray with black facings; and inside, behind the brightly polished windows, sat Maestro Angelini and his pupil
Benedetto. A low autumn sun caressed the maize fields, the gleaming vineyards. On the steep slopes stretched the crooked, faintly blue shadows of
the olive trees.

Maestro Angelini had asked Benedetto to accompany him on his visit
to young Signora Galli, who, with her husband's consent, had retired to the
convent. There the abbess had allotted her a cell such as she had dreamed of.
Was Maestro Angelini so agitated that he was reluctant to be alone in the
coach? Apparently the previous week young Signora Galli had not received him. All the Galli servants (and therefore everyone in the city) had
learned that very same day that, deathly pale, he had immediately left
the convent.

Benedetto willingly concurred in his music master's request — for apart
from any other consideration, it was always worth while to be seen in a
coach belonging to the Galli family. Besides, he was curious to learn how
the Signora in her conventual dress would converse with her beloved
friend.

Also, he had never been in the convent.

With a thoughtful expression full of pain, Maestro Angelini stared through the coach window. The fresh air, aromatic with the scents of the fruitful country, did not rouse him.

When they were halfway on their journey he began to speak. "It's quite possible she won't receive me to-day, again. Last time she asked me not to come so often; but now a whole week has gone by. She is tired — tired. She would prefer to be reminded of nothing. It doesn't astonish me, either, that it should have come to this. Having lived with a man who never showed the least understanding of her finer nature . . . And in the winter guests till late at night, evening after evening . . . Card-playing, which she loathed . . . scandalmongering and senseless chatter, which she abominated . . . It all got to be too much for her. That's why she just embroidered, embroidered the whole day: to keep her mind off things, to give a meaning to her existence. She's a superior woman, Benedetto. Such a woman as I should have met nowhere else, wherever I might have gone. There in the convent she goes on embroidering — she can't give it up now. It must be a passion, as music is a passion. It seems that she makes superb clothes. The abbess told her she worked too much, but that of course is just adding fuel to the fire, and that the old zealot knew very well. She has weak eyes, has Leonilda. She ought to spare them; but in all convents they're stingy with the candles. I've brought some with me, although I know she'll hand them over to the abbess. I believe, Benedetto, that she wants to go blind — in order not to see this world any more. She hopes to be able to see God and heaven all the better."

He brought his large, thin hand down upon his knee. "My God, her magnificent eyes! Her fine, soulful eyes! One day she will turn them upon me without even being able to see me . . . She said they were not necessary to her to retain me in her memory. Do you understand, Benedetto, that I can't get away from here any more? I must at least talk to you about it. You're the only one with whom I can. I want to have you with me, in case she refuses to receive me again. Benedetto — what is to become of me? That house is getting intolerable to me, now that Leonilda no longer lives there. Signor Galli makes me feel very clearly that I'm quite at liberty to go. Up till now, I have not wished to notice, but sometime I shall have to take up his insults, for people without tact know no bounds to their cowardly and gross behavior. And the servants, the rabble, follow in their master's footsteps. They have a feeling, an unerring feeling, for the safe side. The authority in the house is changing. A graveyard atmosphere breathes round the old lady. Signor Galli is trying to be the master in his house, since he's been unsuccessful at the Council. . . . You can see it by the way he sits at table. Rosalina no longer comes to curl my hair — I have to go to the barber on the piazza. They don't think it necessary to warn me when the midday meal is served. They don't bother to remember any more that I dislike the highly seasoned messes that are good enough for the palate of a guzzler like Signor Galli. A day or two ago, I happened to pass the kitchen door, and there sat Franzo with my lute in his confounded paws, making it screech out something to amuse the others."

In his agitation, Maestro Angelini's face had turned gray. Tears sprang into his eyes. He bit his lip nervously.

After a while, he spoke again. "I ought to go before it gets worse. But can I leave this woman? Have I the strength to do it? Now, I should still be taken in the coach as far as Orvieto — a last well-bred attention from that boor. But if I remain much longer, I shall have to take the stagecoach. I had dreamed of another departure — a departure that would have made Signor Galli look up when he was informed of it as he sat playing cards." Maestro Angelini broke into a bitter laugh. "Ah well, what does it matter? It's too late. I know what I ought to do . . . I also know that I shan't do it. If things go too far in that house — after the death of the old lady . . . I shall see if I can't find some other roof, so long as I have money, I can . . . I've got my jewels, my watches, my snuffboxes. If a time comes when my pocket no longer allows me to dress properly, and to have my hair curled like a decent man, — when I have to go on foot like a stableboy to speak to her for a minute or two, — then I can only pray that God will speedily extinguish the light from her eyes."

He gave Benedetto a rapid glance, as if expecting an assurance that it would never come to that. The dreamy, reserved expression on Benedetto's face, however, left the matter in doubt. Maestro Angelini recovered himself a little, afraid lest he had abased himself too much.

"Money!" he said. "I've known some who have got ideas into their heads because they've inherited a great deal. With me it has always slipped through my fingers. I've never counted it . . . I haven't thought it worth while to cling to it. I've squandered it, given it away, wasted it on foolishness, because I think that is the best way to use it. I have been given jewels, — everything I wanted, — and they were proud that I was ready to accept. I used to say to her, How ridiculous it is to worry about money. But she did not dare go away with me. . . . Perhaps she was afraid to get behindhand with her embroidery." Bitter mockery throbbed through his voice. "She elected to go on embroidering, to the greater glory of God, in this abandoned little spot of old Italy."

He broke off on a shrill note. The coach stopped, and Francesco the groom, with concealed derision on his knavish face, opened the door. With lips tightly pressed, Maestro Angelini strode on stiff legs past the rogue.

He was followed by Benedetto, who looked at the groom in amused astonishment, and then suddenly gave him an unexpected kick that made him stumble backwards speechless. Maestro Angelini saw nothing of this short interlude.

An old hag opened the door, a scarecrow in the garb of a lay sister. Iron spectacles hung from her nose. Through an endless passage, the dusk of which was broken halfway by the votive lamp before the small image of Our Lady of Pain, she preceded them towards the reception room. It was a square room, shut off on one side by a grating that could be closed by green felt curtains.

Nobody. Nobody was there. The sister repeated the name that young Signora Galli had assumed in the convent, and slouched away. Whither? Her shuffling feet could be heard for an eternity. Then every sound died.

To dispel the oppressive stillness, Maestro Angelini paced vigorously round the tiled room. He stretched himself a little; his whole figure seemed younger, more triumphant. His stiff walk became more resilient.

Although they had not heard her approach, a young novice appeared on the other side of the grating. She gave Benedetto, who was unknown to her, a rapid glance of astonishment and curiosity. Then she turned towards Maestro Angelini, who, with a strangely fixed expression on his face, came and stood closer to the grating.

They conversed in whispers, but in the stillness of the room hardly a word eluded Benedetto. The Signora had given special instructions that she could speak to no one. When she was not working, she had to rest because of her eyes . . . The young novice turned her own large, dark brown eyes shyly towards Benedetto again, and this time she had difficulty in freeing them, caught as she was, suddenly, by his glance. A dark red flush that became her well spread over her cheeks. Her skin had the bloom of a young peach.

Maestro Angelini coughed and inquired whether there was really no prospect of his having a word with the Signora. Perhaps she thought the reception room was full of people and that was why she . . . It would be for only a tiny moment! Had she perhaps given special instructions in case a certain Maestro Angelini . . . ? Perhaps she had said something to the abbess herself?

The young novice, confused, did not answer at once. Then abruptly she realized that she must speak again, and parried Maestro Angelini's eager questionings with a pitiless: "No. She does not wish to see you. You may believe me. She would also prefer that you do not write to her any more. She now lives entirely among us — with us . . ."

While Maestro Angelini stared at her in silence, a nun scarcely older came in. The novice, afraid to look round, withdrew at her silent command. She fled rather than went, her shoulders raised a little. At the threshold she stumbled.

"Before you go . . ." said the nun to Maestro Angelini, while a feverish flush of unexpected hope spread over his thin, pale cheeks. "The Signora has just heard that it is you. She can't very well come, herself, and begs you not to take offense. She has asked me to hand this to you." From her wide sleeve, the nun drew a little slip of paper upon which had been strung with a needle a few threads of colored silk. "As you are here, she would really very much appreciate it if you would do an errand for her . . . Three skeins of each color, and two of this peacock blue . . . It doesn't matter if it's a little thinner, provided it isn't thicker."

Maestro Angelini looked closely at the little paper. Then folded it haughtily. "Will you inform the Signora, with the assurance of my respect, that I am always prepared to fulfill her every wish? Presumably she wishes me . . . next Wednesday at noon?"

"The Signora is really in some hurry."

"Then I shall have the privilege of bringing it to-morrow in person . . ."

The nun nodded and departed, not without giving Benedetto a suspicious glance. The two men bowed to her.

Far back in one of the passages a bell was ringing. The sound of singing reached them. "It is frightful that that organ is never tuned," said Maestro Angelini, thankful to be able to talk of something indifferent, "and that *she* should have to sing to it."

By the door, the old lay sister was waiting for them with her bunch of keys. As they followed her, down the whole length of the corridor, the sound of the little old organ, growing gradually fainter, accompanied them. They were singing to it in thin shrill voices, and the slippers of the old woman beat time.

Outside, a refreshing autumn storm was brewing. The wind was sweeping up the seared leaves. Benedetto, a curiously brooding expression in his eyes, that had become very wide-awake, again sat beside Maestro Angelini, against whom he was occasionally thrown as the coach rolled on shakily through the storm.

II

"Then it wasn't you at all?" the bishop inquired of Benedetto, who sat opposite him.

With complete unconcern, Benedetto answered, "No, Monsignore."

"The abbess tells a different story, and is prepared to swear to it. She recognized you unmistakably, when you dashed the lantern from her hand."

"Isn't the abbess half-blind, Monsignore?"

"She is shortsighted, but at that moment you were immediately in front of her."

"She must have seen a ghost."

"Benedetto, do you believe in ghosts?"

"Not I, Monsignore, but perhaps she does."

"Let us hope that is not the case — the abbess of a good Catholic convent."

"One never can tell."

Monsignore gave Benedetto a thoughtful look. Then he asked, "Now just tell me . . . How *did* you climb over that high convent wall?"

"Is the wall so high, Monsignore?"

"You're pretending that I ought to know that better than you."

"But it was you who said the wall was so high."

Monsignore gave it up. "Let us assume for a moment, Benedetto, that the wall is four yards high, and decorated at the top with broken glass. How do you think the intruder could have got over?"

Benedetto considered for a moment. "Was a ladder found anywhere?"

"If a ladder had been found, I should not submit this problem to you."

"Well . . . Perhaps a branch of one of the surrounding trees stretched out over the wall somewhere."

"That must be investigated. It would be a piece of unforgivable carelessness not to have chopped off such a dangerous branch in time." Monsignore appeared satisfied with this provisional solution, and asked: "Then you didn't leave the city last night?"

"If I had, Gaetano must have seen me. Perhaps you could ask Gaetano who went out of the gate last night, and who came in this morning . . ."

"I can't do that, very well. This business might do serious harm to the convent, and I've had to promise the abbess to hush it up as much as possible. Oh, yes — there's another small matter. One of the novices has confessed that you broke into her room while the nuns were at midnight matins."

"Then the abbess is certainly lying when she says she recognized me," maintained Benedetto, exasperated. "Everything depends upon the declaration of a young girl, who wants to let her real lover escape free. No doubt it was against her desire that I paid her this visit?"

"She is supposed never to have exchanged a word with you before."

"And the abbess believes these fairy tales?"

"I will ask her that, too," promised the bishop. "To reassure her, can I tell her at the same time where, exactly, you did spend last night? It wasn't at home in your bed, was it?"

Benedetto made a pregnant gesture. His strict duty was silence . . . The honor of a young lady . . .

"Provided you didn't again climb through a window at the house of Racioppi the winemerchant, my mind is at rest," said Monsignore, "for as it happens Racioppi also was here yesterday to complain to me about you."

"Racioppi? Why should I have climbed through a window at Racioppi's?"

As Monsignore looked at him in silence, Benedetto blenched and inquired, "Surely not for the sake of Signora Racioppi?"

"No, by the devil! Not for fat old Signora Racioppi; but for her young niece from Terni, who was staying with them."

Benedetto stared before him. "She was from Narni — but I haven't seen her. Has she perhaps also confessed that, against her wish and unknown to her, I — "

"No, she hasn't betrayed you. But on this occasion a ladder was found at a place where it had not been the previous evening."

"And that is supposed to be a proof that I . . . ?"

"Of course it isn't a proof — with you there is never any proof. But when serious suspicions arise from ten, twenty, different sides — then that is almost as good as a proof. Benedetto: you can't allow yourself everything here. You're in a small city — and, my dear boy, defying people is not without danger. Have you ever thought how this must end, some time or other?"

Discomfited, Benedetto looked up.

He had never considered the end. His only concern had been to see that nothing could be proved against him. False accusations there had always been; but calumny was one thing, and proof was another.

He threw back his head. A little roguish smile, half-triumphant, half-innocent, played about his lips. But the bishop did not allow himself to be deflected from his gravity. His brow was furrowed with anxiety. He seemed to have grown older recently — a fact that suddenly struck Benedetto, who had paid no attention to the matter before: he rarely noticed other people.

While the bishop continued speaking, in grave accents, returning once more to the affair of the convent, pointing out in general terms the seriousness of such an offense, even though it might have its amusing side for

Benedetto, and adding that the intruder escaped imprisonment solely because the convent had a good name to lose, Benedetto's thoughts had drifted away.

He was breathing the air of a winter's night. He saw himself again in the moonlight, slipping down a rope among the sleeping graves in the convent garden. Quietness all around . . . Light from some of the small grated windows of the cells. Three nights he had haunted the place, before he had finally discovered in which one he could find Cecilia, and how and when he could come upon her alone. Then the mad audacious exploit, while the nuns were gathered in the chapel for midnight matins; Cecilia's frightened face, deadly pale; her threats, his soft imploring words to set her at rest, to prevent her above all from shrieking; her tears, her soft averted face under his passionate kisses — and at last her mouth that had longed without awareness. Her terror, terror that had become an intoxicating incitement, giving a tang to the adventure, making of it one that he would never forget during all the rest of his life . . . Then suddenly, returning nuns — escape through the accursed corridors that were like a maze, corridors from which there appeared to be no exit at all. The old woman, that harpy, unafraid even of the devil, a lantern in one gnarled hand, her raised crucifix in the other . . . Her "*Apage, Satanas!*"

"Benedetto," said the bishop, "perhaps you have not the aptitude to spend your life in a little city like this. I can well believe that. But since you have declared to me, yourself, that you don't wish to go away, I must advise you to be a little more considerate of the feelings of the people among whom you have to live. We may be able to laugh about it all, but in the end we shall have to pay heavily for our laughter. Have you ever thought of the grief you must be causing your mother with your daredeviltry?"

Benedetto stared at him. Was he grieving his mother? He did not believe it. The bishop only thought that because he did not know that . . .

Because he did not know anything, anything.

On the other hand, Benedetto was not churlish: he promised to amend his sinful ways, if that would give the bishop any pleasure. Although, of course, he had never committed these sins . . .

"Monsignore," he asked as he was leaving, "what is likely to happen to the novice when you declare to the abbess that it was not I?"

"The abbess will naturally say to her that she has told a lie, and forcibly extract the truth from her."

"Ah well — let the novice have her way. Let us pretend that it was I," proposed Benedetto magnanimously. "Let us maintain that the novice did not know, and cried for help until . . ."

Monsignore took a breath. A smile spread across his somewhat weary features. "My dear boy," he said gently, "did you imagine I should tell the abbess anything else but that it was you? For it was you, wasn't it, Benedetto?"

Benedetto sighed.

"Let us settle it this way," suggested the bishop. "I shall tell the abbess that there was no proof against you, and I shall say that from now onwards I intend to keep a sharp lookout over you. And I shall tell her most emphatically to get sawn off that branch that grows over the wall."

Benedetto nodded, rather less satisfied than he wished to make himself or the bishop believe. Yes, that was all right. The branch was to be sawn off. Then the abbess could sleep in peace again. And for his own peace, it was also better. It would be impossible to scale the wall without a ladder. And how could a ladder suddenly be come by? A moment later, he thought that the one possibility would be this: to loosen a stone near the base of the wall, — during the day it could be pushed back again, so that it was not noticed, — then to throw a rope over the top of the wall, just long enough for it to drop in front of the hole where it opened at the other side. It could then be pulled through and tied to a crosspiece . . . But that would be a risky business with those sharp bits of broken glass on the top of the wall. . . .

III

Rapidly, as if it had been his daily habit, Benedetto mounted the steps of The Three Popes. Coming out of the clear spring light in which the piazza was still bathed, he could not see clearly as he entered the dingy dimness of the inn.

Luigino, leaning across the counter, looked with astonishment at the new arrival who sat down gingerly in the corner by the window.

Luigino came forward, dragging his leg, and winked as he did so at his other guests, who turned round grinning towards the window.

"With what can I serve the signore?" he asked mockingly.

Benedetto returned the stares of his fellow customers. Then, concealing his excitement with difficulty, he whispered close into Luigino's ear, "Who are those people sitting in the next room?"

The room he indicated was reserved for travelers passing through Todi who put up at The Three Popes and sometimes preferred not to mingle with the topers in the taproom.

Luigino grinned. Then he took the liberty of drawing up a chair and sitting down upon it astride, quizzing Benedetto mysteriously. Benedetto, impatient and put out by a familiarity he did not desire, would have liked to order him to stand up again — but his interest, roused and fed by the intriguing rumors that had reached him, made him tolerate Luigino's insolence. That limping fellow must render him a service.

"It is a Roman lady with her husband," said Luigino.

"Young and handsome?" inquired Benedetto.

"Old and ugly," said Luigino, disabusing him.

"What? You mean the man?"

"Yes; and you? Oh!" Luigino smacked his lips coarsely and leered at him.

Benedetto had already heard the news, but now it was confirmed: *la bella e la bestia*. That old billygoat must have a beard of gold. His coach was truly ducal; and yet he was traveling with post horses — without servants. That was strange.

"No doubt they're going on to-morrow?"

"Yes, signore."

"And have they ordered an evening meal?"

"Capon with truffles."

"Luigino — let me wait upon them." His fingers slipped a piece of silver delicately towards Luigino.

Luigino was not taken aback by the request. "Why shouldn't I afford you that little pleasure?" he asked, thoughtfully turning round and round the silver coin as if he had never seen a scudo before, and then casually slipping it into his apron pocket. He gave a little laugh and inquired, "You want me to get you some clothes too, I suppose?"

"Let me have an apron, thread stockings, and a pair of shoes."

"You shall have them, and do you know why? Because you so cleverly stole old Castagnoli's mistress from him. It gave me very special pleasure, because I happen to have a bone to pick with him."

"What did I do?"

"Do you want to deny that he chased you in his nightshirt, stick in hand? And that he stood shouting at the window, making a hellish scene? Wouldn't that alone make anybody chuckle?"

"Every word you say is news to me."

"All right, then. Let's drink together to the health of Signor Castagnoli."

"I shall be delighted to drink to the health of my superior."

When Luigino moved away, Benedetto turned round. The communicating door was ajar. Had he been alone, he could have peeped inside. He could hardly contain his desire to see her. From what he had heard, she appeared to be dressed in very good taste, in a traveling costume of blue satin twill trimmed with silver. She must be young and gay. She had mocked at the old man because he could not alight from their coach quickly. The bystanders were shocked, but Benedetto forgave her in advance. Was it her fault if greedy parents had sold her to Methuselah?

Luigino returned with a carafe of wine. As he poured it out, he said somewhat more seriously: "Look here — it's all very well, but I trust no scandal will come of it. I should never have allowed it, to anyone but you. You're not going to lose me my clients? That's understood, isn't it?"

Benedetto nodded absentmindedly . . . Blue satin twill, trimmed with silver. If he had allowed himself to be announced as a young man of good family, her jealous husband (of course he was jealous) would prevent his making their acquaintance. And would she not prefer a little masquerade?

It was a spring day — April 13th.

In a dim corner of the kitchen, upon whose dirty floor children were romping, Nana was plucking a capon. Benedetto pulled up a rickety chair, and sat down opposite her, his hands crossed. He listened, though his thoughts were far away, to the sad story that fell from her lips. He had divested himself of his lace collar and ruffles, and had bound up his hair in a black rag. He was wearing broken shoes and mended stockings. A soot mark ran along his cheek and chin.

Susanna was moving backwards and forwards in front of the large stove. Her face was tired and sallow, her dress torn and frayed. A small child pulled at her skirts, and on her arm she carried one still younger. It no longer crossed her mind to lay him down somewhere. She carried him with her into the taproom when she served a customer there. Now and again she sat down, in an infinite desire for rest. Miserably, she looked across her pots and pans towards Benedetto, who had come to play one of his pranks. She had a good mind to go in and tell the respectable old signore and his lady. If she refrained, it was because she was ashamed of her appearance, and also from fear of her husband; he was calling her — a short bark: "I say!" She sprang up from her chair.

While she pulled the feathers from the still-warm bird, Nana was saying without looking up, "That's how it goes here. He issues orders, and we all stand to attention. Vacca draws wine in the cellar, or chops wood in the yard, and Luigino has charge of the till. Now and then he stuffs his pockets full of money, and squanders the lot in a week in Orvieto with the common hussies there. Meanwhile, his wife goes on giving him children — she's got that from her mother. But how can the poor lamb stand up to him? Sometimes Vacca does stand up to him. If they should one day set fire to the roof over their heads, it wouldn't surprise me. And if it happened, I'm not sure I should trouble to get up out of my corner. Vacca wants to bring an action against him, because he's already had more than his fair share out of the inn. After all, we have right on our side. But the law? What is that? The law is always on the side of bad men. We have the law already in the house — Carlo lives with us, with his sister Susanna. And what do we get out of that? Luigino just laughs at him. He knows his own brother-in-law won't put him in gaol and abandon Susanna with her unfortunate children to Vacca's tender mercies. Oh, if Vacca got a free hand again, it would be a real spring cleaning. Perhaps he would sweep me out at the same time, and that would be awful, for I haven't a rag to my back that I could show myself in before people. . . . You might tell your mother that, too. That's why I haven't been to see her for an age. . . ."

Nana shook her gray head, and bent lower over the capon. Benedetto listened attentively to the strange confession of this old kitchen sybil, who had once been a sort of mother to his mother, and who used to give him cakes. He was inclined to a vague pity. But it was not to be expected that this evening he should steep himself in the disconsolate old woman's grief — he was too dominated by his own great expectations.

When a few minutes earlier he had gone in to inquire at what time the signore wished to have his meal served, he had glanced rapidly at the wife's profile. Somewhat bored and impatient, she sat looking out of the window across the twilit piazza. Oh, she was quite, quite different from what he had imagined. She had put on a crimson dress that gave great pallor to her complexion. . . . Probably she had made herself even paler with powder, in order to make her eyes appear darker and her mouth redder — almost a cruel red. Her lips curled haughtily upwards. But when the whole world was deriding her because she had such a husband, she naturally had to seek refuge in pride. A monster, with high shoulders and long hanging arms and hands, a repellent mouth and small evil-looking eyes with such a squint that she could never know whether he was looking at her, or at what was happening behind her . . . How rich he must be!

Surely, though, not so rich that she ever actually received him in her arms. . . .

Benedetto brought in a lighted candelabrum and placed it on the little table under the window sill where the young traveler was busy writing. She did not look up.

"When does the post to Rome leave here?" she inquired, while her small hand with its pink nails glided rapidly over the paper.

He waited a moment, deeply stirred, until the sound of her voice had died.

"To-morrow, at your service, signora."

"Then you might hand in this letter for me when you have a moment."

Silently he bowed, and began to set the table with a great air. Sunk in thought over a sentence in her letter, she looked up, and involuntarily her glance swept over him in vague astonishment. Perhaps because of his carefully tended hands . . .

Her husband was sitting by the fire that had been lit at his request, and had thrust his feet so far into the hearth that it was a mystery they were not scorched — only a devil could have borne such heat. Perhaps he was a devil, an old, dreary devil.

The young woman got up. She made for her trunk that had been placed in a corner and extracted from it some toilet article. She signified to Benedetto that he could take away her letter. When he approached the little table, he found a loose sheet of paper on it which he slipped casually into his pocket. Only a few words were scrawled upon it: —

Your hands are too fine for a servant — everything else is right.

He tried to catch her eye, but she did not look round.

Stunned, he returned to the kitchen. He gave the letter to Cesare, Susanna's eldest, who dashed away with it to the postmaster. Benedetto seized a piece of charcoal in order to give an appearance of credibility to his hands. He did not notice that Susanna's brother Carlo had come home, and, while he drew off his heavy service boots, was observing him contemptuously. Nana also looked at him, but with a smile that was like a miraculous bloom in her dreary decline. The whole town said he was a ne'er-do-well, but Nana, thinking of Luigino, knew that there were other and worse pranks than those that made Benedetto a sinner. He could even make her smile in her old age, at the prank he was about to play upon that ugly old man who had not given her a friendly word when she went in to set the fire. All things considered, she thought that Benedetto's faults were perhaps more pleasing to her than Carlo's virtues. A smile still on her ravaged features, she looked up at her husband as he came up from the cellar. Gray now and morose, he barked at her sullenly, but even that did not dispel her momentary good humor. She had plucked the capon, she had done her work: she could allow her hands to rest a moment in her lap and enjoy what her eyes had to offer her this evening.

Madonna! Why was the boy in such a hurry? He almost burned his fingers on the hot dish that held the first course . . . There — he had disappeared on his young, energetic legs. . . .

The old man called his lady impatiently to table, and there they sat opposite one another, like a grandfather and his granddaughter. While the censorious fellow was serving her, the young woman broke a piece of bread with her dainty fingers, and, looking up at Benedetto in friendly, mocking fashion, asked him the questions of a gracious mistress: how old was he, what was his name, was he already married, had he waited upon many travelers?

"Eat, but eat, now," commanded the old man, bending over his steaming plate and blowing at it. She did not obey, but continued to look expectantly at Benedetto as he answered her questions: he waited every day upon travelers who, hearing of the good accommodation at The Three Popes, left the main route before they got to Lake Trasimeno in order to reach Perugia by the road through Todi, which was shorter and at least as safe. As the signora had been kind enough to inquire, he was called *Pipistrello*, and he was indebted for this name to his projecting bat's ears. As for his age, he reckoned it to be that of a newborn babe, because he insisted on counting up his years from the moment he had enjoyed the honor and pleasure of waiting at table upon the young and beautiful signora. Nor was he married, as he preferred to follow the example of the very honored signore and to enter upon matrimony only at a riper age, thus giving himself time to choose the fairest among the fair.

He went to fetch the capon.

When he returned, the old man looked up at him, sullen and distrustful, and as he dismembered the capon with an inexpert hand began to inveigh blindly against the inn. The room upstairs seemed to him far from clean. Instead of a good broad matrimonial bed, he had one so narrow that he would roll from it on to the floor in his dreams. Moreover, the innkeeper appeared to him far from honest. It was the old story: filthy rooms, rascally innkeepers, ill-bred servants.

"Why do you travel?" inquired Benedetto politely.

"Why do you travel? . . . Riper age . . . Why do you travel!" repeated the old man angrily, as he tore at a drumstick with his teeth.

His wife, to whom he had carefully apportioned the white meat, explained to Benedetto that a person who was bent upon spending Passion Week in the Holy City and then upon attending the last first-nights of the season in Venice had no alternative but to travel. She did not mind the discomforts of traveling, either. Highwaymen in Italy were known to be generous and benevolent — they asked travelers for no more than a little ready money on which to live, and — *poveri ragazzi* — defray the expenses of their calling. Nor did it surprise her that innkeepers degenerated into hopeless scamps, considering the inclination of so many travelers to leave unpaid bills behind them. As for the servants, they did not seem to her particularly scoundrelly — especially if one held out the prospect of good tips: which, however, need not necessarily be given. Her husband, unfortunately, had the mistaken habit, wherever he went, of at once abusing the servants as the worst of their species, thus depriving them of all hope of a gratuity.

"*Basta, basta!*" begged the old man. "Here, the carafe is empty. You ought to have seen that. Bring me some more of the red."

In a short time, he had drunk that empty too. He ordered a third, which had gone the same way by the time the capon was demolished. He continued to growl and snarl without rhyme or reason. He leaned back in his chair, his table napkin knotted under his chin. He did not touch the sweet. He beat time with his spoon as he broke out, like a spoiled child: "It's like that, and whoever affirms the contrary is a liar." He ended by breaking his plate in two, and the sweet flowed over the table. Benedetto carried it away and was about to take the spoon from his hand when the old man, to his surprise, closed his hand tightly and refused to relinquish it.

"What's the matter with you, little man? What do you want?" he asked, triumphant and derisive. "With this hand I can still fling half a dozen of your sort to the ground. A half-dozen young rogues like you." Suddenly he opened his hand good-naturedly. "Here you are: take it."

Benedetto turned away: he did not want to get involved in this little game.

The leering eyes of the drunken man followed him about the room. "Take the spoon. Take it if you can." Benedetto ignored him, and then the foolish old man began to expatiate bombastically on his strength. People might not believe it, but one day as he was traveling between Rome and Ostia his carriage had been set upon by three robbers. He knocked one of them down, snatched his pistol and overawed the other two.

His wife nodded gravely, in confirmation of his story. "It's quite true. Everybody's afraid of him in Rome and Venice. No servant in the whole of Italy will come into our house. We have to go to Calabria for them; but the Calabrians are so dirty . . . That's why I noticed your hands at once."

Benedetto took off his apron, and sat down. Looking in the old man's direction, he said to the lady: "Come, come! That must have happened a long time ago!" She glanced at her husband, then looked thoughtfully down at a ring that gleamed on her hand. "No, it happened quite recently," she said in a tone of gentle reproof. The old man, sitting close by the fire once more, seemed to have fallen asleep.

Stillness descended upon the room. After a moment, she said, "He's asleep. Or pretending to be." Benedetto took her hand and looked into her eyes, struggling against a sudden feeling of revulsion. "Tell me," he whispered, "why did you marry that gorilla?"

A bored look came over her face, but she made no effort to disengage her hand. With a smile and a sigh, she tried to conceal that he had caused her pain. "Why did I marry him? I've often been asked that before . . . Not always quite so pointedly, perhaps — but I've always understood. And I've lied so often about it that now I've really almost forgotten why I did. Why do you want to know? I usually say for his money. Oh, he's frightfully rich, you know, rich enough to buy up everything in this little city, including you." Then she compelled herself to seriousness again. "For his money . . . People believe that, at once. Then they're satisfied. They don't ask any more questions, but they spit on me and envy me. Is he so repulsively ugly? I don't see it any more. I only notice it when I see people look at him and then at me. But I'm pretty enough to make them look at me even if I hadn't married him, am I not?"

Benedetto was silent, his lips tight-pressed. She seemed a little disappointed. "Yes . . . Why did I marry him really? He certainly didn't ask me — he would never have dared. He's much too shy for that. I just wanted to have him — nobody was more surprised than he himself. He never looked at women at all: even though I forget it sometimes, he never forgets how ugly he is."

She leaned back, and a smile played about her small, painted, coral red mouth as she looked at Benedetto. He, full of bitter contempt, thrust away her hand. She stroked it gently as if to console it for this harsh rejection, and said: "Once I nearly married a young person like you — young and presumptuous, and a girl at the end of each finger of both hands. But my lucky star spared me such a fate. If I want to amuse myself occasionally, my husband has the tact to drink one glass of wine too many at table and then to close his eyes when the meal is over."

"But doesn't he do that every day? It belongs to his age, surely."

"Well . . . Perhaps it has become a habit by this time," she admitted, coolly. "He leaves me free — and that's another reason that makes people envy me. He only expects my cavalier to wait until he has fallen asleep before beginning to pay his compliments. Surely one should not grudge him that much indulgence."

"He seemed to me to be almost in a hurry to doze off," muttered Benedetto, scornfully.

She seemed surprised by the bitterness that throbbed in his voice. Almost compassionately she looked at him. Then she bent over the table and began to laugh gently, resting her cheek upon her hand. He looked down at her, but her quiet laughter disarmed him: he was defenseless against the artifices of every Eve. He hesitated, then threw his arm about her, and drew her imperiously towards him. He was about to kiss her downy neck when he stopped: Carlo was standing in the doorway, righteousness incarnate in his police uniform with its gleaming buttons.

At the same moment, the sleeper by the fire awakened.

"Can't you knock before you come in?" barked the old man at the intruder, as he felt in his pockets. "Here's my safe-conduct. Read it, if you've learned how to read, and then clear out."

Carlo approached awkwardly and stared at the sheet of paper that was held out to him. "But this *is* your wife?" he inquired.

"Read, read!" snapped the old man. "Rabble!" he snarled as, with a tremulous hand, he put away the safe-conduct. Carlo bowed with exaggerated politeness, cast an inquiring glance in Benedetto's direction, and left the room visibly disconcerted.

The old man got up from his chair with difficulty, and, maintaining a straight course only by the greatest effort of will, walked across the room, past his wife and Benedetto. He seemed somewhat foolishly surprised to see the apron hanging over the back of Benedetto's chair. With his hands behind his back, he went and stood by the window. His dim eyes stared into the complete darkness of the piazza for a while. Then he returned to his chair by the fire, dropped into it with a heavy thud, and averted his face.

Benedetto resumed his amorous advances. She did not demur, though she made no response to the fiery kisses he showered on her neck, her hands, her face. Then, taking advantage of a moment when her lips were free, she asked in her soft, bantering, alluring voice, "But tell me, what did he want here, that fellow with his gleaming buttons?"

"Oh he! He's jealous, but he doesn't know it himself," said Benedetto. "He's convinced himself that it was his duty to enlighten you and your husband about me. Duty might have been invented for him. One of these days he'll take it into his head that it's his duty to free Todi from me."

"Madonna!" She uttered a little cry of terror. "And I've been thinking you're the one amusing thing in this hole."

He was silent, chilled a little. The honor and fame of Todi were also his. He did not wish to be raised high at Todi's expense. Or was she only mocking him?

He asked her whether even Rome, Naples, Venice, or any spot in the five quarters of the globe had anything amusing to offer her; and she admitted that she found it impossible to remain in one city longer than six months. She wanted change, continual change. Then things were new again, at least for a moment — new operas, new plays, new games of chance, new scandals . . .

Benedetto watched the flames on the hearth as he listened to the tale of strange restlessness that filled this pleasure-loving young woman, who — how different from the women and girls of Todi! — accepted his passionate homage without losing her head. Perhaps it had meant no more to her than a welcome break in the yawning boredom that every evening brought her. If that were so, her husband could close his eyes quite safely, and snore in his chair by the fire, for no danger threatened him. Benedetto realized this at the same moment that he decided that he himself was too good to serve as the plaything of one who, even while she casually allowed him to kiss her, was already wondering what distractions the next great city they came to would have to offer her.

She was going to Venice — the town of Monsignore's youthful memories. With some difficulty he overcame his pride. Curiosity, perhaps envy, made him question her eagerly. Of course: theaters — the last first-nights of the season . . .

She shrugged her shoulders contemptuously. All things considered, she was not much interested in the theater. They were usually boring, both the plays and those who played them. It was the people she met, and the scandals about them. At the theater, of course, one had an opportunity to appear in a new dress. She laughed. Oh, she was quite willing to give him more details, if he was curious. The things he thought interesting in a great city were precisely those that were boring. The only thing that was interesting was the unexpected, the happenings that no one could have foreseen one day ahead; the things that were not spoken about, or at any rate only in whispers. In fact, people were the only interesting thing. He might say, of course, that people lived in Todi, but that was his mistake. People did not live there: provincials lived there. They all looked as alike as fishes in a fish bowl. She was acquainted with nobody in Todi, and so could affirm the truth of her observations with complete conviction. No, people did not live there — they would not be able to stand it.

"And you?" She looked at Benedetto as if trying to appraise his exact value. She saw the haughty, expectant smile with which he tried to rise superior to her and her judgment. Did she take a secret pleasure in wounding him? "Yes, I may see you again one day in the Ridotto at Venice, or on the Corso in Rome . . . Yes; but whether I shall recognize you then, I don't know. For there, dear young man, you will just disappear among hundreds of your sort."

This was too much. He got up.

Slowly she looked up at him. "You're surely not going?" Her voice was caressing again. Hesitating, oppressed, he groped for his apron.

"Have I spoiled the game for you?" she inquired mockingly.

With a jerk, he seized the apron, and hurried towards the door. She called to him, and he stopped. A foolish, unforgivable weakness induced him to turn towards her again.

Her eyes were blazing. Hatred and bitter resentment, which had long been gathering within her, suddenly broke out naked in her voice. "And suppose that was just what I wanted, to spoil the game. Suppose I don't care a hang for you, and for all the others who imagine themselves irresistible simply because they're young and my husband is old. Suppose that, in spite of everything, I care only for my husband though he is so ugly and is over sixty, and gets drunk so as not to stand in the way of my pleasure — what then?"

"Then I pity you, signora," Benedetto brought out.

In the kitchen he threw down his apron, and hurriedly changed his clothes under the eyes of them all. Tears of rage were in his eyes. They observed him curiously, and that did not improve his mood. Without a farewell, he hurried away.

"Polished off," declared Luigino with a grin, but with a vague anxiety, too, over what might have happened. Nana shook her old head — she could not understand Benedetto's defeat.

"If the guests have had cause to complain of him, he will hear more of it," averred Carlo, without, however, daring to re-enter the room where the strangers were.

A restlessness, an oppression that he vainly tried to elude, chased Benedetto through the streets. He felt besmirched, affronted to the core. He felt himself a miserable creature. It was no help to assert to himself that she was not worthy of all this disturbance within him. The whole of Todi had suddenly grown as mean as his home had long seemed — a background too narrow for him, that he must shake off in order to breathe. He wanted to speak to Monsignore . . . What was it he had said about Padua, once?

He wanted to get away. She had done that — this woman who had sold herself to an old baboon because she had nothing to lose, since she did not know love; who had spoken to him of the pleasures of the great cities . . . pleasures which, according to her, made one die of boredom, but were apparently all the same worth pursuing restlessly, restlessly.

He could not make up his mind to go home. He felt an increased aversion to the dirty old house crowded with the struggling workers among whom it had been his lot to be born.

Was he perhaps also afraid to look into his mother's eyes?

That day he had not played upon the organ of San Jacopo. He wished he could do so now; but even the sound of the great organ in the cathedral could not liberate him from the sense of intense oppression that was stifling him.

A consoling thought flashed through his mind: he might pay a visit to Giacomina, he, her faithless Benedetto, on account of whom a cruel father-confessor had once refused her the Holy Communion. Little Giacomina, fortunately, had not seen so much of the world that she had learned to spoil the finest game of all. She could still sigh, could weep for love and overwhelming bliss. She could tremble in his arms . . .

He stopped: this was Margherita's home. It was said that Margherita never wanted to have anything to do with boys; and yet once, while still a little girl, she had thrown herself weeping on his neck. He had repulsed her then. Should he go to her this evening and ask her forgiveness? He knew which was her room. . . .

The shadows concealed him as, through an alley, he reached the back of the house of Taruffi the wigmaker. Perhaps he had never been so reckless as he was that evening. He looked round. All the houses were in darkness. On a wall several tomcats were growling and snarling. A stone hurtled through the air, and they resumed their music farther away.

Benedetto piled on top of each other two wine vats that were standing in the courtyard. He reached a flat roof that gave him access to a window. But suppose he had made a mistake in the window? He peered inside, and could make out the line of a bed, a table, a chair. He reached into the room, and his groping hands closed on something: an article of clothing. He held it before his eyes — it was the little red jacket in which he had seen Margherita cross the piazza. He looked round. Nothing. The night watch was going by a few streets away. He sprang lightly onto the window sill, then carefully slid inside. A noiseless step forward . . . He was standing by the bed. Bending over a face framed in dark hair that lay sunk in the pillows, he whispered a name. Drowsy with sleep, the face turned towards him. A soft voice murmured, "Carlo! Why have you done this?"

He shrank back. Her eyes were staring at him aghast. Against the moonlight outside, she could not distinguish his features.

"Who are you?" she muttered hoarsely. "If you have a heart, tell me at least who you are."

Benedetto had no heart; he was silent. Then she had a lover, after all. Think of that!

Away in the darkness . . . Quickly the intruder rolled the vats back into their places, his head bowed to the ground.

Now, away from Margherita, he laughed to himself. No luck this evening. That was very certain. Perhaps the time *had* come for him to get away from Todi.

Carlo. Carlo Who? Susanna's brother? There were Carlos by the dozen. Oh, *basta!*

A little later, a notion crossed his mind that gave him satisfaction. That young woman from Rome *would* meet him again some time, as she had predicted, in the Ridotto at Venice or on the Corso in Rome — and then he would see that she recognized him, him the pseudo-waiter of The Three Popes, even if he *were* like a hundred of his sort.

On tiptoe, he crept into his home. His parents did not hear him enter — they had long been asleep. Would his mother still sleep so peacefully when he had gone?

Next morning, as he crossed the piazza on the way to the secretariat, whither Signor Castagnoli had had him summoned again, he caught sight of the young woman stepping into her coach. The old man was cursing as he paid his bill. From the steps of the city hall, Benedetto watched them a moment.

They were off. The wheels rattled over the cobblestones. The whip was cracked over the bony backs of the post horses. From the little window, the fair traveler gave a parting glance at Todi where no one lived — and suddenly she thought she recognized the young man standing there on the steps. . . .

But before she was able to greet him, he disappeared into the dim interior beyond the open door of the secretariat.

SHADOWS

I

H E'S SAID NOTHING TO YOU, THEN, ABOUT WANT-
ing to get away?" inquired the bishop.

Marietta, staring in front of her, slowly shook her head.
"No. When I asked him — he said he had never thought of going away."
Her voice was agitated. "But he only said that because he knew he would
upset me."

"She doesn't think of me," thought the bishop. Perhaps it was his slight
resentment that made him break the silence after a moment with, "I
predicted it to you, Marietta."

Quickly, distrustfully, she looked up at him. "Have you spoken to
him about Padua . . . Venice . . . ?"

He shrugged his shoulders. Then, with a touch of bitterness, said, "I
can't remember, but it's quite possible. I've renounced the possibility of
returning to my birthplace. You can't expect me to be silent about it too
— after all, I'm only a man, Marietta. In any case, it only needed some
chance to bring about what was bound to happen. Yes: if he grows tired
of us and of Todi — then we shall be here alone, you and I."

She wrung her hands. "I shall tell him — that life will be over for me if
he goes," she declared with chattering teeth.

"You won't tell him that, Marietta."

"I will, I will. He loves me — he loves his mother."

"He will promise to stay; and he will break that promise."

Monsignore stood up, and ran his compassionate hand over her hair.
Then thoughtfully, gently, he said: "A mistake was made. You should
never have come back here. After all, you knew what Todi and the
people here are like."

"I did it for the sake of the child," she sobbed.

A foolish sense of disappointment shot through him, and he withdrew
his hand. "Well — for the sake of the child. But you must not expect your
child to sacrifice himself for you — I may be allowed to be just so cruel.
After all, I too have sacrificed something."

He paced up and down the room. "Looking back, perhaps it would have been wiser, after all, if I had written another letter to Rome."

"And why didn't you do it?" sobbed Marietta. "If you knew that it all had to turn out like this — why did you listen to me?"

Very pale, he stared at her. Then dark rage flooded his being. "I shall see what can still be done," he said in a throbbing voice. "I shall go to Rome myself. I ought to have done that before."

A silence fell between them. Monsignore was standing by the window breathing deep. Restlessness, a desire for action, made him look round the room. "I shall request an audience. I shall see what I can still obtain. If need be, without the help of old friends," he went on, full of somber power and pride — and then, turning to her commandingly: "Send the boy to me to-morrow. I shall speak to him."

Listlessly, Marietta raised her face towards him. She swallowed. "And . . . What about me, then?"

With a jerk he turned round towards her. "What do you mean by that? Do you wish me to think about you, or about the boy? Marietta, there was a time when you were bigger than you are now. I have admired you . . . After all, it was for your sake that I neglected my opportunities in Rome. I must say that now. I've never regretted it — but I should regret it on the day you were no longer the same."

She was silent — she did not know what more to say. "*Babbo*," she moaned softly, "I will be big . . . I will think only of the boy . . . But *can* one always do what one wants to do?"

II

Under lowered eyelids, Benedetto watched his mother as she cleared the evening meal. Her hands were trembling as she seized a dish. It suddenly struck him that she was looking ill. Her eyes looked large and tired in her pale face.

It crossed his mind that he might stay with her a little. His father and Andrea were about to go out for their evening walk. In the squares, the people were sitting together under the balmy, starry May sky.

But an uncontrollable restlessness came over him. He got up, and went towards the door, where, however, he stopped again. His mother was asking him, "Are you going out again?"

He heard the shy entreaty in her voice, but fear welled up in him and dislike of the conversation she wanted to have with him. "Yes, just for a while," he answered.

Ashamed, as if repenting of her effort to hold him back, Marietta devoted her attention again to the half-cleared table.

Sarcastically, Antonio muttered to himself, "Yes . . . for a while. That's very likely."

But Benedetto was already beyond earshot.

He took the direction of the piazza. People were sitting in the streets in front of their doors. Where did he want to go? Lights were burning in every room on the first floor of the Galli palace. Visitors were expected. Benedetto had free entry there: gradually he had come to be considered one of the household. But that did not attract him this evening. He knew all about those evening parties. They had nothing new to offer him. Monsignore would be there, wanting to show him off, and thinking that nobody noticed his intention. Signor Castagnoli would be there — and he saw quite enough of him during the day. For the last two months, Signor Castagnoli had been appearing at the secretariat with unwonted regularity, and the first question he always asked was whether Benedetto had arrived. Signor Castagnoli labored under the obsession that Benedetto had other uncopied documents dating from the feast of Saint Cecilia . . . And Bordoni the cloth merchant would be there — and this person and that — all the citizens of Todi of any consequence; and they resembled one another like fish in a fish bowl . . .

No, he had no desire to mingle with the guests in the Galli palace.

There had been a time when simply to roam aimlessly through the city afforded him pleasure. He sauntered along, glancing up now and again in the hope of catching the eye of some girl leaning from a window . . . He glanced attentively at every pretty face — from how many he had already stolen kisses! How many were very, very well disposed towards him! It had been balm to feel himself surrounded by feminine good will. He sensed the tender glances of the women even through closed shutters — as definitely as he read disapproval, mingled with reluctant admiration of his success, in the eyes of the men.

He had felt himself an uncrowned prince wandering through his domain; and now for a month he had despised all that — despised those who allowed themselves to be conquered so easily, despised himself most of all because such conquests had once given him satisfaction.

He went past The Three Popes, although he had already observed that no lights burned in the room reserved for travelers. Since his unfortunate adventure with the young lady from Rome, he had been drawn as by magic towards the inn. On several occasions since, he had approached strangers and entered into animated conversation with them, expressing himself with lordly superiority about Todi, upon which he hoped soon to turn his back. . . . He watched their faces carefully as he spoke. They appeared to find nothing extraordinary in his remarks; often they insisted

that he must look them up if he ever came to Turin or Milan or Trieste;
and from what he picked up, he was able to reconstruct enough to talk
with an appearance of knowledge to the next travelers who came along
about the San Carlo theater in Naples and about the latest sumptuary laws
enacted by the Venetian Council of Ten.

But what was the use of it? He could not get away from Todi. He refused even to consider any longer why it was impossible. . . . The realization of that fact was so deep in him that he had not even dared speak
to Monsignore again about Padua and Venice.

Why had his mother wanted him to go to see Monsignore a few days
ago? He had not been yet, and she seemed to prefer not to recur to the
subject . . .

Night had fallen. It was the hour when once upon a time good fortune
had smiled on him. Now it seemed only to increase his unsatisfied longings. He had had no sweetheart for several weeks. Perhaps that was why
he felt so empty. Perhaps it would be better if he carried one in his heart
again. Oh, here and there he could safely force his way in, without fear
of rejection. But no lips greedy of kisses could liberate him from the
hunger that was consuming him. Suddenly it occurred to him that he
was being shadowed. His eyes lit up. Had he succeeded in luring Carlo
into a repetition of yesterday's little game?

The Sunday before last, he had seen Carlo leave the cathedral by
Margherita Taruffi's side — Margherita who had had such a fright that
night, and who had whispered with hot breath: "Carlo — why have you
done this?"

He had not been sure which of the dozen Carlos in Todi she had
meant. Now he knew. And it seemed that Carlo, on his side, had a suspicion as to who had intruded by night unbidden on his Margherita.
Perhaps it would have been better if Margherita had been silent. Carlo
had now been shadowing him for days. There might come a time when
this would begin to bore Benedetto, and then his foolish nocturnal spying
might end in unpremeditated murder. The Virgin forbid! Besides, the
jealous creature would have been better advised to feel gratitude towards
the man who had discreetly withdrawn at the mere mention of another's
name. After all, "Carlo" was not the sort of name for which one entertained a blind respect.

As it happened, Benedetto was in the right frame of mind to provoke
and tease his zealous pursuer. He walked rapidly through the deserted
city, choosing intentionally those streets that did not lend themselves
to shadowing. Why should he make it easy for Carlo? Then he crossed

three streets, and turned hastily down the fourth, in which lay the house of Taruffi the wigmaker. He stood still, smiling, until he saw a shadow move on the other side of the way: Carlo had not been thrown off the scent — he evidently guessed that this evening Benedetto meant to try his luck with Margherita Taruffi again.

But Benedetto was not the man to put such a bold project into practice at once. Nervously he paced up and down, up and down in front of the house, until the last doubt as to his intention must have evaporated from Carlo's mind. Perhaps Carlo would not be able to compel himself to remain in the shadow, but would come out into the open in all the pride of his uniform decorated with burnished buttons and ask Benedetto what he was about at that hour. One word would lead on to another — and how that would end depended on oneself.

No, Carlo did not emerge from the darkness. He was not ready to act until he was sure.

Benedetto disappeared rapidly down a side street that led to the court under Margherita's window. But instead of climbing on to the low roof, he pressed himself flat against the wall and was off down the alley again and away into the darkness as Carlo hurried into the courtyard. Carlo searched every corner of the little yard, and in the end could not refrain from softly calling his sweetheart's name, at the risk of becoming involved in a situation that a man like Carlo generally waits for until after the holy sacrament of matrimony. . . . Meanwhile, Benedetto had got clear away and dropped into the lighted kitchen behind The Three Popes, where Nana was dozing, to inquire, "Is it possible I saw Carlo on his way to his sweetheart?"

Nana required a moment to come to her senses. "There he comes, storming into the house again. What have Carlo and his sweetheart to do with you? Is she by any chance yours as well?" And in fear that this might be so, she crossed herself.

But Benedetto set her mind at rest. "I'm only worried about the harm it may do him if he's caught in uniform under a girl's window long after her parents are in bed."

Benedetto heard a laugh behind him, and there stood Luigino with a trayful of glasses.

"Somebody saw the two of you last night, pacing up and down in front of the house of Taruffi the wigmaker," remarked Luigino.

"Somebody who had been here first and drunk your wine, and then saw the world double," suggested Benedetto, delighted at the rumor that was apparently already spreading. Luigino pulled a face as much as to say that he had his own ideas about that.

"Have you any guests?" inquired Benedetto, noticing Luigino's burden.

"Oh, a few latecomers from Perugia. Go and have a look at them," suggested Luigino, who was in a good humor.

As she slowly dozed off again Nana heard, through the hilarity of the few remaining customers who could not be persuaded to leave the tap-room, Benedetto's gay, polished, persuasive voice, to which she always listened with intense pleasure. A woman's clear laugh and the bass of a man's voice formed the echo.

A quarter of an hour later, Carlo entered. He was pale and agitated, and stood in impotent rage in the center of the kitchen. Nana, irritated by this second abrupt interruption of her nap, pointed with a certain mischievous pleasure towards the door, behind which Benedetto was holding forth on the restricted diversions Todi had to offer to the passing traveler and to its unfortunate inhabitants.

III

It was a game he could repeat evening after evening with pleasure. He had to work off his ill humor on someone, and Carlo was a particularly suitable victim. What evil intentions did Carlo imagine to exist behind Benedetto's midnight roamings? Through thick and thin he followed him, clambering after him over a broken section of the city wall, following him out into the country, where he had to slink from tree to tree and crawl through thorny ditches in order to escape Benedetto's observation. With satisfaction, Benedetto noted that Carlo, who after a heavy day's work was wearing out his eyes in the darkness, was looking more unwell from day to day.

He could not help thinking that some time or other Carlo would have enough of this ridiculous nocturnal shadowing. After all, one was not put in prison merely for a gallant adventure with somebody else's sweetheart, and surely Carlo could not suspect him of any more serious offense . . . However that might be, Carlo did not give up. He sacrificed his sleep. With heroic determination he made himself ridiculous in the eyes of the whole city. Yes. . . . But in the end people began to react differently. They whispered to one another that perhaps, after all, he knew what he was about. Perhaps he had certain suspicions that had not occurred to anyone else. And soon Benedetto became conscious of these suspicions, and that consciousness increased his peevishness and ill humor.

Suspicions, once awakened, began to grow. People began to recall Benedetto's earliest misdemeanors, buried as they were in the far past. They remembered that his schoolboy pranks had been of a darker dye than those of his comrades, all of whom had now become more or less serious workers. In the days of his boyhood, opinion at the city well had averred that he was heading for the gallows. . . .

Where did he get the money to buy expensive rings and necklaces from the goldsmith for his little loves? He did not earn it at the secretariat — at least, not honestly. . . . Could it be the bishop who gave him such lavish pocket money? For some unfathomable reason he had always shielded Benedetto. But surely Monsignore would want to know what happened to his money. Besides, Monsignore was probably not rich enough: otherwise he would have had his coach relacquered, and would not be satisfied with such a modest way of living. Was Benedetto in a position to fill his pockets as he liked at the Galli palace? The Gallis were prepared to give away large sums of money when it would raise their prestige in the city; but they stinted on the wages of the servants.

Who knew what Carlo might bring to light?

Marietta had found no opportunity, yet, to talk to her boy alone and warn him against all the wonderful ideas he might be entertaining about the great cities of which Monsignore and others had spoken to him. She wanted to tell him that she would never hold him back if he ceased to be happy in Todi; but on the other hand, she felt it her duty to point out to him how dangerous the great cities were, particularly for anyone of his thoughtless, lighthearted nature. She wanted to ask him whether he was aware of all the antagonism he had roused against himself in this little city of Todi by his boyish presumption. Before he had felt their menace, Monsignore's mighty arm had averted it. . . . But in foreign parts he would stand alone. Did he realize the terrible loneliness that would surround him in a great city, until he found his bearings, seeing that he had been gifted by God with a sensitive heart?

All this Marietta would have liked to say to him, when she noticed, with surprise and thankfulness, that he had not yet given ear to Monsignore's request that he should go to him, a request she had faithfully passed on.

But he avoided being alone with her. . . .

From others, she had heard of the little game Benedetto was playing with the jealous Carlo. A vague smile of contempt played about her lips when she thought of that fellow in uniform who imagined he could catch her boy. But when she observed signs of ill humor and anger in Benedetto, her contempt turned to blind hatred, her quiet assurance to deadly fear. She could not bear it when Antonio, shocked that his good-for-nothing son was now passing for something worse, spoke indignantly about the whole business.

She would not listen to a word about it from anybody.

And the neighbors, who had apparently forgotten her existence for so long, began to come visiting again. Manuela, who these days sold herself to tipsy revelers from Vacca's inn, had the audacity to speak to her, saying she should not make herself anxious about the boy: even as a child, he had been much too artful for his father and his mother and the whole world. Except for Camilla, who, infected with the hostility between their sons, deliberately turned her back on him, the women of the neighborhood came knocking at her door one after the other, as they had done once before. After the usual small talk, they referred to Carlo's foolishness: as if Benedetto *were* doing anything forbidden in the dark! What could it be? No doubt Carlo was influenced by nothing but personal hostility, and if she were wise she would just laugh about it.

Marietta's fears were fanned to mortal terror; but she would rather have died where she stood than show it. She received them hospitably and agreeably; became, for her, very loquacious, telling that her son had been thinking for a long time of sacrificing his magnificent future in Todi because he was consumed with a desire to see the world. Only love of his parents had, so far, held him back from going to Venice, where Monsignore could give him brilliant introductions. . . . Yes, he was not the sort of boy to complain to the podesta about Carlo's suspicions, though they were becoming rather troublesome. There was no reason why he should not, and such a complaint would not be very helpful to Carlo's career. But he was one of those who preferred to fight his own battles. Though, if his life were made too difficult here, he would certainly seek the wide distances — and in that case, she could not but approve.

Thus Marietta spoke about his going away. She heard her own voice, and tried to understand what she was saying. She was intoxicating herself with her own proud words. But when the women had gone, she could hardly breathe — and they kept coming. How much longer could she withstand this oppressive curiosity?

Even Annina, wife of Simone the stonemason, came to see her again — Annina who for years had run past her door because she could not bear it that her Giannino had to shave Marietta's son when it pleased Benedetto to drop into Maestro Pallanza's shop. Yes, even Annina came to see her. When they greeted one another her emotion almost got the better of her. Tears sprang into her weary, faded eyes. Annina said she wanted to make everything right between them again. She recalled their old friendship . . . Had all the ties, then, been severed? Marietta listened sharply to every inflection in her voice. She wanted to know what had driven Annina to call, and suddenly she made the dreadful discovery that it could only be concern and pity for her. Marietta's heart sank; but her demeanor became haughty and very cool. Abashed, uncertain, Annina shrank back, and as she left she said confusedly some awkward things about Marietta's blindness to the dangers and temptations that came from frequenting the houses of the great.

That was the last straw. Marietta decided she could see nobody else. Yes; but on the other hand she wanted to hear what was being said — what tittle-tattle was going the rounds. From Benedetto, she heard nothing. The little he did say was distorted by derision.

She did not sleep. Even when her boy had come home and she could hear his innocent breathing, she could not sleep. True, he was now in her safe proximity; but who knew what he had been doing that evening? He was capable of anything, if only to defy Carlo. Who knew what Carlo would report to-morrow to the authorities?

Her last resource was to go to the bishop. At dusk, while Antonio and Andrea were taking their evening walk, she hurried to him. He was making arrangements for a journey to Rome. His old coach was no longer in a condition to be shown in the Holy City, and was being completely relacquered and repainted and re-upholstered. Michele, his gray coachman, and Sebastiano the stableboy were to be put into livery. Monsignore was thinking of taking his secretary with him. This expedition to Rome must take place with a certain state. He wanted to be met outside the gate. Inexorably, he stood by all his episcopal privileges and rights. All this, however, could only be arranged by much correspondence. In Rome they did not appear to take a bishop from Todi too seriously. It seemed that there were some at the Vatican who were inclined to be amused at the rather excessive sense of dignity of such a provincial prince of the Church. . . . But a time might come when they would cease to smile. His Holiness had answered most graciously the request for an audience that had reached him so unexpectedly from Todi.

Yes, these days Monsignore was almost too busy to receive Marietta. He could usually spare her only a short time; but that did not matter. It was enough if she could just see him and have a word with him. That was sufficient to relieve her anxieties. His forceful energy inspired her with confidence and peace, and it was all the same to her, now, what he did. She no longer dared to judge his actions. She knew that it was all for the sake of her boy, and was prepared to trust blindly, to make a mother's sacrifice — sometimes she even hungered to do so. Now and again, however, she remained a little longer, even though he had told her on her arrival that he had all manner of correspondence to attend to. He had some small success to impart to her, and in his eyes gleamed the re-awakened pride of his younger years. She was grateful that she still meant something to him. She no longer thought of Antonio. Her unfaithfulness to him awoke no sting of conscience, no sense of guilt.

Then, one Sunday, Monsignore departed for Rome behind four post horses. The citizens came rushing out to witness the spectacle. They hardly recognized the sober, solitary man of the episcopal palace. After many years, they felt honored that they possessed such an ecclesiastical leader. They had a premonition of great coming events. Voices were heard affirming that the bishop would not be seen in Todi again, unless perhaps on a ceremonial farewell visit, at which he would already be attired in the red robe.

The bishop expected to be away a month. Would his old friends in Rome still know him? Much depended upon that.

And now suddenly Marietta was alone. Her anxiety increasing from day to day, she simply waited for his return. It was only slowly that she realized what exactly had happened to her.

She could no longer bear the sound of her husband's hammer — some-times it sent her almost crazy. She could hardly remain sitting on her chair. She moved about her home purposelessly, aimlessly, as she had done once before when she had as yet no child.

A few days after Monsignore's departure, Nana came to see her: Nana who had said to Benedetto once that she could no longer show herself be-cause of the rags that were all she had to wear. Marietta was shocked at the sight of her — not so much because of her greasy clothes that reeked of the kitchen, not so much because of her ravaged face and figure: it was the expression in her eyes that frightened her. Nana had come as a mes-senger of ill omen. Nana was bringing her bad tidings; and Marietta be-lieved them, as if Nana were no ordinary mortal, but an ambassador of Destiny. Nana relieved her of her last doubt by coming to the point at once. Nana also was anxious. Carlo was going about the house like the shadow of himself, declaring upon his oath to all and sundry that he would contrive to put Benedetto where he belonged. Nana had at first laughed at him, but in the end she was growing afraid of that madman. She was old, and had a premonition of evil things. She had come to urge Marietta to talk seriously to her boy and, if possible, to keep him at home for a time. Oh, she knew well enough how difficult it would be to get hold of him. He was a rascal. You just had to love him, whether you wanted to or not. He was a breaker of hearts — yes, Nana could cite examples. But he was carrying his pranks too far. For a month now he had been tormenting

Carlo to death by hovering round his sweetheart, with the result that Carlo had become the Devil himself. She could not express it in any other way: the Devil himself.

Marietta stared before her. When she tried to reply, suddenly she could not contain herself any longer, and buried her head in her hands. Nana began to cry with her, but she was too old to bother to conceal her face.

Below, Antonio was carefully putting a coffin together.

"If only he were after Luigino instead of after your boy," sobbed Nana. "That would be better."

That evening, as they were going to bed, Antonio complained that Cesare and Camilla had passed him without seeing him.

"They've probably a bad conscience over what their Carlo is doing to us," said Marietta.

Antonio heard with concern the angry protest flaring up in her voice, and felt bound to say, "They won't see it in that light, Marietta."

"No — that's possible. But do you really love your boy?"

He looked up startled. He preferred to evade these painful and agitating discussions, but now she compelled him to speak. Clumsily he said, "Of course I love him — at least, I've tried to. But he doesn't care either way — and I really don't know, Marietta, whether he deserves to be loved."

Deadly pale, she went on in an agitated voice: "And me? Do you still love me, Antonio? Do you think *I* deserve to be loved?"

Flushing under her scorn, he replied rather stiffly in his embarrassment: "Marietta — is that a question to ask, after we've been married almost twenty years? That's one of the things one no longer thinks about every day. Perhaps I should only come to think of it again — if I hadn't got you."

Oh, Marietta knew quite well. It was foolish of her to have asked that question. He could not answer it. She knew, besides, exactly what she was to him. He had found a safe refuge in his wife. His mother had died, and his wife had become his mother. Such was the fate that had been written in his stars.

Whatever there was of paternal feeling in this man who had never grown up had flowed towards Andrea, because there had been no other outlet. Was that his fault? Benedetto was more alien to him than a stranger. Thus had come to pass the spectacle of a father who ranged himself on the side of those who wished for his boy's downfall.

Thus terribly could a lie avenge itself here upon earth.

Everything around her went black.

Then out of the darkness a voice reached her, a soft timid voice that she remembered having heard long, long ago. It brought her unexpected consolation. And yet it was only Antonio's voice — the voice of Antonio her husband, who lived beside her and had repulsed her boy.

Antonio was saying: "Marietta . . . As you ask me if I still love you — then I wish to say just this: That sometimes it suddenly comes back to me what was between us in the first years of our marriage — the time before Father died . . . Then the year that you were away . . . The days in Rome and our return . . . It was a frightful time, Marietta. But I would not wish to put it out of my life. There is also this I want to say to you, that perhaps that was the finest time of all in my life." He could speak no more, but turned away with moist eyes.

Marietta looked at him. A vague, faraway hope was reborn in her. A faint light broke through the darkness round her. She was aware that he could not save her; but, all the same, she was grateful to him for what he had said. He loved the grief she had brought him: that was how he loved her. He would not have been without that grief — but he could not speak about it every day, if only because he was not a man of words. But in stillness it went on living in him. It had not been dimmed in him, as she had thought.

In the same way he would also have loved his boy. The pain he suffered through him he would have closed in his heart — if Benedetto had *been* his boy.

She would remain with him! If ever she had thought of something different, she renounced it now for good and all.

She must bear her guilt. Whatever happened to her, she had deserved it; and it was one of life's blessings that it had given her a task here when she should be left behind and alone. She turned her face towards her husband. For the first time in years he saw again the smile that took away the hard weariness of her features and made her young — almost as young as when she lay in the Hospital for the Poor in Rome and at last turned her face towards him.

IV

Benedetto was playing the organ in San Jacopo for the evening service; and while his hands glided over the keys, he thought that below, among the congregation, would be Carlo, who afterwards would follow him again. The pride that had deserted him recently returned at this thought. He felt himself inspired — and it showed in his playing. At that moment, he knew he was dominating all the people below in the marble depths. Those who came to San Jacopo's came to hear him play. His playing made vespers something more radiant, more exalted, than in other churches. Since he had taken the place of Geronimo the lay brother, who was ill, the congregation had grown from day to day. The little church was filled to overflowing. The other parishes were becoming jealous, and despite his notoriety tried to persuade him to play for them. And Benedetto was beginning to wonder whether he would not break faith with San Jacopo's for the sake of Saint Clare's, which boasted a better organ . . .

When Monsignore returned from Rome, he would make another effort to get permission to play on the organ in the cathedral. That would be a deep satisfaction for his ambition. Then the people would really get to know their great organ, which was now being done violence to, by that old fogy Father Joshua.

Vespers came to an end. The people stood up and streamed past the holy water stoups towards the exit of the church. The attendants were already extinguishing the candles before the altar, and the verger was going round rattling his keys. Benedetto left the building by a back door. Carlo was no doubt waiting for him on the other side of the street . . . Or was that he coming round the corner? No, it was only Francesco, one of the Galli servants.

"Do you want me?"

"Yes, come at once. The old Signora is dead."

Benedetto stared at the panting messenger. Then suddenly he hastened his footsteps.

"Did she ask that I should come?"

"I don't know — Giambattista sent me."

The report was too astonishing to be immediately believed. No doubt the old woman would come to life again, sit up and issue her orders.

"Dead? You did say she is dead?" asked Benedetto a little farther down the street.

"Yes, this time she is," was the reassuring reply. "And if she isn't, Doctor Barberini will put that right."

With amazing rapidity the news had spread through the city. Throngs had already gathered on the piazza, conversing in whispers, and it had gone round that the last wish of the old lady had been to be buried with all her jewels. Yes, and they also talked about Signor Pompeati the undertaker: after having been tracked down by acquaintances who had hoped to be rewarded for their services to the dwelling of the young Widow Balsamo (what could be his business there?), he had at first refused to go to the Galli palace. He simply refused to believe that old Signora Galli had really passed away. He imagined that the story was a trick of his jealous wife. . . .

Benedetto shouldered his way through the crowd, pressed forward into the entrance and up the stairs. Everyone made room for him.

The upper rooms were even more crowded. Here the notabilities of the

city had gathered; and pressing forward among them in their usual over-
bearing manner were the mendicant friars who had come to collect money
for the souls of the dead. The podesta, pale with agitation, had become
involved in a conversation with Signor Pompeati. Portentous decisions
were being made about the number of horses and bearers — the cost of
the funeral appeared to have risen formidably. Possibly, Signor Pompeati
was including in the reckoning his previous disappointment and exasperation. Possibly also the price increased in proportion to the number of
people thronging around and pricking up their ears at the enumeration of
the charges.

After some awkward hemming and hawing, the podesta agreed to
everything. "Yes, of course, it must all be done in seemly fashion. It must
certainly not fall short of what was done for my father, because after all
my mother was . . ." But suddenly it would not come to his mind what
his mother was, in contrast to her deceased husband. Hesitating, he glanced
towards the discreet faces of the priests who were waiting their turn to
discuss the ecclesiastical side of this burial.

"An exceptional woman," remarked Signor Pompeati, finishing the
podesta's sentence amid the notes and calculations that made the sweat
trickle down his forehead.

People were not encouraged to enter the chamber of death itself. They
were requested to remain only a short time. The doctor was there, the
priest who had administered the last sacrament, the notary, and two other
priests who were trying to discover something about Signora Galli's
eventual legacies to the church. There too was gray, faithful Giambattista
in tears.

On the bed lay old Signora Galli. She viewed the proceedings no less
seriously than the others. Her face reflected to the full the gravity of the
occasion. She was determined that her son should give her the funeral
that was her due. Seen at closer quarters, her stately gravity turned to a
grimace. Her face appeared contorted, still mysteriously alive in the fitful
light of the candles that were flickering in the draught. Sometimes her
face seemed to express anger — a wild, desperate anger that she was dead
and could no longer enjoy these happenings with the others. Perhaps, too,
she had deliberately assumed this frightful expression in order to deter her
son Giacomo from robbing her at the eleventh hour of the jewels in
whose radiance she wished to journey to heaven, so as to be sure of getting
the reception to which she was entitled.

With a fleeting curiosity, Benedetto bent over her. Through her closed
eyelids she stared at him. Her wry grimace could not be meant for him —
he had always stood very specially in her good graces, and in her last will

and testament she had directed that he was to play the great organ in the cathedral during the first Mass sung for the salvation of her soul. The idea had come to her suddenly, after she had heard the bishop drop a word about the organ in the cathedral, and about Benedetto's desire to play it. . . . Yes, and now, still unaware of this, he looked at her. Did old Signora Galli but know, she would perhaps try to smile at him for the last time — perhaps for the last time take pleasure in the fact that again he could not avert his eyes from her jewels. . . . Behind his back people were whispering, overawed by the sight of the dead. As they did not quite know what to talk about, they were saying what a pity it was that old Signora Galli had just missed being a hundred. She would have liked that so much. She had entertained the fond hope of attaining a century, but God had not granted it to her. Everybody knew how modestly and virtuously the old lady had lived, how much good she had done anonymously. Large sums had gone to charity, and to the convent she had surrendered her only daughter-in-law, who had placed at the disposal of the abbess all her worldly possessions.

At that moment, the daughter-in-law herself made her entrance, in conventual attire and accompanied by an old nun. All gave way respectfully, and Benedetto left the bedside of the dead; young Signora Galli did not see him with her shortsighted eyes. Moreover, she did not appear to wish to see or recognize any one of all those people whom she had formerly welcomed as a hostess. In the intoxication of her triumph, she had even had the strength a moment ago to pass her husband, whom she had not met since her withdrawal to the convent. With a flushed face, the podesta continued his conversation with Signor Pompeati.

As he was leaving the room, it suddenly occurred to Benedetto that he had not yet seen Maestro Angelini. He went in search of him. He was stopped every moment as he pressed through the crowd. Everybody appeared to think that he knew more about old Signora Galli than anyone — although as a matter of fact he had not seen her during the last weeks. As he was speaking, his eyes wandered about. He heard the podesta say that already an express messenger had departed for Rome to inform Monsignore of the sad tidings, which presumably would make him decide to return at once in order to give luster to the funeral by his presence. Benedetto thought this doubtful, but did not express his doubt. Where could Maestro Angelini be? Was it possible that he did not know yet that young Signora Galli . . . ?

He found his way to the stairs, hurried up them and knocked at the door of Maestro Angelini's room. No answer came. But the lock sprang open with a snap, and there was his music master staring at him with a pale, worried, tearful face.

"Is it you? Come in," he said hoarsely. Benedetto went in, and the door was locked behind him. Maestro Angelini threw a long arm about him and, deeply stirred, broke out with, "It is good — that you have still come to look me up."

The little room was in hopeless disorder. On the bed lay open a large, heavy traveling trunk, in which were piled higgledy-piggledy shoes, stockings, lace shirts, coats, jewels, torn music sheets, boxes of pomade, scent bottles.

"Are you going away?" inquired Benedetto.

Maestro Angelini slowly nodded.

"I wanted to fetch her," he said in a dull tone. "That was the first thing that crossed my mind when they told me that her mother-in-law . . . Can you understand, my boy, what I felt when I drove out of the gate towards the convent? I hadn't seen her all this time. She always sent a nun or a novice to collect the skeins for her embroidery . . . But now, surely, she must let herself be seen. I thought we should drive back together, she and I. . . . Such was my innocence. I go to the convent, beg them to give her my news — and what happens? She sends back a nun with the reply that she thanks me for my message and will follow immediately on foot. She did not wish to go in a coach with a man. Of course I had it conveyed to her that I should go on foot, although it isn't my habit to walk long distances in the country. Thereupon I am informed that, in that case, I am compelling her to drive back with me, and that she will be there in a moment. . . . For the second time, my whole body is but one beating heart — and true enough she does come, yes; but in the company of an old marvel, a hydra, a Satan's mother under a nun's coif. I bore up well, Benedetto. . . . I put up with this insult. . . . It was better for her to come under her own escort if she did not trust mine. . . . And there they sat, the two of them, opposite me in the carriage, saying their rosaries the whole way, not even raising their eyes once; and her feet were clad in the same coarse woolen stockings as those worn by that Nemesis. I was honored neither by a word nor by a look. . . . Am I then a dog? Tell me, boy, am I? I'm going away from here. Once is enough. I feel I'm a little too good for such treatment. This accursed provincial hole will never see me again. . . . Only my fame will penetrate here later on. Through the thick walls of the convent my name will still penetrate, if God grants me that compensation."

He began to pack again, in nervous haste, stumbling over drawers and boxes, dropping on his knees to look under the bed. "To-morrow morning early, the stagecoach leaves for Perugia. That must have been ordained by Providence. I don't know what I should have done had it been leaving only the day after. I refuse to accept anything from this house any more. I should not allow myself to be driven away in a coach belonging to the Gallis. I have sat in them too often. *I have sat in them once too often.*"

Benedetto listened to all this and was silent while Maestro Angelini went on packing his lace frills and ruffles with his pale virtuoso's hands. When Benedetto went away, his music master called after him, "To-morrow morning, I shall see you again, shan't I? To-morrow morning early, when the coach leaves?"

Downstairs, a few priests only remained. Benedetto shouldered his way through them rather roughly, gasping for fresh air.

On the other side of the piazza, in the shadow of the houses, Carlo was waiting.

V

On Friday old Signora Galli was to be laid in earth. The relatives from Siena were expected to arrive the evening before. Monsignore might be back by then, too, and in any case he would be back by Saturday or Sunday morning, when he would be able to celebrate the first two solemn Masses for the dead. . . . Surely he would not hesitate when he read between the lines of Signor Galli's letter how well the Church had been provided for by the deceased. . . .

Although the will was not to be opened till Thursday evening, Signor Galli was not altogether ignorant of its contents, and he therefore summoned Benedetto to communicate to him the memorable tidings that it had been the wish of the deceased that he should play the organ at the first Mass that was to be celebrated by Monsignore in the cathedral — a distinction to which the ecclesiastical authorities could raise no objection, as they had every reason to meet the wishes of the old lady.

Benedetto could hardly believe that his long-cherished dream was to be fulfilled. The glory of it overwhelmed him. About him he heard already the whisperings of the citizens, who had also heard the news. People looked at him as he passed with raised head on his way to the cathedral to practise on the organ.

The day after the death of the old lady, Maestro Angelini departed as he had said he would. Under the amazed eyes of the women going to the well, he climbed into the stagecoach, where they had given him the front seat so that he should be as little jolted as possible; and there he sat, making

himself slimmer than ever so as to avoid contact with the other travelers.
They were filled with pity as they saw poor Signor Morto-vivo sitting
on the hard bench of a diligence after being used to the soft cushions of
the upholstered coaches of the Gallis.

Benedetto got up late, too late to take leave of Maestro Angelini, whose
dismal bird's eye roamed across the piazza filled with a childish disappointment.

On the organ in the cathedral, Benedetto picked out the melody that
had been singing in him for months. It pursued him day and night, this
melody of distant things. It made him forget the time of day, and where
he was and where he wished to go. It made him moody and impatient. It
deprived him of his amused outlook on men and things, and made him inclined to deeds of cruelty and violence. It accompanied him everywhere,
it was murmuring in his ears and in his heart. Did the others never hear
it, as they complacently followed the dull, even tenor of their ways?
Benedetto was different. There was no melody in them at all. They deserved to be made fools of, to be roused now and then from their bovine
calm.

On Saturday he would play to them.

The family from Siena did arrive on Thursday, in the afternoon; but
they had first made the messenger who brought the bad tidings swear that
there was no possibility of a mistake this time. In the evening the will
was read out, and it proved that Romano Angelini, the music master, had
also been remembered — why had he been in such a hurry to get away?
It appeared that he had had to sell some of his jewelry in Perugia in order
to be able to proceed on his journey. How was he to be overtaken now?

The day of the funeral arrived. The bells were droning over the little
city. The brass band was lamenting on the piazza, where the black procession was forming. Members of the Brotherhood of Christian Mercy
were there donning their impressive hoods with the spectral eyeholes, so
suggestive of the region of the dead. There were also bands of children,
monks, high ecclesiastics, the military authorities of Todi — as if a sovereign were being borne away. The one flaw was the absence of Monsignore, who had written from Rome to say how profoundly he had been
moved by the death of the old Signora, and how regretful he was that there
was no possibility of his being able to disengage himself from an audience
with the Holy Father that had been granted him for that Saturday.

"*Miserere mei, Deus* . . ." chanted the children, as they passed through
the city gates. Skylarks were rising from the fields into the still, early
summer heaven. The throats of the citizens, who sang too as they fol-

lowed, were dry. (Later on, wine would be dispensed.) Immediately behind the hearse, followed the coaches. Benedetto was sitting with members of the family from Siena. There were legacies for all: the whole city inherited, the Church inherited, — although not so much as it had hoped, — all the servants of the house of Galli inherited (old Giambattista inherited the wheeled chair in which he had so faithfully pushed the deceased). It was an impressive funeral. The old lady had wished to reach a hundred, and she had almost succeeded; but now the Lord had called her.

Yes; and now she was lying in her coffin, buried under wreaths and flowers, and was being jolted as unmercifully as Maestro Angelini in his stagecoach — both were used to the same cushions. And in the coaches, the mourning family were discussing the jewelry she was carrying with her to the grave. They knew most of the pieces. Her earrings were famous in the family — she might at least have bequeathed those to someone. It was really deplorable. Her bracelets, her rings, her necklaces, the jewels in her coiffure . . . But it would have been impossible to do otherwise than respect her last extraordinary wish. To disregard that would have upset all the other provisions of the will, and then there would have been no end to the quarrels and recriminations. Even now, tension threatened. . . . Yes; and on the other hand there was something about it that flattered their family pride: the old lady had been like nobody else. The whole city, following in the long procession, talked about the jewels. . . . The Gallis died grandly. That was the least that could be said of them.

Slowly the coffin was carried down the short stairway into the opened vault, while hundreds of eyes stared, fascinated, at the brown walnut lid with the silver ornaments. They could almost picture the radiance of the jewels about which there had been so much talk. Benedetto also saw them, in his mind — and it seemed to him foolish and cruel to deprive their warm luster of the light of day forever.

Something flashed through his mind — an uncontrollable thought that made him look pensively towards the bronze door that would be bolted above this cave of the dead. It would not be easy for the jewels to find the light of day again. He looked about him, unconsciously trying to make sure that nobody else was feeling the same thing. . . . No: none of the eyes that met his expressed a fellow feeling for the mute and lifeless jewels. Suddenly, however, his eye caught that of Luigino Vacca, who was standing a little behind the crowd. In that glance was a curiously questioning look, a strange rapid understanding that affected Benedetto disagreeably. He looked away again at once. But in his imagination he suddenly saw this churchyard deserted, all those voices stilled — completely lost. . . . He was here alone with Luigino. They were working together in a sweat, trying to open that closed door. . . . And as they at last descended into the depths, Carlo — who else? — unexpectedly emerged from behind a tombstone and slammed the door above their heads. That was Carlo's terrible revenge. And now he was alone in the vault — alone with that scoundrel Luigino, with the rotting body of old Signora Galli, with the skeleton of her husband whom he had never known, and with the jewels that in the darkness felt chilly, hostile, worthless. . . .

With difficulty Benedetto brought himself back to reality. He found that they were no longer singing around him, that the speeches were over and done, and that everyone was preparing to go. As he stepped into the coach with the relatives from Siena, he threw a glance behind him. Signor Pompeati, under the personal supervision of the podesta and his now adult son, was closing the grave.

VI

After the funeral feast at the house of the Gallis, to which he had been invited, Benedetto hurried to the cathedral to practise on the organ for the last time.

In the empty cathedral, with its altar still draped in black, the powerful instrument droned and reverberated . . . Carlino, the bent old verger, was at work below on the marble floor. In moments of stillness, Carlino's rusty cough echoed so uncannily through the hollowness that Benedetto, behind the organ, suddenly imagined himself to be in a huge vault. The idea of the Galli vault had haunted his mind throughout the meal. He stopped playing and got up.

He breathed deeply as he stepped out of the cathedral. Then he shivered, and drew his cloak more closely around him. As he turned his back to the piazza, where money was being distributed to the poor, he knew that he had been released by Carlo.

He stretched himself. This evening, he was a free man.

Oh, he had really had enough of it. Enough of Carlo's spying. It had even crossed his mind to dispose of him with short shrift. He might after all have come to the conclusion that he was being pursued by a malefactor with evil intentions, and then he would be exonerated if he waited round a corner and brought him to silence. If people took a different view, then Benedetto would be compelled to flee. . . . Of his own accord, he would never have the heart to leave his mother behind in Todi. He knew very well that apart from him she had little in life; but suppose he *had* to escape?

The same might be said of the idea that was haunting his brain this evening. If he really carried out this insane idea, simply because he was obsessed by it and could no longer resist it, and something leaped out . . . It was true that he had an assignation that night with Lisetta the florist's daughter, and she, *poveretta*, would wet her pillow with her tears if he did not go to her, but would certainly maintain that he had been with her, if that would render him a service; but suppose something leaked out that overthrew her evidence? Then only the far distances could save him — provided he did not wait too long.

Did he already belong to those far distances?

It was a dark night. The moon would not be up till two o'clock.

What time was it now? How long had he been wandering about the city without noticing where he was going?

He made sure that Carlo was not upon his tracks. Nobody was in sight. Everyone in Todi was on the piazza.

He climbed over the city wall.

Just where the path he was following reached the main road to the churchyard, Luigino Vacca emerged from the low bushes.

Benedetto had anticipated this, and it disconcerted him only momentarily. He had counted upon it so much that he had not even bothered to procure tools.

With a laugh, Luigino passed off the awkwardness of their meeting. "So we understood each other," he said in a voice hoarse with agitation. "Have you brought the keys with you by any chance? If so we shan't need this stuff." He waved a sack.

"Who has the keys?"

"Christ, who should have them, if not her son? You're a disappointment. I believe I could have done it just as well by myself."

"Why did you wait, then?" inquired Benedetto.

Luigino mumbled something.

Silently they hurried forward. Luigino did not want to admit even to himself that he would not have cared to do that job in the pitch-black, deserted churchyard without the society of the *pipistrello*.

He walked dragging his foot, and to Benedetto it seemed that the Devil himself was limping beside him. For a second, vague superstitious fear of this limping gait came over him — was it really wise to set forth like this with one thus marked by Destiny?

But they were already bound together by the look they had exchanged at the graveside.

THE

ORGANIST

I

IN THE MORNING BY THE WELL, EVERY DETAIL CON-
cerning the terrible crime was canvassed. The report of it had been
brought to the city at sunrise by the old doorkeeper of the convent.
The family vault of the Gallis violated, the body of old Signora Galli
robbed of all the jewelry! God! that such a thing should be possible under
the sky of Todi. But with the help of the Madonna, the felon would be
unmasked; and then the executioner from Perugia would come — then for
the first time in half a century gallows would be erected on the piazza
in Todi.

Shuddering, the women filled their pitchers and hurried homewards
to tell their husbands all that their ears had just drunk in, with whatever
additions their fancy suggested. Then they returned to the well again,
leaving household duties undone in order to gather the very latest news:
for at the well all news was hatched.

The trio who set the tone at these daily conclaves had lost their leader.
One morning old Barberina had made them all shriek with laughter by
the well; and then, as she carried her heavy pitchers up the many stairs
towards her attic, she had dropped down dead. But the vacancy had been
filled by Manuela, wife of Lascari the cobbler. She would have been well
advised to hold her tongue about others, for there was more to be said
about her than about any other woman in Todi. She lured intoxicated men
to her dwelling so that her husband could win their money from them
with marked cards. Yes; but Manuela did not hold her tongue. She wagged
it so insolently that she won over her audience by the well. They now listened to her as credulously as once they had listened to the vilifications
and prophecies of old Barberina.

Benedetto crossed the piazzetta swiftly, rapt in thought. He was dressed for Mass. The women's voices were hushed as they looked after him.

"Surely he wouldn't have . . ." whispered one of them, with bated breath.

Manuela followed him with her eyes until he had turned the corner. Then she shook her head in contemptuous denial. "*He?* He would have done it in such a way that nobody would have known a thing about it."

Discovery had occurred in the following way: The decrepit old abbess, who had recently been haunted by evil suspicions, was in the habit, when she could not sleep, of wandering through the corridors of the convent. The night before, she had looked through a little barred window, and suddenly she imagined she saw a light in the churchyard. It rose from the earth and had the color of burning sulphur, so that she naturally concluded it was the Devil who had come to fetch old Signora Galli. In her great distress, she could think of only one thing to do: sound the alarm bell and call together all the nuns to pray, not revealing, however, in what shape Satan was roaming round the convent. At crack of dawn, she had gone with the doorkeeper to the home of the father-confessor, the one man in the neighborhood. He had not heard the alarm bell in the night. Scared, his eyes half-closed with sleep, he came peeping round the door, and the three of them went to resume possession of the cemetery in God's name. The father-confessor walked in front, carrying a raised crucifix in one hand and a heavy iron staff in the other, and behind him came the shuddering nuns. By then, of course, Satan had long since vanished; but the vault of the Galli family was open. . . .

The doorkeeper had seen it with her own eyes: the old lady still lay in her coffin, but the lid had been unscrewed. She gave off an odor in which only the Devil could have delighted, and she had been bereft of all her jewels as a punishment for the worldliness of her end. By the abbess's orders, the doorkeeper had set off for the city to inform the podesta, who had immediately communicated with the *bargello;* and now the surrounding country was being searched. Behind the tollhouse lived Il Zoppo, the hunchback; and the *sbirri* had already tapped the walls and the floor of his room, searched everywhere, but found nothing — nothing on his body, either. He was being kept in provisional custody.

Some wondered about the *pipistrello;* but would he still be in the city? Would he dare to sit down at the organ of the cathedral to play for the soul of the deceased, who had always been a kind of protectress to him? God would give a sign, would crush him with a flash of lightning there behind the organ for his sacrilegious act. No. Suddenly they realized who, and who alone, could be the guilty person: someone else who had enjoyed the favor of the deceased, a mysterious, lanky, devilish figure whose nickname served to scare the little ones to bed, and who, as it was whispered, had bewitched young Signora Galli so that she had had to flee to the convent. Nobody had ever fathomed his real self, and he had very good reasons for concealing it. His old protectress was barely cold before he had packed his belongings — he had not even waited for her funeral. Of course he knew then exactly what he was after. He had thought he could lull all suspicion by his ostentatious departure in the public diligence, and the sale of some of his valuables in Perugia, on the pretense of his being unable to travel farther otherwise. . . . In fact, he had then returned at once, and had lain in hiding in the neighborhood of Todi so as to be able to strike his blow in the night. Now he would be caught — he was such a noticeable figure with his specterlike lankiness and his long deceitful face. And when he heard that there was some money waiting for him, he would surely come back of his own accord. In point of fact, it was only necessary to wait, and in the meantime get on with the setting up of some good, high gallows. . . .

II

His head held high, Benedetto crossed the piazza. It was a fine morning in early summer. He could not understand how people took pleasure in talking so long and so exhaustively about such a gruesome subject as the desecration of a corpse.

Wide was the world, and the sun shone upon it. The fields around Todi were saturated with the light of the sun. The young green of the vineyards sucked it in drowsily. The sun bathed in the rivers that flowed past the cities towards the great sea. Cities — distant, great, never seen — basked in that same sun. The sun was also baking the closed shutters of the Todi secretariat, and Benedetto had not the least wish to go in there. Surely Signor Castagnoli would not have the bad taste to have him summoned on the great day when he was to play the organ for the soul of poor spoliated Signora Galli. On Monday Signor Castagnoli might summon him again. . . . But how far would little Matteo have to run to find him?

In an hour and a half, Benedetto must be in the cathedral. He had, therefore, plenty of time to visit Maestro Pallanza. Besides, there he would hear all the latest news. By taking the seat nearest the window in the barber's shop, he missed nothing of what happened on the piazza, and people could see him too — just in case they were expecting him to try and hide himself a little to-day.

As he stared across the piazza, waiting patiently until Maestro Pallanza could attend to him, his fingers played casually with some of the stolen jewels that lay in the pocket of his costly waistcoat.

If anybody was prepared to stake his life on Benedetto's innocence in the matter of this unsavory churchyard episode, it was Maestro Pallanza, who came hurrying forward with his shining, murderous barber's weapons: a pair of scissors, a razor, red-hot tongs. He never failed to show his delight at the honor he felt it was to welcome Benedetto in his shop.

"The whole city will come running to hear you in the cathedral, Sinorino Benedetto," he averred, as he turned industriously about him, impeding Benedetto's view of the piazza by his enormous girth, which had earned for him in popular parlance the nickname of *"Il gran Culone."*

Benedetto begged him to stand a little on one side, and only for a moment got his wish. Maestro Pallanza was growing too agitated over the suspicions that had arisen against the music master who had departed so unexpectedly.

"I can still see him, signori, sitting here in my shop," he said indignantly. "I always attended him in person. If he really had something to do with this crime, there will be nothing left for me to do but to close this shop and go."

In despair, Maestro Pallanza raised his eyes on high. His clients tried to convince him that he was exaggerating the awfulness of his position, but he maintained his point of view, and as he spoke his girth again obliterated Benedetto's view.

A fresh client came in with the news that the *bargello* in person had assured him that a clue had been found, though he had refused to say more. This announcement was received with general skepticism; nor did it disturb Benedetto's peace of mind. But he thought it wise, upon leaving the shop, to drop in at The Three Popes — although he had intended to avoid the inn that day.

The taproom was completely deserted, but it was filled with the sounds of a violent quarrel in the kitchen. Benedetto stood still, hesitating, his hand on the knob of the outer door.

There were sounds of stamping and kicking, and above the row made by two struggling men could be heard Luigino's enraged, muffled voice.

"Tell me what you're looking for. Why have you turned my bed upside down, you old swine? And what business is it of yours how late I come home? Come here, I'll — "

Through the swearing, through the sobs of Susanna and the whimpering of the children, came Nana's piercing voice: "Let him go, you coward!

Do you want to murder your own father? Ghoul that you are! Holy Mary! You accursed scoundrel! Yes, try and deny it was you. The smell of the corpse still hangs about you. Oh, oh, yes, go on. Beat me to death! I don't want to go on living here any longer, now that the smell of corpses hangs about the house. When Carlo comes, I shall tell him. Then I shall tell him . . ."

Benedetto stared upon the ground. Slowly he left the inn.

He took a deep breath of the outside air. Uncertain what to do, he walked against the stream of people coming towards the cathedral.

Where did he want to go? He himself did not know. A taste bitter as gall was on his tongue. In his ears rang Nana's accusation. He who, after that nocturnal exploit, had returned coolly to the city, intending to watch the course of events and to play the great organ for the edification of the faithful, suddenly realized his danger. Nana's words, too, brought back to his senses the revolting smell that had risen from the coffin of old Signora Galli. It had almost made him faint at the time, and he had done his macabre work holding his breath and turning his face away. . . . A few rings that simply would not come off he had left to Luigino. When he got home, he had immediately washed his hands carefully, but perhaps the odor still hung about his clothes, and his hair — or would Maestro Pallanza's perfumes and scents have driven it away?

What was it that the old woman had said: that the smell of a corpse remained hanging about the house?

With a sudden feeling of oppression, he fled into a dark church, the little church of Saint Clare. No one was there — everybody was hurrying that morning towards the cathedral. Hastily he dipped his hands in the holy water stoup. He seemed unable to feel the coolness of the water upon them, and yet the moisture was dripping from his fingers.

He hurried to the side chapel, where the Madonna was enthroned to whom his mother had brought him as a child. Since then, She had never seen him; but She was not angry. Perhaps She had heard about him and about his playing of the organ. Gently She smiled down upon him. Mary, full of sweet compassion. She could not be angry with him — neither could Marietta, Nana, Imma, nor any of the women and girls of Todi. Gratefully he looked up at Her. How beautiful She was!

He confessed nothing to Her. Why should he give Her pain? He only implored Her to have pity on his poor mother. She knew that it had never been his intention to surround his mother's house with the revolting smell of a corpse. It had happened through thoughtlessness.

"O Holy Mother of God!" After all, he was betraying more to Her in his confusion than he had intended. He tried to obscure the truth from

Her, speaking only of his mother whom he had never loved as he loved her at that moment, now that he had brought destruction upon her.

Suddenly he thought he heard the ringing of the bells — and immediately he realized that they must have been booming in his ears for some time. He got up, kissed the feet of the little Madonna, and hurried away.

When he reached the piazza, people were still streaming by. He slowed down his steps and threw back his head. With calm composure, his eyes took in the piazza, including the inn where, no doubt, the quarrel was still going on. Happily, it had not attracted the attention of the churchgoers. His mouth, that but a moment ago had stammered in his great need for confession, was now fixed in a slightly conceited smile.

He was confident that the Virgin would protect him as long as the Mass lasted. When afterwards, in the course of the day, everything came out and people damned him, making his poor mother pay for his guilt — then the memory of his playing upon the cathedral organ would be in strange contrast with their cursing. Even if he had known that the executioner from Perugia would be standing behind him ready to put the halter about his neck as the last chord from the organ died — even then he would have gone to the cathedral, where his mother too was waiting to hear him play.

The only pity was that Carlo would not be among the congregation. Carlo, acting on the orders of the *bargello*, was busy in the churchyard searching for any traces the desecrator might have left behind.

The moment his quick fingers touched the keys, ecstasy flooded through him. If those who knelt below in prayer had ears to hear, then they should hear the devils of purgatory fighting for the soul of the departed that hungered for release. . . . Or was it only the dark passions in Benedetto's own soul? Was the hunger of Signora Galli's guilty soul Benedetto's own longing to get away from here, from Todi that had become a purgatory to him? Against the stormy bellowing of throngs of demons a tenderer melody crept in. Everyone below would feel in it his own sorrow, his own shy, thirsty tenderness. To Benedetto himself, perhaps, came the thought of the grief he was about to bring upon his mother.

Now the light of liberation broke through. Now purgatory was releasing the soul of Signora Galli. The heavens opened wide, wide, to receive the soul of Signora Galli; and all the souls that had contrived to clutch hold of it and were escaping with it from the tormenting devils. There below in the cathedral they could be seen, those golden depths of heaven — or were they the distances far from Todi, haloed in glorious light? Were they the resounding cymbals of oncoming angels — or were they really the clarion calls of this world? But no one noticed the deception, except perhaps Marietta, who was bending forward, her face concealed in her hands.

The older nuns, who had been sent by the abbess to support the prayers for the deceased by witnessing to the magnificent gifts she had made to the convent, saw their heavenly Bridegroom appear in a halo of golden light — as they had imagined Him on the day they took the veil.

The gray, austere priest celebrating the solemn Mass in Monsignore's place picked up the chalice under a momentary hallucination that it appeared to be filled, not with the customary wine from the sacristy, but with the blood of the Redeemer. . . . Not since his youth had such an idea crossed his mind.

The citizens stared into the heaven that Benedetto had conjured up, thinking what a great thing was faith after all. They who had been full of distress over the frightful crime in the churchyard, and over all those things that daily brought restlessness to their souls, felt a soothing balm flow through them; and while the soul of old Signora Galli rose to eternity on the wings of prayer, their own souls were blessed. They made good resolutions, and really thought they would carry them out.

And for these beautiful, pious emotions, they had to thank the devil-possessed organist, who sat above dragging them through good and evil and all the elements of the universe, in order to leave them purified, penetrated by God, as they stumbled to their feet and left the cathedral full of pious humility.

They knew, now, that no one else in Todi could play the organ like that incorrigible sinner Benedetto, and that much must be forgiven him therefor.

But how many among them felt a vague foreboding that they had heard the organ played thus for the last time?

In a few hours, when night had enveloped the world in its velvet mantle, Benedetto — if Fate had not already reached out her hand towards him — intended to abandon the little city forever.

Without a sound, like a bat, he would spread his wings and flutter away into the safety of the dark, fathomless night.

Then the abbess need no longer go her rounds with a lantern through the dim convent corridors, fearful lest some novice were unfaithful to her future Bridegroom in heaven.

Then the young girls still of this world would no longer be sorely tempted to lend the keys of their rooms or to leave their windows open on mellow spring nights.

Jealous husbands would snore deeply and restfully upon the matrimonial couch.

And the pile of uncopied documents beside a certain desk in the secretariat would diminish rapidly under the newborn efforts of some other young coypist.

Oh, yes. Here and there a sigh of relief would rise up, and over the little city would spread a peace, a beneficent, long-desired peace that could barely be improved upon by death itself. And the rich who feared the terrible shame of passing for poor in the hereafter could slumber undisturbed in their chilly mausoleums.

III

Outside, the churchgoers were met by a piece of news that dragged them from the heights of exaltation down to the direst reality. A crowd of men had collected outside The Three Popes. Luigino Vacca was being pushed and dragged outside by his own father, by Carlo, and by two *sbirri*. Blood was pouring down his white, panic-stricken face. Susanna, clinging to her brother's uniform, was being dragged along too. Her dress was torn, exposing the tired breasts that had nourished six infants. But she was as unconscious of that as of the child that clutched at her skirts.

"Carlo! God, why are you taking my husband away? Carlo! He didn't do it!" She shrieked as only a desperate woman can shriek. Carlo himself was as pale as death, but his face expressed unalterable resolution. He looked like the small Carlo who had dared call his father to account. He thrust Susanna angrily on one side, and she collapsed upon the steps of the inn. Vacca, conscious of the crowd's repulsion towards him for acting the part of judge towards his own son, broke out into the most awful curses. "Serve him right! He's no longer my son." Nana pulled Susanna up from the steps, supported her in her old arms, closed her torn bodice.

The crowd watched eagerly: had God revealed the criminal?

"Be careful! I didn't do it," bellowed Luigino. For a moment, he looked over their heads; he thought he could see Benedetto walking rapidly by. "Why should it have been me? Nothing has been found on me. Proofs, if you please, before you can hang me — proofs!" The fear of death glowed in his wide-open eyes.

Benedetto slipped through the entrance to his parents' home, glanced quickly round the deserted courtyard, and hurried up the old worm-eaten stairs. A child wailing in the dusk of the passage interrupted his sobs to

look up at Benedetto, who pressed a coin into his little hand without realizing that he did so. He became dimly aware that it must be one of
Cesare the carrier's children — Cesare's family was sinking into hopeless
poverty. Then, with rapid, careful steps, he strode into the room where
his parents were waiting for their midday meal.

It was his father who had suggested that they should wait for him to-day,
after the great event in the cathedral. He had already remarked to Andrea
several times that probably Benedetto had yet to receive the good wishes
of the church authorities.

Marietta was the first to hear him, and got up to get the food. She looked
at him vaguely. The voice in which she welcomed him sounded strange
and unreal.

She said little, but in her eyes he read the effect of his playing of the
organ. She appeared to be still overcome by it. When she had heard, that
morning at the well, about the robbery in the churchyard, she had been
confused and agitated; but her tormenting suspicions had evidently entirely subsided.

Benedetto took his place at table. It was so strange, to be having another
meal here. He too was silent. Sometimes he seemed to be listening to
something happening at a distance. Then, reassured again, he strummed
on the table. His mother was again invaded by anxiety as she watched this
nervous gesture.

His father was talking. As a matter of fact, he had intended to express
his admiration for Benedetto's performance in the cathedral. Yes; but now
that he saw his boy sitting there, he could not find the right words — was
afraid of expressing himself badly — and thus it was that Antonio, when
he opened his mouth, suddenly heard himself speak about the other great
sensation of the day, which had perhaps made an even deeper impression
on him.

Despite his familiarity with death, he was filled with the deepest aversion
to the very thought of opening a coffin that had once been screwed down;
and he added that although he had thought Luigino Vacca capable of a
good deal, he had not thought him capable of that.

"But how do you know it was he?" broke out Marietta in sudden exasperation.

In astonishment, Antonio looked at her. "But his own father says — "

"His own father? His *father?*"

Antonio felt her taunt, and grew embarrassed under it. Guiltily, helplessly, he looked at his son, who took no notice and bent over his plate.

Suddenly, in the silence, Andrea said softly: "It was fine in the cathedral . . . I sometimes went to listen in San Jacopo's, but . . ."

"Yes, the organ in the cathedral is quite a different thing," said Benedetto, flattered.

"Yes, but you must not put it all down to the organ," intervened Antonio hastily. "Father Joshua is not just anybody, but he can't play it like you. Everybody said so. Yes, and then we came out, and . . ."

Benedetto gave a little laugh, and Antonio thought his son was deriding him because he had thoughtlessly reverted to that other topic about which Marietta refused to hear anything. He had difficulty in getting through his food. He had not really enjoyed it from the start — the day was too exciting and unusual.

Marietta did not touch a thing upon her plate. Benedetto and Andrea both tried to do honor to the meal; but Benedetto was sharply aware of his mother's rising anxiety. . . . And at the same time not the smallest sound that reached the room from outside eluded him, and he was thinking to himself that, while he was quietly pouring out a second — no, a third — glass of wine, the *bargello* was busy examining Luigino under torture. At this moment, perhaps, the *bargello* was saying: "Don't deny it any longer, for the jewels have already been found in your house," and Luigino, by this time dazed and worn-out, would perhaps ask venomously, "*All* the jewels?" And when the *bargello*, unmoved and persevering in mendacity, said, "Certainly, all the jewels" — then Luigino would break into bitter, jeering laughter. As he helped himself to more wine, Benedetto seemed to hear every word of this conversation, and also that laugh. . . .

After the meal, he continued to sit in silence and, without knowing it, resumed his nervous strumming on the table. Several times Marietta gave him a long, penetrating look. She could not take her eyes from those strumming fingers. Finally, she got up slowly and with difficulty, and began to clear the table.

Anxiety rising within him, Benedetto felt compelled to speak.

"I'm just going to the piazza," he said. "I want to hear what they've been able to get out of Luigino." The wine was making him more talkative. "Actually, I don't believe it was he — Luigino is frightened . . . He'd never have dared to go to the churchyard alone by night."

"But who said he was alone?" snapped Antonio.

On her way to the kitchen, Marietta stood still on the threshold.

Benedetto looked thoughtfully at his father. "That we shall soon know," he said, "for Luigino is not the sort to try and save his accomplice when he can no longer save himself."

Behind the kitchen door, a dish fell. Marietta bent down to pick up the pieces with trembling hands. Andrea rushed forward to help her, while Antonio looked round at her in astonishment. Benedetto got up from his chair and left the room.

IV

In the courtyard, he heard somebody call him softly by name, and he stood still with a start. It was Manuela. She was peering through one of the shutters above the shop. She was laughing.

"Just come in for a moment — Lascari isn't in."

He remained standing where he was, strangely bewildered. It vaguely dawned upon him that all this had happened once before. He had been a small boy, and had been unable to resist the mysterious attraction of that place. Once again he would go in — he dared not go on until he had learned what Manuela had to say to him. A finger beckoned him — was it perhaps one of the severed fingers of old Signora Galli?

After casting a rapid glance about him, he bent his head to pass through the low door and went straight in to the back room. Manuela was coming downstairs, wafting about her an unpleasantly heavy perfume.

Paint and powder were useless any longer to conceal the devastation of her face. She laughed again when she saw how full of repugnance was the glance with which Benedetto looked her up and down. She tried to take him under the chin. He thrust away her hand.

"What do you want with me?" he demanded.

And only then did he see that she was drunk. She staggered as she made for the cupboard.

"I want to pour you out a glass of wine," she said.

"You can spare yourself the trouble. I'm going."

"You don't mean that. I wanted to have a word with you. In the old days, you used to sit with me and drink my wine." Disappointment broke through her voice. " 'Wine with sugar in it? Why certainly, little man.' I say — " she cried with bated breath. "Do *you* believe Luigino did it?"

Benedetto was still standing on the threshold.

"I'll never believe it," pursued Manuela. "One moment they say it's this one, and the next it's that. This morning it began by being you. I said at once, 'That's impossible.' Ah well, come here now, and let me pour you out a glass of wine as in the old days."

He approached one step.

Manuela pushed a glass towards him across the table. " 'That's impossible,' I said at once, 'because as it happens I know precisely where he was last night.' "

She laughed at the amazement in his eye.

"With you?" he asked in a flat tone.

She nodded, gulping down the wine. "Yes, and as I said that at the risk of Lascari's hearing about it and of his beating me to death . . . surely that's proof that I have a weakness for you. That's why you might be a little more friendly towards me than you have been up to now. You must know I'm a respectable woman." She nodded her head gravely. "You go and ask if I'm not. Only you I can't resist. You — and Mariotti the tailor. And it's just you two who turn your backs on me. If he hasn't gone again!" she cried out sadly. "That's the thanks I get. Prefers the gallows to having spent a night with Manuela!" She spat upon the floor contemptuously. Then she dropped down beside the table and emptied his glass.

"And how often haven't I lied for him before, in the old days," she complained in bitter self-reproach.

Before the house of the *bargello* surged a crowd of people. Vacca had gone inside to bear witness against his son. Curiosity overcoming repugnance, the limping innkeeper was surrounded and plied with questions as he came out again. He answered hoarsely: "Whatever he may say, he did it. If they let him off, I won't have him in my inn again. I won't have a grave-robber under my roof."

Benedetto just caught what he was saying, and moved away as he had come.

In the little courtyard behind the kitchen of the inn some women and children had gathered. They had been turned out of the inn, which was still being searched from cellar to attic by the *sbirri* under Carlo's leadership. The children were crying. Susanna stared vacantly in front of her, not hearing her neighbors' words of consolation. Nana, her face swollen, was explaining to everyone, and in particular to old Cesare, that no one except Luigino could have stolen the jewels. "What else was he doing away all night? He only got home at daybreak. He took off his shoes downstairs, and came upstairs in his stockings . . ." That was the first thing that had struck Nana as peculiar, for it was quite unheard of, that Luigino should bother about anybody else's sleep. He certainly thought no one had heard him, but, as it happened, Nana could not fall asleep because of the blows she had received the day before. She was thankful now that she had had that beating. She was feeling extraordinarily fit after the extra beating she had received to-day. She wept when she thought of that poor woman there with her brood, for whom perhaps there would no longer be room in the house.

Cesare was nodding, full of care, and saying — more to the people than to Susanna, who could take in nothing — that naturally his daughter could return to her parents. Fortunately, his wife was accustomed to having little children sprawling about the floor.

"They can always come to my kitchen and take away something to eat," said Nana, and several women began to cry. Nana herself had stopped crying. She was dabbing a wound on her thin elbow, and as she looked up she suddenly imagined she saw Benedetto peering from a distance over the heads of the people. . . . When he felt that she had observed him, he slipped away at once. Nana did not know what it was that had struck her as so strange in his look. She was going to say something, and then refrained.

At that moment, Vacca returned from the *bargello*, swearing and raging because Luigino would not confess.

Only a minute earlier, Nana would have echoed him; but now she was speechless. Not a word would cross her old gray lips.

Benedetto wandered here and there. A little later, returning once more to the piazza, he observed the arrival of two travelers, who were denied access to the inn by the *sbirri*. As they had not the slightest interest in a police search, about which they knew nothing, they cried shame on the reception Todi gave to travelers. It was late in the afternoon, too late to reach Orvieto before dark. A bold but almost childish woman's voice, with a foreign accent, resounded from the closed coach. In curiously incorrect Italian, she was saying exactly what she thought of such treatment. The *sbirri* were quite nonplussed.

Benedetto edged his way through the surging crowd, made his bow before the coach door, and declared that the podesta of Todi, not wishing travelers to receive an unfavorable impression of his city, would certainly put them up at his house for the night. Curiously, graciously, penetratingly, a very young woman looked down upon him from the dim interior of the coach, holding back a little dog that barked at him viciously. He hurried away to issue orders in the palace of the podesta. These were somewhat dubiously received: was he really in a position to give orders, now that the old Signora was dead? That did not worry Benedetto. For the last time, he was showing his power here; and the podesta, hearing about it, acquiesced, just as he had once acquiesced in Signor Pompeati's uninvited stay.

After a moment, Benedetto awakened from his intoxication. He had intended to invite himself to the evening meal at the house of the Gallis. He had not seen enough of the fair stranger who, from her pronunciation, appeared to him to be Spanish. Would he ever see her again?

She intended to pursue her journey to Orvieto to-morrow. . . . As soon as darkness made escape possible, that was the direction Benedetto intended to take.

If only Luigino attested to his innocence that long! If only the jewels hidden in the inn were not found until dusk had descended upon the world!

Sometimes he imagined he felt the eyes of the crowd already on his back. He broke out into sweat, and did not know where to go. It seemed as if only now had the imminent danger in which he stood become clear to him. How in God's name could he have been so lightheaded as to return to Todi last night? At all costs, he must avoid being caught in the city. If they wanted to catch him — then he would defend himself to the death.

Everywhere the questions with which the *bargello* was trying to extract a confession of guilt from Luigino pursued Benedetto. "Tell me the whole truth! As the jewels have not yet accused you of being yourself the criminal, a confession may lighten your punishment. Did you have accomplices? Relieve your conscience, Luigino, and think of your own interest. . . . Were you perhaps led astray by another?"

Benedetto was struggling for breath. What time was it? The sun was already hanging low. It was broiling hot: was there going to be a storm? The swallows, however, were wheeling high above the pinnacles of the towers.

If only dusk would fall! Then they might see if they could overtake him!

He simply would not be caught here. He refused to die here. Death, no. Old Signora Galli was dead. That was all right for her, and if she had not taken her jewels away with her into the grave, she would still have all her fingers. . . . Was that a reason for destroying a young life? To avenge a dead person as old as the hills?

He wanted to live. He wanted to see the distances that were calling him.

One moment — his passport! He had almost forgotten his passport.

In the secretariat, the old clerks Stefani and Cesarotti were still copying documents. He greeted them as he entered. They looked up at him with quick surprise. They had heard of the Mass in the cathedral; they had heard of the robbery of the jewels in the churchyard; but they sat there writing. . . .

Benedetto also was writing. The scratching of his pen mingled indistinguishably with theirs. He had taken a sheet of stamped paper, and was writing out his passport by the fading light of day. He added, with an easy flourish, the initials of Castagnoli the chief clerk and of the podesta, scattered sand over the whole document, folded it carefully, and thrust it into his coat pocket.

He went away again, hardly able to contain his satisfaction.

Vaguely mistrustful, the clerks looked up at him over their iron spectacles and exchanged a few words as their pens continued to scratch.

Twilight was settling over the city. The silhouettes of the houses were growing vague, and in the shadow it was already difficult to distinguish the passers-by. The *sbirri* in The Three Popes were using lanterns as they continued their search; still nothing had been found. They were getting discouraged. Only Carlo would not give up, but pursued the search, venting his silent rage upon the house, which he was tearing to pieces.

At the office of the *bargello*, a priest had been led in: he had offered to extract Luigino's secret by the help of the crucifix and the most frightful threats of damnation.

Benedetto had not yet heard this latest piece of news. His passport seemed to be burning through his breast pocket. His anxiety decreased steadily as the dusk increased. At the same time, he grew more careful. He imagined that danger lurked behind every street corner, and continually he took stock of his position, considering how he could make his escape should it be necessary.

In an hour's time darkness would have fallen; and the moon would not be up till three o'clock in the morning. . . .

He thought of the young Spanish woman who was now sitting at the podesta's table. He had seen her for a moment only, and in his feverish agitation his mind had not properly registered her features. He hoped he would see her again in Orvieto, and in the meantime he tried to conjure up her image, but his memory would not serve him. She was infinitely fairer than any girl in Todi. She was the fairest woman in all Andalusia. She was fiery as the sun and tender as the moon. He knew that he must follow her, even to the ends of the world.

Such were the visions that passed through Benedetto's mind. He no longer seemed to hear the bellowing of Luigino, confronted by all the terrors of hell, and afraid to lay his hand upon the crucifix as he protested his innocence. . . .

Then suddenly — there was a sound. It came from here, from there. It swept through the streets, came clattering round the corners, multiplied itself by division: —

"Luigino has unburdened his soul!"

A shadow slipped swiftly across the courtyard of the great house, and now in Antonio's home Marietta and her son were in each other's arms. They exchanged but few words; he tried to wipe away her tears, to console her.

"Mother — forgive me. Say you forgive me. Everything will fall upon you. But I've implored the Virgin to . . ."

"Where did you go? Tell me, quick. Was it to Saint Clare's? I'll go there too. You have been the light of my life — now it is being extinguished. Now it is extinguished . . . But it isn't your fault. Don't ask if I forgive you. My boy!"

Was it his mother or his beloved whom he was pressing to him? Was it her son or her lover whose kisses she was drinking with hungry lips?

He was the first to awaken from their intoxication. He raised his head, listening.

Bewildered, she also tried to listen.

Then, like a hawk, he swooped upon the red bundle in the alcove that her hands had mechanically put together for him that afternoon.

"Mother, they shan't get me!" A wild, cruel jubilation. For the last time he pressed the woman in his arms. Torn with anguish, she surrendered to his fire, and remained standing, impotent and soulless, where he left her.

Somewhere above, just under the roof, hasty footsteps were still creeping. Then all was still. Empty, giddily empty was the house. Marietta had to cling to something to prevent herself from falling.

Slowly she awakened from her swoon. . . . She hurried to the window, and saw below that *sbirri* were posting themselves at the exit of the house. She threw up her head. An insane pride made her blood race again. She felt ready to receive those who willed the undoing of her boy.

Meanwhile, he was at that moment fleeing over the roofs. He sprang across an alley, making a gutter fall just where two women were standing chattering: they fainted, and did not recover their senses again that evening. He dashed into a skylight, and, trusting blindly to his luck, jumped down in the dark, falling through a mouldering table with a dull thud. Down the stairs, through corridors, past terrified women. A man tried to stop him. Then through another window, down a pipe — a cat's spring sideways on hands and feet — away into the night.

A hundred yards from the west gate, which was being carefully watched, he climbed over the city wall.

Under a moonless heaven spangled with stars, Benedetto walked upon the threshold of that wide world for which he had so hungered and which God, or the Devil, had decreed should be his home henceforth.

BOOK THREE

CARNIVAL AND
CONFESSION

AT

GRAZIADEO

THE JEWELER'S

A GONDOLA DREW IN ALONGSIDE THE DARK, deserted quay, and a young man in an ample cloak, a three-cornered hat pulled over his eyes, jumped onto the waterside and walked over to the houses to pick out a few copper soldi by the dim light of a votive lamp.

The *barcaiuolo* threw his fare casually onto the little carpet that covered the bottom of his gondola and inquired, "Shall I wait, signore?"

"Yes — but not just here. Wait for me by San Pantaleone's."

At that moment, the silence was rent by the shrill sound of the bells of that very church. The gondola slipped away noiselessly, under a little rounded bridge on which the moonlight fell. As he entered the blackness below it, the gondolier bent low and gave his warning call.

Stillness. The water plopped against the worn stone walls. In the deep shadow it was invisible. Where it was touched by the moonlight it became a mysterious, living, green viscous substance that seemed to have nothing in common with water.

The young man had disappeared when, a moment later, two women — black figures with flowing skirts and shawls drawn over their heads — appeared from a narrow alley, crossed the little bridge, and glided away into another alley on the other side.

With a gentle, ingenuous smile the little image of the Madonna looked down on the spot where the young man had stood for a second: Benedetto, who had found his way from Todi to Venice.

In the small square near by, he addressed himself to a worthy Venetian taking his evening walk, escorted by a servant who was armed and carried a lantern. He wanted to know the address of a Jewish jeweler of the neighborhood. After an elaborate interchange with his servant, the Venetian gave no less elaborate directions, with many wavings of his ivory cane.

At that moment, two women — one young, the other old and bent — passed hurriedly by, as it happened in the direction he was indicating; and the worthy Venetian allowed his cane to drop as he followed with his eyes the younger of the two, who walked with the gait of Artemis. Benedetto, too, was fascinated by her walk, by her entire appearance. He suddenly lost all interest in the other's further explanations, and, thanking him with a courtly bow, took the direction in which his cane had pointed.

Forgetting for the nonce his Jewish jeweler, Benedetto pursued Artemis, of whose pure profile he had caught a glimpse in the moonlight.

Was she aware that she was being followed, and was she perhaps perturbed at finding herself in the streets at this hour without masculine escort? She seemed to him to be hastening her steps. . . . She bent her head sideways and said something to her duenna, who looked round and, on short misshapen legs, began almost to trot. Benedetto stood still and smiled. He had awakened from the spell under which he had fallen so rapidly and unexpectedly — it had not been his intention to frighten two women.

Bringing his mind back with some difficulty to his Jew, he was about to turn at random into a narrow side street — when lo, the two women stood suddenly in front of him. The duenna groped under her skirts for a key, but her young, agitated mistress could not wait: she began to rattle excitedly at the door knocker, the sound of which reverberated through the deserted alley.

They went in.

Benedetto slowly approached, and came to a standstill in front of the house into which they had disappeared. It was an old house, with barred windows and an iron-mounted door over which hung a signboard: —

SOLOMON GRAZIADEO

JEWELER

The inscription on it was repeated underneath in Hebrew lettering. He had arrived precisely where he wished to be. He let the door knocker fall — a wrought-iron knocker, shaped like some mythical bird. Someone peered through the judas: an old Jew with a thin gray beard — the jeweler

Graziadeo himself. He opened the door as soon as Benedetto mentioned the business that had brought him.

"Come right through here, Cavaliere — and mind you don't stumble," the Jew warned him, preceding him with a candle down a short flight of stairs that led to a corridor. With his tired, sharply chiseled head sunk deep between his shoulders, and his thin old legs that he lacked the vanity to pad, he bore a certain resemblance to a marabou or other exotic, long-legged bird which, to raise a laugh, had donned large felt slippers. "Here we are. Geronimo . . . !" He snapped his fingers impatiently and from a back room came, stumbling hastily, a virile youth of rustic appearance who took the candle and examined the stranger sharply — giving Benedetto the impression that it was his duty not only to carry the light, but also to protect his master's safety.

With a courteous gesture, the old man offered a chair to Benedetto, who sat down and looked about him. He had given up hope of seeing his Artemis again — by now, indeed, she had slipped out of his mind. He attempted to conceal the nervousness that was coming over him behind an appearance of assurance.

Never before had he been in such close contact with a Jew — not even in Florence or Bologna. He had always assumed that a Jew was an inferior being, to be treated with lordly disdain; and he was nonplussed by the strange, subdued refinement of the gestures and voice of this old Hebrew, into whose house he had already, to his amazement, seen the self-possessed young woman and her duenna disappear. He was beginning to wonder whether he had come to the right address, and whether perhaps this Jew might not demand proofs of the origin of the jewels Benedetto meant to offer him.

The room to which he had been led appeared to be arranged with the object of making clients forget that they were dealing with a buyer and seller of jewels. It was more like a study, the study of one interested in natural history, chemistry, and books.

"You are something of a scholar in your spare time, Signor Graziadeo?"

"I am in the habit of being what my clients wish me to be," answered the old man, with a smile and a touch of flattery. Then, coming to the point at once: "I believe you have come to sell me some jewels."

Benedetto nodded, put his hands in his pockets, and silently laid upon the table rings, necklaces, bracelets, earrings, all mixed up, until he could find nothing more. Slowly, his interest roused, the Jew bent over the small gleaming pile, and, without looking up, softly said a word that only his servant understood. He did not at once take the magnifying glass that

Geronimo offered him. He allowed the jewels to slip piece by piece through his fingers, weighed them in his hand while his thoughts were elsewhere, sorted them out according to some system that only he understood, and re-sorted them differently.

Somewhere in an adjoining room a clock ticked gravely. Suddenly, above the oak ceiling, there was the scratching of rats. Then it was still again. . . . Benedetto sat motionless, his face pale against the background of the dim room. In spite of his desire to keep calm, his eyes were gleaming like the stones that lay in front of Graziadeo.

For weeks, Benedetto had given hardly a thought to the way in which he had come by these gems. The early summer night on which he had left Todi seemed to lie in the far — the infinitely far — past. It was autumn now. . . . A world of which he had dreamed with longing had unfurled itself before him since that night, yielded its secrets to him — almost too generously, so that he had already grown weary of it. All that while, he had had these trinkets lying at the bottom of his trunk, and not once had he examined them. When they had happened to catch his eye, he had tried to understand how he could have brought such danger upon himself for the sake of a few bracelets, earrings, rings, necklets. . . . Why had they, now, suddenly regained the luster that had lured him irresistibly towards old Signora Galli's grave? Was it the magic of the candlelight reflected from a thousand facets? Was it the way the Jew took them in his hands and fondled them?

Graziadeo began to inspect each separate piece under a magnifying glass. As he did so he murmured to himself as though he were talking to the jewels: "They include a few doubles. That's a pity. And Cassius-purple paste is scarcely a ruby. . . . The lady to whom these earrings belonged was cheated. Cassius-purple paste! If a Jew were to sell such 'rubies' he would be sent to the gallows, and wouldn't that be his proper place? But this pearl and emerald necklace is a magnificent piece. . . . How can you bring yourself to part with so beautiful a thing for a handful of ducats?"

Benedetto was almost reassured: in that last sentence he recognized the Jew as he had always been represented to him from his childhood. Instead of allowing himself to be excited, however, he maintained a cool reserve and, with a faint suggestion of mockery, said, "I'm inviting you to make an offer for the whole collection."

The Jew raised his eyebrows thoughtfully as if this request took him somewhat by surprise. Piece by piece he examined the jewels again, and such was the time he took that Benedetto began to grow impatient. The old man might at least say something!

At last Graziadeo said, in a voice that seemed to struggle with some deep-rooted hesitation: "You cannot expect more than a thousand sequins for the whole collection."

Among the jewels on the table there were, to Benedetto's knowledge, single pieces that had cost more than that — large, tasteless pieces, thick with magnificent gems; but he also knew that he would not gather the jewels together to take them to another dealer. It would not be safe to go hawking them about the city. For four months he had not dared to let anyone touch them. He had now been bold enough to do so only because Venice was a city of a thousand strangers who gambled away their money in the Ridotto of San Moisè, and then had to sell or pawn their jewels. Besides, he was in need of money, and at once — money to repay a debt of honor before midnight, money for a new passport on which he intended to change his name for the fourth time, money to settle his account at the inn where he had lived for a month so that he could free his trunk and take a private lodging somewhere. It had come to his ears that, as soon as carnival began, — and it began next day, — the sbirri were in the habit of searching the inns at dead of night; and he preferred to sleep undisturbed. For a thousand reasons, he must get rid of these jewels that he had carried about with him so long. Besides, as they lay there gleaming on the table, some curse seemed still to deny his ownership of them, though he had placed his life in the balance for them. As for the Jew who hoped to buy them at a receiver's price, they would belong even less to him. They were ownerless, as intangible as the twinkling stars in heaven, and it seemed incredible that a man could be found prepared to count out a thousand sequins for so illusory a property. Benedetto was tempted to agree to Graziadeo's offer at once, and eagerly. He trembled at the possibility that fear and suspicion might take possession of the Jew, and cause him to change his mind; and it was only because the simplest of tactical rules ordained that one should never and nowhere accept a first offer that he said, "I was making a serious proposal, Signor Graziadeo."

"And do you think, Cavaliere, that the offer of a thousand sequins is not a very serious business for me?" retaliated the Jew, pretending that his feelings had been wounded.

"For you? A serious business? But another jeweler might laugh to hear you say that."

Graziadeo hesitated. Then suddenly he elected to abandon the little game: Benedetto had gone too far. The Jew pushed the jewels towards him across the table, and his decision to renounce the purchase seemed a relief to him. "Very well. Go to another jeweler, and have a good laugh together at my expense," he said, without anger.

Benedetto, disconcerted, hesitated to gather up his treasure again, and the Jew gave him a slow, penetrating, sardonic look: the disdain that played about those proud young lips only amused him now.

"No jeweler cares to buy so many valuable pieces from a stranger unless he produces guarantees and references," said Graziadeo gently, almost confidentially. "All that I know of you is that you do not belong to Venice — I can see that by your dress, and I hear it in your speech. I can understand very well that the Cavaliere does not wish to mention his name in this house. . . . But then, on my side, I may be allowed to refer to you as a stranger." He paused, as if to give Benedetto an opportunity to speak; but Benedetto remaining haughtily silent, the old man continued: "To affront you is the last thing I desire, Cavaliere. But I cannot forbear to mention one thing. It needs some courage to venture upon this purchase. At any moment the *sbirri* might be standing at one's door and turning the whole house upside down, because they expected to find I know not what. . . ."

The *sbirri*. He had spoken of the *sbirri*. For weeks on end Benedetto had felt them behind him, but they had never been so close as they were at that moment when the jewels of old Signora Galli lay upon that table for sale. Invisible, but present, were the *sbirri*. They were lurking there in the dark, waiting only for a sign from the Jew to come forward and lay their hands upon his shoulders. He had known that this moment of danger waited him inevitably unless he could be strong enough to rid himself of the jewels unseen, to throw them into one of the canals when nobody was about. Was old dead Signora Galli in the room too, perhaps? Was he merely selling the jewels on her behalf?

By an effort, Benedetto shook these insane imaginings from his mind, and said: "The profitableness of the transaction must be your return for the risk you are pleased to attach to it, Signor Graziadeo. I can give you no guarantee, and so far I have no references here in Venice. Still less can I compel you to trust me."

"Oh, but I trust you completely, Cavaliere," the old man hastened to declare, and he sounded almost genuine. "I'm not asking for any explanation. Suppose you were, however, to tell me, for instance, that these jewels belonged to your sister who has just sought refuge in a convent where her trinkets are no longer any use to her . . . Then I should believe you unconditionally. I was only wondering whether the *sbirri* would believe me, in my turn. You don't know what they are like. How could you? But ask a Jew about the *sbirri*! I don't mean to say that they've ever crossed my threshold; but I know their little ways all the same, the least obnoxious of which are the breaking-in of doors and the overthrowing of cupboards. . . . I was about to make you an offer of a thousand sequins. Fortunately, you did not fall in with it." With almost revulsion, he began to sift some of the gems through his fingers again, and as he did so he came under their spell once more in spite of himself. Suddenly a new doubt rang in his voice.

"There are some fine pieces here. I don't deny that. But there are also others . . . See here, what is one to make of a piece like that?"

Benedetto threw a hurried, astonished glance at the heavy dull silver ring that the other was putting on one side so contemptuously. Then he realized that his familiarity with the jewels was being put to the test. Oh, he could withstand *that* test. He knew them, these jewels. He could at least show the Jew that he had not stolen them from some passer-by in the street. That topaz set in old silver was antique, and was perhaps the most precious piece in the collection, modest as it looked beside some of the other flashy, fashionable jewels. If the Jew put him to no severer test . . . !

"Have another look at it before you dismiss it so lightly," said Benedetto. "This ring is a thousand years older than you are, and you're not going to tell me that you have often seen a more magnificent topaz."

The quiet disdain in his voice made an impression — it obviously inclined the old Jew to further thought. Graziadeo tried to conceal his momentary embarrassment by assuming a subtle, somewhat tired smile as he picked up the trinket again and inspected it more closely.

As he did so, his attention seemed to be drawn to something on the inner side of it — a happy accident that saved him from the necessity of answering Benedetto at once. He examined it with his magnifying glass, and carefully, with some surprise, deciphered aloud: "*Respice finem* . . . Think of the end!" He raised his head rapidly in order to read the reaction on his youthful visitor's face.

In silence Benedetto took the ring from him, and stared at the half-erased motto of whose existence he had been unaware. It seemed to have come to him as a message from a remote past. . . . Deeply stirred, he closed his hand over the ring and put it back in his pocket.

The old man watched him under half-closed eyelids, convinced too late of the authentic origin of these jewels. Smothering his disappointment with difficulty, he said warningly, "Bear in mind, Cavaliere — if you don't sell this ring with the rest, I shall have to revise my offer."

"You must do that in any case, if you want me to consider it," answered Benedetto pugnaciously.

Running his blue-veined, delicate hand protectingly over the rest of the jewels, Graziadeo asked with weary humor, playing the part of one vanquished to whom mercy should be meted out: "Well, now . . . How much am I to give you for what is left?"

Benedetto demanded fifteen hundred sequins.

A moment later, they agreed upon thirteen hundred.

Benedetto assumed that the Jew would pay him his money and escort him to the door. But something else happened. Graziadeo, as though aware of what had lured this client from the dark towards his house, invited him into his living room to receive the thirteen hundred sequins and seal the transaction with a very rare wine that had been specially consigned to him from Spain. Curious to make the acquaintance of the beauty, whom he now suddenly recalled to mind, Benedetto accepted the invitation and, relieved at quitting the room where old Signora Galli's jewels would soon lie hidden behind bolts and bars, he followed the jeweler turned host. Geronimo preceded them with a light.

As soon as he entered the living room, Benedetto felt an unusual atmosphere of quiet, secluded intimacy. By the light of a lamp sat Signora Graziadeo and a young girl of not more than eighteen, in whom he recognized with some difficulty the self-possessed young woman he had followed in the street. The old servant was easier to recognize. Tucked away in a shadowy corner, she was busy running blue and pink ribbons through freshly laundered night caps. The young girl, almost too slender, had remarkably large, dark, peaceful eyes set in a fine pale face which, with a complete disregard for the fashionable powdered wigs, was framed by black, gleaming curls. As they entered she closed a book from which she had been reading aloud, and looked up inquiringly. Then she got up to greet the stranger, whom she had no further cause to fear — if, indeed, she recognized in him the pursuer of a while ago, on whose account she had hastened her steps in the dark. Her mother (for surely the young girl was the daughter of the house?) nodded sideways, with a certain reluctance and distrust, in the direction of the unexpected guest. Signora Graziadeo was large and portly, and appeared to be one of those who suffer under their girth.

"Leah, my child, pour out a glass of Alicante for the Cavaliere, and offer him a chair — if he has no objection to stretching his legs under a Jew's table," said the old man, as he opened a money box. Then he asked with satisfaction, "What were you reading to your mother as we came in?"

The clear, serious eyes of the young girl were still directed inquiringly towards Benedetto, as if she were trying to settle in her mind in what

AT GRAZIADEO THE JEWELER'S   547

category of mankind to place him. Dutifully, she answered, "Jean Jacques Rousseau, Father: but Mother was just saying she had heard quite enough." Her voice sounded vivacious and alert, like that of an industrious, attentive schoolgirl well aware that she was the pride of her teachers.

Oh, yes, the old man was proud of his child, who read the French contemporary masters and translated their ideas as she went along into Italian. "And on whose side are you? With your mother, or with Jean Jacques Rousseau?" he inquired, full of eagerness to hear the answer she would make before his guest.

The girl laughed as she looked towards the woman under the lamp, who was clearly not pleased at being bantered in the presence of a stranger. Then she said, "Of course I'm on Mother's side. Only there is one thing I should like to convince her of: that the world cannot stand still because she wishes it to. Isn't that so, Father? The world must be influenced by the new ideas."

"The world? Must *we?*" said the old man with a fire that struck Benedetto as peculiar. What was it that was exciting this gray Jewish jeweler, and how did his child come by such eyes? Who was this Jean Jacques Rousseau? People talked and disputed here in Venice, even in the cafés and the public squares, about Goldoni, the two Gozzis, about Metastasio, Ariosto, Plato, about the Abbé Chiari; but of this writer, with his French-sounding name and his new ideas, Benedetto had never even heard.

What kind of unknown world was this that he had suddenly discovered? So far Venice had shown him nothing but rooms in inns, and the wings of theaters. And what was the mysterious attraction that made him reluctant to leave this warm, caressing lamplight, and step out into the night?

Slowly he emptied the glass of dark red wine that he had taken from the hands of the young girl.

"Leah, just ask the Cavaliere to show you what I am not allowed to buy from him," said the old man.

Ensnared by her gaily questioning eyes, Benedetto handed her the ring.

When Graziadeo saw how entranced was his child with this jewel, and how she noticed the half-erased letters on the inside even more quickly than he had done, he was overcome with regret, and made another attempt to secure the jewel.

"Cavaliere, for that ring alone I offer you another two hundred ducats," he said, and there was a lack of control in his voice that clearly betrayed how easy it would have been to induce him to make a higher bid.

But his daughter prevented further discussion by returning the coveted object to its owner, and saying, mildly reproving, to the old man: "No, Father. You must respect the Cavaliere's wishes, if he does not want to part with it."

Benedetto, at these words, was seized with an almost uncontrollable desire to give her the ring; but a curious diffidence towards this cultured young Jewess, mixed with a distrustful fear that he might be laughed at behind his back for allowing his feelings to run away with him, made him restrain the impulse.

Without counting it, he slipped into his coat pocket the money the Jew had handed him, and got up from his chair to go. Graziadeo offered his servant as escort to his inn: the Cavaliere was carrying enough money on him to rouse some robber's covetousness, and the bad lighting of the streets of Venice was notorious. . . .

Benedetto was on the point of expressing gratitude but refusing the friendly offer, on the plea that he feared no night marauders and that his inn was not far away, when it occurred to him that this was the moment to broach another subject. As they were on the subject of inns — he was looking for a room in a private house, a house such as the one he was in, for instance. Did Signor Graziadeo happen to know of any that might suit him?

In a house like the one he was in. . . . "Do you by any chance know of a room, Wife, in this neighborhood or elsewhere?"

In a house like this, the Cavaliere had said. . . . Then he would not object to living with Jews. Leah looked at him, astonished and thoughtful.

Benedetto's last words still hung in the quietness of the room. Graziadeo did not know why the jewels came back to his mind again, and why he felt renewed doubt as to their unexceptionable origin.

Signora Graziadeo did not reply immediately to her husband's question. She went on with her embroidery, trying to turn a deaf ear to him, but her peace of mind had gone. Her needle seemed to lose its way. The things that women consider passed through her mind. How much could she save on the housekeeping if there were a paying guest in the top-floor back room that was used as a guest room and was therefore empty? They so rarely had guests . . . It was true that their paying guest would be a Christian, a hated *goy;* but it might be possible to arrange matters so that they would see little of him. It would only be for his money. . . . Still, it was her husband's business. If he would not say anything, was it her place to open her mouth? He had asked her whether she knew of anything that might suit the Cavaliere in their neighborhood or elsewhere. . . . She knew of nothing, and everything in her seemed to fight against making any mental effort. Perhaps Susanna might know of something.

. . . At that moment the old servant was sitting with her hands on her lap, her shortsighted eyes fixed inquiringly upon her mistress. Old Susanna, also, was thinking of that top room, apparently quite forgetting that the prospective lodger was a Christian, and that they were not in the habit of letting rooms to the first comer. No; but all the same, Susanna's inquiring, half-blind look seemed to act as a spur to Signora Graziadeo.

She suddenly put down her work and unexpectedly came out with, "In a house like this? The Cavaliere might perhaps like to rent the top room overlooking the water."

She refused to notice her husband's dubious, astonished glance. She had spoken, and she proceeded blindly on her course, telling Geronimo to show the room to the Cavaliere, and adding that he could take possession that very evening if he were so minded — a bed could speedily be made up.

Not Geronimo, but Graziadeo himself accompanied Benedetto upstairs. His wife had taken him completely by surprise with a decision the responsibility for which would ultimately fall upon his shoulders. He knew exactly what had actuated her in this decision; but he also knew that it was as much beyond his power to oppose her as it was to suppress within himself a treacherous feeling of self-congratulation because this young Christian Cavaliere was prepared to take up his abode in a Jewish household.

There was something about this young Christian that had a mysterious attraction for him, although he found it at present impossible to analyze precisely what it was.

Benedetto, for his part, had already made up his mind to take the room whether it were large or small, lofty or low-pitched. He meant to sleep under Graziadeo's roof that very night.

The room turned out to be large and airy, well furnished and very clean — a pleasant surprise. When he looked out of the window, he saw that it gave on to one of the smaller canals of Venice. On his return downstairs, he at once declared himself satisfied with the price that Signora Graziadeo, not without some diffidence, mentioned. The old servant had resumed her work, and nodded in silence as the bargain was struck.

"Geronimo can go with you at once and bring your luggage here," said Graziadeo, thus concluding the negotiations.

"I have only a trunk — he might pack it for me, and bring it along. I shall return later — if that is in order."

"Come as late as you like. You need only knock, Cavaliere. Geronimo will open for you. We are used to being disturbed in our sleep. I often receive clients at the most unusual hours, or they send their servants to me, and then I have to get up, at any hour of the night!"

Benedetto understood at once that the old man was not yet prepared to trust him with the key of the house, but he was not affronted.

"Very well. I will knock. Is your servant ready to come along with me now?"

The gondolier was still waiting at the appointed place. He came running out of an *osteria* with an incredulous greeting; apparently he had scarcely anticipated the return of his passenger. If it had been only a question of Benedetto's safety, Geronimo could now have turned back: Benedetto had nothing to fear under the protection of this *barcaiuolo*. His shoulders were impressively broad under his thin blouse, and over his dark, audacious face played an impertinent, haughty, challenging smile.

Swiftly, with a soft lapping sound, the gondola shot away through the narrow, cavernous canals. Now and again, a gondolier's cry, sharp as the cry of a bird, rang through the night.

Benedetto stared before him, over the *ferro* of the gondola, wondering when he would see the Grand Canal shimmering between the overhanging walls of the houses. He was still under the spell of this city where, homeless, he had arrived a month ago. In the wide spaces of Venice's sky and water, his restlessness, the undefined longings that consumed him, had wandered awhile and found rest.

When he left Todi, he had immediately made his way to Florence — having first thrown out a false scent in the direction of Rome. On horseback and by stagecoach, he had journeyed through Italy faster than the *sbirri* could follow him. By the time he reached Florence he had already lost his name, the name of the coffinmaker Buongiorno, thrown it away like an old, useless garment that he had never liked to wear.

"Buzzi" he called himself when he entered the gates of Florence. Buzzi — that was the name of the bishop of Todi. Giambattista Buzzi was Todi's bishop. Benedetto might have chosen a thousand names when he laid down that which was his by inheritance. A thousand names, one more resounding than the other, his fancy might have conjured up; and the ambitious young clerk in the City Hall of Florence, who made a lucrative practice of writing out more or less true passes, would have given him the necessary papers for any name he cared to take. Why had Benedetto — without a moment's hesitation, without the slightest effort of the mind — why had he chosen the name of Buzzi that, by its sound alone, might have raised the suspicions of the sleuth-hounds who might still be after him?

He had adopted this name, and boldly attached to it the aristocratic prefix "Cavaliere," without troubling to analyze the feelings that had driven him irresistibly to take it.

"Cavaliere" Buzzi! "Cavaliere" — a title scattered lavishly up and down Italy, and, as Benedetto was soon to discover, arrogated to themselves from self-esteem by many who had not inherited it. No mortal bothered to investigate a man's right to it, so long as he was not born and bred in the city where he resided. With his assumption of this title, he assumed also the privilege of wearing a sword. . . . He aroused the enthusiasm of his fencing master in Florence, the small, famous Maestro Bracciaforte, by his natural aptitude and lightning passes; and shortly afterwards he fought his first duel under the stone arcades of Bologna, the students' city. What did it matter that the occasion for it had been the defense of the dubious honor of a courtesan notorious throughout the city?

He had had to flee from Bologna after that successful duel, in order to avoid the vengeance of the affronted students. But why had he left Florence, where fortune had smiled upon him to the last? There seemed to be no fundamental reason for his ingratitude to that city. In July, when the old roofs of the palaces and patrician houses lay broiling in the ruthless glare of the sun, when at night heat hung in the streets and squares like some slow liquid that one half-drank and half-breathed, when even the mornings brought no refreshment — then, his rich friends and acquaintances took pity on him and invited him to their green summer homes on the bank of the Arno, their villas on the wooded slopes of Fiesole. The young stranger, who could play the harpsichord like a maestro, could dance the minuet with equal talent, and could acquit himself manfully at the gaming table, was welcome everywhere, and he had only to reach out his hand: the world in all its luxuriance offered itself to him. Pretty women of old Florentine families invited him to their feasts, to their merry masquerades and theatricals, to their impromptu meals on the soft moss under the shady trees. They took him into their confidence, prized his advice. They invited him to drive through the surrounding countryside. An adventure with a scatterbrained lady of high standing threatened to have an unfortunate ending; but it was hushed up by the prefect of police himself, who had taken an almost paternal interest in him. If there was anywhere in the world where Benedetto would have found protection and support against a surprise attack from his past, then that place was Florence.

He did not remain, however. For him it was but an intoxicating episode in a journey he had yet to conclude. At Ferrara, whither he fled from Bologna, he took ship on board a felucca for Venice.

His heart found rest only when he saw that city rise up, white and superb, from the mother-of-pearl mist of early morning: the dream picture that Monsignore had so often described to him.

Florence, Bologna — the wounded, longing gaze of loved ones left be-hind — all was as nothing against the mysterious allurement of this city.

Other cities were precisely limited and divided off by intangible bar-riers: one remained a stranger in them. In Todi itself, though he had played there as a child, he had never been at home. Invisible walls closed him in, suffocated him, so that in the end he had been forced to break away. Venice, however, seemed to him to belong to all who could fathom something of her secret, to all who had dreamed of her before seeing her. Perhaps Venice belonged only to herself, and to the black gondolas that glided noiselessly over her canals, leaving no trace on the waters that closed behind them; and it was not so much a city as a labyrinth, a maze of meandering alleys, small squares, narrow waterways, and bridges.

For days on end he roamed the city, seeking to know its most hidden corners. He spoke with this person and with that, and familiarized him-self with the singsong of the Venetian dialect. He was told that he had arrived at the wrong season of the year. All Venice that counted was *in villeggiatura* on the banks of the Brenta, celebrating the feast of the gath-ering of the grapes. During the first days of October, when the theaters reopened and masking time began, these sojourners in the country would return in stately procession, tired but full of energy, to inaugurate the winter carnival, which, as the Cavaliere must know, lasted in Venice for six months of the year. Those who remained in the city breathing the poisonous vapors that rose from the lagoons during the month of Sep-tember — they were only the common people, the lower bourgeoisie, and the impoverished nobility of the San Barnaba quarter, who counted among their forefathers senators and even doges, but who, ruined by prodigality and gambling, now lived on gifts and small pensions and their remaining investments, shamefully selling their votes in the Great Council, in order to provide their daughters with dowries for any who would buy them.

No, the Cavaliere must remain in Venice during the winter, if he wanted to see Venice as she was.

Benedetto, however, had the impression that Venice was really itself only in the dying stillness of the month of September, when he seemed to hear her hidden voice, to revel in an intimate contact with the city in her nakedness, unadorned by the sport and frolic of carnival time.

The poisonous vapors of which they spoke seemed to him the very breath of death spreading round the old, deserted palaces. He inhaled it deeply with a strange delight — this real, sweet, intoxicating aroma of a dying Venice, that had once ruled the world and now served only as a great ballroom where men made revelry.

Soon they would come: the hundreds, the thousands of strangers —

the fortune-seekers and the crooks — the Polish counts and the Russian grand dukes, the Spanish grandees and the French marquises, the English lords with or without their ladies — the traveling scholars, the tutors with their grown-up pupils who were seeing the world to acquire wisdom and had already learned to squander their money. They would fill the inns, the casinos, the theaters, the concert rooms, the cafés near San Marco's and the Rialto bridge; and they would hurl themselves into the carnival of Venice; but by that time Benedetto would have ceased to be a stranger. By that time, he would have learned to know the true face of Venice, the voice of her silence.

Whether he wandered through the maze of alleys, bridges, and quiet squares, or whether he absorbed the proud glory of the Piazza San Marco, or took a gondola out on the Lagoon in the evening, he never ceased to feel that he was mysteriously linked with this city. It was *his* city: at last he had found his own city. Here his forefathers had lived — had not his mother been left behind in Todi by a company of Venetian players? That company had long since broken up. Nobody knew anything about it any longer. But what did that matter?

Now he himself was in Venice, and he hoped to secure a foothold there. But suppose he were not successful; suppose he had to flee from there as he had already had to do from Todi, and from Bologna — what then?

For some time after he left Todi, he was obsessed by the nightmare that his life might become one long flight, a flight without purpose or object, a flight in a fatal circle that would end in Todi once more by the desecrated tomb of old Signora Galli, towards which he would be beckoned irresistibly by one of her mutilated fingers. The obsession passed, and he did not give it a thought for weeks when, in the intoxication of life in the Tuscan countryside, he forgot the past and went about bearing confidently a name that he felt to be the completion of himself. But in Venice the nightmare had recurred.

He had had to renounce the name that seemed to belong to him, he had had to sacrifice it to Venice, where there were surely living relatives of Monsignore whose existence might land him in unforeseen difficulties.

In Venice his name was "Cavaliere Bussoni"; but that was not the same thing. He ought not to have given way to the foolish weakness of trying to derive his name from "Buzzi." Any name bearing no resemblance whatsoever to it would have been better. "Bussoni" — it had a senseless, ridiculous, dead sound. It had nothing in common with him, and he could not believe in it himself. At times he was assailed by the insane idea that he might suddenly forget that this new name was his.

He thought it might become familiar if he could see it written out in black and white on a pass . . . That very evening he would go to a Greek on the Giudecca who had promised him the precious document on payment of two gold ducats.

It was at any rate reassuring to have escaped from the dangers of an inn and a garrulous landlord into the security of a private house.

The house of a Jew . . . If anyone had predicted that to him yesterday, he would not have believed it. But now he could not imagine a better, safer roof under which to sleep.

Besides, nobody need know.

Somewhat relieved by this quiet brooding, he turned his eyes towards Geronimo, who was sitting at the other end of the gondola, and, either from good breeding or innate taciturnity, had not opened his mouth. Simply to hear himself speak, Benedetto asked, "Geronimo, — that's your name, isn't it? — how long have you been in that house?"

"Six years, Cavaliere," Geronimo answered promptly.

"But you're not a Jew, are you?"

"I'm an orphan, Cavaliere."

"Yes, but you might be a Jewish orphan."

Geronimo bent down as the gondola shot a low, dark little bridge. When he raised his head again, he said, "But my parents were Christians, at your service."

"And how did you come to take service with a Jew?"

Geronimo moved a little nearer and sighed. Then he said, "Everybody wants to know that, Cavaliere. Some folks won't believe that Jews are human beings. But anyone might be pleased to serve Signor Graziadeo. And as for Signorina Leah, I'd better say nothing at all, or I shall get angry. I used to think that sort of thing too. I'm prepared to admit it, and that's why I ought not to take it in bad part if others think a Jew and the Devil are one and the same thing; but I . . . But I'm talking too much, Cavaliere."

"Not at all. But you haven't answered my question — how you entered that house."

"Oh, I owe that to Signorina Leah. She used to live in Padua. Her aunt had just died — But I ought to tell you, first of all, that I was in an orphanage in Padua. I had permission to seek work outside, and I worked for Signorina Leah's aunt. At that time Signorina Leah was scarcely twelve years old, but she so contrived matters that I could come and take service with her uncle here in Venice. It was as though I had fallen from hell into heaven, if I may permit myself the comparison, Cavaliere."

Her uncle in Venice — to whom she said "Father." Benedetto assumed that Leah herself was also an orphan — hence perhaps her sympathy for the simple orphan boy from Padua.

Benedetto did not pursue his inquiries and Geronimo fell silent again. Benedetto's thoughts wandered from Leah, with her eyes like dark jewels, who was perhaps an orphan like Geronimo, to the morrow. He had written some music for a poor play — the first work of a young abbé, which was to be presented to the world next evening, when the theaters reopened. Benedetto had known nothing of the text until the play was in rehearsal, and it was with some misgiving that he was looking forward to the first performance.

But whatever might be the fate of the play, its author, and the unfortunate players, the mere writing down of the gay tunes he had composed to accompany it had stimulated him. It had begun as a joke: an airy promise over a glass of wine to Rossi — a sighing, complaining theater manager who, having heard Benedetto improvise, had expressed emphatic belief in his talents. He had held Benedetto to his lightly given promise, however; and so, much as he regretted the poorness of the text, he had felt the thing must be done. And who knew what might come of it?

At the inn he asked for his bill. The innkeeper, reckoning busily, deplored the departure of a guest who had spent without thought and who, in spite of all the host's misgivings, was about to pay. With many bows, he presented the bill. Benedetto glanced contemptuously at the total, and, looking at his watch, left the inn: his luggage would be attended to by Geronimo.

With a practised hand Geronimo folded garment after garment, slipping them into the one large black trunk in the room. The expensive silk shirts with lace ruffles earned a respectful glance. At the top of the trunk, he placed the oddments that still lay about the room — flasks and painted boxes — and the pink and blue bows and ribbons that he brought out from the back of a drawer: these, so far as Geronimo had understanding of such things, appeared to have belonged to ladies — perhaps to the ladies whose miniatures he also found. He closed the heavy trunk and carried it downstairs as though it had been a feather. The same gondolier was waiting outside: Geronimo boarded his gondola and returned with him to Graziadeo's house.

When he reached home, he was called upon to make a full report of everything the Cavaliere had talked about on the way. Geronimo was at a loss to understand why he remembered so little of it.

"Geronimo must have held the floor himself," insinuated David, Leah's betrothed. He had arrived for his usual evening visit after closing his shop and making up his daily account. David had just heard the whole story, and considered they had been irresponsible to let a room to someone of whom they knew so little — of whom, indeed, they knew nothing: had the Christian even given his name?

Signora Graziadeo, more sensitive to a reproach from David than from her husband, said that the times were bad, and referred to Leah's dowry: her parents were not there to provide it. The room was free, after all, and the Cavaliere appeared to be of good family, to judge by his dress and manners . . .

"And he paid his bill at the inn without checking it," said Geronimo, happy to be able to communicate something about the Cavaliere.

"A frivolous-minded person," declared David, disapprovingly. Signora Graziadeo was annoyed, but did not know whether it was with David, with the Christian, with her husband, or with herself. She fidgeted upon her chair while David, satisfied with the effect of his words, repeated obstinately: "Yes, a frivolous-minded person. After all, what do we know of him?"

They knew nothing of Benedetto. David did not stay much longer — old Levie, who lived just inside the ghetto gate and had the keys, smuggled him in every evening after his visits to his sweetheart, and he did not want to keep him waiting. When he had left, Signora Graziadeo began to question her husband in a roundabout way about the new inmate of their house. Solomon, however, made her very little wiser: just when she would have liked him to stay with her, he retired to the large back room that held his books and where for his pleasure he read and studied.

As she lay alone in her bed, Signora Graziadeo regretted too late her hasty action. She could not sleep for worrying about it.

Leah also thought awhile about the young Cavaliere with the haughty but sensitive lines round his thin lips, the dreamy but watchful expression in his strange, restless eyes. He had excited her curiosity. She would have liked to know more of him; particularly since, for the sake of her dowry, Aunt Rachel had taken him into the house. It was true that David did not appear to approve, and, other considerations apart, Leah was not displeased to see Aunt Rachel rebuked. How strange that here, in this quiet house, in that top back room that had always been empty so long as Leah could remember, suddenly someone had come to live — a Christian, too. Strange also that it should have been Aunt Rachel who had thought of that room, Aunt Rachel who, like old Susanna, had bitterly regretted leaving the ghetto after Uncle Solomon, by dint of heavy pecuniary sacrifices, endless patience, repeated hush money, and stacks of petitions setting forth the argument that most of his clients came to him when the gates of the ghetto were already closed, had at long last gained permission to take up his abode in the city among the Christians who were at that time complete strangers to them.

Uncle Solomon had always felt drawn towards the Christians. The ghetto was too narrow for him. The dogmas of the synagogue were too stark for him. It was he who had pressed into Leah's hand books by modern writers who preached liberation and the brotherhood of man, books that were spurned in orthodox Jewish circles, where they wanted to hear nothing of brotherhood with Christians and where — in the common prison of the ghetto — the only liberation dreamed of was that of Zion by the coming of the true Messiah.

Her uncle had had her taught French as well as Hebrew; and when upon feast days she went to the temple and was surrounded by a throng of unwashed, ill-fed children who pulled at her skirts impertinently or begged insistently for a soldo, with sorrowful eyes full of precocious wisdom, as though she were a stranger to be exploited — then she felt a stranger, and could not believe that one day she, as the wife of David, would return to the ghetto to live.

And Aunt Rachel — did she want to return? Aunt Rachel was a peculiar case. She hated and despised Christians; yet she was intimidated when she came to live among them. She had noticed the deep impression it made in the ghetto when their removal at last became a fact and their furniture was carried away through the narrow gate. She knew how much evil had been spoken of the few Jews who had gone through that gate before them, and she also knew that behind those calumnies lurked envy. An obstinate pride awoke in her: she went less and less to the ghetto. She no longer visited her former friends; and in the end she came to live within the four walls of her home as in a fortress of her pride. She hated the Christians, whom she did not know; but she also began to hate and despise the Jews, whom she had almost ceased to meet. And now, thought Leah, it had come to this: that Aunt Rachel had no insuperable objection even to letting one of her rooms to a Christian!

These and other thoughts came crowding into Leah's mind, and kept her awake for a long time.

Only old Susanna, on whom the things of this life no longer made a deep impression, failed to hear the knocker an hour or two before sunrise. Geronimo had also fallen asleep; but he jumped out of bed to open the door.

"TRAGHETTO D'AMORE"

IN

REHEARSAL

I

BEHIND THE DOOR STOOD LEAH, A TRAY OF CHOCO-late in her hand. She had already knocked twice and was listen-ing. A quarter of an hour before, she and her aunt had heard the Cavaliere moving up and down, and as Susanna had gone out she had hastily prepared the chocolate. Surely he could not have gone to sleep again. She did not dare peep through the crack: should she knock a third time? Then suddenly the door opened, and the Cavaliere stood before her, in a hastily donned dressing gown. He seemed agreeably surprised. Gallantly he took the tray from her hands, and laid it on the table for her.

"I had not dared count upon this," he assured her.

In her confusion she hastened to explain: "Susanna has gone to market, and Aunt and I heard you getting up."

"Does this mean, Signorina Leah, that if I get up earlier I shall have my chocolate served by Susanna as a reward?"

She had to laugh. She recovered her self-possession, and answered, "I doubt if you will get up early enough for that; but if you really so very much prefer me to bring you your chocolate, I shall see that I get permission to do so every morning."

They laughed together. Benedetto was delighted with her natural, carefree manner. He had slept well, — a deeper, more peaceful sleep that he had had the whole week, — and he was charmed with this morning's visit.

"And who must give you permission for that, Signorina Leah? Your betrothed?" He did not know yet whether she had a betrothed, but her answer would, he thought, enlighten him.

Benedetto's question brought back to Leah's mind David's objections to the Cavaliere, whom he had not even seen. She thought to herself that Geronimo was inclined to babble. . . .

"No, not my betrothed, but Aunt Rachel," she said with more reserve.

So she had a betrothed. Well, to the devil with the fellow. Benedetto evinced a courteous interest in him, inquired who and what the lucky man was.

As if she feared his mockery, she told him with a sort of deliberate obstinate pride in her voice: "A worthy young man, Cavaliere, who has a hosiery business, which he started with practically no means: when the shop brings in enough we shall be able to . . ."

"I'm in need of some shirts," said Benedetto.

Leah, momentarily surprised, tried to compose her face to a grave, businesslike expression. "Good: if you want him, I shall have him summoned."

"I want stockings, too. In fact, I want stockings more than anything else."

She did not know whether to take him seriously, and suddenly she grew embarrassed: from which Benedetto deduced that she was in two minds, and that she did not belong exclusively to this worthy young vendor of shirts and stockings.

"Signorina Leah, I really am in need of stockings." He looked about him as if in search of proof of what he said. "Who would have mended my stockings here in Venice?"

Leah met his eyes, and then smiled. She asked, "Were I to tell you that David also sells pills and ointments, perhaps you would need them too?"

"No, Signorina Leah. I should prefer to hear that he is also a barber and could come and shave me."

"That would be a meager calling for him, Cavaliere. The old Jews let their beards grow, and the young wait till the eve of Sabbath before going to the barber. And Christians don't mind going to a Jew for a shirt or a pair of stockings if they know that they will get them cheaper from him — but as for entrusting themselves to a Jew's razor . . . As soon as Geronimo comes home, I will send him upstairs at once to shave you. He is out now with Susanna, to carry the market basket."

Leah moved away. Benedetto looked after her until she had disappeared down the stairs. Then he bent over his chocolate: it seemed to have been carefully prepared.

A quarter of an hour later, David appeared. He was a young, slim Jew, all attention for his silk shirts and stockings, and barely conscious of the presence of his young sweetheart, who stood in silence by the door, looking on.

"Am I to believe him, Signorina Leah?" asked Benedetto. "Doesn't he fleece his clients by the price he puts on his shirts?"

Before Leah could answer, David was assuring Benedetto that his Christian clients would not come back to his modest shop in the Jewish quarter again and again if they did not know that he gave them equal quality for half the price they had to pay in the Merceria. Without listening to his asseverations, Benedetto bought both the shirts he had brought.

"They are the two best shirts in my shop, Cavaliere. Ten years hence you will still be wearing them: may you be in health — and remember me!" predicted David. The day had begun well — he would depart in a few moments with empty hands. If he had brought more with him, perhaps he would have got rid of them too. This Christian was a blockhead who paid what he was asked, at once.

"Leah, if the Cavaliere needs anything else, call me right away," he ordered his betrothed, as he was busy folding up the shirts and stockings. Benedetto got up to get some money from his coat, which was hanging over a chair. Leah looked after him, and then involuntarily her brooding glance shifted to the industrious David as he knelt upon the ground, and to the chair upon which the Cavaliere's clothes were hanging. A sword covered them protectingly. (Had a sword ever before lain over a chair in this room?)

David thanked him for the money, which he counted carefully. Then, with a somewhat awkward bow, he withdrew — indicating by a severe glance at Leah that she was to follow him. Leah had had no intention of remaining. She felt that her betrothed had made an unfavorable impression upon the Cavaliere, and was affronted by the fact; but she was more deeply wounded by David's peremptory glance, which she obeyed only because at the moment she had no choice.

Downstairs, in the presence of Aunt Rachel, David reiterated his wish that she should not be alone in a room with the Christian. Leah looked at him with cold astonishment.

"Gently, now. We take good care of her," said Aunt Rachel reassuringly, full of understanding and forgiveness for his jealous agitation.

Then she asked how much he had sold. He told her the handsome amount, and added sneeringly that the Cavaliere did not know that every vendor had to be beaten down. Aunt Rachel nodded, satisfied, and smiled. David was the only one who knew how to bring a smile to her face.

"Ah, well, my boy — you'll have a client like that every day. Off with you now!"

"I'm going at once. They may be standing in front of my door wanting to buy, and no one to attend to them," said David, giving free rein to his fancy, and eager to get away. He waited just long enough to kiss Leah on the forehead, with almost pious solemnity. As he did so he suddenly noticed her reserve, but he had not the time . . .

In his haste, he forgot to say good-by to Aunt Rachel, who had packed up some bread and meat and grapes for him — he did not get much to eat at old Levie's. She looked after him lovingly as he rushed away with her little parcel under his arm.

This betrothal between her husband's niece and her own nephew had been her doing. She had brought it about.

She had observed Leah's exasperation, but she did not take it very seriously. "What do you say of our David? A lamb, you'd think, and then suddenly he roars like a lion. But that's how a man should be. If he were different he'd be worth nothing," she said, trying to smooth things over. She hoisted her heavy body from her chair and went towards the kitchen, leaving Leah to recover herself.

Leah gave herself up to her work, but her thoughts were elsewhere. David's veto continued to exasperate her. She would have preferred him to leave such matters to her own delicacy of feeling. Besides, there was no reason for him to worry about the way her aunt was looking after her. And in Leah's ears still rang the words David had used to mock at the Cavaliere who, from pride, had refrained from haggling in her presence over the price of shirts and stockings. She almost regretted having spoken to him about David and his business, however profitable it had turned out to be.

As always when troubled, she felt drawn towards Uncle Solomon. He calmed her by his mere presence. She remembered something that needed doing in his room, thinking she would find him engrossed in his beloved books. He was, however, packing jewels in wadding, making them ready for dispatch to Uncle Nathan in Trieste. He showed her the precious pieces over which he was bending, telling her that they had come from the Cavaliere. She slipped a magnificent bracelet onto her shapely wrist, and tried as she did so to solve the mystery of how the Cavaliere had become possessed of all these valuable feminine trinkets.

Had some eminent Venetian lady, not wishing to expose herself personally, entrusted him with the sale of them?

Did he know many women intimately?

When Leah had returned to the living room, her mind was somewhat eased; but her aunt's first words roused fresh rebellion and annoyance in her.

"Where is Geronimo?" Leah inquired. "Is he back from market? The Cavaliere is waiting for him to shave him."

"If the Cavaliere had thought fit to get up sooner, he would be shaved by now, and already out in the street," replied Aunt Rachel, to which Leah retorted, "The Cavaliere knows best when it suits him to get up."

Aunt Rachel stared at her niece, and was preparing a further sally when she suddenly felt that she ought not to annoy Leah any more that day, and that it would be wise to drop a hint to David that evening, to make things right again with his betrothed.

Fortunately, at that very moment Susanna slipped the key into the outer door.

II

Cunningly shaved and curled, Benedetto left the house and went on foot to the Piazza San Marco for a last meeting with the Greek who had promised him his pass on that morning. He then intended to go on to the San Samuele Theater, the smallest and least conspicuous of the seven theaters of Venice, to witness the dress rehearsal of "Traghetto d'Amore."

He was thinking with some irritation of that hosier's visit. He could not reconcile himself to the thought that Leah had chosen such a man, and he made up his mind to sound her sometime, carefully and tactfully.

Then the infinite variety of Venice distracted his thoughts. His way led him through one of the Sunday markets with their appetizing, brightly colored stalls of fruit and greens. The shrill cries of the market women blended with the warning shouts of approaching gondoliers and the sing-song calls of the bargees who were throwing bundles of greens to one another from the sides of their heavily laden barges: in this city of marble and water, only the markets announced the full triumph of autumnal fruitfulness. The morning sun glittered on the broad canal; the heavy bell of San Salvatore's was ringing for High Mass, scaring the pigeons up into the blue heavens. Along the Riva del Vin a procession was moving in honor of some parish feast day — maidens in white, crystal-clear children's voices, flaming red banners embroidered with figures of saints. . . .

Full of color, full of music was the city; it was only necessary to wander in the street and write down what one heard. And behind the many-voiced noise of the Grand Canal and the markets murmured another hidden music that was eternal: a faint melody wafted from the blue sea and the sun-gleaming heaven. A darker strain rose from the murky, reeking water of the meandering inner canals. Both were magically woven together in Benedetto's ear. He heard them everywhere and always. . . .

Benedetto hastened his steps, but in the Merceria he was brought to a standstill: a crowd had gathered to see "Madame from Paris." "Madame" was a doll. She had just arrived from France, where she had been dressed by the modistes of the Tuileries. She was being displayed for the first time, and during the entire season she would set the fashion. By a circuitous route, Benedetto reached the Piazza. It was more or less deserted; but the proprietors of the cafés under the Procuratie had already set out their chairs by the dozen, and by the Molo hundreds of moored gondolas bobbed up against one another. Under the white arches of the Palace of the Doges, liveried servants and *barcaiuoli* were killing time playing at cards and dice.

Behind the Campanile, Benedetto found the Greek, who unobtrusively handed him the promised document and then stood waiting at a discreet distance until Benedetto had examined it. The pass was marvelously forged. It looked worn and much used, and it was so generously sealed that it would deceive the most quick-witted *sbirro*. Satisfied, Benedetto nodded towards the Greek, and the talented calligraphist departed at a dignified pace.

Benedetto got into a gondola and was rowed to the little piazza opposite San Samuele's. There he bade farewell to the golden day, slipping out of the burning sunlight into a sort of cellar, a windowless room that was the San Samuele Theater.

Darkness reigned. At first, he could distinguish nothing as he groped his way forward across overturned benches. Then he heard his name called, and gradually he began to make out one or two gesticulating figures, — dark shadows against the dimly lit stage, — and he knew that the creditors had come to disturb the rehearsal again.

Upon the stage, the actors and actresses were talking together as though no rehearsal was in progress. They nodded to him, and Rosetta, who was so unhappy because her entire rôle consisted of three words, came down the steps into the hall to welcome him and explain their difficulties to him.

The Brighella of the company, who had a duet in the second act with his master Pantaloon, had almost lost his voice and was running up and down between the wings like a hungry lion, oblivious of everyone else, practising scales in order to clear his throat. In the small space reserved for them, the members of the orchestra were tuning their fiddles and wind instruments and studying their parts in little groups. But all this cacophony was drowned by the violent altercation between Signor Rossi, manager of the theater, and the raging creditors, who threatened to close the theater before the first performance that night unless they received their money forthwith.

"Very well. Close my theater," shouted Signor Rossi bitterly. He was completely hoarse and waved his fat arms temperamentally as he spoke. "Close my theater, if you think that's to your advantage. That's certainly the way to serve Art, gentlemen. I only want to point out that in that case their money will have to be returned to all the true patrons of the theater who have reserved their boxes in advance."

"*Mi-mi-mi-do-re-mi!*" sang Brighella in full-throated ease on the stage. He had recovered his voice.

But the creditors bellowed furiously: "And where is the money for the booked seats? We ought to have received it. That's what we've come for. What have you done with it?"

Rossi pulled a face at once sorrowful and angry, threw his arms round the two creditors nearest to him, and raised his chin on high as if to signify that the money had somehow gone up in smoke.

"Are we going to begin soon?" thundered Benedetto suddenly through the hall. There was general silence. The manager nodded, grateful to this unexpected and powerful voice from the darkness; and while the creditors turned round infuriated, he clapped his hands and called out, "Begin! Begin!"

"Marcolina's disappeared again!" replied a voice from the stage.

"Where has she got to, *per Bacco?* Who gave her permission to run away in the middle of a rehearsal? Bring her back!" commanded Rossi, and tried once more to make the creditors see reason. "Gentlemen, show a generous spirit. We're going to show you a performance this evening such as Venice has never yet seen. People will stream to it, and we shall be able to repay you. Cavaliere Bussoni from Florence is standing there: he has composed the canzonettas. There's the author, the Abbé Baccherini of the Academy Granelleschi — Venice has not heard the last of him," he cried pathetically, as he pointed to a forlorn figure that looked the picture of despair. "Not a word can be said against my actors and actresses . . . But what *has* become of Marcolina? Gentlemen, you must surely see for yourselves that we're fighting against odds. We're acting in old costumes, against a background of patched-up scenery. We're rehearsing by the light of two candles, and we've been fasting the whole week."

From the stage, someone called that Marcolina refused to come. She had her rich friend with her in her dressing room, and she could not afford to affront him.

"Tell her she's to come immediately, or she'll be dismissed," bellowed the irate manager, and then added in a tone of entreaty: "Tell her the creditors are sitting here waiting to hear her sing the finale of the second act. Cavaletti, you're her husband," he added, suddenly remembering the fact. "Go and fetch your wife."

"Yes, Carlo, you go yourself!" came an echo from the stage as they tried to push the unhappy Harlequin through the door that gave access to the dressing rooms. Their efforts were not very successful, for Harlequin resisted wildly. Benedetto was growing heartily sick of the whole situation. Was he the only one to realize the importance of these last hours? The play might fail, but he was determined that his canzonettas should be properly sung. Carried away by annoyance, he jumped on the stage and disappeared into the wings, to appear a moment later with the Columbine of the play who, under her paint, was white with rage. She hurled a withering look at the manager there in the hall; but he remarked that he assumed the play might now proceed, with the help of the gods. New hope sprang up in the abbé's breast. He stood up in his dark corner, and began speaking in a protesting nervous voice; but the players paid not the least attention to him.

Rossi was producing, and also playing the part of Pantaloon. "Put life into it, life!" he thundered, drowning the irritable remarks of the exasperated abbé, who was trying to group his actors according to prescribed rules. "The public won't inquire whether we're all in our proper places. It wants us to *live*. Our backs are as good as our faces, provided they *live*."

He, at any rate, was alive in every nerve and sinew. His blind, stormy passion, his ridiculous grief, his pitiable loneliness when he discovered how his young wife had deceived him — all was real, and filled the bare, empty hall. He carried his players along with him, lifted them up by his titanic power; and thus in the world of appearances behind those feeble footlights the miracle of truth in art was accomplished.

The creditors, considering among themselves how to deal with that shameless debtor Rossi, were silenced as they watched.

They could not but respect Art. . . .

"Silence, there!" Rossi, wholly absorbed in directing and acting, had the audacity to bellow into the hall when one of the creditors suggested in a muffled tone to the others that justice should be tempered with mercy and they should after all wait, in God's name, to see how the first night went.

The rehearsal proceeded. "Traghetto d'Amore" ("Love's Ferry"), the play was called. The title and the plot were both forced in their facetiousness. Columbine, just out of a convent, and the coquettish young wife of a jealous old Venetian merchant, Pantaloon, demands that the semi-demure abbé who gives French lessons in the houses of well-to-do Venetians should explain to her the exact meaning of the word *adultère*, which is always cropping up in her French novels. In order to avoid uttering so indelicate a word as "adultery," the gallant abbé translates it into "love's ferry." Even though this translation should be clear enough to a Venetian ear, Columbine pretends she does not quite understand. She says that if there is a ferry there must, after all, also be a ferryman. The abbé, no longer able to resist her seduction, confirms this, and adds that every man would be happy to be the ferryman of such a ferry, if so bewitching a woman as herself were to come on board for a trip to the Isle of Cytherea, and, to make his meaning plain, offers himself as ferryman. Columbine is so delighted with her first crossing, that she spends all her time looking for ferrymen — of whom there are many in Venice, that city rich in canals. To the annoyance of her husband Pantaloon, who has become suspicious, all the visitors to his house talk of nothing but this or that mysterious ferry, until, in his anxious dreams, he sees whole ballets of ferrymen dancing round his young wife. In the end the innocent fool Harlequin, who really is a ferryman on San Giorgio Maggiore, and is afraid of the excessive competition about which he has heard vague rumors, forces his way into Pantaloon's palace, refuses to listen to reason, and with wild threats and curses drives all the guests out of the door. Peace returns to the house, the abbé reappears as the contrite teacher of French, and adds to the disconsolate Columbine's vocabulary a new word that gives her far less pleasure: *la résignation*.

Rossi himself was anything but delighted with the plot. He had accepted it only because he had been unable to obtain anything better for his modest little theater, and, as the creditors had left, the whole company gave free rein to their feelings. (Whatever hopes of success they had were centered upon two canzonettas: *"Traghetto — traghetto d'amore"* and *"Rassegnazione, che cosa stupenda"* — the only moments when, thanks to Benedetto's forceful efforts, orchestra and singers worked completely in harmony.)

The author, who had this play upon his conscience and was at last beginning to realize what a responsibility he carried on his shoulders, was wringing his hands and clutching desperately at Benedetto, who shook him off. Marcolina, the prima donna of the company who was saddled with the rôle of Columbine, suddenly burst out sobbing, and, pulling off her pointed shoes, was about to hurl them at the head of the abbé when he ducked under a bench. Harlequin, trying to bring her to reason, was rewarded for his courage by a resounding slap on his face. Rossi decided that the moment had come to interrupt the rehearsal for an hour, and suggested that they should all go out and take their midday meal together. The only question to be considered was whether they could still get a meal on credit. At The Wild Man and The Four Bronze Horses, the slate was already full — and Rossi's story of boxes booked and paid for in advance was merely an invention intended to exasperate the creditors. Benedetto put an end to these discussions by inviting them all to eat at *Il Pulciaio* at his expense. Benedetto invited the musicians to come, too. They put their instruments away in haste; and when the stage-hands and the prompter politely inquired whether they also were not . . . Of course, they too.

The city was dead at the midday hour — the only living things they met on their way to the *osteria* were some cats gnawing fishbones. The sun fell scorching on their heads.

Il Pulciaio — The Nest of Fleas — had its name to thank for certain rumors concerning the condition of its beds; but its cooking was beyond all praise, and its wine cellar was famous throughout Venice. Benedetto composed a long menu, and then sat down at one end of the table, with Rosetta on one side of him and Marcolina on the other. Rosetta thought she had acquired certain claims on Benedetto, and was annoyed when Marcolina, who had her rich friend, and whose interest in Benedetto had begun exactly a quarter of an hour earlier when he blossomed out into a Mæcenas, took no heed of these supposed rights of hers. Marcolina's rich friend and gray-haired protector was not present, and she always needed someone in her immediate vicinity to protect her. That afternoon the only person in a position to fulfill the part of her protector was the lavish host. She suddenly recollected that it was he who had come to fetch her from her dressing room, and had actually made her follow him. As she thought the situation over, she could hardly believe it. Pouting coquettishly, she reproved him for his victory; but, these coquettish reproofs apparently making no impression upon him, she tried the other well-proved weapons in her armory of seduction upon Benedetto — so that she could later avenge herself. After her third glass of wine, however, she began to imagine that she was really quite mad about him. She flirted with him shamelessly: but perhaps only to annoy Rosetta — she was not sure, herself. To capture his attention, she paid him little compliments about the two songs he had written for her. She crooned them softly to him, and, her face close to his, looked at him like a Circe. Her handsome velvety eyes stood out, a shade tired and expressionless, in a face from which the first bloom had faded. About her mouth, which must once have been as alluring as a ripe red cherry, there was a permanent line of regret and discouragement even when she smiled. Once, no doubt, she had dreamed of rising to be prima donna of the first theater in Venice, where the Doge had his box and where the first nights of Goldoni's plays were given; and instead she found herself in Rossi's cellar behind San Samuele's.

At the other end of the table sat Rossi, stately and imposing in the guise of paterfamilias of this great family of artists. He saw to it that the empty bottles were immediately replaced, and that no dish was taken away until it was empty. He raised his glass and in his loudest voice proposed a toast to the composer favored by the muses now sojourning in their midst, who had disinterestedly placed his art at the service of the theater, which embraced all the arts. The gods reward him! The muses crown him! Let Venice show herself worthy of him!

Life was smiling on them again, and, as they sat at the richly furnished table, they began to feel more cheerful about the evening before them. After a brief struggle with his conscience, Rossi even rose to propose a further toast, — to the writer of the wretched play, — but, laughing uproariously, the others pulled him down on his chair again: the abbé had not come with them. He had said he was not hungry, and had remained behind in the dark theater. . . .

The wines of *Il Pulciaio* appeared to be even better than their reputation. White wine cooled in ice was drunk with the fish, and a dark fiery red wine with the fowl. Rossi's urge to propose toasts to any person to whom he had ever felt obliged in his life became quite irrepressible. In the end, they let him be, and each time he rose clapped their hands, shouted "Bravo! bravo!," and emptied their glasses at a gulp. The two princesses of the footlights sitting on either side of Benedetto were both by this time hanging about his neck, laughing and whispering into his ears nothings that were incomprehensible because of their laughter. He joked with them and filled their glasses.

At the end of the meal he insisted upon liqueurs for all, and anything else they fancied . . . And as he did so, he tried to imagine that he was as ingenuous and carefree as they. But suddenly a longing still new to him swept over him: did those two who hung about his neck and kissed him not sense it . . . ?

In Todi he had been lonely, but there his loneliness had been his escape. The girls and women who had given him their hearts there had been incapable of freeing him from his loneliness. Intentionally, he had armed himself against them, because he had wanted to be bound to nothing and to nobody in Todi; he wanted to be free, so that at any moment he could depart.

But now he had reached the goal of his longing. He was in Venice, searching for happiness; and still loneliness escorted him, loneliness that he could not lose, even now that he wished to.

Not one of the company sitting at table gave a thought to the afternoon's rehearsal. Rossi held forth to some of the other guests of the inn, who, attracted by the noise and revelry, had joined the actors. He poured contumely upon Gozzi and Goldoni, and directed their attention to the latest play of the well-known Abbé Baccherini, "Il Traghetto d'Amore," which, as they were doubtless aware, was to be performed that very evening in the theater behind San Samuele's.

"Pay attention to the name, signori! A rising star, a new comet who to-morrow will be gleaming over Venice. What a privilege for me to have the means at my disposal of bringing such a work before the footlights, with a cast worthy of it!" And he actually managed to sell a number of seats to his listeners.

At that moment, the unhappy abbé, the new comet, rushed in, and declared that he shook off all responsibility for the evening's performance, seeing that producer and actors could find nothing better to do than drink themselves drunk. Rossi tried to talk him over, to persuade him to join them, and to listen to the toast he was about to propose to the author. Then suddenly his own conscience pricked him. He got up from his seat, and, instead of raising his glass as the rest laughingly anticipated, clapped his hands curtly. With a start, the company awoke from their carefree enjoyment, and remembered the first-night ordeal before them.

They all stood up to go, but Benedetto remained seated. He had no particular desire to return to that dark cellar in broad daylight, and watch the disheartening preparations for an evening doomed to failure. The wine had made him languorous. He thought of his room, which must be cool and quiet, and vaguely before his mind appeared the figure of Leah.

Rosetta gave him a sidelong glance, and asked whether she should stay with him—Rossi would hardly notice her absence if she missed the rehearsal. She knew her part! It consisted of the words, *"Grazie, Signor Conte."* Her bitterness found expression in mockery.

Her mood was dreamy and at the same time impatient. The wine had got into her limbs and roused vague longings in her. She would have liked to go out on the Lagoon in a gondola to be kissed, and she was faintly disappointed when Benedetto refused to understand her.

Oh, he understood her well enough, even felt a momentary responsiveness to her mood; but he was afraid to be alone with her that afternoon — he might have been tempted to say more than was good for her to hear.

Something urged him to go home. He had always fled from his room at the inn; but now he was drawn to his home. He excused himself to Rosetta, speaking of urgent business that he had to attend to at once. Of course she was wounded all the same, and he tried to salve the wound by buying from her a dozen seats that Rossi had given her in lieu of salary: she forced herself to see a proof of his tenderness in that gesture, and ceased to be angry with him.

Benedetto summoned the innkeeper and paid the bill (the shameless cheat swore that more than a hundred bottles of wine had been emptied, and that the ladies and gentlemen had consumed five-and-twenty chickens). Then he escorted Rosetta to the theater. On the way, she could talk of nothing but of how the innkeeper had fleeced him. Her tongue wagged unfalteringly until, reaching the cellar, she left him with a lingering parting kiss.

When she had disappeared into the darkness, he immediately stepped into a gondola: he had suddenly decided what to do with the seats he had just bought.

III

He found Leah and her uncle alone together — Aunt Rachel was having her midday nap. He asked her whether she was interested in the theater as well as in books, and whether her interest was strong enough to incline her to accompany him, with the escort of her betrothed or of her uncle and aunt, or indeed of all three, to the first performance of a mediocre play with a very mixed cast. If she did feel inclined to go, she should prepare herself for the worst: the stage was so small that the dancers scarcely had room for their jumps, and when three of them stood together, the boards creaked. Also, some bungler or other had written a couple of impossible canzonettas that would surely drive the audience away.

Leah had little difficulty in deducing that he himself had something or other to do with the play: was he perhaps playing a part in it? She assured him that, after his description, she was burning to see the performance, and with smiles and thanks accepted the tickets he offered. When, however, she saw how many there were, she looked up in astonishment; but he entreated her to keep them. "I can do nothing with them, Signorina Leah. I have been saddled with them. Perhaps with the extra tickets your betrothed might care to oblige some of his customers."

She hesitated a moment, rendered ill at ease for the second time that day. Flushing, she turned to her uncle and said, "David could perhaps oblige his best clients with them, and so put them under an obligation to him."

She did not know herself whether her sudden happiness was due to the fact that Benedetto was heaping coals of fire upon David's head with these free tickets or whether it was only the prospect of going to the theater in the company of the Cavaliere, whatever the play or the actors might be like.

"And suppose the play is hissed and the audience yawns with tedium? Will his best customers still be under an obligation to him?" inquired Benedetto, whose conscience was pricking him.

"Of course they will: David couldn't know that in advance. People always enjoy going out when they haven't to pay, and David's customers are not accustomed to buying seats for the theater," said Leah, reassuringly. "Isn't that so, Father? And you'll come too, to-night, won't you? And you?" she asked of Aunt Rachel, who had just come in, her eyes full of amazement.

Benedetto decided to leave matters in Leah's hands: it was sufficient for him that she had accepted the tickets. He went upstairs to his room, and lay down on his bed for a while — he had had but a short night, and wanted to collect his strength for what awaited him that evening at the theater.

IV

When twilight descended upon Venice, he was already in the street again, sitting outside the busy Café Florian on the Piazza San Marco and watching the crowds saunter by. The bells had long finished ringing for vespers, and over the spacious white piazza the only sound in the evening air was the buzzing of many voices.

Young women passed: they had just left the cathedral and had no

desire to return home — there was so much to see on that first evening
after their return to the city. The summer residences on the mainland
where they had spent the summer were many of them miles apart.
In the heat, people visited only their nearest neighbors; but now they
had all gathered together again, for Venice, fashionable Venice, was
small: it consisted of the Piazza San Marco, and the adjoining Piazzetta,
the Molo, and the Riva. Inevitably the whole world that mattered
gathered there and exchanged their thousand scraps of news, the minutest
particulars of all the scandals that had been only vaguely rumored in
the country. Every woman had rushed to her dressmaker to order a
new dress in the latest fashion, and to pay a part of what was owing
for the old. Every woman had tried to make an appointment with the
hairdresser, who, however, refused to be caught: where could he have
got to? Before what appreciative audience was he busy tittle-tattling?

They greeted one another, they embraced one another. They laughed
and they whispered. Here and there, a figure wandered forlorn and sad:
she had not yet found among the crowd the friend for whom she had
longed the whole summer. Was it true, then, that he was inconstant — that
he had become the *cavaliere servente* of another?

They did not want only to see; they wanted also to be seen, to be
pointed out. Only when darkness fell did the first masks emerge. Some
of the women wore small oval patches of black satin that rendered white
and seductive the part of the face left uncovered. But others carried
chalky white masks that covered the whole face; worn with a black lace
veil hanging from the rim of the hat onto the shoulders, these suggested
death itself, and seemed to have been invented to scare children to bed.
Grotesque, unbelievable beings drifted past, their three-cornered hats,
adorned with ostrich feathers and gold lace, pulled well down over their
faces or cocked with arch impertinence over one ear, coquettish little
slippers peeping from under their ample cloaks and flowing skirts.

Benedetto watched them. Every face had become a mystery that
might be worth solving. Dark, gleaming women's eyes answered his
hesitating, inquiring glances with sudden boldness from behind the safe
protection of their masks.

There was something new in Venice that evening: there was a growing suspense in the air that was becoming oppressive. Perhaps Benedetto
had been wrong: perhaps Venice was only herself when carnival had
begun. He got up, a prey to restlessness, and roamed among the throng.
Against the white marble of the Palace of the Doges, against the purple
depths of the Lagoon that was spangled with little golden starlike lights,
dark spectral figures flitted by. Along the Riva crept the undulating mul-

titude, like a thick, black, indolent caterpillar. Still more masks . . .
Under the dead-white satin, the voices sounded strange, as though they
no longer belonged to this world; a laugh became ominously loud.

On the Molo and the Piazzetta blared the toy trumpets of the hawkers
selling syrup and wafers, oranges and burnt almonds. On a platform the
tooth-drawer from Verona was bending over a patient; he was flanked
by the four best-known characters from the *commedia dell' arte* who
shouted in unison and beat pots and drums to smother the cries of the
victim. Jugglers . . . Some acrobats who had unrolled a carpet before
the doors of the sacred cathedral in order to perform the "Forze di Ercole"
there . . . The learned doctor who sold a potion that ensured long life;
behind him stood the Seven Deadly Sins and Death himself, who held
an hourglass like a clyster-pipe under his arm and with a knucklebone
counted off the people who tried to pass hastily by. Parties in fancy dress,
joined hand to hand in long queues, forcefully broke a way through the
dawdling crowd: Pierrots, Harlequins, dominoes and gay Columbines,
Turks with waterpipes, rat-poison sellers trailing behind them a dozen
dead rats with which they made the girls scream, Savoyards with their
marmots, Calabrians who played the bagpipes. Devils and monks, stilt-
walkers and veiled women, Chinese and lansquenets, and fallen-girls-
with-the-child-of-their-shame-in-their-arms. Farther on were many red
noses with wild moustaches under them. Squibs crackled, and on San
Giorgio Maggiore fireworks were going off, their reds and greens and
pale blues reflected in the shimmering waters of the Lagoon.

The usual haunters of the Riva — Orientals, Negroes, Slavs, Greeks
mingled in this masked world as if they formed part of it. Even the beggars in their rags, the gondoliers in their red caps, the vagabonds collecting bits of glass in baskets for the factories of Murano no longer
seemed real. For anyone wishing to escape the eyes of the *sbirri*, there
was no safer city in the world than Venice. Benedetto had thought of
Venice and her eternal carnival when he fled from Todi.

Now he was in Venice, and it was carnival time. Surely he should be
delighted to join this chaos, to live as carefree as the others about him.
He had bought a mask and he had it with him. What strange hesitation
deterred him from putting it on?

He felt a curious reluctance to lose himself in nothingness, an aversion
to complete anonymity.

It was as if this city, which he had learned to know in its stillness and
its beauteous nakedness, had masked itself from him this evening, disguised itself in order to evade him and break all ties with him. Only
yesterday she belonged to him — to-day she belonged to carnival, to all

those others who shrieked and shouted along her waterside. Surely no other city in the world was so perfidious!

In the midst of these crowds he felt again the loneliness that had overcome him that afternoon. An undefined menace hung like a cloud about his thoughts. On the Ponte della Paglia, which spanned the dark canal between the Palace of the Doges and the prison, he stood still, his back to the multitude, and peered out at the little groups of gondolas decorated with Japanese paper lanterns, which were moving toward the Lagoon. There was singing and the playing of guitars.

It seemed to Benedetto as though each one knew all the others. And so indeed they did — was it not in that fact that the whole joy of this masquerade lay? Again the fruitless longing gnawed at him: that he were not a stranger in Venice, that he had been born and bred there, that he had no past to conceal. He had gone masked so long — he yearned to be able to put down his mask. The little scrap of satin worn by the revelers that evening: that, he could don with pleasure. . . . What was this sudden quietness invading him? What mysterious feeling of anxiety warned him, at that moment, not to turn toward the throngs streaming past behind him?

Of course he did turn round, quick as lightning, and his eye lighted upon an ample matron who, thrust forward by the unregarding crowd, stumbled across the bridge, weary and protesting, and leaning upon a stick. When she reached the top, she stood still, trying to get her breath, at arm's length from Benedetto. She spat upon the ground; and with dull, empty eyes glanced at the motionless man who was staring at her. Cursing and mumbling, she was pushed on again. She descended to the other side of the bridge, and made her way to the dark arcades of the prison, where the crowd was less dense. Then she disappeared.

It was some time before Benedetto could take his eyes from the arcades. He breathed deeply. Then, recovering suddenly from his alarm, he tried to smile at the foolish vision: he had imagined that old dead Signora Galli was haunting Venice, that it was she who had just passed him and had looked at him, wanting to know what he had done with her jewels.

But it was merely an old woman — there were thousands in Venice, hobbling about with or without crutches. Only his morbid fancy had made him think that from the gnarled hand with which the old woman held her black shawl together under her chin some of the fingers were missing.

A while longer he stared into the crowd, seeing nothing and no one. Then slowly he groped in his pocket and, turning away from the people, drew a mask over his face.

THE FAIR MASK

IN

THE BOX

BELOW IN THE BODY OF THE THEATER LEMONADE
and sherbet were being served. People produced comfits and
offered them about. Friends and acquaintances who had arrived
late were hailed with lively gestures. A few seats remained empty. Those
who met expressed surprise at seeing one another again — it was weeks
since they had had any news of one another. Absent members of the
family were inquired after. Snuffboxes were handed from one to the
other, and good wishes greeted the resulting sneezes. People chatted at
length, and sometimes in whispers because the person being discussed
happened to be sitting only a row in front. Some of the men ogled the
comely girls and hastily scribbled little notes on their knees.

At the same time a play was being performed. It was called "Traghetto
d'Amore," and it was the first work of a young abbé who had been fired
to imitation by the thought of the laurels won on the Venetian stage by
a certain Abbé Chiari. Pantaloon was good, remarkably good. When
Pantaloon was on the stage grumbling at the whole world, at the hard-
ness of the times, at the price of meat and vegetables, at French cooks
who, with their accursed sauces and herbs, had spoiled the good old
Venetian cooking, at the convents that had become abodes of pleasure,
at children who these days were so free and familiar with their parents,
and at his servant Brighella who cheated and robbed him in his very
presence — then it was not surprising that the public roared their amusement, shouting in unison for Pantaloon to stay. Stay, *caro*, we like to see

you. Do not abandon us to tedium; we did not come here to be bored to death.

The Harlequin was as saltless as a bad Harlequin can be. He was a ferryman on San Giorgio Maggiore, if he spoke truth. Well, he was welcome to stay there — he would have done better not to show himself on the boards. A Harlequin who could not be merry should be sad, and everyone would be satisfied. The sadder he was, the merrier his audience would be, for a sad Harlequin always provokes mirth. Columbine's voice was so-so, but her legs were shapely, and she knew how to show them too — there was something temperamental in the way she waved her skirts. *Bravo, Colombina!* She was like a peach in the warm glow of the footlights. If only her voice had been as soft as her throat and her bosom, Venice would have idolized her, adored her more ardently than the Madonna and the saints. But her sole adorer in fact was a lonely mask who sat in the side box with a bouquet in front of him, from which he threw her a handful of roses each time she reappeared.

No; she *had* some other adorers: they were standing behind the orchestra — several gondoliers and a dozen young men of the people. With brooding eyes they stared across the footlights towards Columbine. They listened admiringly when she conversed with the abbé in French, waiting patiently for the moment when she would whirl her skirts again, and show the round curve of her pink thighs to such of her admirers as had sharp enough eyes. . . . These simple souls would have stood there even had the performance lasted till next morning. With their large, heavy hands they applauded thunderously every time Columbine entered from the wings. They stamped their feet peremptorily, demanding silence every time she opened her mouth to speak. They were not only adorers, but also protectors — as surely as was her rich old friend in the box.

Then suddenly stillness descended upon the theater, without the intervention of stamping feet. Suddenly there was something to see that was really worth while: someone was entering the center box.

A masked woman took her place. About her were grouped a half-dozen masked men, among them one older than the rest who sat at her side while the others lost themselves in the dimness at the back of the box.

The actors on the stage interrupted the performance until the new arrivals had settled themselves. Then Pantaloon came forward, and wished them welcome; for besides being Pantaloon he was also Rossi the manager, and he was honored when distinguished patrons arrived.

The play proceeded; but the audience was more interested in trying to overhear what was said in the box — for the author of "Love's Ferry" had come rushing round from behind the scenes. He kissed the fair lady's hand, and volubly assured her that the best scenes were yet to come: the end of the second act, and the ingenious dénouement. The public listened with a certain skepticism to his declarations.

The lady in the box accepted his assurances in silence, and for a while followed the play attentively. Then suddenly she ceased to pay any heed to it, and began to whisper behind her fan of magnificent Venetian lace to the gallants who formed her escort and immediately bent eagerly over her.

The occupants of the box laughed and tittered, and the saddened abbé was sent back behind the scenes, on the plea that they wanted to be able to speak ill of his play freely. . . . They called for cooling drinks — it was so warm and oppressive that they would not be able to hold out very long.

On the floor of the house, beside Signora Graziadeo and her young niece Leah, sat Benedetto. He had filled his pockets with sweetmeats, and showed himself an attentive host to his guests. (Graziadeo himself had preferred to remain at home.) David sat on the other side of his betrothed, who was looking quietly in front of her in the direction of the stage, although she was no longer following the play. Leah was disappointed. Benedetto's description had not led her to expect a great deal, but she had not realized how wearisome it would be to watch a bad and tasteless play for hours. Benedetto tried to make amends by talking to her, but she could not pay attention to him, either — the talk on the stage distracted her, and her thoughts wandered. She asked herself why the Cavaliere, who must have known what was in store for them, had offered her seats for this performance. She guessed the truth, but she hesitated to admit to herself that he had simply seized the first available opportunity of spending an evening in her company. She was afraid, too, that her aunt would speak her mind about this invitation later on, and could not help feeling restless and annoyed in anticipation. One thing she knew, that in that case she would have to stand up for the Cavaliere, would have to try to make Aunt Rachel believe that he himself had had no idea of the sort of evening to which he was inviting them.

Yes — but if her aunt and David had not been sitting here at that moment, she would have been inclined to reproach him herself.

Halfway through the first act, David had made up his mind that the play was hopelessly bad, and, having taken careful soundings as to whether the Cavaliere was in any way connected with it, began to criticize it witheringly. He looked round continually to see which of his customers had made use of the tickets he had given away, and at last jumped up to present his compliments to them and to express his regret at their disappointment — it could not be greater than his own and that of his betrothed. In his anxiety, he was so neglectful of Leah that Aunt Rachel began to make signs to him, with the result that he hurried back to his place, and resumed it ostentatiously, casting a suspicious look as he did so at Benedetto who, with cool friendliness, offered him sweets. David did not accept them, nor did he leave his seat again. He remained sitting stiffly by Leah's side, silent as a fish. As the time wore on, he began to yawn behind his hand. Every evening it was the same: he was so tired from standing hours on end behind the counter . . . He turned white with sleepiness and, unaware himself of what he was doing, leaned against Leah's shoulder and fell into a doze.

But suddenly he opened his eyes wide in astonishment: thunderous applause had wakened him with a start. From a hundred throats came the shout: *"Bravo, Colombina! Encore! Encore!"*

Everyone pressed forward towards the front. On the stage stood Columbine, her eyes glittering. The violins took up the refrain again, and in a radiant voice, through which the sun seemed to break unexpectedly, she sang: —

> *Traghetto — traghetto d'amore!*
> *Matto m'hai fatto il cuore . . .*

She repeated all the couplets, and again the audience went mad.

Benedetto sat there benumbed, surprised by a completely new sensation. He felt Leah's glance, and was about to turn his face to her when he heard someone behind call his name. Would that name after all acquire significance for him?

"Bussoni!"

It was the abbé, who appeared to be highly excited and was beckoning to him, with excessive gesticulation, to come to the large center box.

Benedetto hesitated. He did not particularly want to be called away just at that moment. Besides, he felt out of sympathy with the bungler who was capable of writing such a play. Did he want to introduce him to his friends in the box?

Then suddenly Leah said — and there was a deep gravity in her voice and on her face that, in this moment of bewilderment, moved him profoundly — "Someone's calling you!"

He nodded. Then with a smile he got up slowly and begged the ladies to excuse him for a few minutes.

He was standing before the fair lady in the box. She offered him a soft and perfumed hand, to which he pressed his lips. Two haughty eyes gleamed through the black satin mask. Nobody mentioned her name to him — it was apparently assumed that he would know it. She spoke to him directly, wished him happiness with his success, and invited him to her house after the performance in a fashion that brooked no refusal. "Rio di San Felice; any gondolier will take you. You will meet people there who are interested in you. Your Columbine will be there too, and will sing the canzonetta for us again."

He bowed. Her strange alluring voice, with its seductive exotic accent, sang in his ears. Fresh applause broke out — but he was scarcely aware of it. At that moment, he could think of only one thing: that when they called "Bussoni" Leah knew at once that it was his name, and that she had sensed his triumph almost more quickly than he himself had done. She seemed, indeed, to partake of it. His mind elsewhere, he received without understanding them the compliments of the men who bent forward from the box in order to make his acquaintance.

They raised their masks hastily, because he had uncovered his face. In his excitement, the abbé boisterously introduced them one after the other as though all of them were his bosom friends. There was pathos in his voice as he said of the gray-haired Baron Barbaresco, who sat at the lady's side, "Our celebrated judge!" — which did not seem to gratify the scowling Venetian *nobile*. Again he shouted, "Signor Galuppi, glory of our younger painters!" and a sad, neglected figure bent forward.

The last to be introduced was a grotesquely lanky creature, who came forward from the depths of the box. Behind a sharp, prominent, aquiline nose, a pair of shifty, evasive eyes leered at Benedetto, and about an ugly mouth without lips a vague mocking smile formed itself: presumably this gentleman's method of intimidating those to whom he was introduced. Benedetto responded with an angry, penetrating glance, and at once Cavaliere Maniscù, for that was the foreign-sounding name the abbé had pronounced, changed the expression on his face.

In spite of that, however, a feeling of discomfort began to pervade Benedetto, and he could not rid himself of it. He began to wonder why he was allowing himself to be robbed of his cheerfulness. His thoughts wandered back to Leah. He longed to hear her speak again. He gave only vague and disconnected answers to the flippant questions the fair mask put him concerning his musical past. His restlessness suddenly made it impossible for him to listen any longer, and he excused himself: he would be pleased to place himself entirely at her disposal later in the evening — but for the moment he was in company . . .

The inquisitive charmer seemed taken aback for a moment. Then she gave him permission to go. As he hurried away, she followed him with her eyes, and when she observed the company for whose sake he had deserted her, she could not resist the temptation to pick up her opera glasses and study his companions more closely. Her interest centered first on the dark, slender young girl at whose side he had taken his place. She refused to be disturbed in her investigations by the teasing remarks of her jealous cavaliers, and laughingly prevented them from turning the hand that held the opera glasses in another direction.

The elderly judge put an end to this innocent badinage by getting up abruptly and reminding them that they must see an act of Algarotti's latest play at the San Cassiano Theater. Jarred by the unmistakable annoyance in his voice, they all waited to see what the lady in the company would say or do. At first she said and did nothing at all. When she noticed that they were all waiting for her decision, she sighed, got up, and, after a last glance at the stage, turned her shapely back upon it. With some embarrassment, the elderly man followed her, and then, with many compliments and civilities, the rest of her cavaliers.

As soon as he was back in his place, Benedetto felt that he ought to have remained there and allowed the abbé to go on winking and gesticulating. Leah gave him a hasty, constrained look, and when the curtain went up again for the ballet, just at that moment, she seemed relieved that she could look in front of her and need not speak to him. In fact, she saw nothing of what was happening on the stage.

Benedetto glanced at David: in that glance aversion seemed to have grown to hatred, for he blamed her betrothed for Leah's change of attitude. David did not notice his glance: he was staring with wide, unbelieving eyes at the sparsely clad dancers. The ballet awakened in him a longing at once shy and fiery, for Leah. He could think only of Leah — his Leah, the prettiest girl in Venice, whom one day he would carry back in triumph to where she belonged, and where no further dangers would threaten her; his Leah, whiter a thousand times than all those *goy* ballerinas put together. His eyes would rest upon her in all her pride and glory on the night that followed the solemn celebration of their marriage. David turned dizzy at the thought of it, God forgive him! Why did the whole of Venice not buy stockings and shirts at David's, stockings and shirts at David's?

Benedetto, burying his disappointment sullenly, also stared at the stage; and, having nothing better to do, he began to wonder about that gaunt Beelzebub sitting at the back of the box. Where in God's name had he seen him before? Where had his ears been filled before with the nasal, glassy voice of that Satan's bastard who, in his diabolical majesty, seemed worthy to be a spy of the Inquisition?

Cavalicre Maniscù. . . . He could not recall the name. Neither in Florence, nor in Bologna.

The third act brought the inevitable catastrophe. The bored audience began to express its disapproval with loud cries; but, so long as it refrained from throwing rotten eggs, the actors continued to perform their duty faithfully insofar as they could make themselves heard above the uproar. The abbé tried to save a hopeless situation by calling out *"Sh!"* and "Silence there!" and he found some support among the creditors, who were sitting side by side with somber faces; but others were so annoyed by him that they ran out to provide themselves with projectiles from the street.

Benedetto thought the moment had come to suggest that they should leave the theater for the sake of the ladies' safety. David accepted this view at once, and begged and implored his betrothed to heed the Cavaliere when he himself spoke of danger. Leah, however, her face pale and set, obstinately turned a deaf ear to him and to her aunt, saying that she wanted to see the end: they, after all, had nothing to fear, for they had not written the play.

Benedetto admired her composure, and the authority with which, at this decisive moment, she exerted her influence not only over her agitated aunt, but also over her betrothed. He guessed that she wished to remain to the end only out of loyalty, because she knew he himself was interested in the fate of that unfortunate play. A warm, compelling feeling for her rose up in him. He had difficulty in restraining himself from throwing his arm round her and, under the very eyes of her aunt and her betrothed, dragging her with him into the street and safety, away from this place where he should never have brought her. And perhaps it was only diffidence towards Leah herself that prevented him.

But another occurrence took place that put an end to the evening: the first rotten cabbages and apples went hurtling against the scenery. In the body of the theater, men and women in their Sunday clothes began to scramble for safety. Aunt Rachel hoisted up her heavy body determinedly, and veered towards the exit, leaving David rushing anxiously backwards and forwards between her and Leah, with the result that Leah had no alternative but to stand up herself and allow Benedetto to throw her cloak round her shoulders.

And so the public missed both the canzonetta *"Rassegnazione, che cosa stupenda!*" and also the most interesting portion of the performance: the improvisations at the end. Only the creditors stayed so long – they had gathered together to debate what was to be done.

Benedetto was lucky in his attempt to secure a gondola. Singing and shouting, a party of costumed revelers stepped onto the Campo San Samuele, and as one of the *barcaiuoli* sprang after a passenger who had tried to escape without paying, and caught him by the collar of his Pierrot costume, Benedetto jumped into the empty gondola and prevented others of the audience joining him. David approached with his betrothed and their aunt, and the *barcaiuolo* returned, putting away the soldi he had extracted by the threat of his fists.

They set off, Leah beside her aunt on the back seat. Her face, on which shone the light of a lantern hung high on the *ferro* of the gondola, gleamed from the darkness of the awning. Her eyes met Benedetto's and then looked away over the black water under the walls of the houses. He cursed the presence of her aunt and her betrothed, which prevented her from speaking her mind to him about this unlucky evening. He hungered for some intimate converse with her. He wanted to tell her about himself. For the first time in his life, he wanted to speak to somebody about himself. He sensed that she knew and understood a great deal about him – perhaps everything – even before he had spoken a word to her. He glanced with angry contempt at David, who was staring vaguely in front of him and yawning.

They left the bustle of the Grand Canal behind them. In the part of Venice they were traversing, quiet reigned in spite of carnival. Quiet also reigned among the four of them. The gondola stopped before the iron-mounted door of Graziadeo's house, and Benedetto offered his hand to the ladies as they stepped out.

"Oh, are you going out again?" asked Leah abruptly. She stood there on the quay, enveloped in her cloak, her whole attitude expressive of hesitation and conflict.

"The Cavaliere has no need to be at his business at eight o'clock tomorrow morning. The Cavaliere can amuse himself," said David, drawing his betrothed away.

Benedetto took his hat off.

It was at least balm to his wound that Leah evinced an interest in his movements. Of course he was going out again. Could he sleep now, and under the same roof with her? That he left to David, for whom his aunt had provided a camp bed so that he need not rouse old Levie from his sleep. David could close his eyes and dream in comfort of his Leah –

he had no need to fear that all his dreams would vanish into thin air. Benedetto watched her follow her aunt into the house, supported solicitously under the arm by her betrothed; when the door closed behind them, a sudden dull despair took possession of him. Everything seemed foolish and hopeless; Leah could never belong to him. Like a chasm there yawned between them differences of blood and origin, the deep seriousness of this Jewish betrothal, however stupid in itself; and even if those difficulties had not existed there was still something else: never would he dare confess to Leah who and what he was. A moment ago he had thought he could, but now that she had gone he realized that to do so would be a grave injustice towards her. What business was it of hers that he had once appropriated jewels from a vault in order to get away into the wide world, and that now he could find no rest, no happiness in this world? He shrank back at the mere thought of the bewildered look that would come into her large, handsome eyes. At the mere thought that by a foolish, unasked confession he might shatter the quietness of her pure life with its thousand ties, self-disgust filled him.

He gave instructions to the gondolier to take him back to the theater. He did not know what he wanted to do there — but in any case there would be carnival on the Grand Canal.

For a fugitive moment, he remembered the invitation of the fair mask in the box. He would have gone to her if he had been sure that he would not meet in her house the lanky Cavaliere dressed in green whom he still could not place in his memory. Besides, he was not attracted by the prospect of a closer acquaintance with that old Venetian judge. Since the spring of that year, anyone connected with the law had ceased to have attractions for him.

Or was it only the ridiculous apparition he had seen that afternoon on the Ponte della Paglia that was making him shy of meeting a bad copy of Satan and a judge who could not possibly know anything about him?

Black as the infernal regions themselves was the water through which the gondola was cleaving its way; and in the eddies it left behind, strange shapes moved.

In the theater, the curtain was still lowered. Pieces of melon and reeking egg-yolks were slowly dripping down it. Behind the curtain, Marcolina had fainted. Harlequin, and her rich friend from the box, who was on the stage as if he formed part of the company, were rushing about to fetch water for her. Her friend returned from a fruitless expedition in the dark; he was still carrying some of his red roses, and looked completely helpless. Against the backcloth, a blue heaven sullied with cabbage and tomatoes, the creditors stood like funeral guests in somber silence. They did not reproach Rossi, nor did Rossi make a pathetic oration for their benefit. They were reconciled by the common blow of fate.

Benedetto felt no desire to become involved in the situation. He made a sign to Rosetta, who was observing Marcolina and her satellites with quiet and supercilious satisfaction. She was so engrossed that she did not notice him at first. Then she came hurriedly towards him.

"Are we going out together?" she asked in glad surprise – she had ceased to count on that.

"Yes; get ready to come."

"I am ready. It's carnival time. I'll keep on my costume. Don't you want to dress up? Come with me: I'll get a domino for you."

She dragged him through the darkness behind the scenes. She was struck by his docility – she had never known him like that before: was he in love with her after all? Had his heart driven him to her? She helped him to cover his clothes with an ample red domino, and could not refrain from giving him a kiss. She was exuberant, and not without reason. She, too, had a friend who had come to fetch her in order to celebrate with her the first night of carnival, and Marcolina, her hated and envied rival, had been unable to sing the end of the third act. That was more important than the fact that Rossi would have no money on the morrow to buy them food.

"Are we going to eat somewhere?" she asked.

"At The Wild Man, if you like."

"I believe you're a wild man yourself this evening," she said, and hoped that it was so. As they went out and up the street, she hung on his arm and sang close to his ear, as she had seen Marcolina sing that afternoon, the little air that had brought him success. "Why don't you let me too sing something like that on the stage?" she asked reproachfully.

The host at the well-known eating place to which he took her conducted them with many bows towards a private apartment where they would be completely undisturbed. There Rosetta could find out whether Benedetto was really a wild man that evening. . . . Oh, and so he would be, if only his thoughts were not elsewhere. A darkness was hanging over his whole being. She had noticed it a while ago behind the scenes. She jumped on his knees and put her arms about him, determined to chase away his somber mood with passionate kisses and foolish prattle. She mixed liqueurs with her wine – and yet she succeeded in carving the pheasant with a practised hand, and dividing it fairly between them.

"I should like to know whether Marcolina's enjoying herself as much," she said, revealing that she had created for herself the illusion of complete happiness that evening. "She'd been invited out somewhere," she added.

Benedetto thought he remembered something about that, and in order to be of service to Rosetta, he made an effort of memory: "Yes, to a palace on the Rio di San Felice."

She looked at him, astonished and distrustful. "How do you know that?" Before he could reply, she had worked it out for herself. "Oh — you've spoken to her too, to the Spaniard in the box. Don't deny it, for I saw."

Why should he deny it? So she was a Spaniard: that explained her curious accent. At the mention of her, the sound of her voice came back to his ears; but the strange thing was that he at once began asking himself where he had heard that voice before. Was he seeing nothing but apparitions to-day? He ransacked his memory; but this time his brain would not obey him.

Rosetta tried to read in his face what was passing through his mind. Into her eyes there came an anxious and imploring look as she said, "Be careful of her."

When he looked up at her slowly and inquiringly, she added emphatically, as if she feared that he would not believe her: "Do you know what they call her here in Venice? They say she came into the world without a heart."

After this mysterious and effective warning, she would have been well advised to say no more about the Spaniard. She knew this herself; but to her own annoyance she felt compelled to go on speaking about her, and the more she talked of her the more she was convinced that she was rousing Benedetto's interest in her. Oh, of course he was already in love with her, although he had only seen her in passing, and wearing a mask.

The Spaniard had arrived in Venice that summer, and since then, according to report, half the men in the city had run after her. To be the talk of the town after only a few months — that was a really exceptional occurrence in Venice.

When Rosetta had said everything she had to say about the Spaniard, she fell silent, and suddenly began to feel a desire to cry. It could not be the fault of the wine, for wine never made her sad. It could only be her exasperation with the Spaniard, and her disappointment because she had thought she was so happy this evening.

To conceal her tears from Benedetto, she leaned her head against his shoulder, and now and again brought her glass to her lips.

Laughter and shouts reached them from the other rooms. Rosetta was melancholy as she listened to them. Songs were being sung to the accompaniment of a guitar. . . .

In the end Benedetto drew her softly to him. Since she had grown silent, she had come nearer to him. Perhaps he mistook her for Leah. Perhaps he was dreaming, and his dream would be shattered by the first word she spoke. She felt this, and dared speak no more. If it was his desire that she should be another — that she should be the Spaniard — that was right too. She resigned herself to her part. After all, she *was* an actress.

As she continued to remain still, just sipping her wine in silence from time to time, the desire rose up in him to speak, to break through the loneliness that surrounded him. He had to make a great effort not to commit such an act of folly.

Only one person could have liberated him, but she was not there, and that was just as well. Leah . . . Leah! Then suddenly he recovered himself and shook away the cobwebs from his brain. He wanted to seek oblivion to-night. Perhaps life could offer him no more than oblivion. He must be satisfied with that.

"Come," he said hoarsely, and stood up.

She looked at him incredulously. "What a queer one you are," she said. Then with her diminutive lace handkerchief she wiped away the tears from her eyes.

It was only now that he observed them. He was moved. She noticed this, and immediately fell into his arms. He kissed her blindly, passionately.

"Well — where shall we go?" she asked. The miracle of his sudden change she accepted without wishing to understand it. "To the Piazza? It must be crowded now." But wait: Rosetta knew of something better. "Let's go to the gardens of the Giudecca! They're lit up with Japanese lanterns. There's music and dancing — "

"Yes, and don't forget, you've still got to pay here," she reminded him as they departed, she hanging on his arm with renewed hope.

When Benedetto returned homewards in the first gray light of the morning, a few vegetable barges were already gliding through the gleaming water over which the mists of the nights still hung. Gondolas filled with masks, also returning homewards, floated up the Grand Canal. Some of the revelers were trying to keep the dying carnival spirit alive by song and shouting instead of waiting for the coming of a new evening. Others, like himself, sat mute and motionless.

All about Benedetto was Venice — Venice — But did he see it?

Yes. When he had nothing left, Venice would still be there. A little

Jewess under whose enchantment he had fallen could not take that away from him.

His coming to Venice had been no accident; but it was an accident that he should have found his way to the house of Graziadeo the Jew. An accident, nothing but an accident that he must try to forget, that he *must* forget.

And suddenly there appeared before him an apparition more threatening, more concrete than that of old deceased Signora Galli.

The repellent, shameless face that had pursued him since he had seen it disappear behind a pallid mask in the dark box of the theater had risen up again in his mind. He cursed it, but could not banish it, and from this face his thoughts wandered towards Todi.

Feverishly, he sought in his mind for someone in Todi with a face like that. Nobody — nobody. But while he assured and reassured himself of this fact, he wiped the clammy sweat from behind his mask with a handkerchief.

The piazza of Todi stood before him. It was the evening of his flight, and the *sbirri* were searching The Three Popes. The cries of Luigino, who had been taken into custody, resounded as loudly in his ears as if he were hearing them for the first time. Outside, the crowd was whispering excitedly, and waiting upon events. He himself was among them. He wanted to flee, but something still held him back.

The tramp of hoofs was approaching. A vehicle, a great traveling coach, stopped before the inn, to which, however, no travelers were admitted. The multitude surged back. . . .

He himself strode forward — and now he asked himself whether he would have done it even if he had known then that those few steps would cost him his life. A woman's laughter resounded from the dark coach, and a young, proud face stared in amazement at the *sbirro* posted at the door of the inn. He advanced in order to relieve the attractive traveler of her difficulties by offering to put her up at the house of the Gallis. A few moments later, and he would have lost the power to do that. She nodded to him in joyful gratitude, and then out of the dusky depths of the coach emerged a long, lanky creature — a sort of Beelzebub — who, for both of them, accepted his offer. . . .

And here the rapid sequence of visions ceased.

Motionless, he sat in his gondola. Through the holes of his black mask, his eyes stared across the gleaming water.

THE LITTLE GOTHIC PALACE

ON THE

RIO DI SAN FELICE

I

PALE GRAY AND SLENDER ROSE THE LITTLE GOTHIC palace out of the green-black water of the Rio di San Felice. It had small rose-windows and a balcony of carved stone tendrils and foliage. It was a delicate late-Gothic jewel, and, such was the delicacy of its construction that it would probably have collapsed if, some couple of centuries after its erection, the massive, strongly built Renaissance palace that was its neighbor had not been built for it to lean against.

On the other side it was quite detached. Behind a low wall of the same tender gray stood several austere cypresses, black as ink. In Venice, the few square yards of ground behind that wall and the half-dozen cypresses it nourished ranked as a garden. The adjoining palace could boast of no such luxury. The garden opened onto a miniature harbor just large enough to contain a gondola, and protected by a gate that autumn had covered with bright red vine leaves.

The little palace itself was wonderfully quiet. Behind the windows and the small door to which a short flight of steps gave access from the water, all life appeared to have died. The gently swaying cypresses rustled a barely perceptible threnody over the mossy roof, and a thin wraith of smoke that rose slowly from the towerlike, bombastic chimneys was the only indication of life in this house that seemed to have fallen asleep.

Twenty years before, *"lo Spagnuolo"* — "the Spaniard," a shipowner — had bought it from an impoverished aristocratic family whose daughters, if one could believe report, offered themselves for money to rich foreigners.

The whole neighborhood thought that the new owner would pull down the decrepit, dark old house and build another on its foundations; but he disappointed these expectations, and confined himself to overhauling it. Workmen came to mend the leaking roof, to replace the broken glass, and to remove the paper stuck against the window panes. When all was done, *lo Spagnuolo* married a Titian blonde, eager for life's pleasures. He himself was dark and dignified, a real Spaniard. Like a gravedigger risen from the black, somber earth, he moved by the side of his blooming young wife, exposing her to the mockery of her former friends who, according to Venetian custom, were accompanied, in the street and at church, at feasts and at balls, by their chosen *cavaliere servente* — some pleasure-loving young fool who amused them from morning to night with his lovesick prattle and assiduous gallantry.

Lo Spagnuolo would not hear of such a *cicisbeo* for *his* wife, and denied her all those innocent little pleasures without which no Venetian could live. He guarded her with angry jealousy and a suspicion that was wounding. The old Gothic house with the dark cypresses that rustled softly by day and by night became a prison in which she soon began to pine away. When, after a year, she brought her child into the world, a fever took her to the grave. The dejected widower followed her coffin alone to the churchyard that lies halfway to Murano. "Gracias Dolores," he called the little daughter she left behind, and, confiding her to the care of his old servant Catarina, who found a wet nurse for the infant, he turned his back upon Venice and took ship for a long voyage to the distant Indies.

He continued to travel, visiting his Eastern factories regularly; and he removed the head office from Venice to Malaga, to the house of his unmarried sister Concha, who held the reins for him like a man.

Years later, he returned to Venice to see his child. Old Catarina showed her to him, full of pride. She had the pale, sun-kissed hair of her mother, but a shade redder: owing to the mixture with the black hair of the father, explained old Catarina, who had talked so much of her father to the child that the little girl realized who he was. *Lo Spagnuolo* was strangely moved by the sight of her.

He decided to take the child away with him, and show her to his sister. He considered selling the old house on the Rio di San Felice, since it was now of no further use to him; but he came to realize that he was deeply attached to it — perhaps he had some premonition that he would yet return to Venice. He kept the old palace, and allowed Catarina, who had looked after it so long for him, to go on living there in company with her large tomcat. Sobbing with gratitude, Catarina kissed his hands.

Concha, however, was somewhat perturbed when he landed in Malaga with his small daughter. She had not even enough tact to pretend to a little feeling for her. She had never known the child's mother, and she felt almost as though her brother had brought an illegitimate child under her severely pious roof. The child was not like him either. She had a free, debonair way with her, as one would expect of a child from so simple a city as Venice, and she spoke a language her aunt did not understand. Even the father could converse but imperfectly with her.

After much consideration, and a short but acid dispute with his sister, *lo Spagnuolo* decided for the time being to take little Gracias Dolores with him on his travels. "*La muchacha*," — "the little girl" — the Spanish sailors called her, and among them she learned to pick oakum, make sailors' knots, and climb the mast. She soon knew the four points of the compass, and all the oaths the men used — even those in using which it was necessary first to spit on deck and then to cross one's self; and she also knew that these must not be uttered in her father's hearing.

It was as if the old spinster in Malaga sensed this hidden knowledge in her. Aunt Concha's distrust of her increased with every homecoming; and on her side she was as distrustful of Aunt Concha, who decided that she ought to keep her little niece at home, and heaped reproaches upon her brother for the way in which he was allowing his child to grow up. She brought her old father-confessor's influence to bear upon him, and when in due course there were clear indications that little Gracias could no longer be left solely in the company of men, her father's obstinate objections broke down and she was left behind. Gracias did not weep when her father sailed away — in some ways she was like him, after all. She only looked very pale and disturbed, and did not appear to hear what was said to her. Concha was radiant at this separation, radiant as her brother would have liked her to be eight years earlier, when he had first brought his child to her. This time he had been unable to bring himself to give her the customary brotherly kiss as he departed. Nor did she expect it: her triumph was enough for her.

This first voyage without *la muchacha* made him realize that he was growing older — too old for constant traveling in distant parts. Desire for a settled home came over him, and his thoughts went back to Venice, where he had found a wife and buried her. The wonderful, quiet little palace on the Rio di San Felice rose before his mind. In Alexandria, he took ship on one of his vessels that was bound with a cargo for the city of the lagoons.

To his sister he wrote that, full of gratitude for the great services she had rendered him, he wanted to relieve her of her business worries so that she could devote herself entirely to the upbringing of his daughter, which lay so near her heart. He had decided to resume the reins of authority again, and intended to remove the head office once more to Venice, where he still had many connections. As the main reason for this sudden decision, he alleged, at the end of his letter, that he had had an unexpected and grave attack of the gout which had deprived him of his freedom of movement.

Concha replied that she would accept no thanks for services that had been rendered from sisterly love, and that she would send the book-keeper and one of the clerks to him with the books and all the correspondence. She had not been aware that the Venetian climate was favorable to sufferers from the gout, but of that, no doubt, he was himself the best judge.

She also sent him a letter from Gracias that bothered him and filled him with grave anxiety, although it was friendly in tone.

He sought in vain for some valid motive to take his child, so recently entrusted to her, away from Concha. Upon re-reading Gracias's letter several times, he had to admit that it contained no single word to justify his anxiety.

Meanwhile the old bookkeeper arrived, and laid the accounts before him.

Now, six years later, his ships continued to sail to the Levant, to the harbors of North Africa, and to the distant Indies; but increasing doubts had spoiled for *lo Spagnuolo* even his pleasure in watching from the quay of the Dogana the departure of one of his ships, seeing it rowed to the Lagoon and there unfurling its white sails against the blue of heaven. The short walk to his office on the Rialto was almost too much for him. One of his clerks brought the post daily for him to annotate. For the rest of the day he sat bent over bills of lading, as though he were the bookkeeper of his business. He received his captains at home when they reached Venice with their rich freights, and tormented these men, bronzed by sun and sea air, for hours on end, holding them responsible for all damage and every unexpected charge. For six long years he remained in the quiet little palace on the Rio di San Felice with old Catarina and her tomcat, now gray and blind. He allowed her, rather unsuccessfully, to massage him for his gout, and, while he bit his lips in order not to shriek with pain, made her account for every item in the household expenses. But an almost morbid longing for his daughter suddenly came over him.

The heart he had closed against the world overflowed with memories. He sat down and wrote to his sister.

Concha was disinclined to release her prey. A second letter in which he addressed her, as in the days of their common youth, as "Conchita," was no more effective; and he threatened to enforce his paternal authority through other channels: an ultimatum that led at last to the desired result. Gracias, now a young lady, came over from Spain on the *Santa Cruz*. . . .

The first surprise was that she arrived before the ship that was to bring her. The second was that she did not come alone, but in the company of a cavaliere whose appearance inspired little confidence — a long, lanky, cadaverous creature who, with remarkable unconcern, delivered her at her father's door, and then retired with a bow. This cavaliere turned out to have been a fellow passenger, and Gracias had come upon the original notion of getting off with him at Naples and, as his way took him also to Venice, traveling with him overland, leaving her heavy luggage to the care of the captain of the *Santa Cruz*, and taking with her, as her only chaperon, Toto, a minute, yapping Maltese dog.

The old man, still counting on his calendar the days that would bring the ship to Venice, reconciled himself with difficulty to the fact that his child had upset all his calculations in so simple a fashion, and had interpreted his fatherly instructions so freely. An overcharged atmosphere reigned in the little Gothic palace, and darkened the joy of their meeting.

And then there came a third surprise. During those six years, little Gracias had outgrown his paternal authority. She had not become the sort of young girl he had expected, but a young lady, and she appeared already to have outlived a number of prejudices. What sort of upbringing had she had in Spain? Was it for this that Concha had deprived him of his child? He recalled to his mind the dried-up, bigoted face of his sister, and tried to understand this miracle. The clothes Gracias wore could not have come from Malaga, where the women still went out demurely cloaked. She must have procured them in Naples or in Florence, using the travel money he had sent with too lavish a hand.

Besides, it was not her clothes that deprived him of his authority. It was the complete unconcern with which she allowed the storm of his wrath to sweep over her. It was the faint quiet mockery in her eyes, the wordless disdain of her comely, proud, hostile mouth. Beautiful she had become, his daughter, even more beautiful than his wife, whose form seemed to be miraculously resuscitated in her.

When the old man halted for a moment with flushed face to get his breath, she took this to be an indication that the subject was now closed, and informed him that she had done business for him on her journey, handing over in Rome, Florence, and some of the smaller cities that happened to lie on her way letters entrusted to her by the Naples factory. She had good news for him, and orders for an amount that she had not been able to reckon out precisely, since she had no aptitude for that sort of thing, nor ambition either. In any case she hoped she had given satisfaction to those in Naples who had entrusted her with these commissions. She doubted whether all that she had done could have been effected so rapidly and smoothly if the letters had been carried in the usual way by a courier. She fumbled in her little traveling case, and, finding the precious freight orders, handed them over to him.

As he fixed his eyes upon them, trying to decipher them, suddenly he was aware only of his child, his Gracias, and the desire welled up in him to ask her forgiveness for a fault he sensed — he could scarcely have put it into words. He hungered for her, longed to close her in his fatherly arms, and press her to his heart — had he but dared.

Old Catarina was not more daring, and when she noticed that Gracias no longer even expected her embraces, she turned against her.

Toto, the Maltese toy dog, slept with his young mistress and yapped angrily at Catarina when, with an aggrieved face, she took up the chocolate on the morning after Gracias' arrival. He barked more angrily still when the old man, after a night of conflict, shambled into his daughter's room to wish her good day. An oppressive smell of perfume and powder greeted him.

Lo Spagnuolo had intended to unburden himself of much of his bitterness and disappointment when the captain of the *Santa Cruz* landed a week later. While the shipowner heaped reproaches on his guilty head, the captain, instead of trying to justify himself, unexpectedly made a surprising gesture, more eloquent than any words, of complete helplessness and discouragement, and the old man halted in the middle of a sentence. Then, unexpectedly, Gracias entered the room and greeted the captain laughingly. He turned paler than the documents he had placed before the shipowner. Only as he was about to depart did his courage come back, and he begged her to have the kindness to accept a trifle as a memento of their journey: a small gold Byzantine cross set with jewels that he had bought from a monk in Corfu. He hoped it would please the young lady.

Gracias accepted the costly ornament and wore it round her neck as long as the captain remained in harbor. The evening before he was to sail on a long voyage to the West Indies he called to take leave; but he was unlucky: she had gone out with friends, said the old man, dismissing him curtly, with rising fury.

Before his daughter's arrival *lo Spagnuolo* had had the whole first floor of his house refurnished as a bedroom, a boudoir, a salon, and a library for her use. The walls were hung with silk, and the rooms were furnished in the latest fashion. Now, downstairs in the room to which he had completely withdrawn himself, he wrote an angry letter to his sister Concha. With uncommon friendliness, she replied that Gracias had left her house a God-fearing, severely brought-up young lady, and that to her the voyage under the protection of a sea captain had seemed from the beginning a curious proof of his consciousness of fatherly responsibility.

Upon Gracias' entry, peace had deserted the little Gothic palace. To begin with, Toto and Mutu, Catarina's gray tomcat, could not bear one another. Toto yapped as soon as he saw Mutu. The cat spat and arched his back, grown stiff with old age. It was impossible to keep them out of each other's way. Neither the one nor the other forgot for a moment that its mortal enemy shared the same roof. It was a feud that was to remain undecided until the end of their days, since neither dared approach the other nearer than half a yard. The old man raged and threatened to put an end to the intolerable situation. Catarina, rushing upstairs to carry Mutu away from the scene of strife, had to catch at the banisters halfway up, overcome by palpitations of the heart. The only person who was not bothered by this perpetual feud was Gracias. She did not leave her rooms, and when she was alone with Toto she encouraged him and spoke evil to him of his enemy.

At last *lo Spagnuolo*, hearing once more the angry yapping and spitting, lost his self-control, seized the two animals by the scruff of their necks, and threw them through the window into the canal. A gondolier who happened to be passing saved Toto, and handed him in at the door in hopes of a reward. Blind Mutu he had not noticed, or else he had taken it to be one of Venice's too numerous tomcats. When Catarina returned from market an hour later, she found the consolation of her old age sitting by the side of the canal, to which he had scrambled by his own powers. He was shivering as he licked himself clean. She pressed him to her narrow bosom, and swore revenge.

More animals came into the house. A young, ambitious, newly appointed ship's captain brought a parrot for Signorina Gracias straight from the primeval forests of the Amazon. During the long voyage, the bird, avid to learn, had picked up a number of ship's orders, and also unfortunately a number of words that sounded less seemly in a lady's drawing room. The donor, however, was sure the bird would soon forget them. But the parrot, whose name was Socrates, did not forget them:

he immediately began to direct them at Toto, who barked furiously in response.

Gracias, through the same captain, ordered a little Moor for her drawing room, after the fashion of the day. He promptly brought from North Africa a twelve-year-old Christianized Negro boy, whom she dressed like a prince in blue shot silk with silver stitching, a garb that was wonderfully flattering against his tawny complexion. Furthermore, she hung round his neck a small golden Byzantine cross. (The giver of that gift was at the moment steering his ship, the *Santa Cruz*, through a hurricane somewhere in the latitude of Haiti.)

At first Annibale, the Negro boy, was as shy as a caged animal, and tried to hide from everybody in the house. He had to be lured from his hiding-place with sweets and friendly words. Panic fear lurked in his large moist pupils with the chrome-colored whites. But all that soon changed. His fear of white people departed. He became free, bold, finally shameless — and spoke to Marianna, Gracias' lady's maid, with an air of superiority in his smattering of ridiculous, muddled Venetian.

Before very long, young *nobili*, poets, painters, parasites, began to frequent the quiet little Gothic palace by the dozen. Over *lo Spagnuolo's* head there seemed to be perpetual merrymaking. To old Catarina's mute amazement, he did not protest. He seemed afraid to take action, appeared unable to adopt an attitude. Perhaps it flattered his vanity that half Venice, after having shrugged their shoulders about him, now came to his house as his guests. For, as he had to pay the bills, they were in reality his guests.

During the six years since his return, he had restricted himself to those few luxuries which were obvious and indispensable to every Venetian of his class. His daughter, however, put things to rights. She rented the most expensive box in the theater of Sant' Angelo when it happened to become free halfway through the season. She bought a richly ornamented gondola of her own, and engaged the services of a liveried gondolier.

And as the summer progressed and the poisonous vapors of the Lagoon penetrated into the city, she expressed cool astonishment to her father that he had no villa on the Brenta, as had every self-respecting Venetian who prized a long life.

Lo Spagnuolo fought the matter out with himself for two days before he sent his bookkeeper to look for a suitable summer residence. When, however, he saw his daughter depart with a gondola full of trunks and a rollicking company, he felt that he had been merely discharging a debt he owed her.

He himself, as in former summers, remained in Venice. He expected some of his ships to arrive shortly; and besides he was not invited. He paid the bills that reached him from the summer residence, and his only concern was that they should not fall into Catarina's hands. Her expenditure he continued to check with an iron hand, paying no heed to her increasing protests.

In her villa by the Brenta, Gracias gave small and large garden parties. The grounds were hung with lanterns like an orchard with ripe fruit. Against the violet night sky rose the red and golden flare of fireworks. There was dancing under the oak trees, and flushed young faces laughed in their frames of powdered wigs. In the dark depths of the garden, in the cool dusk of the grotto, sighs and whispering voices blended with the sound of distant music. While Catarina on unwilling feet had to ransack the whole market to provide her master with a cheap though young and tender chicken, two thousand wax candles were burned during the night from Saturday to Sunday in the villa on the Brenta. Concerning this business of the two thousand wax candles, *lo Spagnuolo* decided to ask Gracias upon her return whether she deemed his wealth inexhaustible; but he knew he would never find the necessary words once she stood before him. The stillness of his house that had once been dear to him began to oppress him. He wanted to hear Gracias' voice, the voice of his child in which he seemed to hear again the voice of his wife. He therefore waited impatiently for the festival of the vintage that brought to a close life in the summer residence.

When, however, Gracias returned with a great following, he was put out to meet in this company a worthy Venetian judge who ought to have known better than to mix with all these young people — a man of his own age, who helped her out of the gondola and, so it appeared to a suspicious and jealous father, seemed to arrogate this privilege to himself on other grounds than his sixty years. And he was disturbed even more by a cynical, mocking glance that he caught in Annibale's eyes.

Stillness had departed from the house once more. *Lo Spagnuolo* should have been satisfied. Next evening, after the first performances of the season in the theaters, all the windows of the first floor were brightly lit, and in the black cypresses next to the little palace gleamed gold paper Chinese lanterns. Long, narrow, somber gondolas brought boisterous masked guests who pressed into the house, filling it with their wanton noise.

The Chinese paper lanterns in the garden died out one by one when the midnight hour had expired, but upstairs in the little palace the candles continued to burn — their warm glow would be dimmed only by the light of the rising sun. Through the oaken ceiling the sounds of revelry and dancing feet pressed upon him.

In anxious suspense, Catarina listened: her master had gone upstairs. What did he want among all those young people who had not called him?

Through the open windows music was wafted into the night, and passed over the heads of the gondoliers waiting below in the shadows. Among them Silvio was first. Yesterday a mere *barcaiuolo* whom anyone could summon, that morning he had entered the service of Gracias, who had had to dismiss her former gondolier because he could never be found. Among the thirty who presented themselves, her choice fell upon Silvio. He recommended himself to her favor immediately by his Herculean frame, and his insolent eyes. A giant he was, now distinguishable from his former equals by his too tightly fitting livery and his broad, red silk sash. Under the narrow jacket his athletic shoulders showed impressively. A few black curls fell boldly over his brown rogue's face.

With a broad, mocking laugh he looked up towards the illuminated window from which his mistress had bent for a moment to cast a glance into the impenetrable darkness. Swaying his head gently to the rhythm of the minuet that was being danced upstairs, Silvio bit greedily into the salami sausage in his brown fist, and took a long draught of red wine.

II

For two days Benedetto roamed through Venice without being able to reach a conclusion. As if by magic, he was always being drawn towards the Rio di San Felice, which he would have been wiser to avoid. From the shadow of the quay beside the monastery of the Misericordia he stared across at the little Gothic palace on the other side as though he could see, through the closed door, whether his fate awaited him behind it.

Of course, the wisest thing would have been for him to say farewell to Venice. But it was as if there were no world outside Venice.

He felt a little self-pity, too: at the very moment when he was about to take possession of this city towards which his longings had flowed for so long, it seemed that he must already give her up, on account of a thoughtless act committed in the past. He could not shake off the obsession of that act, which in its lurid reality contained its own punishment. On account of a deed already repented a thousand times, to which perhaps he had been unconsciously tempted only in order to reach Venice, he ought to leave her again.

Quite apart from the fact of whether that maypole of a man in the box would go to the *sbirri* or not, Benedetto felt himself betrayed by his birth as the son of Buongiorno the Todi coffinmaker, by his upbringing in that provincial hole where he could not breathe, by old deceased Signora Galli who, as if with devilish intent, had ever and again made her jewels glitter before his eyes.

It seemed to him that his bitterness over his past was gnawing at him more deeply than concern about present danger. It was true that he had recognized the lanky companion of the Spanish woman, and he would have recognized her, too, as soon as she had lifted her mask; but that was natural, since all the impressions of his last afternoon in Todi had been ineradicably engraved on his memory, as if in the fierce light of a feverish vision. But was that a reason why they should recognize him? The boorish manner of Cavaliere Maniscù proved little or nothing. Would the fellow have looked at him like that if he *had* recognized him? No. Benedetto had little to fear from that Beelzebub.

And the Spaniard herself — he would have liked to know what had been in her mind that evening when, in the house of the Gallis, they described the whole crime in all its details. In spite of everything, she must have remained grateful to him in her heart that, with the *sbirri* so hot on his tracks, he had still allowed himself to be allured by her laugh, and had used the last of his power and influence in Todi to help her to obtain the best lodging the Umbrian mountains could offer. Would she betray him if she recognized him?

Oh, why not? What did he know of her?

But he could not bring himself to leave Venice. The more conscious he became of the danger that lurked for him there, the surer he was that he would not flee.

Venice had, if anything, become even more his own now that it contained his fate, and ever and again, blindly, he took the same way, ever and again by a different approach he found himself by the Rio di San Felice peering across the water towards the pale little Gothic palace on the other side.

He went home only to sleep. As he got up at irregular times and took his coffee in one of the coffee houses on the Riva, he hardly ever saw Leah, and that was just as well: it was better she should pay no heed to him . . . With her David she was safe and sheltered.

He kept his solitary watch by the monastery of the Misericordia until at last it came to be noticed. Had the young Spaniard observed him from her window? Upon one occasion he saw her returning home. As she stepped out, she was helped by that giant of a gondolier of hers. Benedetto wondered whether by any chance he had not met *that* fellow too, formerly.

Should he let the door knocker drop and go in? If he had followed up her invitation of that unfortunate evening in the theater, he would at least now know where he stood. That would have put an end to this accursed uncertainty, which was threatening to become an obsession.

Suppose he challenged his fate, went to meet it face to face?

III

Unexpectedly the miracle happened, and liberation came from an unforeseen quarter.

First it was a few notes that made Benedetto look round in astonishment — a gondolier, high on the *poppa* of his slender craft, was gliding by, pressing the long blade through the water with all the weight of his body and singing: —

> *Traghetto — traghetto d'amore,*
> *Matto m'hai fatto . . .*

A *barcaiuolo* who, some evenings before, had witnessed the disaster in the San Samuele theater and had saved from it a few bars of Columbine's song. A baker's boy, balancing a Turk's-head on his head, picked up the tail end of it and disappeared with his acquisition into a little alley: —

> *Matto m'hai fatto il cuore!*

And with him the fragment of Benedetto's canzonetta was lost once more in the carnival revelry of the evening, and one might have assumed that it was lost for good.

But a new air that haunted the ears of several theater-going gondoliers could not be lost in that city, where they needed a new popular song every day. Benedetto might have known that, for Monsignore had often talked of it in Todi.

Another *barcaiuolo*, two canals away, remembered the tune his brother gondolier was singing. In three, in ten different places, the little mischievous canzonetta sprang up; and then suddenly it spread with unbelievable rapidity through the whole city.

Next day it was ringing from all the gondolas as they went out onto the Lagoon where it was the thing to watch the evening glow die behind the cupolas of San Marco's. Lutes and violins accompanied and echoed the swinging melody, the printed text of which was on sale that afternoon in the Merceria for two soldi.

Benedetto hurried with intoxicated feet to the little San Samuele theater. He thought he would find it closed: instead he found enraptured faces. A full house was watching the performance. The whole of Venice wanted to hear Columbine sing "*Traghetto — traghetto d'amore.*" She sang it now in the first act, in the second act, in the third act. As she sang it, it was no longer a song, but a pæan. In the stage box on the right, her rich friend sat with his bunch of red roses, but from the left and from above, too, flowers rained on the stage.

The song of the moment was sung as a duet, as a trio, in chorus. Pantaloon sang it, Harlequin sang it. The orchestra played it in the intervals. The ballet danced to it. The public sang, whistled, and bellowed it. The theater rocked to the ditty. The play itself was rushed through, at breakneck pace, with ruthless cuts, so that it should be noticed as little as possible. Besides, each of the actors surpassed himself. Brighella improvised until he had to be dragged from the stage by force, leaving an audience behind him that was rocking with laughter. Pantaloon polished his text until it sparkled. Rossi wanted only one thing — that Benedetto should write songs, ballets, operas for him. Everything would be welcome. He could make use of everything. He was prepared to hire whole orchestras, dozens of singers . . .

Benedetto had suddenly found himself again. Success had come at the right moment. Every hesitation, every inner weakness dropped from him when he saw Venice intoxicated by his song. Because he could not bring himself to believe it, he had come to the theater. Now he was forced to believe it.

Then he heard his name, Bussoni. *His* name. Apparently his presence had been grasped when Rossi was seen talking to him so excitedly, embracing him with his large fat hands. "Bussoni — Bussoni!"

Slowly Benedetto looked round. It no longer seemed to matter if the *sbirri* were waiting for him. Of infinitely more importance was it that he should bestow more songs upon Venice.

He had a feeling that they would come to him now. To-morrow he would write others and bring them to Rossi. . . . To-morrow! But he was too elated to go home at once and retire to his room to work. He had a foolish desire, impossible of fulfillment, to go carefree among good friends. . . .

And then Fate ordained that at that moment the little abbé should come rushing up to him, as excited as himself, and averring that he had a dozen ideas for new plays in his head. In his overflowing joy and emotion, he flung his arms round Benedetto's neck and kissed him on both cheeks.

The audience noticed their meeting, and broke into laughter and applause. A deep gravity compelled the abbé to silence for a moment. A flood of tears streamed down his cheeks. Then suddenly he rushed after Benedetto, who had shaken him off and was hurrying from the theater. He overtook him, angry and panting, and said, "Where are you off to? Why are you in such a hurry? Come along — We're going to Gracias'. She said I must look you up. Why didn't you come that evening and drink with us to the success of my play? After all, it might have been foreseen — The public was mad about it at the end of the second act."

Benedetto stood still and stared at him. What was the fool saying?

To the Spaniard's this evening . . . ? For a moment fear came over him again, deeper and more acute than it had been — a paralyzing fear of detection, of the destruction of everything that was just glimmering so magically before his eyes. And then this fear itself made him suddenly decide to go with the abbé. He must know now whether he could go about in Venice safely.

"Good," he said, still fighting against a last hesitation that turned to anxiety as he heard himself utter the deciding word.

The effect of this word upon the abbé was strange: he was visibly disappointed at the success of the mission he had undertaken.

He fell silent, seemed disconcerted and out of humor. Then he assumed an empty enthusiasm. "Bravo!" he said, and clapped his hands joylessly.

While he dragged Benedetto by the arm in the direction already so familiar to him, the abbé looked before him, worried and abstracted.

"A WOMAN

WITHOUT

A HEART"

I

WHEN THE GONDOLA THEY HAD TAKEN AT THE little square in front of San Samuele's had left the Grand Canal by the Ca d'Oro and drifted into the little Rio di San Felice, the abbé suddenly broke the odd silence in which he had enveloped himself. It seemed a relief to him, now, to have somebody with whom to talk.

"There won't be so many this evening. . . . This evening, we're among ourselves. There'll be a dozen people, perhaps. She had to see you, she said. I really can't understand why you didn't come after the performance . . . ?"

Benedetto, his eyes raised to the lighted windows above, was conscious of the puzzling agitation in the voice of the portly little abbé. Before the gondola had properly put in, he jumped onto the waterside, and began to drum on the door with the knocker.

"That's our prearranged signal. That's how we recognize one another," he explained, with a sort of childish elation, as Benedetto paid the *barcaiuolo*.

And then they waited. The prearranged signal had no immediate effect. The abbé repeated it, more loudly and excitedly. They must surely hear him upstairs. "And Catarina, the lazy old bitch, just doesn't open the door," he said reproachfully, wounded in his pride.

Behind them lay the silent darkness of the water, from which an autumn chill was rising. The disappointed abbé shivered, and began to rattle wildly with the knocker. "Francesco!" he shouted, in bitter reproach to a pale face that came peering round a chink, and he pushed the door wide open so that they could enter.

In front of them, a lantern in his hand, stood the somewhat seedy apparition from the box whom the abbé had introduced as "the glory of our younger painters." The apparition said never a word, but preceded them up the stairs with his lantern, holding on to the banisters.

"Galuppi, how do you come to be drunk again?" began the abbé in a moralizing tone, and then worked himself into a sort of ecstasy as, with an air of superiority, he informed Benedetto: "We're at home. We do everything ourselves. No lackey crosses the threshold. We're all pressed into the service of *la muchacha*. We're her proud servants, and if she were to order us to sweep the stairs . . . Just make yourself at home. You can hang your hat and cloak here, and we enter through this door."

As soon as the door was opened they were met with a hurlyburly of voices. In the golden shimmer of the superabundant candlelight was gathered a company that seemed to consist almost entirely of *Barnabotti* — poor aristocratic parasites from the quarter of San Barnaba; but this deceptive impression was due to the fact that the well-furnished sideboard stood just next to the door. The abbé carried his prey inside, crying loudly above the clamor: "Here he is, the fugitive. Here he is at last!" and he was not abashed by the fact that only one or two turned round, with palpable indifference. It was enough for him that his voice appeared to have reached the youthful hostess herself where she was sitting in a circle of admirers all trying to speak to her at once. She put her fingers ostentatiously in her ears, and turned her face towards the new arrivals. With a surprised little smile, she recognized the Cavaliere who had needed so much begging before he would enter her house. She offered her hand graciously to both of them, and advised them to get chairs for themselves somewhere.

"I'll see to that," cried the abbé despotically. "You're commanded, Bussoni, to stay here and wait until I bring a chair for you. Are there no more chairs? Wait! I'll go downstairs . . . "

The company turned out to be larger than he had expected. With the exception of a young girl who was waiting upon such guests as were disinclined to make their way to the sideboard, it consisted entirely of men. In a faintly ironic tone that sounded charming in her mouth, the hostess introduced the composer of *"Traghetto — traghetto d'amore."* Several guests came forward to compliment him. Others bowed with an unmistakable absence of interest. One or two told him that they themselves were musicians or members of Arcadia, the academy of poetry . . .

"Marianna! Where can I find chairs?" wailed the abbé, still running vainly backwards and forwards, and, already discouraged, clutching at the young girl as she crossed his path. He had not been able to make up his mind, after all, to go downstairs. As though afraid that somebody else would take the floor, he himself spoke on uninterruptedly, telling them unbidden, in a loud excited voice, about his new play that had not yet been written.

"I'm dedicating it to you, Gracias! The whole of Venice is bound to recognize you, in any case. It will succeed through the gossip it will excite; and its success will be complete if you yourself will play the part of Columbine. I think I can expect a courageous young woman like you to do that. I shall only tell you the title: 'A Woman without a Heart.' "

A few began to applaud wildly, blindly, apparently simply to prevent his speaking further. Others, misled by the applause, came running up inquisitively. "What did he say? What is the play to be called?" Nobody enlightened them, so they looked expectantly at the abbé, who at once began to relate the plot. One guest, not wishing to hear, jumped up from his chair and fled. The abbé swooped upon the seat thus freed and sat down, entirely forgetting that he had gone to look for a chair for Benedetto . . .

"Columbine has thirty-three lovers, three-and-thirty lovers has Columbine. Pantaloon does not sleep, neither does he eat or drink. He is pining away. He seizes a hammer. He would like to break the necks of his wife's three-and-thirty lovers. But for lack of a better use for it, he shivers the looking-glass in the house to fragments, so that she can no longer see how beautiful she is, and thus be led away by lighthearted thoughts. But it is all no use, *povero Pantalone!* He begins to go mad, crackbrained, signori; he loses his senses completely, and kills his pretty little wife, his Columbine. May her soul be saved from hell-fire, amen. The soul of Pantaloon, however . . ."

From the sideboard half a dozen cavaliers approached with the somewhat disconcerting proposal that they should dress themselves up as devils or something, and in that guise penetrate into the reception room of the convent at Murano. The abbé, wrathful at this intentional interruption, shouted: "The soul of Pantaloon, however — "

"What do we care about Pantaloon's soul?" shouted the young cavaliers. "To hell with the soul of . . ."

"Let him tell us about his play," decided the hostess, sending the noisy interrupters back to the sideboard.

"The soul of Pantaloon finds no rest," proceeded the abbé, eagerly. "He rushes to a famous surgeon, and begs him to open Columbine's heart for him. Perhaps after all he will find in it only the image of her good, elderly husband. But the surgeon finds nothing! No heart at all! Columbine never possessed one. Poor Pantaloon grows madder still. He takes the road as a penitent to a monastery famous as a place of pilgrimage, and inhabited by thirty-three brothers. He confesses his murder to the prior. The venerable father grants him absolution, which in any case could not be denied to a madman, and gives him a heart for his Columbine: the heart of a newly killed hind. What heart could be more tender, more devoted, more true? A happy man, Pantaloon hurries home. The surgeon knows how to plant it in Columbine, and recalls her to life by secret remedies and incantations. She stands again, God be merciful to her and her good man. Result, a joint pilgrimage of thanks to the monastery. Three-and-thirty days Pantaloon sojourns there in prayer, with his little wife. A new miracle: all the brothers change into deer. Too much of a miracle! Back to Venice! Third miracle: deer are waiting on the Molo, deer are racing across the Piazza San Marco. . . ."

The ultimate solution of the miraculous occurrence was not yet quite clear in the mind of the abbé himself. Nevertheless, he dared to foretell success: the audience would be unable to contain itself for delight when they saw the venerable gray-bearded prior running round like the rest carrying formidable antlers.

Those few who had listened to him to the end with genuine or simulated interest adjured the young hostess to create the rôle herself. Any producer would be only too pleased to engage her for the part. The public would be jubilant at the sight of her, alone. Besides, the theater would be packed with her friends, and as a surprise they would all put on antlers for the last act.

Her eyes wandered towards Benedetto, and, as if she were trying to fathom what he thought of his company, she continued to look at him while she answered her friends without troubling to keep out of her voice unmistakable boredom, even distaste. "Oh, are there thirty-three of you? I hadn't counted."

Benedetto met the look with which she was trying to read him. So far she had not recognized him. Or at most but vaguely, and without being able to place him. It was improbable that she would take the trouble to search in her memory for long. There was too much to distract her in her life from day to day, he thought. . . . So much reassurance had his visit already produced.

Besides, if she supposed that he thought the atmosphere around her somewhat childish, she was not mistaken. Were they really enjoying themselves, or were they only pretending? He was wondering why she

— Gracias — surrounded herself with a circle of such admirers, if she was so mortally bored among them.

She might not have recognized him; but he had recognized the fiery, dissipated eyes in that comely face, the laugh that had struck him when he heard it resound for the first time from the interior of a closed traveling coach. In the four months that lay between that memorable meeting and this, that laugh of hers had acquired an added fascination for him. Whenever he recalled to his mind his last hair-raising hours in Todi, her laugh sounded through them crystal clear, and for a second chased away the dark menace of that afternoon. . . .

The old judge who had sat next to her in the box appeared suddenly in the doorway that led to the adjoining room. For Benedetto there was something almost uncanny in the unexpected appearance of this man of threescore in the company of these young fools. He felt that the gray-haired *nobile* was driven to Gracias' house by some inner restlessness, that he was in a way mounting guard there by the door. The Venetian dignitary, so oddly out of place in this company, tried to keep himself in countenance by a barely perceptible smile of superiority. He looked at all those irresponsible young things as if it amused him to observe them unobserved. But the sullen fire that glowed in his weary eyes, the involuntary expression of misery in his whole being, betrayed that he could not have torn himself away even had he wished to.

At last his youthful hostess appeared to take pity on him. She summoned him with her eyes, and he came closer to her, fearing to hasten his steps and thus show how great was his gratitude for this privileged glance.

Was a cruel little game being played with the old man? *La muchacha* seemed to Benedetto to be quite capable of it.

She was tormenting the foolish abbé too. Behind his agitated, idle prattle lurked some concealed grief. Who of those in the room besides these two, were also suffering through her?

Most of the others were young *nobili* without a care in their minds. Benedetto knew a few of them by sight. When he arrived in Venice, he had aimlessly wandered the streets with them by night in his desire to make this city his own, until their senseless heroics had repelled him.

Looking slowly round the room in which the correct taste of *lo Spagnuolo* was blended curiously with Gracias' more airy fancy, he rested his eyes incredulously upon a little Moor decked in scarlet who, as he leaned against one of the high window seats, stirred a glass of sherbet, and met his glance with one grotesquely bold and unashamed.

II

Gracias had not recognized him. His previous concern struck him now as having been exaggerated, and he almost despised himself for the feeling of relief that came over him. During the abbé's recital of the plot of his foolish play, an entirely new and audacious plan had come into Benedetto's mind, a plan for something far more ambitious than the composing of a few simple canzonettas . . . But this was not the place to mature such a scheme.

But what had become of the long, thin fellow of the box, whose existence in Venice had filled him with restless anxiety for days? He suspected that he might be in the adjoining room, where play seemed to be in progress. Unobtrusively he moved to the door by which the old judge had stood a while back, and discovered that his surmise was correct. There he saw Cavaliere Maniscù in the rôle of banker, and he could not have said why he had expected him to be in precisely that position.

Maniscù's roving eyes noticed him at once. This time they brightened as they saw him, and Benedetto despised him no less for this than for his previous attempt at intimidation. He responded with an almost insulting coolness. The lanky Greek, however, was not to be denied his enthusiasm over this second meeting. With elaborate compliments he introduced him to the other men, and invited him to join in the game. With the firm intention of winning money from him, Benedetto accepted the cards.

Only when he had lost several times did it occur to him to mistrust the persistent luck of the bank. Perhaps his mind had not been entirely on the game, but suddenly a vague warning sounded in his brain. As if he no longer trusted his luck, he took no part in the play for a few turns while he studied the banker's hands. They were uncommonly large, pale hands, with long, bony, knuckled, mobile fingers. There was something unattractively expert about those hands, but something also of the down-at-heels actor. Behind the little wall of gold and silver pieces that he had won, the incredible quickness and ease with which they shuffled the cards and slipped them were almost imperceptible.

Deep astonishment invaded Benedetto. He could hardly believe his eyes. Was it in the company of this cavaliere that the petted and only daughter of lo Spagnuolo had traveled? He must work it out. . . . Meanwhile it just crossed his mind that the position might be reversed, and that he was about to acquire power over those whom he thought he had cause to fear. He only needed to get this virtuoso of the cards into a corner. . . . Oh, he would do it, too. He would avenge himself for the anxiety that he had suffered on account of this arrogant fellow who now thought he could get his money out of him with the help of a few double cards.

He was under the impression that his careful watching had not greatly disturbed this cavaliere. Nevertheless, Benedetto expected that he would come to him during the next of the short intervals in play that were the rule in all private houses of standing. When the moment arrived, he stood somewhat aside to make Cavaliere Maniscù's approach to him the easier, and true enough the banker did come up to him — not, however, because he was troubled by an uneasy conscience, unless he were adopting a truly masterly pose. With an air suggestive of wounded feelings, he inquired in a soft, unctuous voice why Benedetto had ceased playing.

Benedetto stared at the lean cheat in silence. Then, by way of reply, he made a surprise movement and lifted an ace of spades out of Maniscù's cuff. The other, his face turning gray, snatched it back almost in the same fraction of a second and, casting a disconcerted look about him, buried it once more in his broad damask cuff, over which he ran his hand pretentiously as though he were merely adjusting his dress after a brutal assault. He seemed to be on the point of pretending to be affronted. But Benedetto put his hand softly upon his arm, and the cavaliere turned to him, with a contempt that was as foolish as it was audacious, and said disdainfully: "Give me your address. I shall see that you get your money back."

"No — instantly."

The other hesitated, momentarily at a loss. Wild hatred flickered in his small, shifty eyes. Breathing deep, he asked: "How much was it?"

Benedetto had not yet given that a thought.

"Two hundred gold ducats."

"Good. Wait." With recovered dignity, Cavaliere Maniscù moved away — a weedy, somewhat unsteady shadow through whom Benedetto could almost see. Leaning his back against the table, he conversed with the sons of one or two rich merchants out of whose pockets he had spirited the gold; they were in a hurry to lose more money, and asked him how long the interval would last. He looked at a watch gleaming with diamonds. "Another minute," he said, with a weary smile. When they were all seated again, Benedetto returned to his place, and there he saw his two hundred ducats lying.

From that moment the bank was out of luck. After having raked in his winnings three times in succession, Benedetto thought he had had enough, and got up with the intention of moving to the adjoining room; but he had not yet reached the door when a young man of wealth who had that summer inherited two glass factories on Murano broke the bank with a bold stake. The penurious banker got up and seemed almost relieved that he was at last able to throw down the cards; probably he feared that the shaking of his hands might be noticed by others besides Benedetto. Hastily, he retired from the field just as Gracias came in with another group, declaring that she wished to play. With a wry smile, and a gesture that he attempted to make airy and chivalrous but which was merely tragic, he signified his bad luck, bowed, kissed her hand, and begged her to excuse him: he had another appointment.

If he had hoped that she would pretend to believe him, he was greatly mistaken. It did not occur to her to act in a way that would facilitate his departure. Struck dumb with astonishment, she stared after him and did not attempt to conceal that his abrupt departure was one of the great puzzles of her life. Then she decided to regard the matter humorously, and slipped her arm through that of the old judge, who had already offered to replace the departed guest. She rewarded him by going to sit beside him. As she guilelessly stretched out her hand for some cards, she suddenly discovered that the young composer of songs who had entered her house for the first time that evening was in a chair opposite her, and she could not refrain from observing him with attention and a certain suspicion, as though she felt some vague connection between his presence and the sudden departure of Cavaliere Maniscù.

Play was resumed, and she looked away from him.

His victory had roused in Benedetto a lust for battle that threatened to go to his head. He felt capable of any recklessness; he had found himself again. What had been the matter with him during the month he had spent in Venice? What sort of ghosts had estranged him from himself? Now he had awakened from his nightmare. He wanted to watch the young Spanish girl's cards, too.

Behind him, half against his chair, leaned enamored young *nobili* and young men of wealth, their one anxiety to be in her line of vision. Benedetto could scarcely refrain from smiling. How did she contrive to keep a whole regiment of adorers on a sitting? What was her secret?

Certainly she was young and beautiful. There was no gainsaying that. She had the magnificent pale complexion of the red-haired, — though her coiffure had been fashionably powdered, her skin betrayed the original tint of her hair, — and in the tender pallor of her face burned fierce, dark, seductive eyes. But her witchery could not be due to that alone — there were many pretty young women in this city. It was something fascinating and unfathomable in her being; though in truth there might be little enough to fathom. The playful, mysterious, almost stereotyped little smile about her still childish mouth had at the same time a line of disillusion-ment. If one looked at her mouth for long, one almost wanted to obliterate that teasing smile that had something wounding about it. Instead, one would have liked to see an expression of pain about her lips. Did she know pain? It would be pleasant to get rid of all these adorers for a while, to be alone with her, eye to eye.

Perhaps her whole secret was that so far she had protected herself from being alone with any one of her many admirers.

Every movement of hers, even the smallest and least remarkable, had something challenging about it, something contemptuous and yet alluring. One wanted to seize her wrists and say, "Don't move a moment, just to please me."

He would have liked to be able to discover whether she knew of the practices of her departed guest and travel-companion of the spring. If she knew everything — then that childish something about her whole being was but a deceptive mask, more dangerous than the silken mask of the Venetian carnival, and a man might think himself lucky to have seen through it in time.

But stop: there was another possibility. That ingenuous quality about her was perhaps unsimulated. Even though she knew everything, perhaps she moved like a child between good and evil, a little smile of mockery about her mouth, without feeling the necessity of discriminating between them. If that were so — it changed everything. If that were so — she be-longed to him, to nobody else in this room. If that were so, she might well hear everything — about Todi and about his past — from his own mouth.

What feverish thoughts were these? A deep discomfort came over him. A moment ago he had been unable to observe her quietly — could he do so no more? Why did he himself conjure up again the menace of his fate when it had seemed to subside? Or was this also but a possible way of conquering his fate: by evading it no longer, by binding himself to it voluntarily and defenselessly?

Was he then so tired of strife that he was thinking of surrender? A short while ago he had been glowing with the brave dream of dominating this city through his music. But perhaps he must first conquer his fate.

Or was this weakness simply due to that dangerous sense of loneliness he had carried about with him ever since he had come to this city?

He tried to recover his self-control. Before his bewildered mind rose the image of Leah: perhaps she could help him and guard him against a danger into which he was going open-eyed, unless someone held him back. Oh, Leah was far away, and Leah belonged to another. If any woman in Venice were to belong to him, then something told him it could only be the woman now opposite him, if she were indeed what he thought her.

Like a child she took part in the game of chance, regretting her stakes too late and changing them when the game had gone too far. She was elated when she won, downcast when she lost. She pretended to regard Fate as her especial enemy. Everyone at the table treated her as though she were a child: boisterously they wished her luck in unison, or, bewailing her ill luck, they gave her more good advice than with the best will in the world she could have followed. The sixty-year-old judge, whose duty it was to pass sentence in the Palace of the Doges on erring mankind, and who seemed singularly out of place as banker at a gaming table, treated her like the rest, palpably happy when he could push her winnings towards her.

Benedetto thought the whole company about her ridiculous. With difficulty he restrained the biting words that would have revealed his irritation and restlessness. The longing, the hunger to reveal himself to her, however perilous the step might be, was growing within him minute by minute. Only thus would he gain certainty regarding the mysterious bond that seemed to him to link them. If he found it to be but a figment of his mind, then he must make the effort necessary to wrest himself from it.

Why did she not glance at him? Was she no longer aware when a man looked at her as he had been looking at her this half-hour, this hour? He did not know how long he had been sitting opposite her. Did this game of chance mean more to her than that other game of chance in which he wished to offer himself as the stake? Or had she observed his glances, and was she merely playing with him?

When he noticed that he had no more money in front of him, he felt automatically in his pocket. He must have done that several times already, for his pocket was empty. Vaguely he knew that he must have lost a great deal, although now there could be no other reason than that fortune no longer smiled on him. He felt in his waistcoat for more money. He did not withdraw his hand immediately: what decree of Fate brought his fingers at that moment into contact with the silver ring that had completely escaped his mind since the evening when Graziadeo the Jew had attempted in vain to acquire it from him? For the fraction of a second he hesitated; then he accepted the sign. Alleging that he had no more ready money with him, he handed his find to the banker, and asked how much he deemed it worth.

The old judge, whose thoughts were elsewhere, gave it but a passing glance. By the tone of his voice, he made it very clear that only good breeding led him to allow the curious silver ring to count for a hundred sequins.

At the same moment, Benedetto's secret wish was fulfilled: Gracias stretched out her hand towards the gem. Suddenly his suspense became unbearable: would it say anything to her? No, she had only been struck by the peculiar quality of the antique trinket. She could not refrain from slipping it on her finger to study the effect. The old man at her side noticed this typically feminine gesture and turned, with the abruptness that betrayed his complete lack of inner control, to the owner of the jewel, saying: "How much do you want for the ring?"

Benedetto saw that this question had roused general interest, and his answer was directed not to the banker alone, but to the whole company who were waiting expectantly.

"I want nothing but what you have already given me, Baron: permission to stake it at the value you have placed on it."

"But I'm prepared to offer twice as much, if you will allow me . . ." Realizing his own mistake, the old man broke off in the middle of his sentence. Benedetto merely smiled. The judge flushed with embarrassment, then his face became sallow and colorless as before. His mouth twitched: one could not look at him without pity.

Slowly, wonderingly, Gracias drew the ring from her finger and laid it before Benedetto. He thanked her with an inclination of the head.

"The Cavaliere has declared a hundred sequins an acceptable valuation," said the old judge at that moment, so that all at the table could hear. Then he handed cards to those who wanted them.

His face showed bitter disappointment when the bank lost, but it brightened again when Benedetto put the gem on the table, together with the hundred sequins he had won.

Two hundred sequins upon a single card: it was a larger stake than anyone had dared to risk that evening. The others, forgetting their own game, and putting down a gold or silver piece merely as a matter of form, watched the duel between these two men.

A soft cry went up among the watchers; for the second time the dusky golden brown scarab brought luck to its owner. The bank would need more capital if it intended to invite a third defeat. As it lay there gleaming on the table, the ring appeared suddenly to be more valuable than any other single object in the room. The three hundred gold pieces that now lay beside it seemed of little or no significance compared with the mysteriously gleaming topaz whose value could perhaps not be expressed in terms of money at all.

All but Gracias fixed their eyes on the ring: her attention was riveted upon the man who had staked it. Gradually her eyes took on a thoughtful expression, and for the first time the little mocking smile about her lips died away. Benedetto felt her glance and dared not look up as he reached for fresh cards. Was she ransacking her memory? But now he knew that he did not want her to recognize him simply from that one evening in Todi — he wanted more! He wanted her to recognize him from all the others, as he had recognized her behind the deceptive appearance of her little mocking smile. Suddenly doubt of her filled him again, and sweat stood on his brow. Hastily his eyes sought the window: if need were, he could reach it in two steps, knocking aside everything that might stand in his way. At the back the wall of the garden gave on to an alley. Armed with this knowledge, he could take the risk of continuing to play.

His ring had won twice in succession. Fortune, who had turned her back on him through most of the evening, now favored him, thanks to his ring. If he had to make his escape, he would first whisk it from the table — this ring of his with its mysterious motto, of which nobody here knew, not even Gracias.

Twice in succession the ring had won. The gray-haired banker was pale as he stared at the mysterious, dangerous trinket, towards which Gracias had stretched a hand so covetous that he had been overcome with a wild longing to give the jewel to her. He had not known, then, that within a few minutes he would be prepared to place in the balance, if need be, his entire fortune. He would open a new bank if this one broke. In case of absolute need, he would send his servant to a Jew to borrow ready money.

Luck must come the way of the bank some time or other, and once would be sufficient provided the jewel still lay on the table.

But what if the other were to win once or twice more, and were then to slip the ring back into his pocket?

But that did not happen. The devil withdrew his hand from the game. Upon a breathless silence, there followed a sigh of relief, then a sudden buzzing of voices. A number of those who had been watching left the gaming table, and scattered through the room in animated talk and laughter.

Luck had deserted this young cavaliere. It had been a mistake to ascribe some mysterious power to him and to his ring. With the gold that had been piling up beside it, the trinket had gone to the banker, whose courage deserved this success. Slowly, attempting in vain to conceal his perturbation, Benedetto got up and mingled with the others.

His first emotion was bitter regret and anger at the loss of his ring, and a passionate desire to recover it. His ring should have won just once more, just once more — that would have been enough. Then he would have put it away, and got up from his seat in the expectation that Gracias would come to him.

To her he had wished to present it, if she had come to him. Now it belonged to that repellent old man who was angling for her favor, who had put a value of a hundred sequins upon it, and who in his heart had at first thought even that too much. A somber foreboding welled up in Benedetto when he asked himself what the old man intended to do with his ring. Curse him! His impotent rage made him almost ill.

Those still about the gaming table wanted to inspect the ring more closely; but the old man was reluctant to satisfy their curiosity: he seemed to fear that someone might filch the treasure he had gained at so great a risk. Hardly able to restrain his tears, Benedetto observed the scene from a distance. Then he suddenly noticed Gracias, approaching him casually. He waited, trying to control his breath.

She looked for him with eyes in which a strange glow was burning. She stood in front of him and tapped him playfully on the shoulder with her fan. She looked round hastily, to see if their meeting was being noticed and discussed, and then said in a low, teasing voice, "You still owe me the story of the ring."

Their eyes met as he answered, "I will discharge that debt this evening, if I can speak with you alone."

She nodded — nodded also towards the old judge, who looked in her direction at that moment. "Why shouldn't you be able to speak to me alone? But they need not know. Wait in the garden until they are all gone."

She left him with a smile, and hurried towards Baron Barbaresco, in order to set him free from his troublesome besiegers.

A prey to stormy feelings, Benedetto remained where he was. Overwhelming joy flooded his being, almost stifling him. If she did not yet know everything, her intuition had nevertheless revealed enough to her to make her think it advisable to conceal their sudden familiarity from the others. She had given him a sense of assurance that she would be silent if he confided his secret to her. By that silence, she would become his accomplice. It was for that he had longed. He would cease to be alone. Already he had ceased to be alone in Venice.

Later in the evening, Gracias' eyes once or twice rested on him, thoughtfully and as it were by accident. He seemed to be engrossed in conversation with her father.

III

A Spaniard. Dignified and conceited, gruff by nature and not simply to mask shyness. A thin and rather unhealthy face, in which lines of grief were bitten deep. Even though he was perhaps less erect than he had once been, he still had an air of authority that failed of its effect only in the rooms where his daughter reigned. It was not age that had dealt this blow to his pride; it was some inner defeat above which he was still trying to rise. Under his bushy gray eyebrows lurked a pair of jet-black, tortured eyes.

It would have been difficult to decide whether he had come upstairs to insist on a little peace over his head, or whether he had been lured from his joyless isolation below to the liveliness about his daughter; but that second possibility he would never have admitted.

There was something mysterious and over-grave about him. No wonder the children of the neighborhood ran away from him on the rare occasions when he ventured from his house. It was rumored in Venice by the superstitious seafaring folk that a voyage with him on board was always unlucky. A menacing cloud loomed over his whole being. By his manner and the clothes he wore, he seemed to have stepped out of an earlier century.

His daughter was the first to welcome him. Her guests looked on jealously as she embraced her somber father. *Lo Spagnuolo*, however, embarrassed and suspicious, looked over her head to see whether the comedy of this embrace had been realized, whether it was giving rise to quiet mockery of himself.

He perceived the judge, and the two men of mature age exchanged a hostile, courtly bow: one of them felt ashamed and despised — but not this time *lo Spagnuolo*. To him, the forced respect of the judge brought a bitter-sweet compensation, and he hardly troubled to conceal an expression of derision that passed quickly over his stern features.

The young *nobili* and merchants' sons greeted him with the joviality youth is accustomed to employ towards old age, which it no longer takes seriously. Some of them brought him wine, and wanted to drink with him. He pushed back their arms, and in his sonorous and still exotic-sounding Venetian inquired after their parents. The young rakes, nonplussed, reassured him, but felt obliged to say that since their return to the city in connection with carnival, they had not been much at home, and during the summer and autumn they had seen little of their parents, since their attention had been too much engrossed by his incomparable daughter Gracias . . .

The old man nodded slowly, and looked without a word at these young people, so fundamentally alien to him, who did not scruple to talk to him about his child in such tasteless fashion. He turned his eyes from them to Benedetto, who was introduced to him.

He felt at once that here was something different from these Venetian *nobili*, these timekillers and wealthy idlers, among whom were to be found also the sons of serious men with whom he had had business dealings. In Benedetto he found a man who, like himself, stood outside this crowd that made him a stranger in his own house. He invited him to sit by him and drink a glass of wine with him. Benedetto was delighted by such privileged treatment from Gracias' father — indeed, he would otherwise have been hard put to it to fill in the evening until there was talk of departure.

Everyone else was grateful that *lo Spagnuolo* had selected his victim, and no further attention was paid to him. A few late guests dropped in — actors and musicians. Like hungry wolves, they swooped upon the sideboard, and as they ate greedily they uncorked a dozen bottles of wine. Some of the young *nobili* who could play the violin or the guitar picked up, without troubling to ask permission, the instruments brought by the musicians, who made no objection.

Meanwhile, *lo Spagnuolo* conversed in dignified and measured tones with Benedetto. He said no word of what he saw around him — he even tried to avoid seeing anything, by sitting with his back to the company. He asked Benedetto what he thought of this city, which, drifting as it did upon the waters, seemed a refuge for rats rather than for men. He confessed that he had lost his heart to it thirty years ago, when as a young merchant he first viewed it.

"The world still opens from here — even though it is no longer ruled from here. Where can a merchant establish himself better? It is true that one has to get used to stepping out of one's front door into the water. It is impossible to grow altogether accustomed to Venice; one remains a stranger here. It's a treacherous city. It has a more hospitable appearance than any other, but in fact it accepts nobody."

Benedetto was not so sure of that; but why should he try to convince the Spaniard? As if guessing at Benedetto's unspoken disagreement, the Spaniard repeated dictatorially: "Nobody. A man may have a house here for thirty years, for thirty years he may pay his taxes faithfully — and they're not low. He gives to the Church, and to charity. He provides work for some hundreds of seamen from Chioggia and Malamocco. He even marries a Venetian, and his child is baptized in San Marco's. . . . But in spite of all that he does not acquire Venetian citizenship."

As he spoke his eyes wandered. Something stronger than himself compelled him to look in the direction of his child, who was conversing with the old judge.

It was some time before he managed to resume his subject, and then it was with difficulty. "Gracias can become a Venetian if she wishes — she need only marry a Venetian. That's a privilege she has which her father lacks. But with her everything is unpredictable; she may not care to take advantage of her privileges. And I often ask myself what is to become of Venice when I see the youth of the present day. Thirty years ago, the young *nobili* were not very different from what they are to-day. They were unmoved by the slow decadence of their city, thinking, 'If Venice goes under, the whole world goes under.' Yes — but in those days, the young men belonging to the aristocracy of wealth still had pith."

He forgot the youth of the person to whom he was speaking with such bitter disappointment. Perhaps he forgot Benedetto altogether, and was really speaking to himself. Without expecting any answer, he asked: "What do you think of the way a young girl behaves these days among her friends? Must a father accept such a situation? Can he rely upon it when she says she knows how to look after herself? Won't she become the victim of her own thoughtlessness? How can she attract an old man like that to her . . . ? He is as old as I am, or older. I didn't ask him here. Had I selected a man of that age for her, she would have turned away from him with disgust. The world would have cried shame on me, and the world would have been right."

Lo Spagnuolo took a deep breath. The hand that lifted his glass to his lips was trembling. The look he could no longer withdraw from his daughter and the judge contained so much bitter disgust that he might almost have been taken for a rejected lover of his daughter Gracias.

At that moment, her maid glided past him carrying a decanter of wine. Involuntarily, she gave him a pitying glance. He looked after her, vaguely astonished and a little suspicious. Then suddenly he seemed to wake up. There was a light in his eyes, and hoarsely, like one thirsting, he called her name: "Marianna!"

She stopped, turned round doubtfully. There was something strangely shy and melancholy in her appearance. Her face, figure, and demeanor suggested that she belonged to some good but impoverished family. Benedetto looked at her with attention — up to then he had paid little heed to her. Nor had anyone else.

"Pour us out more wine, Signorina Marianna!" begged *lo Spagnuolo*, half gruffly, half humbly. He wanted to please her, and continued to look up at her as she poured wine for both of them. "How old are you? You seem to be much more sensible than my daughter. I should like to have a word with you some time about her. . . . What? Twenty-two? In my young days a girl with your looks did not remain unmarried so late."

She tried to hurry away with a little abashed smile, but he seized her with his hard, old hand. Frightened, she looked round, but was partly reassured when, with downcast eyes, he merely said, "Leave us the decanter."

He emptied his glass and poured out another for himself and Benedetto. He broke an awkward silence by saying in a bragging tone that seemed alien to him: "She's one who would like to be friendly to a lonely old man. I wonder whether the judge has noticed it. She's good-natured and not at all unattractive, but nobody looks at her. They look at my child. I have to look at her myself, whether I want to or no."

His child. Perhaps he had seized Marianna's hand only because it was the hand that helped his daughter to dress. "Isn't it so? Isn't there something fascinating about her?" he asked with an almost irritating vanity in his voice. "One must forgive her a great deal. I forgive her everything. She makes a mockery of my thirty years' hard work. She fills my house with people to whom I cannot talk. I sometimes ask myself what I come up here for. But it's to see her — I'm filled with a restlessness I never knew before."

There was no need for him to say that. The torment of this restlessness was unmistakably apparent in the look he fixed upon his child. He was no longer aware that he was speaking.

"She knows no pity. It's an idea that has not yet penetrated to her. Just once or twice in my life I've felt pity for this person or that. But Gracias does not succumb to such foolishness. She's a complete egoist, in all innocence, without being aware of it, and with no uneasy conscience about it. Oh — but I do not wish her different from what she is. I don't believe anyone would wish her different from what she is. She is herself, but we are no longer ourselves when we come into contact with her. And when I see the sort of people who hang round her, then it consoles me to know that nobody approaches her unpunished."

Slowly *lo Spagnuolo* got up to go.

"Are you going, Papa?" inquired Gracias, and her voice sounded clear and ingenuous; but he did not reply. He bowed stiffly to the company, and the door closed behind him.

A little later, the old Baron, in whose eyes there was a glow of mysterious agitation and triumph, made the proposal, which was at once greeted with general despair, that they should bid their hostess farewell and retire for the night. Benedetto was the first to kiss her hand and take leave. The others, all somewhat under the influence of wine, followed his example, showering flowery compliments upon her as they did so.

Only Galuppi, completely inebriated, insisted upon staying, determined to be alone with Gracias. He had to be spoken to at length and with tact before, leaning on several friends, he could be persuaded to depart. He was in tears as he went down the stairs.

Below, the gondoliers jumped erect in their craft.

IV

Gondolas were drifting through the night. In a long procession, they came out of the narrow, dark mouth of the Rio di San Felice into the Grand Canal, where they scattered in all directions.

In his own gondola sat Baron Barbaresco, the judge. He leaned back and closed his tired, feverish eyes. In the protecting black shadow of the *felze*, he saw nothing of the fireworks that were going up from the basin of San Giorgio Maggiore. Nor did he hear the faint sound of distant shouting that greeted each shower of colorful, starry rain. His thoughts took their own course.

A day was about to break that would be longer than any day he had ever lived. The hours would drag and the sun would appear to be riveted in one place; but at last twilight would fall — and the night that was to follow would compensate for the almost intolerable torture of that one day, for the ordeal of months.

Would she whose name he need no longer utter to himself, since there existed no other woman in the world for him, would she keep her promise?

From the moment that his stars had brought him into her proximity, and she had laughingly accepted him as fatherly friend and protector, she had played with him. She had confided her sorrows and her joys to him. With sighs she had talked to him about her young courtiers. She had flattered him, and made him happy by assuring him that only in his company was she not bored, and that his friendship was of more value to her than the meretricious calf-love of a dozen of those others. Thus, slowly but surely, she had poisoned his blood. When he had become aware of it, it had been too late. The first time that, losing control of his senses, he had in an unguarded moment bent over her and touched her shoulder with his lips, she had hastened to evade him. Thereafter she had always taken care to surround herself with ten, twenty, of those young rascals and idlers in whose company she felt so bored. And they allowed themselves to joke at his expense. Yes, they seemed even to wait until he was within hearing before they cracked their best jokes; and she listened to them and smiled, in spite of all the assurances she had given him. Ever and again she soothed him with vague promises that robbed him of his sleep and his power of clear thought, which he still needed in his capacity of judge.

He was sixty. In his youth he, like everyone else, had had his adventures. When he had risen to the dignity of judge, however, he had decided, with some difficulty, to put an end to all that. For fifteen, twenty years, he had then lived in the delusion that he had been successful. He had begun to believe that he was proof against emotional shock. He thought he could look back upon his life with a detached smile; and for this presumption life was taking its revenge. Whatever unknown dregs had settled in his blood during those twenty years now swirled up and robbed him of his wisdom, of his proud self-possession. Once again his blood had been stirred, more turbulently than in all the years of his youth. His brain glowed feverishly. He no longer knew himself; had he done so, he would have had to cover his face for shame.

He realized the danger to which he was exposing himself. The Republic looked askance on such of its servants as made public laughingstocks of themselves. She did not even like it when they went too regularly to the houses of foreigners, even though those foreigners might have lived in Venice for thirty years. If too much were to leak out about his visits to the house of *lo Spagnuolo*, if too many droll stories were circulated concerning his strange adoration of a twenty-year-old girl, then the Senate would ultimately find itself compelled to deprive him of his toga, even though it recognized his capacities to the full. . . .

But to-night he had ceased to care. He had settled his account with life — provided he were allowed to celebrate his leavetaking of it, provided that life granted him this last favor, that *she* should come to him next evening as she had promised, that he should be alone with her one night within the safe refuge of his own four walls, kiss her mouth but once, quench in the glory of her young body the wild, cruel fire in his blood, still that eternally teasing little smile, which he had come to curse, in an embrace such as she had never expected from a graybeard. . . .

In this one night he would regain his ascendancy over life, would be able to look down disdainfully once more upon that old sour Spaniard and those young coxcombs. That night would reveal to her who and what he was, and if she still thought to continue luring and tormenting him, then her dangerous little smile would glance off on his own broad one.

For a moment his thoughts rested on this dream vision. Then they ran forward again feverishly. Where would he best receive her? In the *salotto* with the little bay window giving onto the canal? Once upon a time it had been arranged precisely for such charming visits, but it was long since he had sat there. Those evenings when he did not go to the opera, the theater, or the Ridotto, he was in the habit of spending in the Palace of the Doges, bending over legal documents.

How would his servants behave? The only one he could rely upon was old Zaza, who had cooked for him in his student days in Padua. She would want to prove to him that she had forgotten nothing of her craft. He would go down into his wine cellar himself — he belonged to those wise people who never entrusted the key of the wine cellar to servants. Giacopo and Achille could begin at once to get things ready, dust the silk furniture, renovate the chandeliers, remove every dull parchment that, in the course of years — oh, desecration! — had strayed into his former love-nest, and reeked of the judge's bench. Giuseppe would have to doff his gondolier's dress and serve at table. He looked less like a gallows bird than the other two, and the Baron felt reasonably sure that he would at least be able to refrain from smirking, and would not empty the sauce-boat over her dress.

The whole house would be in darkness — a discreet semidarkness that would put her at ease. Only in the little *salotto* would the candles burn, and with their golden light illuminate the feast.

The very last, dearly bought feast of his old age.

V

In the garden, in the deep shadow of the cypresses hung with golden lanterns, another was waiting — waiting and listening to every sound. From the distance, dull reports of fireworks reached him from time to time. Then for a minute or two he heard nothing but the mysterious rustling in the dark foliage above his head. In the sky, the stars gleamed and twinkled.

On this side, the house was shrouded in complete darkness. Perhaps a window was still lit up on the side facing the *canaletto*, but it was invisible from the garden. No sound reached Benedetto. The whole of Venice seemed suddenly dead. It stood about him — dead, quiet, gray, risen out of the water that was unfathomable as the Styx. He heard nothing but the beating of his own heart.

When would the door be opened for him? Surely he could not have misunderstood her? Surely she had realized that he must go away with the others and return by a roundabout way? Should he knock . . . ?

He had been sure of her while he had been in the same room with her and, as he listened courteously to the effusions of the old Spaniard, had been able to observe her and smile quietly at her band of turbulent admirers, among whom was one not far removed from the Biblical threescore and ten. The consciousness of what he had just risked for her sake gave him a feeling of precedence over them all. Surely they had been invisibly linked together ever since they had met in Todi. He had been sure that he could extend his power over her the moment he found himself alone with her.

But now that he no longer had her before his eyes, now that he could no longer see what was happening above, his fancy began to play him dangerous tricks. Supposing the front of the house, too, were plunged in darkness. Suppose she had simply gone to bed. Had all those whom she had consoled to-night with her little mocking smile once waited in vain in this dark garden?

A wild suspicion rose up in him: That long lanky cheat — where had he gone? Had he really left the house? Was Gracias whispering in his ear at this moment that he need not worry over his unmasking because he, if he so wished, could run to the *sbirri* and make his dangerous opponent innocuous?

When he recalled Cavaliere Maniscù's tragic air as he departed, however, these suspicions evaporated. He wondered whether, after all, it had only been his overheated imagination that had made him think Gracias had recognized him from Todi. He tried to remember, word for word, what she had said to him. "*You still owe me the story of the ring.*" Yes — but what did that amount to? It all depended upon how she had said it. How had she said it? He could no longer recall the tone of her voice. Suddenly he was overcome by longing for her, the longing to hear her voice, to recover the certainty that she had recognized him. . . .

Was he always to be martyred by such a senseless restlessness the moment she was no longer under his eye?

He took a decision, made almost an oath to himself: In the event of her knowing nothing about him, he would be silent. Now and always. But if she had recognized him, then he must find means to curb her, to keep her curbed.

He ran his hand over his forehead, and noticed that it was covered with the sweat of anxiety. And then suddenly the door opened.

He stepped forward swiftly and stumbled against Marianna who, almost too constrained to speak, preceded him with a candle. Holding his breath, he followed her up the stairs. The maid led him to one of the rooms he knew already, and with a gesture and an inaudible word re quested him to wait.

He stood motionless in the middle of the room, almost intimate now that most of the lights had been extinguished: only one heavy silver candelabrum was still lighted. Lost in a corner in the half-darkness, gray with sleep, stood Annibale. Benedetto did not notice him until he yawned. As Benedetto turned towards him with a jerk, Annibale interrupted himself in the middle of a new yawn, and disappeared.

Gracias entered, and if a last doubt still remained with him, now he felt sure: she had recognized him. In her eyes, mysteriously directed towards him, full knowledge lay hidden. If she kept silence, her knowledge would stamp her as a voluntary accomplice of his guilt; for such a silence he would be madly grateful to her.

She herself was aware that she was bringing him a gift. To play with him a little longer — that was no more than her right. As if in fear of him, she did not come to him at once, but glided past some chairs before she sat down and appeared to be on the point of offering him a chair, too. But she did not defend herself when, from behind her chair, he drew her towards him, passionate and masterful. Only when he was about to kiss her mouth did she bend her head backwards and begin to moan softly. He hesitated, bewildered again and afraid. Like a mischievous girl she looked at him, pouting. He might only kiss her mouth after he had first kissed her hand. She pressed her small kittenish hand to his lips. There now!

On her hand she was wearing the ring he had lost in play that evening to the old judge.

He let her go, and shrank back, asking doubtfully: "How did you come by that?"

That was the surprise she had wanted to give him. She threw her arms wildly round his neck. "Nothing, he will get nothing in return," she averred, laughing and whispering with hot breath. Her eyes lit up with an almost devilish triumph as she looked at him mockingly, and said: "How did *you* come by that ring?"

MUSIC

IN THE

NIGHT

I

NOT WITHOUT DEEP, SECRET REASON HAD BENE-detto been driven irresistibly into the arms of the young Spanish woman. Even had his feelings beforehand not told him so, that night proved that they belonged to one another.

She had listened to him, leaning back and staring at him wide-eyed. She could hardly draw breath for suspense. And round about them was stillness: the old house, the whole dark world held their breath to listen too. He evoked Todi before her eyes — not the charming, primitive little city buried among the mountains where for one evening and one night she had stayed, but the tedious, dying, provincial hole, in which he had been doomed to spend his youth, and where he heard of the live world beyond just enough to long for it with an almost morbid longing, and to break a way out for himself, if need be by force. He described decrepit old Signora Galli, as she sat waiting for him all day on the first floor of the massive, brown *palazzo*, buying with money the story of his latest adventures. Under the guise of protecting him, the son of parents without standing, she had sucked at his youth like a poisonous vampire; and while he mocked at her and at himself by the fantastic stories with which he titivated her senile fancy, he had not himself realized in how devilishly cunning a way she had ensnared him. She had closed him in her heart and, with the madness of a gray Fury, wanted to possess him too — if not in this life, then in death. Since she herself had nothing left with which to lure him, she had lured him with her accursed jewels, which she had dangled glittering before his eyes again and again. Her jewels, which he could not forget even after she had taken them with her into her coffin. What diabolical inspiration had compelled her to add a clause to her will that she was to enter the Beyond with all her jewels? An involuntary, fateful glance into the squinting eyes of a gallows bird on the other side of the grave had completed his circle of destiny. Looking back, he realized that the old woman in her coffin was a party to the plot. That night she had waited for him there in her tomb as she had waited for him when alive in the more spacious chambers of the Galli palace; and she had triumphed when, defying while loathing the odor of the dead, he had bent over her by the glimmering light of a torch. Then she had gladly surrendered to him the jewels she had formerly locked away with exaggerated care in the secret box of which she herself carried the key. But she had seemed to want to keep her rings. His companion of that night had found a way. . . . Luigino had been caught by the *sbirri*. What had happened to him? Gracias should know — she was still in Todi the day after his arrest; what had they done with him? Quickly and without hesitation, she spoke the word he expected. He had never thought anything else possible; but nevertheless he swallowed and could not forbear to give a hasty thought to Nana, and to Susanna with all her children. Then, feverishly, he put such thoughts out of his mind. Luigino had been bound to end that way; no Signora Galli had been necessary to bring that to pass. Besides, she had not wanted to have anything to do with Luigino: it was he, Benedetto, she had wanted. She had been waiting for him again in Venice after giving him a few months' respite. Nine-and-ninety years she had been allowed to live and spread her poison. On her hundredth birthday she hoped to celebrate her third wedding by moonlight in the city of the lagoons.

But she had miscalculated. He no longer feared her pitiful ghost, now that Gracias also knew of its existence. From this night, she would have to abandon her earthly phase and retire for good to the kingdom where the spirits of the dead sojourn, remote and innocuous.

To satisfy him, Gracias gave him an account of the evening she had spent in the house of the Gallis. She had at once seen through the gruesome comedy enacted there, had realized that they were merely discomfited by the filching away of the jewels they themselves would have liked to steal from the dead, if only the will could have been spirited out of the way in time. She had seen the absurdity of the pompous, corpulent podesta of Todi. He had forgotten his complicated feelings of grief in an effort to seduce his unexpected guest; and she on her side had been scarcely able to conceal her amusement when he had tried to soften her by ridiculous stories about the wife who had fled from him to a convent, and at the same time had tried to convince her of his impressive virility. During the few hours she had spent in it, she had sensed the oppressive atmosphere of that little provincial city, where a thunderstorm from time to time must be in the order of nature. She declared she had felt an immediate curiosity about the audacious raiser of this storm. While the good podesta was trying to describe to her all that this incredible desecration of a grave meant to his whole family, and to himself in particular, — himself, the only son of the deceased, — all that she had wanted was to find out more about the youthful perpetrator, of whom she had had but a fleeting glimpse when, emerging from the crowd, he had come forward to offer her lodging in the Galli Palace. Everything she heard of him pleased her. It pleased her that old Signora Galli, who had decided to make her journey to Eternity arrayed in her costly jewels, had always had a weakness for him, and, little thinking that she was nursing an adder in her bosom, had given him the blessing of her protection. It pleased her that he had also enjoyed the protection of Monsignore, the bishop; and the nickname — *il pipistrello*, "the bat" — under which he must since have become a legend in Todi: she liked that, too.

She drew him to her. *Pipistrello* — now you are mine.

Another woman, full of abhorrence, would have crossed herself again and again as he made his confession — that is what he had always imagined. But she, she broke into frivolous laughter, the laugh he remembered so vividly, a laugh expressive of her contempt for mankind and of her unconcerned gaiety. It chased away the last menace of old Signora Galli's ghost. Instead of sinking into the chilly, dead arms of his centenarian mistress, he sank gratefully into arms warm and alive. . . .

Life had come back to him.

Through the shutters fell the first shy light of day. It touched the silken curtains and the furniture and conjured up from the dimness the indistinct figure of a young woman. She sat, her face turned towards the light, telling him of her life. Now it was Benedetto who looked up at her, guessing sometimes at the expression on her still half-invisible features, sometimes perceiving only the sound of her voice that seemed to come to him from afar.

She told him of her childhood, of the time when the sailors called her "*la muchacha*." The first time she remembered seeing her father was when she was five years old. He seemed to her the lord and master of the tall ship, manned by powerful, bronzed, rough fellows, that carried her away. Till then, old, bad-tempered Catarina had been to her the highest power on earth; but that power collapsed like a pack of cards the moment her father appeared upon the scene. On board, after a time, she was aware of a similar situation. The captain commanded the ship in name, but behind and above him rose the somber, hated figure of her father.

"I believe there was nobody who did not hate him. He affronted almost everyone with whom he came in contact, and often he expected the impossible; but there was nobody who dared tell him so to his face. Some of them were rough fellows whom one might have expected to use their fists when he tormented them too viciously — but they didn't. After all, their livelihood was at stake. They were afraid of him, because they knew he was afraid of nobody, not even of the Devil. They feared above all the invisible power that dwelt within him. He would say, 'We're going to the East Indies, little one,' and after weeks and months of sailing, the Indies rose from the endless sea. Everything happened exactly as he said and wished. Everybody carried out his orders, however unreasonable. And I didn't protest either when an hour or so before we were about to leave Malaga he said to me, 'This time you're to stay with Aunt Concha. You're too big to be on a ship any longer.' I gathered my things and meekly allowed myself to be rowed to the quay, although I had just felt so delighted at parting from my aunt for another short year.

"From the moment my father delivered me up to her, she considered me her prisoner. That prudish old maid was born to be a gaoler. I was allowed to speak to nobody, to see nobody except my old father-confessor. I was accustomed to freedom, and day and night I prayed for revenge. *Ave Maria, give me my revenge!*

"At first I hoped he would come back soon — but he didn't. His ships came, but he was never on board.

"When I was fifteen or sixteen, a day arrived when my father-confessor confessed to me, instead of my confessing to him; but I gave him no absolution — that was the difference. I refused to see the old Franciscan again. Aunt Concha, who thought him a living saint, insisted that he should come and drive the Devil out of me; but I had had enough of his beard with the remains of *olla podrida* in it, and defended myself tooth and nail like a mad thing . . . At that time, I was learning to read and write from a nun who brought me 'The Lives of the Saints,' and while I was supposed to be deep in study, I allowed myself to be kissed by the gardener's boy, whose pale face appeared at the grating of my room that was, in truth, my cell. The window was high, and he was small of stature. He had to hoist himself up by his wrists to reach my mouth. I stood on 'The Lives of the Saints.' Aunt saw the entire performance, and came running across the patio, but he was only aware of her presence when she began pulling at his breeches. He kicked out behind him, and it cost her a front tooth or two. He was driven from the door at once, but he prowled about the house like a lost dog. He did not care about being hungry, or that people laughed at him. When the letter came that brought me release, my gardener's boy was found on board the *Santa Cruz*. He lay hidden under a coil of rope, and sprang over the bulwarks with a frightful oath before they could seize him. Dressed as he was, he swam ashore, and stood looking from the quay as the boat left. I waved my handkerchief, but he did not wave in return. Perhaps he couldn't see me any more.

"During the journey the captain showed me on the map the course we were taking, but even without a map I could see what course he was trying to make. He pleased me more than my father-confessor, that living saint, and one evening when the moon was shining and the ship was gliding gently, soundlessly over the water, it seemed as if my captain's chances were not too slender. But then, unluckily, he spoke of my father. Why couldn't he have left that subject alone? He said that he was such a strange, unfathomable man. I looked at him and asked, 'Don't you like my father?' If he had confessed that to cool his vengeful feelings he would have liked to blow up the ship that very day with all its costly cargo, supposing he were not its captain, I should probably have told him that I had hated my father for five long years with a hatred beside which his was insignificant, because he had delivered me up to Aunt Concha and her father-confessor — though perhaps I should just have slapped his face for his shameless honesty. But he lied. That, in any case, was the stupidest thing he could have done. I turned my back on him, and that night the moon shone in vain.

"At Palermo a passenger came on board, a long, lanky creature with large, creepy hands. At first he paid no attention to a living soul, least of all to me. He spoke to nobody, except to the wind, for he was in a hurry to reach Naples. At last I made bold to speak to him, although I had learned from Aunt Concha that a lady waits until a gentleman speaks to her, or better still sees to it that it doesn't get as far as that. He seemed to be flattered by my curiosity. In confidence he showed me tricks he could do with cards. The wind dropped. We hardly moved at all, and then morning, noon, and night there was card-playing in the cabin. We played for money, although ship's orders forbade it. The captain himself set the example. He played and played, and lost to his mysterious passenger all his wages for that and his next voyage.

"In Naples I went ashore with Maniscù. He had confessed to me that Sicily had grown too hot for him, and now he proposed that we should cross the Italian mainland in triumph together. We did! My good Maniscù always saw to it that he did not scoop up so much profit as to arouse suspicion. He was satisfied with modest gains, and once in a while the bank lost. He was equally modest in his demands upon me. The nearer we got to Venice, the more he was oppressed by the fact that he had carried away the trophy of my virginity. That was more than he had wished or expected. Besides, he was afraid that in my childish simplicity I might talk too enthusiastically about his little card tricks. Why did he show them to me in the first place, if he was going to get afraid? Had I made the same journey in Aunt Concha's company it could hardly have been more tedious."

She sighed pathetically and, her thoughts elsewhere, looked down in silence for a while on Benedetto. At last she said: "I'm glad you unmasked him. I always knew he was only a bungler. I was expecting somebody to turn up who would do it. I haven't betrayed him, although he more than deserved it; I just didn't come upon anybody for whom it was worth my while; and with you it wasn't necessary. When Maniscù went off of his own accord, I knew everything. He's never done that, so long as there was anything to rake in without danger. When once or twice I asked him to spare my guests for an evening because I happened not to be in the mood to see him rook them, he came all the same and opened a bank. He clung to me like a leech. My house was the purse from which he found it safest to draw. When things went badly with him, he didn't forbear to rob even me with his false aces and kings that he could juggle from nowhere. As it happened, I didn't care how much I lost, because my father had to pay, and I wanted to revenge myself upon my father. Perhaps that was the main reason I landed in Naples with that mopstick. When I saw my father, I noticed soon enough that his moneybags were his weak spot. So that was where I attacked him. At first, he spluttered over the flourish with which I threw into the Grand Canal the ducats he had scraped together, but now I'm afraid I've overshot the mark — he's become enthusiastic over it himself! That wasn't my intention. The higher the bills I send him, the greedier he is to pay. I've ransacked my mind to know what to do, but I can think of nothing better than to go on in the same way. I've grown accustomed to it, anyhow.

"It is the only thing I have left. Formerly I was never bored, not even at Aunt Concha's, for there in my prison I could at least dream of revenge, and of my future freedom here in Venice. And now I've obtained this freedom; but it disappoints me, and my revenge seems ineffectual. The young *nobili* and pleasureseekers who swarmed round me at once seem so much alike that I could exchange one for the other without noticing it. Then, there's the abbé who wants to dedicate a play to me — a play doomed to an early grave at the very first performance; and I'm to play the leading part in it! There's the painter who wanted to make a sensation with a daring nude of me. But when it came to the point, his hands trembled too much, and he reeked of alcohol. Besides, I heard he has a wife and child somewhere in Venice whom he has to support with his art. Since then I always send him away, but it doesn't help much. . . .

"And then there's the old judge, who is risking his position for my sake and who is still sufficiently clear in his mind to realize himself that he does so. He put his fortune in the balance because a ring had pleased me. Oh, he's certainly the best of them all, and far and away the most entertaining. Besides, I assume that during his long life he has learned how to receive a woman in his home, and . . . But was I born for a graybeard? He has made me a present of the ring, in return for a promise I shall not keep, although that's probably the worst act I've committed in my life. Perhaps, looking back, he'll realize that at his age even a promise is a gift. I wanted the ring. He thought he could ask for what he wanted in exchange, and he asked for everything. That was too much, and he ought to expect to be deceived. Besides, who knows what I mightn't have done a little earlier? A woman has never yet refrained from trying to make a man feel young again, if she is well disposed towards him. And it seemed to me that youth was the only thing he lacked. But he had no luck — for you came."

She stared in front of her. Was she waiting for him to speak? Slowly uneasiness gripped Benedetto. It was something that was not an unreasoning jealousy of these men of whom she had spoken, not an aversion to the old judge and the promise with which she had obtained the ring. It was rather a vague fear of a misunderstanding that might have fatal consequences.

Doubtfully, distrustfully, he asked, "And — what do you expect from me?"

She laughed when she heard his voice and his strange question, and bent over him. She could not answer at once. Perhaps, too, she wanted to tease him a little for his faintheartedness, which surprised her in him. Had the story of her life so impressed him that he had grown afraid of her? She laid her head against his shoulder. "What should I expect from you? It's enough for me that you're here. For the first time since I came to Venice life is tense again — thanks to you. I don't know whether the *sbirri* are still after you; but to-morrow I shall go and pray that it may never come to that. I want only to see you — every day, and for preference every hour of the day. And if nothing happens to-day or to-morrow — that makes my breath fail — then I shall know that the Madonna has listened to my prayer."

He was reassured. For a moment he even forgot the judge and all the others. Oh, he would make her breath fail, but in another fashion. He did not want to speak to her about it yet, about his opera. He left it to Galuppi and to the abbé to reveal their plans before they were ready. She should sit unaware in her box and grow dizzy under the unexpected rushing magnificence of his work. From the night, the first notes were wafted in to him through the open window — confused and undefined but, as he greedily snatched at them, already forming themselves into a whole. They filled him entirely, made his heart swell almost to bursting point. In the darkness, tears came into his eyes. He was conscious of pain. . . . He still had no libretto. How could he come by one quickly? He would not have the patience to wait for it. He had an idea that any text would be good enough. He could even reconcile himself to one by the abbé. He only wanted words that could be sung and would constitute a modest plot. If only he could get a plot, he would begin to write the overture that very day, for he had everything ready except the unhappy libretto. He would turn Venice herself into music — Venice, dying Venice, with her pale palaces reflected in dim canals; Venice with her bells — the last living voices out of a great past; her decorative, noiseless gondolas gliding by — precious black coffins; her odors of decay and corruption, that came up from forgotten *canaletti;* her poisonous fevers from the autumn lagoon; her dark cruel inquisition, her spies; Venice with her wanton carnival visitors who tried to drown her stillness because it reminded them too much of death . . . Thus and not otherwise Benedetto saw this city, and thus she would be recognized by all.

Figures grew up before his mind: The Doge! The Doge of Venice, in gleaming purple, in radiant gold and a blind glittering of diadems, in ceremonial robes too heavy and ample to be any longer worn as they should be worn, magnificent ceremonial robes in which only a spirit dwelt, hollow-eyed. He would express this in the language of music, the language eternally free; would he be understood? A spirit as Doge of Venice — and in the vicinity of the Palace of the Doges and the prison, Death itself, in the shape of a centenarian witch who, with a withered hand from which several fingers were missing, held a black shawl round her skull. The Dogaressa! Old deceased Signora Galli had not thought of that, she who wanted to deprive him of his peace of mind even in Venice; she had not thought that he would one day raise her to such exalted rank. She had been sufficiently flattered by her position as mother of Todi's mayor. But — Dogaressa of Venice, that was quite a different thing.

Would he succeed in setting down his dream in music? At that moment he had no doubts. But how was it that this proud consciousness of power over melody and harmony had come to him only that night?

Maestro Angelini had done his best to stifle at birth the composer in him. But when in Florence he had witnessed an opera for the first time, he had thought the difficulty of writing such a piece not inordinate. Only in Venice, however, had the urge come to him to try his own hand; when Gracias had talked of something that might make her breath fail, she had thought of some new irresponsible act on his part; but *he* — immediately thought of his opera.

It was getting lighter outside. The hour of separation was approaching. But Benedetto could not make up his mind to go. That they must part already bewildered him, seemed incomprehensible. He drew her to him; but his embrace did not hold back the inexorable day. The thought of leaving filled him with an indefinable fear, as if he would suddenly again lose the ground from under his feet.

In the end, she had to send him away. "You must go now. You must sleep. I also want to sleep. I don't want to look ugly and tired this evening when you come back. Come early. Come early in the afternoon." She rang for Marianna.

He looked into her eyes that looked back at him glittering and a little weary. Had he fathomed them entirely, those eyes? Could he go with a tranquil heart? He tried to recall the deeper accents in her confession, clung to them tenaciously. . . .

Marianna knocked and entered discreetly. "See the Cavaliere to the door, Marianna."

Abashed by the presence of the maid, he tried to regain his composure. With bowed head, he went quickly past her. When he stood masked on the steps and called a passing gondola, Silvio was just opening the gate of the little harbor overgrown with vines that adjoined the garden. The fellow did not look at him. Nevertheless, this accidental occurrence disturbed Benedetto. A vague warning reached him through his dreamy condition; but when he was sitting in his gondola he forgot Gracias' gondolier. Other things were in his mind. Nor was he conscious of the world about him. Only with difficulty did he recognize the points they passed. Venice, his Venice, he carried within himself, and he would pour it out and give it shape. He would reveal Venice to herself. He could no longer wait for a libretto. He would begin to build up this city in sound in the expectation that the characters of his opera would of themselves take possession of it.

II

At home he saw Leah, who was already up and about her work. To avoid a conversation, he slipped by her and hastened upstairs. Slowly, in pained astonishment, she looked after him inquiringly. Why had he barely greeted her? Was he annoyed? Or did he want to have nothing more to do with her? What had been the matter with him all these days? Since that one unfortunate evening at the theater, she had scarcely seen or spoken to him. Ah, well — in that case, he could not have noticed the change that had come over her, either. Formerly, she had been calm and self-controlled. Now, she felt agitated and uncertain in all she did or left undone. She jumped up in the night with a start when she heard the knocker of the outer door. She asked her uncle to trust the Cavaliere with the key of the front door, and he did so. But since then even the grinding of the lock had wakened her. She heard Benedetto's footsteps on the dimly lit stairs. A thousand thoughts beset her mind these days, depriving her of peace. Her path, that path drawn out for her by her uncle and aunt, had been clearly marked, and she had followed it with childlike obedience. But now she was beginning to feel doubt and anxiety. She was discovering in David characteristics and habits that were unpleasant to her, that might in the end repel her, perhaps were already repelling her. She suddenly shrank from the idea of becoming his wife. She tried to forget about it altogether, consoling herself with the thought that for the next year or two his shop would certainly not bring in enough. Her mind was kept busy with thoughts of the Cavaliere upstairs. She tried to guess where he spent all the time he was not at home. It was carnival, and everybody in Venice who had the time and money was bent upon pleasure. Was he, too? He seemed so withdrawn into himself. The fair mask in the box came into her mind. She felt that she might seek for the solution of the puzzle in that direction, and yet — just for a moment — it had seemed to her that she, Leah, meant more to him than the rich, comely lady from whom, in the theater, he had returned to her, so quickly.

His strange restlessness, the reason for which she had tried to fathom, communicated itself to her in the end. She went about the house during the day, and at a given moment could not remember whether she still had to dust the front room or whether she had made up old Susanna's market accounts with her. In the mornings she went upstairs to take the Cavaliere his chocolate. As she held the tray, her hands trembled. He thanked her, quietly and distantly. She had an idea that he started up when she came in after she had knocked. The presence of danger, the menace of some strange fatality penetrated to her consciousness.

She wished he would talk to her. Had she dared, she would have told him that he could trust her. If she were to say something like that, would he not look at her in genuine amazement? He had asked her for nothing.

Sometimes she feared, without being able to explain her fear to herself, danger for the whole house, for Uncle Solomon. Upon one occasion she sounded her uncle to know whether the jewels which he had bought from the Cavaliere were still in his possession. No, he had forwarded them to Uncle Nathan in Trieste, through whose safe hands all the jewels he bought passed. Why did she ask? Her uncle looked at her sharply: he knew her well. She glanced away. Oh, it just crossed her mind — she would have liked to see them again. Had the Cavaliere by any chance spoken to her? Had he told her where the jewels came from? In that case, she ought to tell him, her father. From him nobody else would hear a word of it. Oh, no, it was not that. She scarcely saw the Cavaliere. She knew nothing of him, or of his jewels. Nothing . . . She left the room.

He had never been so late home as he had been this morning. She assumed that he would throw himself upon his bed all dressed, and drop off to sleep at once. But after an hour or so she heard him pacing up and down his room and closing the window. Closing the window? Did he want silence? Was the noise outside disturbing him in his sleep? When somewhat later she had something to do on the landing, she heard him move his chair: he had not gone to bed. Suddenly she caught herself standing still by his door and listening. She did not move away at once, although she was fully conscious how contemptible it was — to be listening at somebody's door. Her heart beat loud. But what was he doing? Was he writing letters? A letter, perhaps, to the lady in the box? A soothing thought suddenly flashed across her mind: he was writing music. She might have thought of that sooner. He was writing a new canzonetta after the success of the previous one. Was not everyone in Venice singing "*Traghetto — traghetto d'amore*"? Everything was explained: his restlessness, his abstraction. She would ask him when she saw him — he could not take that amiss. She wanted to congratulate him on his belated though well-deserved success.

Should she take him his breakfast? Perhaps he would enjoy a cup of warm chocolate or coffee. But perhaps she might be disturbing him at an inopportune moment. And how could she really know that he had not gone to sleep? It might cross his mind that she had been standing listening at the door. Suddenly, flushed with shame, she hurried downstairs.

Then, when the time came for the midday meal, she went upstairs again. After all, she must ask the Cavaliere now whether he wanted something to eat. If it was only his chocolate he wanted, she would take him that.

As she stood by his door again, she trembled like an aspen leaf. Was it consciousness of guilt at having hung about there a little while ago? She struggled to control herself, and knocked. She heard nothing. She knocked again. No reply. After a hesitation, she half-opened the door. He was no longer sitting at the table; he had taken off his coat and shoes, and was lying stretched out upon his bed asleep, his face tucked away in his arms. Should she wake him and ask? But he would not want to eat now. He must be dead tired. She overcame all her inner shrinking and walked in. He had gone to sleep with windows closed and in full daylight. It would soon be oppressive; indeed it was so already. Carefully she opened the windows and drew the blinds — everything creaked and cracked in this old house, but he heard nothing: it was unnecessary for her to look round in fear. His deep though agitated breathing could be heard through the stillness of the room. On tiptoe she moved about, satisfied in her maternal feelings. Lying on the table in disorder she saw sheets of music paper, filled with writing. With difficulty she refrained from going up to the table: perhaps he would not like her to see what he had done. She wanted to put the papers in order; but perhaps he would not like that either, and perhaps she would do it wrong.

When she went downstairs again, she was a different person. A vague little smile of relief was playing about her face. Her thoughts were suddenly brighter.

Aunt Rachel, looking at her distrustfully, asked, "Is the Cavaliere eating at home to-day?"

"No, he's still asleep," Leah informed her, and ignored the look of scorn on Aunt Rachel's face. Perhaps she did not see it. "I'll call Father," she said, and disappeared towards the back of the house where her uncle was experimenting with this and that. It was the first time for days that she had had an appetite.

III

For several minutes, Benedetto had been staring at the heavy oak beams of the roof. It was twilight . . . through the closed blinds the daylight came only faintly. It must be evening already. Evening? With a start, he jumped up.

He rushed to the window, drew up the blinds — who had lowered them? It was evening already. He slipped on his coat and shoes. On the table the sheets of music were scattered as he had left them; had Leah noticed them when she came in to close the blinds? He had better put it all away — it was but a beginning, a first groping and searching. He could not get on very well until he had a libretto.

This painful longing for a suitable libretto had made his sleep feverish. He still felt dazed and disconcerted. Now he must go to Gracias. It was evening already, and she had asked him to come to her in the afternoon. What had happened during his absence? Nothing . . . nothing. But all the same he would not feel reassured until he had seen her. And then he must find a libretto.

The gondola was not going fast enough. He was peering in front of him beyond the high *ferro*, watching for the Grand Canal to come in sight. "*Fa presto, barcaiuolo!*"

At last they reached the Rio di San Felice. Upstairs lights were burning. Several gondolas were waiting; of course she had visitors again. Had he come earlier, he would perhaps have found her alone. Would this continue — visitors every evening?

He paid the gondolier, and let the door knocker fall. He did not yet know the prearranged signal that the abbé had mentioned with such an air of mystery. Presumably any of the gondoliers could have given it him. But the door opened.

The young *nobile* who came peering round the door greeted him exuberantly, wishing him luck. Luck with what? Had she been talking? He ignored these congratulations, and preceded the other up the stairs. The sound of many voices reached him — how many were with her already?

When he entered, there was a clapping of hands. "At last! Doña Gracias has just been wondering for the tenth time whether you would honor us this evening."

Benedetto bowed stiffly and went up to Gracias. As she offered him her hand to kiss, she looked at him half-guiltily, half-poutingly. "We were on the point of going to the theater without you."

He made a resigned gesture of regret. The whole atmosphere seemed strange, almost hostile.

"We wanted to go to the San Carlo Theater, and then all have some food together at The Four Horses." Gracias leaned towards him. In her teasing eyes still lurked the passion of last night, and his ill-humor and distrust subsided. Good — to the theater, then. This company would at least disturb him less there than here in this room.

Rivalry threatened to break out as to who should accompany Gracias in her gondola. The judge, to everyone's surprise, was absent that evening; and Benedetto's rights, in spite of the congratulations he had received, did not seem as yet to be considered unassailable. Gracias, however, put her arm through his, and that was the end of the matter. A flicker of pride and asperity about his narrow lips, Benedetto conducted her downstairs. The others followed, accusing Gracias the while of being untrue to her old, well-tried friends for the sake of one who still had to prove his preparedness to walk through fire for her, as they would all gladly do.

Silvio the gondolier put out his hand to help his mistress into the gondola, but Benedetto robbed him of this right. Indifferently, the huge unmannerly fellow pushed off, and while he pressed his blade so powerfully through the water that the others were left farther and farther behind, however much they urged on their own *barcaiuoli*, he looked angrily and with unconcealed contempt at the Cavaliere, that interloper in satin clothes who had dared to push away a hand that could have knocked him down, if its owner had not had his wits about him sufficiently to refrain.

They took several boxes at the San Carlo Theater, where a piece by Algarotti, the Bolognese count and protector of the arts, was being played. Benedetto sat beside Gracias — nobody else now thought of claiming that position.

In the gondola, she had told him that she had been to church that afternoon to pray, and had interceded for him with Saint Anthony, the patron saint of lovers. She had asked Benedetto whether he was very annoyed that they all knew how things stood between them. She swore she had betrayed nothing — at least, not intentionally, only through her impatience over his coming so late. He reassured her, saying that it was just as well, as now they all knew what limits to place on themselves.

Oh, he was proud that she was going to the theater with him. He wanted to show her that too, her and those whose envy and growing hostility he felt at his back, even though they tapped him on the shoulder with patronizing joviality. His friends they could not be; then they must be his enemies. He responded to their unasked patronage with a cool haughtiness that must have been wounding. He would have liked them actually to hate him, and to stay away from Gracias' house — they had nothing more to do there now that he entered as lord and master. He regretted that Baron Barbaresco was not present: he would have liked him to see how things stood, and deduce the necessary consequences.

The only one who did not seem fully aware of his new position was Galuppi, who was trying to whisper to Gracias. He was drunk again, and spoke ill to her of this cavaliere whom she had now chosen for herself. Who was he, this newcomer . . . ? A day or two ago, nobody in Venice had ever heard of him . . . His talentless songs would soon be forgotten again. On the other hand, anyone who had the least understanding of painting knew at once who and what Galuppi was — only that boor did not know. If he had known, perhaps he would have realized that he was putting on too many airs. Gracias laughed and told Benedetto, who was not very far from striking the drunkard, that he must not be angry with Galuppi. Once one came to know Galuppi, it was impossible to be angry with him. "What are you doing here again this evening, Galuppi? How often have I sent you away already?"

The abbé had disappeared behind the scenes: he liked to be complimented in theatrical circles on his success. Soon he would return and tell Gracias that the director and the actors of the San Carlo Theater had again been imploring him for a play.

Everybody was looking at Gracias. Her mask did not prevent her from being recognized: no other woman in Venice surrounded herself with such a following of young cavaliers. They were trying to guess who was sitting at her side. They would soon know that the composer of "*Traghetto — traghetto d'amore*" had taken over the dignity of the old judge.

Benedetto did not think much more of this play than of the abbé's trumpery work. It did not hold his attention. His thoughts were roving. His longing for a suitable libretto returned and gnawed at him.

Gracias glanced at him sideways and whispered something into his ear behind her fan. Those who were sitting behind him noticed this with annoyance: it was a more hateful privilege than had fallen to the lot of the old judge. Quietly, some of them decided that they would begin to neglect Gracias. She would notice that, and reflect on it. They were still ready to go to The Four Horses; but only because they were hungry and had light purses, and *lo Spagnuolo* was accommodating enough to pay for the meal.

They filled the large wooden guest room with their shouts for wine. While they waited for the food, they started drinking and challenged Benedetto to keep pace with them. Could he be so unmannerly as not to listen to them? They were confident that the hour of their revenge would strike. This evening when he left Gracias (for it was certain that that was what the two had been whispering about a moment ago — what else could it have been?) they ought all to wait for him and teach him manners. Yes, they would do that.

That was what they would do, if by that time in their drunkenness they had not forgotten all about it. Meanwhile they called others to their table, including several actresses, in order to annoy Gracias. But she did not even notice. In the eyes of all, she was flirting shamelessly with that fellow, humiliating herself before him in order to gain his favor. Leaning her head upon his shoulder, she looked up at him with adoration. He looked down at her without speaking. He did not kiss her, although her eyes implored him to. He must be thinking there would be time enough for that later on, when he had her all to himself. Curse him!

Rossi, the manager at the little San Samuele Theater, came in with some of his people. The abbé rushed up to him, and, so loud that all could hear, asked whether the house had been sold out again for the performance of his play. Of course it had. Rossi counted upon full houses for the remainder of the week. His eyes wandered down the table until he discovered Benedetto. He brought up a chair and sat down behind him and his lady. Throwing his arm round Benedetto's shoulders, he asked him in a flattering and impatient tone what had become of the new canzonettas. Benedetto retorted that if only Signor Rossi would have a little patience he would bring him something better than canzonettas — a complete work that would fill the whole evening. As soon as he could say more about it, he would come and talk to him about a larger orchestra and the engaging of the singers; but it was too early for that yet. Good — Rossi thought it a fine idea. A larger work. Excellent. He would be patient. But the public? Would the public also be patient? Here in Venice a ditty was sung one day, and another half-day — but then they wanted something fresh. He urged Benedetto to go on writing his big work, but also to let him have, in the meantime, a canzonetta or two to keep people's interest alive.

"You can just shake them out of your sleeve. Doña Gracias, speak to him, tell him that he must help a poor theater manager, and the couple of dozen people dependent on him, who all have to live with the help of a canzonetta."

Gracias smiled. She looked at Benedetto in silence: he had bewitched her. What did she care about the music he wrote, whether it was canzonettas or anything else? That was Rossi's affair. He must do the best he could about it. All she wanted was to be alone with Benedetto, now. She would tell Silvio to take them home as quickly as possible, so that the others could not keep up, and would arrive to find a closed door.

Benedetto's mind was no longer upon writing ditties for Rossi. Only the day before they had come to him without difficulty; but now the vision of greater work was ousting the smaller, the source of which seemed to have dried up.

He might as well speak to Rossi — perhaps he might know of something suitable. "I'm looking for a text, Signor Rossi: a little plot with its action in Venice; something that couldn't happen in any other city — otherwise it doesn't really matter what the plot is."

Rossi looked at him. With the artist's intuition, he read in Benedetto's eyes the seriousness that contrasted so strongly with the casualness of the request. He read in them the wild longing for this libretto; the lady beside him might well be jealous of such a passionate preoccupation. He sensed, too, almost exactly what the other was seeking. He ran his large fleshy hand over his furrowed brow. "A suitable libretto? The action must be in Venice? It must be typically Venetian? Wait a moment! Upon my life, if I haven't something for you! This very night I'll ransack my papers until I find it. But I am to perform it, with my company — you're my witness, Doña Gracias; and as a reward for my pains, if the libretto really turns out to be first class, then in the meanwhile a canzonetta, a little canzonetta, something like the 'Traghetto — traghetto.' I knew at once that people would go mad the moment they heard it."

He had done what he had set out to do, and now returned to his own party. Precipitating himself upon a plate of macaroni, he imparted the good news between two great mouthfuls. At that table sat one actress on whom Rossi's news appeared to make little impression. Sadly she looked towards Gracias and towards Bussoni the young composer, who paid no heed to her. Rosetta knew now that her suspicions had been justified; but the knowledge did not make her any happier. Ah, well, he must know best himself. She had warned him. She would have nothing more to do with him; he did not deserve it.

Then Cavaliere Maniscù came in. Resting his hand thoughtfully on his thin cheek, he wandered about aimless and distrait, avoiding Benedetto's line of vision, casting looks of glowing hate at him meanwhile. Sullenly he replied to the greetings of some of the young *nobili*, who beckoned to him to sit beside them at the table. He did not seem pleased at being observed. His restlessness increased. He paused by the door a moment, considering whether he should after all go up to Gracias and greet her. Then, after a desperate inward struggle, he decided that he had best eclipse himself, and departed on his long legs — unsatisfied, hungry, lonely as he had come.

"Come," whispered Gracias, pulling Benedetto's hand. The others did not notice their flight. They had drunk a great deal, as they always did, and they were standing round Rossi's table clapping their hands while Marcolina, accompanied by singing and the stamping of feet, danced in a sort of intoxication, lifting her skirts high. The only one to notice their departure was Galuppi, who, his head upon his hands, had not left the large empty table. In his eyes was a deep melancholy, a bitter reproach against Gracias. He did not condescend to glance at Benedetto. Nor did he sound the alarm — why should he? What had he to do with those others?

Outside, Silvio was waiting, as if he had foreseen that his mistress would want to go home earlier this evening. They got into their gondola and moved off; they could no longer be overtaken — Silvio's powerful arms were surety for that. Like an arrow from a bow, the slender craft shot forward.

Gracias had been conscious of Benedetto's rising restlessness, but she felt that he was already a little calmer. She asked him if he was, as she leaned meekly against his shoulder.

In silence he pressed her to him. There was a restlessness in him even deeper than she knew, and it would subside only when he saw the great work of which he was dreaming grow under his hands. He felt it like a wound, this lack of a libretto that was preventing him from starting. It made him suffer physically. He hoped that Gracias would be able to still this pain until the cause of it had been removed.

Could she do that? Slowly there was reawakened in him that deep feeling of solidarity with her. He wanted to speak to her again about Todi — it had been such a relief to do so the night before. He had not been able to put Luigino Vacca's fate out of his mind. She must liberate him from that, too, as she had freed him from the ghost of old Signora Galli. Oh, why could she tell him nothing of his mother, who had taken upon herself the whole curse of his act in Todi without his being able to relieve her of one iota of this terrible burden? When his mind reached the possibility of rehabilitation through his work, it was of his mother he thought in the first place. . . .

Was it possible, too, that Gracias understood the great import underlying that short conversation between Rossi and her lover? "Not a word did you tell me about the opera you intend to write," she said reproachfully. "Are you afraid that it won't be a success? But it will be a success. Everything you want must succeed. To-morrow Rossi will bring you a libretto. It's to his own interest, and failing that I shall provide you with one. Had you said a word to me, you should have had one already — of course not by my abbé. . . . Silvio," — suddenly she interrupted herself, and raised herself a little as she looked round, — "take the way through the Rio della Madonnetta!"

Benedetto was struck by what she had said to him about his libretto. So she had understood something of what was gnawing at him. In a moment, when they were alone together, he would try to explain to her what it would mean to him if he were successful. He would tell her about Maestro Angelini, and how he would only allow the virtuoso to grow in him, suppressing the other deeper, shyer urge with his full authority as a maestro. But in Todi, what could have developed in him except the virtuoso? There had never been any room for him there. . . .

But he had got away from Todi. Gracias might imagine that he was still the same person who had come up to her carriage in Todi after having spent the previous night robbing an old lady in her grave. . . . With the great work that was to be the justification of everything he had done so far, he hoped to cure her of this error. Besides, only in this work would he at last find himself again. If he were successful in painting Venice, the hidden soul of Venice in his music, then that city would have to surrender to him; and as he had once offered Gracias the palace of the podesta of Todi as a lodging for the night, so now he would place Venice at her feet — that, surely, would be enough for her.

In the sudden fullness of his heart, he could not refrain from telling her in a few words how, round a simple plot, he would create the gray shadow of this city ennobled through the centuries. . . . The mysterious sounds that came whispering from the depths of the canals and the obscure *canaletti* would permeate the whole action, and finally embrace it completely until it was absorbed into them, and Venice herself would rise before the audience, built of marble yet drifting like a wraith upon the wide Lagoon.

Gracias listened to his subdued voice, in which he was trying to repress the emotion. This same Venice had also constituted the background of her dreams when she had lived, a prisoner, in Aunt Concha's house, and now he wanted to set it all to music for her. That was a marvelous idea. Yes, but he must not run away, and hide himself for days on end. She would see to that. She was determined to make him understand that at an opportune moment. She would tell him this evening that he must play to her sometimes: she had not heard him play yet. Oh — but she did not know whether she would remember to ask him, once they were alone together. She was so happy. She wanted nothing more, not even that he should write operas for her. . . . What was he talking about?

The Rio della Madonnetta provided her with a small triumph that she enjoyed, although her conscience gave her a pang, and although she herself felt that her triumph over Benedetto was sufficient in itself. Oh, but she was greedy. Had she ever felt pity? Certainly not for her judge, who, in the dangerous infatuation of an old man, had thrown his dignity overboard for her sake. But as she glided past his house, by the side of her lover, full of a sweet happiness, and saw that there was a light burning inside, she could only conclude that he still hoped she would visit him, though it was more than improbable that she would arrive at that hour. Then, she was inclined to a little pity for him. That was what she had wanted to know. Now she was reassured. She would never have forgiven him if he had realized in time the stupidity of this waiting, and had gone to sleep; but since he was sitting there so faithfully waiting, she had pity for him. Never had she been better disposed towards her old judge. Should she send him a little note by Silvio, with a few words of consolation and a promise that she would explain things to-morrow? Or should she simply write that she had suddenly fallen madly in love with the young fool whom, for her sake, he had beaten in the duel of the gaming table? Should she write to him that her lover was a tiger who stood no nonsense and watched her every hour of the day and night? After all, was he not — a tiger? What would he do if she had the courage to deceive him? Supposing she were to do it, simply to make him show his claws once?

But whatever she did, she would never return the ring to Baron Barbaresco. She would not wound him even more deeply by returning to him what he had once given her. Besides, he would only send it back to her at once, and that would be as well, for she did not want ever to be without it, this ring. Anyone who wanted to deprive her of it would have to wrench it from her finger. Thoughtfully she looked down at her hand with the ring on it, and softly caressed it, to console her fingers for what anyone would have to do to them before depriving her of this jewel.

IN A GARDEN

BY THE

BRENTA

I

ALMOST SOLEMNLY ROSSI HANDED OVER TO BUSSONI the opera libretto he had managed to extract from dust-laden piles of manuscripts that had been hastily turned over once and never sent back to their authors.

"Here — read it: 'The Revolt of the Gondoliers.' I tell you it's just what you want. I spent the whole night looking for it, but I wouldn't have minded searching for a week. I knew it was about somewhere. Sit down there, and read it, and get the thing ready by Christmas so that I can have a full house to the end of the season. Then I shall consider myself rewarded for my pains."

Benedetto sat down by the window with the manuscript. The title pleased him at once. Meanwhile, Rossi threw off his clothes and threw himself with a bump on the poor hired bed that, if he was to be believed, he had not seen for thirty-six hours.

The libretto was partly written in verse, and partly sketched out. Benedetto soon realized that he had found what he was looking for. He was thrilled with deep joy and thankfulness. He was grateful to Rossi, to the unknown creator of the text, to the good fairy who had sent him this libretto.

The plot was simple, but every scene offered an opportunity to conjure up Venice afresh. The action could not occur anywhere in the world except in Venice. Pantaloon, grown newly rich, was ambitious to ally his daughter Filomena to a young aristocratic idler. The old *nobile*, however objects—he places the celebrated name of his race far above merchant gold; but his degenerate son is of the opinion that money has no smell. Filomena herself, who has not been consulted, is in love with Vittorio, the simple-minded son of a merchant. Dressed as a gondolier, he elopes with her on the eve of her pompously prepared bridal feast. Pantaloon hurries to the Doge with the terrible news that his daughter has absconded with a gondolier. The Doge, wishing to make an example, sets a price upon the head of the guilty man. When, however, the gondoliers of Venice hear of this uncommon severity, they band themselves together. Harlequin, a noisy and rebellious *barcaiuolo* who likes very much to hear himself speak, takes the initiative. The gondoliers know all the secrets of the city, and they know also the hiding-place of the pseudo-gondolier and his sweetheart. They conceal the fugitive pair, who move from gondola to gondola. Whenever the *sbirri* are on the scent, the gondoliers contrive to put them off. The lovers have lost courage by the time they have stepped on to their hundredth gondola, but Harlequin still produces words of consolation and finds a priest to bless their wedding in a rocking gondola, on the wide, dark Lagoon, both of them being sick meanwhile.

Harlequin also contrives to enlist the co-operation of the young ladies of Venice. They are equally indignant over the ruthless decision of the Doge, and in order to circumvent it, and to make it ridiculous, they all decide to allow themselves to be abducted for one night, each by some young gondolier. Harlequin, however, their leader and no longer so very young, must swear that the night will pass in all honor and virtue. There follows a night of thunder and lightning and stormy waters. In their small rapid craft, the gondoliers roam through the darkness of Venice, and wherever they see a candle burning behind a window, they enter and by force or by cunning carry off the expectant young woman within. Only Harlequin has no luck. He has formed the bold plan of eloping with the daughter of the Doge himself, famous for her beauty. Instead of which, he finds he has eloped with the Doge's old kitchen maid who, thirty years before, had listened too trustingly to his pretty speeches. Her young mistress supports her in this innocent retaliatory deception. In the end, the Doge has no alternative but to make mercy prevail over justice, and acquit all the gondoliers of Venice; but old Zazarella brings an action against Harlequin, her seducer, for having broken his pledge of good behavior: as he was abducting her he blew the candle out. That is sufficiently indicative of his scarcely honorable intentions. Harlequin, sobered and disappointed, avers that Zazarella herself blew out the candle, so that he should not notice the intentional substitution. The Doge, however, now working off all his severity upon poor Harlequin alone, condemns him to matrimony with old Zazarella. . . .

Benedetto stared at the yellow, crumpled manuscript. Entirely forgetting Rossi, who peered at him from under the bedclothes, he buried the manuscript in his pocket and hurried away. He gave Rossi no time even to call after him and extract some sort of promise as to when it would be ready. Benedetto was already down the stairs. Rossi turned over on his right side, fell asleep, and began to snore loudly. He felt he had well earned his rest.

II

Benedetto had been working two days at his opera, "The Revolt of the Gondoliers." He had already sketched out the overture. His only fear was that it would be too heavy, too full of somber menace as an introduction to such lighthearted happenings. Where had they come from, those dark harmonies that refused to be repressed, and stifled all the airy melodies he wanted to produce by way of contrast? He breathed more freely since he had written them down.

Maestro Angelini — where was Maestro Angelini, so that he could put this before his eyes? But no: it must not be revealed until the whole work was ready. No one must know of it.

Sometimes he paced up and down his room overwhelmed by the joy of creation, and for an hour at a stretch was rendered incapable of working by his wildly ambitious dreams. He saw himself famous not only in Venice, but in the whole of Italy. His name had reached even such provincial holes as Todi, and one day, when the time was ripe, he would proclaim his past to the world. Then the world could judge. Great commotion would reign in Todi. People would join their hands together in amazement and talk of nothing else, and one among them would weep for pride and joy. . . . One among them would know who and what was her son, whom they had once wanted to hang. His imagination ran on unchecked; and he saw coming from Todi, instead of *sbirri* seeking to arrest him, ambassadors to do him honor, to present him with the apologies of the city from which he had once had to flee. Among them would be the chief clerk, Signor Castagnoli, and Cesarotti and Stefani, the two old clerks, his obsequious satellites, and all the surviving members of the council who had once provided his mother with the bread of charity. He would be seated on a platform, round about him the Procuratie of the Piazza San Marco with their rhythmical arches of pale marble. From the sky, the golden sun would flood the majestic spaciousness of the Piazza where tens of thousands — but why mention a figure? — had gathered together. All the bells of Venice would be ringing in his honor, and beside him would sit his mother. And of her, yes, in the first place of her, would they have to implore forgiveness.

He returned to the regions of common sense. A little bitterly, he tried to smile at his foolish fancies — in which, however, he still retained a slight, vague, unreasoning belief. He was confident that his work would triumph. With renewed inspiration he bent over his sheets of paper again.

When he could work no more, he left his room and hurried straight to the Rio di San Felice, eluding anyone who might have recognized him. Rossi had not seen him for days, and was nursing great expectations from the fact. Benedetto no longer heard his canzonetta sung in the streets, and that pleased him too. People must have ceased to think of him: the first notes of his overture must fall into complete stillness.

He found Gracias as usual surrounded by friends. She could not get away from them, and at that moment he was inclined to forgive her. The blessed sense of creation filled his heart, and he saw no evil. He was even glad that she found distraction during the day, and was himself pleased to join the throng of youthful merrymakers. But they, they had thrust him out of their circle, and would not let him in again. If he was prepared to be forgiving, they were not. They heard from Gracias that he had not shown himself the whole day, and they took the view that he was already beginning to neglect her. Greedily, they fed her self-pity, and they were wondering whether they could not allow themselves certain liberties at the expense of a lover who fell short so gravely. But they soon recognized, however regretfully, that they had been premature: Benedetto did not leave Gracias' side, and they, despite their hopes, were forced to give way.

Gracias gave a sidelong glance at her lover. . . . He had not shown himself the whole day. It was as though he had already begun to feel indifferent; but it had not come to that yet. It might come to that, if she did not always surround herself with friends. Laughingly, growing bolder as her friends grew more careful, she lured them to her. They must feel that she was jeering at them. Oh, they were not afraid of Cavaliere Bussoni. If she thought that, she was mistaken. They merely respected her preference, that was all. But if she proved ungrateful for that, all of them together would show that little song composer . . . !

Later in the evening, however, they had as usual drunk so much that they forgot their thirst for revenge.

Benedetto waited impatiently until they left. Then there was nothing in the world for him except Gracias, nothing except their being together. The abbé, half-drunk, came reeling towards him and asked him whether his opera was not almost finished. "I must get you to write one or two canzonettas for me again," he said, in the jovial tone he felt entitled to use since their successful collaboration. It annoyed Benedetto that the abbé knew about his opera. It did not occur to him that Rossi might have trumpeted this piece of news abroad. He suspected Gracias of the indiscretion, and when he was at last alone with her, he could not forbear to reproach her.

She looked at him in astonishment. "But surely it is the best excuse I can offer for your absence," she said reproachfully.

"If you did not receive them every day, you would have no need to search for excuses for me."

That was better. She nestled against him and in a small voice, as though she feared his wrath, she asked, "Do they bore you? They've always bored me too, but at the moment somehow they don't. At present I'm glad when they come, because I like to see how exasperated they are and how they shrink back when you show your teeth. In the afternoons they come and fetch me for vespers or to take the air in a gondola. They speak ill of you, and they try to get me to talk, but I only make them more curious to know. I tell them that I had met you before, and then they want to know where, but that I can't remember. They threaten to give you a thrashing when you go home alone in the night. I say to them, 'But do. Why should I care? Why don't you?' You see yourself they don't do it. . . . No, if I had girl friends that would be more dangerous for you. In all the months that I've been here, I haven't found one. Perhaps I haven't looked for one either, and that's lucky for you. For now, just this once, I wish I had girl friends, so as to make them green with envy over you. Over you — and the ring I got from you, and perhaps also over its story."

Painfully surprised, he released himself from her embrace: his past continued to fill her thoughts. Perhaps after all it would be wiser if he let her share in his great work. He had thought he would fight his battle quietly and alone — he would have liked to surprise her with his victory; but suddenly he was aware of the danger of such a protracted isolation. He simply had not reckoned with the possibility that renewed and direct danger might threaten him again from his past, while he was plunged in creative work. A strange anxiety caught at his throat.

He stood motionless before her and did not himself know what made him say unexpectedly and with deep inner conviction: "You will betray me. A day will come when you will betray me."

For a second she was impressed by his prophecy. She wavered inwardly before she said triumphantly, "What a good thing you're afraid of that, at least." She sat down upon the divan, and pulled Toto onto her knee.

"Have you heard, Toto? A day will come when I shall betray him, he says. Ah, well, you'll surely do all you can to postpone that day as long as possible, won't you? Or did you think you could go on as you're doing now, leaving me alone here from morning till night? If I should betray you one day, you'll know you have yourself to thank. At this moment, I would still defend you against the *sbirri* with my own body — I've done that already in my dreams. But perhaps a time will come when you'll no longer be moved by that, and you'll regret having told me everything. Then . . . then you must be on your guard against me. I may as well tell you that now."

He overcame a hesitation and then suddenly went to the harpsichord. The instrument had not been tuned for some time. Sitting down, he played for Gracias the motifs of his overture: somber melodies welling up from the depths. Gracias opened her eyes wide as she stared at the harpsichord player and saw him lost in a world of sound that belonged to him, that he controlled with virile assurance.

When he let his hands rest, she hung round his neck. "And I was to hear nothing of all that? I should have heard it only when I was sitting in the box with the others? And you write all that at home instead of writing it here at my side? I want to be beside you when you're composing. I won't disturb you — I swear it. You can have the quietest room in the house, and not a soul shall enter it so long as you're working . . . Nobody, nobody."

A dull, almost painful satisfaction came over Benedetto at his victory. But at the same time he felt ill at ease. What did she want of him? Here? In her house? With the old man downstairs, and in the afternoon those signals at the front door? Oh, she only wanted to have him near her in order to keep him from his work. . . .

Passionately she tried to win him over to her plan. In her excitement, a wonderful idea suddenly crossed her mind: "Listen, we won't remain here. We'll go to the country — the weather is still mellow. You haven't seen how we live on the Brenta — a large garden, a peaceful old house, quiet. We shall be alone. I'll look after you. You'll be able to work. We'll remain in the country until you're ready — even longer if you wish. If they forget about us here, so much the better. They'll remember us soon enough when we return and your opera is performed."

He listened, impressed. The country, alone with her. She was really prepared to abandon her swarm of admirers for a time for his sake. It would be a palpable, immediate advantage to be able for a while to avoid their company every evening, to be able to forget their very existence. He would be away from Venice, but only a few hours away, and besides, did he not carry Venice about with him in his soul?

"They will follow us — your judge, your abbé, your painter, and the rest," he said weakly, still hesitating.

Gracias clapped her hands for joy because she had won her case. "No, no, no. We'll tell them nothing. They'll feel wounded, angry, and that's just what I want. As for Baron Barbaresco, you know yourself he hasn't appeared the whole week. . . ." Now that that fact came to her mind, it almost gave Gracias food for thought; but she did not let Benedetto notice that. So she went on to say quickly, "And if they come all the same — then we'll set Toto on them."

III

Next day, in the little Gothic palace on the Rio di San Felice, trunks were packed under Gracias' supervision and with her personal co-operation. Old Catarina was sent to market to purchase provisions, and returned with a gondola full — Gracias might have been about to undertake a voyage round the world. Besides Toto, Socrates was to accompany them — he would have no one with whom to converse if he were left alone with surly, silent Catarina, and Gracias' still more silent father. And Annibale went too, because Gracias thought she would give him Italian lessons in her spare time. She could no longer bear his gibberish lingo now that she herself spoke Italian perfectly.

Just at the right moment, the signals of the abbé sounded on the door below. He appeared to have come on behalf of all her friends, to deliver a sort of ultimatum: they were at the end of their patience, and if she continued to receive Cavaliere Bussoni every evening, she must resign herself to seeing nobody else.

While the abbé talked, delivering a decisive speech prepared in advance in collaboration with the others, he was forcibly made to sit upon a trunk that without the involuntary help of his rounded corpulence would never have closed. Affronted, he jumped up and demanded an explanation: Was she thinking of leaving Venice? Where was she going, and for how long?

Instead of answering his disturbed questions, she merely looked round to see if there were no other trunks that needed . . . Suddenly it was too much for the abbé. Sweat broke out on his forehead, and he implored Gracias upon his knees to tell him her plans. When he got up, he threatened that she would be forgotten by all her admirers within a week if by any chance she intended to stay away so long.

"But *you* won't, *you* won't?" queried Gracias, running backwards and forwards with her arms full of clothes and thrusting everything haphazardly upon Marianna, who had some difficulty in sorting what had to be packed from what had not.

At last, between tears and wrath, the abbé went; but not before he had cravenheartedly admitted that he would not have forgotten her after a week. When he had gone, Gracias suddenly felt a little pity for him. She asked the silent Marianna whether perhaps she had not treated him rather cruelly, and she went towards the window to look after him. Should she call him back and whisper into his ear where she was going, just to see whether he and the others would be foolish enough to follow her? She might also invite them for a day — just one day; just long enough to show them how well she could do without them.

Oh, but how foolish she was! But if she was, it was due to her senseless passion and to her fear of losing him, her tiger. . . .

The "*burchiello*," the large, roomy towboat that regularly connected Venice and Padua, and on the way drew up by request at any of the villas lying on the Brenta, left at break of day. Gracias herself had proposed that they should not take ship at the Rialto bridge, where hundreds of idlers watched every departure; and so it was that Benedetto got himself transported with his trunk by gondola to Fusina, and waited there. Soon, in the semidusk of the Lagoon, the sail of the *burchiello* emerged. But a gondola bringing Gracias was as yet nowhere to be seen.

Benedetto paced up and down, looking out for Gracias in rising uneasiness. There was also another restlessness within him that blended strangely with it. Vague expectations filled him. What sort of adventure had he begun? Would he be able to work any more to-day? Had he been at home, that little motif that had come into his mind a moment ago on the Lagoon could have been written down immediately; he thought it would constitute the beginning of the first act. It was the motif of Filomena's love for her Vittorio. It was to be interrupted a little further on by her father, when he entered with his Conte della Luna. . . .

In the meantime, the towing horse had appeared, and on the *burchiello* controversy had broken out among some of the passengers, who had decided that they were in a hurry, and that the skipper had been bribed by Benedetto to wait. The first hour of the day had rung from the little church of Fusina, and behind the misty towers of Venice the sun was rising, a fiery red.

Just as the skipper appeared on the gangway to talk with Benedetto again, with a view to extracting at least another silver coin from him, a gondola approached; already from that distance the gigantic figure of Silvio was easy to distinguish. Another gondola, which was manned by two rowers, and seemed to stagger under the weight of luggage piled up in it, followed with difficulty. With a little cry, Gracias sprang on to the moist grass by the waterside. Benedetto caught her. It appeared that she had been almost unable to get out of bed that morning — Marianna had had to call her three times. Marianna, Annibale, and Toto stepped out after her. Silvio hastily moored his gondola — he could afford to be more casual about such things than another: no one had yet stolen from him — and came alongside, carrying Socrates in his cage, which was covered with a red silk cloth against the cool of the morning.

When Gracias heard that the *burchiello* had nearly left without her, she uttered a little cry of dismay: she who had once visited the coasts of the Indies seemed thrilled by the adventure of a trip on a towboat. The passengers all listened with great interest to her excited chatter, and nobody regretted that the skipper had tarried awhile for such a passenger. Nothing delayed their departure further except that Silvio was having an altercation with the other two gondoliers, who refused to be satisfied with the ordinary tariff: owing to their cargo of trunks, they had endangered themselves and their gondola on the treacherous Lagoon, and besides they would have to rest at least an hour after such furious efforts so early in the morning. Silvio laughed in their faces. Gracias called to him to give them a little extra because they were sweating so; but instead of carrying out her instructions Silvio jumped and, without using the gangway, landed on the deck of the *burchiello*. The two disappointed *barcaiuoli* cursed, but everybody else laughed. The skipper spat, and goodhumouredly uttered a gross word as he drew in the gangway and gave the signal to proceed.

Gracias clapped her hands, and called at once for hot chocolate, which could surely be obtained on board. Marianna had been seasick on the Lagoon, and she herself had eaten nothing that morning — she had been in too much of a hurry. Shortly afterwards, the aroma of chocolate, the materials for which had been extracted by Marianna from the luggage, reached them from the cook's gallery. Greedily Gracias swallowed it, almost burning her lips, and sent Annibale with much success round to the other passengers: nobody refused her chocolate. Suddenly she remembered something she wanted to tell Benedetto. The previous morning, Cavaliere Maniscù had appeared unexpectedly at her house. He wanted to come every night again and rob her friends, and she must negotiate with Benedetto over the sharing of the winnings. After this communication, to which she expected no reply, she nestled against her lover's shoulder and dozed off almost at once, after having said with a roguish glance, "I told him to come this evening in any case, as you would not be there. . . ."

The sun was falling aslant through the little windows of the craft that glided slowly, almost imperceptibly, between low green banks. It was an October morning. Across the blue sky white clouds were drifting. The skipper raised the sail again to profit by the wind, but it fell back in long folds: it was going to be a hot day.

For a long time Benedetto stared at all the green around him that had become strange to his eyes. Trees glided past. . . . It was as if the trees were moving and the boat were standing still. Then he looked down at Gracias, who had fallen asleep like a child on his breast. The name of Maniscù in her mouth had disturbed him again; but he could not help smiling at the trick she had played on the thin, pitiable devil by inviting him for that evening. She played with all of them, out of an ingenuous desire for revenge. Was he to upset her little game? A loving tenderness filled him. His longing for his work blended with his longing for her. She was as irresponsible as the plot of his opera; she was his Filomena. Behind her lighthearted exuberance smarted the grief she had confessed to him. Perhaps after all she was so lighthearted only because she felt happy. She was trying to amuse him from fear lest he should be bored. Oh, he loved her as she was. She was the bearer of his secret, and he knew that secret to be safe with her so long as there was love between them. She would not betray him to a rueful knight like Cavaliere Maniscù, nor to the abbé, nor to any of the others.

When he looked up, he noticed, not without satisfaction, that all the travelers were fascinated by her, and that they were trying to conceal from him how busy they were devouring her with their eyes. Wherever she appeared in the world, she would always and immediately gather about her a host of adorers. She bewitched everybody, as she had bewitched him.

There was another who watched the sleeper uninterruptedly, but Benedetto did not notice him at first. Silvio was sitting half-concealed behind the pile of luggage that had been entrusted to his care. Only his head with its bronzed face was visible. But Marianna's odd behavior struck Benedetto. He was accustomed to her silence and abstraction. Now, however, her whole appearance suggested an uncommon misery that she could not conceal by keeping her eyes lowered. Deadly pale, she sat in a corner, her hands trembling on her lap. Morosely she thanked him for the bottle of perfumed water he offered her, to help her over her indisposition.

He could not put her conduct out of his mind. Without thinking, he looked behind him and discovered the gondolier's head: Silvio returned his glance quietly, cynically, brazenly. Suddenly Benedetto realized that the moment was not far distant when he would request Gracias to discharge the fellow from her service.

Leaning against the trunks, gray-brown and sallow as a dying monkey, Annibale slept with wide-open mouth. All his ridiculous hauteur had left him. Socrates under his red silk cloth thought the moment had come to introduce himself to the still invisible company, and gave vent to several impertinent squawks. Toto was shamelessly begging for lumps of sugar from all the passengers, as soon as he had been lured away by one of them from his sleeping mistress.

Gracias woke refreshed, and filled with her lively chatter the empty silence that had descended upon the travelers. She offered them dainties that Marianna had to fetch from the luggage under Silvio's guard. He watched her approach, half-kindly, half-ironical. . . .

Gracias began whispering to Benedetto: sarcastic remarks concerning those about her, interspersed with tender words about the miracles she anticipated from their sojourn in the country. It would be as though the whole of nature existed for them alone, for everyone else had returned to Venice. If the weather became too cool, they could light a fire in the *salotto*, as well as the huge stove in the kitchen.

Towards midday, when they had passed Malcontenta and many other marble show villas and pleasure parks belonging to the first Venetian families, she could no longer contain her impatience. She was on the lookout for a spire that would soon rise above the foliage on the horizon. She talked to the skipper, who tried to allay her impatience, begging her to hold out another short half-hour. . . .

At last the house loomed up behind dark old trees. It had a friendly, quiet air — dignified also, with its impressive square tower. But Gracias was annoyed that it seemed so indifferent to their arrival: she was afraid her lover would be disappointed. In the summer, the house looked over the river through living, shining windows. Now all the shutters and blinds were closed. The house was asleep, sunk in a deep dream. It had not expected to be reawakened till the winter was over.

A few hours later, smoke was rising from the damp chimney, and circling slowly round the ruddy crowns of the autumnal trees. Teresa, a buxom peasant woman who had helped the cook during the summer, had been summoned by Silvio from the village near by and came running to welcome the Signorina who had returned so unexpectedly. She started preparations for the evening meal at once, while at intervals she rushed upstairs to make up the beds, for which Marianna had given her clean bedding.

She enlisted Silvio's services: "Silvio, — that's your name, isn't it? — are all the shutters open upstairs?" "Indeed they are, Signora Baronessa." What a foolish creature; but they were all like that in the city — one never knew where one was with them. Teresa ran into the garden, to convince herself with her own eyes that he had spoken the truth. All the shutters were wide open. The house could breathe again.

In an upper room sat Benedetto working. He threw himself upon his sheets of music paper as a starving man upon meat, and Gracias made no effort to stop him. On the contrary, she wanted the house to be put in order before she showed it him, and he could take possession as lord and master of it. Later on, at sunset, he must admire the view with her from the balconies: between the trees gleamed the Brenta, over which every now and again a sail glided slowly by. He must see everything, including the large country kitchen with its high vaulted fireplace and its impressive stove upon which, if need be, one could cook for a hundred guests at a time. Graziano the cook, whom she had hired for the summer, had actually been kept busy with three assistants. Yes, but now she had only one guest, and she liked it better so.

The setting sun was turning the water blood-red, and still Benedetto had not appeared. Gracias was impatient and disturbed, but she did not dare to call him. She wanted him to be in good spirits this first evening that they would be really alone together, and she also wanted to show him that she had meant everything she had said — for to-day at least. Ah, well, surely he would soon come of himself.

She went into the kitchen to see how Teresa was progressing with the evening meal. "Do your best, Teresa. Nothing must go wrong this evening." Teresa swore that she would rather fall down dead where she stood than let anything burn or be overdone. She would have liked to fling her arms round Gracias' neck. She was simply delighted that the Signorina had returned. She had earned good money during the summer, but now the long winter would soon be upon them. Perhaps the Signorina remembered that Teresa and her husband were ambitious to send their little son to the seminary in the city, so that he could become a priest and a glory to his whole family. God had given him the brains for it, so the parish priest had said.

"Here, Teresa, take this for your little son, the priest."

"May God reward you, Signorina Gracias. How long shall I have the pleasure of serving you this time?"

"That depends upon the Signore, Teresa. He alone will decide that."

Gracias contrived to make her voice full of suspense. "Have you seen the Signore yet? He is upstairs working in his room."

"Madonna, Signorina, nobody has ever worked in this house, except me. May I ask whether the other gentlemen are coming too? May we expect them to-morrow perhaps?"

"No, this time we shall be by ourselves, Teresa, and that's why I didn't bring a cook with me from Venice."

Teresa joined her hands in incredulous surprise, picked up the hem of Gracias' skirt and pressed it to her cheek. "May Jesus and the Saints bless you, Signorina. It's what I've always said. One is better than three dozen. May we yet celebrate your wedding here — then I shall know I have not lived in vain!"

With these words, Teresa began to peel the onions for the sauce. Her mistress made for the door at once, tears already smarting in her eyes. Teresa threw kisses after her, and with her fleshy arm wiped the moisture from her face.

Laughing, Gracias reached the garden, where she found Silvio raking up the leaf-strewn pathways. Lifting her skirt a shade because of the dew on the grass, she went up to him. "Have they made a gardener of you, Silvio?" He leaned on his rake and looked at his mistress with the quiet, insolent smirk that had intimidated her when he came with twenty other gondoliers to offer his services. She thought it better to resume with a little more dignity: "In a moment the Signore will be coming downstairs, Silvio, and by then the paths should be raked."

"Yes, Signorina, it'll be dark by then." He had the audacity to mock her. She looked at him in astonishment, and walked away. While she pretended to go on inspecting the garden, she tried to see nothing disquieting in this reply, or better still, to forget it.

Why did Benedetto not come downstairs?

Some two weeks earlier, the farewell feast of the summer had been celebrated in this garden — was that possible? Years seemed to have gone by since then. Surely it had always been autumn here. The paths that Silvio had not yet raked were littered ankle deep with brown, black, and yellow leaves. The sad remains of a burned-out lantern hanging from a bare branch conjured up visions of nocturnal revelry long since dead.

At last Benedetto got up and stood by his open window: there was no longer sufficient light to work by. He stared down into the garden, and she looked up at him and tried to smile through her tears of impatience. In the quiet twilight, a bird was singing somewhere.

Another moment, and he was standing beside her.

"Marianna could have brought you a candle," she said hypocritically;

she could not keep a faint mockery out of her voice, but surely that was her due. He did not even notice it. He shook his head, and suddenly she felt that he belonged to her again. He had been longing for her upstairs. Her waiting was rewarded.

Eagerly she seized him by the arm. Now he must do all that she said. He must go with her to the balcony and to the kitchen. . . . "Come, now you may see the house! We shall just have time before the evening meal. Look, Silvio is raking the paths. He wanted to get them right before you came downstairs, but did not expect you till it was dark. You can leave off for the day, Silvio!" She smiled at the gondolier as if there were a mysterious understanding between them.

At the evening meal, Marianna sat with them — she could not very well be sent to eat in the kitchen. With bowed head she took her place at the small round table that was decorated with autumnal asters and late roses from the garden. She did not utter a word, and ate no more than a bird. Gracias' appetite seemed particularly healthy, and she almost monopolized the conversation. Enchanted, Benedetto listened to her lively babble and her bright foaming laughter. She had him enthralled again completely, had snatched him from his absorption in his work. He felt exuberant and in good spirits as he drank the fiery wine of the country that ran with a warm glow through his veins. This was the modest feast with which they were celebrating their first complete and undisturbed night of love. That was how he felt, and that was how Gracias felt also. Perhaps Marianna felt it too, and that might account for her obvious embarrassment; but that morning already she had looked so pale and abstracted. . . . Benedetto tried to liberate her from her sense of intrusion: he talked to her and urged her to empty the glass she had not yet touched. He asked her several well-intentioned questions, but had to wait so long for her replies that in the end Gracias, full of impatience, answered for Marianna. When the dessert arrived, Marianna begged to be allowed to withdraw: she was tired and would like to go to bed.

They were alone, and Benedetto forgot that he had meant to question Gracias about the peculiar behavior of her maid.

Teresa returned to the kitchen with the remains of the feast, and placed them before Silvio, who accepted all that was offered him. She stood, arms akimbo, watching with amazement his truly enormous appetite. "I've never seen the like of it in my life, but I may as well say at once that I've not often met a fellow like you."

"Give me all you've got! And I wouldn't mind having you into the bargain," Silvio assured her, smacking his lips.

Teresa could not help laughing. "Yes, I can see that. You don't like to let anything pass your mouth — at least, not if you can come by it."

Silvio did not respond to this sally. He went on guzzling and breaking the hard country bread between his formidable fingers.

Teresa continued to watch him in silence, impressed in spite of herself. Then she said, because her thoughts happened to wander in that direction, "Now they're sitting alone together upstairs. . . . Signorina Marianna has gone to bed."

Teresa had had such pleasant talks with Graziano the cook that summer in the kitchen. She had brought him scraps of news from upstairs, and Graziano had commented on them in a way that had made her laugh and filled her with respect for his ever-ready wit. She waited, eager and curious, for what Silvio would say.

He said nothing. He only looked at her, suddenly absent-minded and obtuse, and wiped his hands upon the tablecloth as if he were about to get up.

"Where are you off to?" she asked him in surprise.

Immediately he recovered himself. He laughed casually, thinking thus to still the suspicions he had roused in her. "Where am I off to? Nowhere. Bring me my dessert — at least if they've finished with it upstairs."

Teresa, however, had her own quick thoughts and exciting combinations. He had given himself away too plainly. "So, my little man, you didn't want to go anywhere, didn't you?" she said scornfully, swaying her hips alluringly, and then she demanded impertinently, "How many sweethearts has a person like you in the city?"

She hoped he would say, "Twenty a week and we'd better say nothing of Sundays, and although you with your peasant's understanding may not understand it, there are fine young women among them — maids who serve distinguished ladies and do not scorn a simple gondolier in their bed, if he's as well set up as I am. . . ."

Such a reply would not have astonished Teresa. How often she had discussed with Graziano the prudish, over-reserved Signorina Marianna who went about with her nose in the air as though she were not one of the staff. "Still waters . . . ," had said the wise Graziano.

But Silvio was not lavish with his confessions. Slowly he helped himself to more wine, and nodded.

Ah, well, it was better so. Besides, what had she been talking about when she said, "They're sitting alone together upstairs?" Teresa could not help feeling ashamed when she thought of the gold coin Signorina Gracias had pressed into her hand a short while ago so that her boy could go and study in the city. Besides, there sat Annibale too. She looked round at him suspiciously as he lounged half off his chair with circles round his lackluster negro eyes. During the summer she had grown accustomed to this, the first Negro she had ever seen in her life. In spite of her ever-recurring repulsion, she could not help feeling motherly towards him, the sort of feeling she might have had for a domestic animal; and if only he had been a domestic animal, it would have been much easier. It bothered her anew that he was after all a human being and a Christian too. How could one grasp that?

The unconcealed hatred in the look he now gave her and Silvio almost frightened her. Why did he hate them so intensely? Was it simply because his mistress had condemned him to eat in the kitchen that evening?

Suddenly constrained, Teresa ran upstairs — it was time the dessert was removed. A few moments later she returned with an empty dish: nothing had been left, and Signorina Gracias and the Signore had left the table.

Silvio uttered a hoarse curse that he tried in vain to make sound humorous. Teresa crossed herself swiftly and murmured appeasingly, "I'll bring you a little more wine." She did not know why she was exerting herself so much for this man. She seemed possessed by a strange desire to make him feel at home, able to do as he wished. She felt happy and excited in some unaccountable way, and at the same time vaguely anxious. The blood crimsoned her cheeks, and her hands were trembling. She dropped the wine decanter — a thing that had not happened to her during the whole summer. "Oh, it doesn't matter. I'll tell the Signorina that . . ." She spoke reassuringly to Silvio, who was indifferent to her assurances. She bent over the fragments, and cut herself as she gathered them up.

Then she placed another bottle in front of him on the table, and sank into a chair beside him, wrapping her bleeding hand in her apron. He did not even notice that she had cut herself. As he sipped the wine slowly, he looked at her. Surely his thoughts were elsewhere. He seemed to be brooding over something that was tormenting him — but at the same time, he peered at her over his beaker, until she could hardly control her breathing.

It was coming — that towards which she had herself been steering. His thick lips formed themselves into a slow, mocking smile. . . .

Now that it was too late, her dizzy thoughts flew in despair and confusion towards her worthy husband who, but a few hours ago, had had such a happy face because she was going to cook again at the large house and bring home good wages. With all the strength at her command, she tried to think of her boy, who was to become a priest, and she actually heard herself asking Silvio more or less sensible questions about the matter. Perhaps he could tell her, as he came from the city, something about conditions in this and that seminary . . . And whether it was really advisable to send a thirteen-year-old-boy from the country to the great city, where so many temptations lay in wait . . .

While she talked like this, no longer expecting a reply from Silvio, she looked round in exaggerated fear towards Annibale. Was he asleep? She had told him to go to bed, but he did not understand her, or would not. Besides, he obeyed nobody — not even Signorina Gracias, to whom he owed everything.

Teresa did not remember him again until she was smoothing back the hair from her red, flushed face as she looked round the kitchen with a shattered far-away expression, as if she no longer knew what sort of a kitchen this was, and how she had got there. When she softly muttered the name "Annibale" as she stared at him open-eyed, Silvio also remembered him, broke out into a coarse laugh, and went outside. Then Teresa had to cry, and now Annibale's repulsion became too great, and he also slowly left the kitchen.

Teresa sat on a long time, trying to understand what had happened to her. She had only known the fellow since that afternoon, and they had scarcely spoken three words to one another. How could she look her husband in the face? How could she kiss Giorgino, who must steel himself against the temptations of life in order that he might stand unsullied before the altar and bless his fellow men?

In the night, unable to sleep, her thoughts went back reluctantly to this gondolier, and to his coarseness in running away laughing without consoling her or helping her over her guilty feelings by so much as a single word. Had he just gone to his room and there thrown himself upon his bed to sleep, the pig? She would have nothing more to do with him. To-morrow she would not put food and wine before him: he would have to help himself.

Oh Lord, and would she not sink into the ground for shame when she met that black monkey again?

IV

Leah could not understand why the Cavaliere had left Venice so unexpectedly, without giving notice, without telling them of the purpose of his departure, without even giving them any idea when he would be back.

She had done everything to give him satisfaction in his lodging. She had forbidden old Susanna to enter his room so long as he was working there. She herself had taken his meals upstairs, and had quietly departed again when, lost in his music, he scarcely looked up. Their house had always been quiet, but she had taken despotic measures to make it quieter still. She had received her music master, Signor Bontempelli, in a downstairs room from which no sound could reach Benedetto. She had even been tempted to rush outside and forbid the *barcaiuoli* to utter their warning shouts as they went under the bridge. And for all her pain and trouble, her only recompense had been to cast a shy, discreet glance every evening over the sheets of music he had left spread carelessly on his table.

When in the evening he got up from his chair, paced up and down excitedly awhile, sat down again, and then suddenly got up and hurried from the house, greeting her hastily as he passed with bowed head, instinct had told her that he was going to a woman; but she had ceased to be jealous. She had known that he would come back so long as those sheets of music lay upon his table. To-morrow, during the whole day, she would have him under her care, just as at that moment she had his music under her care. To-morrow he would find his work-table tidied up and dusted, and he would have no need to fear the disappearance of a single slip of paper. He would sit there again bending over his overture and only take leave of it in the evening, after long self-conflict.

Leah had thought a great deal about this strange, mysterious being. She had tried to imagine in what circles he had grown up, and by what circumstances he had reached Venice where none of his relatives seemed to live — nobody in the city bore the name of Bussoni, and nobody ever came to inquire for him. Her intuition had told her that the beautiful woman of the theater had become his sweetheart when, during the previous week, he had been tortured by so much restlessness and had only come home to sleep. Looking back, Leah got the impression that she had noticed that evening in the theater that the woman had deliberately set out to make him her lover. Oh, that could not have been difficult: he was not the sort of man one lured in vain. How many women had he already come to know in his young life? It would have interested her to know.

Sometimes it seemed to Leah that in spite of his gallant connections an oppressive loneliness overshadowed his whole being. Perhaps it was this loneliness that had so fascinated her and aroused her maternal feelings. For Leah was certain of that, and it reassured her deeply — her feelings for him were only maternal. Otherwise, how could she have seen him go every night to another, without envy? How otherwise could she allow herself to be kissed by David?

But now he had suddenly disappeared and taken his music with him. All that remained of him was a pile of clothes, and the room itself, the rent of which he had paid in advance. Was that, in his case, a sufficient guarantee that he would come back?

Leah had not realized that maternal feelings could occasion so much pain when suddenly deprived of all satisfaction, that they could rouse such restlessness and confusion.

Her obsession did not escape her aunt's observation. Aunt Rachel asked her sly, underhand questions, which, at once on the defensive, Leah evaded as slyly with vague, ingenuous replies that defeated her aunt.

Rachel consulted her husband. He listened patiently to her recital of what he had long observed with his own eyes, and advised her to wait until the child brought herself, through some inner need, to pour out her heart. Aunt Rachel sighed: the burden of her responsibility as a foster-mother oppressed her. In her youth everything had been different. Then, a young girl was not allowed to harbor secrets. Fortunately it was not difficult to guess at Leah's secret. She was simply under the spell of that Christian, that *goy*, who had kept on his room in her house and did not scruple to turn the head of an affianced Jewish maiden. They ought never to have taken him as a lodger for the sake of a handful of silver. But he had been, so to speak, forced upon Aunt Rachel. . . .

This last thrust did not quite tally with the facts, but Solomon Graziadeo did not contradict her.

That evening Leah waited for David's arrival with a strange impatience. Thus does a drowning man clutch at straws. It was true that she could not tell him her trouble; but perhaps he would understand. Perhaps he could give her back her peace of mind. If he could do that, then she would be grateful to him for the remainder of her life. Oh, she would be grateful to him if he could do no more than protect her against Aunt Rachel. . . .

He was so visibly surprised and moved by the reception he got that evening that she wondered with a start whether she had been receiving him very differently of late. He kissed her tenderly, and for a time seemed quite confused. Then, as though he had wanted to do so for a long time without having had an opportunity, he began to speak about their wedding, and to tell her of the slowly but surely increasing returns from his shop. He could tell her the exact amount for the last few months. He hoped that in two years, perhaps a year and a half . . . ! She listened to his figures, nodding slowly, prepared to believe; but after a moment she noticed that all David's figures could not fill the void, the terrible void that yawned within her — could not exorcise her grief at the departure of the Christian upstairs. She would have preferred it a thousandfold if a depressed David had told her that the returns from his business simply refused to increase, for all the trouble he took. Then she could have consoled him, and fired him with courage; but now she had to listen to him talking with triumphant certainty about their marriage. In two years, or a year and a half, he was saying, and he took it for granted that she also . . .

Suddenly he broke off in the middle of his childish figuring, and stared at her, afraid and suddenly distrustful. "What's wrong with you these days?" he broke out, angry and bitter. She could not speak. She only shrugged her shoulders and turned away. David found nothing more to say. He was so downcast that he did not notice how Aunt Rachel leered at him and tried to convince him with her guilt-conscious eyes that it was not so bad as it looked.

David decided that for once he would make his betrothed feel how unjust she was, by taking up an ostentatiously angry attitude. But stronger than any other feeling was the treacherous fatigue that came over him. He still could not endure standing on his feet all day in the oppressive atmosphere of his shop, and after a time, in spite of himself, he began to struggle against his yawns, until the tears came into his eyes. Severity was impossible, and he grew dejected with the sadness and the burdens of his race.

Leah could hold out no longer either. She told David that he ought to go home to bed. She, too, was tired and wanted to sleep. After a moment of weak protest, he left her, with a solemn chaste kiss that was merely a form.

No, he could not liberate her from her obsession. It was too much to ask of David. But a day or two later, Uncle Solomon succeeded in doing so. He had only been waiting for a moment alone with her. Then he turned the conversation in the right direction by asking her ingenuously whether she happened to have any inkling as to where the Cavaliere had gone. He got precisely what he wanted when Leah, wounded and angry, looked up and asked him in her turn how *she* should know: the Cavaliere had not thought it necessary to tell her one word about it. Of late even a greeting had seemed almost more than he wanted to give her. Besides, she no longer cared where he had gone. She did not tell Uncle Solomon what she had learned secretly from Geronimo — that Benedetto had taken a gondola for Fusina early in the morning, and that at that moment he had been still alone. . . .

Graziadeo looked at his niece, at his child, as she stood there before him, flushed and rebellious. Rather than show her grief, she curled her lips scornfully, contemptuously. Gently and thoughtfully, weighing every word beforehand, he said as he looked away from her: "Good. No doubt he'll turn up again. I think you're quite right. There's no point in our racking our brains to discover where he has got to. Probably at this moment he's not giving a thought to what we are about — why should he? He'll be amusing himself; that appears to be his chief occupation, in any case." Almost in spite of herself, Leah wanted to protest, but she lacked the courage. She prepared to let Uncle Solomon go on. He waited a second as though he expected a protest, and though none was expressed, one seemed all the same to have reached him unuttered, for he went on: "I don't know what has kept him these last days in his room, but I have a feeling, and I had it the first moment I saw him, that he has never in his life busied himself seriously about anything, whatever passing enthusiasms may have possessed him. There's no point in getting engrossed with people like that, Leah my child, and it's just as well you've come to realize it already. We waste our time with people like that. He's a young Christian, and takes life as lightheartedly as one would expect a young Christian belonging to a rich family to do. I could stake my life that he came to sell those jewels — they must have belonged to his mother or sister — to settle a gambling debt. I recognize a gambler at sight — I've seen many. And probably he gambles with life, too. But life doesn't allow itself to be played with, even when the player is quick-witted, and a young, attractive-looking Christian of good family. Even the proximity of such a scatter-brain has its dangers. For who knows whether to-day or to-morrow, if it should serve his turn, he won't make one of us his stake? Perhaps we should only notice it when it was too late!"

Uncle Solomon ran his handkerchief over his forehead. He shook his head thoughtfully as though he were himself still in doubt, and wanted to reconsider what he had already said. Then he looked up at Leah shyly, almost ashamed, and when he saw her pale, fixed face he was overcome by his own feelings. He put out his hand and drew her to him. Then whispering, as though he feared his wife might be standing listening behind the door, he said: "Leah, never forget one thing if you want to avoid unhappiness. Never forget what you are. However friendly a Christian may be with you, — even though you were as brother and sister, — a day will come when he will remember that he is a Christian, that his family and all his friends and acquaintances are Christians. It is better, Leah, never to forget what you are yourself. Just say to yourself, 'I am proud to be a Jewess.' Say, 'If centuries of grief ennoble a people, my title to nobility is as great as that of a Christian who writes "cavaliere" before his name.' Be friendly, be gracious, be without resentment towards a Christian, if he is of goodwill towards you; but never forget that it is only a fairy tale, that it will last only as long as a fairy tale lasts. Reality is different: reality for us has always been stern and bitter. Reality for our race has been tears and blood and blood and tears. A young Christian who has means can perhaps permit himself to ignore reality — but we are compelled to look at it from the moment we open our eyes and see the light of day. When you go to the temple on the Sabbath, observe the gravity of those little children's faces in the ghetto. You have had a good life with your aunt and me. But when I think of my own youth — No, let's rather talk about David. Before he was ten he had to work for his mother and himself. When his mother was dying, there was not enough money in the house to call in a doctor. At twenty he already looks worn out. Life has marked him. It is for his wife, Leah, — for you, — to erase those furrows from his brow."

Thus Uncle Solomon liberated her from her doubts and hesitations, by reminding her, "You are a Jewess." She had almost forgotten that. Safe with her uncle and aunt, she had not touched the reality of life. She knew the world only through books, especially through the books of the new writers in France who preached the brotherhood of men. She had been carried away by that ideal, believed in it, thought its realization was no longer so far off; and even now she was still prepared to add her contribution towards the realization of it. But she was equally prepared to hate the Christians with all the strength of her flaming young heart if these Christians thought they could despise a Jew simply for being a Jew. She was prepared to hate the Cavaliere if he had thought he could play with her because, after all, she was only a Jewess.

Had he played with her; had he thought that he could safely play with her? No, but he had left her without a word, without saying whether and when he would return, and he had taken away the sheets of music that she had put in order for him each evening. . . .

She longed to tell David as soon as possible that she wanted to stand by him as his wife, and the sooner the better — that she was prepared to live more modestly than she had always done with her uncle and aunt.

She told him that very evening, and, trembling for joy, hardly daring to believe his ears, he calculated the earliest moment at which they could marry. It was rumored in the ghetto that old Aaron behind the German synagogue was thinking of closing his hosiery shop at the end of the year, and retiring. Then David would come into his custom and, God willing, they could perhaps go to the rabbi in the spring to discuss their marriage. They would have to begin in a small way, would have to count every soldo . . . He had never dared suggest that to her, because he could see for himself how she lived at her uncle's. Besides, she deserved nothing less. She was, after all, a lady — there was not such another in the ghetto. She could read French and play upon the lute and sing to her own accompaniment. . . .

Next spring. Leah's breath came faster in a sudden strange oppression.

Next spring . . . She did not know herself what it was she had to repress within her, what it was that required such heroic courage to overcome. Good, next spring. She was not afraid. She knew what she wanted: she wanted to share David's cares. He would see that she could do something else besides read books in foreign tongues and practise exercises with Signor Bontempelli.

Oh, protested David, she must not give up Signor Bontempelli's lessons. He had always included them in his calculations. It was his pride to have a wife who played upon the lute — for the sake of keeping that up, he would gladly go without a meal from time to time if necessary. That could easily be done. But it was not even necessary, for he had included Maestro Bontempelli in his reckoning — at least, if he was prepared to give lessons in the ghetto; and if he was not, they would have to find someone else instead — a Christian, so that those in the ghetto could see what sort of wife he had brought there!

David began to pour out his whole heart. He had recently been so full of doubt and fear that he had even sometimes asked himself whether she still wanted to follow him to the ghetto; and where would she be safer and better? But he had not known how he stood with her. Sometimes he could not eat; old Levie said, "We've a cheap boarder in you. We shall grow rich on you yet. But if you're sad don't bury it in your heart. Just tell old Levie . . ."

There was a faraway look in Leah's eyes, about her mouth a smile of delight was playing. David could not stop watching her. Uncle Solomon remarked that the amount of Leah's portion might be a surprise after all, and Aunt Rachel nodded, although she did not usually approve when her husband let fall such admissions.

Next spring . . . Leah was alone that night with those words. She tried to close her mind to them; she simply would not think about it. Reckoned in weeks and days, it was still far away. Behind the humble figure of David loomed large the words with which Uncle Solomon had warned her against a perilous error. Behind David rose the centuries of sorrow that had ennobled the Jewish people, and therefore him also.

Leah had no wish to be accused of forgetting her race for the sake of a thoughtless, thankless young Christian. Leah wanted, before it was too late, to understand the seriousness of life.

V

Gracias was spending the whole morning in bed. Resting upon one seductive arm, she stared with half-closed eyes into the sunlight that penetrated into the shadowy room through the chinks of the shutters, and scolded Socrates and Toto. As usual there was trouble between the two. Marianna came in to ask what her mistress wanted for breakfast.

"Chocolate, Marianna. And coffee for the Signore."

Marianna said that she had taken coffee to the Signore two hours ago: he was up and working in his room. Gracias heaved a sigh.

Later, as she broke a cake into little pieces and made Toto beg for them, she inquired what had become of Annibale: she wanted to give him an Italian lesson. She was in the right mood this morning. What, he was still asleep? His mistress was awake and at breakfast, and he was sleeping still? Marianna said she would have him wakened, but Gracias forbade that: if the boy was still asleep it was a proof that he needed sleep. How late did he go to bed at night, or rather where did he roam in the night? Did Marianna know by any chance?

Gracias derived a mischievous delight from teasing and affronting Marianna in this way that was not perhaps very kind, but Marianna annoyed her too much for her to exercise sensitive tact towards her. She wanted to provoke Marianna, if necessary to wound her grossly, in order to lure her out of her reserve. Why was this young woman so haughty and reserved? Formerly Gracias had not minded, because Marianna obviously had no secrets; but ever since the girl had fallen in love with that rough gondolier . . . Did she really imagine this had escaped Gracias? It was only necessary to look at her to see how things were with her. With a glance of his impertinent eyes, he had contrived to turn her into his helpless tool — a well-bred, finely tempered girl who had never allowed herself to be fondled by any man. Gracias had chosen her among twelve because it flattered her to have such a maid in her service. Oh, but nature avenges itself on those who try proudly to deny it. And if only Marianna would honestly admit everything, Gracias would have been all compassion for the poor little thing who, moreover, appeared to have been spurned by the fellow after he had seduced her. But why did she say no word about it? She might have been amazed at the good advice she would have received, and at her mistress's readiness to jump into the breach for her. Gracias, out of revenge, teased her about that brown Negro boy. She asked her what she was to make of the fact that Annibale spent half the day sleeping, and that Marianna herself looked greatly in need of the same cure?

She knew well enough that she had wounded Marianna, even though her victim felt it beneath her dignity to give so much as a contemptuous twist to her lips.

Ah, well, if Marianna refused to say a word about her lover, Gracias her mistress was not so proud. She must talk about Benedetto, and there was no one to talk to except Marianna.

Had he again gone to his study early this morning? He seemed to be able to do without sleep. He only looked a little pale with fatigue. In his eyes was a fire that glowed, a fire within him that could not be extinguished. He was busy writing an opera. He must just be given his head. He was going to conquer Venice. His spring was as the spring of a tiger, Marianna — as of a tiger. He made her tremble, he stopped her breath — then he was away again, at crack of dawn; and then he forgot everything but his work.

Benedetto had his midday meal in his room. He hardly touched it. He was working as if possessed, as if his life depended upon it.

Gracias ate with Marianna, and Annibale was allowed to sit at table with them. He was put out by all sorts of known and unknown causes, and was more impudent than ever. He had had no desire to come to the country, but his preferences had not been consulted. In the city, he knew what to do with his time. He brought all this out in his ineffable Arabic Italian. Gracias knew very well how he spent his time in the city. At twilight, he sauntered along the Molo, saying shameless things to the women and girls passing by. Once some girls of the street had taken him with them as a sort of plaything. Gracias, to whose ears this had come, had questioned him the next day about his adventures, and had been much amused when in his inadequate language he gave her a stammering account of them. But in the country he had no adventures. He was in poor spirits; and his humor did not improve when his mistress, after feeling a vague pity for him and putting up with his tantrums for a time, at length had had enough of them and began to poke fun at him. Marianna sighed: she felt she could not stand much more of this, and was gasping for fresh air.

Gracias made her accompany her upon expeditions to the village near by. She visited the simple families she had come to know in the summer. The people who furnished supplies to the summer villas had learned of her return with joy, which was turned to disappointment when they discovered that she was giving no great parties. Gracias considered it necessary to excuse herself: she told all of them about Benedetto and his opera, and tried to make everything right with presents. But it was not only for the sake of her royal ways that she was eagerly received in every house. She was liked for her gay, lighthearted manner, and for her very unusual appearance. She wanted to see the children, she allowed them to talk endlessly of their troubles and worries, she tried to alleviate them.

And then suddenly she had had enough of it all, enough of the bad air in those stuffy, dark houses, enough of sitting on rickety benches at broken

tables over which flies crawled, enough of the worries and the obsequious-
ness of these peasants. Suddenly she longed to get back to the large house
on the Brenta with its spacious airy rooms. From her sedan chair, she
looked with hatred and aversion at the boorish yokel who, with a comrade,
carried her through the ruts of the almost impassable road. The sweat
streamed over their brown, glistening, unwashed necks. For a few soldi,
or for the honor alone, they were prepared to become beasts of burden.
She longed for the pure cool of the evening after the heat of the day. She
longed to be alone with her lover with the wide, dark night outside the
open window. Lying in each other's arms, they listened to the gentle wind
in the autumn foliage that ever and again detached a leaf and sent it
whirling to the ground. Outside it was autumn, but in her arms he found
summer.

The evenings, the nights were hers. The days were her enemies. She
tried to fight them bravely. She fled to the kitchen, talked with Teresa
about her little son who was to become a priest. But Teresa did not speak
of him with the same proud joy as she had done in the summer. There
was doubt and hesitation in her voice. Gracias tried to remember whether
she had given her money to help in the realization of this dream of hers.
She had meant to, but perhaps she had forgotten.

Teresa had grown humbler. She said that perhaps it was too presumptuous of people like her and her husband to wish to make a priest
of their son. The boy himself talked only of the monastery, not of the
seminary. It was really only because the parish priest had said he was so
good at learning . . . What was she to do?

"You must bring him along one day, Teresa, and let me see him. I shall
be able to tell you whether he's likely to grow into a dapper young friar,
one of those for whom it would be a sin if he were to belong exclusively
to heaven. You surely won't make a Franciscan of him, a Franciscan with
a dirty beard? Far better make him a Dominican, a blushing young Dominican in a cream-white cowl."

Teresa did her best to evade her mistress's request that she should bring
Giorgino to the house. She agreed vaguely — some time or other, when it
happened to be convenient . . . Her boy was not really good-looking;
but he had a kind heart and was righteous and very severe with himself.
He was only three years old when . . . But Teresa suddenly broke off.
Gracias looked round and saw Silvio come in. She fancied she had guessed
something, and asked Silvio whether he knew what to do with his time in
the country.

Certainly: he had just put the fountain in the garden in order. The pump
had been working badly, and the reservoir was stopped up with leaves.

"Excellent, Silvio," said Gracias. "I want to have a look at the fountain. I want to see all you can do."

Together they went through the garden. The pebbles crunched under their feet. Gracias threw a stealthy glance up at the window behind which Benedetto was busy working. He was not looking out. Music had him in her toils. But behind another window the shadow of Marianna glided by.

They had to cross a little brook that ran across the grass and provided water for the fountain. Silvio offered her his hand as he used to do when she stepped into her gondola; he looked at her and she was somewhat disconcerted by the boldness in his eyes. She wondered whether to dismiss him. Perhaps it would be better if she did. He was too insolent. He smelt very like an animal too, like Annibale and Toto. She noticed it as she jumped over the brooklet: he had put his face unnecessarily close to hers.

She marveled at the result of his activities: the fountain had not spouted so high the whole summer. Benedetto still did not look up from his work. Only Marianna watched, invisible behind a curtain.

"Annibale!" called Gracias. "You'll be ill if you lie like that in the wet grass!"

And the strange thing was that Annibale, who, thinking himself unseen, was resting his head on his brown wrists, half-concealed among the roses and the grass, got up at once, shook himself sulkily, and drifted away, instead of remaining where it suited him.

Silvio looked up and muttered with a rather forced laugh, "That little serpent is spying all day long!"

Gracias looked up at the gondolier in astonishment, and asked, "What is there to spy on here?"

VI

Benedetto was sitting upstairs in his room — working. How long did he think he could go on with this? Gracias was beginning to feel self-pity. They had been a week in the country. For seven days on end she had been bored, and he had not even noticed it. And it had not occurred to him to ask her how she was dragging through the days. Every day she got up later — there was nothing to do. She no longer wanted to give Italian lessons to Annibale: he would never learn it. She had gleaned all there was to know about everybody round about. She knew the life stories of all the villagers, and had no curiosity about them left. She knew everyone who had falsified or spirited away a will during the last thirty years. She knew which wives had deceived their husbands, and which children sprang from unlawful fathers. After much insistence, she had contrived to meet and admire Teresa's little son — an ugly child, precocious and affected, who looked at her as though he were Ignatius of Loyola in person. She had advised Teresa not to make a Dominican of him after all — her child already had the eyes of a Jesuit; and while the future priest distrustfully inspected the whole household, and in particular the converted Annibale (who, on his side, manifested boundless contempt for the little yokel), Teresa sobbingly confessed that Silvio had made an attempt upon her virtue. Yes; but she had given him a piece of her mind. What was she sobbing for, then, Gracias asked, exasperated by the lie; and later she told the story to Marianna, who pretended she did not hear.

Gracias wondered how she had managed to spend a whole summer at the villa. She had been bored then — but she had less time to realize it. She had never been alone as she was now. They played cards, and disputed about nothing for hours on end. They were always busy preparing some mad jollity — only afterwards did they realize it had not been amusing. They killed time with round games, playing blindman's buff by the light of the stars that did not penetrate into the deep shadows under the trees. They set off fireworks, they organized absurd competitions among the peasants. They danced and they kissed in arbors, and who was kissing whom they did not know until they raised their masks.

Now, to make matters worse, it had begun to rain. Arrayed in a nonchalant negligee that made her even more seductive than usual (oh, it was not fair of Benedetto to lock himself up in his room!) Gracias wandered about the house, seeking refuge at last in the kitchen, where she discussed with Teresa the preparation of the dishes. Gracias insisted upon preparing the greens herself, for once: she grew quite excited wondering what Benedetto would leave on his plate after the midday meal. But Gracias triumphed. He left nothing.

When Benedetto was beside her again in the evening, she forgot the tedium of the endless day. She could not help it. She was more in love with him than she would ever be again in her life with any man. Meanwhile, however, the day had to be lived through.

One faint hope remained with her: that her friends in Venice would after all find out whither she had fled, — it ought not to be too difficult, if they set their minds to it seriously, — and that then they would suddenly all come trooping off the *burchiello*, cursing the rain, and the puddles through which they had to wade because no one had thought of putting down a plank or two for them (but after all, they had not been invited, had they?). If Benedetto heard their voices below in the garden — would he not then leave his study a little earlier?

Suddenly the fear overcame Gracias that perhaps her friends in Venice had altogether forgotten her. Perhaps they were all doing as Baron Barbaresco had done — he had never reappeared after that one evening when he had waited for her in vain. Apparently it was possible to go too far with a man, after all. She had not realized that.

She would like to return to Venice for just one day, to see if anyone turned up when the news of her arrival spread through the city. Of course, she would say that she was not at home, because she would still be supposed to be at her villa in the country . . . Alas, Marianna was not the sort of person with whom she could stand behind a curtain and get some fun out of such a situation. She ought never to have taken Marianna into her service. With someone else she would not have been so lonely in the country. She would have liked to give notice to Marianna that very day. But first she wanted to hear from her own mouth her story about Silvio. Marianna, like Teresa, might tell her a story that was half lies, if she wished: Gracias was prepared to be satisfied with half a confession, with half the truth.

Perhaps she would send Silvio to Venice for a day or two, to pick up the latest scraps of news; and while he was away, perhaps Marianna would at last grow soft and break her silence.

No, Silvio must remain at the villa. She could not do without him. He had to chop wood for the kitchen; and these last few days she had been amusing herself observing how far he would dare to go with his insolence. If Benedetto knew everything about that gentleman . . . Should she go and tell him how the gondolier was following her about everywhere and watching her? But had he no eyes in his head? Did he not see that she was exposed to a perpetual menace?

Oh, if only she were not so madly in love with that sleepy man! To make him less peaceful and self-absorbed as he sat in his room all day, she had a good mind to pretend she was deceiving him with her gondolier. She would like to make both him and Silvio look foolish. Perhaps such a little game with Silvio would not be entirely without danger. Ah, well, so much the better; and after all, a gondolier could always be dismissed if it seemed advisable.

Outside the rain was falling gently, gray in sound and in color; but in Benedetto there behind the open window lived the colorful happenings of his opera. To-day he hoped to finish the first act. He was working excitedly, at high pressure, because his music was dragging him along, but also because the time at his disposal was short. Not Rossi, but the indefinable danger he felt all about him urged him on. He knew that he must hurry. He tried to shut his eyes to the sense of vague menace that grew and grew within him. He wanted to be aware of nothing but his work. He hoped to finish it before danger completely encircled him. When it was finished he could rise and look the danger, wherever it was, straight in the face.

Why did Gracias not support him? Why was she not patient with him when she saw how hard he was working? She knew of his great purpose, and she wanted to join him in the day of his triumph. In the evenings, exhausted by his work, he fled to her, hungering for the young fiery life in her arms that quickened him and enabled him to gather fresh forces in short, deep sleep. In the night he knew he was safe; but during the day, when he had to abandon Gracias to herself, he felt his danger afresh. He knew that his work, his great struggle, did not occupy her thoughts. She was bored, and longed for Venice and for her friends. For him, Venice was far away — a quiet, gray shadow that would begin to live again only when he returned there for the performance of his opera. For Gracias, Venice was the world where life went on, and she was having no part in it. She was afraid she was missing something here in the country where there was no life. Suppose she were to go back alone, and leave him here long enough for him to . . . An absurd notion that could only have arisen in a distracted and exhausted brain: in that case, he would have no peace at all, quite apart from the fact that he could not do without her, her kisses, her voice, her laughter. He wanted daily renewed assurance that he still dominated her. So long as he was at her side he dominated her, but his power over her did not endure while she was alone all day. Oh, he had known that already on that first evening when he had waited for her in the dark garden, waited until someone came and opened the door for him, he had known that he would have peace only when he was beside her, when he had her within sight of his eyes.

In the evening at table, when Marianna was with them, Gracias told him of her plans — all the amusements she was planning for the time when they would be back in Venice. They would not have to wait very long now, would they? Madcap, silly plans they were. She was much madder than when he had first come into contact with her in Venice: she felt she had to make up for lost time. She wanted to be talked about, and she demanded that he set his powers of fancy in motion and provide her with bright ideas. She was possessed with a strange lust to torment people. She wanted to amaze and challenge the virtuous, notable ladies of Venice. She seemed to feel restricted as he had felt in Todi. He might have been of greater service to her then than now. She searched within him continually for the image she had made of him in Todi. She wanted him to go further, beyond the point at which he had halted and come to his senses. In her impatience, she looked as if she might destroy what he was building up by straining all his powers. She looked as if she might betray him and bring about his downfall merely because she was bored and was curious to know how he would act. But he could do nothing, nothing, if she betrayed him. All would be over. Did she not know that? This evening he would tell her that he could not begin all that afresh. . . .

VII

Although the rain had stopped an hour before, he did not find Gracias in the garden, where she usually waited for him at the end of the day. Full of impatience and passionate longing, he sought her all over the house. His vague restlessness almost overpowered him. Meeting Marianna on the stairs, he asked her where Gracias was. With barely concealed reluctance the girl answered that he would find her mistress in the kitchen; and true enough there she was, in the company of Teresa and Silvio, instructing them in the preparation of a specifically Spanish dish of which he was to taste later on.

In a corner sat Annibale, watching. It did not occur to him for once to get up and run away as he usually did when the master who had been imposed upon him made an appearance.

Something in the whole atmosphere of the room made Benedetto feel uncomfortable as soon as he entered. Gracias' exaggerated gaiety struck him as unreal. He noticed Teresa's sadness and anger. Silvio tried to defy his cool, investigating glance, and then looked up innocently at the beams of the ceiling.

Gracias suggested that this evening they should follow the country custom and dine in the kitchen. Benedetto looked surly and remained silent; whereupon she dried her hands on Teresa's apron and accompanied him out of the room. If he were annoyed, that was just what she wanted. He had annoyed her.

When they were alone and he still did not speak, she asked, "How much longer do you think of remaining here?"

He breathed deeply, — it sounded like a sigh, — and said wearily, "We could return by the *burchiello* to-morrow if you wish. If I go on working this evening, I shall finish the first act to-day."

Back to Venice to-morrow! He himself was suggesting it. Gracias had obtained what she wanted, and felt almost guilty. Well, if he wished to finish the first act at the villa, of course he had better go on working for an hour or so in the evening. "But the other two acts?"

"I can write those in Venice." Suddenly, in a vision, he saw before his eyes his room in the house of Graziadeo the Jew, and dimly he felt the comforting protection of Leah's hand. He was so tired. . . .

Gracias seemed to see through him in a flash. She had never questioned him about his dwelling in Venice — it had never interested her. But now she thought she heard in his voice that a return to Venice would not be unwelcome to him. In a sudden spasm of undirected jealousy, she thought: "If you think you will find more peace there than here you're mistaken. I shall see to that."

"Very well, go on working this evening, and Marianna must see to it that everything is packed by to-morrow morning, for the *burchiello* goes by at nine o'clock . . ."

At these words, they both suddenly felt the completeness of the failure of their flight together to the country. Gracias' irritability subsided. A feeling of melancholy longing came over her. She wanted to cry; but there was no need for him to notice that. She overcame her weakness. Lust for revenge welled up in her again. "Very well, let's go back to-morrow, if you prefer to write the rest in Venice."

That evening at table Marianna was not the only one to be silent and agitated. Benedetto could not eat for nervousness. Only Gracias did honor to her Spanish dish — she assured him that she was enjoying it more than any dish that had been prepared for her in this house. She was determined to regale all her friends in Venice with it. They would know how to appreciate it; and if they were to die of it, it would be no great loss either.

As soon as the meal was over, Marianna fled upstairs to pack the trunks. Gracias said she did not see why everybody else should be tired and not she: she, too, was tired and would go to bed early — what else was there for her to do, anyhow? Benedetto went back to his study.

There he rapidly lost all conception of time and place. The morning might have surprised him at his writing table without his being aware of it. The tense close of the first act (Filomena's flight with her lover disguised as a gondolier) carried him away. He gathered together all the earlier motifs — the fiery longing of the enamored young man, the hesitations of the maiden educated to obedience who implored the Virgin and all the saints for forgiveness and support while she followed the call of her heart. Hardly had the gondola disappeared into the darkness when . . .

With a trembling hand he was writing, writing, bewitched himself by the power of his music that soared far above the feeble inadequacy of the libretto . . .

And then . . . suddenly . . . there was a disturbance. The magic web was broken. The disturbance of which he had had a vague anxious foreboding, and which he had hoped to be able to evade by working feverishly at his task, had come to pass. The great liberation he had almost reached was denied him. Out of another, smaller world that he had tried for a moment to forget in the great dream world within him, came a warning.

Something had been thrown through the window into his room. With throbbing head, he looked on the floor beside his table. Something glittered there in the light of the candle: a pebble. Music still sounded within him, but the motifs that had been forming themselves into one thrilling whole disintegrated, were lost in a senseless chaos of sound. He stared towards the window: probably he had been sitting there for hours — did somebody want to remind him of that? It took him a moment to collect his thoughts. Then suddenly he was awake. He threw down his pen. Yes, he was awake.

Like a flash of lightning he leaned out of the window and saw a figure that apparently had been on the point of disappearing into the adjoining room from a ladder, but that, thinking better of this plan, was slipping down again like a sack. It did not seem to be to this figure's liking when almost at the same moment (thanks to an insanely daring jump) his master stood beside him.

Silvio was so disconcerted that he was on the point of retiring quietly, his ladder on his back. Roughly, Benedetto knocked the ladder down before Silvio had a chance of letting it drop upon his head.

"Where are you going with that ladder?"

"To Marianna," lied the gondolier, stammeringly.

"Through your mistress's window?"

Silvio recovered himself: he lied for the pleasure of lying. "I made a mistake in the window," he said, and looked up at the window to which he should have gone.

Benedetto stood a little too close to him. The giant thought things were coming to a fighting bout, in which he knew he would have the advantage. To disabuse him of this error, Benedetto took a step backwards and the half-yard he thus put between them restored his authority. Silvio's shoulders drooped almost submissively after he had arched them in conscious strength. As Benedetto had no pistol with which to shoot down the gondolier on the spot, he had no alternative but to say: "We shall talk about this later. Now clear out."

Silvio bent down and picked up the ladder.

"Ask Marianna," he said feebly, annoyance and shame breaking through his voice.

When Silvio had disappeared, Benedetto returned into the house, after searching vainly for the person who must have thrown the pebble. He went back to his room and picked it up. In the adjoining room he found

Gracias asleep. He took the candle and stared at her face awhile attentively. Peacefully her breast rose and fell: she was really asleep.

He undressed and went to bed.

But he lay awake, listening in the night. An arrangement between Silvio
and her was out of the question. Or was she so giddy-minded that even in
that case she would fall asleep? Probably she had merely played with the
fellow from boredom and thoughtlessness. His senses were too dull for
him to order his ideas.

An hour later Gracias woke and saw him lying motionless beside her.
She raised herself upon one arm and stared, astonished and incredulous,
into his open eyes that refused to look at her.

"What's wrong with you?" she inquired, and upon his evincing no inclination to reply, she asked, "Have you done as much work as you intended?"

When he shook his head slowly and indifferently, she knew that in one
way or another she had won her case.

She said nothing further, and continued to watch him silently and in
suspense until of his own accord he came out with, "A little while ago I
caught Silvio trying to force his way into Marianna's room."

Then she knew a little more — the whole truth. But still she wanted to
find out why he was trying to conceal the whole truth from her. Did he
suspect her? Or was he trying to discover her secret by cunning? What
did she care what he thought? She had him beside her now, and he preferred to speak no more about his work. She had him, and she had Silvio
to thank for that.

"Ah, well — and suppose Marianna had invited him?" she asked impertinently, and looked at him laughing. She was delighted that Benedetto
had caught the fellow. He had been just awake enough for that! She would
have liked to know what had happened between Silvio and him. She would
have liked to watch — but alas! she had been asleep. But suppose that she
had been awake when he had caught Silvio . . . What would he have
done to her then?

There had been a struggle between him and Silvio, who was powerful
and ferocious as a bull, and he had won, apparently without requiring to
use his hands. He was the stronger, and she rejoiced in it; she was grateful
to him.

But in the night — which in the country was so unfathomably deep, so
black and deserted — there suddenly came over her the first feeling of
anxiety about this gondolier whom she had lured towards her playfully
to-day and yesterday, and perhaps from the moment he had come into her
service, until he had been on the point of slinking into her room. In her

mind's eye she saw that great animal standing by her bed, and it turned her blood cold in her veins. . . .

Nobody, nobody but Benedetto could protect her against him, once Silvio had gone so far as to think of setting foot in her bedroom. She opened her eyes wide in a dismay for which she could find no name, and with a stifled cry sought protection in Benedetto's arms.

At that moment he knew she still belonged to him; but as he drew her to him and felt the soft warmth of her face in his neck, he was overcome by grief for his work that had remained unfinished. That suddenly interrupted end was like a wound, a raw mutilation.

No — it could never come right. It had been disturbed and destroyed. That was the price he must pay for his confession to this woman.

DEFEAT

I

NEXT MORNING ANNIBALE LIMPED; BUT ON HIS flat sallow Negro face lay a glow of bitter triumph. Silvio, not doubting a moment that he would be dismissed and would have to return to his old standing, was sitting in the kitchen half-dressed, waiting for his bread and wine. He looked as though he had not slept. As the bread and wine were not forthcoming of themselves, he reached into the cupboard to take what was not given him, cursing the while. Teresa was standing before the charcoal fire in tears. The news of this unexpected and overhasty departure made it unnecessary for her to put any constraint upon herself. At Silvio's dreadful curses she crossed herself, sniffed away her tears, and shivered. How jumpy she had become these last few days!

With downcast eyes, Marianna knocked at her mistress's door and collected the toilet articles and last knickknacks. She must have worked far into the night, for all the trunks were ready to be carried downstairs by Silvio. Had she heard or noticed nothing of . . . ? Benedetto gave her a shrewd look, but her face was like a mask.

When Gracias noticed that Annibale was dragging his leg, she drew him apart and listened with interest to his story of how he had hurt it: in the dark he had not noticed the last step of the stairs. She answered that she had supposed the accident to his leg was due to the fact that perhaps he saw too much in the dark. How could she have been so mistaken?

At nine o'clock the *burchiello* put in, and they all went on board. Only Teresa remained behind, sobbing her heart out, one arm about the future Jesuit, as if she wanted to protect him and at the same time find support in him. With her other arm she waved as long as the boat was in sight. Unmoved and motionless, Silvio looked towards the old country house that was now definitely about to enter on its winter sleep.

It disappeared behind the red-brown and purple foliage of autumn.

Venice lay broiling in the two o'clock sun. Out on the Lagoon, there was still a faint coolness, but in the city the quays and canals were blazing hot. Venice had continued to live its daily life during Gracias' absence; perhaps it had forgotten her already.

During that one week, the little Gothic palace on the Rio di San Felice had recovered its former peaceful quiet; but that was at an end now. Gracias was in despair the moment she heard from Catarina that none of her friends had shown themselves during her absence. She usually suspected every word that came from Catarina's mouth to be a lie; but this time she believed her, and vented her annoyance upon her father who, stiff and dignified, came from his room to greet her and to inquire after her well-being. Benedetto bowed but the old man took no notice. Nor did he appear to notice the ill-humored ungraciousness of his daughter. His dark eyes roamed through the room looking for another — for Marianna. When she came in, he spoke to her and inquired with genuine interest how she had been during her absence and whether she was glad to be back in Venice again. She excused herself, and fled from the room. His eyes followed her with a faraway look in them.

A change had come over *lo Spagnuolo*. It seemed as if during the week he had spent alone he had thought deeply and had arrived at a definite conclusion: his whole deportment expressed determination. At first sight he seemed to have grown younger. In his voice, formerly so cold and measured, throbbed a certain warmth. Gracias noticed it with astonishment as he spoke to her maid. He was trying to put resilience and suppleness into his walk. For her, there was something ridiculous in this deliberate attempt by her father to recover his youth and liveliness. She would have been almost inclined to pity him had she not been put out by something that seemed to contain a curious menace for herself.

Gracias being safely at home, Benedetto went to hail a gondola to take him and his trunk to Graziadeo's. Silvio, still uncertain of his future, offered to take him — an offer that might be considered as an expression of cynicism but also, possibly, as a somewhat primitive effort to bury the past. In any case, Benedetto ignored it, and summoned a passing *barcaiuolo*. Later in the day, he would suggest to Gracias that it might be a good thing for her to discharge from her service a gondolier who climbed into her window at night by mistake. On the other hand, he felt a certain indifference as to what she did in the matter. From her despair a moment ago when she found that no one had inquired after her, he could easily deduce how things would go. He would have preferred not to return to her house that evening, had it been possible. He felt tired and defeated — a new and disquieting experience for him.

He longed to see again his room in the house of the Jew. Perhaps he could rest an hour or two there, and gather up his strength in order to confront the danger that he felt was growing, growing. . . .

He was slightly stirred, too, at the thought of seeing Leah again.

He had given up his key when he went away, and so had to use the knocker. Geronimo opened the door, and welcomed him with unconcealed pleasure. He immediately took charge of the heavy trunk and said that the Cavaliere could go straight up, as the room was waiting for him. Benedetto was moved by a somewhat childish feeling of gratitude. Good Geronimo! And his room had been kept for him. True, he had paid the rent in advance.

He saw no one else. Halfway up the stairs he stood still. "But where's the family, Geronimo?"

"Signorina Leah has gone out with Susanna," Geronimo informed him, "and the master has a visitor. Would you like to see the Signora?"

With a gesture, Benedetto conveyed that he would not disturb her. He asked Geronimo how matters were in the house generally, and received the most satisfactory account of affairs. But why did Geronimo not understand that he was primarily interested in Leah? Yes. . . . Geronimo realized this suddenly, and brought out the great news that he had almost forgotten to tell him. "Signorina Leah is to be married in the spring. She's gone out now to buy things for her house and her linen cupboard."

Benedetto stared at him. The puny hosier rose before his mind, and in a sudden gust of disappointment he thought: "In the spring . . ."

Suddenly he seemed to lose interest in Geronimo's company. "You can go, Geronimo. You might unpack my trunk this evening if I'm not here."

He was alone in his room. A moment earlier these walls and these pieces of furniture had welcomed him in friendly, familiar fashion. Now they seemed different: it was as if Leah had already left the house.

He opened his trunk himself, took out the sheets of music that lay on top, and spread them before him on the table as if he hoped that the mere sight of them could give him joy, could fortify him. But at that moment he saw nothing save written notes. He had got so far; now it was over. He would not be able to go on. Strength failed him. It was over, over.

He gathered up the sheets higgledy-piggledy and threw them back into his trunk.

Then, dressed as he was, he dropped upon his bed, and stared at the beams of the ceiling in quiet, gnawing sadness, listening for any consoling sound that might come from the silent house.

What was he waiting for? When the twilight came in through the window, making the furniture in the room unrecognizable, suddenly he could no longer breathe there. He sprang up and went downstairs, where he met Graziadeo, who welcomed him, but hesitatingly and in a minor key. He excused his wife — she had gone to bed with a headache. Benedetto felt he was lying, but he had no desire to see Signora Graziadeo. He wanted air and light. He was about to leave the house when old Susanna, her arms laden with parcels, slipped the key into the door, and preceded Leah into the house.

Leah uttered a soft cry and stared at him in amazement as if he had been away not seven days, but seven years. She was still out of breath from walking rapidly, and was apparently completely lost in the activities of the day: buying for her coming wedding. With transient bitterness, he realized this. He was successful, however, in concealing his bitterness. He greeted her. For a moment the temptation came over him to congratulate her on the news he had just heard from Geronimo, but he refrained.

"So you are back?" she asked, disconcerted. He only nodded slowly and tried to smile. And as she saw him standing like that, trying to appear indifferent, she felt suddenly something of the defeat he must have endured, and her eyes that a moment ago had expressed only intense surprise, and something almost of ill will, took on a gentler expression.

Old Susanna rattled her keys busily, and said with unconcealed hostility in her voice, "Come, my child! You're warm with all this running about."

Leah still hesitated a second; then she bowed her head and, passing Benedetto, went in.

II

Giddy, dreaming, he walked for a while in the direction of the Rio di San Felice. He did not call a gondola until he reached the Grand Canal. Just as Gracias' dwelling came in sight, he saw a long thin shadow appear on the steps and get into a gondola. He tried to collect his thoughts. It was high time to wake up. He recognized also the gondola and the gondolier: Silvio, still in Gracias' service. Disquieted, somber, he noted that fact. He must take action that evening, make his authority felt, before it was too late.

Silvio appeared to have noticed him too as he drifted away, and drew his passenger's attention to him. Maniscù, who sat tucked up in a black cloak that enfolded him and made him look like a large bat, glanced up a little too hastily, so that the mask he had just put on dropped again. In the half-light, Benedetto had the strange momentary impression that his face itself, pale as the mask, had dropped from him, and there was something unspeakably macabre and ghostly in the gesture with which he readjusted his mask with his large, skeleton hand.

As Benedetto paid off his own gondolier, he gave a quick glance at the pair of them as they disappeared into the twilight, and a feeling of approaching disaster possessed him more and more strongly.

After knocking several times, his anger and suspicion increasing every moment, the door at length opened a crack. He thrust it open forcefully, almost knocking down Galuppi who stood swaying on drunken legs, carrying a lantern without a light.

Bendetto strode past him up the stairs, and entered the room where twenty, thirty people were all speaking at once. They looked round at him, and one or two who were standing near him took it into their heads to welcome him with applause. That had happened once before – how long ago?

Bewildered for a moment, he stood still and looked about him. Were they taunting him? He encountered vacant, almost mirthful eyes that met his determined stare with some difficulty. Only a few of his enemies showed more courage. Gracias walked up to him, a raised glass of wine in her hand and a smile on her lips. Her walk, which she was trying to make seductive, betrayed that she had drunk more than was good for her. She was going to bewitch him with her glance: she wanted them all to see what a Circe she was. But he saw only the hostility in her eyes: she had ranged herself with these others and thought she could make game of him.

He bowed to her, and then turned abruptly away, intending to go to the adjoining room, hoping blindly that he would find somebody there with whom he could enter into conversation. But before he had reached the door, laughing women's voices reached him: several actresses from the San Carlo Theater were calling him to them: it was the first time he had come upon women guests in that house.

Gracias looked after him, the glass of wine she had intended to invite him to drink still in her raised hand. Her face expressed deep astonishment that turned into almost childish disappointment; and when she saw these princesses of the theater, whom the abbé had thought fit to bring along with him, dragging Benedetto down by them, a line of anger appeared upon her mouth and something dangerous glittered in her eyes. Oh – she too could be a prima donna, if that was what he wanted, and the next moment her glass was dashed in fragments on the floor, and with a shrill laugh she turned to her friends, who shouted "Bravo! bravo!" and almost fell over themselves in their hurry to fetch a fresh glass for her. She allowed them to fill it, merry and melancholy at the same time.

"And when is your opera coming off?" the actresses were asking Benedetto, paying little attention to a scene that was commonplace to them. "Will it soon be ready? They talk of nothing else in Venice."

That was probably exaggerated – but their own interest was genuine enough. A shock ran through him, "My opera? . . . One act of it is written," he said hesitatingly, "and the overture."

Titia was one of them, *la bella Titia* of the San Carlo Theater, a famous beauty in Venice. She was not present by Gracias' desire. It must have been out of revenge that her friends had brought this woman along. *La bella Titia* looked at the successful young composer out of her velvet-black eyes that glowed magnificently in her softly powdered face framed in a silver wig. Then she said plaintively: "Rossi is telling everyone that you've promised him your opera. Surely you haven't been as foolish as that."

He drank in her look, the calculated allurement of her seductive red mouth, and tried to make excuses for his arrangement with Rossi. "Ah, but he's going to increase his orchestra for it. He'll have fresh scenery, and if necessary he'll add strength to his cast. I shall tell him — " Titia knew already what he would say to Rossi: she looked round triumphantly as he finished his sentence. "I shall tell him he must engage you for the part of Filomena."

"That is, if I'm free," broke in Titia at once. He did not hear her. It flashed across his mind that there was something too powerful and heroic in her soprano for his Filomena, who was, in his mind, shy and girlish. But he did not regret his promise to her — so long as Gracias had heard him make it.

Titia, with sober matter-of-factness, inquired as to the subject of his opera; for even if she were not in the position to sing the part of Filomena, still it had become her rôle, and she had the right to know what it was about.

The subject of his opera . . . ? He began to talk — and rather loudly, for surely Gracias was listening too. He talked also about his music. Up to now, he had been silent about his work, self-consciously silent.

A circle formed itself about him. One or two who had been standing by Gracias came forward to listen, and then the drunken Galuppi came swaying nearer and insisted upon telling them all about the painting he had in mind. They ignored him, but suddenly, for some unknown reason, Benedetto could not proceed with his story. They thought, anyhow, that it had come to an end. The other actresses, jealous of Titia's success, pressed round him, demanding, "And when are you going to write parts for us?"

A group of musicians came in: Gracias had hired them, since she wanted to be merry and dance to celebrate her return to Venice. She wanted to prove to her friends the first night she was back that no one was bored in her house.

The company also increased. Countess Bogliasco appeared on the scene, accompanied by her little friend Antonia in whose eyes there slumbered a strange shyness and unapproachability. She was known to the whole of Venice by her pet name of "Nina." The Bogliascos, the two of them were called. A chaperon accompanied them: Marchese Dolcetti, a little old gentleman, ridiculously made up, who was worshiped throughout the theatrical world as a harmless, perpetually misguided Mæcenas. The moment he entered upon his stiff shaking legs, he rushed towards the actresses, who received him with loud cries of enthusiasm, and began to stroke him under the chin. This new trio must also have been invited without Gracias' knowledge. Countess Bogliasco herself, a large mannish woman who must once have been very handsome before her features were ravaged by age and passion, had a reputation to maintain in Venice for her whims and sallies. In her somber husky voice she announced the impending arrival of an interesting Greek with a prayer book. Everybody wanted to know more, but she refused to give away her secret. Strangely enough, she still found adorers for her overblown beauty. Twenty-year-old cavaliers hung about her, trying their utmost to appear interesting in her eyes. She treated them like naughty boys, and smiled goodnaturedly at their not always discreet allusions to her inclinations, which were universally known in Venice. Meanwhile, with the watchfulness of an aging lioness, she guarded her Nina against them.

But as the evening went on, Countess Bogliasco's interest was gradually diverted to Gracias, whom she was meeting for the first time after hearing much about her.

The musicians played and Benedetto danced with Titia. With satisfaction, he felt Gracias directing towards him a look full of hate. She was sitting in the midst of a small band of the faithful and did not dance — she was plotting instead. And the more he grew conscious of his danger, the more carefree did he become in his surrender to the dance. He danced with everyone except Gracias, and he reveled in the whispers around him. He made his bow in all innocence to Nina, unaware of her relationship to Countess Bogliasco. He asked her why she had not even danced the minuet, and then before the eyes of a half-dozen speechless cavalieri a miracle happened. With a few hesitating words, Countess Bogliasco let her go. The young girl herself was so surprised that she did not know what was happening to her. As they danced, Benedetto tried to amuse her; but she gave him no reply on any subject. She danced stiffly, and kept her shattered gaze fixed upon Countess Bogliasco, who flushed under her paint and tried to explain her mysterious conduct by an unctuous smile. Benedetto reproached himself for being unable to get her to talk. His own words sounded empty and hollow in his ears. He went on dancing, and did not know why. When he escorted Nina back to her place, the Countess bent towards him behind her fan. Everybody thought she was saying that she had allowed him the privilege of dancing with Nina once, but could not allow it again: whereas she paid him a compliment, and then rebuked him for not having danced with Gracias. "She is sad. See for yourself. She would like to cry. How can you behave like that to her?" But her voice did not sound genuine.

The interesting Greek, for whose arrival the company had been prepared so mysteriously, made his entry, and true enough carried a prayer book, but not for the purpose of edifying his fellow men. On payment of a gold or silver piece, anyone could stick a pin into the closed book after announcing in advance at which page it would open. The player who aimed correctly received back his stake a hundredfold: a fair bargain, since the first and the last thirty pages did not count, and this, since the holy book contained a hundred and sixty pages, left a hundred pages only for the players to choose from. The Greek had also altered the sequence of the specified hundred pages here and there — just as a surprise, and because otherwise it would have been too easy. Everybody had drunk too much wine. All wanted to try their luck. Gracias was determined upon choosing the right page, once at least. Thanks to his prayer book, the Greek rapidly raked in the gold. The place vacated by Cavaliere Maniscù was triumphantly filled by his fellow countryman, who was asked to return next evening: Gracias would invite the whole of Venice. But he must first give his word of honor that he had never been anywhere else with his prayer book. Nothing was easier than for him to give his word as to this with the clearest conscience: he had only arrived yesterday, by sea, straight from the Piræus. Besides, the fact that Countess Bogliasco had introduced him this evening was sufficient proof. If he might be permitted to introduce himself to the company: Cavaliere Cirigottis.

Next evening there were to be more guests — Venice would know that Gracias was back. Benedetto would be able to see that she still had friends and admirers in Venice.

Annibale had heralded her return, by taking a walk along the Molo where he had been seen by everybody. (He had not yet come back.)

They went on drinking; only the Greek with the prayer book did not drink. The musicians played melancholy old Venetian airs that were still sung by the fishermen of Chioggia at sunset. Ancilla, one of the actresses, knew the words and sang them. The Greek sighed.

Lo Spagnuolo came upstairs. He stood listening by the door. His eyes followed Marianna, who was serving wine. When Ancilla had finished singing, he sat down by the side of Countess Bogliasco, conversing with her about his daughter, and waited for Marianna to serve him too. He intended to pay her a charming compliment he had long been preparing. Why did she not come? Surely she was not afraid of him. . . .

Gracias came up to him with slightly uncertain steps. To show him that his sudden rejuvenation had not escaped her, she spoke to him gaily and challenged him to dance a Furlana with her. She wanted to dance the Furlana, the mad, risky Venetian folk dance, before them all. The old man, turning pale, felt compelled to relinquish this privilege to another. The abbé offered himself, and the music struck up a slow measure. The dance began almost draggingly, increasing in tempo all the time until it ended when the powers of the dancers were exhausted. The abbé stood up bravely to it. He still went on dancing with the same energy even when the sweat was streaming down his face. Gracias' playful smile gradually grew fixed and then disappeared. When she threatened to collapse, her friends supported her. Countess Bogliasco rushed up with a smelling bottle. After a few moments, Gracias opened her eyes and looked, bewildered, into the face of the woman bending over her. Then horror seemed to take possession of her. She brushed aside the hand with the smelling bottle, and came to at once.

With glowing eyes, Benedetto watched her as she danced. He noticed that her eyes were searching for him; it was for him she had danced. For no one but him. But why had she made him spend such an evening? Why was she plotting with his enemies? He knew — he felt — that danger approached him very close this evening, and that the fault was hers. He would have liked to throw himself into some sort of intoxication, as she had done, and forget everything; but the intoxication would not come over him. He had vainly attempted to drown his grief in wine.

Gracias was crying, leaning against some of her friends, but assuring them the while as they tried to console her that it was not from grief. She was so pleased to be among her friends again this evening. She was grateful to all of them for their presence. . . . Suddenly she called to the abbé, who was still panting for breath, that he must go and fetch Baron Barbaresco. She was longing for her old judge — he always knew how to console her when she was sad. The abbé tried to hide himself, but the others dragged him from behind the sofa, clapped his hat on his head, put on his mask, and threw his cloak around him. Forward, out of the door — could he disobey the command of *la muchacha?*

On the sofa, between *la bella Titia* and Ancilla, sat Marchese Dolcetti, still applauding indefatigably by way of expressing his admiration for Gracias' dancing performance. Perhaps he was enjoying himself more than any of them. Little could be seen of him except his pointed raised knees and, under the caressing fall of magnificent Brussels lace at his wide damask cuffs, his hands: two thin gouty hands blazing with jewels that, tired with clapping, were now resting on the soft knees of the two dainty creatures on either side of him, beneath whose opulence he seemed to be buried alive. His lady friends called him "the mad marquis."

Benedetto struggled against his desire to get away. He felt an almost morbid longing to be alone, to have quiet around him. He was beginning to dream of his music again, too, since he had talked about it a while ago. But he could not get away. If he got up now, and fled from the torture of this evening, Gracias would betray him. Nothing would then hold her back from wreaking her vengeance upon him, and this very night the *sbirri* might come. . . .

Suddenly he noticed that Galuppi was sitting next to him, quiet and mute like himself, a dull fire gleaming in his weary, drunken eyes. Now that Benedetto no longer strode through these rooms in triumph, now that Gracias was making him suffer as she had made Galuppi suffer, Galuppi felt drawn towards him as to a brother. Even in his drunkenness, he hesitated to throw his arm round Benedetto's shoulders, or to show him any other mark of sympathy; nevertheless, Benedetto was made suddenly aware that Galuppi was on his side, while all the others were plotting his downfall.

The wine had taken possession of everybody's wits. No one spoke a single sensible word. Nina was weeping bitterly. A half-dozen cavalieri were standing round her, trying in vain to get out of her the reason of her great sorrow. Countess Bogliasco, who herself seemed a prey to agitation, was saying that it was just one of Nina's whims and would blow over as soon as she breathed the fresh air again. She suggested that they should go and see the sun rise over the Lagoon, and the plan was greeted with wild enthusiasm. They all got up, clutching at one another to keep their balance. As a joke, they exchanged cloaks and hats. Several cavalieri disappeared and returned in women's attire: they had ransacked Gracias' wardrobe.

Then the procession made its way downstairs, carrying Antonia, still sobbing hysterically, with them. The only guest left behind was the little old marquis, who, feeling suddenly unwell, had remained in the inner room, and now lay prostrate and alone in an armchair, his face distorted. Nobody gave him a thought: even the actresses, for whom his purse had always opened wide, forgot him. Not until the next night, as the curtain was about to rise, did they hear that they had harbored among them a dead man, or at least a dying one.

The musicians packed up their instruments and disappeared, stuffing themselves at the sideboard hastily, and with the casualness bred of habit, as they passed it. In the old palace were two people only: Marianna, who began to clear up nervously, and *lo Spagnuolo,* whose eyes followed her as she came and went. He was not drunk; but his eyes were those of a drunken man. Catarina had gone to bed some hours ago: she shut herself into her little room downstairs with Mutu, as though she feared for her virtue. Marianna, in increasing anxiety, had hesitated as to whether she should speak to Benedetto and Galuppi, who had left just before the musicians. She had gone up to them once, but at the last moment her courage had failed her.

And now these two were alone. *Lo Spagnuolo* sat there staring at her, as she hurried to and fro with the dishes and glasses; he was pondering how to address her without frightening her. In his complete uncertainty of how to act in these matters, he thought it would be a rather happy idea to ask her whether he could not help her by any chance. "Signorina Marianna — " he began huskily, but at the sound of her name on his lips she dropped to the floor the dishes she was carrying, and fled in panic terror to the adjoining room whither Marchese Dolcetti had retired to die. (Of that fact, however, neither Marianna nor *lo Spagnuolo* had an inkling.)

Lo Spagnuolo looked towards the door she had hastily bolted behind her, but he did not get up from his chair — as if he feared lest even that might frighten her. When, however, he suddenly heard a piercing shriek from behind that safely closed door, followed by the fall of a swooning body, he did think her behavior rather exaggerated. He said to himself softly that he could not go to her aid without forcing a door in his own house; and besides, if she opened her eyes and saw him, to be consistent she must faint again immediately; and, since she must look upon him as the devil incarnate, she would be justified in so doing.

There he sat, staring at the floor in front of him. His thoughts turned to his ship, the *Trinità,* which was expected to arrive next day, and of all he would say to her captain. . . . After a while, slowly, stiff and dignified, *lo Spagnuolo* got up from his armchair and went downstairs.

Benedetto stepped into the last gondola moored by the steps. He tried in vain to be by himself — Galuppi refused to leave him. Those ahead of them were singing and shouting. Other gondolas joined them — merry-makers who had intended to go home after celebrating carnival all night, and changed their minds upon seeing this procession. Some of the gondolas fell out of the company again, dispersing to right and left: their occupants were feeling sick with too much wine, and decided that after all they had no wish to see the sunrise, but wanted only to get to bed.

A solitary gondola met them. It contained one small passenger: Annibale returning homeward. He lay back like a senator, and stared at his mistress and her guests with weary eyes. They recognized him, and called to him laughingly to come too and see the sun rise above the Lagoon. But he shook his head carelessly and snapped to his gondolier to go on: "Rio di San Felice, Number 7."

Benedetto had no desire, either to continue the game. He hoped that Gracias, surrounded by her friends, would no longer miss him. Galuppi's melancholy and unwished-for company was more than he could stand. He told the gondolier to draw in somewhere, as he wanted to go home. "Don't let that disturb you, Signor Galuppi. You go on."

Galuppi, startled, sat bolt upright. There was no doubt a certain lack of clarity in his drunken head. He said, "I'm coming with you."

"Thank you, Signor Galuppi. I'd rather go alone."

"Let me see you home . . ."

Benedetto was not prepared for a friendly altercation; even before the gondola had put in, he sprang ashore, raised his hat, and hurried away. Galuppi tried to follow him, but he had difficulty in getting to his feet in the light, rocking craft. His legs would not obey him; and besides the *barcaiuolo* held him back for payment.

"Wait at least until it's light," Galuppi called after Benedetto as he walked rapidly away. He then felt in his breeches' pocket, but found no money. As he went on searching, the gondolier pulled him down. With his head still turned in the direction in which Benedetto had disappeared in the half-dark, he continued to mutter to himself. The *barcaiuolo* could make nothing of what he was saying, and decided to pretend that he thought his passenger wanted to be rowed after the others: if the signore had no money, his friends and acquaintances could pay for him. The gondoliers of Venice constituted a united robber band well able to get the better of a company of drunken ladies and gentlemen. If the signore was unaware of that fact, he would know it soon enough.

Benedetto tried to find his way home through dark little streets and alleys. It was not easy. He ought to have gone home in the gondola. It was all the fault of Galuppi, whose presence he could no longer tolerate.

He must take measures to save himself. In his feverish brain, belief in the possibility of saving himself had reawakened. He thirsted for his music, as for something living to which he could cling. His work was the one thing that could perhaps save him, if he were quick. . . . He would throw himself into it at once, and finish the first act before his absence was noticed by Gracias. He felt capable of it. She would certainly sleep till the next evening. Then he would go to her and say he had resumed work on his opera, of which the whole of Venice was speaking. Then he would ask her what she wanted, whether she wanted to betray him and expose him to the ridicule of her friends, or to stand by him.

He hoped to win her over again, to prove his power to all. He still hoped to triumph over this city, to win a victory through his music. Maestro Angelini in Todi had asked him once, "Do you understand what that means, to stand in a blaze of light? Nobody understands that here. Do you?" Oh, yes; he understood what that meant now. To stand in a blaze of light — with me — would you like that, Gracias?

A sound. Away in the country, on the Brenta, another little sound had put a cruel end to everything. He looked about him sharply. Where was he? Giving rein to his fancy, he had wandered on, but surely this was the corner by the house of Graziadeo the Jew. The sound had come from a doorway on the other side. Suddenly it flashed across his mind that a dark figure had slipped in there. . . .

He hesitated a moment, then turned round. He did not want to be disturbed in his flood of thoughts and sensations. What did he care at that moment if some Venetian merchant *was* being robbed of his best silver?

With quick, soft steps he walked away. A minute later, he had reached a little alley running parallel with the other, and leading to his home almost as quickly. He had forgotten the suspicious noise — it had perhaps been merely his fancy. He was thinking only of his goal: the room where his work awaited him.

But before he reached the corner he heard a sound again. For a second, a sense of oppression came over him. With a jerk, he shook himself free of it, felt instead anger and annoyance. He drew his pistol, and took a step forward that brought him to the corner of an alley from which subdued voices reached him. Shadows sprang back. He fired at a light directed towards him to blind him. The shot misfired; but the light was blown out. He drew his sword, sprang forward, and cried, "Halt, there!"

No answer. Instead, a frightful blow on his head. The alley — Venice itself — sank away, and he with her.

And now suddenly the sun rose above the Lagoon. In its stark light moved dark shadows. Gruff voices, kicks, blows from invisible fists . . . Once or twice a sharp, acute, cutting pain . . . Dragged along. A hand, pressing stinking mud into his thirsty open mouth — Go to hell!

Then an infinite silence. One of his legs was throbbing with pain. He felt only the throbbing, not the pain. Music: now he had got it — the close of the first act . . .

The music lost itself in oblivion, and he lay by the side of the *canaletto,* empty and pitiable and slowly bleeding to death, when a familiar voice reached him from afar. He vomited: his mouth was full of filth. He felt himself supported, his face was washed with water. He was not yet dead. He even opened his eyes, and looked into an old, narrow, bearded face — into a pair of melancholy, anxious eyes.

"Come! Quick!" said the old man, whom he knew well. Then strong arms picked him up.

In the first gray of dawn, Geronimo carried the wounded man carefully into his master's house. The master, meanwhile, pressed into the gondolier's hand five large silver pieces.

The *barcaiuolo* stared in amazement at this lavish payment, and then rowed away with unobtrusive haste, under the mistaken idea that a bewildered old man had made a mistake and would call him back again. When he had gone some distance, he felt reassured that this mistake could not be rectified and was able to appreciate the situation better. He smiled at the thought of that Jew who, guiltless as a child in the whole episode, had unfortunately and against his will come upon the scene and set to flight the band of *bravi* in the very act of dispatching a fellow. What a Jew! To lift the victim into a gondola instead of abandoning him to his possibly well-deserved fate! Had he been caught, this Hebrew, in a gondola with a half-dying Christian, what a hornet's nest he would have had about his ears! That was why he had trembled and his voice had been shaking as he ordered the gondolier to push off quickly. But why had this Jew meddled with a dying Christian who could constitute nothing but a danger to him?

What a Jew! To think that he had given him five silver ducats so that nothing should leak out! But was it even worth talking about? So long as the victim was not one of the state inquisitors or the Doge himself, not a single one of his boon companions would bother to listen to such a story; and the victim certainly did not look like either the one or the other.

He had been bleeding like a pig. It might be advisable to wash the gondola at once. Fortunately he had managed to save the little carpet from damage. Yes, the trouble he had been put to was certainly worth something extra.

But five silver ducats . . .

Jew!

LEAH

I

VOICES MURMURED ABOUT HIM. HE KNEW THEM well; but when he tried to establish clearly in his mind to whom they belonged, they sank away again into a thick fathomless oblivion.

Sometimes darkness turned to a pale gray twilight inhabited by dream faces. Then the voices came back and took shape. There was the monotonous singsong voice of a tired old man, encouraging him to patience and confidence. It calmed Benedetto. Then there was the worried, heavy voice of an irritable woman who did not like him — he wished her to the devil. He liked best of all the clear, subdued voice of a young girl who gave decisive orders in a friendly way to an obstinate, ill-natured old creature who had to be told everything twice. Occasionally he felt a desire to take action himself and bring her to reason, to remind her that she might stamp a little less. Her hands seized everything clumsily, and she brought with her an unmistakable and unpleasant odor of cooking and frying.

From time to time the young girl with the friendly voice bent over him and pressed something wonderfully cool upon his forehead. For a moment he vaguely perceived a filmy contour against a patch of light. Mustering all his strength, he was able to see two almost unnaturally large dark eyes peering into his face. He recognized those eyes, and a sound tried to form itself in his throat. But he could not bring it out. Then darkness enveloped him again. He had tried to raise his head; a heavy hammer was thumping at it, and in the deep stillness there was a dull boom, boom . . . Through his left leg that was like a lead weight ran a sharp pain.

He would have liked to cry, to sob; but he could not. He was deeply unhappy.

Then he grew calmer, but still he could not muster his thoughts. His mind seemed to be occupied with one picture from the far past. He wished he could remember all that had happened since, but he could not. He saw his mother in the semidusk of the alcove packing a bundle for him, for her only son who must leave Todi because of the *sbirri*, because of that accursed Carlo who had been after him for so long. She stood with her back to him in the dim alcove. He could see what he had done to her by the way her shoulders were hunched with grief. He would have liked to put his arm about her so that she could cry her heart out against him — him who had no fear of the *sbirri*, or of the world beyond, where he must seek refuge in flight. Yes; but it was beyond his power to get up from where he was. Something held him in the middle of the room. He must be on the alert, in case the *sbirri* should come. Motionless, he stood and listened. . . . And by the window stood Buongiorno the coffinmaker, whom they called his father. His calloused hands folded behind his back, he was looking through the window into the empty courtyard, and had not the least suspicion of what was taking place behind him. He had finished a good long day's work, and was looking peacefully back upon his own quiet life. But suddenly from across the courtyard resounded the shrill, hoarse voice of Manuela, the cobbler's wife: "*Addio, addio per sempre — è l'ora della partenza.*" Oh, Manuela was aware of the terrible appropriateness of her song. "Farewell, farewell forever — it is the hour of departure." She meant her song to be heard in the room. His mother turned large frightened eyes towards him — if only he could say one word to set her at rest. But his throat was closed as by a vice. The ditty, long ended, still reverberated in the air and would not die. It reverberated like the cry of despair of a lost soul in the silent kingdom of the dead, echoing endlessly against the gray naked walls. Suddenly, with one step, he was at his mother's side, closing her in his arms — a great moment of which Buongiorno the coffinmaker perceived nothing. Sobs shook Benedetto's frame — liberating, beneficent sobs. His heart that had threatened to burst from drought began to overflow, and the woman in his arms was crying too. Wonderful harmonies such as no earthly organ could have sounded seemed to come from heaven. Through them Manuela's voice could still be heard; but now it expressed all the human sorrow of this world. Everyone, even Carlo, must recognize it, and bow his head. And suddenly a gleam of light broke through Benedetto's benighted brain, and he knew that this was the close of his first act that he had never been allowed to write down. He wanted to write it down quickly, before he forgot it — Where were his sheets of paper? Who had taken them away?

"What is it? Tell me what you want!"

With wide-open eyes, he stared at the young girl who was supporting his trembling body. He recognized her: "Mother!" he moaned, and clung fast to her.

"Still! Be quiet! You must lie down."

His rebelliousness over, she let him slowly fall back upon the pillows again.

"Leah," his lips muttered.

Then terrible pain extinguished consciousness.

II

He knew where he was again, although he did not recognize the room. He remembered everything. He remembered too much. He wished he could forget again. He had been saved by a miracle. Why had this miracle been wrought upon him? What was there left to wait for? Knaves had lain in wait for him near his home, and had felled him in cowardly fashion. He feared Gracias had known of the plot. What had he done to her to deserve that? He would ask her — if ever a day came when he could.

Thinking still tired him, nor were his thoughts encouraging. While he lay there safely, under Leah's loving care, he tried to think of nothing, and sometimes he was successful.

He said a few words to her, but she told him he must be quiet so that he could get well more quickly. Had he said he wanted to get well quickly?

She came back, closing the door carefully behind her, and stood watching him — he could see it through his half-closed eyelids. She stood there like life itself that had returned to him. The sun shining in the bare little courtyard cast a greenish reflection on her face.

He tried to smile at her, but the left corner of his mouth refused to obey him, and a pain shot through his whole cheek. In any case, she could not have seen the smile through the bandages on his face: it was useless to try to smile at her.

To show her how his interest was increasing, he asked, "But why am I lying in this room?"

She came nearer, and answered, because he had asked her a definite question: "We did not dare carry you up the stairs — besides, it's quieter here. If only you would keep still . . ."

He tried not to move. "How long have I been here?"

"Two days and nights. I'll tell you all about it later on. We're all so pleased you're coming through. Things looked bad with you. We had to watch by you, but now you must also . . ."

"Who watched by me?"

"Aunt and Susanna and I — and Uncle acted as surgeon. He knows more than all the barbers and doctors put together. And besides, we didn't dare summon anyone to the house so long as we were not sure . . . Fortunately nothing is broken."

Slowly Benedetto put his hand to his bandaged head. Gently but commandingly, Leah pushed it away. "Don't touch that. You had a wound in your face . . . Uncle stitched it and hopes it will not show . . . But you must do your part, and it isn't good for you to talk too much yet. Just tell me this: is there anything you'd like?"

His throat was quite dry from the few words he had uttered. But he said nothing of his thirst, afraid that Leah would go away again. She realized his need, however. "Wait a moment," she said, and disappeared. Hungrily he looked after her slim, dark figure, at her delicate, slender neck with the two plaits of hair black as night.

Benedetto's eye roamed slowly round the soberly furnished room where Leah had received her music master in the days when he sat upstairs composing. He went on staring almost lifelessly without being quite aware himself what was passing through his mind, staring at the dark, warm outline of the thickbellied lute that hung against the cool white wall. Behind a book that stood up on the little table beside his bed, he could see the ear of a candelabrum: during the night watch, the light of the candle was shaded from his eyes.

What care had been lavished upon him! And yet it might have been better if they had allowed him to bleed to death there on the side of the *canaletto* — he would have known nothing about it. Instead, he was lying here . . . Slow tears fell from his eyes.

He wiped them away: Leah must not see them.

He waited and waited: why did she stay away so long? Was someone keeping her? A gray world of sadness closed in upon him, giving him rest yet depriving him of all faith.

In a few minutes Leah was by his bed again, offering him upon a little dish an orange from which she had neatly cut the peel in four. "That will refresh you," she said.

III

Benedetto was still unable to move his left thigh: a knife had been plunged into it twice, gravely damaging a muscle. But the wound in his face that had been stitched by Graziadeo gave him the greatest trouble and pain. It extended across his cheek, and the corner of his mouth, and interfered grievously with his speaking — even more with his eating: and his appetite was returning.

Two weeks he had been lying here, and nobody in Venice knew it. Did they take him for dead? If so, Gracias must now be receiving her friends undisturbed.

When he was well again, he must get away from Venice; it did not matter where. It was safest that they should think him dead, that he should never be seen again.

Away from Venice . . . He could not quite conceive of that yet.

He preferred to imagine the face of Gracias and her friends, supposing he were to drop the knocker again and enter. Would they be afraid? They might have good reasons for being so. He would look at one and then at another, and he would know soon enough who had done this thing to him.

How foolish! To flee from Venice was desolation; and to rise up as an avenger was madness. He had lost — lost.

Now and again his thoughts dwelt on his opera. He had once been on the point of asking Leah to bring him his work; but as he was about to make the request, skepticism and discouragement came over him again. It was as though he were about to make himself ridiculous in the eyes of Gracias. It was all over with his opera. Had he really once dreamed of seeing Venice at his feet?

There had been a time when so humiliating a happening as being beaten to death in the dark by hired scoundrels could not have happened to him; he would never have fallen into such an obvious trap. He had always been accustomed to being on his guard, and had always in the past avoided any danger that threatened. Now he had run open-eyed to meet destruction: he had made up his mind to continue with his work that night. That the scum of the street lay in wait to kill him had seemed no serious impediment. And at the first treacherous blow, his strength had been broken: the presentiment of defeat lay in his limbs and paralyzed them.

He would have done better to forget all that; but against his will his tortured thoughts still took the same direction. When Leah sat beside him he was at peace, and only then. In her eyes the humiliation of his defeat counted for nothing, and for a while she could make him forget the hopelessness of his future. The whole day he looked for her longingly.

He wished she sat beside his bed in the evening so that he could fall asleep peacefully in the quiet, deep dusk; but it was in the evenings that David came to see her, and her aunt wanted her to stay in the living room.

Geronimo was not as a rule free in the evening either, and so it was Susanna to whom was delegated the task of looking after him and shaking his pillows, even though he did not ask for this service. On his bed post she hung a large, mysterious basket that held an inexhaustible supply of work. When she tired of knitting, she turned to mending. She held her work at a distance, because of her farsighted eyes. Had she thought Benedetto capable of it, she would have asked him to thread her needle. She preferred, however, to miss it a half-dozen times. She opened her mouth only in order to hold a couple of pins between her thin, bloodless lips. And he liked it better so. Now and again she threw a searching glance at the patient entrusted to her care, or at the bed in which he lay, and then she got up from her chair and tucked in his blankets where he had loosened them because they pressed on him. As she busied herself with this work of charity, in which he did not disturb her, — since it would be less trouble to loosen the blankets again later, — she bent over him sighing and groaning in her tight bodice.

Benedetto was thinking that at that moment David was sitting by the side of his betrothed in the living room, and that together they were probably talking of their coming marriage. He recalled that a few weeks ago there had been no question of such a hasty marriage. Then it had seemed to lie in the distant future. There had been an evening when Leah's eyes had rested in his, and for a while she herself had forgotten her coming marriage with the stocking-seller. Oh, that was past too. That was when he had taken her to the theater. Even though the play had been hissed, he had triumphed. And now he lay here, utterly defeated. Probably she did not even see him as a man any more.

How long must he continue to wear those accursed bandages round his head? What had those scoundrels done to his face? He could feel more or less how the cut ran, and he feared the worst when he remembered that it had been stitched as a first experiment by a jeweler interested in surgery and healing. Ah, well, any disfigurement would be better than these rags about his head that made him ridiculous — he would have torn them off if that had not seemed too ungrateful towards his saviors.

One evening he could hold out no longer. He turned to Susanna and said, "Bring me a mirror!"

He might just as well have addressed this request to the workbag hanging at the bedpost. It was only when he repeated his request with rapidly rising anger that Susanna looked up, annoyed and distrustful, and asked, "A mirror? What do you want that for?"

He felt no desire to enlighten her. As she appeared disinclined to defer to his wish, he shouted, without however any hope of being heard, "Geronimo!" Instead of allowing his cry to fall quietly upon the desert air, Susanna herself grew angry. "What do you want with Geronimo here? Am I not here?"

"Geronimo!" he called with all his strength.

Whereupon she got up angrily, pushed her mending into the bag with trembling hands, and, muttering to herself, disappeared, to return a moment later, shuffling and stamping her feet, with a broken, disfigured little mirror.

Benedetto took it from her and sat up to see himself in it.

He stared into the small, somewhat distorted glass. Was that he? He looked like a dying man, so pale and thin. It was his eyes that had changed the most. There was no glow left in them. They looked at him, grave and desperate, like those of a stranger. With an uncertain hand, in spite of Susanna's protest, he tore away the bandage from his cheek and chin. Across the dark hairy skin ran a revolting red scar a hand's breadth long, disfiguring the left side of his mouth.

Then he felt Susanna's glance on him. In that glance was anger, dislike, and at the same time something vaguely like pity. It was this pity that affected him most and made him realize the completeness of his defeat. He pulled the bandage over the half-healed wound, handed the mirror back to Susanna without a word, and, more listless than before, sank into the pillows and closed his eyes.

IV

Old Graziadeo came to look at him, examined his leg, upon which he still could not stand, and removed the bandage from his face. According to Graziadeo, the cut across his cheek had healed magnificently. No surgeon in the city could have improved upon the stitching. So satisfied was the old man with the clean closing of the skin and the mending of the muscles under it that he had no eye for the changed, fixed expression of that side of Benedetto's face. He congratulated his patient (and therefore himself), and Benedetto thanked him, thanked him too for saving him. That nocturnal rescue had so far involved no unpleasant consequences for the rescuer, and the old Jew had almost forgotten it. But he thought he did deserve a word of thanks for the successful healing of the wound. Benedetto asked whether Geronimo could not come and shave him.

"Why not?" answered Graziadeo, and a modest pride rang through his voice. "He will be careful enough."

And so it was that Geronimo came and did the work with the most meticulous care. "When that patch still had to be stitched, I shaved you — but then it wasn't so easy," he said, and as he lovingly admired the effects of his master's stitching. It occurred to Benedetto that this scar had increased Geronimo's esteem for him.

Later on, Leah looked at him shyly. He tried to read in her face whether his appearance filled her with aversion — but no, he read only retrospective fear in her eyes at the way he had been knocked about. "Perhaps it may disappear altogether," she said, to console him. But the scar did not matter so long as Leah did not avert her eyes from him. He would keep his scar — those who had made it might see it and have a care for themselves.

As his strength returned, his gloom increased. In the evenings, when he was alone or when old Susanna kept him company, he nursed his bitterness and feelings of revenge.

But Leah's presence softened him again. She had only to come into the room, and already things seemed brighter to him. On one occasion he got her to hand him the lute that had hung all this while unused upon the wall, and he played to her. It was a cunningly contrived instrument. He had only to put his ear to it to discover how excellent was the sound that lay hidden in it, to know that he would part from it reluctantly. He asked Leah to sing something to him; he would accompany her. She said she could not sing, at least not sufficiently well for his hearing; but by his persistence he persuaded her, and she sang one or two French ditties she had practised with Maestro Bontempelli, and then a Venetian air. Her voice, still insufficiently trained, had a fine lower register. Besides, she was singing now — she admitted it quietly herself — as she had never sung before: he supported her so wonderfully with his playing of the lute. He led her, inspired her, increased her self-confidence. She thought that if she were to devote a lifetime's study to it, she could never play upon this lute as he could, after having had it in his hands but a few seconds; and yet in the vainest corner of her heart she did not think herself ungifted. Maestro Bontempelli had assured her too often and too fervently . . .

Behind the door stood Signora Graziadeo, listening. She did not know whether she ought to be annoyed at their playing together or proud of her husband's young niece, who seemed to have a fine voice, and had not therefore taken all those expensive lessons for nothing except form. If only David had been there, Aunt Rachel would have had a better idea what attitude she ought to strike. In any event, David must hear this once also, and her husband too — he happened not to be in the house at that moment. Suddenly afraid of being caught now that the singing and playing within had stopped, she moved away with a swaying motion of her heavy body.

In the kitchen down below old Susanna interrupted her cooking and stared upwards. If Signorina Leah had begun to sing with that fellow who had been brought in half-dead, and who no doubt was not without blame for finding himself in the company of such nocturnal riffraff — yes, then Susanna did not know what attitude to take. All this time she had been in doubt as to how to treat him — whether as an uninvited guest received out of Jewish charity or as an old friend of the house. Her master himself made it difficult for her. She trusted Benedetto less and less as he moved towards recovery. This playing together was a new milepost in the healing process, and for Susanna an indication that she must sharpen her watchfulness. From that afternoon, she began to show an inclination to look after the patient unasked in her spare time. It was with reluctance that she got up when duty called her back to the kitchen.

Benedetto and Leah often felt themselves hampered in conversation, and this playing together was a relief to them. Sometimes old Susanna herself was not sure whether she had been driven upstairs only by the watchfulness she had imposed upon herself as a duty, or whether from a desire to hear a pretty piece of music and to take a nap over her mending. Leah increased her doubts by singing old Hebrew songs in her deep, tender voice; Benedetto found exactly the right, sober accompaniment for them. Old Susanna, who had dared to suspect something sinful behind this being together, began to think she was the sinner, and suddenly she felt reassured again. But later, when the music had died, her obstinate, sinful distrust reawakened.

Benedetto no longer needed watching in the evenings. He was often alone, and then he picked up the lute and played to himself, to distract his thoughts. But he missed Leah's voice. Foolish, bitter words came to his tongue when he thought of David, who was now exercising his right to her company, regaling her probably with stories of his clients, — what else had he to talk about? — and waiting for the moment when Aunt Rachel's back was turned in order to steal a hasty kiss from his betrothed. Leah! It occurred to Benedetto that she also was a fine, dark instrument on which not everyone could play. He would have liked to wound her, in order to hear, once, the very deepest note at her command.

Actually the whole house had within it a deep, hidden sound that one came to know only after a time. It seemed lost in stillness and loneliness. In the living quarters of the house, Graziadeo always wore felt slippers. Leah, as if afraid lest she should make any noise, went about in velvet Oriental mules. Her aunt made no sound at all: she preferred to remain in the living room. The only noises he heard were Susanna's movements and the rattling of her pans, and the firm ingenuous tread of Geronimo, the Christian orphan, who, despite his faithfulness and devotion, struck an outlandish note in the quiet, colorful, peculiar harmony of this Jewish household.

Nobody from the city came about the house. Graziadeo must have thought the young unknown cavaliere who had dropped one night from the blue to offer valuable jewelry for sale an object of great curiosity, to have hit upon the idea of showing him to his wife and daughter. Not one even of the regular customers had access to the sacred living room. Graziadeo led them through the long passage towards the back of the house where his storeroom was and where Geronimo kept watch while he did this or that useful thing.

Rabbi Isidore, thin and stately, sometimes came to visit them. Then Signora Graziadeo herself cooked, standing before the fire with flushed face. Susanna went about out of humor, her honor thus impugned; but as she was often out of humor, no one noticed; and when the august guest arrived, her old face beamed all the same with the glow of respectful joy. Her master behaved himself towards this exalted guest upon a footing of complete equality — he might well have become a rabbi himself. There was much of the rabbi in his whole appearance, and in his quiet wisdom; but instead of reading the Talmud, alas, he poked his nose halfway through the night into books of worldly wisdom which, instead of being in Hebrew, were usually written in French.

Apart from Rabbi Isidore's rare visits, there was the regular weekly visit of shy little Maestro Bontempelli, who, scattering endless compliments about him, appeared every Wednesday at five o'clock precisely to initiate Signorina Leah into the mysteries of music.

He was amazed at the rapidity with which she had recently learned by heart the pieces he gave her to study.

Leaning back on his pillows, Benedetto listened to the singsong prayer that introduced the evening meal in the living room, which was situated slantwise on the other side of the passage. On ordinary Sabbath evenings, Graziadeo was in the habit of saying the prayers, but on this occasion the cantor of the Spanish synagogue was a guest, and there seemed to be no end to the melancholy singsong hum of his voice. Beside the modulated voice of the cantor, which was growing more ecstatic every moment, he could also hear Graziadeo himself, the monotonous, dreary noise that came from David, and occasionally also Leah's voice — crystal clear, firm, and grave.

That evening Geronimo came to keep him company — he was free, because his master was doing no business. Geronimo thought the cantor insufferable, and had therefore fled from the living room to Benedetto. He brought his basketwork with him: it was one of the few things he had learned to do in the orphanage, and he was weaving a more habitable cage for Leah's pompously named finch, Signor Bomboni. As he worked, Geronimo talked upon his pet subject, the haughtiness of Christians towards the Jews they so misjudged.

"Former acquaintances of mine turn away and spit upon the ground when they see me, and yet they too only come from the orphanage just like me. 'There goes the Jew-servant,' they cry out. Jealous, that's what they are, because they see for themselves what a good place I have. I only laugh at them, and let them see it too. I don't know, Cavaliere, what you used to think about the Jews, but now that a Jew has saved your life . . . I assure you, of ten Christians (at least as they are in Venice) nine would have let you lie where you were because they would rather not burn their fingers. But my master, without even knowing who you were, told the gondolier to draw up. Only by the light of the lantern did we recognize you. And Christ in heaven! What you did look like! Happily you were still breathing. My master told me to carry you to the gondola, and then home, boys . . . I'd rather not think what we should have done if, after all, you'd died in the end; but my master saw to it that it didn't get to that length. If I should ever get into a similar mess, it would be my pride to be pieced together again by him, and by nobody else."

Benedetto listened to him with pleasure. Later, when he was alone and the whole household was asleep — except Graziadeo who, after a long and profound religious discussion with the cantor, was fingering the Talmud by way of relaxation — he still lay awake thinking that he also felt strangely at home in this Jewish house, just like Geronimo, and that he was tempted to put the world beyond almost completely out of his mind.

V

He knew that the moment would come when he must again have dealings with the world outside this room, outside this house; but he tried to close his eyes to the fact. He no longer gave much thought to the wound in his face — it gave him little pain, and nobody in the house paid any attention to it. With the help of a stick, he could take a few steps in the room, and Leah came to admire his first efforts.

She still refrained from asking him any details concerning what had happened to him; nor did she inquire whether he had any definite suspicions. Nobody in the house asked about it. And after all, it concerned only himself. At first it had occupied his own mind, and ever and again the picture flashed across his brain of Cavaliere Maniscù looking round at him, startled, and hastily replacing his fallen mask — Maniscù, who had that last evening paid Gracias a short visit and then, before his arrival, gone off in Silvio's gondola. Silvio also, that dangerous giant, came to his mind; but so long as he was here, he need not bother to think of either of them. They were for him the almost incredible figures of a feverish dream in which he must have lived and from which he was only now slowly awakening.

Or was he rather surrendering to a dangerous dream now?

David, who had not once been to visit him, was, like the world itself, becoming a distant shadow, inspiring him from day to day with less interest. Leah spent her evenings with this shadow, but Benedetto no longer strained his imagination to conjure up their companionship before his tortured eyes. The evenings were of no account — she sat by his bed for hours on end during the day.

Guided by her intuition, she herself contributed towards making only an inoffensive shadow of David. In her conversation, she never mentioned him or their coming marriage. She herself thought less and less of this marriage. When David spoke to her about it, she considered the matter sensibly, but it did not appear to touch her. This self-deceit went so far that she sat beside Benedetto doing needlework, and to neither the one nor the other came the thought that the piece of needlework growing under her industrious fingers was perhaps destined for her trousseau. As she worked, she chatted with him, told him of her early youth, about her uncle and aunt, and about Geronimo who in the beginning had made them laugh so, and of old Susanna who in her way was no less amusing. These hours belonged entirely to him. Every disturbing element was eliminated from them.

Up to this time he had still sometimes imagined that there was in Leah a certain deliberate reserve towards him, and that she looked after him only in order to fulfil her duty of neighborly love. But if that had been so, it was no longer true. A comradeship was growing up between them, almost as if they had been brother and sister. When in a bold moment he called her "Leah" or "little one," it gave her obvious pleasure — even though she blushed, even though she refused to address him by his name. Longingly he tried to press this familiarity upon her; but when he saw that she grew more thoughtful, quieter, he gave up the attempt. Immediately she brightened up again, became even unusually bright. Only, just before Susanna was due to come upstairs, she begged him to forget for the time being that he had called her Leah and had said this and that to her.

Next day it was later than usual when she came in to him, and he was tormented with the idea that she might be angry with him. At last she appeared, and something certainly seemed to have disturbed her, made her silent and constrained. But this mood gradually passed again. She herself desired too much the return of their intimacy.

When Susanna tactlessly remained too long with them, Leah revenged herself by reading aloud passages which the self-constituted chaperone could not possibly understand. Not that she allowed herself to be driven from her post by that; but she was exasperated, and that compensated Leah richly for her reading — which, at that moment, did not greatly interest her either.

Benedetto could not help wondering, occasionally, whether Leah's coming marriage was in her mind at all. Upon one occasion, when he sounded her carefully, himself the prey to a curious agitation, she appeared to know the exact date of the wedding. But as she talked of it quietly, it seemed that this wedding was not hers at all, but concerned someone else; and it was with some amazement that Benedetto noted that the working of Leah's mind seemed at times to be even bolder than his. Silently he admired her courage. He remained awake all night brooding over what seemed to him to be the altered condition of things. He felt almost irresistibly driven to take her in his arms, to make her dream complete. But then he feared that she would wake from this dream with a shock, and that much would be spoiled between them. Thus he lived between fear and dim hope, and all his thoughts on the subject were fruitless.

VI

Upon one occasion Graziadeo came in while they were together. He inquired after the patient, and asked Benedetto whether, seeing that he would be all but well again in a week, he would care to spend the last evenings of his enforced confinement in the family circle.

Both looked up with astonishment into the acute, kindly face of the old Jew, then thanked him for his friendly suggestion and agreed to it; and Leah added hastily, as if foreseeing awkward pauses in the evening conversation, "Then the Cavaliere will bring his lute with him, and we shall make music for you."

And so it happened that that evening Benedetto joined the family table. It was a patriarchal family meal, which old Susanna and Geronimo shared.

Leah was excited and ill at ease. Her aunt made no attempt to hide her hostile feelings towards her guest, although Solomon had begged her beforehand to restrain them for this once. Benedetto talked in lively fashion, and paid endless attention to Aunt Rachel, who sat at his right. He held the heavy meat dish for her, and poured out her wine. But the elderly woman accepted these friendly attentions clumsily, uncivilly, struggling with embarrassment and with her increasing dislike for the Cavaliere, whose *goy* courtliness she did not trust.

Fortunately Uncle Solomon was an attentive host. He kept the conversation going, and seemed to be in excellent spirits. The ingenuous Geronimo occasionally laughed out loud when his whole attention was not concentrated on the impressive helpings placed before him. Old Susanna, at Aunt Rachel's other side, did not raise her head from her plate.

How Leah would have liked to see Benedetto at their table in the intimate atmosphere that usually prevailed! This evening her uncle had not prayed before the meal, lest he should embarrass his guest. Her aunt and old Susanna took that in bad part, and felt they were being defrauded of their rights by the presence of this Christian; but Leah also would have preferred it if her uncle had prayed as usual. It was as though they did not like to show themselves before the Cavaliere as they really were. Leah liked Uncle Solomon's voice and the way he uttered the fine old prayers. She much preferred his way of saying them to that of Rabbi Isidore. She even preferred it to the ecstatic way of the cantor, for whom her aunt had the profoundest admiration. When Uncle Solomon said the mealtime prayers, he seemed to love them for their simple wisdom, their comely poetical form: that was how she was accustomed to hearing them; and she would have liked Benedetto also to hear them from his mouth, even though he could not understand Hebrew. At least, then, he would have seen how they began their evening meal. It struck her as a little crude to start upon the food at once when there was a guest sitting with them. She did not enjoy it either this evening, although her aunt and Susanna had done their best in honor of the stranger, the *goy*, the enemy who could now see how guests were received in this house.

Leah brightened up at an idea that gave her the bitter-sweet feeling one experiences when carrying out a noble revenge. Uncle had not prayed: but she knew what songs she would sing later on with the Cavaliere. She would show them all that it was not necessary to omit the mealtime prayers for the sake of this guest. She wanted to show them that a Christian was capable of feeling the beauty of the old Jewish poetry, and that the rigid hostility of her aunt was a prejudice, an injustice. . . .

After the meal, Geronimo retired to the back of the house, where his basketwork was waiting for him, and David knocked at the front door.

It was the first time he had seen Benedetto since the attack on him, and he stared at him doubtfully, stared at the scar that disfigured his face. David had a Jewish dislike for brawls that resulted in such wounds. If a man got knocked about in such a frightful, such a revolting accident (he had heard the particulars from Leah), then he were better dead instead of returning to life patched-up. Had anything like that happened to

David, which God forbid, he would have called so loudly for help that the scoundrels would have cut off his head — dead and finished with.

But the Cavaliere was alive. He was a Christian, and a half-dozen stabs with a knife were but a small matter to him which after a while he forgot. He was on his feet once more, ready no doubt to resort to fisticuffs again. And this evening he was playing the lute, and Leah, David's Leah, was singing to it, the Kol Nidre.

David sat stiff as a poker, listening. He felt an irresistible desire to turn upon his chair, to put his fingers in his ears, and to ask Solomon Graziadeo and his wife Rachel whether this was supposed to be fine; but he did not ask that, neither did he stick his fingers in his ears. He was afraid of the Cavaliere. Of course he was afraid of a Christian with a scar across his cheek and mouth as long as his hand; one who, moreover, played the lute and made no reference to his awful adventure instead of telling it over and over again a hundred times. Yes, David was afraid of this Christian, but he also wanted to make him aware of his dignity, of his unassailable dignity as the betrothed, the future bridegroom of the Jewish maid who was rendering the old Hebrew songs with a voice that heaven had given her, and that had been perfected at great expense by a music master — a voice such as David hoped to hear again on the day he was summoned before God's throne by the blaring trumpets and had to take leave of this earthly vale of tears.

Aunt Rachel watched David anxiously as he sat there, pale and formal and stiff with self-esteem. She understood him perfectly, and was satisfied with his attitude. Thus, and not otherwise, should a respectable Jew behave when his betrothed sang old Hebrew songs to the lute accompaniment of a *goy*. She knew it, and that was why she wanted David to hear it once, and to tell Leah what he thought of it. Solomon — how could Solomon bring himself to introduce this Christian into their midst?

Rachel was always in opposition to her husband. Never could she see the wisdom of his decisions. Leah understood him better. Leah divined that Uncle Solomon had intended to defeat her and the Cavaliere by bringing them into the midst of the family group.

She saw David sitting there, waiting in silence for justice to be done him. She was about to awake from a dream in which she must have lived without being aware of it herself.

Annoyance at what she considered almost a betrayal of her pure friendship for Benedetto flared up in her. She felt that her uncle had been too severe, too cruel, to do this to her. With her proud rebellious nature, she was almost inclined to range herself openly on the side of the Cavaliere, the Christian who was being unfairly treated. But what made her weak was the doubt that came to her, as to whether Benedetto desired her to range herself on his side.

When she said she could remember no more songs, he did not help her to find others. He evaded his audience's enforced compliments by getting up and declaring that he would like to go back to his room, as he had tired himself more than he had expected. Nobody held him back, and he went with scarcely a parting word for her with whom he had made music that evening.

When he had gone, an oppressive, uncomfortable atmosphere hung about the room. Uncle Solomon, a prey to a strange feeling of guilt, retired to the back of the house. Perhaps he hoped Leah would join him there. Disturbed and annoyed, his wife looked after him. She had a feeling that he was taking flight, abandoning her to David's wrath.

Leah did not join her uncle, but at that moment she recalled the words he had once spoken to her — was it only a few weeks ago? Had the Cavaliere remembered this evening that he was a Christian, and that his friends and acquaintances were Christians? But no reproach could be made to him for that. Not he himself, but the others here in the house had reminded him, tactlessly, of that. Was he thinking perhaps that she had wanted this? That she had been in the plot, when her uncle had come to him with an invitation, apparently so ingenuous, to spend his last few evenings at home in their midst? She had been happy over the invitation. Had he remembered that as he left the room with scarcely a word for her?

Leah wanted to revenge herself upon David by eluding his parting kiss, which had in any case become very perfunctory during these last weeks. This was made easy by her aunt who, after a short hesitation, followed her fugitive husband, not knowing herself quite whether she was going to find him in order to reproach him, or whether she wanted to let the young people settle their difficulties by themselves. And so they were left alone under the supervision of old Susanna, who, half-blind and half-deaf, was engrossed in her mending.

Her aunt had barely left the room when Leah said to David, who sat looking foolishly and drearily in front of him, that she also was tired, and wanted to go to bed; but he seemed not to hear her. When she left him without further words, he continued to sit stiffly on his chair, and as Leah closed the door behind her and went to her room, she wondered uncomfortably whether he himself had not wanted to give her a parting kiss this evening; and if that were so, had he intended to refrain from delicacy, because he felt she did not wish it, or did he think he could play the judge towards her and punish her by his coolness?

This last possibility roused a storm of anger and indignation in her, and when the storm was over she was left only with tears. She cried all night, even in her sleep that did not come to her till daybreak.

VII

Benedetto continued to treat her distantly. In the evenings he said he was tired and preferred to remain in his room. One evening, Leah made bold to defy her aunt's wrath, and went to keep him company. Her aunt could tell David what she liked; Leah was indifferent. And so Signora Graziadeo explained to her nephew that his betrothed was feeling unwell and had gone to her room. Silently, full of self-control, he listened, and went away at once, before Aunt Rachel had time to press him to her ample bosom, and sobbingly confess the truth to him. Leah, on her side, hoped that Benedetto would pour out his heart to her, and complain about the way he was treated by her aunt and David; but he seemed to have no desire to talk about that. Discouraged, she fell silent too. Brooding somberly, he stared in front of him, and she guessed that his fixed, grave look was directed towards the day when he would go outside the house. What could be waiting for him when he showed himself again to Venice?

Leah felt compelled to look at him. He had from the very first arrested her fascinated gaze, but he seemed to her to have changed. Had the mutilation of his left cheek altered him? She had scarcely noticed it before; but suddenly she recollected the mysterious, triumphant little smile that often used to play about his mouth — it seemed to be gone for good. She could not even imagine it upon that cruelly mutilated mouth.

He was friendly to her, but kept a distance between them that had once seemed to be bridged over. She felt he would have preferred to be alone with his thoughts.

Once he asked her for the written sheets of music that must still be lying in his trunk upstairs. He had been on his feet all day, but climbing the stairs still gave him pain and difficulty. Moved to hopefulness, she brought him what he asked for. Then, in the sudden fear that he might tear everything up, she hesitated to go away and looked about the room for something to do. He did not even notice her. He read through his music as he sat at the table, and muttered to himself. Then he paced up and down the room, noticed her, stood still in front of her, and said, "I have been here longer than I ought to have been."

There was in his eyes a strange, hungry, desperate fire.

"Wait at least another day or two before you go among people," she said, and then suddenly could not refrain from putting a question inspired by premonition. "Are you sure something won't happen to you again?"

He laughed, but it was a laugh that only increased her fear and anxiety for him.

Why did he not speak to her? Again she felt that loneliness about him, the menace of fate above his head. She would have liked to implore him to tell her everything. Were he to do this, were he to make her his confidante at this moment and allow her to help him, to think of him — then perhaps she could reconcile herself to the great and final change that would come over her life next spring through her marriage with David.

But he did not speak. He did not give her a look. He turned hastily from her, and she struggled with the tears that sprang into her eyes from sheer nervousness.

Next afternoon, he came unexpectedly to the rear of the house, where at that moment she was talking to her uncle, and said to his host, without looking at her, that he wanted to go up the street a little, just to find out whether he was fit enough to do so.

COMPENSATION

I

CONCEALING THE UNCERTAINTY OF HIS FOOTSTEPS, Benedetto sauntered under the arcades of the Piazza San Marco, then crossed over towards the Piazzetta and the Molo. He was masked, and had gathered his cloak about him — it was cooler since he had last been out. Thus, in the twilight, nobody would recognize him.

He looked at Venice. It was as though he had returned from a distant journey in a strange land, and must find his way again in this city.

Slowly he shook his head as he strolled along the dark Riva when a gondolier insistently demanded his custom or when some idler clutched hold of him — him, the stranger — to take him to the Ridotto.

He had been observing the women, who had attended vespers in San Marco's, and were now streaming out accompanied by their cavaliers, hurrying towards their gondolas, or towards one of the cafés where they intended to eat while they waited for the hour when the theaters would open. He had looked at their dresses, and had tried to divine their features behind their masks: this much was certain, Gracias was not among them. He would have recognized her, if by nothing else by the host of cavaliers with whom she always surrounded herself. And if she had been there, what would he have done? He would have sunk deeper into his cloak to escape recognition. He wanted nothing more to do with her. If she thought he had been murdered, so much the better. He had merely been curious to see if she was still amusing herself as pleasantly as ever. He wondered whom she had about her, who had triumphed with her once he was out of the way. Several of the cavaliers he had met at her house passed him, walking arm in arm in high spirits. They did not notice him until they were right upon him. He looked at them intently, and even then they did not recognize him. They did look round, but it never crossed their minds that it could be he. They laughed among themselves as they went on. He had been lucky again.

He wandered along the Riva until he reached a part where few people walked. Then he noticed that he had gone on without thinking, and retraced his footsteps. He had overtired himself, however; so he rested awhile outside an *osteria*, asking the innkeeper for his best wine. He raised his mask a trifle to drink. He stared, lost in thought, at the multitude streaming by, groping every now and again for a copper coin to throw to a persistent beggar. Orientals of all kinds passed by, seafaring folk, some of them singing as they swayed drunkenly along by the dark waterside, or disappeared, a dozen of them together, into the *osteria* — casting bewildered glances at the lonely mask outside.

Away from Venice . . . ! Perhaps on board a ship. He did not know what he was doing there now. Gracias had betrayed him. And what foolish dreams he had woven round Leah, who belonged to another man, even to another world! If he were to remain here, one last woman friend would be his: a faithful friend would appear once more about him — the shade of old Signora Galli. Perhaps he would chance upon her again, when in a moment he crossed the Ponte della Paglia near the prison, which she appeared to have chosen as her haunt.

Away from Venice, no matter where . . . ! But before going, he wanted to see Gracias just once more, to convince himself with his own eyes that she was amusing herself well, and to discover with whom in particular she found her pleasure now: that interested him still.

How long had he been sitting there? On the wharves, work had already stopped. The proprietors of the little popular shops had taken their stalls inside, and were bolting the wooden shutters over their windows. They were all about to sit down to their evening meal.

Benedetto emptied his glass slowly, as it grew more deserted about him. Suddenly it crossed his mind that there had once been an evening when a song had echoed over the canals, the proud rollicking song of "Love's Ferry." Or had he only dreamed that? He could scarcely believe it, now. This Venice about him appeared to him so mute, so still and sad. Was it because the winter was coming? Or was it the winter within himself?

It was too cold to sit outside any longer. The *Borina*, the chill wind from the snowy mountain tops, was blowing across the water. He shivered under his cloak and got up. Moving his feet with difficulty, sometimes lurching too near the waterside in spite of himself (could he no longer carry two glasses of wine, or was it the fresh air and his fatigue that were making him drunk?), he returned to the center of the city.

Out of the shadow of the arcades, near the Ponte della Paglia, an apparition did loom up; but it was not old deceased Signora Galli: it was Rossi, the theatrical manager, hastening to the gondola landing-stage. He stopped abruptly and stared at Benedetto.

"Bussoni? Is it Bussoni I see?"

Finding himself discovered, Benedetto silently met Rossi's eyes. Rossi could hardly control his emotion.

"But it isn't possible! They told me . . ."

"What did they tell you?"

"All Venice thinks you're dead."

Benedetto uttered a grim laugh, and could not refrain from saying, "They may notice their mistake yet!"

"God be praised, man! Come and have something to eat with me. You can pay for my gondola too, for I haven't a soldo. Bad times, my boy."

He seized Benedetto and dragged him along. But Benedetto pushed his arm away and asked, "Where are you going to eat?"

"Somewhere where nobody will see us," said Rossi reassuringly, understanding instantly what was in Benedetto's mind. He was enthusiastic over the sensation he already pictured. "That's fine. Everybody must think you're dead. Not a word will cross my lips. That I can swear. You'll work in secret . . . How far have you got? Then you'll hand over your opera to me — and then I shall say that it's by Mr. So-and-So from Abracadabra behind Messina. I'll tell the same to my actors, because you can't expect an actor to keep his mouth shut, and of my actresses I prefer to say nothing at all. And on the first night I shall appear before the footlights and tell the audience that the celebrated composer has just arrived, and then I shall drag you forward. . . . I tell you, the tears will pour down the cheeks of both of us, so great will be the applause!"

Hesitating, bewildered, Benedetto listened to him. He could not bring himself to smile. They stepped into a gondola together. Rossi gave his address to the *barcaiuolo*. As they moved off, he told Benedetto with a sigh that on Saturday the abbé's new play "A Woman without a Heart," was coming on. It was hopeless. He did not know how they were going to get a laugh out of the audience — the author had done nothing to that end, and this time there were no canzonettas either, to save the play from certain failure. Rossi had accepted it because he had nothing better, and also because everyone had pressed it on him, blinded by the undeserved success of the previous play. His creditors had agreed to give him further credit, because they expected a sensation, and therefore a good box office. The ecclesiastical authority had agreed for the time being to pass the text with heavy cuts, but once it came on the boards, it was bound to create an uproar. That did not matter to him, but if a definite prohibition followed, that would be the end of the fun. But in any case . . . Was that the sort of success an artist strove after? What did a real actor want? He wanted to act, to believe in what he was acting. But what sort of playwrights were these? Rossi was growing excited, and his agitation did not fall upon deaf ears. Once more, though feebly and under moral compulsion, faith in his opera welled up in Benedetto. If Rossi still had confidence in him — if he could finish his work, unknown perhaps and undisturbed, even though he would have to forgo the first-night sensation Rossi had in mind . . . He was not a playwright, but parts that could be made to live — these could be created in music, too; and Rossi, after all, was not expecting more from him.

Dizzy, Benedetto followed him into his house. They had to climb many flights of stairs, each more winding than the last, and then they arrived. The door was open. In the small kitchen behind the room Rossi inhabited, a little girl of about twelve years old with unshod feet was busy cooking. The master of the house poked his head round the corner and inquired whether the macaroni was done.

"*Sissignore.*"

"Good; serve it up then."

He fetched the wine himself, took two bethumbed glasses and poured in the grand manner while he inquired how far Benedetto had got with his opera. "You've done the overture and almost finished the first act? That's fine. Go on writing. It'll come right. I tell you it'll come right. I'll have it performed blindly. I can see with one eye what a man's worth. I shan't mind engaging good principals, whatever the cost. Giaconda, my lovely flower, what's happened to the macaroni?"

His spirits rose when he saw the large dish the little maid brought in. Her face was soiled with soot, her hair bedraggled. Strumming upon the table with knife and fork, Rossi instructed her: "First the guest, Giaconda. I have to tell you that every time, and I see you haven't got your slippers on again. You'll catch cold, and I shall have to stand cooking in the kitchen for both of us. First the guest, then your master, and what remains over you can have yourself or take home to your family. I don't think much'll be left over to-day. Help yourself, Bussoni. Help yourself well, my boy! There's no occasion to hold back. Here, drink! Now tell me, have you got a room somewhere where you can work quietly unseen? Otherwise come and work in my room. I'm away all day, and my little cook will look after you so well, you won't want to go away again. I'll have to show you the door forcibly when I've got your opera in my hands!"

He was famished, and in the twinkling of an eye had devoured the mountain of macaroni that stood piled up before him. Then he made short shrift of what Benedetto, whose appetite was poor, had left upon his plate. "You're lucky, Giaconda! My guest isn't eating. More than half the onions will remain. It'll be a gala day in your home."

A moment later, without thinking, he helped himself to the remainder of the onions, but then he remembered and put back a few. He looked at his watch and jumped up from his chair. In half an hour, he must be at the theater, and he still had to change. While he was preparing to do that, in the middle of the room, Giaconda hurried backwards and forwards collecting his evening clothes. As he stood before the small broken mirror in his underclothes, hurriedly arranging his jabot, he said to the little maid who stood just behind him holding out his breeches in the expectation that he would step into them, "As for your wages, child, you can tell your mother that that'll come right. Tell your mother we're about to do our new play on Sunday — a week earlier than first agreed upon. Say the same thing to the tradespeople to-morrow morning. Tell them we're going to make it the success of the season. They'll all see their money on Sunday, and of course you can also promise them free seats for the first performance. Free seats always. You'll get a free seat too, and then you'll see your master different from what he is at home. Now my breeches. Did anybody call to-day? Remember, you mustn't let in a living soul, even though they were to show you sealed orders from the Doge! Tell them you can't read — you'll only be speaking the truth. As we came up, the door was wide open. Anybody could have entered and robbed us of everything, yourself included. Even though there's no silver and gold lying about here, there are precious documents in the cupboard, that from my point of view . . . Precious documents! Tell that also to the tradespeople. Tell them I've confided that to you, but that nobody must know about it. My coat! Where is my coat? Yes, I can see it's hanging there, but you ought to have had it ready for me. Valuable documents . . . It's high time, Bussoni. We must go. The audience is already sitting waiting in my theater. At least, if anybody turns up this evening . . ."

As he was leaving, he discovered Giaconda's slippers behind the door and between thumb and index finger carried them to the kitchen, this time with strict orders that they were to be put on at once.

When they were in the street, the nearer they came to his theater the more his haste seemed to diminish. He walked in more stately fashion, with growing self-sufficiency. "I don't want people to get the impression that I'm rushing to the theater to be told how big the receipts are to-day," he declared. "Here we are! Here we part company. We might be noticed if we were together, and then our whole plan would be upset. That's right, isn't it? I can count upon it . . . ?"

There was now something more faltering in his voice, but he tried to make that right again by saying: "When shall I see you again, to hear how far you've got in the meantime? And by the way, you haven't told me yet what actually happened to you. I thought I noticed something on your cheek — What, are they standing there again? The moneychangers in the Temple . . ."

Wrathfully, he bore down upon a half-dozen fellows who were waiting for him at the entrance, and with wild gesticulations shouldered his way through his creditors. "Is this necessary, gentlemen? When every minute is precious to me? The audience mustn't be kept waiting any longer. Good! and suppose there are only seven? Even if there were only one, our duty towards the one would be the same. I must request you to have patience till after the performance. Meanwhile, you can take your seats."

The pitiable absurdity of this exhibition did not kill Benedetto's reawakened illusions. On the contrary, the poverty and the humiliating worries of Rossi and his company acted as a spur to him to resume his work. For the sake of one canzonetta, half Venice had already poured into this dark little theater. Only the badness of the play itself had prevented the success from being lasting.

He felt grateful towards the theater manager who had provided him with a meal and spoken to him warmly. On the Piazzetta, he would take a gondola and have himself rowed home, and then to-morrow, refreshed after a good sleep, he would muster all his strength again and . . .

Was it a sudden feeling of physical exhaustion or one of deep inner weakness that made him, as he crossed the Piazza, enter San Marco's by an open side door? He hoped to find peace there — peace was the one thing he still lacked, in order to be able to go on with his music. He dropped on his knees before a side altar, and, his head buried in his arms, tried to find himself again.

Was there any music left in him? Oh, yes, as he rested there in the quietness of the deserted church, melody softly stirred again within him. But as emotion caught at his throat, he felt that there was no longer any connection between this music and his unfinished opera. The motif of his opera, which had filled him with such rejoicing, had become strangely indifferent to him. His imagination refused to be engrossed by it. Did that mean that he must look for some new motif?

The dusk of the magnificent Byzantine cathedral lay about him. Speaking and laughing in whispers, some church officials passed him, carrying silver candelabra towards the sacristy: a body had been lying in state. Benedetto stared after them in dull despair. A little later an old beggarwoman shuffled into the church and lit a candle at the side altar, near which Benedetto was sitting; and when suddenly out of the dark a friendly little Madonna smiled at him, he thought of the Virgin in the little church of Saint Clare at Todi where his mother had taken him as a child. He could scarcely master his tears. He only recovered when the beggar mumbled for alms. He gave her something, and went out.

He would go home, lie down and sleep. Perhaps Leah was growing concerned about his remaining away so long. Was that true? Would she really . . . ? David was with her at this moment.

He went to the Molo, intending to call a gondola, but as he peered across the water his attention was arrested by something: a gondola drifted past him very close, in it a man stretched out complacently, his seemingly endless legs extended along the sides. Over his ugly Beelzebub face, which Benedetto could see in sharp profile, there lay an expression that appeared to the silent onlooker on the quay to be one of devilish satisfaction, though that he might have imagined. . . .

Benedetto entered the gondola that pulled in for him, and with a gesture of the head indicated to the *barcaiuolo* that he should follow the gondola that had just glided by. The fellow understood him at once.

He wanted to see where Maniscù was going. He wanted to keep his eye on that thin Satanic silhouette for a while, in order to be able to pour out all his hate towards him — his hate, of the depth of which he was only now conscious; and he wanted to confront his enemy face to face, to see how he would bear himself . . . He no longer considered whether that was wise.

Maniscù had no idea yet that he was being followed. Pretentiously, as if he were a thinker, from time to time he ran his long, slender hand over his forehead, looking up at the houses on either side as they glided by.

His *barcaiuolo* did not begin to feel suspicious until, following first the short busy inner way towards the Rialto Bridge, he turned right towards the Rio dei Santi Apostoli and still saw the same gondola behind him — the gondola of his uncle, Gaetano. Gondoliers met each other too often to bother about greetings, but this time he did send a greeting to the *barcaiuolo* behind him which was also a question in the secret language of the gondoliers. Behind Benedetto's back the secret question was invisibly answered.

Benedetto knew where Maniscù was going, and he gave instructions to his *barcaiuolo* to turn left before the Rio Gesuiti, and to see to it that they should reach Number 7 of the Rio di San Felice at the same time as the other gondola, which had taken the shortest way, through the Rio di Santa Catarina. He promised an extra tip. His *barcaiuolo* nodded in silence. The gondola swerved and shot viciously into the narrow, dark canal.

The other, however, was too far in advance, and was already putting in to the steps of Gracias' house when Benedetto's *barcaiuolo*, eager to earn his lire, came grazing round the corner. Maniscù got out and paid, then looked up involuntarily to see who was in such a hurry to visit Gracias and lose money to him.

He did not recognize Benedetto until they stood facing one another on the steps. Behind his mask, it was impossible to see the expression on the cardsharper's face; but his behavior was sufficiently eloquent. He shrank back and uttered a stifled cry. He made an uncertain, grabbing movement at the *ferro* of Benedetto's gondola, as it was about to glide away from the steps — and, thanks to the unbelievable length of his arm, he just caught it. He drew the gondola to him, not even noticing that he had put one foot into the cold, turbid water. "Careful, signore," the gondolier warned him, as he eagerly backed and, for the sake of a new fare, contrived to conceal the hidden mockery in his voice.

Maniscù, to his own surprise, found himself sitting in a gondola again; but now he was not lounging back luxuriously as he had done before. Neither did he pass his hand over his forehead like a thinker. He sat bolt upright, his trembling hands clutching at the sides of the vessel as if he were ready, clothes and all, to jump out of it. Thus he stared up at Benedetto as at an apparition. Meanwhile, the gondolier pushed off, without pausing to inquire where his passenger wanted to go. He plunged his oar into the water and pressed against it with the whole weight of his body, as he glanced hastily behind him to see if the other signore was by any chance furnished with a pistol and had a mind to shoot.

The first gondolier, who had watched the development of events with curiosity, came up again: he was prepared to continue the pursuit, the other way round — and to engage in a life-and-death race with his own blood nephew Marco. It promised to be a thrilling race in which, according to a silent understanding between them, they would have followed hard upon each other's heels for an hour or more, so that both signori would have a long bill to pay. Yes — provided they did not attempt to shorten the distance with pistols, and shoot holes in the precious gondolas, or, almost as bad, in a brave and zealous gondolier.

For a moment the unsuspecting Benedetto was tempted to get into the other gondola: had he not let his prey escape too quickly? But then, with a perhaps exaggerated optimism, he decided that Maniscù could no longer evade him in Venice. He was now sure that Maniscù was one of those who could if they wished tell more of what happened on a certain evening. Instead of pursuing his enemy, he decided to surprise the others, before they came to hear of his resurrection indirectly.

The *barcaiuolo* Gaetano, rejected by Benedetto, slipped away again, and darkness swallowed him up. The stillness in the little canal was undisturbed, except for an obstinate knocking on the door, which opened after a time. A yapping dog emerged, and in the dimly lit doorway a small, dark figure loomed up: Annibale, who, evincing greater presence of mind than Cavaliere Maniscù, tried to slam the door to again. But Benedetto slipped his foot between the door and the doorpost, hurled it open, and swept past Annibale, who cowered angrily by the stairs. With a few long strides Benedetto was up the stairs, the barking dog at his heels.

He was in Gracias' room. Those nearest to him broke off in the middle of a sentence. Those farther away, who did not immediately realize what had happened, also fell silent. Everyone stared at him and, speechless, rose to their feet. Restraining his panting breath with difficulty, he looked about him. At first he could not distinguish a single face. Then, he recognized Gracias.

She uttered a soft cry, and was about to throw herself on his breast. But he turned quickly away from her, and greeted the abbé, who stammered a few words. Benedetto paid no attention to him, but looked about him again for other familiar faces. There were no women, except Countess Bogliasco, who had been sitting next to Gracias when he entered, her arm about her. He noticed *lo Spagnuolo* — the one person upon whom his unexpected intrusion and the oppressive silence that followed it appeared to have made no impression. Indeed, *lo Spagnuolo* seemed to be altogether unconscious of Benedetto's entry: his eyes were riveted on the door leading to the adjoining room. Benedetto approached him, but the old man, quite unaware of the fact that all eyes were now on him, got up from his chair and went towards the communicating door at which Marianna had appeared, and stood as one rooted to the ground. Benedetto glanced round sharply, to see if any dared mock at him for this involuntary affront; but he saw only disturbed, fearful faces that were almost strange to him. What were they to him? They were not his murderers. Maniscù, yes. he was one of them, and he had let him escape . . .

And, just as he was turning, suddenly uncertain of himself, away from the cynical glance that *lo Spagnuolo* at last gave him, — *lo Spagnuolo*, for whom he had no interest alive or dead, — a giant loomed before him, holding a tray of drinks under his nose.

Silvio, who now apparently served in the house also, and seemed to have risen in favor — Silvio was the second.

A head taller than Benedetto, Silvio stared down at him with a roguish grin, stared with interest at the scar on Benedetto's cheek, which had turned an angry red.

Benedetto's arm stiffened convulsively in an almost uncontrollable desire to hurl the silver tray with everything on it from the coarse fellow's hands, although such theatrical manifestations were repulsive to him. With some difficulty, he recollected that he had a servant in front of him. Why had he come here? Maniscù — he need not meet anyone else, and fortune had favored him with that meeting on the steps. Instead of taking the opportunity offered him, why had he brought down the knocker just to convince himself that Gracias was enjoying herself among a group of people who were indifferent to him, who had not threatened his life — even though they had not bemoaned his death? He would have liked to slip away again unobtrusively, if that had been possible. He noticed Galuppi, sitting in a lonely corner: the painter signed to him to come and sit down on the empty chair beside him. Galuppi, an expression of misty compassion in his sad eyes, watched Benedetto as he approached with hesitating steps. Then he looked past Benedetto towards Gracias, who seemed to want to join them, but was being held back by friends who were whispering agitatedly.

"Let me go!" cried Gracias. "Why have you told me lies? Why did you tell me that he . . . ?"

Benedetto, already half-sitting in the chair, jumped up again and measured them all with his glance. Galuppi tried to draw him down; but Gracias rushed to her former lover and flung herself on his breast. A feeling of weak emotion swept over him. He could hardly refrain from throwing his arms about her protectingly. It was only with the greatest difficulty that he contrived to control himself. He pushed her away from him, and over her shoulder asked, "Who said — that I was dead?"

Nobody could or dared reply. Then suddenly the abbé was pushed forward by some of the others, who were apparently under the impression that he was most likely to be able to calm Benedetto. The unfortunate abbé looked round him helplessly, but it was too late. He could no longer evade the task that had been forced upon him, and so he stammered: "All of us here are guiltless, Bussoni! After all — you know yourself — we were with Gracias on the Lagoon when that accident happened to you. We only heard of it the following evening. I can't remember now who first reported it. I swear to you, I bemoaned your fate. . . ." He looked round in search of witnesses to this fact, but they were all staring at Benedetto. Sweat stood on the abbé's smooth forehead as his eye returned to the closed, scarred face that was regarding him with strange mockery and contempt.

"Come, Bussoni," said Galuppi, dragging at him, and this time Benedetto did not resist, but sat down with his back to the rest.

Countess Bogliasco had followed Gracias and, with an expression of grief and silent rage, waited for her to abandon her foolish attempt to soften one who had risen from the dead. Then she supported and consoled the rejected Gracias, who gave way to bitter complaints. "He will have nothing more to do with me. Why then did he come back? They lied to me . . ."

At that moment Silvio appeared before her with his silver tray, and offered her wine. She took the fortifying glass, and looked into his eyes as she emptied it at one draught.

Galuppi, afraid Benedetto might have noticed this strange relationship, pushed a glass towards him across the little table. "Drink, Bussoni!"

Benedetto drank eagerly, and Galuppi, calling Silvio, took a decanter from the tray, to the gondolier's astonishment.

Suddenly music filled the room — had Galuppi given the forgotten musicians an unobtrusive sign? As he poured wine into his own and Benedetto's glasses, he said, "It was not wise of you to come back here. You might have known she would have learned to do without you. To come back was to walk straight into the arms of your adversary. And then to turn away from her, when she wanted to throw herself round your neck . . . She will never forgive you for that, and it wasn't nice of you, either. She is innocent. As it happened, some of them had bragged, in front of her, that evening that they intended to read you a little lesson; but you should not expect her to take such chatter seriously. And, in any case, nothing came of that, either. Danger threatened you from another side — I felt it, though I was not sure. Perhaps she also felt it, and perhaps she would have said something to you about it if you had not been so ungracious to her that evening. Why didn't you stay with us, and see the sun rise above the Lagoon? It was the finest sunrise I ever saw in my life; but perhaps that was because we were just in the mood for it . . ."

Benedetto did not answer. Galuppi did not expect him to, either. He looked about him, and then after a pause continued: "And here you are, back again, and you can see for yourself how some of us are slowly going downhill. I come here only to drink, now. Do you know who is the new rising star? Countess Bogliasco! She has dismissed her little friend — the poor child has gone into a convent to save her soul, at least. And then there's this gondolier: for the last day or so, he has ruled the roost here — after he had been dismissed by *la muchacha!* And her father, the old fool, has grown more foolish still. He's been unable to withstand the spring his daughter has brought into the house. Marianna can't find a corner to hide away from him. The other old satyr — I need not mention names, you know whom I mean — has never turned up again. He must have got wind of a painting I intended to do, in which he was to figure. Incidentally, my studio hasn't seen me at all recently. Ah, well, we won't talk about that now. We're talking about you. Save yourself, if you still can, if it isn't too late. Don't show yourself here any more — there are other women in Venice. I can no longer persuade myself of that; but perhaps you can. Remember your music — your début was glorious enough."

He was speaking more slowly, because his attention was distracted by something. "Wait," he said. "Come with me to the next room."

When Benedetto got up hesitatingly, Galuppi took him by the arm and said with rising agitation, "Come along — if she wants that, you must grant her wish. Do you want to repulse her again? Then I've finished with you. She wants to speak to you; she's made me a sign."

Listlessly, Benedetto let himself be led away. She wanted to speak to him. What had she to say to him? Everything was lost — everything was lost. What had happened could no longer be put right. He ought to have gone home, and carried out his promise to Rossi. When they reached the adjoining room, Galuppi said nothing, but looked expectantly towards the communicating door. When Gracias appeared, he moved away.

She took a few steps towards Benedetto, and when he did not stir, she stood still, saying, "You think I betrayed you; but you're mistaken."

He allowed these words to sink into him, then shrugged his shoulders. Betrayed him? Was she alluding to his past? He had not given a thought to that yet. But she could do that, too — he was ready to flee from Venice, and to be upon his guard against her forever; and what did it all matter, anyhow? Nothing was as it had been before he was waylaid. Then he had had something to guard besides himself.

Why had he allowed himself to be drawn into this private conversation with her? He did not dare look at her. Her voice alone made him feel weak. He was afraid lest he might take her in his arms all the same — that he might remain on, and in her arms forget his revenge, so that those who had plotted his downfall would actually be in a position to jibe at him. Oh, she had not betrayed him. But his triumph, his liberation through his music — of that she had deprived him. His work she had killed in him when it was ready to come to birth. That was worse than betrayal.

"Look — see for yourself. I still wear your ring," she said, speaking with difficulty, and like a child showed him her small white hand. "Perhaps that was why I was silent, even when everybody told me you were dead. I don't want to make myself out better than I am. Perhaps I was only silent because I was afraid of losing the ring. Those last days, I tormented you because I was jealous — jealous of your work. I wanted to have you for myself, entirely to myself. I refused to believe, at first, when they told me you'd fallen into an ambush. I said to myself: 'That couldn't happen to him. He will come back again. Suddenly he will stand before me again, and they who are now so glad about his death will not know where to conceal themselves from him.' I dismissed Silvio, because I knew that had been your wish. Father showed him the door for me. I wanted you, when you came back, to see that I had sent Silvio away. But you did not come — weeks passed — it lasted so long — it was too much for me. Nothing must ever last too long, with me. Your opera lasted too long, also. I could see you were working at it; but I could not wait for the end."

She had never spoken to him so humbly before. He turned towards her and drew her to him — there were tears in her eyes. He wanted to say something, but he could not find his words. Everything was dull in his head.

At last he brought out, "Perhaps I shall come back to you. Now I must get away. I cannot stay. I must settle accounts with . . ."

"Maniscù did it!" she whispered hoarsely, passionately. "He came early that evening, and left again, to collect a dozen scoundrels to carry out what he hadn't the courage to do himself."

Benedetto seized her wrist with a wrench. "Confess — You knew of it!"

She defied his glance, and answered, very pale and in a trembling voice, "He did tell me, but I only laughed at him." She went on quickly, imploringly, "And I wanted to warn you. I swear it, but then you came — and immediately turned to others. Was I to shout it to you from the housetops? Maniscù — I spat in his face, and I went for him tooth and nail when he came next evening and reported that everything had gone off well, and that I should not see you again. For three days he stayed away from terror of me — and then he came back. I could not prevent it in the end — he has no shame, no sense of honor. He has been here every evening until to-night. He must have heard something. Benedetto, I will tell you — I will tell you who helped him."

"I know."

She stared at him in amazement. "You know?" she stammered; and when his words appeared to have sunk in, "You know? — and yet you tolerate him here?"

Cool and cutting, he replied, "But you have retained him in your service. One can't settle accounts with a servant as one would with an enemy. In the case of a servant, one sends for the *sbirri* or shows him the door."

"But I did do that," she sobbed. "Because he helped Maniscù, I got him put to the door. Didn't I tell you that?" She rubbed her eyes as though to awaken herself from bewilderment, to be able to see more clearly. Then a tremor swept through her whole body. "I did not want to take him back into my service, but he kept hanging round the house. Oh, he knew better than I — I have always been afraid of him — in the country on the Brenta,

Marianna was afraid of him, but so was I. I have felt him come closer, always closer; and when last Saturday he made his entry again he entered as though he were master of the house. There's no other master here now. Father has lost his head, and his sole interest is to run after Marianna, who is Silvio's slave; and the fellow wants to make me his slave, too. He already behaves as if he expects me to obey him. And a day will come when I shall obey him, too, Benedetto, my love — if you abandon me again." She shuddered; her eyes were full of tears. "I had to take him back into the house again. You must try to understand me. Because of Countess Bogliasco. Yes, for if *he* isn't here, devouring me with his terrible eyes like those of an animal, behind me all the time watching and waiting until my resistance is broken, and his day has come — then it is that frightful woman. She sends me flowers and cakes every day, and writes me letters such as I have never received from any lover, so passionate, so tender, so mad they are. And she comes to see me every evening, and kisses me before all these men, makes jealous scenes, and looks upon them all as her rivals. And I can't defend myself. I open her letters instead of tearing them up. I bury them under my pillow and read them again in the middle of the night, and forget they come from a woman — I dreamed once they were letters from you. I don't send back her flowers, but their scent poisons me. I took Silvio back into the house, because then I hoped to be safe from her — but since he is here, the beast, I seek refuge now with her from him. Only if you stay with me now, only then shall I be able to laugh in both their faces."

He was still listening to her, but her words had already eluded him. He only heard the fearful anxiety in her voice. The urge to protect her welled up in him. But then his aversion to her sinful weakness, to what was unfathomable in her nature, grew too strong. The perverted atmosphere of this house oppressed him, drove him to flight. For a moment, in striking contrast, the image of Leah, clear and pure, rose before his mind. Oh, how fruitless that was! No pure power in the world could save him now. He could not save Gracias either — if she was so weak, so vacillating. He could not forgive her for having known that evening, and for having left him to his fate.

He shook himself free from Gracias' desperate embrace, and hurried from the room; everything went red before his eyes. He went past Galuppi; he shook off the abbé, who stood in his way to assure him again that he had bemoaned his fate. Most of the others had gone — they had elected to leave the house earlier than usual, and they had not cared to disturb their hostess when they went. *Lo Spagnuolo*, Countess Bogliasco — they were still there. Silvio opened the door for him.

He called a gondolier and gave him Cavaliere Maniscù's address, though he had a presentiment that he would not be able to overtake the cheat.

The keeper of the little inn knew nothing except that the Cavaliere had departed. He had come home an hour earlier, and while his gondola waited below, had hastily packed a few necessities, leaving the rest of his luggage behind as a guarantee for his unpaid account. He had gone without mention of the day of his return. The innkeeper was none too pleased, and would have been delighted if the signore had perhaps come to exchange the trunk for the money that was owing?

No, Benedetto had no such intention. He sought the fugitive here and there, although he was convinced that by this time Maniscù had left the city. In the end Benedetto himself was not quite sure whom and what he still hoped to find that evening. He allowed himself to be taken to the Ridotto, and wandered through the various rooms; but Maniscù was not there, either. He paid the *barcaiuolo* with almost the last of his money, and, finding himself in the Ridotto, listlessly allowed some cards to be pressed into his hands. The blind Goddess of Luck was on his side. In a few minutes, he gathered a pile of gold pieces, and then he left. In some unaccountable fashion, this satisfied him — it was as though the fifty or sixty ducats he had won would give him the power to overtake Maniscù.

Outside, he walked into a masked woman who first rated him for his inattention, and then suddenly uttered a cry: she recognized his voice as he stammered an apology. It was Rosetta, and she tore the mask from his face to make sure of his identity. She noticed his exhaustion: he could scarcely stand upon his feet, and was unable to utter a sensible word. Full of commiseration, she forced him into the gondola in which she had intended to go to the public gardens for the fireworks, and dismissed the youth who was to have escorted her.

She sat close to her protégé to warm him: his teeth were chattering. He rested his head on her shoulder. She stroked it gently and, tears streaming down her face, spoke to him encouragingly with a thousand endearing words, to which he made no reply.

She paid the gondolier. It needed all her strength to help Benedetto up the narrow, dark staircase to her room. She laid him on her bed, undressed him, and covered him with the blankets. They were not thick, and it was a chilly night; but he would not feel cold: Rosetta would see to that. She threw off her light clothing, and lay down beside him. There was nothing special about that: he had been beside her before . . . Now he had returned.

She was full of love and attention. She had screened off the light of the candle, and lay motionless, resting on one arm, at his side. She could not quite believe, yet, that he was with her again, after all Venice had taken him for dead. She had swooned away like a diva, when she heard of it, and she had cried for three nights, although he had deserted her for the sake of that Spaniard, and did not deserve so many tears. A quarter of an hour, half an hour she lay motionless, until he ceased to tremble and seemed more at rest. She stared at the scar on his cheek and wondered, with indignation, who could have so ill-used him. He really did seem to have risen from the dead. There must have been a time when he had ceased to belong to the living — she could see it in his face.

When at last he opened his eyes and looked at her in silent gratitude, she could no longer contain herself and overwhelmed him with questions. It was no matter that he did not reply. She understood, and answered her own questions, and then, as he was still too exhausted to tell her what had actually happened to him, she began to tell him all that had been said about it in Venice. She pitied him for the scar on his cheek, and looked at it shyly by the candlelight: but immediately she assured him that she would no longer like him without it. It gave more gravity to his face. People would feel compassion, but at the same time admiration, for him when they saw that terrible scar. She covered it with kisses: if kisses could have healed it, after that night Graziadeo himself would have been unable to find it again.

Rosetta asserted bluntly her suspicion that the Spanish woman who lived on the Rio di San Felice had played a part in what had happened to him. But when she noticed that this subject engrossed his thoughts too much, she tried to steer clear of it again. She was annoyed with herself that she had again spoken to him about that woman, when he ought to be thinking only of her, of his little Rosetta, in whose arms he was resting safely, whose body and soul belonged to him.

Oh, he was tired. He must rest, must sleep. She would question him no more, nor trouble him. She felt she pleased him better by speaking ill of the abbé's new play, in which she had again been allotted an impossible part. The abbé must be his enemy, after having shared his success in "Traghetto d'Amore." Wasn't that in the nature of things? There had been talk of an opera Benedetto was to write. Would anything come of that? And would she have a good part? Her voice had developed recently. She was taking lessons. She waited for him to speak; but it occurred to her that he had not even understood her. Ah, well, if he preferred not to talk about his opera . . . She would remind him of it later on.

He was asleep. Like a mother, she looked down upon him. She could not sleep yet, nor did she want to. She did not dare to move, either. Her arm, on which his head was resting, would soon be numb. She listened in the night, fearful lest, as so often happened in carnival time, drunken revelers might come stumbling up the stairs and begin to bellow an air outside her door. Then there was the lame beggar who lived in the room opposite her. He was said to be as rich as Crœsus, and to conceal his money in his wooden leg — otherwise, why did it tinkle at every step? One day he would be murdered. She was terribly afraid of that. It might happen in his room, and perhaps he would come stumbling in upon her without his leg, and with his throat half-cut . . . And suppose the murderers mistook his room . . . It might happen to-night. Well, at least she was not alone. Would the light of the candle disturb his sleep? She must remember to buy another to-morrow. Usually a candle lasted her a week, because she was in the habit of dropping upon her bed dead tired, and now she wanted to burn up a whole candle in order to be able to look at Benedetto all through the night. She looked down upon his face. She thought it a handsome face, and that scar really suited him well. She had not just said that, she meant it. He struck her as being almost too precious for her. She felt that this night was a very special night, was perhaps more illusion than reality.

And yet — who could tell what he had gone through, and what difference it had made to his life? If she were patient enough, perhaps the saints would so dispose things that he would need her consolation for longer than this one night — consolation for what another had done to him, another whose name she would have done better not to utter a little while ago.

The candle went out. For a long time she gazed into the darkness of her small, wretched attic, and considered what other purchases she must make on the morrow, besides a candle, supposing her guest remained longer with her. Her greatest concern was to know where to find the money. As she tried to solve that problem, sleep overcame her too.

In the little Gothic palace on the Rio di San Felice, Gracias was at that moment sobbing out her grief in the arms of Countess Bogliasco, who whispered the harshest accusations against Benedetto into her charming little ear, and finally had to struggle against tears, too.

In desperate anxiety, the abbé clutched at the last remaining guests. "He suspects me," he wailed. "By God, truly he suspects me! And just because they made me their spokesman. It was Romano and Giulio who pushed me forward, and now they've vanished. How can I even cross the street in safety?"

"Flee from Venice for a while, until he has calmed down a little," suggested some.

"But how can I leave Venice at this moment?" cried the abbé, disconcerted by such hypocritical advice, "when my play is to be performed in three days' time? I must be present at the rehearsals, and I can't miss the first night, even if it costs me my life. Do you others know what that means, to see one's play performed for the first time, and to hear it applauded . . . ?"

When the party broke up at dawn, he insisted upon being taken home in Gracias' gondola under the protection of the giant Silvio . . .

II

Rosetta woke at dawn. Carefully, she withdrew her lifeless arm from under Benedetto's head — but in spite of her care he awoke. She whispered to him that he must go on sleeping. He could remain in bed the whole morning if he wished. At midday she would return to cook a meal for both of them, unless he had disappeared by then — in which case, she would cook for herself alone. He might also like to take a breath of air. She would leave him the key of her room. Look, she would leave it for him on the table. If he did not want to come back, he could give it to the vegetable woman downstairs.

She would tell nobody that she had met him. Instinctively, she felt that this promise of silence was welcome to Benedetto; but perhaps it merely gave her pleasure to share a secret with him that was known to no one else.

On her mules, she skipped about the room, lit the fire and prepared chocolate, which she put before him with a piece of bread. He could help himself, and it would certainly do him good.

Then she dressed rapidly, and in the semidarkness put on powder and rouge — she did not open the blinds, because she wanted him to fall asleep again. Just one kiss before she left: did he think he would still be there when she got back? Ah, well, she would see him soon.

With light tread, she was gone. Her lawn skirts rustled in the door as she closed it softly. She had gone, and to Benedetto there in bed it seemed that a good fairy had departed.

At midday, after the rehearsal, she came rushing home. She put her head in at the door of the vegetable woman's to inquire whether by any chance a signore had left the key of her room — she did not want to have to drag up all those stairs twice. The vegetable woman, interested in the fact that Rosetta had apparently entrusted the key of her room to a signore, asked in her turn what sort of a signore he might be? Her question, however, was enough for Rosetta. She flew up the stairs to her room, and flung herself on Benedetto's neck. He was sitting on the side of the bed. Quick: what did he want? She would buy eggs. She still had some macaroni, but she must fetch greens and onions and butter and a candle, and some fruit, and a bottle of wine — red or white?

The brightness, turmoil, and vivacity that came into the room with her shook him awake. Being alone must have made him sad: but why had he not gone out to take a breath of air?

"Have you money?" he asked, as she was hurrying off again, and he felt in the pockets of his clothes, which she had hung hastily over a chair that morning.

She made a gesture of disdain. "There's no art in buying with money. You just see all I can get without it."

She was already halfway out of the door, laughing, but he called her back peremptorily. "Take this," he said casually, turning out his pocket so that the gold pieces rolled from it. She kissed him, took one, and hid several more under a loose board. "I'll keep that in case we need it," she said.

With astonishing speed she was back again from her marketing. He got up and helped her to set the fire, blackening his wrists in the process. A small girl brought a heavy pail of water upstairs, and stretched out her grubby little hand for immediate payment. Benedetto had only gold pieces. Rosetta signed to him to leave the matter to her, and, feeling in her market bag, found a copper piece. Then she sent the child for charcoal. And what about a little vinegar? She would pay her mother in cash to-day. She had a rich signore with her. Quick, quick! and don't fall down the stairs, my little heart.

As she cooked, Rosetta told Benedetto she could safely have mentioned that she had met him, for all Venice was talking of nothing else but his reappearance. At least, at the theater it was the first thing that had been talked about that morning, and the abbé must be involved in the business, for he dared not set foot in the street unless he was surrounded by friends. Even while he was supervising the rehearsal, he peered into the dark hall continually, as if Nemesis might strike him from there; and if reports were true, somebody else had already fled from Venice, from that same Nemesis. The abbé would have been quick enough to follow, if it had not been for his play: he insisted upon being present when it was hissed. Of course, Rosetta had not told a mortal soul that the Cavaliere Bussoni was sitting waiting for her in her room. Nobody need know that; and besides at the moment she herself had not been sure whether he would be. Of course, she could have told them where he had spent last night. She could have made all the others jealous with that: it had been extraordinarily difficult to keep it to herself while they were all talking about him. But she had succeeded: all the more so because they would not have believed her.

Besides, she had promised to be silent.

By this time, the food was ready and they sat down to table. Rosetta saw to it that he helped himself well. She poured out his wine, anticipated all his wishes. She talked about the theater, about Rossi, and about her stage rivals, whom she hated with a deadly hate, without exception, without one reservation.

Benedetto did not listen to all she said. She spoke too quickly for that, and most of what she said did not interest him. But he was delighted by this intimate companionship with her. He was grateful to her for the safe little harbor to which she had piloted him when he had not known where to go.

Later on, when it grew dusk, he would go out into the street again. He could not sit indoors all day. He had been shut up for more than a month. The fresh air had been like wine yesterday, when he breathed it again for the first time.

So long as he did not meet anybody who recognized him! How could he control his feeling of shame, of deep shame that he had been so foolish as to become the defenseless victim of an ambush that had, besides, left him visibly disfigured? And over and above all was the shame that he had allowed Maniscù to escape.

Rosetta was beginning to hope that she would keep Benedetto under her roof another night. Perhaps after all the fairy tale would become reality, and she would get him entirely to herself. The coming night could not be like the last one, when he had fallen into her arms exhausted, and slowly recovered in them — it could never be as fine as that again, but she had known that at the time, she had enjoyed those hours to the full, and they would remain in her memory forever.

She was crazy about him, and her vague assumption that he had something on his conscience on account of which he must lie in hiding with her only made her feel crazier. If she had ever wished to expose herself to danger for the sake of a man, that man was certainly Benedetto, with whom she had fallen in love so terribly from the very first moment because of his dark, faraway eyes, his whole figure, his hands of a *nobile*, his mysterious reserved mouth with which he could kiss so wildly and passionately that she felt herself dying away in his arms.

Most of all she loved the scar that disfigured this mouth, and the sorrow expressed in his taut face, about which, through pride, he was silent to her and to the whole world — whose business, besides, it was not. Did that other woman in her *palazzo* know about his sorrow? Had he told her about it? She must be crying her eyes out — if she was not tearing her handkerchief to bits with regret. Oh, if she only knew to whom he now belonged! If need be, Rosetta could be silent to the whole world — but if she should meet *her*, she would be unable to hold her tongue in leash, God and the saints forgive her.

She had to go, quickly, because there was another rehearsal during the afternoon. She left the key of her room with Benedetto again. As she left, she kissed him; in sudden superstitious fear, she preferred to ask him nothing.

III

In the shadow of the houses, Benedetto walked slowly up and down. Then he stood still for a while and waited.

He could not recall that he had often waited for a woman; but now he was waiting for a little actress whose miserable dwelling had been a refuge to him. He was waiting. It was getting dark and cold, and he drew his cloak about him, sinking into it.

Suddenly he saw the abbé come out of the theater with a half-dozen friends. He was talking and gesticulating excitedly. As he spoke, he looked round timidly, peering into the shadows so that Benedetto drew back a step or two.

The new and absurd thing about the abbé was that he was wearing a sword. Benedetto could scarcely refrain from smiling — but his smile had acquired a something that was bitter, almost unfriendly, owing to the distortion of the left corner of his mouth. A sword! Did the abbé feel himself so menaced? And if he were really menaced, what use would that sword be to him? What help would those half-dozen friends be to him if Benedetto meant business? Suppose he were to emerge from his hiding-place now and request him to draw his sword — what would these friends do, except courteously range themselves on one side and wait to see what would happen to the poor abbé?

Basta . . . !

Rossi came out of the theater. He was even less desirous of being seen by him. Nobody, nobody must see him.

Benedetto wondered whether, if nobody saw him for a time, Maniscù might return to Venice. . . .

Rossi passed him, in a hurry as usual, and, just like the abbé, anxiously looking round — not for a possible enemy who might have challenged him to a duel, but for his creditors, the nightmare of his life.

And then Rosetta came out. In front of the theater, she hurriedly took leave of some of her colleagues, who tried in vain to persuade her to go with them. She came straight up to him; she had noticed him at once. In her joy, she kissed him in the middle of the street under his mask.

She would light the fire again in her room, and prepare the evening meal for him, and coffee, unless of course he preferred to go out with her somewhere. As not a soul now came to the theater, Rossi had canceled the last performances before the first night. They could therefore stay at home for the rest of the evening, and go to bed immediately after their meal if he thought it was too cold to join a while in the carnival, or if he was afraid of being recognized even though masked.

Rosetta shivered under her thin cloak.

He seemed absent-minded. Instead of telling her what he had decided, which she was burning to know, he asked her suddenly whether she had seen that the abbé was wearing a sword.

Unwittingly he disarmed her with this question. She was seized with a fit of laughter. "Yes, we had to hold on to each other in the theater in order not to fall in a faint: although actually we haven't much to laugh about as things are at present."

Benedetto dragged her along with him. People were already looking round at them, and her exuberant merriment found but a dim echo in him. Immediately Rosetta grew serious, too. She lowered her voice as she said, "Yes, he carries a sword. Surely he must feel guilty. In any case, that's what everyone thinks now."

"What — what does everyone think?"

With a sudden premonition of danger, she said, speaking carefully and emphatically, "Well, this is what they say! That he knows something about it. At least that's what everyone at the theater thinks now." She hesitated, and then added, "He must have dropped hints himself, too."

Benedetto stared in front of him. So now they were thinking in Venice that the abbé had brought about his downfall. And the abbé was running about freely, and when he felt safe allowing himself to be tempted into bravado and the dropping of hints, according to Rosetta. Why need he do that, why of his own accord was he filling the place Maniscù had left vacant by his flight? Did he not understand what a dangerous vacancy it was?

In his mind's eye he saw the short, somewhat portly figure of the abbé, and something almost like compassion welled up in him. He wanted to remove him from the place he was so unwittingly occupying.

"What sort of hints?" asked Benedetto dubiously of Rosetta, who was walking in silence beside him in growing agitation.

"Well — hints! That you had stood in his way with a woman — and that you wouldn't do that a second time."

She brought out the words with difficulty. Excitement made her tremble. Unexpectedly she had hit upon the notion that she too, if she wished, could be demoniacal, like the Spaniard who had been his love, to possess whom he had allowed himself to be very nearly murdered; and besides, there was not an untruthful word in what she had told him. The abbé really must have said something of that kind; and that he had regretted it afterwards, when he was in the dark street, she could well believe, without having actually witnessed it. But why had he said such things? If fatal consequences followed his words, he had only himself to thank; and she had proved that it was not necessary to be "a woman without a heart" in order to blow up the fire that smouldered in Benedetto, the glow of which she had seen in his eyes from the moment he entered the theater with Rossi, still a stranger to her. . . .

Rosetta felt that something big was about to happen in her life. The thought of what might happen to the poor abbé crossed her mind fleetingly, and she had to call up all her fiery feelings of revenge for the impossible parts allotted to her in his plays. Towards that aspect of the matter she preferred to shut her eyes. She wanted to prove to Benedetto that she too was a woman of whom Venice might think it worth while to speak, as well as that hated Spaniard who still dwelt in his heart. She had felt that a moment ago when she told him about the abbé and a woman in connection with whom Benedetto had stood in his way. The abbé had never said anything of that kind at all. She had made that up, just to see how Benedetto would take it, and now she knew. He still thought and dreamed of his Spaniard, even while he was sleeping under her roof, in her bed; even while he was kissed and fondled by his Rosetta, after she had picked him up half-dead from the street.

IV

The abbé also carried a pistol concealed under his cloak, just in case he might be attacked by someone not chivalrous enough to challenge him to draw his sword. The lines of his play haunted his brain, but they were only words that he heard spoken at rehearsal without grasping their full meaning. They no longer lived in him: how could it be otherwise? Only anxiety lived in him, the frightful fear of an enemy conjured up by himself alone. Anxiety robbed him of sleep, robbed him of joy over the rapidly approaching first night of his play, to which he had been looking forward so eagerly.

His anxiety had also prompted him to the foolish step of arming himself — and his friends, false, dangerous flatterers, whom he would have done better to avoid instead of calling on them for protection, admired him for carrying these weapons, admired him for his palpable preparedness to defend himself like a man. Romano and Giulio, who on that fatal evening had pushed him forward when they did not dare speak themselves, now zealously offered themselves as seconds. They seemed most anxious to be present at the kill. They talked of his excellent chances, though they knew quite well that these existed only in their imagination . . . And if he should survive this terrible adventure (but deep within him he knew that he would not), he could write a play in which he held up a mirror to mankind — so true that all would shrink back in horror.

Although he knew that their words were mendacious, their encouragements the inspiration of the Devil, who was waiting impatiently for his soul, his limitless vanity compelled him, nevertheless, to let it be known in covert words that he had actually participated in the ambush of his enemy, though that distinction had been thrust upon him long after the event. In his heart he already loved that enemy, as a man loves his murderer, because of the terrible loneliness they share at the moment when death makes a third with them. The one person with whom he could still have talked honestly, upon whose word he would still have dared to depend, the sole person who knew mankind as he knew it at that moment, was Benedetto. But Fate would have it that they did not meet. Those about them wanted this tragedy of stupid misunderstanding to evolve to its bloody end, according to the rules of all tragedy. Fate would have it that their next meeting was to be the fatal one, and their last.

The abbé saw his enemy everywhere. He could not sleep, he could not eat. He grew pale and hollow-eyed. Soon he would be a ghost. It sometimes crossed his mind that he had already ceased to belong entirely to this earth. He was becoming familiar with Death as with a brother. He was beginning to long for it. He had had enough of mankind, enough of life. He had but one true friend left — death, whom he had always imagined as terrifying in the old days before he came acquainted with it. With death would come peace at last. With death he would have nothing more to fear, neither his enemy nor his friends.

But first he wanted to live through the great triumph of his play. That would be his honorable leavetaking of this senseless, deceitful life. His vanity still wanted that tribute. He was still vain, and therefore still clung to life . . .

At other moments he tasted the sweet joy of feeling himself a hero.

Who had come forward that evening, and by that bold step taken upon himself all the blame and all the danger? He had done that, in the full consciousness of what he was doing. And now death was hanging — a somber, impressive apparition of glory — over his head. All could see it, all were fascinated by it; their attention was riveted by it.

And Gracias — what of Gracias? She had always regarded him as one of those at whom people merely poked fun (he knew that too, now: was there anything he did not now know?); but suddenly Gracias was looking at him with other eyes. She was pale and troubled. For the first time, life had done something to her, even though she would not admit it. Oh, Gracias! She wanted them all to come visiting her as usual, and anyone who stayed away she stigmatized as a coward. She behaved as though she could not contain herself for gaiety. She hired musicians, she drank and laughed; but she could not prevent herself from sinking continually into silent, somber abstraction. Then she looked round with a mocking smile that curdled the blood in their veins. The abbé now understood life, and he understood exactly what was happening within her. He could have told her, if she had wished. But of course she had no desire to hear the truth about herself. Indeed, she actually looked at him as if she were trying to fathom him. Then she asked him about his enemy; and suddenly he was again the less wise of the two, for while he gave vent to all his feelings about the man to whom her heart belonged, she was silent and about her lips played a little smile that should have made him fear instead of feel flattered.

While he boasted, she saw his anxiety, his terrible anxiety, and derived pleasure from it. A truly devilish idea awakened within her; and he who thought he had seen through the whole game of mankind, he did not see through this little game of Gracias'. What availed his wisdom, then?

She noted that he had destined himself to be the prey of Benedetto's desire for revenge, and in her awakened the inclination to throw this prey to her vanished lover. Perhaps she could thus lure him back to her again; but in any case, this little game would for the moment still her own dark instincts of hatred and revenge.

Behind her fan, a glass of wine in her small, soft hand, she ogled and smiled at the abbé; and when, weak and vanquished, he knelt before her, she whispered something in his ear.

Suddenly he saw through her; but he still tried to close his eyes. He wanted to believe in this fairy tale that had come to him too late. He was prepared to pay with his life for this first rendezvous with her; and he did not want to wound her. Trembling all over, he drank from the glass she held out to him.

This evening he was to come to her. She wanted him. She could wait no longer, now she had seen who he was.

This evening — when was the first night of his play? To-morrow — but he would no longer be there. Bewildered, he looked about him. This evening was the last of his life. Already he saw the friends about him as through a haze. Their voices reached him from afar with a sound of unreality.

He drank and laughed. Gracias must see how drunk he was with joy at the prospect of this night. All must see how merry he was, with the halo of death about his head.

When he left with his false friends, he threw his arms about their shoulders and pressed them to him; and as he took leave of them before his house, he revealed to them his sweet secret with Gracias, in words that could not be misunderstood. And he said to them that they must not be jealous, for in the presence of perpetual danger, surely he deserved the favor of so superb a woman.

And his friends, who realized that this evening he would be a lost man, nevertheless still grudged him his rendezvous with Gracias.

But they had all drunk much wine, and they went away singing in their gondolas.

The abbé was alone.

At the door of his rooms, he stood still, his head buried in his hands. He was trying to think. It crossed his mind that he still had various matters to settle, but he could not remember exactly what. He moved about aimlessly, lighting candles here and there: why should he stint over a candle? The air was oppressive in the house. He threw open a window, but even then there was no air. It was uncommonly warm this evening. The atmosphere itself was oppressive. A heavy thunderstorm threatened — there was lightning already in the distance. Would that distant flash of lightning and the flickering flame of these candles be the last light his eyes were to behold? Would he never see the coming day, the sun above the Lagoon?

Upon his table lay a sheet of paper with stage directions. He threw himself upon it. With a trembling hand, he wrote a few words destined for Rossi. He could hardly form the letters.

He also wanted to write to his old mother who lived in the country, but he could not find another sheet of paper. He doubly underlined what he thought was most important in the stage directions. He placed the sheet so that it must be seen immediately.

Then he looked at his pistol, and stared dubiously into the mirror in front of him, where he saw something interesting: a man about to die. Later, he forgot the pistol again.

When there was really nothing else for him to do, he threw his cloak round him, walked out, and breathed deeply in the warm, languorous air. He had never closed the door of his dwelling behind him with such feelings before.

He could not take a gondola to the palace itself — Gracias had told him to wait in the garden. He would have to climb over the wall from the back. Upon reaching the Ca d'Oro, he paid off the *barcaiuolo* and continued on foot.

As he reached the garden wall, a masked figure stepped out of the darkness, threw open his cloak, and called upon the abbé to draw his sword.

He obeyed instantly. He stared at his enemy, behind whom, grand and gray, rose the familiar shadow of death.

Through the eyeholes of a mask he saw Benedetto's feverishly burning eyes. Through the mask he saw his whole face, with the scar and an expression of pain on the thin, closed, determined lips. . . .

At that moment, he could not help recalling their first meeting when Benedetto had promised Rossi to write some music for "Traghetto d'Amore." Were he now to remind him of that, with a word, with a cry, surely all hostility between them would suddenly vanish?

The abbé lifted his sword high, as though he wanted to thrust it straight into the heart of the pale shadow behind Benedetto.

A short, festive glitter and tinkling of steel glancing off steel. Then, cold and sharp and quick, death glided into the abbé's body. He sank down and felt his own warm blood streaming over his groping hands.

A

STRAY

SHOT

I

AS BENEDETTO BENT OVER HIS VICTIM, THE FIRST tepid raindrops began to fall, and a gust of wind swept through the narrow alley. In the dark foliage that rose up behind the wall, there was a rustle of falling leaves. The oil lanterns at the corner of the house, by whose feeble light the duel had been fought, were suddenly extinguished.

Over the face of the poor abbé, however, glided another shadow than that of night.

Quickly Benedetto covered it with the black cloak that had been blown open, looked about him in the darkness, and with his hand that had grown suddenly shaky slipped his sword back into its scabbard.

What had he done? What had driven him to this act of madness? He had imagined he could no longer evade this act of retribution; but now that he had carried it out, suddenly he could no longer believe that it had been necessary. It had brought him no liberation. His throat was dry. Something even heavier weighed upon him now, a curse more oppressive than before. In an urge to implore forgiveness of somebody, the idea crossed his mind to knock at Gracias' door and throw himself down upon his knees before her; but immediately he saw the triumphant glow in her eyes, the sensuous, wild longing of her moist, red mouth. . . . *She* had willed this: she had intentionally played the abbé into his hands. In his imagination he shook himself free from her, free from her deadly embrace. This evening she would wait for him in vain.

As he hurried away, he tried to direct his bewildered thoughts towards his own safety. Nobody had witnessed the duel, which had taken place without seconds. Nobody could swear that the abbé had fallen by his hand. The rain would come down in a moment and wash away all traces. Why had he not thrown the dead body into the neighboring canal? Should he do that now? The slow movement of the waters would carry it to the sea; and people would think that the abbé, like Cavaliere Maniscù, had merely fled from Venice.

Hesitating, he began to retrace his steps; but then he imagined he heard voices, and resumed his flight instead. Only later did it occur to him that what he had heard was the distant rumbling of rapidly approaching thunder. But then he did not dare go back again.

He must mix with the crowd, try to find an alibi far from the site of the tragedy. He might also be able to maintain that he was with Rosetta at the time — she would be willing to support any lie of his by perjury. But in that case he must go to her at once, and not show himself anywhere else — and he still wanted to see people. He could not take leave yet of this night of misfortune. He was haunted by a blind hope that this night he might still come upon Maniscù, that he could make him pay for the injustice done to the abbé. God grant him yet a worthy opponent! Only in a life-and-death struggle, in which the chances were equal, could he smother his self-loathing.

Above the pale walls of the city, black clouds had gathered. It was as close and oppressive as a July night. The storm would break at any moment. There! An impressive sheet of lightning tore the sky asunder, set it on fire. At the same moment, the thunder rattled and cracked.

Still the real rain did not come, despite the few drops that had fallen.

As fast as his feet could carry him, Benedetto walked to San Moisè, where he took a gondola to the main entrance of the Ridotto. There he must show himself to everyone, a quarter of an hour after the abbé had been overtaken by his fate. Should friends of the abbé be there, they would be able to see that he was calm and composed. Was he?

With a few strokes the *barcaiuolo* steered him to the gaming hall, where lights burned all through the night; but they were not gambling at the moment. At the open windows, silhouetted darkly against the gold of the flickering candle flames in the gilded chandeliers, the guests had gathered to enjoy the impressive spectacle over the Lagoon and the basin of San Marco. Benedetto sank back into his gondola. A strained imagination made it seem as though they were all waiting for him up there and were looking down upon him as his judges. At the very last moment, courage to enter failed him, and he told the *barcaiuolo* to go on to the Campo San Vitale. Without a word, the gondolier carried out the new order as he had done the first.

Through the darkness Benedetto hurried on, with no further object in view. When he heard a confused sound of voices approaching, he crouched against the wall of a house. A group of noisy merrymakers dressed in carnival attire passed him. They were excited by the stormy night, bent on brawling and hooliganism. They were too busy to notice him. They shouted and whistled against the noise of the thunder. Slowly Benedetto followed them; then suddenly he joined them, clutching his sword under his arm like the rest.

Lonely, somber, he walked among them, not knowing himself what he sought in their midst, not knowing why he was in this nocturnal Venice. In a moment, perhaps, this band would meet another band of young fools. Then a confused fight would begin, and those on either side would run from each other's swords. What was he doing among them? He must get away. Why did he not leave them? Was he afraid to be alone? He did not belong to them; although they were his age, he was far older than they.

Instead of leaving them, he pressed forward until he was in the front of the group. When they reached the Piazza, where a meeting with another group was likeliest, he found himself at their head, and without a word they chose him as their leader. They felt a dark urge in him and became infected with it. In this stormy night, they were preparing for once to give a serious turn to their frolics.

He noticed this and stood still. But it was too late. Immediately confusion arose. They surrounded him, heads reached forward, masks stared at him. Behind the masks voices were asking, "What is it? What are we going to do? Can't we try to knock down the columns on the Piazzetta? The reward for that is death, or at least the 'pozzi.' Or shall we foul the great staircase in the Palace of the Doges, or attack the shirri or . . . ?"

At that moment, for the duration of a second, the whole Riva and the Molo stood out in a blaze of lightning. Ten steps in front of them a long, thin figure with shoulders bent passed hastily, about to take a gondola at the landing stage. But one of the young people, desirous of showing his lack of fear, turned round, drew his pistol and wantonly fired it. The shot went off at the same time as a clap of thunder, so that it was not heard. The marksman himself thought his weapon had misfired; but no, the bullet appeared to have found a home. The hurrying figure fell from the quay into the water just before the gondola he had summoned had put in. The barcaiuolo bent forward, but already the dark water had closed upon the drowning figure. There was nothing left for him to do but to push off again. As he rowed away into the night, he shouted a half-amused, half-regretful and annoyed curse at the drunken young hooligans who had shot down his prospective fare — and that at a moment when God was manifesting his wrath from above.

The young hooligans themselves stared at the vacant spot on the quay; then the one who had fired the shot stammered something, and dashed away wildly while the others called after him.

At last the sluices of heaven opened. They scattered before the downpour, seeking refuge under the arcades of the Palace of the Doges.

Their headlong flight gave Benedetto the opportunity to choose his own way. He hurried towards the Riva, turned into a dark little side street, and only stopped in front of the faintly lit entrance of a house known as "The Seven Heavens."

A woman in night attire, candle in hand, stood on the lookout behind the door. "I say, won't you come in? It's dry in here," she called to him.

When he followed her up the stairs, she threw her long bare arm intimately round his shoulder, careless of the fact that he was drenched with rain. "Don't you know me?" she asked him, genuinely astonished. "Then you must be a stranger. I am Lucrezia, 'Red Lucrezia' of The Seven Heavens. If it hadn't poured so, I suppose you wouldn't have come in here at all?"

II

Rosetta lay listening in the night, wondering when Benedetto would return. She had almost given up hope that he would. Her pillow was wet with her tears. She crossed herself at every flash of lightning, and at every thunderclap that followed, and she looked upon this storm as God's punishment because she had excited her lover against the abbé. The abbé and his friends must have laid a second ambush for him, and this time he would not get off with a scar that only made him more attractive in her eyes. This time his enemies would make a better job of it. He was lying somewhere in the shadow of a long bare wall, bleeding slowly to death. The rain was pouring down upon him, and together with his blood was flowing away from his soaked clothes. She could see his waxen pale face with its thirsty open mouth that still faintly called her name. . . .

Rosetta could not bear to remain longer in her bed. She must do something to distract her mind. She lit the fire and began to prepare coffee: if he were to come in in a moment, he would be glad of a cup to fortify him, and he would want to dry his clothes — he must be drenched to the skin.

She paced up and down her room, racking her mind to think what else she could do for him. At intervals she peered through the window into the night, where the terrible storm was subsiding and the sky was brightening a little — or was it the first glimmer of dawn? The coffee was ready. Why did he not come back?

Should she go into the street and look for him? A woman, alone at that hour in the street! And suppose he were to come home in the meantime, and not find her.

Morning came, gray and drab, more terrifying in its sobering clearness than the wide dark night with its stormy violence. She dressed, scarcely able to fasten her clothes with her trembling fingers. She went downstairs, left her key with the vegetable woman, requesting her to hand it over should a signore come and ask for it. The vegetable woman, who had just got up, held a broom in her dirty fat hands. She nodded silently — she knew now what kind of signore was meant. Half-compassionately, half-mockingly, she looked after the little actress as she buried the key under her torn grimy skirts.

Rosetta ran through the city in all directions. She felt hate rising in her bosom against this Venice that was pursuing its everyday life, this Venice that, washed clean by the rain, was preparing to disport itself anew in the clear sun while Benedetto had not yet returned to her, to his little Rosetta, and probably was no longer even alive. Then she heard, from stray conversations in the street, that two people had fallen dead during the night. She stopped and listened. Her heart stood still. The woman who had been talking was delighted with the increasing interest around her, and she summed up her story thus: an abbé had fallen in a duel, near the monastery of the Misericordia, and somebody on the Riva had been about to step into a gondola when . . . But little Rosetta did not wait to hear more. She was not interested. The abbé had fallen near the monastery of the Misericordia . . . just next to the Rio di San Felice. Which of the two, then, Benedetto or the abbé, had been going to the Spanish woman when the other stood in his way in blind jealousy?

It was as if all the blood left her veins for a moment. Dizziness came over her. The abbé had fallen. Then Benedetto lived. And she thought she could guess to whom he had gone for his conqueror's prize. At the same time, she knew why he had not dared return to her. That was also the wisest thing he could do. She hated him, as she had never hated a man before. She would like to see him dead at her feet, as she had seen him during the night in her dreams. Her eyes would not shed a single tear.

But why did she still cry as she turned away and went to the theater? She was a quarter of an hour late — that had not been necessary.

It was the last rehearsal of the new play. Everyone had arrived early, and had already heard what had happened to the abbé, whose anxiety they had all made such fun of, in anticipation. Now his anxiety appeared in another light. Silent and pale, Rosetta listened to the story that several of them rushed up to tell her. She gave no sign of any surprise or emotion, and some of her colleagues looked at her with surprise and suspicion. It was known that she had had dealings with Cavaliere Bussoni — perhaps she herself could tell more of the story? Messer-Grande ought to summon her, and interrogate her.

Rossi entered. In his hands he held a crumpled sheet of paper that had just been handed to him. It was with difficulty that he controlled his emotion. His disciples listened, eager to learn, to the exact correctness of the throb in his voice, and watched his face for the reflections there of his emotions.

Solemnly and with dignity, he told them what they already knew. Then he read to them the last stage directions left by the author, at the point of death. It went without saying that these sacred instructions would be carried out with punctilious piety. Then he folded up the artistic testament of the poor abbé, and brought out, at last, the sentence for which they had all been waiting: "This terrible accident means a packed theater for a week!"

III

The Seven Heavens had three exits and so many invisible eyes that a surprise attack by the *sbirri* was almost impossible. In stormy weather like that of the previous night, at least a dozen votive lamps burned before the various saints to whose protection the girls had entrusted themselves. A few, however, dared to defy the Almighty by singing with drunken guests and playing on the guitar. They did this merely to give vent to their godlessness, for they could scarcely hear their own voices in the rolling of the thunder and the downpour of the rain.

Just as Lucrezia was about to open the door leading to the reception room, Benedetto laid his hand upon her arm and looked at her in sudden fear; but before he had brought out a word, she understood him.

"Come along here," she said, "there's another room behind. Those who go there do not talk of what happens here."

They went down a further passage. Lucrezia leaned several times against the wall. She seemed as though she would set her wig on fire with her candle. "I've been drinking," she said with a laugh, "but we'll drink together all the same, won't we? I'm still thirsty. I can stand more, and the matron likes it. You've got money, haven't you? Otherwise you'll be thrown out again, rain or no rain. They know no pity here." Smiling at him, offering her body, she threw open a red curtain and signed to him to enter.

There in the dim room sat a man leaning his arms upon the table, a bottle in front of him. He was talking to two half-dressed girls, one of whom was leaning against him and the other staring at him across the table, her pale, consumptive, sphinxlike face, with its bright red patches of paint, resting upon her hands.

The girls turned their heads towards the doorway, and the man also looked round slowly and indifferently. It was Galuppi. He recognized Benedetto, but did not seem surprised to see him there.

"This is Beatrice, and that is Antea," said Lucrezia, introducing them. "Oh, the signori know one another? I'll get some wine."

"Bring some for us too," shouted the girls after her, as she went away. They paid no further attention to Benedetto, since he belonged to Lucrezia. "Go on! Tell us about the painting," they said to Galuppi. But Galuppi continued to look at the newcomer, who had sunk down beside the table, and was staring straight in front of him in a strange, miserable fashion.

Slowly something like a smile appeared on Galuppi's lips. At last he asked, "And so you've run up against the abbé?"

Benedetto started, but continued staring in front of him and did not answer. Galuppi, however, thought he knew enough. He poured out some wine and sighed. "It had to come to that, and she had destined this night to be his last. How long had you been after him? What do you think of doing now?"

Lucrezia came in with the wine, and noticed that they were all looking expectantly at her new friend. "What is it?" she asked. But nobody answered her.

"I believe I ought to advise you to fly, if what I think has happened to the abbé is true — *what we all think*." Galuppi said these last words with some emphasis.

But as he could not get a word out of Benedetto, he addressed himself to the girls again. They raised their glasses to him. In lavish good humor, like an older uncle, he poured wine for them, and they began a general conversation as to how and where one could most safely flee. Antea, with the consumptive complexion and the faraway sphinxlike look, mentioned America, the large new world on the other side of the ocean. Many went there these days. A man could choose his own land there, as much as he wanted. He had only to fight against the Indians, whose treachery must cry to heaven. Two girls from The Crowing Cock had gone there and married. Nobody asked questions. They had written to say that the only things they missed were *polenta* and wine and *pasta asciutta*. Oh, it must be fine, first to cross the sea in a ship — and when you reached the other side to be waited upon by Negro slaves whom you could thrash to your heart's content. Antea moved the tip of her small pointed tongue carefully over her lips. "I should so like to have been able to whip a few in my time, even though they weren't Negroes; but instead . . ."

At that moment, the curtain was drawn aside. She was called away. With a stifled curse she got up. Then she looked at herself in the mirror, emptied her glass, and departed listlessly.

Lucrezia sat down next to Benedetto. By helping him to wine and more wine, she tried to get the truth out of him. Why ought he to flee? What had happened to that abbé, and what abbé were they talking about? There were so many in Venice. Lord! one would never be missed. Must he escape to America because of an abbé? He was leaning forward with his head over the table, and did not even stir when she ran her hand softly over his head. Thinking that he had fallen asleep, she began talking to Galuppi and Beatrice.

Slowly, gradually the dawn broke, shedding over the brothel the discouraging, catastrophic atmosphere that every morning brought. Galuppi staggered up and was accompanied to the door by Beatrice.

When Beatrice came back, she brought the news that had just reached her from outside: Abbé Baccherini, the writer of the play that was to be performed that evening in the San Samuele theater, had been found dead in the street with a sword thrust through his breast.

Lucrezia, who had dozed off, looked up, her eyes drowsy with sleep. Other girls who had heard the news from Antea came peeping round the curtain inquisitively. Protective and proud, Lucrezia, suddenly quite awake, threw her arms round her sleeping Benedetto.

IV

During the day, it was noticeably still and quiet in that house. The blinds were drawn to keep out the sun. In the large room where guests were received in the evening, the girls sat mending their silk clothes in the dim light, and spoiling their eyes at the same time. In whispered tones, they talked with one another about the news that reached them from the city in which they lived without ever seeing it. A few were playing cards. Others were sleeping. Antea sat staring in front of her, with her sphinxlike look, dreaming of America, where she could whip Negroes.

In the back room, Lucrezia was keeping Benedetto company. She was both submissive and haughty. She had hung out his damp outer garments, but she wanted to convince him of her very special worth. She wanted to appear interesting in his eyes. She spoke contemptuously about the *sbirri*, as if she knew all their secret methods and slinking ways, and told him how wise he had been to choose this place as a refuge: the *sbirri* never came there, because they had been bribed by the matron. Above all, he was under the safe protection of Lucrezia, "Red Lucrezia" of The Seven Heavens. It was true that she was red-haired and therefore had the right to call herself thus: but when she gave herself this appellation she tried to endow it with a deeper meaning, as though the "red" were applicable to her bloodthirsty, Borgialike being. She told him a man had once lain in hiding at The Seven Heavens for a whole week. She had looked after him all the time, and opposed the matron when she wanted to turn him out because he had no money — "But you've got some money, haven't you?" Yes; and thus the ungrateful dog saved his skin, but he had never been heard of since. Oh, what hadn't he promised her: that he would come and fetch her, that she should sit in his carriage like a princess. And she was still sitting here. Fortunately she had never believed him. "Never believe a man," she concluded, staring with a melancholy expression at the table. "I don't believe you, either."

There was nothing, so far, for her to believe or disbelieve — he had barely said a word to her. His first complete sentence had been addressed to the matron, who had come in at midday with a honey-sweet face, wishing to see his money. Lucrezia was radiant as with downcast eyes and uncertain gesture he laid a handful of gold pieces on the table. "For that amount you can stay here a month," she assured him, in her delight probably a little optimistic in her reckoning.

When it grew dusk, Benedetto intended to get away. He was dimly aware that Rosetta might be anxious about him, and that he ought to go back to her. It was not quite clear to him — nothing was clear to him. He had an oppressive feeling of inferiority within him. No, he was not sure that he would return to Rosetta. It was not his fear of the *sbirri* that held him back. It did not occur to him that he might run straight into their arms by going to her. The idea of surrendering voluntarily had crossed his mind, but he decided to wait until they found him. It was not likely they would look for him in The Seven Heavens: how could they guess he was there? Ah, well, so much the better. He did not see why he should make things easy for them. Things had not been so easy for him, either, recently.

What did this woman want from him? Why did she not leave him alone? To be left alone — that was all he wanted. He had shown he was prepared to pay. He wanted to think things out, but his brain was too weary. It had been another, just anybody, who had shot down Maniscù last night as he was about to take a gondola on the Molo — for it had been Maniscù, surely? He had recognized the figure, but when he looked back he was not sure whether . . .

It was already dark outside, and Rosetta was probably feeling anxious about him; and still he sat on.

The first guests arrived with the twilight. Their voices penetrated from the large room to the smaller one at the back. Occasionally, Beatrice and Tonina and Rosalinda came rushing into the small room because they wanted to get away for a moment from all the jollity, to yawn and to belong to themselves. Half-inquisitive, half-annoyed, Lucrezia looked at them every time they came in. They brought with them the stale remains of the chatter from the other room, and Lucrezia was quite eager to listen; but on the other hand she would have liked to be alone with Benedetto, for she was occupied in telling him of her romantic descent. None of the other girls there could prove, black on white, that they descended from a duke and a nun. She still hoped to get him to talk, too. If he remained silent much longer, thought it unnecessary to reply to one of her questions by so much as a single word, when in addition she heard that he had something on his conscience for which the *sbirri* were on the watch for him . . . It would be too much for her, too much for Red Lucrezia. She could not but fall in love with him, as she had done with that other, the dog who had allowed her to look after him for a whole week, and had promised her the world. This one would of course be ungrateful, too. She was waiting to hear him make her all sorts of promises. This time she would not believe a word of them. But she would like to listen to them.

Carlotta and Zanetta, the only girls apart from herself allowed on the Molo and the Riva, to attract clients to the house, brought Annibale the Negro boy with them. He had been there often before, and always had money to spend. He was the youngest guest of the house, and much in demand. The girls marveled at his early maturity. They derived much amusement from him, and had an almost maternal weakness for him. "Little one," they called him tenderly — but in the same breath readily admitted that he was already quite a man. They gave him something to drink; he was always half-tipsy on arrival. When he was thoroughly drunk, he allowed himself to be raised upon a chair and sang a wild African song that made the blood curdle in their veins. His eyes stood out of their sockets — he really made them tremble. He was in love with Rosalinda, the prettiest girl in the house, and the most foolish and the vainest. She was blonde, and a shade too ample in body for some tastes. She was almost twice as big as he. In her rage she would give him a resounding slap on the cheek when he dared to choose her, but as he paid well the matron insisted upon his obtaining his right, and made her apologize to him. While Rosalinda sulked and made a scene, the others laughed. Only Annibale looked gray and pale and trembled in his whole body until in the end they went away together.

To all except to the pretty blonde Rosalinda he behaved currishly and shamelessly. Again and again they had to burst out laughing at the coarse things he said; he seemed to be unaware of their gravity, as he uttered them in his queer Venetian. Like a little black hero, he sat among these white women and angrily refused to surrender the intimacies of his dusky body to their curiosity.

He talked in the most cynical fashion about his mistress Gracias, about her old father, about her guests. He seemed to have seen through them all. He had his own opinion, even about Countess Bogliasco: it was preposterous to hear the things he said about her, coming from his boy's mouth. This evening, his victim was the dead abbé, whose posthumous play was about to be hissed as it deserved. If only Annibale could be as sure that the *sbirri* would catch his mistress's former friend this same evening! Under cover of darkness he had made the abbé cold, and was now wanted for a double murder.

In spite of themselves, some of the girls glanced in fright towards the back room. Others bent in anxious curiosity over the little know-all. "A double murder? But he seems to have given his enemy the opportunity to draw his sword, for that's how the abbé was found, with his sword in his hand, and we haven't heard anything of a second murder yet."

Annibale swelled his chest and, sure of his facts and of his ascendancy over these women, said portentously: "Oh, really? And isn't it murder when a man raises his pistol and shoots down a passing Jew for the fun of the thing?"

The girls knew a Jew had been shot dead on the Molo, but they were amazed to hear that Benedetto was supposed to have done that, too.

"Oh, well — a Jew in the streets at night is bound to be a usurer," remarked Beatrice, in an attempt to gloss the matter over. Antea got up unobtrusively and went to the back room. The other girls all started speaking together. "For my part, they can shoot all the Jews. If the

matron were to tell me to go and sleep with a Jew . . ." Zanetta did not finish her sentence: what Zanetta would do in that case was to remain a mystery
forever. Nanetta reassured her with, "The matron never allows a Jew here,
even though he were to cover you with gold as you sit there. . . ."

At that moment, Antea entered the back room. She stopped by the
curtain and, speaking almost casually, said to Benedetto, "Listen — they
are after you also on account of an old Jew you shot dead on the Molo."
As she spoke, her eye was riveted, calm and cool, upon him. She was determined to be the first of the house to discover whether he had really
done it. When she saw him get up deadly pale, she was certain he had —
as well as of the power of her glance to unmask the truth. This power
was her secret pride, though she did not want anyone to know that. She
could return satisfied to the others; but she was so overcome by her own
triumph that she remained a little longer leaning against the red curtain,
in a weary, wanton attitude; she was waiting to see what he would do.

Lucrezia watched him furtively. He seemed shattered by Antea's news,
and jealousy welled up in her. Where was he rushing to now? She wanted
to hold him back, but, striding past Antea who stood on one side to give
him free passage, he was already out of the room. Softly and sadly,
Lucrezia muttered something to herself. Had she dared, she would have
upbraided Antea sharply; but she was afraid for her eyes.

Where had he gone so suddenly, this second man she had loved and
shielded? Would she ever receive any thanks?

She still hoped that Antea would go away, but when she continued to
stand by the curtain waiting for her, she got up, full of aversion and silent
resentment. Together they returned to the large room, which had been
full of noisy gaiety for an hour past. Perhaps she could manage to join in
the laughter.

V

As the door knocker fell, that queer door knocker in the shape of an
allegorical bird, David's thin, sallow face peered through the judas. Two
dark, anxious, Jewish eyes stared at the man waiting outside. Then David's
face disappeared, the door opened, and behind it stood only old Susanna,
small, shriveled, bitterly hostile. David, farther along the passage, was
about to enter the living room; but before doing so he spat upon the stones
and said in a loud voice so that Benedetto should hear, "He has come! The
goy has come."

Benedetto swept past old Susanna, who tried to hold him back when
she saw that he was not going straight upstairs to his room, and entered
the living room. But Leah was not there. Some low chairs that he had not

seen before stood in the room. On one of them sat Signora Graziadeo. In that position she seemed more ample than ever. She looked up at him with tearful, dark-rimmed eyes. Behind her, like a guard, stood her nephew, pale and rigid. Both were silent, and stared with abhorrence at their unbidden guest, who seemed bewildered by their glances, and could find nothing to say but the pointless question, "Isn't Leah here?"

Leah's aunt was on the point of saying something, but David stopped her, and snapped at Benedetto: "What is that to you, whether my betrothed is here or elsewhere? What do you want with her?"

Benedetto measured his enemy. Then, uncertain again, he turned to the woman on her low chair. "I wanted to come and say that I am guiltless of what has happened to Signor Graziadeo."

The woman burst into sobs. Old Susanna, crying herself, went up to her to console her. David, however, unmoved by these tears and annoyed that his future mother-in-law should reveal her grief so unmistakably before this Christian, this accursed dog who had come to tell them he was innocent when the whole ghetto pointed at him as the criminal and the *sbirri* were already after him . . .

David said icily, "I wish you joy if you are innocent of this cowardly assassination. I shall inform my betrothed. If you have no further message, I must request you to leave us here alone with our grief."

"I will go," said Benedetto. "When I have spoken to Leah herself, I will go."

"You can't speak to her," snapped David. "She doesn't wish to receive you. I must request you . . ." To his unspeakable annoyance, his aunt raised her head and, pushing Susanna away from her, moaned, "But why don't you tell him so that he may know too? Leah is not at home. She's been in the streets since early this morning, looking for her uncle. She wouldn't believe it when people came to say he was dead. She wanted to see him with her own eyes—the child can get no peace without that; and I sit here praying that for God's sake she may not find him. I said to her, 'But don't you understand? They've shot your uncle. They've shot your uncle with bullets, and he fell into the water and is drowned. They haven't recovered the body. What more do you want? God has taken him to Himself. Why must you see him like a strange man, stiff and dead and with dripping hair?' But no—she had to go looking for him. Old Levie saw her—she was running along the quays by the water's edge like a sleepwalker. She may yet fall in and drown herself!"

The woman ran on unintelligibly. Benedetto turned to David. "And is she wandering about alone—still?"

David, hurt, answered only with a look of unspeakable contempt. His

aunt, however, observing that her protégé was being reproached, recovered herself, and passionately jumped to his defense.

"What do you mean, alone? Geronimo is with her. Could David have
gone with her? Could he just close his business to go and look for the
drowned father of his betrothed? Do you think a new business could
stand that? But what do you know of such things? Geronimo returned
from Padua early this morning, and he was able to go with her at once.
If only he had been with my poor husband last night, this frightful misfortune would not have happened. Geronimo would have jumped after
him into the water, and, who knows, we might have been able to keep
him alive. . . . But here they come," she cried, and hoisted herself up.
David hurried away, and old Susanna toiled after him.

There was whispering in the corridor, and then Leah came in, pale,
with weary lines upon her comely face. Her eyes had acquired a strange
expression. She did not greet her aunt, who looked at her anxiously. Exhausted, she sank down upon one of the low chairs.

David came in behind her, devoted and submissive. He did not dare
to touch her, or even to go and sit beside her. He looked at her in great
compassion, prepared to read her every wish in her eyes. Signora Graziadeo made desperate gestures to old Susanna to indicate that she must
bring something for Leah, hot coffee, chocolate . . .

"You'll eat something, child?" she implored. "You've been running
about all day and had nothing. You might have fainted in the street.
They've all been here, Rabbi Isidore with Isaac, and Sarah and Judith,
and Levie with Rebecca his wife, and the cantor of the Spanish Synagogue . . . They condoled with me because I was here alone. If your
uncle were still alive, he himself would wish you to remain at home,
and eat something — a plate of soup at least."

Slowly, shaking her head in loathing, Leah signified that she could
eat nothing. But her aunt was not to be put off by that, and she made
another sign to old Susanna, who went to the kitchen to heat soup.

Then for a time there was no sound in the room, except Signora Graziadeo's sighs and nose-blowings. Benedetto stood by the door, and had
not the strength either to go or to speak to Leah. David cleared his
throat. Was he going to say something? He had completely lost his
proud demeanor of a while ago. In his despair, he even debased himself to the point of summoning his deadly enemy to his aid by saying
suddenly, "The Cavaliere has come, Leah, to tell you that he knows nothing about last night — about your uncle . . ."

Leah looked up swiftly at Benedetto, who tried to meet her glance,
and with difficulty corrected David's words, "It is true I am innocent —

and I did not know about it, either. But it is also true that I was there . . ."

David broke into a cry of horror. Leah buried her face in her hands. Her aunt, turning her head disconsolately towards the kitchen door, wailed in Susanna's direction, "He was there. He saw it."

Benedetto, his hands behind him as if to support himself against the wall, defended himself passionately. "I did not know who it was that had been hit by the bullet. I don't even know who fired the shot. I only happened to be there accidentally. Leah, could I have wished your uncle's death? Hadn't I to thank him for . . . ? Leah, say something."

Leah did not look up. She bowed her head lower still. He thought she was weeping, and it was with the greatest difficulty that he could prevent himself from going to her. At that moment Susanna came in with a table napkin and a plate of steaming soup. The aroma wafted from the kitchen appeared to have reached Leah also. Suddenly she jumped up and fled from the room. All looked after her — nobody dared to follow her.

"Where has she gone?" asked Benedetto in alarm.

Signora Graziadeo, sniffing and wiping away the tears from her cheeks, was affronted by Leah's unreasonable flight. It was as if this behavior, exceeding all bounds, had suddenly brought her to herself again. "Where has she gone? To her room, to be alone. Listen — the door upstairs. If only she would have a good cry, like anyone else, so that it would be possible to speak to her again! To think of all the things that must be talked about and decided!" She looked towards David, who was sitting huddled in a chair, with his eyes covered. "And just look at him sitting there," she moaned, overcoming a hesitation within her. "I ask you now, as you've said you did not wish my poor husband's death and were grateful to him for what he did for you . . . I ask you, oughtn't we all to begin talking things over sensibly? There's so much to settle. The house must be sold, for I refuse to live here any longer. Leah has a third-interest in it. That was to be a surprise for her; but now she will have to agree to the sale. David doesn't dare talk to his betrothed — or rather, shall we say, he refuses to. And really I had far better keep my mouth shut, for every word of mine is fuel to the fire."

David, bitterly wounded by all these words, said, "But you must have patience, aunt. Uncle is only just dead. I shall talk to Leah when she has got over the worst. It isn't as if we've done nothing. We've sent the news to Ancona and Trieste . . ."

"Oh, yes, if only Uncle Nathan from Trieste were here, everything would be better at once," admitted Signora Graziadeo. But she said nothing of Samuel, her husband's brother from Ancona. "When my brother comes . . . But will he be able to get away at once from his business?

Still, he'll have to come for the funeral, and what sort of a funeral will it be without the body itself? Lord, what shame! If only we'd remained in the ghetto, then perhaps we shouldn't have had so much misfortune. This is our punishment for coming to live among the Christians. It was in the minds of all those who came here to-day. They didn't say it, to spare me . . ."

She was wringing her hands, and relapsed once more into hopeless grief. Her thoughts, that a moment before had been directed clearly upon realities, lost themselves in a mist. David jumped up and began pacing up and down the room—his hands upon his head, which he was rolling nervously backwards and forwards. Irritated, she said, "David—do something. Go and speak to her . . . If you mean to be her husband, you must have the courage to make your will felt. If you can't do that now, you'll never be able to."

Under her prodding words, David was on the point of going to Leah, but her closed door filled him with too much fear and respect. In his terrible perplexity, he broke out: "Aunt, what do you want now? I know her better than you do. Yes, yes, I tell you, you don't know her. If I were to speak to her now about such things, I should have to pay for it for the rest of my life. I won't have her thinking I don't respect the death of her uncle. I won't have it, do you hear?" Hysterically, he brought down his thin, pale fist upon the table. "I won't lose her, for you and your house. And if you understood that, you wouldn't tell me now, and in the presence of a stranger too, to go and speak to her."

"Oh, not about that, not about the house immediately," moaned Signora Graziadeo. She seemed to be on the verge of anger. Instead, she gave an unexpected turn to the situation by turning to Benedetto. "Cavaliere—you have influence over her. Don't say you won't. I know what I'm talking about. You speak to her, for her sake and for the sake of all of us. Tell her she must see reason, that her betrothed and everybody in this house wish her well, and that we have the same grief as herself. Tell her she must think of her health, that she must come down and have something to eat, and not go out into the streets again to-morrow. Geronimo is still running about because she has told him to—if you have a heart, you won't be able to bear to see it. Help her, help us all. If you think you are still under obligations towards us . . ."

Leah made no reply when Benedetto knocked. He found her sitting in the half-dusk at her table. When she saw who had come in, she got up and, turning away from him, went to the window, saying nervously and reproachfully, "What do you want again here?"

He dared not approach her, and it was only with the greatest effort that he found his words. "I only wanted to tell you, Leah, that I wouldn't have waited to come here till this evening, but should have come at once in the middle of the night, had I guessed that that accident had befallen your uncle."

Leah looked down for a long time as if lost in thought. At last she asked, "Did they downstairs send you here?"

"Yes. But for me that was only a pretext so that I could tell you that."

"What do they want of me?"

"To remind you of the fact that you have a betrothed and an aunt who are bowed under the same grief as yourself."

She ran her hand over her forehead, as though something prevented her from understanding this. Then she spoke, and hatred echoed through her voice.

"I know," she said, "I know I have a betrothed and an aunt, and I also know what they want with me. I see it in Aunt's face. I see it in David's. They're thinking of themselves, not of Uncle Solomon. I have always known Aunt did not care for her husband, and that she didn't deserve to have him at all. Now she's afraid of having to see him again. That was her greatest concern this morning, when I wanted to go and look for him in order to make quite sure that he was no longer in need of our help. She wants to save herself, and I must serve her to that end. She wants to go back to the ghetto, to sell this house as soon as possible. The purchase money will make it possible for me to marry David. Then she wants to come and live with us, so that she won't be alone, nor have to mourn her dead husband. She wants her life to be bearable again. But I don't want it to be bearable again. I hate her, I despise her for all she did to my uncle while he was alive, and for her cowardly betrayal of him, now that he is dead . . ."

Suddenly a sob broke through her voice. At last she was weeping. So grievous, so passionate, was her sorrow that she did not notice it at once when Benedetto, carried away by his feelings, threw his arms about her. It was in vain that she dried her tears—they flowed on as she sobbed: "I don't want to marry David. I can't, any more. And I don't want to go back with the two of them to the ghetto. It just happened that I got engaged to David. Uncle wanted it. Perhaps it was only Aunt who wanted it—I was too young to know. I had never come to know anyone but David. I thought he would be good to me later on—but now he repels me. It's his own fault, and Aunt's. Perhaps that was why I ran out of the house this morning, in order not to have to be at home alone with Aunt and with those who came to condole with her. From shame and fear I ran away, and to think things out. It even crossed my mind to run away from the city altogether, had I but known where, and if I hadn't been hoping all the time to be able to speak to somebody else besides that good Geronimo . . ."

Starting up suddenly, perplexed, she tried to free herself from Benedetto's embrace, but he prevented her, and when she looked at him with amazement, she saw that there were large tears in his eyes also.

"For the love of God — what are you doing? What are we doing?" she moaned. His only reply was to press her against him hopelessly. Only when she had ceased to defend herself, crying bitterly the while, did he let her go. She buried her face in her hands.

He looked at her and tried to think what he could say to her. Could he save her still, he? Could he hold out some prospect to her? He could say to her that he loved her, that after his mother she was the only woman in the world whom he had really and sacredly loved, that he was prepared to sacrifice himself for her. Would that help her?

As she stood there, he could hardly refrain from throwing himself at her feet, clasping her knees, and confessing to her, telling her everything, everything, so that she should know with whom she had to do. But still he did not dare. He was still held back by the petty fear that she would feel aversion to him, would have nothing more to do with him. He tried, therefore, to hold his weak knees in control, and only said in a whispering stammer, "Forgive me!"

"What have I to forgive you for?" she sobbed, "I too love you. Don't move. Don't come near me, I implore you. I only want to tell you that I was looking for you to-day in Venice — you. I reproach Aunt for her selfishness, and I am no better myself. David came along this morning with that awful report that you had murdered Uncle. I did not believe him. For that report, for that lie, I hated him even more than for all the rest. I simply could not believe you would have picked up a weapon to direct it against my uncle. I felt at once that it must be some terrible mistake on other people's part, or on yours . . . I know I should have forgiven you even for such a terrible, unintentional murder if you had come at once to tell us of it last night. But we had to hear of it from others, and I did not understand, myself, how I could have been so weak as to go into the city looking for you. For you — or for uncle's dead body — I don't know myself which, any more!"

Wavering, he took a step forward and whispered hoarsely: "Leah — couldn't we flee together? Up to now, I haven't been able to make up my mind to escape. I haven't been able to get away from Venice. But with you . . ."

She looked at him, struggling with a terrible hesitation within herself. "Flee together . . . ?" she asked tonelessly, and without daring to believe in the thought.

Weakly, in spite of his own lack of faith, he tried to convince her. "If you don't come too, Leah, then I don't know whether I shall flee, although — "

"Although you ought to flee," she said quickly, starting up. "Why must you? If you say you didn't kill Uncle?"

Catching his breath, he confessed, "There is something else."

She tried to read the whole truth in his eyes. "If you were to escape — if we were to escape together, were able to . . . Would you still have reason to fear they might find you, elsewhere? Even if I were to say I had come with you of my own free will?"

"If we were to flee far enough away, they wouldn't be able to . . ."

"Yes; but supposing they found you after all?" she insisted with a strange obstinacy. He was silent, but she pressed him further, despair in her voice: "I want to know. That is all I want to know. You must answer this question. If they were to find you — what would happen to you then?" So great was her tension that she could hardly draw her breath.

He bowed his head, still tried to make himself believe that much would depend upon whether Garcias had given away something of his past — she had said she never would. She wanted to keep the ring . . . Oh, but what was all that to Leah? She had asked him a question, and she had the right to the only answer he could give.

Almost inaudibly, suddenly with the full, clear consciousness of his early end, his irretrievable doom, he declared, "Then I should be lost."

She seemed to have foreseen this reply, and she nodded, almost imperceptibly. She tried to conceal from him the fact that this reply meant the end for her also. She had no wish to question him further about the heavy crime to which he must be alluding: that was his affair. She had heard what she had wanted so much to hear.

"I wished to know that before I decide something," she said, wearily. "Let me think it over. I must think it over first . . ."

From such further thoughts he did not anticipate much good to himself.

There was a silence between them. Was Leah, perhaps, still waiting for his confession? Did she perhaps long for him to fall upon his knees, pour out his confession, confide to her the gruesome thing she did not wish to know? Oh, in that case her longing was in vain. At that moment he knew again, as clearly as he had known that first evening in the gondola, that with her eyes looking at him he would never be able to get his Todi crime over his lips. He knew that his past was only now completely revenging itself upon him, and that the hour could no longer be far away when he would give up the struggle, give up his vain flight from it.

Suddenly he remembered the others who were waiting below for the result of his conversation with Leah. Consciousness of them made him so uncomfortable that he could no longer stay where he was.

"I must go back to them now," he said, and she made no effort to hold him. Apparently she assumed that he knew best where to seek a refuge from temporal justice. Supposing she should come to know, one day, where he had temporarily found such a refuge!

She did not know, neither did she ask him; but when his hand was already on the doorknob he heard suddenly a soft cry — "Benedetto!" He hurried back to her, and kissed her. She offered him her mouth. "Come back to-morrow; I will see," she moaned. Then gently she pushed him away. He obeyed her and, weak with emotion, departed.

In the passage he fell into Geronimo, who had just returned home and was waiting for him after having heard of his presence from those in the living room. Geronimo only made a mute gesture expressing despair. He hoped Benedetto would occupy his room again; he ran by his side, and tried to keep him back even at the door.

"I'm so glad you have come, Cavaliere. You're surely not going away again? I've been looking for you the whole evening, so that you could speak to Signorina Leah. She has been crying, hasn't she? Tell me, Cavaliere — I won't tell the others there inside."

Benedetto looked at him. Instead of replying, he asked, "Were you in Padua last night?"

Geronimo raised his hands to heaven. "Yes, just last night. The head of the orphanage had died, and I simply had to attend the funeral. I never told them here that he used to beat us and keep us hungry. This, this is the last thing he has done to me." Geronimo's voice broke, and he shook his fist impotently against the invisible powers of darkness. "Why did I have to go to that funeral? Why did they almost all go who were still in the neighborhood? Now we're all out in the world, we've learned to see with our own eyes in what beastly fashion he treated us when we were children and in his power! And we wanted to curse him among ourselves after his death. That's why we all gathered in Padua. But out of the grave he has avenged himself. Master promised me not to go out, as I wouldn't be there — and this awful thing happened. You don't know what it feels like now in the house, so empty, so empty it is everywhere, here and in the back rooms. And now you're going away too. I had hoped you would have been able to console Signorina Leah. . . ."

Slowly, Benedetto freed himself: Geronimo had so far forgotten himself as to seize him by the arm.

He refused Geronimo's insistent offer to escort him at least to a gondola. As he hurried through the dark, deserted little streets alone, he saw only Leah as she had stood by the window when he held the doorknob in his hand. He heard the voice with which she had first called him by his name. On his lips her kiss still lay.

It seemed to him to be the parting kiss of Life.

THE

NOTE

I

THE CAVALIERE HAD GONE. . . . THEY HAD HEARD
Geronimo speak to him in the passage, and then the outer door
had slammed. They expected Geronimo to come and tell them
what had happened, but, as though he wanted to keep them in uncertainty, he went straight to the back of the house to hang up his funeral
suit.

They had been listening in the living room to all that had passed. They
had heard the Cavaliere's agitated voice, and Leah's sobs. Aunt Rachel
had wanted her to cry, but when Leah's weeping penetrated to the
living room, her aunt had forgotten this desire of hers, and began to behave like one in despair. David clutched at his chair with trembling hands
to prevent himself from rushing upstairs, and deaf Susanna, unable to
hear a thing herself, but reading everything in their faces, repeated at
short intervals: "Let us go to her — let us go to console her — the *goy* is
making her cry, the poor child!"

The Cavaliere had gone, and Geronimo had not come to report. Therefore Signora Graziadeo said to her nephew: "Now, David, no more nonsense. You go upstairs. If she was willing to receive that Christian, she
won't shut the door against you."

David had already made up his mind to go upstairs, and it annoyed
him to be thus instructed. Without a word or a sign to his aunt, he left
the living room. He was pale, but had already assumed the dignity with
which he meant to appear upon Leah's threshold.

Halfway up the stairs he stood still: someone was knocking at the front
door—who could it be? Had the Cavaliere had the pitiful courage to re-

turn? Or had the body of Leah's uncle been found, after all? In that case, he would be able to carry the news to her.

With rapid steps, he descended the stairs again, went to the front door, and peered through the judas. Outside he saw several figures dressed in slovenly uniforms.

Only now did David feel to the full the curse that had descended upon the house since a *goy* had entered it. The *sbirri!*

They rapped with the knocker again more loudly, and David hastened to open the door. Immediately one of the men pushed his boot into the opening. Others pressed against it with all their might, so that David staggered back against the wall. He stared in deadly fright into the barrels of a half-dozen pistols.

"Keep your eyes on this one!" said the captain of the band. "Two of you remain here. The others must come with me. We must search the whole house."

David thought of Leah, alone upstairs. He forgot all danger of death, and cried out, "He whom you seek is no longer here. He has just left the house. I swear it, captain!"

The *sbirri* paid no more attention to him than if he had been a piece of furniture. Two men felt in his pockets for weapons, put away the money they found there, posted themselves next to him, and gave him a powerful prod in the ribs when he was going to call out something to their leader. "*Sst!* Be quiet or . . ."

David was quiet as, with hollow eyes, he watched a dozen men hurrying along the passage as quietly as their footgear allowed, until they came to the door of the living room.

Signora Graziadeo and old Susanna had heard the noise at the front door. Paralyzed with fear, they remained sitting on their chairs, staring at the *sbirri* as they entered. The captain considered one man sufficient for watching the two women. The rest went to the back of the house.

Their search there took up some considerable time. At last they returned, dragging Geronimo with them, his hands tied behind his back. The bruises on his face testified to the kicks and blows he had received. One of his eyes was almost closed, and he found it obviously difficult to move forward as quickly as they expected him to. In such plight, he was dragged into the living room, where he collapsed upon a chair, and with the one eye that still served him sought his mistress's forgiveness for appearing before her in his underwear — he had been busy changing. Neither of the women, however, dared to look at him.

"Tie *his* paws together too, and bring him in here," said the captain, pointing to David. "Then we have them all together." While David's wrists were, with rough gestures, being bound behind his back, his eyes followed the *sbirri* as they started to go upstairs: at the first cry he heard he would tear himself away from his guards and hurry to Leah's help. He would be able to do nothing for her, but he could die for her. That was at least something.

There was no cry — nothing. The *sbirri* kicked him before them towards the living room, and he did not see Leah as she came downstairs softly, with staring eyes.

The quarter of an hour that David spent in the living room, hearing no sound above his head but the shuffling backwards and forwards of heavy boots, haunted his memory for many a long day.

At last the men came downstairs again. In the passage, near the front door, there was a loud and sudden uproar. "Did you leave the door unguarded?" "But we were ordered to take him into the room." "Idiots! Fools! Swine! One of you could have remained here. And didn't you even notice, *mille fulmine*, that the door was open . . . ?"

One of the *sbirri* called David: he was wanted by the captain. David followed him trembling. The leader of the *sbirri* came and stood before him, straddle-legged, and looked at him threateningly as he said, "You told us a lie!"

"Told you a lie, captain?"

"Don't pretend you're stupider than you are! He was in the house. Deny it if you dare!"

"He had gone, I swear it. I heard the door. Geronimo!" He looked round helplessly.

The leader of the *sbirri* took a grim delight in misunderstanding him. "Oh, you heard the door, did you? Then you heard more than we did! You ought to have told us that, Jew. Here, take that!" He gave David a resounding slap on the cheek, turned round, and kicked the front door to.

David, his cheek flaming where he had been struck, stared in amazement at the angry officer. Had somebody escaped since the police entered the house?

Suddenly he moaned, "Leah! Didn't you see her upstairs? Then she must have fled into the street." He wanted to rush upstairs to convince himself with his own eyes that Leah was in her room, but the *sbirri* seized him and threw him on his knees.

His arms akimbo, the captain bent over the pitiable specimen of humanity lying before him on the stone floor, and, somewhat relieved, inquired, "Whom are you talking about? Your sister?"

"My betrothed," panted David.

The leader looked round towards his men, who were trying to meet his glance. "His betrothed? While we were searching the first room, she must have passed across the landing, and there wasn't a soul down here to watch the front door! You'll pay for this!" He turned to David again. "Has she run away to go and warn him?"

David ran his hand over his head. Could that be true, that she had rushed out of the house to go and warn that Christian, leaving them all behind in terror and anxiety, exposed to the wrath of the *sbirri?*

"Stand up when you speak to me!" thundered the officer, and immediately his satellites hoisted David up like a sack. "Now go on: I'm waiting for a reply."

Trembling in his whole body, David could think of nothing to say except: "She won't find him. We don't know where he is."

"We know where to find him, but we can't catch him there," growled the captain, exasperated, as he turned to his men again. "At least with such bunglers as you, I can't!"

David had recovered. Suddenly he visualized the possibility of being useful to the *sbirri*, of bringing to his downfall that thousand-times-accursed Christian: that would be some small compensation, at least, for the fact that Leah was wandering alone through the city in the dark. "Captain: I'll get him to come here, if you tell me where I can write."

Astonished, the leader looked at the young Jew to whom life had so unexpectedly returned. The thought of a possible deception, which had crossed his mind, left him as he looked into David's eyes.

"Good. Write," he said — and to his men: "Unfasten him, for he can't do it like that, and take him into the room if there's ink and a quill there."

"Not in the room," implored David quickly, afraid. "To the back of the house."

"To the back of the house," commanded the captain, without making any effort to guess why David preferred not to write this little letter under the eyes of the others.

A few minutes later, he read through with heavy mockery the hastily scribbled epistle. "Leah?" he then inquired, vaguely astonished. "I thought that was a woman . . ."

David ventured to cut him short, and as a counter-service for writing the letter of his own free will, almost insisted on a promise from him: "May I depend upon it, Captain, that my betrothed will never know who wrote, using her name?"

The captain, taken by surprise, nodded in spite of himself. Then he folded the sheet of paper, and said, "We'll see that it gets into his hands as soon as possible. And perhaps we shall have him here within the hour, for what you have written is rather urgent. Are you sure he doesn't know her handwriting? Good. Meantime, we'll wait here to see what happens. Luigi, take this. You know the address. Try to smuggle it in without being seen yourself. I entrust it to you, because you're less of an impossible ass than the others. . . . Off with you!"

He was now well disposed towards David. He patted him on the shoulder and said he could return to the living room. "If we are able to catch the bird, we shall still want you," he said. "You can open the door to him."

Four men were posted at the front door. The others, while they waited on events, made themselves comfortable in the living room. One of them, preceded by the trembling Susanna, descended with a candle to the cellar and returned with a dozen bottles of wine. The captain tried to enter into conversation with Signora Graziadeo. He sat down on one of the wailing stools, and asked her with genuine interest why Jews liked to sit so low. . . .

By this time, Signora Graziadeo had learned that Leah had run out into the streets again. Not knowing what to do, she sighed and moaned and tried to get some word out of David; but he merely stared before him, and now and again passed his hand over his forehead, as if in severe pain. The captain of the *sbirri* laughed consolingly — "It will soon pass, my friend!" For he imagined David was suffering from the blows he had received. David did not even hear him: he only heard what had been said a moment before — that he must open the door for the Cavaliere. He realized now that it would be useless to ask for permission to go and look for Leah. In his imagination he saw her roaming about in the dark, searching for that *goy* who, God willing, would be undone by his hand (but that, Leah must never know). In his mind's eye he saw her the victim of an accident — saw her assaulted by some scoundrel. . . . He bent his head and prayed, swaying backwards and forwards in his grief; and when his aunt saw that, it was too much for her, and she began to sway in unison; loudly she began to wail a Jewish lament.

The chief of the *sbirri* raised his head in amazement, and, unable to believe his eyes and ears, watched this performance. His men had emptied their bottles of wine. It was heavier than the wine to which they were accustomed. Feelingly, they bellowed in concert; but this profanation scarcely penetrated to Signora Graziadeo and her nephew.

Susanna, old and deaf, was in the kitchen, preparing coffee for the gentlemen of the police, and although she was trembling all over, she was also inclined to think that this was a great moment. So many uniforms in the house, and all to get a criminal Christian into prison — where he belonged, where he belonged. If only nothing happened to Leah! Need she have run out into the street? The *shirri* escaped from the jeremiads in the living room and came to watch her at work in her kitchen. They nosed round in all the saucepans, and for once Susanna did not dare say anything. There was some goose left, because no one had been able to eat to-day . . . And then there was a tart for to-morrow, when more guests were expected. Here — would the gentlemen care to have some?

The gentlemen did care to have some; and the one who had gone down into the cellar with her a while since knew the way again.

II

For several weeks Galuppi had been going every night, more or less tipsy, to The Seven Heavens. The matron would have liked him to come during the day, because she had arranged with him that he was to do some mural paintings for the large reception room. He had brought several colored sketches that had been placed on chairs in the room on the ground floor where the matron led a respectable life with her husband and little daughter. But it had remained at that. By way of payment in advance, he came every night and drank for nothing. He then talked to the girls about Naiads and Tritons, instead of painting them. He had a marvelous idea for representing The Seven Heavens: the first a heaven in the blue depths of the ocean. He told the girls that he wanted to paint the matron as Neptune's wife, a crown of seaweed in the elaborate head-dress that was her pride, riding upon a dolphin to which he would give the physiognomy of her husband. She would be surrounded and supported by a bevy of lusty mermaids, in whom they would be able to recognize themselves.

That evening he was earlier than usual. He had attended the first night of "A Woman without a Heart," which had proved a hopeless fiasco, in spite of the moving words Rossi addressed to the audience before the play began. Those who had been present at the beginning were the last to hiss; but the catastrophe had been provoked by the unfeeling spectators who had arrived halfway through the first act. Galuppi did not deny, however, that he had hissed with the rest, confident that the author could no longer hear. Had he still been alive, he would have thrashed him for his tasteless play in which a woman who was high in Galuppi's esteem had been made to appear ridiculous on the stage. When the penetrating odor of rotten eggs began to predominate in the theater, Galuppi had left. Besides, he was anxious to know whether Cavaliere Bussoni had fled from Venice. He was no longer here? That was fine.

He was cheerfully playing cards with Beatrice, Rosalinda, and another drunken client, when Antea came slouching out of the back room and asked, "Where is Lucrezia? Her friend is back."

Galuppi broke off in the middle of a deal, stared at Antea for a second, and then said to the others: "Wait! I must speak to him."

He got up and staggered away. In momentary curiosity, the girls looked after him. Then they wanted to continue playing. "Let's go on! You take his place for the time being, Antea." Slowly she shook her head, and disappeared again.

A quarter of an hour later Galuppi returned with a flushed face. "I have told him, but it's no good," he said in answer to their questioning glances, and picked up the cards again with an uncertain hand. "I've told him he must fly from Venice this very night, if he's wise . . . The *shirri* are looking for him everywhere. There's a woman who's interested in him, too," he added a moment later, "but I don't know whether her interest will bring him luck. What are trumps?"

The game engrossed them too much for them to pay any particular attention to Galuppi's half-drunken chatter. Some new arrivals wanted to know how the first night of the dead abbé's play had gone off. Galuppi, now completely drunk, could only repeat over and over again: "The abbé is really dead now, gentlemen. Now he's really dead."

Her old Norwegian captain, who was so stiff with the gout that she had to help him on with his shoes, had just left Lucrezia when Antea came to tell her that her friend had returned. This news gave her a shock (he could see for himself, then, with whom he was safest from the *shirri*), but she wanted to show Antea that it left her cold, so with an indifferent expression she pulled up her stockings and powdered and rouged before joining Benedetto in the back room.

To make him conscious of his ingratitude, she adopted a more or less hostile attitude to him, and tried to raise his jealousy by talking of the dapper young Dutch seaman who had just left her with a promise to write to her from the Indies. "He wanted me to go with him, or, failing that, that I should join him in six months. He will send me the money for the voyage. But of course he won't. What man can one trust?"

She had once had a young Dutch seaman whom she had been unable to forget for months, and she had watched for his letter until all the others had begun to jeer at her: a letter he had certainly promised her.

She was afraid she had annoyed Benedetto. He did not react at all to the story about her young Dutchman, and her wounded pride gave place to humility. To make things right with him again she said, after some lengthy brooding, "Well — I shan't go anyhow, even if he does send me the money. I'll send it back to him or give it to the Church. All that way to the Indies, and then with a Dutchman! After all, we couldn't even understand one another."

Lucrezia sighed. She would have liked to know where Benedetto had been earlier in the evening. Something must have happened to him. He was no longer sullen and broken as before. A hidden glow smouldered in his eyes. He was restless. Perhaps he would like to be rid of her. But she was not going to leave him, even if he had got another woman in his head. Full of contempt and bitter jealousy, she said warningly, "You mustn't think you can depend upon another as you can depend upon me, as you can depend upon all of us here. Not one of us will betray you to the *sbirri* — we don't like them enough for that. But you would be making a mistake if you thought others would be so good at keeping their mouths shut. I'm only telling you because you should know. You mustn't think I'm jealous. . . ."

He buried his head in his hands in order to hear no more, to see no more. Why could they not leave him alone? A moment ago, Galuppi had actually tried to compel him to flee. . . . But he could not go, now that Leah had told him to come for her decision to-morrow. He had returned to The Seven Heavens because he did not know where else to hide. He would like to be alone, so that he could call up before his eyes his parting with Leah. It crossed his mind that he might expect something from her decision, since she had nothing more to lose. She was a stranded soul like himself. He felt a longing to surrender to his dreams; but out of every word that the woman beside him spoke sounded the vanity of dreams.

Lucrezia broke off in the middle of a sentence when Benedetto buried his head in such a pained way. It stirred her profoundly. She hoped that he was feeling compunction, and that, helpless, he would allow her to console him after all. If he were to promise her that they should fly to-gether, she would swear eternal troth to him. . . . Slowly she got up, leaning her hands upon the table. Her eyes were moist and large. She thought she would go to him, round the table, noiselessly. It was quiet; she held her breath. . . .

Then the curtain opened. From the reception room came the sound of voices, and the thrumming of Nanetta's broken guitar. Lucrezia, who had almost reached Benedetto, turned round startled: Antea was standing there. Yesterday she had been a messenger of evil, with her story of the Jew who had been shot down, and Lucrezia felt that she had come in in-tentionally, just at that moment. Her tender feelings changed to dull rage. Antea, however, subdued her with an icy, unnatural stare.

Defeat was in Lucrezia's voice: "What is it? Why have you come?"

Antea felt herself affronted, and did not answer. Passing Lucrezia, she went up to Benedetto and threw down a note under his nose.

"Here; they've brought this for you."

He looked up, bewildered. Hesitating, he unfolded the little sheet of paper. Lucrezia saw the emotion upon his face as his eye ran over the contents. Suddenly she could contain herself no longer and snatched at the note, intending to throw it through the window. But he was too quick for her, and snatched it back.

Now he was awake. He groped for his cloak and hat, shook off Lucrezia, who tried in foolish despair to throw herself round his neck.

When he had left the house, she got up slowly. Antea still stood there, upon her face a lifeless smile. As she turned to go, Lucrezia ceased to fear her: loudly, so that Antea should hear, she spat after her.

Antea, on the point of entering the large room, looked round with raised eyebrows — the eyebrows that, with a cunning hand, she penciled a little, to heighten the effect of her sphinxlike expression.

III

Benedetto was scarcely in the street when it was thrust upon his consciousness that the note was a forgery. He stood still by a lantern and excitedly unfolded it again, after making sure that no one was observing him. No; this could not be Leah's handwriting. He had never seen her writing; but it must be a freer, more decorative hand, and she would have chosen her words differently — unless she had written these lines under dictation.

The whole note breathed a lie. He could not understand how he had been misled, even for a moment.

It was a snare. Even as he was rushing madly out of The Seven Heavens, he might have been overpowered. He considered whether he should go any farther. For a few seconds, he was shattered by his own suspicions.

Then he decided, after all, to take the risk. Anything was better than not to obey a summons that bore her name.

He went on his way, though he slowed down his steps. His brain, which for a second had been so clear, had grown dull again. He had ceased to look round to see if he were being followed. He fancied that he was quieter, and could face calmly whatever awaited him that evening. As he was being ferried across the canal by San Samuele's, a dozen gondolas drifted by carrying carnival merrymakers. He watched the procession pass, and the thought struck him that the whole of life was like a theatrical performance — at any moment the curtain might fall.

Then he reached the neighborhood of Leah's house. This was the spot where he had once been left bleeding by the water's edge. Graziadeo, who had rescued him then, had now himself found death in the water.

He felt a moment's uncertainty. A chill shudder of vague anxiety ran down his spine; but he overcame this last weakness and hastened on, as if he suddenly were afraid of arriving too late.

Now he was standing at the front door. He laid his hand upon the knocker: it gave him a peculiar sense of familiarity this evening — surely the allegorical bird must recognize the pressure of his hand by now. There was no one in the little street. His knock reverberated through the stillness. . . .

The door was not opened so quickly, this time, as it had been a couple of hours ago when he had come to assert his innocence of the murder of Graziadeo. The same face, however, did appear, after a few seconds, behind the judas.

The door opened, but before crossing the threshold Benedetto waited until he could see David, the new master of the house, in the semidarkness of the doorway. David was trembling so violently that he was unable to inquire what brought Benedetto there at that time of night.

Benedetto could see the treachery in those dark, fearful, birdlike eyes. It was ridiculously clear — and behind David he heard a boot scraping against the floor. There stood the traitor who had laid the snare into which he had willingly flown. There stood the writer of Leah's letter; and behind him were waiting the *sbirri*, waiting for his victim to enter.

Had Benedetto turned and run as fast as his feet could carry him down the street, round the corner, towards the little square onto which five other passages debouched — then the labyrinth of Venice would certainly have saved him again.

But stronger than the longing to escape rose the urge to fly at the throat of the traitor standing before him, to deprive him of the last little bit of breath he still possessed.

With a penetrating cry of "*Help!*" David fell like a log. A catlike figure had hurled itself upon him, and now knelt upon him, throttling him with iron fingers.

At the same moment the front door was slammed to, and in the halfdarkness of the entrance blows fell on attacker and attacked. Only after a confused and lengthy struggle were the half-drunken *sbirri* successful in overmastering the devil who had sprung in from the street.

Groaning and bleeding, David got up and groped his way towards the living room, where his aunt fainted. To old Susanna, who was clasping both hands at her heart, he said with the sullen satisfaction of a man who has carried out a difficult mission at the risk of his life, "They've got him!"

When the *shirri* had gone with their prisoner, leaving the house behind them in complete confusion though unwatched, David had recovered sufficiently to throw his cloak about him and go out to look for Leah in the night — an almost hopeless undertaking.

Excited and blustering, the *shirri* led Benedetto away. His hair was disheveled, his clothes torn. They called for a gondola, pushed him in, and sat down beside him with their carbines between their knees. When they knew themselves to be safely on their way to the prison with him, they began to brag to each other about their share in the capture. By the light of a lantern, they looked at his face as at a curiosity. A cool, dangerous fellow! But he had fallen into the right hands! They would have to be careful, however, lest he made his escape as they stepped out. The safest plan would be to enter the gaol from the waterside.

Benedetto was not afraid of prison. There at last he would be left alone. He had never been in one, and was almost curious to know what it would look like inside. The one thing he would have liked to know was how things were with David; and he would also have liked to ask Leah's forgiveness. She would never know about the note. David would certainly not confess his heroic deed to her. She must be thinking his attack on her betrothed an act of wanton brutality. He would not rise in her estimation through it; but it did not matter. Everything was over. Perhaps at this moment she was consoling David, and binding up his wounds.

Had they not reached their destination yet? Longingly, impatiently, Benedetto looked over the water he was traversing for the last time. A ridiculous fear suddenly welled up in him: they would have to go under the Ponte della Paglia; would *she* not be standing there, and grinning down at him — his centenarian lady friend?

No. Instead of old deceased Signora Galli, another apparition waited for him there on the bridge by the gaol: dark and slim, her eyes riveted on the gondola that was approaching with rapid strokes of the oar.

Benedetto stared into those great dark eyes, and he was trembling as David had done at the door of her house.

"Leah . . . !" he wanted to cry out, but he could not find his voice.

Instead, the *shirri* raised their heads and called something to her: they took her to be one of the girls from The Seven Heavens or The Falling Star.

With open mouth, a prey to the most wonderful stirrings of anxiety, shame, and joy, he looked up at this magical apparition until the gondola glided into the darkness under the vault of the bridge, beyond which gleamed the little canal that ran past the gaol.

When they cleared the bridge, he looked up again; and Leah had fulfilled the prayer he had sent up from the darkness: she had run across with the gondola, and was now standing on this side of the bridge. She looked at him as she had done when he held the doorknob in his hand as he was about to leave her room; but this time she did not speak his name.

With rough force, the *sbirri* threw him through the watergate of the gaol. At the last moment, he would not obey, and tried to offer resistance to all of them. With a piteous cry, he gave way at last to their united efforts.

The gate was slammed to; the heavy rusty bolt was shot into place.

When Leah, there on the bridge, heard the crash, she slowly bowed her head between her shoulders. Thus she stood, her slender hands on the broad stone parapet of the bridge, and stared down as the gondola that had brought Benedetto returned to the large canal, until the eddies it left behind under the bridge were stilled. Then she was put to flight by a noisy carnival procession approaching along the Riva.

She shrank into a dark corner, away from the foolish merrymakers. She had no purpose any more. All she knew was that she could not return home, where her aunt and David were waiting for her.

Benedetto she would only see again in a world where there were no more Jews and Christians, and where earthly ties ceased to count.

There she would meet Uncle Solomon, too. Uncle Solomon had been flung into one of the canals of Venice, and his body had drifted out to sea. . . .

The water lured her with a magical power. She felt the temptation to look into it, to run along the uttermost edge of it, dizzily, with closed eyes.

Why should she seek God's wide, safe distances longer, when she was so tired — so tired? Surely they were close — close in the magical depths of every canal?

A quiet, deserted quay . . . No lights in any house, on either side . . . No footsteps, no voices . . . Stillness. A star looked down through a hole in the clouds. At first the water would be cold and dark; but then, suddenly, the golden sunkissed fields of God would open out.

Forgiveness, David. If you have loved me, you will also forgive me.

Forgiveness, Aunt. And you too, old Susanna, and good Geronimo —
forgiveness.

The clouds thickened; and the water, opening like a black crater, and
pressing up in eddies against the stone quayside, closed again, shimmered,
and was still.

CHRISTMAS

BELLS

I

CURSING BETWEEN HIS TEETH, SILVIO CLOSED THE door of Gracias' room behind him, and angrily went down the stairs past Annibale, who made way reluctantly for him. She had given him a note to deliver to Baron Barbaresco, her old judge, and he felt a great desire to crumple the bit of paper, tear it in pieces with his teeth, and spit it out.

But he recovered control of himself and with an angry grimace tucked it into his red silk sash.

He shot past all the other gondolas on the Grand Canal, gliding by without a word of greeting to any of his fellow gondoliers who steered them, and as he did so vowed to himself that he would have her yet. He had only made a mistake in choosing the moment — that was all.

The one remaining person who could have stood in his way, she had had thrown into gaol — and it was unlikely he would re-emerge from there. She had given information in the right quarter about that gentleman, and when Messer-Grande had been unable to catch him quickly enough, she had helped. Galuppi, the sot, had had to tell her where he had spoken to him; and after that Silvio had enjoyed the pleasure of investigating Cavaliere Bussoni's comings and goings at her behest. He had acquitted himself well in his task: a few hours after he had started to keep a watch for the culprit, in the neighborhood of The Seven Heavens, the *sbirri* had captured their man.

It was because of this rapid success, and the certainty that the only person he had occasion to fear was safely locked up, that he had been unable to keep his hands to himself. She had bitten his wrist. But on second thoughts, perhaps this might be described as their first intimacy.

She had accursed sharp little teeth, but he had always suspected that. It rather pleased him. She had cried for help, and of course Marianna had come into the room at once— she had been standing waiting.

His insane ambition had gone to his head. But she herself had tempted him. She ought to have realized that a man of his kind would take the whole hand when a finger was offered. He knew other gondoliers who slept in beds where no one would have expected them to be. In the eyes of the world they were servants, but secretly they were kings who guzzled the best wines in the cellar, gambled shamelessly with their mistresses' money, and, by way of thanks, thrashed them when they felt like it and there were no witnesses.

Why, when she was about to cry out, had he not seized her by her slim throat, and pressed her back against the wall, his face upon hers, so that she would have realized at once what sort of man she had to deal with? Was he less of a man than Marco and Zeno and those others, of whose heroic deeds he had heard tales?

When, however, things got as far as he intended, he would not boast about it as they did. It would be sufficient for him that he and she, the two of them, knew about it. He wanted to inhale her perfume, the perfume of a young lady — that pretty, costly little animal, who spent half the day before her toilet table, and for whom the most expensive scents and soaps were not expensive enough. He wanted to bury his head in the soft stuffs in which she arrayed herself, and, drunk with that, he wanted to see and feel the soft, white woman's flesh she concealed under them. Those pearls and diamonds of hers, and those other shining stones of which he did not even know the names — he would tear them from her, and slip them into his pocket, to teach her to whom it all belonged. He would make her beg and implore him to return them to her, one by one — if he had not already taken them to a Jew. And, by God, perhaps he would be unable to refrain on occasion from casually taking a handful out of his pocket, as did Marco and Zeno; from hurling an emerald necklace across the pavement when the others tried to persuade him to take part in a game of dice.

Oh, he would humble her pride. He would make her pay for pointing him to the door, white with mortified pride. He would make her pay for being a lady while he was only a vulgar gondolier. He had made her feel it already: she was afraid of him, and she had good reason to be. Did she imagine her old judge would offer her a refuge from him? Otherwise why had she remembered him again so suddenly? It was all one to him. He could wait until she was cured of that fancy, too. She would certainly not dismiss him again. She had done that once, and she had discovered that it did not help. She belonged to him. She had lured him to her, and now she could no longer hold back the course of events. Because he knew that, it suited him to exercise patience. A smile, nothing but a smile, deprived her finally of tranquillity . . .

When, half an hour later, he returned with the old judge's reply, he found Marianna at the foot of the staircase. She tried to make it appear that only coincidence had brought them together there. Poor Marianna! As if he did not know she had been waiting for him since the moment she expected his return. She had been listening there in the half-darkness, trembling at every sound that reached her from above, from the back of the house, from outside. And at last she had heard the scraping of the gondola's *ferro* against the poles by the steps, the clink of the mooring chain, the crunching of a footstep on the marble.

The smile he had destined for her mistress he directed to her maid: he did not want her to imagine he had not seen through her. Besides — she was beginning to weary him. He had made it plain to her, often enough, that he had had enough of her. Did she imagine she could lecture him about what had happened upstairs before he went out?

He had long since forgotten why he had once lain in wait for her and kissed her in the neck, breaking her resistance quietly, stubbornly. Probably she herself had wanted it, even though she had struggled against it when it came to the point. Perhaps she had pleased him only once — that evening when, hungry, he had come home and seen her slender figure flit softly, rapidly down the half-dark passage. Perhaps any woman would have tempted him that evening. He only knew that the minute he held her prisoner in his arms he felt a sudden aversion for her, an aversion for her false primness, for her furious struggle against something that appeared to him not worth talking about, perhaps even more for the wild feverish fire that seemed to smoulder in that prudish, tender body.

Then she noticed that she had served merely as a rung upon the ladder that led to her mistress's boudoir, and she began to hinder him with her morbid suspicions, her hysterical jealousy.

He was tempted to kick her — that would get her out of his way for good. He was exasperated by this calculated meeting at the foot of the stairs. Only an involuntary respect for the refinement in her appearance, a latent fear that she might avenge herself at a moment when he least suspected it, held him back: with those thin, pale, hysterical girls, in whom a hidden fire smouldered, it was necessary to be careful.

He did not bother, however, to conceal his disdain and annoyance. "What are you doing here?" he inquired, and then affronted her by looking past her down the passage and saying warningly, "Be careful that the old man doesn't see you here with me!"

Yes, that had wounded her. She came and stood straight in front of him with flashing eyes. At that moment, hatred had almost conquered her despair. She elected to ignore his warning, and instead of answering it, she retaliated with, "Suppose you tell me what *you're* doing in this house!"

He stared at her, and had a mind to strike her a blow on the head that would fell her to the marble floor. He could not speak.

When she saw he was unable to reply, she said, "You were talking about the 'old man.' Are you sure you've taken sufficient account of him? Perhaps he's not so old as you think."

This, happily, gave him a way of escape from his mute rage. "Yes, you ought to know that, better than I do!"

She swallowed this fresh affront: she had her purpose, and she pursued it determinedly.

"What would you say — if one fine day he were to marry me? and we went off together?"

Silvio could hardly restrain his laughter.

"Is that the sort of fairy tale he tells you?"

"I asked what you would say."

"Ah, well . . . I should wish you luck from the bottom of my heart."

"And perhaps you'll have good reason to," said Marianna, weak and suddenly helpless, because she felt she had spoken too soon, and her words had only revealed her inner misery.

Silvio had had enough of this conversation. He pushed her to one side, and was about to hurry upstairs, when suddenly she clung to him, clasping his knees with her thin arms.

"Silvio, don't think I'm telling you lies. He wants to go away with me! Haven't you noticed how he goes out again, in spite of his stiff leg? He watches the departure of his ships again these days. . . . He wants to leave secretly with me, settle up his affairs here, and leave his daughter a definite income on which she can just live. He wants to revenge himself, and save himself before she ruins him completely. He still wants to take from life what it can offer him — and he has chosen me as the woman with whom to end his life. Silvio, I'm betraying this to you. I know it won't help . . . You don't care for me any more; and yet, if you wished, I would keep him here — him and his money! Silvio . . . !"

She wanted to say more, but the words would not come. Sobs rose in her throat.

In astonishment, he stood a moment listening to her boastful words. He only grasped from her foolish story that she was trying to play off the old man against him. What did it matter to him if *lo Spagnuolo* wanted to hasten his death by a little honeymoon trip? And if she liked to go with him, he would not prevent her. She hinted something about his taking his moneybags away with him too, and at the end of the riotous living in the little Gothic palace. But that, Silvio thought, remained to be seen. For the time being he was not inclined to take it too seriously. In any case, she was mistaken if she thought he was after his mistress's money: it was the woman herself he wanted.

He looked down at Marianna as at a patient who must be treated carefully. Then he bent and resolutely freed himself from her pitiful embrace with the very hands that had once seized her, abased her, and turned her into his slave.

Without paying her any further attention, he went upstairs and handed his mistress the reply to her note. But he forgot his little smile.

II

A quarter of an hour later, as darkness was falling, Gracias was on her way to her old judge — who had agreed, courteously and without pausing for consideration, to receive her at once. She sat huddled in the gondola under the dark shelter of the *felze*. When she stepped out, she ignored the hand that Silvio with quiet impudence extended to her. With bowed head, she disappeared quickly through the door a liveried servant opened wide.

Inside, in the brightly lit salon, she found a Baron Barbaresco who had recovered from his recent dangerous aberrations. If she had imagined that she could renew her former little game with him, she saw at once that she was mistaken. She noticed quickly, also, that he had understood that it was not for his sake, but for the sake of another, that she had come to him that evening. Ah, well, in that case she need not trouble to attempt to delude him. She was grateful to him for the purity of his feelings and the tact with which he tried to conceal that he had seen through her. He was no longer angry about that other evening. He had forgiven her, and was glad to have the opportunity to prove that to her. He wanted her to see the victory he had obtained over himself, and he pretended not to notice that this victory rather saddened her — though that she would not have admitted, even to herself. He tried to be an amusing, entertaining, attentive, entirely disinterested host. He brought the conversation round at once to the young cavaliere whom the hand of justice had cast into prison the previous night, thanks primarily to her denunciations. Gracias' feelings immediately got the better of her: she began to sob, bending forward in the broad, old-fashioned armchair in which he had made her sit down. He looked at her quietly for a moment, with a smile. Then he ventured to run his hand over her head. She seized it and pressed it against her moist cheek. Then she confessed to him that in a moment of rage she had wanted to bring about Benedetto's undoing, but that now her desire for revenge was dead, now she wanted to save him; and in her despair she had come to the judge, because only through him could Benedetto possibly be saved.

In the course of her confession, Giuseppe peered discreetly round the door. Could he serve? His master nodded acquiescence.

To Gracias, he said that she expected a great deal of him, but he would think it over while they sat at table, and after they had eaten he would give her his answer and his advice.

She was sure he could easily save Benedetto, and, half-consoled by the mere fact that he now knew her wish, she allowed herself to be comforted by him. With her little lace handkerchief she wiped away her tears as he took her gallantly by the hand to show her several paintings that were his pride. She stood entranced before a small Tintoretto, representing an elopement in a gondola by moonlight. For a moment he was tempted to make her a present of it — it was his own favorite; but he felt he could not, after all, part with it, and led her to the table.

For weeks she had been living under unceasing pressure, but only now did she realize this. She would have liked to stay with her judge longer than just an hour or two. She had almost a mind to seduce him after supper, as a reward for his exemplary conduct and to make good her former mean deception. Should she? After all, it would not be so difficult. But first he must drink with her to Benedetto's speedy release — the release of *il pipistrello* — her tiger. He must first swear that he would put that matter right to-morrow. After all, was he not a judge? He merely had to say the word; and besides — justice, in Venice! The innocent were clapped into prison, and the rogues left free. He would manage it for her! He had always been her good friend, the best of them all, and she had treated him outrageously. She regretted that. Later on, after she had seduced him, she would ask his forgiveness. She would like to call him "father" — would he be affronted if she asked him whether she might?

During dessert, Gracias remembered that she had told Silvio to wait for her outside. She wished she had sent him home again; but how could she have known that she would find her old judge in this mood? She had expected simply — and in all courtesy — to strike a bargain with him. But time was passing, and there had been no negotiations over such a bargain.

In fact, it had slipped her mind. She thought she had drunk a good deal: her thoughts were no longer very clear. She still had to make Barbaresco swear, glass in hand, that he would free Benedetto for her. Yes, but had he not promised something of the sort a while ago? She was tired, and, closing her eyes, she laid her head on his shoulder. She would have liked to fall asleep, and only wake again far, far away from Venice. . . . In the old days she had gone on long voyages with her father, as far as the coasts of the Indies. . . . In the old days, when she had still been a child . . . Had she ceased to be a child?

Baron Barbaresco did not move, but allowed her to rest quietly against him and think of the past. Why did he not lift her up and carry her, half-asleep, to the sofa? She was beginning to pity herself. She decided to rouse his jealousy. Softly, poutingly, she began to tell him about her lover whom she had helped to bring to gaol, how passionate and fiery he was, and how he allowed himself to be tormented by her — no man would ever again allow himself to be tormented by her like that; and he was writing an opera: she had heard the beginning of it. He had played portions of it to her; for it was for her that he was composing his opera. It would have had a different sort of first night altogether from that unfortunate play dedicated to her in which she was supposed to be able to recognize herself. Three-and-thirty lovers! She had never had more than one at a time. She had only loved two men in her life, and those two she had tormented most. Was it really so dreadful that her friend had struck down the unfortunate abbé? It had happened in a proper duel, and the abbé ought not to have provoked him. And as for that other matter, about which she had written to the tribunal, the thing that had happened long ago — she would recant that to-morrow; and in that case she would like to have her ring back, the ring that he, Barbaresco, had presented to her one evening. . . .

As she went on talking in this fashion, looking up into his eyes every now and again caressingly and helplessly, his eyes rested on her small hand from which the ring was missing. Unconsciously she ran the other hand over the place where she had worn the gem; and because he so disliked to disappoint her, he considered seriously whether there was anything that could be done in this hopeless affair. It was clear that Gracias had made up her mind, before coming to him, that she was prepared to pay a price — not too high a price, when one thought of the risks he had already run for her sake. He felt, too, that she would pay that price gladly and from the heart. Yes; perhaps she would even be affronted if he did not demand what she was prepared to offer him as a pure gift. Oh, he was justified in any case in considering it as repayment of an old debt.

And it was not so easy for him, either, to renounce what had so unexpectedly fallen into his lap. He had waited for her — longer than that one night. While she had remained in his debt, he had still dared to hope, had waited in secret for her — not perhaps, in the end, in actuality; but certainly in his dreams. Reality had been filled with other matters; but his dream had grown dear to him. He would not like to be without it. If he were to accept from her, after she had drunk rather too much good wine, the gift with which she had originally meant to effect the liberation of her lover . . . Would he have anything more to wait for in life? In his dream, she could make him happy: he would be satisfied with his dream. He did not want more. Probably she would feel a little affronted and angry; but he knew what he wanted — thank God, he knew again what he wanted. He was not going to be deprived a second time of his self-esteem, recovered with such difficulty, and of his ascendancy over life.

So, gently, and with wise words, he tried to make her understand that she could not expect a judge to coöperate in effecting the liberation of a guilty man; but he would see that the matter was properly investigated, that guilt — if there was guilt — was conclusively proved. He would try to see that all extenuating circumstances were taken into account. He would inquire into the prison conditions of the accused, and have it conveyed to the gaoler that things were to be made as easy as possible for him in every respect.

Gracias listened doubtfully to all these words: Barbaresco did not speak of Benedetto's release. It was true that he gave the whole affair a milder, less dangerous cast. She saw before her eyes a lenient tribunal — and things would be made pleasant for him, there in prison. . . . Then suddenly she was aware that this did not help her at all, that this was not the way to bring him back to her. She had gambled him away; this was the punishment for her betrayal. Barbaresco could not help her, or he would not. . . . He no longer wanted her either. He who still wanted her was waiting outside in his gondola. Oh, he could wait! She would not go yet. She would remain where she was a little longer. She *must* seduce Barbaresco.

She pretended to be completely reassured by his words. Here — he got a kiss for that. She was quite relieved. She wanted more to drink. And he must kiss her on her mouth — he had never done that. He must console her, for, merry as she appeared, she had her troubles. And not only about her friend in prison . . .

Then she cried and laughed again. She threw her arms round Barbaresco's head and pressed it to her bosom. It looked as if this poor Antony in the desert, despite his heroic resistance, was going to succumb to temptation, after all. . . . Then suddenly there was a knock at the door, and Giuseppe came to say that Silvio, the gondolier, had insisted on his coming to inquire whether he was to wait any longer for his mistress. . . .

The master of the house raised himself from the sofa with as much dignity as he could muster, and turned an interrogative glance towards Gracias, who tried to collect herself. She turned pale, and for a moment she, too, could find no words. Then she asked for her cloak. He need not escort her — she would be safe under the protection of her gondolier. Could she count upon seeing him at her house again? He gave the required promise, and knew that for self-preservation he would not keep it.

As he went to fetch her cloak, she cast a melancholy glance round the empty room where she had hoped to find help and salvation. She had merely found a friend who could not help her.

Outside, Silvio was waiting: he offered her his hand again, as though she had not already more than once ignored this gesture. Silently, with his wild brute force, he drove her gondola, with her in it, through the dark fathomless night. . . .

III

Samuel Graziadeo, Solomon's twin brother, had come over from Ançona. He was equally thin, and of the same aristocratic Jewish type, but he looked infinitely older, more worn. Life had been less easy for him. But he did not speak of the cares that had bowed his shoulders. Indeed, he spoke but little, and shyly eluded his sister-in-law's boisterous despair. Apart from his many and faithful prayers, he opened his lips only to ask a dreamy, absent-minded question now and again about his dead brother or about Leah: he had seen her once as a child during a previous visit to Venice years before. He inquired whether she had not grown into a very pretty young woman . . . ? She had had such exceptional eyes. He could still recall them. It would have been more to the purpose if he had been able to occupy his mind with Signora Graziadeo and David, who were still alive, lost in grief and in need of advice and support. But Samuel was not a man to give them support. Rather he seemed to require it himself, though of a different kind: he had come without money for his return journey — and the money for his journey to Venice he had had to borrow. This was the only good he did his sister-in-law, and that was involuntary: he made her forget her grief for a moment, in exasperation over the brother-in-law who had appeared simply to claim his inheritance from his wealthier brother, so that he could provide a meager dowry for his four daughters. Signora Graziadeo was waiting impatiently for the notary to hand him his money, so that he could return to Ancona. Why had she summoned him? From respect for her husband, who had always loved his only brother, and had sent him money from time to time (though *she* had never heard of that before). Rachel could not restrain herself from throwing that into his teeth, and he bowed his head, muttering shamefacedly.

They were sitting on the low chairs, praying by the subdued light of a lamp. In his almost intolerable grief, David was rocking his slim body backwards and forwards, backwards and forwards until he could bear no more, and then he gave vent to his great sorrow in a wailing cry in which the two women joined, sobbing miserably. Even Rabbi Isidore could get no word out of him. Half the day he sat there, neglecting his business. There was no one for whom he need work now, said he. In the ghetto they predicted that he would go off his head with grief, because his pretty sweetheart had drowned herself for a *goy*.

And then, like a refreshing west wind, Rachel's brother Nathan from Trieste blew into the house and cleared away the cobwebs of despair. Merciful heaven, he had come after all! It was as his sister had thought: he had been too busy when the news reached him to leave at once, but now he had arrived. He had had a terrible crossing on a wretched felucca. He had thought it was all over with him — such a storm! He meant to return by land. Where was his trunk? Sara had given him a few trifles to bring along with him. Something for Leah too: everything had already been packed when the second news arrived from Venice. Also a home-made cake of which his little Sara knew the secret. He could not eat it on the way because of the storm. And now they must tell him how in God's name all this had come about.

In almost every respect, he was a contrast to his relative by marriage from Ancona. He was pink and well-set-up, spoke with excited gestures, and liked to hold the floor. When his sister had sobbed out the whole story to him once, it was enough: he knew everything. With a somewhat childish ostentation he played with his heavy rings and watch-chain ornaments; he maintained that the solitaire in his jabot had not its equal in Trieste. He wore showy and expensive clothes, and an uncommonly luxuriant and much-curled wig, from under which, when he had talked loud and long, drops of sweat came rolling and a little rim of his own red hair showed. Oh, he had always been the pride and glory of his sister Rachel. Immediately he breathed fresh life into the house. Plans were immediately considered and rejected. He looked at David as he sat there broken, and tried to instill new life into him by talking about his shop in the ghetto. It really pleased him that the boy was grieving so genuinely for his betrothed. He must be industrious — Rachel had assured him as much; but it was not apparent now, in his listless manner. And when he did manage to drag out of David the details of his business, Nathan was not impressed: he had a better idea for him altogether than running a fiddling hosier's shop in the ghetto here. David must go with him to Trieste. There a Jewish business man did not have to rely solely upon his own race, as he did in Venice. There Jews and Christians mixed. . . . Well, it was an offer. He could take it or leave it. David could come into his, Nathan's, business, if he wished — it was not likely he would have a second chance like that in his life. He would be like one of the family. His wife and his daughter Rebecca would be like a mother and a sister to him, and he would have no occasion to complain about the food. Oh, Venice was nothing — a dying city, a dead city, a city that had survived itself. Trieste! Trieste was a city with a future . . .

As he talked in this breezy fashion, at a loss to understand why the boy had not already thrown his arms round his neck, Rachel drew her brother into the adjoining room and asked him in a bitterly reproachful tone whether she must be left alone simply because he wanted to find a good husband for his daughter Rebecca. No, she would not be left alone: Nathan had thought of that. She was fond of David: he was as a son to her. She must move to Trieste too, away from this Venice that had been of no use to her. At first, until she had got over her grief, she could live with him.

Rachel, taken aback, did not know what to say. Certainly she could not and would not live alone in this large house. She must return to the ghetto. That had once been her dream, and with David and Leah she would have been glad to return. But Leah was dead (the shame of it, a betrothed Jewish maid who flew out of the house at night to throw herself into the water!), and if David were persuaded to go to Trieste . . . In Trieste she would certainly enjoy her brother's proximity, but of course she would fall out with Sara . . . And then she would feel more isolated than here in Venice with her old Susanna. Besides, in the ghetto here, everyone knew who she was and who her husband had been. For his sake, they would perhaps forget Leah's offense. . . .

For the time being all Rachel said was, "And what about this house? Has this house been sold? So long as that hasn't happened, we can't begin to talk about anything at all." No, this house need not be sold: it would remain her property. She could draw rent for it to the end of her days. Nathan had thought of that also. Who would live in the house? Samuel from Ancona. What sort of life had he in Ancona? He did not live there — he starved there, with his wife and his four daughters — who would never find husbands there, either. Ancona! Why, even Venice was better than Ancona. Samuel must come to Venice and take over Solomon's business. S. GRAZIADEO, JEWELER — that could remain. Who would notice? For a Christian, a Jew is a Jew. He could earn money here, just as well as his brother. He would grow stronger. His wife Miriam would get fat and round, and his daughters would find husbands and not become a burden to the family — as they otherwise would, as sure as fate.

Rachel had to admit defeat. Her brother had arrived, and his every word was a word of wisdom. She had never been able to withstand him, had always been a helpless tool in his hands. Thirty years ago, he had chosen a husband for her and she had taken him, although she had preferred another; but Nathan had turned out to be right. The other had departed for America, and nothing had ever been heard of him again. And now that her good Solomon was dead, her brother was taking her life into his hands for the second time, and she adapted herself thus: she would let David go to Trieste, to please her brother Nathan, and she would remain here herself. She would keep a room for herself in this large house. Thus she could live for nothing. Nathan nodded, satisfied, and on his thick red lips a smile appeared: he had understood that she wished him to have peace in his house.

In the evening the plan was laid before Samuel, who was at first a little distrustful. This plotting of brother and sister seemed rather formidable to him — life had made him fearful and skeptical. Gradually, however, he was won over, and in the end grew quite enthusiastic. A light awakened in his dull, weary eyes. Slowly running his hands backwards and forwards over his thin thighs, he looked at the ground in front of him, and saw himself liberated at last from the cares that had weighed him down all his life. He saw a satisfied, smiling Miriam, and her four daughters married to good Jewish husbands. His only hesitation now was about the costs of removal. . . . But with a large gesture Nathan dispelled this objection at once. Money would be advanced for the removal, and he need only pay rent when he was able to. Rachel wanted to add something, but Nathan looked at her inquiringly, and the words stuck in her throat.

Thenceforward, Rachel had a thousand things to talk over with Samuel. When Rabbi Isidore came to pay his visit of condolence, he found a widow who had returned to the things of this world, and he could go back and report to the ghetto that, with God's help, David also had been saved. . . .

Samuel had already returned to Ancona, and Nathan's departure was also drawing near. He and his sister sat together in the living room discussing the last necessary details. Geronimo was so abstracted within himself that they forgot his presence, and when the conversation turned upon Christians, they talked as freely as though no Christian had been present.

Signora Graziadeo blamed all her misfortunes upon Benedetto. Her smouldering hatred of the Christians had been fanned to a living flame. She hated them, madly, boundlessly. She scarcely noticed the signs Nathan was trying to make to her. Oh — because of Geronimo! She did not reckon him among the Christians. He had been in the house so long that it was not necessary to hold their tongues for his sake. Besides, he was only an orphan. Solomon had taken him into his service out of pity; and she could no longer be silent. If he was uncomfortable with them, he must go. Then they would all be Jews together. . . .

Geronimo scarcely heard what was being said; but for the first time since he had been in this house he felt himself alone. He felt as if he had strayed among people who were different from him and in whose midst he could never be at home. A vague, restless feeling came over him that whereas all these others were saving themselves from the frightful catastrophe that had befallen them, none thought of his predicament.

That evening, as the Christmas bells were ringing over Venice, he awoke from his apathy. They had been booming and reverberating for some time before he became clearly aware of them and realized why the bells would not be silent that evening. It was Christmas. His master and Signorina Leah had always honored the day for his sake. They had always tried to make it a feast day for him. His master had been in the habit of making him a present of a silver Venetian ducat, and Signorina Leah had made something for him every year with her own hands. He had always had the day off, and at midnight he had been allowed to go to San Marco's to attend the service, and see the crib.

But his master was dead, and misfortune had overwhelmed Signorina Leah too, and there was nobody in the house to remember that it was a feast day for him. While the bells were droning over Venice, these Jews, these unbelievers, sat together, and did not dare to show themselves in the streets because of what the Jews had once done to the Saviour. In this house, where they thought themselves safe, they dared to affront Christ by speaking ill of the Christians. As the golden light of the Star of Bethlehem shone over Venice and over the whole world, the owls were skulking together in the dark, blinking their eyes against the light that was too strong for them. . . .

Geronimo felt this for the first time in his life, as though he too were as foolish and ignorant as had been his comrades at the orphanage who had so infuriated him in the old days.

It was Christmas Eve. Must he continue to sit here listening to their blasphemies? His master had always given him leave this evening; this year he would give himself leave. He could not bring himself even to ask his mistress's permission. He meant to go out. Let them stop him if they dared.

Suddenly he got up and left the room without a word; but he noticed, not without satisfaction, that Signor Nathan broke off in the middle of a sentence. He was not displeased that they should know they had wounded him.

He went to the back of the house for his cloak, and as he was extracting his rosary from his working clothes, he thought again of what Signora Graziadeo had just been saying.

"My husband simply would let a room to that ill-starred *goy*. Solomon insisted upon having him in the house. He wouldn't listen, and it wasn't enough for this *goy* to plunge our house into mourning: if the *sbirri* hadn't interfered in time, David wouldn't be sitting there alive, either. He jumped at his throat like a raging animal. . . ."

Up to that moment, Geronimo had scarcely given a thought to what might have happened to the Cavaliere — his mind had been full of Signorina Leah and his master; but now, on this Christmas Eve, his thoughts turned to him again, and suddenly he guessed a truth about which there was a scrupulous silence in the house: Signorina Leah had loved the Cavaliere. Her pure heart must have belonged to him, for she had gone to meet death on the night that the *sbirri* had dragged him to gaol. Had she cared for Signorino David, her betrothed, she would still be alive. That she had thrown herself into the water from grief for her dead uncle, that she had been drowned accidentally in the dark, that she had been assaulted by some villain who had afterwards tried to hide his deed of shame by throwing her into a canal — these were the things they said in the house, and they said them because anything was better than that she should have chosen to die for the sake of a Christian.

It was clear to Geronimo that David had never deserved her love, and the discovery that she had in truth loved the Cavaliere was almost a satisfaction to him. He realized, too, that he had ill fulfilled his duty towards Signorina Leah in not having troubled himself further about the Cavaliere.

As he left the house, he decided that, before going to San Marco's, he would try to speak to the Cavaliere in prison: perhaps he could do something for him. They surely would not refuse a visitor to a prisoner on Christmas Eve. How was it possible he had not gone at once to the prison, if only to let the Cavaliere know of the terrible misfortune that had overtaken Signorina Leah? Had he heard already, from some other source?

Geronimo did not believe in the Cavaliere's guilt. He had never seriously believed, even for a moment, that he had shot down his master; and Signorina Leah had not believed it either.

Suddenly he knew that he would speak to the Cavaliere only about Signorina Leah. His heart began to beat loudly, almost joyously. By his decision to go to the prison, he felt purified from the contamination he had suffered these last evenings.

People were streaming towards the churches. Christian people — Geronimo was walking among Christians; and the Christmas bells were ringing.

OLD

ACQUAINTANCES

I

IN A GONDOLA THAT HAD JUST TURNED FROM THE
Grand Canal into the Rio di San Felice sat Amadore Galli and Carlo,
the young captain of the Todi *sbirri*.

Amadore Galli had grown heavier and puffier than ever. The bored,
dull expression in his good-natured eyes betokened the fatigues of a student's life. His features were already somewhat flaccid, and involuntarily
expressed a certain disgust with life and with the things of this world. He
looked as if he disliked the unpleasantness that lay just ahead of him. He
would have preferred to visit Venice exclusively for the carnival, and
in the company of his friend Fortunato Cecchi, who found his way about
everywhere, and had a way with the girls: he was always pleased to rele-
gate his leavings to Amadore, who was quite satisfied with them — even
Fortunato's leavings were not to be despised.

All that Amadore knew of Venice was that it was the city where
pleasure reigned supreme. But he noticed little of that this morning — because apparently every proper person was still lying in bed asleep after
the previous night's revelry. He would not be able to see much of that
side of things so long as he was tied to this ruthless sleuth-hound, this up-
start bumpkin — whose one idea was to better himself, who knew nothing
and did not want to know anything of the pleasures of life, those pleasures that were the only things that made life worth living.

Immediately upon their arrival in Venice, instead of first looking for
some decent lodging, Carlo had dragged him to Messer-Grande, where he
had had to look at a ring that was supposed to have belonged to his dead
grandam; and true enough he had recognized the ring at once, and had
been amazed to come upon it here so unexpectedly. His grandam had

thought she was going to take it away with her into eternity, but on its own account the ring had returned to these sublunar regions and found its way to Venice even before Amadore.

And he was also to be confronted with Benedetto, who had always been the best pupil at the dancing class and had often prompted him at school. He was not at all averse to seeing him again, and, if there had been a few students about, he would perhaps even have asked him with deliberate casualness, "I say, what sort of a prank was that you played on my grandam?" Yes; but to have to visit him in gaol, where the bird of ill omen was now lying, presumably in chains and half-gnawed away by the rats — that Amadore did not relish in the least. He felt sure he would not dare to look him straight in the eyes.

Further, Carlo insisted upon Amadore's accompanying him to the lady who had handed over the aforesaid ring to the police, presumably because she thought that it did not suit her. What was this lady to him? She herself had declared that the ring came from Benedetto. Amadore had recognized the ring. That surely cleared the matter up. No, it was not enough for Carlo. Carlo wanted everything that had already been proved to be proved over again. He wanted to be praised, to be thought much of. He wanted Todi to admire him even more highly. He wanted Amadore's father, the podesta of Todi, to attest his satisfaction with him.

But perhaps the strongest driving power of all was still his hatred — his blind, senseless, repugnant hatred against the desecrator of that Todi tomb, who had had the temerity to slip through his fingers. Amadore would have liked to tell the rotter this to his face, if he had been the sort of person to say anything to anybody's face. If only he were not so timid, even in the presence of such a wretched martinet as this vulgarian! If only Fortunato were with him! He could let fly at his dog for five minutes on end without once repeating a swear-word. He could have told Carlo the truth, and then have taken Amadore away to some pleasure haunt. When Amadore ceased to be a student, he would miss Fortunato. He would never find such another friend. He was glad to pay all the expenses of such a friend; he ought to have brought him to Venice. But that accursed sleuth-hound from Todi had swooped down upon him so suddenly that he had not had time to think of it.

This was Carlo's first visit to Venice, too. He did not trust this city that floated upon the waters, but not a word of comment on all that he observed passed his lips. With a certain disdain, he had talked to some of the *sbirri* chiefs, indicating to them that Venice would have to hand over this prisoner to Todi, which had the oldest and gravest accounts to settle with him.

Amadore was very sensitive to ridicule, and he did not like Carlo's company, or feel proud that they had both come from Todi. But it never occurred to Carlo that people might secretly poke fun at him. He only felt exasperated at the obtuseness of these people, who spoke an almost incomprehensible Italian, and seemed to take scarcely any interest in the important matter that had brought him specially from Umbria.

In the palace of the lady to whom they were indebted for the arrest of the fugitive, they were received by another vulgarian, a Hercules who had the presumption to behave like the lord and master of the house, and barked at them that the lady had made a statement to Messer-Grande and wished to hear no more about the ring or Cavaliere Bussoni.

" 'Cavaliere Bussoni'?" cried Carlo, gnashing his teeth with rage. It was difficult to know which irritated Carlo more: Benedetto's change of name, by which he had put his pursuers off the scent, or his unlawful assumption of the prefix "cavaliere." Turning to the Hercules, who was a head taller than himself and looked dangerous, he snapped: "We'll see about that. It is not unknown to the police that the lady spoke to this 'cavaliere' in Todi, and afterwards spent the night in the house of the despoiled family. But the police really want to know whether the lady received that ring, and perhaps some other jewels as well, on the day after the robbery."

There was nothing that Carlo did not know, nothing that he dared not say. The other vulgarian stared at him for a long second in amazement. Then he shrugged his broad shoulders mockingly and went away.

Carlo wandered about the room in which they were waiting, examining everything — the furniture, the pictures on the walls.

A young woman entered. Amadore introduced himself clumsily, and made an attempt to enter into conversation with her; but Carlo did not think it necessary for Amadore to talk. He kept in the background for a second, thus giving precedence to his highest superior's son, and then shot forward, bowed with the awkwardness of a servant, begged to be excused, and began his examination there and then.

Graciously she answered the questions he put to her. She admitted at once that she had reached Todi that very evening. . . . Had she guessed that this fact was of the least interest, she would have communicated it to Messer-Grande. She had lodged in the house of the podesta. The ring she had received in Venice as a present from Judge Barbaresco, after he had won it in play from Cavaliere Bussoni.

Carlo laughed angrily as he heard his name for the second time — it exasperated him unspeakably. The lady looked at him in astonishment. Then she turned graciously to Amadore, down whose glowing red cheeks the sweat was streaming, inquired after his father the podesta, and begged him to convey her special greetings to him.

Amadore stammered that he would. He would have liked to protect her against Carlo's insolence. For the second time that day, he felt ashamed at being in his company. Rather helplessly, he tried to make that clear to her, and he believed she understood. At that moment, he cared less than ever about his grandmother and the robbery of her jewels. He would have preferred the crime never to have been discovered rather than that this lady, with her dark seductive eyes and her small red mouth, should be implicated in it. . . .

But perhaps she stood in no need of his protection. With a smile difficult to decipher, she looked at the boor. Amadore felt there was something more behind this look. Quietly she answered Carlo's further questions: whether she had met Benedetto before she met him in Todi, and when precisely she had seen him again, and in what circumstances. Amadore had the impression that she thought a little longer than was necessary over her replies to these wounding questions. The whole affair became infinitely more mysterious as she talked of it. Presumably she was making a fool of the fellow, just as he deserved. "Idiot! Fool!" thought Amadore. She put an end to the irritating performance by getting up, excusing herself, and promising that someone would come to see them out.

The giant whom they had previously seen appeared again. Downstairs in the doorway, Amadore did the bravest thing of his life: he instructed the fellow to inform his mistress that he would give himself the privilege of waiting upon her again that evening. In the afternoon he would send his servant to inquire whether it would be convenient. . . .

Carlo would have liked to arrest her at once. As he left the little palace, he cursed the slackness of the Venetian *sbirri* who allowed her to move about freely — of course only because she was a great lady.

"And the ring was actually found upon her," he cried, and struck his knee in annoyance.

Amadore stared at him. Then, foaming with rage, he snapped, "But she handed the ring over to the authorities herself!"

"She chose the wisest course in time," answered Carlo the implacable.

Amadore was almost inclined to pity him. Carlo would have liked to put her on the rack, and, a hot iron in his hands, ask her the most indiscreet questions about her relations with Benedetto. Was he by any chance jealous of those relations? Did he grudge Benedetto that he had taken too much from life, even now that he had been thrown into prison to pay for what he had taken? Oh, no; Carlo had seen nothing of the bewitching charms of the young woman. He was merely possessed by what he considered his duty. He would have liked to place the whole world behind barred windows in order to act as their gaoler. He was a dangerous fellow. Amadore decided he ought to be careful, to be sure that Carlo never came to know anything about *him*.

As Amadore's rage gradually subsided, and was transformed into vague lovesick brooding, Carlo began talking of the chief feature in the program of the day — the visit to Benedetto in prison.

The moment when he finally met Benedetto face to face was one of the high lights in Carlo's life. He had longed for that moment for months. This meeting signified more to him than the whole of Venice with its carnival and its many pretty young women.

"Carlo!" muttered Benedetto tonelessly, as they crossed the threshold of his cell, and then he looked at them both fixedly and in silence.

It was Carlo who broke the impressive silence by saying humorously, "Thus we see each other again, after all!"

A strong feeling of pity suddenly rose in Amadore. Would it look too foolish if he went up to Benedetto and gave him his hand? If only that accursed Carlo were not there! He would not have bothered about the gaoler who stood behind them, a bunch of keys in his hand.

He scarcely recognized Benedetto: was it he? The fire that had formerly glowed in his eyes and had been secretly feared by many of the boys seemed dimmed. And what was that great scar across his cheek? Amadore had a sudden feeling that something else must have happened to Benedetto, and he did not know why his thoughts suddenly went out towards that pretty lady whom he had just met, and who had sent the ring to Messer-Grande. . . . If it had been only that the *sbirri* had caught him, he would not be so changed. In spite of himself, Amadore's eyes wandered towards the bars above. They were certainly thick. But if Benedetto had been bent upon his freedom, would he not have managed to break through them? Even as a boy, he had been capable of anything.

For Amadore, life had still a great deal in store, even though he was often tired and listless. He wanted to enjoy himself for a long time — drink and sing and take girls of the people upon his knee: their heads were so easy to turn. "Signore," they still said, even when you had them beside you in bed. Yes. But for Benedetto the joy of life seemed to be over for good. That was what his eyes seemed to say. Who would have predicted that, a year ago in Todi?

Even Carlo sensed something of this — and it put him out rather badly.

If Benedetto no longer attached to life as much value as he once had done, then Carlo would not see him grow pale with terror before the vengeful fist of justice — and that was the prospect that had so rejoiced Carlo. Benedetto was making a new treacherous escape. He was again slipping through Carlo's fingers. Carlo felt it, and he himself grew pale. He tried to believe, however, that Benedetto's attitude was only comedy, that he was only feigning indifference in order to deprive Carlo of the satisfaction of complete triumph. Wait a bit: he would still cry "*Ow*" when things grew serious.

"You see, there is little more that can be done," he said slowly, as he observed the prisoner standing before him with tormenting composure. "There are so many proofs that we shall soon have too many. It would have been too bad if we had come for the wrong person." Carlo looked round the relatively roomy cell, and observed, "You're not too uncomfortable here. I don't know whether we shall be able to offer you as much in Todi. What really became of the other jewels?"

This last question made Benedetto start vaguely. He gave a quick look in Amadore's direction, then turned his eyes on Carlo again and replied, "I shall say what I have to say before the judge."

"Before that time, however, you will be interrogated by Messer-Grande upon one matter and another," snapped Carlo, annoyed because Benedetto realized that he need render no account to Carlo here. "Ah, well, we shall have a word together in Todi."

"In Todi?" asked Benedetto, anxiously.

Carlo did not bother to reply: he knew Benedetto's tender spot now. Go back to Todi — that the fellow would rather not do; just what Carlo had thought.

"Haven't they examined you at all yet?"

Beaten, Benedetto shook his head.

Carlo would have liked to say what he thought of this remissness if a gaoler had not been standing behind him. Instead he made an excuse for this unforgivable slackness. "They want, no doubt, to collect material against you, but now that there are witnesses from Todi . . ." He meant, "Now that I am here . . ."

The official reason for this visit had been that Amadore Galli, having recognized the ring, ought also to recognize the thief. He now made a written confirmation of these two facts.

Benedetto paid no further attention to Carlo. With a strange expression in his eyes, he looked at Amadore Galli, as if he had only now realized who he was. Amadore for his part was afraid of only one thing: that Benedetto would ask forgiveness for what he had done to his family.

This fear suddenly became so unbearable that he made a deprecatory gesture of the hand as if to convey that that business was already forgotten and forgiven, and then cast about for something to say; but no subject of conversation would come into his mind.

The gaoler was now urging them to go: he wanted his food, and Carlo, despite his handsome dark green uniform, did not strike him as a person of authority.

As they left the cell, Carlo hinted at a further visit to Benedetto. Amadore said that he would probably return too; and both meant that each would come without the other.

Amadore was scarcely outside the prison door when, with a decisiveness unusual in him, he freed himself from Carlo, who raised only a passive objection by asking how they were to find one another again, as they had not yet got a lodging.

"I shall look for one for myself. You do the same. We shall be seeing each other again," said Amadore. Carlo shook his head doubtfully — and his doubt was justified, for their ways now definitely parted. But he said nothing more. He withdrew with a bow.

Sad and aimless, Amadore was rowed in the direction of the Piazza San Marco, where in the twilight something of a carnival atmosphere was already noticeable. He started back when suddenly Angelo, his servant, appeared in front of him. He had forgotten that he had told him to await him here.

"I've booked a room for you," said Angelo, who was not averse to telling Amadore what he must and must not do. For once, Amadore accepted the situation — he would not have to tire himself looking for accommodation.

"Where is it?"

"Just round the corner, but let me take you there."

"No, only tell me what the inn is called. At the Lion of San Marco? That's fine. I shall find it when I'm ready to go home. You're free for this evening . . ."

Still doubtful, he looked after his servant as he disappeared rapidly in the throng.

Amadore let him go. If he wanted to send somebody to the lady he had met a while ago to ask if it would be convenient for him to visit her, he could send any idler in the street. Besides, he knew he would never dare. In the first place, it was questionable whether her servant, who struck him as being a scoundrel, had so much as given his message to her. In the second place, was he so witty and entertaining as to fancy that he could amuse a spoilt woman for a whole evening . . . ? Besides, there were pretty women here on the piazza. They had just been attending vespers, and were coming masked from church. Oh, if only Fortunato had been with him! One or two of them smiled at him behind their black silk masks. Perhaps they could see by his bearing that he would never dare speak to them. Would he gain in courage if he were masked too? On the Riva he had seen a little shop. . . . Should he put on a large, impertinent nose? Fortunato would have had one long ago.

As he passed the prison on his way to the Riva, he thought of Benedetto with sudden compassion: he was lying there locked in his cell while the whole world outside was amusing itself.

But was Amadore amusing himself?

He came out of the shop with a pink mask that did not really greatly change his appearance. He had also bought a Harlequin's rattle. If he should come upon Carlo again, he would flap it in his face. . . . As he stood there waiting, peering longingly through the eyeholes of his mask over the Lagoon, as if he might expect to see his friend Fortunato looming up from that direction, a tall, thin, red-haired girl whose youth was a little weary took pity on him.

"I am Lucrezia," she said, quietly and confidentially. "Red Lucrezia, of The Seven Heavens."

And although he would really have preferred something different, and need not have provided himself with a mask for an adventure like this, he allowed himself to be carried off passively into a dark side street at the end of which a red lantern was burning. . . .

II

Next day there was another arrival in Venice: Monsignore Giambattista Buzzi, for years bishop of Todi, and a few months since translated to Feltre in Friuli. From Todi a cry of despair had reached him — a letter written hastily by Marietta. Immediately he had had his traveling coach made ready, and had set out for Venice, which he had not intended to visit before the spring. Then, he would have arrived in state as guest of the Patriarch, an old friend and fellow student of his who, fully aware that he had made a greater success of his life, probably wanted to do Monsignore this special honor for that reason.

As it was, he arrived in simple priestly garb and took up his abode at the same seminary where he had once studied. In itself, he could have wished for nothing pleasanter than to be rowed through the canals unobtrusively as a simple priest, and to feast his eyes upon the familiar pride and glory of this city which he had always carried with him in his heart.

Only the people he saw reminded him of the flight of time. His former friends were either dead or had grown old. The handsome young women of former days were now ample dignified matrons. . . . An awful thought — to be introduced again in company, and to recognize one another only because of the names! But the city herself was pure, undiluted joy to him. The years could not change her. Her palaces rose up as beautifully, as eternally young. The Lagoon was the same gleaming expanse of water that invited to boating and merrymaking. It brought the tears to his eyes.

His emotion at seeing Venice again blended strangely with the great anxiety that gnawed at him from hour to hour and would not let him close his eyes at night.

As he drifted through Venice, recognizing every palace and muttering automatically to himself the name of the family to which it belonged, — at least, had belonged forty years ago, — he reviewed quietly in his mind those upon whose support and help he could reckon. On the dread tribunal itself, he still had one good acquaintance. Oh, he had neglected his most useful connections, stifled as he had been in the sleepy atmosphere of that provincial hole. How he regretted the lost years. . . .

Still, Giambattista Buzzi hoped he would succeed in his quest. His self-confidence had increased again since his audience with the Pope and his nomination to Feltre, Feltre in Friuli, his native land. After his successful visit to Rome, his powerful figure that had begun to stoop had grown erect again. He had let himself grow slack in Todi, and he thought that he had been punished for that, but God had kept something in reserve for him: he had still to go through this ordeal in Venice. He could not evade the responsibility he had taken upon himself, the responsibility he had towards the woman in Todi whom he had loved. He must succeed, and to that end he would employ all his powers. His purpose accomplished, he could return to his diocese, and think at last of himself — look back no more, but forward only, to the future, his future.

He was still young — not so very much past sixty. In Rome, they had been surprised. They had not expected such a man from Todi. The Pope himself had been impressed when he suddenly saw before him the forgotten man from the provinces, who stood a head above the tired, old-womanish cardinals and appeared to have a different bearing, a different voice, a different will from them. The Holy Father had received him graciously, and had conversed with him familiarly and vivaciously for a whole afternoon, while some of the prelates at the Vatican put their heads together, envious and anxious. (That had not escaped Giambattista Buzzi's notice, either.)

If need be, he would go to the Pope himself, to the very steps of the Vatican, to save the irresponsible young rogue, the youthful madcap who had found his way to Venice to come to the gallows here.

The way to Venice? Perhaps because *he* had once pointed him the way. Or was it the even deeper urge of his blood? If he should ever again open his heart to that dangerous rascal who had already given him so many anxious hours — then it would be for that reason.

Buzzi, the young devil had called himself in Florence; as the bishop had passed through on his way to Feltre, they had mentioned to him a young Cavaliere Buzzi who played several instruments, including the viola d'amore, and some of the escapades in which he had been involved. . . . He had run a student through in Bologna, and had had to flee from that city, and then nothing more had been heard of him.

Nothing more had been heard of him. . . . It had been kind of him to divest himself of his name in Venice, or rather to give it a twist — "Bussoni." "Cavaliere Bussoni" — "Cavaliere Buzzi." In Todi he had fled from the *sbirri;* in Florence from an affair of the heart; in Bologna from the results of a duel. And now in Venice the *sbirri* had run him to earth for another duel. But before that he had written a canzonetta that had been played and sung for three whole days everywhere in the city, and once he had been so mercilessly attacked for the sake of a woman that he had been thought to be dead. Buzzi!

Of the duel in Bologna nobody in Venice except Monsignore knew anything, and he would not shout it from the housetops. That Benedetto had run an abbé through in Venice, in an honorable duel or otherwise, was a suspicion — presumably a correct one. But proofs were lacking, and he must certainly have provided an alibi — the heroic deeds of his boyhood seemed to guarantee that. There remained the grave accusation from Todi. But that was precisely what had brought Monsignore to Venice.

Were he, with the help of God, to succeed once more in wresting the scoundrel from the claws of justice, he would talk to him. He had spoken to him more than once before, and it had not helped; but in those days the young knave had not stood in danger of the gallows; and Giambattista himself had been a sort of grandfather, leading a retired life in Todi.

Perhaps it was only possible to speak to this youthful Buzzi within the four square walls of a prison cell. He would make those walls reverberate; the saints above should be his witnesses. If once in his life it was to be given him to set right a youngster for whom, in spite of himself, he had a feeling — then might it be this time. If his powers were insufficient for the purpose, then he wondered to what end so much trouble and money had been expended that he might wear the garb he wore.

"Buzzi!" he would say — "*You* want to be a Buzzi?"

Oh, he would get him out of prison as certainly as one could get anything done in Venice by good connections and hush-money; and then he would take him to Feltre and keep an eye on him — a different eye from the loving, paternal eye he had kept on him in Todi.

And then, perhaps, he would be able to breathe again after the shock Marietta's note had given him. Had he really thought that he could tear that boy out of his life, put him out of his heart after his horrible misdeed in Todi?

Upon his return to Todi from Rome, he had expected to hear covert reproaches about his absence from the funeral of old Signora Galli; but he had not expected the news that had greeted him. Giambattista Buzzi had anticipated that he would never again in his life hear or see anything of the boy — and on that premise had imagined that he could draw a line through all his life in Todi. He had been in the mood for that kind of ruthlessness. The diocese had deplored his transference to Feltre, but Marietta, in her pitiable apathy, had uttered no reproaches. She thought that possibly, somewhere else in this wide world than in Todi, he might again be a refuge to her boy.

And he had scarcely reached Florence when he came to hear something of a certain youthful Cavaliere Buzzi. . . .

Now it had come to this; and he was taking action as she had expected he would when, with a trembling hand, she wrote the brief letter that penetrated to his heart like a knife. He would see whether he could still put things right for that boy, who needed protection not only against the hand of justice, but also against himself.

That boy, possessed by all the devils.

His boy.

Monsignore established contact with the youthful student Amadore Galli, who seemed somewhat weary with the delights of Venice. After a few minutes' conversation Amadore appeared no longer to be quite sure whether he had actually ever seen the ring in question on the hand of his deceased grandmother, the old, venerable, and beloved Signora Galli. As for Monsignore, who had enjoyed such frequent visits from the old lady, he could not remember the ring either, from Amadore's increasingly vague and confused descriptions.

Monsignore's next move was to summon Carlo, who seemed to have slept better, although he confessed that the noises in the night had disturbed him. Monsignore had only to look at the ambitious young captain of *sbirri* to see that here he had a harder nut to crack. He began by obtaining from Carlo a comprehensive report of how matters stood. With a rigid bearing, Carlo obeyed the one-time bishop of Todi; his report was in the nature of a challenge, for he had not forgotten in whom Benedetto had always found a powerful protector in his Todi days. When Giambattista Buzzi had listened to Carlo's magnificent marshaling of the facts, of the carefully collected evidence, he regretted that he had not in his own service this conscientious zealot, and he could not refrain from saying to Carlo that he would have been a useful soldier for the church, and might well have become more than a soldier.

Oh, Carlo was vain enough, but he was watchful and suspicious too. He waited for what was to follow.

Carefully Monsignore began to criticize points in the report. On second thoughts, Amadore Galli was no longer quite sure whether he had seen the ring in question on his grandmother's hand. It was true that he had made a written declaration to that effect, but perhaps that had been under the influence of suggestion?

Taken aback for an instant, Carlo looked at his impressive opponent. Instead of flushing scarlet with anger, however, Carlo remained calm, and merely remarked that the ring was in the hands of justice, and in case uncertainty as to its authenticity should arise it need only be sent to Todi and submitted to the podesta.

"Yes, that's what would have to be done, of course," admitted Monsignore, and then was silent, as if he were weighing all the objections attached to that course — the possibility of its being lost on the way, the expenses involved in having it sent by special courier. "But everybody here will be skeptical about the whole affair from the moment young Signor Galli says he doesn't recognize the ring after all. Besides, we must reckon with the possibility that the podesta may not recognize the ring either. What has become of the other stolen jewelry?"

"The other jewels have not yet been recovered," said Carlo, full of dark resentment. "But even if the podesta should no longer remember the ring, the servants, after all, would be — "

"It is improbable that the courts of Venice would rely upon the testimony of servants, if the son and grandson of the robbed lady are not sure they have recognized the ring. On such slender grounds they will never be prepared to surrender a prisoner with whom they themselves have a serious account to settle."

Now Carlo was sure: the mighty were banding themselves together to check the sacred course of justice. To please Monsignore (how could Monsignore attach so much importance to the life of a young criminal?)

the podesta, like Amadore (whom he ought never to have given the chance to move freely in Venice), would declare that the ring had not belonged to old Signora Galli. The Gallis were not sufficiently interested in unmasking the desecrator of her tomb; for even if the jewels were recovered, they would have to renounce them in favor of the dead. But he, Carlo, he was interested in it.

"Meanwhile, there is also the testimony of Luigino Vacca," said he, in a sort of dull despair, wondering how this also was to be dismissed.

"The testimony of a criminal . . ." murmured Monsignore, scarcely interested.

"But what about the flight from Todi?" cried Carlo, losing his self-control. "If he had nothing to do with the robbery of the jewels, why did he then . . . ?"

Carlo restrained himself again. He realized that he had gone too far, had lost sight of the respect due to Monsignore.

Monsignore looked at him, but made no comment on his having raised his voice. Monsignore just looked up at him, and his glance was not even unfriendly — rather, it was filled with genuine respect. Carlo expected he would be told that Benedetto had only fled from Todi because he had heard of Luigino's false accusation.

But no, this time Monsignore gave the matter yet another turn.

"Yes, that flight from Todi, of course, continues to be suspicious. He will have to give a plausible explanation of that."

Oh, that could safely be left to Benedetto. He would make as many plausible explanations as the courts could wish. His apathetic bearing in prison had been only a snare. Carlo was to be lulled into a false security.

Carlo's thoughts were busy working quickly, feverishly. He must get on the track of the other jewels. He knew that Benedetto had lived in Venice with a Jewish jeweler. The *sbirri*, when they arrested him, had turned the whole house upside down; but they had found nothing. Of course not. If anything had been found, the Jew would have been no Jew. But something more could have been done. For instance, the business connections of this Jew could have been gone into. The Jew himself seemed to have come to a sad end; but his wife was still alive, and she could perhaps be brought to remember quite a number of things she had forgotten, if a thumbscrew were properly applied. There was, also, a young Jew who frequented the house and had a hosiery shop in the ghetto. Other members of the family had come over from Trieste and Ancona, and they had been allowed to depart again unhindered. The best plan would be, perhaps, to try to befriend that Christian servant of theirs who appeared to know all about his master's affairs and who, over a good glass of wine, might be prepared to reveal even more that he still remembered. . . .

"That will do. Thank you. You can go, Carlo," said Monsignore; and Carlo kissed the hand of the former bishop of Todi, and left the room backwards, saluting stiffly by the door.

Carlo had scarcely departed when Contessa Foscarini was announced. Monsignore looked up in surprise upon hearing this celebrated Venetian name. It was true that in the old days he had come into contact with several members of this house, but he had kept up no connection with them. . . .

A lady in the forties, still youthful-looking, came sailing in. She greeted him exuberantly, and then raised her mask to reveal a pretty, smiling face. He was delighted, but still did not recognize her. Oh, but she recognized him. She had been a novice in the convent of Saint Clare near Todi when he had made his glorious entry there as bishop. It was so long ago that she would be forced to blush if she tried to reckon out how long. "Virginia" she had been called in those days, and before his entry she had embroidered an altar cloth for him, over which she had almost ruined her eyes. When he visited the convent, he had come to see her in her cell, and had brought her to tears by talking of Venice. Now, fortunately, she was back there again, married and the mother of three children. She had heard of his arrival by accident, and had hurried to throw herself at his feet and to thank him for the good deed he had afterwards, apparently unconsciously, done her. Her vanity ought to have prevented her from appearing before him again after so many years; but nothing and nobody could have kept her back, not even her husband, who had said that Monsignore would probably be none too pleased over such a visit.

On the contrary, Monsignore was in the seventh heaven. He remembered very well the pale novice who had hungered for Venice and Venetian life, and in particular he remembered what had subsequently happened to her. Happily the old abbess had been of an especially tough constitution and had managed to rise above even such a shattering event as the disappearance without trace of one of her nuns. . . .

At this sally, his visitor flushed and broke into a guilty laugh. She had grown into a blooming woman: happy the man for whom she had fled from the convent!

Monsignore inquired after this person and that. He promised to visit her and her husband; and then, having quietly but quickly considered the matter, he told her something of the reasons for his presence in Venice.

He had come to save, if possible, a young man accused of having killed an abbé in a duel. . . . Perhaps she had heard something of the affair? Yes, precisely. Proofs were missing; but he was also suspected of a graver crime which he was supposed to have committed in Todi. Primarily because Monsignore was concerned about the fate of the mother, he was trying to save the ne'er-do-well from the gallows. . . . It would perhaps interest her to know who the mother was. Could she recall a young girl at the convent who had later gone to live with him as . . .

"Marietta!" cried she who had been Virginia, and immediately her pretty eyes filled with tears. She wanted to know about Marietta, and she wanted to help save Marietta's son. "Cavaliere Bussoni!" She could never have guessed it. She had played his canzonetta upon the lute and sung it. He could not have ambushed the abbé. He must have been victorious in an honorable duel. That abbé wrote such rubbishy plays! The last one had been dedicated to a young Spanish woman who imagined she could get all the men in Venice after her, and who was no longer received in decent society. Wait a moment! Piero, her brother, must help — he had just become a senator; and her husband was distantly related to the Doge himself. Marietta . . . !

"Let's write her at once that her son will be freed, and then she herself must come to Venice . . ."

Virginia, now Contessa Foscarini, was perhaps taking a too optimistic view of things; but her heart was of gold. That was clear to Giambattista Buzzi, and her faithful and warm feelings for Marietta went to his heart. He had pricked up his ears at what she had said about her brother. Had that madcap become a senator? He who twenty years ago had forcibly carried off his sister from a convent where he himself had locked her up! Venice was fortunate if her senators were cut from such wood, provided a little wisdom were joined to so much spirit and power of action.

"Oh, you wouldn't recognize him, Monsignore," cried Virginia, who, married and three times a mother, was still in love with her brother. "He has quieted down so. When he dons his toga and rises to speak . . . ! He must help us."

When, half an hour later, Giambattista Buzzi had her escorted to the door, — after promising faithfully that he would really and truly go to make her husband's acquaintance and admire her three boys, of whom the eldest was already so big that she was almost ashamed at having to admit that she was his mother, — he felt almost completely at rest as to the prospects of his mission in Venice.

The women were going to help him. He had never underestimated their help.

He was about to prepare for his first visit to the accused himself when another lady was announced. He had begged for the favor of this visit: the lady was she who had provided the courts of justice with the fatal evidence against Benedetto. In her voice and manner of speaking, she tried to make him feel that she had come only in order not to refuse a friendly request, certainly not because she was in any way still interested in the matter.

When, however, she discovered that he was anxious for the liberation of the prisoner and did not want to pile up further evidence against him with her help, she abandoned her feigned indifference. After he had talked to her for a few minutes, courteously and gallantly, she seemed already prepared to declare to the courts that Benedetto had never said a word to her about a jewel robbery in Todi — at least, not about his alleged participation in it. She seemed prepared also to declare that she had received the ring from Spain as a souvenir of her old father-confessor, the report of whose death had reached her as a painful surprise barely a week ago; but that, unfortunately, was impossible, because a couple of dozen people had been present when Cavaliere Bussoni lost the ring at the gaming table to Baron Barbaresco. But, making use of the old truth that the dead cannot speak, she could suddenly recall that the unfortunate abbé had told her in advance of a duel he was to fight with Cavaliere Bussoni over a lady — it was immaterial what lady was involved. That would dispose of the suggestion that there had been a cowardly ambush: though, even in that case, there was the mitigating circumstance that Cavaliere Bussoni himself had shortly before been the victim of such an ambush.

So Giambattista Buzzi had got the original accuser on his side. He forgave her the excess of temperament and the thoughtlessness that had caused her to send her friend to prison through spite and rage, and now prompted her to want his liberation — not only because she had made a good impression upon him, but also because he imagined she was trying to conceal a secret sorrow from him. A spontaneous warmth welled up in his heart, mixed with an anxiety not easy to define. He noticed, under her almost childish smile, an expression of pain that would not subside, and in her voice a secret agitation and restlessness that showed in every word. As she talked to him, she turned her head from time to time towards the door, behind which there was no one except her gondolier — an uncouth fellow who had escorted her upstairs, and need only cough in the passage to make her start up anxiously.

Monsignore, too, was disturbed by his presence: it must be a recent fashion — in the old days a gondolier waited below in his gondola.

When his visitor got up to go (there had been a great deal of coughing again outside) he thought he noticed something like hesitation in her, and for a moment had almost a desire to ask her to sit down again, to look upon him for this once as her father-confessor. . . . Perhaps he would hear other interesting things.

But he had not come to Venice for that. Oh, in what complications — for what sort of woman — had the young rogue dared to involve himself! Perhaps he was to be congratulated upon having been safely shut up by the *sbirri* between four walls.

He would now go and see how the young man was faring.

After Monsignore had obtained a pass that enabled him to talk with Benedetto in private, with no gaoler present, he began to realize how little he was looking forward to the first moments of their conversation. A half-minute would be sufficient for him to get the upper hand of the situation, but that half-minute of uncertainty — as to whether he would meet the same boy again, or a cold-blooded adventurer grown cynical and hard — unnerved him more than he was prepared to admit even to himself.

He was led through dark, chilly passages, then had to bend his head as he entered a stone cell.

Immediately, he knew that his vague fear of this first moment of meeting had not been unfounded. Somewhere deep in his heart, he must have entertained the foolish hope that upon his entry the boy would break out into a cry of joy and relief, would hurry up to him as a man rushes to his savior, to his father upon whom in the hour of his greatest need he can still rely. Instead, he came upon a pale stranger who got up slowly and shrank back towards the wall against which he leaned as he waited there, hostile.

Monsignore could find no words of greeting. He straightened himself up, then turned silently towards the gaoler, who, realizing that he had only remained from curiosity, withdrew.

When Monsignore felt sure he was alone with Benedetto, he asked him, concealing his disappointment under his customary kindly mockery, "Can you remember who I am?"

Quickly, fearfully, Benedetto asked: "Why are you here? What — what have you come to do?"

"Yes, what have I come to do?" said Monsignore. "We must needs consider, in the first place, what I still can do. What do you think, yourself?"

"Nothing," whispered Benedetto, agitated.

For a moment Monsignore was taken aback. Then he abandoned his more or less humorous manner, and inquired, "Were I to tell you that I have come here in the name of your mother — would that mean something to you?"

A tremor went through Benedetto, and there was a pause before he managed to bring out the words, "Does she know everything?"

"How can you ask that? Haven't Carlo and Amadore Galli been here? That should have been a proof to you that . . ."

"I just hadn't thought about it," said Benedetto shyly and gently, and seemed far away with his thoughts. Suddenly he cried out wildly, "I didn't ask you to come here. I want to be left in peace."

Monsignore came a step nearer. He could not stand the light that was shining straight in his eyes from the grated window as he stood there by the door. Neither could he stand those four walls about him — no wonder the boy had lost his senses.

He took a deep breath, tried to restrain the angry grief that was welling up in him. "Just tell me one thing, my young friend. Would you really like to see your mother again in this life?"

"Is she coming here?" stammered Benedetto. It looked as if the sweat of death were breaking out on him.

That was not what his question meant. Why were they talking at cross-purposes? "In this life," Monsignore had said — surely that was clear enough. Or did the young rogue not realize that it was a matter of life and death for him?

"No — she won't be coming here herself. She asked me to come to you, and at the same time she is relying upon my getting you away from these four walls. I really wanted to wait before telling you that. We haven't come to that yet, if that's what you mean."

Oh, no, Benedetto did not mean that. Prey to a terrible emotion, he stood there, deadly pale, against the gray stones of the prison wall. Why did he say nothing? It was as if he were intentionally pressing his narrow lips together to prevent himself from speaking. He tried weakly to defend himself when Monsignore laid his heavy hand upon his shoulders and looked at him closely. Panting, he brought out, "But I want nothing. . . . Leave me alone!"

A strange, deep emotion ran through Giambattista Buzzi. Then a feeling of dread took possession of him, dread of something he had not thought of before — that the prisoner himself might stand in the way of this liberation, which was in any case none too easy. What had happened in this cell, or earlier in his life? What had happened to the boy he had lectured in Todi, had talked to about the seriousness of life? Did a man stand before him in whose life he could no longer interfere, a man who deliberately willed his own undoing and would allow nobody — not even Giambattista Buzzi, bishop of Feltre — to hold him back?

He had hoped to hear a confession — a confession, made in the fear of death, of all that had happened. Instead, he was confronted with a desperate opposition that rendered him powerless — powerless and speechless. A feverish anxiety filled him.

If he had ever loved this boy, then it was at that moment when the young madman turned away from the hand extended towards him to pull him to safety. What did that increasingly hostile expression on his face signify? Those eyes had seen through life, and behind life they had seen liberation through death. This embittered, scarred mouth had known kisses that had left a bitter after-taste. . . . Perhaps the young Spaniard had helped him to this untimely wisdom. Perhaps with a smile she had given him that poison to drink from which he now must die.

In sudden angry despair, he shook Benedetto. "Boy! Wake up! Give up your folly. I'm more than forty years older than you, I tell you. You're twenty. Tell me everything. I shall understand! I swear it. I've received confessions before. If you're so keen on self-destruction, you can do it away from these prison walls, when you have breathed fresh air again. Here it's like a tomb. . . . The atmosphere of the grave has warped your senses. Return to the light of day, and you will get well. In the old days, you relied upon my help. You dared to torment the world, because you knew I stood behind you; but now I want you to repay me for that. Now I want you to rely upon me again, and upon the forty-odd years I've lived longer than you. Think it over to-night. To-morrow morning I shall come back. In Todi I still have friends who for my sake will save you from the gallows. All you need do is to deny that you had anything to do with what happened there. As for your flight, you must give an acceptable reason. You had a duel with that abbé. You gave him time to draw his sword. Everything will come right, if only *you* don't work against me. They will be satisfied here with exile from the city. Here in Venice, I still have some influence. . . . Let me use it on your behalf. . . ."

In answer to all these words, Benedetto only shook his head and closed his eyes in order not to see the face, drawn with grief, of the angry old man before him. What did Monsignore want with him? To get him out of prison and have him exiled from the city? But he did not want to leave Venice any more. He wanted to remain there, where Leah had gone to her death for his sake. He had fought everything out with himself. He did not want to see his mother any more, either. That would put him to infinite confusion, and might make him weaken again. He did not want to begin life afresh. He was tired, tired. . . . That other one could not imagine that. He was over sixty, and not yet tired. But Benedetto had nothing more to expect from life. His one remaining wish was to be united with Leah. If Monsignore could not understand that, let him go to the house of Graziadeo the Jew and ask Geronimo who Leah was.

For almost a year he had lived under a burden of guilt and had no-where found peace. He did not want to shoulder a new and greater guilt, by breaking his vow to Leah.

When Giambattista, a prey to nerves, left the prison, having obtained nothing with all his desperate insistence except that the boy turned against him with ever-greater obstinacy, he carried away with him something of Benedetto's revulsion from life. In the gondola that took him back to his lodging, he looked beaten.

To-morrow morning, of course, he would go again to Benedetto, and try afresh to break down his insane opposition; but suppose the boy really knew why he had had enough of this life? Suppose he carried about with him some secret sense of guilt more dreadful than that known to the authorities and to him, Giambattista Buzzi?

That woman who had come to see him . . . He ought not to have let her go before she had confessed to him. All he need have done was to send away that gondolier, and she would have spoken. Perhaps he would have been better prepared, then, for his visit to Benedetto in his cell. He would do it yet! He would get the truth out of her, and in exchange she might, if she wished, leer at him mockingly, and triumph as a woman. He would play every game with her until she had told him everything, and he could hurry to the prison with his knowledge.

That same evening he sent round to ask her to receive him, but she appeared to have gone out with friends; and in the mornings she did not receive. If Monsignore would care to call to-morrow afternoon about five o'clock . . .

In the night, his courage failed. It seemed to him that he, and no one else, bore the blame for this bankrupt young life, just as he had been guilty towards the mother; and all his subsequent protection had been useless to counteract that guilt.

Did the boy's quick intuition realize his guilt also? And was it for that that he turned away from him with revulsion?

During that night it seemed to Giambattista Buzzi that but one thing remained for him to do: to go to Todi and confess to Marietta herself this guilt.

Oh, of course he would do nothing so absurd. When it was light again, he would see the impossibility of it. If his mission failed, he could do nothing but return to Feltre and keep his glance fixed on what lay before him, even though he could see no future for himself now.

He would finish the race, and others would be envious of something that was not there.

Yes, the boy was braver than that. Ought he not to be proud of him instead of wanting to lecture him, to point the way that, for himself too, led nowhere now?

III

In the dusk of the early evening, Benedetto paced up and down his cell: he had not been so afraid since Geronimo had come to tell him of Leah's death.

At last he began to thump with his fists against the heavy iron-mounted door, and when he had bruised his knuckles to blood, the rattle of a bunch of keys approached, and Marco, one of the older gaolers, showed his pockmarked face behind the judas.

"What's the matter?"

"I want to be taken before someone who can take down a statement . . ."

The gaoler had many years of service behind him, and saw that Benedetto was serious. He also knew that he had been visited by an ecclesiastic that afternoon: perhaps, owing to this visit, the prisoner had come to reconsider things, and wished to unburden his soul by a voluntary confession before being examined.

"Is it so urgent?" he inquired, but only in order to avoid acceding to a request immediately.

Benedetto nodded, clutching at the grating with his thin hands. Gratefully he panted, "I've something important to say."

When half an hour later he returned to his cell, a wonderful calm had descended upon him. He found his way in the dark to his plank bed, fell down upon it, and slept almost at once. Neither the sounds of carnival nor the knocking of his neighbor, who for a week had been trying to establish contact with him, disturbed his sleep.

The first few nights of his imprisonment Benedetto had made plans for reaching Leah. He had received help from outside: Rosetta had come to visit him. On the afternoon that preceded the night in which with her help he had hoped to escape, he had been unexpectedly transferred to a better cell. The gaoler informed him that one of the judges was well disposed towards him — he could not mention names. From the front of the prison, however, an escape was a thousand times more difficult; and his file he had left in his previous cell behind a stone that had with difficulty been loosened. Then, on Christmas Eve, Geronimo had come and brought him the tidings about Leah. . . .

That night he dreamed of her and of his mother in Todi, both of whom he hoped to see again.

But not here.

Next morning Geronimo came to visit him. Monsignore did not appear: perhaps he was too busy with his efforts for Benedetto's liberation; perhaps he had already heard that his efforts were vain, since the previous afternoon the prisoner had confessed his guilt, voluntarily and without pressure, in connection not only with the jewel robbery, but also with the criminal attack upon the abbé — and that last in itself involved the death penalty, so that there was no longer any question of his being handed over to Todi.

Geronimo had become his confidant — more than that, his friend. In the face of his approaching end, it no longer mattered that Geronimo had grown up in an orphanage for the poor while Benedetto had had the advantage of dancing lessons in the Galli Palace at Todi. Geronimo looked anxious and disturbed when he heard that the former bishop of Todi was trying to influence events; and then he heard with profound satisfaction that, immediately after his visit, Benedetto had made a written confession of his guilt in both crimes.

With Geronimo, he spoke of nothing but of Leah and of death. There was nothing else about which he could still talk to Geronimo. Geronimo had promised that he would save him from the terror of the gallows. Not as a hanged man would Benedetto appear before Leah.

Geronimo had formed few notions in his life, but those he had he held to; and one of Geronimo's notions was that the Cavaliere must not appear before Signorina Leah as a hanged man. That was why he had been so pleased with an idea that had come to him in his sleep one night, and that he had communicated next morning to Benedetto.

The head gaoler had a feeling that these visits were without danger and allowed him sometimes to be alone with Benedetto, whom he supposed to have been Geronimo's former master. He noted Geronimo's moving devotion, and, when he remembered that this servant would probably shortly be masterless, he had half a mind to offer him a place as gaoler in the prison. . . .

Marco also, the gaoler on that corridor, had developed a liking for Geronimo. He often asked him to spend the evening with him and his wife, if he were free. Oh, yes, Geronimo was free. He was always free these days, pending the arrival of Signor Samuel from Ancona. Besides, he was not at all sure yet whether he would enter Signor Samuel's service. He had not yet said "No," but he was so indifferent to his future that he had not given the matter a thought.

At Graziadeo's house they sometimes looked strangely at Geronimo. Signorino David in particular appeared not to trust him. He had a way of asking him suddenly where he was off to. "To church, to pray for Signorina Leah," Geronimo answered. It was difficult for David to say anything to that. Even though Signorina Leah was not a Christian, the prayers of a Christian could do no harm to her soul. David gave him an aggrieved and cunning look; but Geronimo did not notice it as he closed the front door behind him.

And true enough, Geronimo did go to church from time to time. He was afraid again lest Benedetto should awake from his feverish longing to do penance, to die. That was why Geronimo prayed for a rapid end to the affair; and to-day he lit an extra candle before the Madonna, for he had heard with thankfulness that the bishop of Feltre, after having in vain and for the third time tried to persuade the Cavaliere to see reason, had at last left Venice.

At the corner, Geronimo was spoken to by a stranger in a dark green uniform who first asked him the way, and then, as they proceeded together, tried to make him believe that he had come especially to Venice to drink a glass of good wine with him.

"What is it? Better tell me at once what you want with me," said Geronimo, testily.

Oh, nothing. The stranger only wanted to know — he was prepared to give several silver ducats for correct information — whether by any chance a certain Cavaliere Bussoni had sold some jewelry to the deceased Jew Graziadeo.

Geronimo considered for a second. Then, true enough, he remembered something of the kind. Yes; and the jewels had been sent to Signor Nathan in Trieste. . . . Signor Nathan's surname he did not know.

Oh, that did not matter. The stranger in the dark green uniform could find that out. So pleased and satisfied was he with Geronimo's information that he hurried away without giving a thought to the reward he had promised.

Geronimo did not think of it, either. As he looked after the horrid creature with his treacherous *shirri* eyes, there appeared upon his face an expression of hate and of almost devilish satisfaction that made him look very different from the old Geronimo.

Would the Madonna still accept his candle?

IV

During the night that followed Epiphany, Monsignore, who had returned to his diocese to give luster by his presence to the feast of the
Three Kings, wrote a letter to the Pope. He expressed to His Holiness
once again his profound thanks for all the favors of which he had recently been the recipient. As the condition of his health, however, was
suddenly no longer what it had been (for instance, the festivities of this
day seemed to have put too great a strain upon him), he made bold to
request the Holy Father, in the most submissive obedience, to release him
from his administrative functions and in his infinite goodness grant him
permission to retire to a monastery.

Meanwhile Venice was celebrating carnival. In honor of the Feast of
the Three Kings, a bullfight was held on the piazza. Strangers were pouring into the city of the lagoons, for it would soon be Lent. The theaters
were packed — even Rossi had better houses and was actually able to
mollify his creditors. Rosetta was having a great success in "A Thrifty
Father of a Family," an old play new to the strangers. They applauded
Rossi as the Thrifty Father and Rosetta as the daughter who extorts
money from him. Actually, *la bella Marcolina* ought to have played this
rôle, but during the rehearsal she was always fainting and could not look
at food, and in the play they had to eat all the time. So little Rosetta had
become the happy successor of her unlucky rival. She was completely
bewildered by her unexpected success. She cried, and did not know
whether it was from joy, or from anxiety and concern over her imprisoned friend Benedetto. An Englishman, no longer very young (a Lord
at least!) sat in the stage box night after night, and sent her expensive
presents. . . .
Strangers filled the Ridotto, the casinos. The brothels, too, profited by
them. Lucrezia, "the Red Lucrezia," received a happy Three Kings' surprise: a visit from her well-set-up young Dutch seaman. He had been as
far as Australia — and all that time he had been unable to forget her. Now
he was off to America. He would write her a letter from there. Lucrezia
kissed him like a mother seeing her son after an absence.
One sensation was almost unnoticed in the rapid sequence of carnival
festivities. A seventy-year-old Spanish shipowner, known throughout the
whole city to be afflicted by the gout, had taken a new lease of life and
had unexpectedly sailed away to the East Indies in one of his own ships;
and to wile away the tedium of the voyage he had carried off with him
his daughter's young, attractive maid — and who that daughter was, every-

body in Venice knew also. A gondolier was now master in her house. It was rumored that he beat his former mistress, and that he had boasted he would send her on the streets to earn money for him, as the old man her father had not left a soldo behind him. And it was said that the intrepid, gray-haired Countess Bogliasco had hidden herself one night in the house in order, if need be, to protect the young woman. Whether she had actually done this would be forever in doubt; but it was certain that the *barcaiuolo* had picked up the old Contessa and thrown her through a window. Another gondolier, who happened to be passing, just succeeded in fishing her out of the canal. She was now laid up with an ague. The ruthless villain, who had imagined her to be a bird with wings, had had no alternative but to leave the city in haste — for after all, there was such a thing as justice in Venice. But he had taken his sweetheart with him. She had followed him, willingly or otherwise: God be merciful to her. And now over the little Gothic palace on the Rio di San Felice a serene stillness had descended once more. Nobody lived there but old Catarina and her blind tomcat. They had both reached a respectable time of life. The Negro boy who used to live there had been shown the door by the *barcaiuolo*, and the girls of The Seven Heavens, taking pity on him, had got him made doorkeeper. Thus he had something to eat at least, and occasionally he earned something extra by singing an African song for the guests.

On the Piazzetta, a seven-year-old boy who formed the top of a human pyramid had fallen from a height of twelve yards to the pavement, where he lay dying. More than a dozen of the ladies who witnessed this scene swooned away and had to be carried into San Marco's. The accident happened just between the two famous columns, on the spot where a gallows was to be set up that very night — for a young stranger who had written a successful canzonetta and had run through an abbé in the dark. He had also stolen some jewelry that had been captured at Trieste. Contessa Foscarini, the sister of the popular senator, had turned heaven and earth to save him, but the law in Venice cannot be fooled.

Executioners' assistants were proverbially craven-hearted, and it was not surprising that one of them could not get over the fact that a little acrobat had met with his death between the two columns where next day an execution was to take place. He had been completely shattered by it, and had begged to be released from his duty.

In the first glimmering of dawn, while the gray light of a winter morning still hung over the Lagoon, a great throng gathered to witness the event: apprentices who hoped that it would soon be over, so that they could get to their work; public women from the brothels near by. Lucrezia was among them, and she was indeed Red Lucrezia, for the man who was about to be hanged had been her friend. Annibale also was present. He was trying to find a high place, because otherwise he would be able to see nothing. Several women giggled excitedly when they noticed him. There were masked ladies and gentlemen returning from a carnival feast and wanting just one more sensation before going to bed. They were shivering in the chilly morning air, and there were tears in their eyes as they concealed yawns behind their hands.

How many executions had there been this year? There had been more the year before; the year before there were . . .

The representatives of the law approached; the *sbirri* and soldiers who were keeping a clear space saw to it that the gentlemen with bowed heads passed unhindered.

An actress fainted and had to be carried away. The gentleman who was with her shouted to the crowd in English to make way for them. On the base of the Campanile, pressed against the tower, a thin young Jew had found a place from which, over the heads of the multitude, he could see the scaffold with his dark, restless, birdlike eyes. He did not deserve his good place, for as soon as there was something to see he fainted and spread his thin limp arms about the neck of a fat butcher who, with a startled curse, shook him off.

The death bell began to sound shrilly. The crowd trembled, and was silent. Under the arcades of the Palace of the Doges the condemned man was brought up.

Women began to cry, because he was so young. His eyes were the eyes of one who had spent a long time in prison and had retained no real conception of the world outside.

Farther back in the crowd, they talked in whispers. Some wanted to know of what he had really been guilty. A harlot cried out that he had been hers — she was a drunken, red-haired thing. She also called out his name, and tried to press forward; but the soldiers pushed her back. Moaning, she began to curse and weep.

The condemned man ascended the scaffold. Everybody could see him. "What a handsome fellow!" cried several women, and fell fainting. Hesitating, he looked over the multitude, then hastily turned his head towards the Lagoon. Did he hear the death sentence as it was read out? In his restless eyes there was suddenly an awakening — a longing, a fear.

Right in front, within the enclosure, a young man wrapped in a cloak looked at him keenly. His face was gray, pale. This privileged man, who was not pushed back by the soldiers, must surely be a blood relative. . . .

When the eyes of the condemned man lighted on this young man, he seemed suddenly to realize what was happening about him. He even listened to the death sentence. Beside him knelt his father-confessor, praying for his soul. He too sank upon his knees and folded his hands.

Gondolas came floating up swiftly, bringing the last of the curious. Strangers were still inquiring what was afoot, when they must have seen that a gallows had been set up. . . .

The sentence had been read to the end, and the accused man was asked whether he had a last wish. He did not answer. He only stared with wide-open eyes at the young man in the wide cloak, there within the enclosure.

There was a breathless silence, followed by a low murmur from the executioner's assistants: they deemed their moment had come.

Then suddenly, as if he had only now succeeded in overcoming a paralyzing hesitation, the young man in the cloak raised his arm — and before anybody could prevent it a shot rang out.

Soldiers hurled themselves upon him before he could reload.

Terrible confusion broke out among the public; and cries rose up from those who were being trampled upon, as the condemned man sank into the arms of his confessor. The executioner's assistants, in a raging zeal that justice might still be done, seized the dying man, threw a halter round his neck, and hoisted him on high.

The morning red had just begun to paint the cupolas of San Marco's, and one of the two bronzed giants on the Torre del Orologio was about to raise his huge hammer in order to sound the first hour of the day.

But in the general commotion nobody heard the blow fall.

Neither did Benedetto.

THE END